LEONIDAS OF SPARTA

A HEROIC KING

LEONIDAS OF SPARTA

A HEROIC KING

Leonidas of Sparta: A Heroic King

Published by Wheatmark®
2030 East Speedway Boulevard, Suite 106
Tucson, Arizona 85719 USA
www.wheatmark.com

ISBN: 978-1-60494-830-1 (paperback)
ISBN: 978-1-60484-831-8 (ebook)
LCCN: 2012948111

rev201701

CONTENTS

Part III

THERMOPYLAE

CAST OF CHARACTERS

(Those marked with * are historical figures)

Spartans

Agiads:

Leonidas,* son of King Anaxandridas
Cleombrotus,* his twin brother
Cleomenes,* Leonidas' half brother and Agiad king
Chilonis, mother of Cleomenes, wife of Nikostratos
Gorgo,* daughter of Cleomenes, wife of Leonidas
Agiatis, Leonidas and Gorgo's daughter
Pleistarchos,* their son
Pausanias,* Cleombrotus' firstborn son

Eurypontids:

Demaratus,* the Eurypontid king
Percalus,* his wife, sister to Alkander
Leotychidas,* cousin and heir to Demaratus

Agoge Officials:

Epidydes, Paidonomos (headmaster), later councilman
Alcidas, deputy headmaster, later Paidonomos
Alkander, deputy headmaster, later Paidonomos, ephor
Hilaira, Alkander's wife
Thersander and Simonidas, their sons

Elected Officials:

Nikostratos, Spartan treasurer, later councilman
Talthybiades, magistrate, ephor, later councilman
Orthryades, councilman
Technarchos, ephor, later councilman

Appointed Officials:

Asteropus, priest, Agiad ambassador to Delphi
Euryleon, chorus master
Sperchias,* politician and ambassador
Bulis,* guardsman and ambassador

Army Officials:

Kyranios, one of five lochos (regimental) commanders
Dienekes,* Spartan officer, later Guard commander
Oliantus, Leonidas' quartermaster
Eurybiades,* Spartan mariner, later admiral

Young Men:

Temenos, a Spartan Peer, lover of Chryse
Maron,* eirene, later citizen
Alpheus,* his younger brother
Eurytus,* son of Lysimachos
Meander, agoge dropout, Leonidas' attendant
Aristodemos,* his younger brother, a Spartan citizen
Philocyon, a Spartan citizen

Other Spartans:

Prokles, son of Philippos, Spartan exile and marine
Lysimachos, conservative Spartan citizen

Perioikoi

Phormio, Leonidas' estate steward
Eukomos, royal steward of the Agiad kings

Helots

Pelopidas, principal tenant on Leonidas' kleros
Laodice, his wife
Polychares, their eldest son
Melissa, Polychares' wife

Pantes, Pelopidas' second son
Crius, his third son
Chryse, his youngest daughter
Pelops, her first son by Temenos
Kinadon, her second son by Temenos

Corinthians

Archilochos, Corinthian aristocrat
Lychos, son of Archilochos
Kallias, his younger son, attends the agoge
Adeimantus,* Corinthian commander in 480 BC

Thespians

Arion, a bronze master
Demophilus,* son of Diadromes, Thespian gentleman
Dithyrambus,* Thespian citizen

Athenians

Miltiades,* Athenian general, commander at Marathon
Kimon,* his son
Xanthippos,* Athenian aristocrat and general
Aristides,* Athenian aristocrat and general
Eukoline, his wife
Themistocles,* son of Neocles, Athenian politician, commander at Artemisium and Salamis

Persians

Xerxes,* the Great King
Artaphernes,* Persian satrap of Sardis
Zopyrus, Persian cavalry commander, interpreter
Tisibazus, Persian ambassador

Others

Danei, Chian youth enslaved by the Persians
Teti, an Egyptian scribe
Taiwo and Kaschta, his slaves

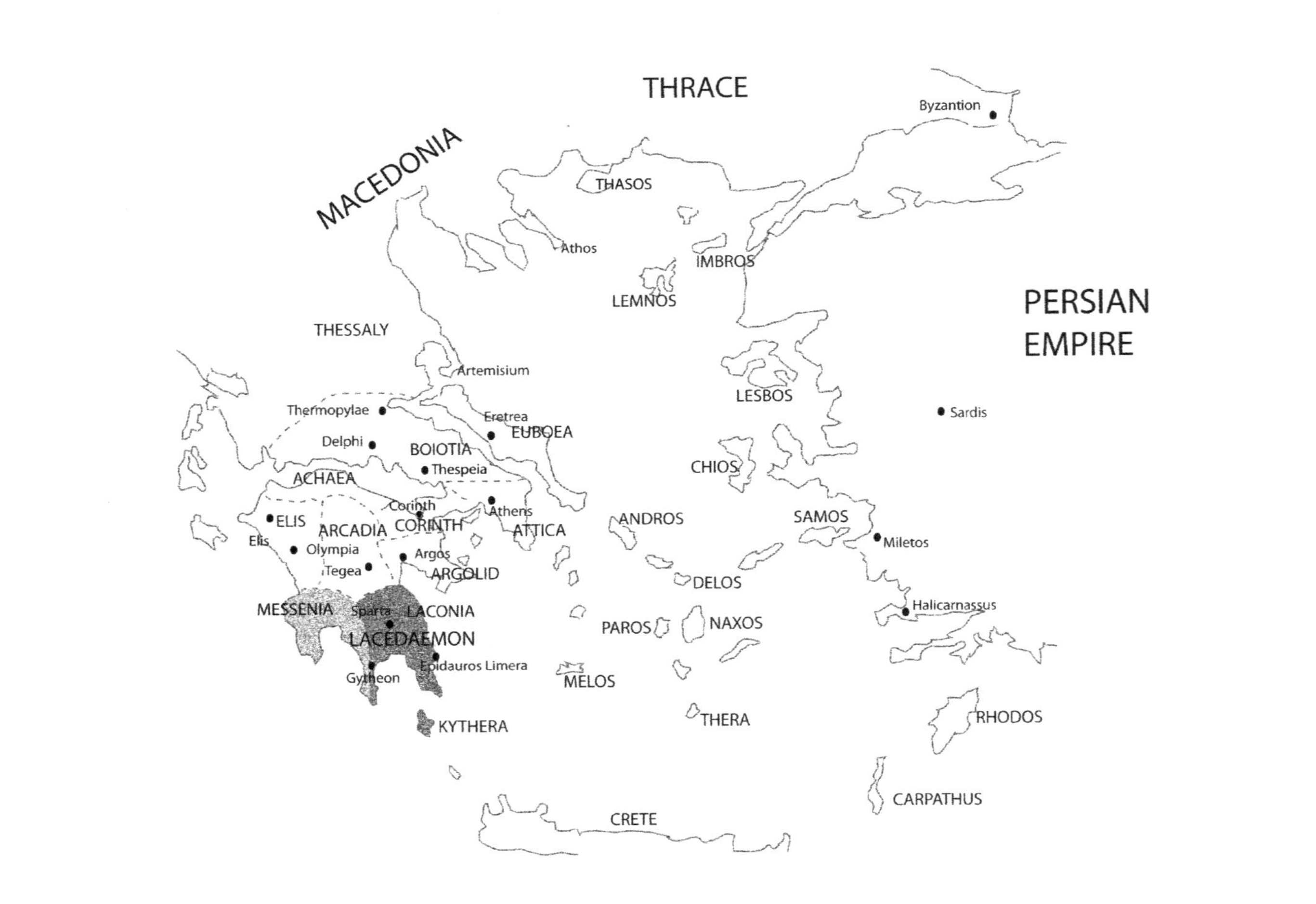
THRACE
Byzantion
MACEDONIA
THASOS
Athos
IMBROS
LEMNOS
PERSIAN
EMPIRE
THESSALY
Artemisium
LESBOS
Thermopylae
Eretrea
Sardis
EUBOEA
Delphi
BOIOTIA
Thespeia
ACHAEA
CHIOS
Corinth
Athens
ELIS
ANDROS
SAMOS
ARCADIA
CORINTH
ATTICA
Elis
Olympia
Miletos
Argos
Tegea
ARGOLID
DELOS
MESSENIA
Sparta
LACONIA
Halicarnassus
PAROS
NAXOS
LACEDAEMON
Epidauros Limera
Gytheon
MELOS
THERA
RHODOS
KYTHERA
CARPATHUS
CRETE

INTRODUCTION AND ACKNOWLEDGMENTS

THIS IS THE THIRD BOOK IN the Leonidas trilogy, a biographical novel in three parts, dedicated to reconstructing and depicting the life of Sparta's most famous king. Leonidas is legendary for his defiant defense of the Pass of Thermopylae, with just three hundred Spartans and roughly six thousand other allies, against a vastly superior invading force, in 480 BC. As in the earlier two books in this series, I have made maximum use of the available ancient sources, relying as much as possible on Herodotus and the sayings attributed to Leonidas and his wife Gorgo by Plutarch and other ancient scholars.

This book also reflects extensive secondary research on ancient Sparta as well as a dozen trips to Greece to visit Sparta, Athens, Corinth, Delphi, Argos, Messenia, Olympia, and the site of the Battle of Thermopylae. Over the years of research and writing, I have evolved an understanding of Spartan society that stands in sharp contrast to the often simplified, sometimes fantasized portrayals found in other works. Sparta was a complex and far from static society, and readers interested in a systematic discussion of my interpretation of Spartan society should refer to my essays on Sparta as well as my website and blog "Sparta Reconsidered," all of which can be accessed via my personal website: www.helenapschrader.com.

The first book in this trilogy, *Leonidas of Sparta: A Boy of the*

Agoge, focuses on Leonidas' boyhood and education in the Spartan public school, the agoge. The second book, *Leonidas of Sparta: A Peerless Peer*, concentrates on his years as an ordinary Spartan soldier and citizen, working his way up the ranks and developing leadership capabilities. *A Peerless Peer* also introduces Gorgo, the daughter of King Cleomenes, who in the course of the novel becomes Leonidas' wife. In this final book, the narrative turns to Leonidas' years of greatest influence. It describes him as a diplomat as well as a soldier, and above all as a king. The last part of the novel, naturally, follows Leonidas to Thermopylae and provides an account of that battle, based rigorously on Herodotus, yet presented through the eyes of the characters of this novel, both historical and fictional.

I realize that fans of the film *300* may find it hard to think of Leonidas as a diplomat. In the Hollywood cartoon, Leonidas is portrayed as the brutal antithesis of a diplomat: he personally throws a Persian ambassador down a well. But there is no more historical evidence that Leonidas committed this crime than that Xerxes was a monster. The historical record, foggy and imprecise as it is, suggests that far from being a tactless brute, Leonidas was a savvy diplomat. During his brief reign, Leonidas managed to forge a coalition of Greek states willing to oppose the Persian invasion *and* to convince this loose coalition of independent and proud city-states to agree to a unified command. (Remember, ten years earlier, Athens was so suspicious of unified command that no less than ten generals shared command of the Athenian army at Marathon.) Equally notable, while Leonidas' brother Cleomenes alienated Lacedaemon's Peloponnesian allies to the point of provoking revolt, Leonidas won over new allies, such as Mycenae and Tiryns.

Leonidas' accomplishments as king were probably even more significant, if harder to document. It is clear when looking at Spartan history from the Messenian wars to Sparta's dismal and ignominious end under Rome that the reign of Leonidas was a turning point. Archaic Sparta saw not only the establishment of a new, revolutionary form of government (arguably the first democracy in history), but also a significant flourishing of the arts and trade. Sparta's most significant monuments (for example, the Menelaion, the Amyklaion, the Canopy, and the bulk of its temples) were constructed in the archaic period. Sparta's most famous poets—Tyrtaios and Alkman—lived and worked in the archaic age. Sparta produced internationally renowned sculptors, export-quality pottery, and exquisite bronze works in the sixth century. Not least important, Sparta's most admired statesmen in the ancient world, Lycurgus and Chilon, both lived in the archaic period.

In contrast, Sparta in the classical period is characterized by artistic stagnation and a dramatic end to Sparta's competitiveness in trade and manufacturing. Based on descriptions of the Spartan state and constitution written at the end of the fifth century and later, Spartans in the classical period disdained all forms of luxury and by inference, art itself. In short, Spartan society underwent a radical, indeed revolutionary, change in the mid-fifth century BC, immediately following Leonidas' death.

Leonidas was the last of the archaic kings not just in terms of timing, but in terms of policy. Sparta obtained its reputation for opposing tyrants and built up the Peloponnesian League in the second half of the sixth century. Significantly, that was during the reigns of Leonidas' father and half brother. These policies reflect on the one hand an interest in world affairs, and on the other a willingness to negotiate and compromise rather than rely on brute force. Likewise, during Leonidas' lifetime Sparta took an active interest in world affairs, and led an international coalition of forces opposing the Persian invasion.

Even more significant is the possibility that Leonidas' domestic policies were tolerant and liberal. Although we have no documentary evidence of this, we know that in 479, only a year after his death and before his successors could make any significant changes to Spartan policy, the Spartans were able to deploy thirty-five thousand helot auxiliaries outside of Lacedaemon. This suggests widespread support for the Spartan state among the helot population. (The hypothesis that the Spartans took thirty-five thousand *rebellious*, hate-filled, and untrustworthy helots with them, when marching out to face the undefeated Persian army, is ludicrous.) In short, in 480 BC Sparta had a fleet of at least sixteen triremes, requiring almost three thousand helot oarsmen, *and* thirty-five thousand helot light infantry so loyal to Sparta that the Spartans could—literally—entrust their very existence to them. Leonidas, if not his predecessors, must have done something to win that loyalty.

Yet little over a decade later, the only recorded helot revolt against Sparta erupted. This is highly significant, because we know that revolutions do *not* occur when people are most oppressed, but rather when *rising living standards decline sharply and rising political expectations are abruptly disappointed.* My thesis is that during Cleomenes' reign helots enjoyed a slow but steady increase in living standards and political rights, a trend that accelerated under Leonidas. In the post-Leonidas era, however, helot hopes and expectations were bitterly disappointed by Leonidas' successors, leading to the explosive situation that culminated in the helot revolt of 465 BC.

Could Sparta's archaic golden age have continued if Leonidas and his closest companions had not died at Thermopylae? Probably not indefinitely. Athens was on the rise; conflict was almost inevitable. Yet there is little doubt that the helot revolt of 465 BC traumatized Spartan society and set it on a course toward brutal internal repression. The revolt caused Sparta to create despicable institutions such as the kryptea and to commit acts of brutality such as the "disappearance" of thousands of helots who had been led to expect reward. In addition, the helot revolt led to mistrust of Athens and increasingly rabid xenophobia. At least some of these changes might have been avoided had Leonidas remained at Sparta's helm. It is not too far-fetched to hypothesize that had Leonidas survived longer, he would have continued the enlightened policies of the archaic kings, who had lived in harmony with the helot population for well over a century. Certainly if Leonidas had lived longer, neither Pausanias nor Leotychidas would have been given a chance to turn Sparta's allies into enemies.

This, then, is the historical backdrop for *A Heroic King.* The portrayals of Leonidas, Gorgo, Themistocles, and other historical characters are literary interpretations of these historical persons. Many of the incidents described, and virtually all of the dialogue, are fictional. (Quotes drawn from ancient sources are clearly identified.) Despite the historical setting, the focus of this novel—as with all my novels—is the characters, which I hope will come to life and inspire the sympathy of my readers.

I wish to express my thanks to my dedicated editor, Christina Dickson, who as always has done a magnificent job cleaning up my erratic spelling and grammar. In addition, I wish to thank two graphic designers, Charles Whall and Mikhail Greuli, who together created this brilliant and evocative cover. Last but not least I wish to record my appreciation to Paul Bardunias for advising me on ancient warfare and tactics.

Helena P. Schrader
Leipzig, Germany
May 1, 2012

PROLOGUE

Thermopylae
480 BC

"YOU DARE TO CALL THAT CREATURE a king?" Xerxes screamed at the men who laid the corpse at his feet. They had come triumphantly, proud to have the trophy at last—after losing it no less than three times in the course of the fighting and paying a high price in others' blood.

But there was no mistaking Xerxes' fury. Even his kinsmen and senior officers were intimidated by the intensity of his rage. They knew him well. They had seen him rage before—and they had seen him fake rage for the purpose of intimidating. A furious Great King could strike terror into the hearts of even the bravest men, and satraps no less than officers had often found themselves sweating from sheer terror at the potential consequences of the Great King's rage.

No one in the Great King's entourage had the least desire to provoke the Great King's rage, and they all kept their eyes averted in the hope of diverting his fury away from them. Even his brothers Artabazanes and Masistius and the trusted Mardonius judged the situation dangerous and avoided eye contact, much less comment. Xerxes' anger was, after all, directed at the impertinent enemy that had dared to delay their advance into the heart of Greece by three whole days. The real target of the Great King's fury was the leader of the Greek defenders, the Spartan King Leonidas—now dumped at his feet, dressed in battered bronze and a ragged cloak stained with blood, mud, and other filth.

Xerxes' eyes swept across the faces of the men around him, and their passivity infuriated him further. "He is no more a king than that donkey over there! Our spies saw him working on the wall with his own hands. Stinking and filthy like the rest of these primitive Hellenes. What true king fights like an ordinary soldier? Not even mounted, much less in a chariot. In the end, there was nothing at all to distinguish him from the lowest slave!"

Nothing except the fact that his men fought so fiercely to defend even his corpse that it had only been recovered after the very last of them was dead.

Because the very silence seemed to belie his words, Xerxes was enraged further. "I will not allow this slave to be honored as if he were a king—even a petty king!" He kicked out at the corpse with his foot, causing it to roll a bit, and an arm fell off the chest onto the dirt. The hand was filthy, the fingernails black with dried blood. Only a heavy gold ring on his left hand still gleamed like a hint of lost rank, wealth, and station. But Xerxes had a thousand rings like this simple one with a carved lapis surface. He shuddered to think that the toe of his slipper had touched the vile thing.

"Cut off the head and put it on a stake! Leave it there for the crows to feed upon, so that the whole army will see he was nothing as they march past. He was absolutely nothing! Why, if his subjects had valued him at all, they would not have sent him here. They knew the oracles. They knew he would die here. They discarded him like an old cloak. That's how much of a king he was to them. Completely dispensable! A dispensable king!"

The thought was so absurd that Xerxes started laughing. Mardonius and Masistius exchanged a worried glance. Xerxes' laugh sounded slightly hysterical. But no one was willing to risk defying him, and so the order was carried out.

PART I

THE AGIAD THRONE

Chapter 1

THE DESCENDANTS OF HERAKLES

"A bastard?" the chairman of the ephors exclaimed in horror. "You're saying that the ruling Eurypontid king of Sparta is a bastard?"

"I'm saying more than that," Leotychidas replied coolly. Leotychidas was a tall, lanky man with the large nose typical of the Eurypontids. He was the ruling king's closest male relative, albeit only a second cousin. He was also officially his heir—because Demaratus, at forty-nine, had yet to produce a son. Leotychidas continued in an aggressive and self-satisfied tone, "I'm saying he does not have a drop of Herakles' blood in his veins and has no right to sit upon the Eurypontid throne."

"That's impossible!" a second ephor protested, no less outraged than the first. "He was born to King Ariston's queen in the royal palace and immediately acknowledged as heir. He never attended the agoge, and at his father's death, almost seven Olympiads ago, he ascended to the throne without question. He has no brothers. He is the only child King Ariston ever sired."

"Ariston never sired anyone! He was as sterile as a mule!" Leotychidas sneered. "Have you forgotten he had three wives and the first two, maidens of good stock, gave him no sons, but produced children by their subsequent husbands?"

There was dead silence in the Ephorate, the small but venerable building adjacent to the more imposing Council House and backed up against the Temple to Fear. The five men sitting in the throne-like marble chairs at the center of the chamber were just ordinary Spartan citizens. They had each been elected by the Assembly to a one-year term as ephor. Each man owed his election to a combination of a distinguished career in public service, an effective election campaign among his fellow citizens, and the endorsements of influential members of Spartan society. Once elected, however, these ordinary citizens collectively became extremely powerful, which was why the law prohibited a second term. Each man served for one year and one year only. While in office, however, their duties included receiving and dispatching ambassadors, issuing fines to citizens found guilty of breaking the law, and the dismissal of magistrates or commanders convicted of wrongdoing. The ephors also served as advisers to the kings, and in extreme cases could bring charges against them.

The men gathered in this room were prepared for these duties. They were not prepared to hear that one of the kings, one who had reigned for a quarter-century already, was illegitimate. Yet what Leotychidas said was true: Demaratus' father Ariston had had three wives, all of whom had had children by subsequent or previous marriages, but only one of whom had ever given Demaratus a child.

Technarchos, the chairman of the five ephors, was a man respected for his hard work and common sense. In the army he had risen to the rank of enomotarch, but was passed over for promotion to company commander. On attaining full citizenship, he had been appointed deputy headmaster of the public school—the agoge—with responsibility for the twenty-year-old eirenes. For twenty years he had fulfilled this demanding position with firmness and fairness, but he was not credited with particular subtlety or wit. Recovering from his shock, he protested simply, "Demaratus was Ariston's issue by his third wife."

"Indeed!" Leotychidas agreed eagerly. "A woman who had been the wife of Agetus, son of Alcides, and had borne *him* children. There was no question of *her* fertility—but she produced only one child in her entire long marriage to Ariston, and that son—Demaratus—was born too soon to have been sired by the king. He was the son of Agetus."

"That cannot be!" a third ephor protested. This man had benefited from Demaratus' patronage, and he asked rhetorically: "Why would Ariston raise another man's son as his own?"

"Because he was ashamed to admit his impotence, and because he wanted to deny me *my* rightful place," Leotychidas retorted, adding in a tone of beguiling innocence: "But you need not take my word for it. I have a witness, a man who was ephor the year that Demaratus was born, and he can testify to the fact that King Ariston knew Demaratus was not his son."

The ephors looked at one another in astonishment. It was forty-nine years since the birth of Demaratus. Since the legal minimum age for election to the office of ephor was thirty-one and ephors were usually men in their forties or fifties, any surviving ephor from the year of Demaratus' birth would now be close to ninety years of age. None of the men present were aware that such an ancient citizen still lived.

Leotychidas opened the door leading directly into the Temple of Fear, and called into the darkened temple. He held the door open while a very decrepit old man, bent with age and clutching the arm of a young helot, entered the chamber.

The old man had so little hair left that he could not plait it from the forehead in the Spartan fashion; it was simply combed back over his scalp until it could be bound into a single, thin, wispy braid at the back of his neck. The skin on his face and neck was discolored with age spots and sagged on his fleshless bones. His eyes were gray with cataracts, and his mouth seemed to cave into his toothless mouth. He shuffled forward until the helot holding him up came to a halt in front of the five city officials. There he waited.

Technarchos cleared his throat and asked politely, as was appropriate when faced with a man of such venerable age, "Who are you, father? And why are you here?"

"I am Diophithes, son of Paidaretos," he said in a surprisingly firm voice, although his words were slurred somewhat by the lack of teeth. "I am almost one hundred years old, but I am here to be heard."

"We are listening, father," Technarchos assured him politely.

"Then listen well! I was ephor in the reign of King Ariston. On the very day that Demaratus was born, we ephors were attending upon King Ariston in the palace when a messenger burst in upon us to announce the birth of a child to Ariston's new queen. Ariston was most astonished. In front of us, he counted on his fingers the months since his marriage and—with an oath—declared: 'The child cannot be mine.'"

"But he accepted Demaratus! He brought him to the Council of Elders! He doted on the boy!" protested the ephor who owed his post to Demaratus' patronage.

"That may be," the old man admitted, pressing his lips together so that they completely disappeared into the cavity of his mouth. "But that does not change what he said," he added stubbornly, repeating, "He counted on his fingers and declared Demaratus could not be his child!"

"But why did you and the other ephors keep silent about this?" a fourth ephor asked skeptically. Although this man owed Demaratus no particular favors, he found it hard to believe such a significant utterance would have been ignored for half a century.

"We did not! We told the Gerousia, but they were displeased. They were all Ariston's men!" the old man spat out bitterly, and his foul breath made the ephors recoil involuntarily. The old man continued passionately, "They said the Eurypontid king had need of an heir, and if the Gods had seen fit to give his queen a healthy son, then a month or two did not make any difference."

Since a man had to be over sixty to be eligible for election to the Gerousia, all members of this body at the time of Demaratus' birth were long since dead. No one could prove or disprove the accusation of the old man, but there was no denying that there had been a period when the Gerousia was dominated by supporters of King Ariston. They had been elected when the Agiad King Anaxandridas was still too young to have much influence with the citizens. Only after they died off one by one was Anaxandridas able to get some of his own candidates elected to the Gerousia.

"I say the Gods have made it perfectly clear that Demaratus was not meant to become king, since he too has failed to produce an heir," Leotychidas took up his appeal. "I, in contrast, have three fine sons. That alone should tell you where the Gods stand in this dispute!"

The ephors looked at their fellow citizen with varying degrees of alarm and discomfort. Although Leotychidas was not without his supporters, he was far from popular, and he had never distinguished himself either at arms or in other forms of public service. What he was asking seemed utterly impossible to these five ordinary men, who for more than a quarter century had seen in King Demaratus a descendant of Herakles and representative of the Gods on earth.

The situation was particularly delicate because the Agiad King Cleomenes was clearly mad. Last year, after a decisive victory over Argos, he had mindlessly slaughtered captives, burned down a sacred wood, and ordered the army to withdraw rather than follow up the battlefield victory with the sack and humiliation of the city of Argos. If Cleomenes was no longer sane, Demaratus was effectively Sparta's only king. If Demaratus were not a rightful king, than Sparta had no mentally competent king. Since only Sparta's kings could command Sparta's armies outside of Lacedaemon, Sparta's army could not take the field even if attacked.

The more he thought about the implications, the more Technarchos felt as if his head were spinning. He was a man with an acute appreciation of his own limitations, and he recognized that this dilemma was beyond him. He resolved to speak privately with the one living descendant of Herakles who had repeatedly demonstrated good character and leadership capabilities: Leonidas. Out loud he declared, "We must consult with the Gerousia."

Leotychidas smiled a crooked, sinister smile and shrugged as he replied, "Of course. Consult the Gerousia. But I am the rightful Eurypontid king, and when I have been recognized, I will remember who sided with me—and who tried to stand in my way."

The youth half-raised his hand to signal surrender, but the boxing coach pretended not to see it and shouted to the boy who was winning, "Don't let up on him! Go for him! Beat him down!"

The victor needed little encouragement. He lashed out with renewed fury, confident of victory, pummeling with both fists as his opponent sank down into the sand, dazed and bleeding from his nose and one ear. Only when he fell face forward into the sand with a dull thud did the other youth let up and turn to grin at the coach.

"Well done!" Cleombrotus praised. "You have potential, Philocyon." Cleombrotus, known better as Brotus, was an Agiad prince, half brother to the ruling king Cleomenes and twin brother to Leonidas. In his youth he had won the honors at the Feast of Artemis Orthia by running the gauntlet of cane-wielding seventeen-year-olds the greatest number of times. At eighteen he had followed up this local victory with a crown in youth boxing at the Pythian Games. Although an incident as an eirene blemished his record and disqualified him for officer rank, his athletic prowess was confirmed when he took Olympic laurels as a youth of twenty. Three years later he triumphed in boxing at the Isthmian Games. At twenty-five he was selected for the corps of Guardsmen, Sparta's three-hundred-strong elite unit. At thirty he won the laurels in boxing for a second time at Delphi. Now, at thirty-six, Brotus filled his free time coaching the next generation in boxing, while biding his time for an opportunity to bring down his half brother Cleomenes.

"I thought I saw Maron signal surrender, sir," one of the younger spectators ventured.

"Spartans don't surrender!" Brotus retorted with a sneer. "So you must have been mistaken, Alpheus."

Alpheus was only fifteen. He glanced at Brotus, but his thoughts were carefully masked. He stepped into the sandy exercise pit and knelt beside his brother. When he realized Maron was unconscious, however, he looked up, alarmed. "He's out cold! Can somebody bring me water?"

Unfortunately, an exciting wrestling match was taking place in the next courtyard of the palaestra, and this had drawn the attention of the helots who were supposed to attend the athletes. At fifteen, Alpheus had no right to give orders to any of the older age cohorts, much less any of the citizens, and he couldn't spot anyone younger than himself. To his surprise, however, one of the citizens, who had been watching the wrestling from the back of the crowd, heard his appeal and walked over to the fountain, took one of the waiting jugs, and scooped water up to bring to Alpheus.

Brotus, who had been chatting to the victor as he unbandaged his hands, glanced over as the citizen slowly poured water over Maron's head. He laughed and called out, "Temenos! I knew you slept with helot sluts and sired helot brats, but I hadn't realized you'd started acting like a helot as well!" The boxing coach laughed loudly at his own joke, echoed by his admiring juvenile pupils.

"I'm sorry, sir," Alpheus muttered to Temenos, taking the jug from him.

Temenos shook his head to indicate it didn't matter and used the end of his himation to wipe the blood off Maron's face, holding the youth's head gently as he inspected the damage done to his nose and jaw.

"He makes a good helot, doesn't he?" Brotus continued jovially, enjoying the success his joke was having with the nineteen-year-old meleirenes, who had come to watch the fight between their colleagues, Maron and Philocyon, and had not yet dispersed. "Makes you kind of wonder if his mother didn't—you know—enjoy the dick of one of her household helots a little too much just about nine months before our friend Temenos was born."

This kind of remark was guaranteed a good reception among the nineteen-year-olds, so Brotus again harvested laughter, while Alpheus gasped and glanced again at Temenos. Although the young citizen's face was rigid, he still refused to acknowledge the provocation.

"Not even willing to defend his mother's honor! That can only be a helot for you," Brotus continued, although by now the joke was getting old and some of the meleirenes had turned to watch the wrestling instead.

Maron's eyes fluttered and then opened. Remembering where he was, he tried to sit up, but fell back dizzily onto the sand. "Just relax a moment," Temenos recommended.

"Helot! Clear that coward out of the sand pit so we can get on with the boxing!" Brotus ordered.

Alpheus looked nervously over his shoulder. Two eighteen-year-olds had stripped down and bandaged their hands in preparation for a round. Alpheus whispered, "Sir, we'd better get him over to the side."

"In good time," Temenos answered.

"Helot! Didn't you hear me?" Brotus bellowed, stepping nearer to loom over the trio in the bloody sand. The eighteen-year-olds flanked him ominously, evidently enjoying the opportunity to intimidate one of their elders in the guise of supporting their coach.

Maron rolled over onto his side and tried to crawl away. Alpheus had hold of one arm and was trying to help him by pulling him to the side, but Temenos turned and looked up at the man looming over him. "I never knew twins could be so different."

"You're right!" Brotus retorted smugly. "Little Leo may be as timid as a kitten and as easily led astray as a helot bitch, but I'm not like him at all."

Temenos got slowly to his feet and stood eye to eye with the stocky boxing coach before agreeing profoundly, "No, you're not like Leonidas at all."

Brotus had always been compact and now he was very square, with massive shoulders over a flat but far from slender waist and thick legs that were a little too short for the rest of his body. His dark hair was already flecked with gray, as was his black beard—which he wore longer than most men to cover up an ugly chin scar from a broken jaw he received in his one Olympic defeat.

"Get out of my way, helot!" Brotus dismissed Temenos, with a contemptuous back-handed flick of his fleshy hand.

Temenos saw the blow coming and drew back his head enough for Brotus' hand to glance off him harmlessly, but he stood his ground. "I'm no helot, and if this youth was seriously injured—"

"Brotus!" The voice calling his name came from behind, and Brotus recognized it as Orthryades, one of his intimates. He looked over his shoulder, and the expression on Orthryades' face made him forget about Temenos altogether.

"What is it?" he asked, pushing the two eighteen-year-olds aside.

Orthryades didn't answer verbally. He grabbed Brotus by the elbow and pulled him to the far side of the courtyard, away from the crowd still cheering the wrestling match. "Leotychidas just laid claim to the Eurypontid throne!"

"What?" Brotus barked, his brain only slowly able to shift focus.

"He's found a man who swears King Ariston denied Demaratus at birth. The old man claims Ariston said outright that Demaratus could not be his son!"

Brotus thought about this for a moment, his eyes narrowed and his jaw working unconsciously. Then he looked hard at Orthryades. "Did you know about this? Did you know he was going to do this? Why didn't he warn me?"

"Does it matter?" Orthryades counted. "This is what we've been waiting for! First Leotychidas replaces Demaratus, and then he will help you bring down your mad brother Cleomenes."

"Where's my twin? Where's Leonidas?" Brotus asked.

"How should I know, and what does it matter? We've got Demaratus at last!" Orthryades believed he had been passed over for promotion because Demaratus opposed his appointment. He had hated Demaratus ever since and had worked for years with Leotychidas and Brotus to see Demaratus discredited.

"Leonidas is an ass!" Brotus insisted. "He will try to find a way to protect Demaratus!"

"What can he do against evidence like this?" Orthryades countered, full of excited triumph. "Ariston himself declared that Demaratus could not be his son! Demaratus is nothing but an ordinary citizen, sired by Agetus on his wife before she was forced to marry King Ariston."

"How should I know what Leonidas will do?" Brotus retorted, frowning. "But I tell you, he will try to interfere."

Hilaira was in the stables on her husband's kleros. Her father had raised racehorses and even now, as a matron of thirty-two and mother of three, she was transported back to her childhood whenever she spent time with the few horses her husband Alkander kept. Alkander could afford only four, and they were not spoiled racehorses but working horses that had to perform many tasks, from serving as riding horses for Alkander and chariot horses for Hilaira to hauling produce to market in the cart. Today they were providing new hair for the crest of Alkander's helmet.

Rich people, of course, could afford to go to the crest-maker in the agora. He produced very fine, stiff crests, waxed to perfection, and sometimes stiffened with bronze or silver wires to make them gleam. But Alkander was just an ordinary ranker, and he could not afford such crests. In the decade and a half since their marriage, Hilaira had become increasingly adept at fashioning Alkander's crest herself.

Hilaira hummed as she brushed out the thick tail of a big bay gelding in preparation for clipping it. Some people preferred to wash the horsehair after it had been clipped, but Hilaira's father said the natural horse oil helped keep the hair stiff and shiny. He recommended brushing it to a natural gleam, and then twisting and binding it with tarred twine in the middle, before folding it in two and stuffing it into the ridge of the helmet to fix it there. This gave the crest a thick, bushy look, although it was also shorter and stiffer than the tall, soft crests some men preferred.

The sound of hooves in the courtyard and the stirring of the horses in their boxes interrupted the peace of the afternoon. Hilaira looked up. The sunlight streaming through the open windows of the stables caught the dust particles swirling gently in the air, but she could not see into the yard. She looked toward the barn door in time to see a chariot roll past, but not who was driving. Her first thought was Gorgo; Leonidas' bride of four years, although a decade younger than Hilaira, had become a good friend, and Gorgo often drove over to visit.

Hilaira put the curry brush down on the nearest bale of straw and started out of the stables. As she emerged, she squinted and put a hand over her eyes to shade them from the bright spring sunlight. She was astonished to see a heavy chariot with a professional driver at the reins, and Alkander's sister, Percalus, dismounting from the chariot car.

Percalus had been considered a great beauty in her youth—so much so that men had been willing to marry her without a dowry and despite the fact that her brother had been too poor to pay his own school fees. She had been clever, too, Hilaira reflected, at playing her suitors off against one another until she obtained the ultimate prize: the hand of a ruling king. So Percalus was now a queen—and it was rare for her to come visiting her humble relatives.

At the sight of Percalus in her bright-colored and elaborately decorated peplos, her arms and neck laden with lapis lazuli jewelry, Hilaira tried to tidy her own attire. She could do little about her everyday peplos of natural wool with gray and brown stripes, but she removed her snood, brushed her hair back from her face with her fingers, twisted it together, and reaffixed it to the back of her head with the wooden clip. There was no time to do more. Percalus fell into her arms. "Where's Alkander?" she demanded. "Where's my brother?"

"He's at the agoge," Hilaira replied, confused by the question. Alkander had been an instructor at the agoge ever since he attained full citizenship at the age of thirty, six years ago. He spent every day at the agoge.

"Oh, why is he never there when I need him!" Percalus protested in a dramatic wail.

Hilaira could not remember a time when Alkander had failed his sister, nor a time when Percalus had done anything for Alkander. Percalus had preferred to forget all about her relationship to the impoverished Alkander as soon as she became queen. But Hilaira saw no utility in pointing this out and asked instead, "Why do you need him? What's going on?" As she spoke she guided her evidently distraught sister-in-law toward the house, out of sight and hearing of the helot children, who were naturally staring wide-eyed at the Eurypontid queen.

"Haven't you heard?" Percalus asked in disbelief and irritation. "You must have heard! The city is talking of nothing else. That snake! That vile, treacherous bastard Leotychidas!"

Leotychidas, too, had once been one of Percalus' suitors, Hilaira remembered. In fact, Percalus had promised herself to him—but then Demaratus had come along. More recently, in her despair over her barrenness, Percalus had sought out an old priestess in the mountains of Mani, and this woman claimed Leotychidas had put a curse on Percalus' womb. "Leotychidas has produced some old man," the queen continued in a frantic voice, "who claims King Ariston *said* Demaratus was not his child! The senile idiot says Ariston *swore* Demaratus could not be his child. Leotychidas is calling Demaratus a bastard and has laid claim to the Eurypontid throne!"

"After all this time?" Hilaira asked, finding it hard to credit. Demaratus had been king for a quarter-century.

"Don't you see?" Percalus demanded irritably. "He's found a witness! Some toothless old man who was ephor the year Demaratus was born. I'm sure Leotychidas has bribed him to say this. I'm sure of it!"

They had reached the back door of the main house. Hilaira held the door for her queen and sister-in-law, then guided her into the hearth room and offered her a seat on a wooden bench.

Percalus looked at the simple furnishings with obvious disdain. She was used to thick Persian rugs and Macedonian goose-feather cushions with bright, woven covers. She did not belong to the faction of citizens who interpreted Lycurgus' laws against the hoarding of wealth to be a prohibition against all forms of luxury. Hilaira didn't belong to that faction, either; she and Alkander simply didn't have much extra income. They had only this one kleros, and from its solid but not excessive earnings they had to pay Alkander's mess fees and the school fees for both their sons, twelve-year-old Thersander and eight-year-old Simonidas.

Hilaira brought her sister-in-law two of her homemade cushions with linen coverings, and sent her helot housekeeper to fetch water and wine. Then Hilaira eased herself down on the stone facing of the hearth and asked Percalus, "What does your mother-in-law say to these accusations?"

"The old fool!" Percalus exclaimed. "Holding the entrails of a sacrificed ox in her hand, she has sworn that on the third night after King Ariston brought her to the royal palace as his wife, she was visited by a 'phantom'—that's exactly the word she used. A phantom! Who—she claims—looked exactly like King Ariston. After lying with her, he left a wreath he had been wearing on his head and vanished. Only a few moments later, Ariston himself came. He demanded to know who had left the wreath, and they quarreled until they took the wreath to the priests for interpretation. According to the old idiot, the priests told her the wreath was made from twigs of a tree only found in the shrine of Astrabacus, and suggested that she had been visited by Astrabacus himself—a story which the hare-brained old fool insists Ariston believed."

"No one else will," Hilaira commented dryly.

"Of course not! But as my mother-in-law pointed out, women don't *always* carry a child to the tenth month. There is nothing odd about a child being born after only nine months, or even less. You know that!"

Hilaira nodded. Her second son, Simonidas, had been born earlier than expected, and he had always been small and a bit dreamy. He was in his second year at the agoge, and she worried about him. She tried to meet him in town at least three times a week to be sure he got some affection and some of the sweets he loved so well. But now was no time to think of him; she focused again on her sister-in-law. "What do you want of Alkander? He can hardly say anything about Demaratus' birth, since he was not born himself at the time."

"Of course not, but surely he can talk to Leonidas."

"Leonidas is the same age as Alkander."

"I'm not an idiot!" Percalus snapped back. "I *know* how old Leonidas is! But he's Cleomenes' brother and son-in-law. He must have influence with him! The ephors have referred the matter to the Gerousia, and with Demaratus charged of usurpation, Cleomenes alone will chair the meeting. Leonidas has to be sure Cleomenes dismisses these ridiculous charges and supports Demaratus."

That was never going to happen. Cleomenes and Demaratus had been at each other's throats for as long as Hilaira could remember. Cleomenes blamed Demaratus for his most spectacular humiliation: the defection of the allies during one of his invasions of Attica. Cleomenes had been plotting with Leotychidas to ruin Demaratus ever since. In fact, Hilaira strongly suspected that Cleomenes might be behind this latest attack. Still, there was no point telling Percalus that, so Hilaira instead promised that Alkander would talk to Leonidas.

Phormio was getting very heavy these days. Sometimes, when he noticed how much his weight slowed him down, he would tell himself he had to lose weight. But then his wife would put a delicious pork chop on his plate, encrusted in bread and parsley, and open the basket with white bread fresh from the oven, and all his resolve melted away. Besides, he told himself, he did not need to get around so much these days. He was extremely wealthy and could afford messengers. Furthermore, he was an important man, one of the Council of Forty who administered perioikoi affairs and represented the perioikoi to the Lacedaemonian government; people generally came to him, not the other way around.

The exception to that rule was his most important client, the Agiad prince Leonidas. For the last sixteen years, since Leonidas had come of age and into his inheritance, Phormio had served as his steward. It was a highly lucrative position, since his advice could be used to further his own business interests as well as those of his employer. Phormio had done very well by Leonidas, and vice versa. Due in no small measure to Phormio's careful guidance, Leonidas was now substantially wealthier than his twin Brotus, although both had received identical shares from their father's estates at the time of their maturity. But Brotus was a conservative who took no interest in his estates and refused to own shares in manufacturing and trading enterprises. Brotus claimed that Spartans should draw their wealth from agriculture alone.

Leonidas' attitude was more flexible. He did not personally engage in any kind of trade or manufacturing, but he put land and capital at the disposal of perioikoi who did, and collected an agreed share of their income in return. Not that he was all that interested in business, Phormio reflected, as the heavy chariot pulled up in front of Leonidas' lovely kleros on the west bank of the Eurotas. As he let himself down off the back of his chariot before the wide colonnade that fronted Leonidas' country home, Phormio admitted to himself that Leonidas was not so much interested in business as willing to give Phormio a free hand running his affairs. The person who was *good* at business was Leonidas' wife, Gorgo.

Phormio had been skeptical at first. Like all perioikoi, he grew up surrounded by Spartiate women running their husbands' estates, but most of these women had run just one kleros. They understood the essentials of overseeing the planting, the harvest, the slaughter, and the production of common household products such as cheese, preserves, bread, wool, wax, and honey. Phormio had seriously doubted, however, that a woman could understand the more complex aspects of industrial production and commerce. Perioikoi women certainly didn't!

Gorgo had rapidly taught him that she could. After he got over the initial awkwardness of reporting to a very young woman (from the day of his marriage Leonidas had referred Phormio to Gorgo), he had quickly discovered that dealing with Gorgo was far more satisfying than talking to Leonidas himself. Gorgo was genuinely interested in what he had to say. She asked good questions, was eager to learn, and quickly grasped the relationship between risk and reward. She recognized the multifaceted components contributing to profit, and she developed an astonishing appreciation of long-term over short-term gain. She could comprehend complex relationships and think things through to logical conclusions. Increasingly, Phormio looked forward to their weekly meetings and the questions she would put to him. She challenged him to be better than ever before.

Phormio mounted the steps to the front porch and called a greeting through the open door. He was answered from the far side of the house. So he passed through the large, paved formal hall to the back terrace.

The terrace was surrounded on three sides by the whitewashed two-story house, but the fourth side looked out across Leonidas' fields to the Eurotas, with the panorama of the Taygetos mountains beyond. At this time of year the view was particularly spectacular because the peaks of Taygetos were still white with last winters' snow, yet Leonidas' pear orchards were already in bloom, framing the central field on which barley had been planted.

The terrace itself was paved with local terra-cotta tiles set in a simple but elegant pattern in which only the shapes and positioning of the tiles, not their colors, provided the design. There was a simple free-flowing fountain with a bronze lion-head spout backed up against the right-hand wing of the house. This emptied into a terra-cotta basin in the shape of a large shell before the overflow filled a trough for washing and watering animals. There were also large terra-cotta pots containing palms and flowering plants framing the terrace and ascending the outside staircase to the second story of the house. Although Phormio's own house was considerably more decorated, with colored mosaic floors and frescoes on the walls, on days like this—when nature provided an abundance of color and sunlight glittered on the dribbling water of the fountain—he recognized how beautiful this understated kleros was.

Gorgo was sitting behind a large loom set up under an awning in the corner of the terrace. A dog, going gray at the muzzle, slept at her feet, while two puppies cavorted about on the edge of the terrace. Gorgo did not try to rise for Phormio, but she broke into a smile and gestured for the steward to come sit beside her.

Gorgo had never been considered a great beauty like her mother. Her hair was the color of chestnuts, her eyes green, and her mouth too wide to fit society's ideals of beauty. But she was by no means unattractive. She was slender, but with well-developed breasts. Her arm muscles, exposed as she worked at the loom, were firm, and her skin an even light brown. She was barefoot here in her own home, and the slit of her peplos revealed a lovely, well-shaped leg propped under her as the other worked the pedal of the loom.

Phormio settled himself comfortably and asked, "How are you feeling?"

"Fine," Gorgo smiled. "I've never had problems with pregnancy." She was pregnant for the second time, having given Leonidas a daughter two years earlier.

Phormio nodded again. "That is good. I have made a sacrifice every week since you told me the news, begging Eileithyia to give you an easy birth and Athena to give us all a son. You have heard the news?"

"About Demaratus?" Gorgo asked back.

Phormio nodded. "It is very bad news."

Gorgo looked over at the round-faced perioikoi manager, and only now noticed how worried he looked. She stopped weaving and turned to face him. "Do you believe these accusations, then? You think it possible that Demaratus is not King Ariston's son?" Gorgo found it hard to believe. In fact, she strongly suspected her father was behind the entire affair. She suspected her father had somehow found this forgotten citizen, old enough to have been an ephor the year Demaratus was born, and had bribed him to tell the story he had.

"My lady," Phormio addressed her formally, "perioikoi do not presume to know what is right when it comes to the kings of Lacedaemon. We pay homage and taxes to whomever the Spartans recognize as king. But between the two of us, my dear, I am deeply worried. If Demaratus must step down and Leotychidas becomes king, the consequences for Lacedaemon will be grave."

"Why?" Gorgo asked earnestly, her eyes fixed on the fat perioikoi she had come to respect and admire for his business acumen, common sense, and humanity.

"Because Leotychidas is backed by men such as your uncle Brotus and others who think Lacedaemon is better than every other nation in the world and that her army can solve every problem. They see

Lacedaemon as a fortress of virtue that will be contaminated by contact with foreigners. They want to cut themselves—and so the rest of us—off from the world. They want to stop the sun in the sky and keep everything the way they think it was in some forgotten past. They are frightened men, afraid of change, afraid of anything unfamiliar, afraid of new ideas."

Gorgo did not like her uncle Brotus. Brotus had frightened her as a child because he had always seemed to be frowning. More important, she knew that he coveted her father's throne and, until she had a son, he was the heir to it. Even if she had a son, Leonidas said, Brotus would argue that the crown could not pass through a daughter and insist he was still her father's heir. Leonidas would defend her rights and those of her son—she knew that—but she knew, too, that he was only an ordinary citizen and that there was no guarantee of success.

"Let us talk of pleasanter things, like the profits we made from the yearling sales. I did not come here to bring dark thoughts to a lady in your condition," Phormio declared with a smile, feeling only slightly guilty. He knew that a man did not give his wife as much authority as Leonidas gave Gorgo without respecting her opinion. He knew that Gorgo would pass on to Leonidas the concerns he had expressed, concerns that the perioikoi dared not voice officially. Too many Spartiates would take it amiss if perioikoi dared to express an opinion concerning the legitimacy and prestige of the Spartan kings.

But Phormio put his trust in Leonidas. Leonidas knew how dangerous Brotus and Leotychidas were, and it didn't hurt to remind him that the vast majority of Lacedaemon's citizens, those who did *not* vote in the Spartan Assembly, had a stake in this dynastic crisis, too.

Nikostratos was seventy-two. For most of his adult life he had served as Sparta's treasurer, elected year after year to this position. Ten years ago, however, he had been elected to the Gerousia, and he had soon found the double burden too much. Four years ago he had surrendered the burden of the treasury to a younger man to focus on his duties as councilman.

His eyesight was weak, so he was almost always accompanied—if not by his second wife, Chilonis, the mother of the Agiad King

Cleomenes, then by a young helot boy with sharp eyes, quick legs, and a cheerful temperament. Not only did the boy lead Nikostratos where he wanted to go, he called out to anyone impudent enough to block his master's path, and commandeered horses if Nikostratos was in a hurry.

The boy cleared Nikostratos' way from the Council House across the square and down the street beside the Canopy, the stoa in which the Assembly met monthly. They passed the rotunda dedicated to the Olympian Zeus and the Olympian Aphrodite, and turned left at the corner on which Kastor's Grave stood. Ahead of them stood the massive building complex that housed the headquarters, barracks, stables, and storerooms of the Mesoan lochos, one of Sparta's five regiments. In peacetime, the lochos consisted of two hundred men on active duty, who were required to live here in the barracks. In wartime, up to eight hundred reservists could be called up by age cohort to swell the ranks until, in a full call-up reactivating men up to the age of forty-five, the lochos could field one thousand men. Leonidas commanded this lochos in peace and war.

The helot boy led Nikostratos up the steps, through the colonnade of Doric columns, and past the meleirenes on duty at the door. No one dreamed of stopping them; even those who did not know Nikostratos on sight recognized the purple-trimmed white himation of a councilman. Furthermore, Nikostratos wore the himation over a long chiton with a border of lambdas, another symbol of his office. The energetic helot youth and the dignified Spartiate elder proceeded down a long corridor toward the high-ceilinged, breezy anteroom before the chamber of the commander.

Several other men were already waiting, perioikoi purveyors and contractors for the most part, but also one ranker. Nikostratos presumed the young soldier was here for disciplinary reasons, since he looked distinctly nervous as he paced the room. The boy led Nikostratos straight to the paneled and bronze-studded door that gave access to the commander's office, knocked loudly, and without waiting for a reply opened it to announce, "Councilman Nikostratos!"

Leonidas was standing behind a table. He had evidently just returned from somewhere; he still had his himation over his shoulders, and his light brown hair was wet from sweating in the helmet that now stood on the desk in front of him. The ties of his leather corselet had been loosened but not undone, revealing his sweat-soaked beige chiton underneath. His hands were dirty from sweaty reins.

Leonidas looked up sharply as the door opened, but his expression eased at the sight of Nikostratos. The councilman sent the helot boy to wait outside with a word and gesture, adding, "And close the door behind you." Then he focused on the man in front of him.

Leonidas was five foot ten, three inches taller than his twin but not a giant. A wrestler rather than a boxer, his body was well proportioned. His naked arms and legs were tanned and muscular, the result of spending most of his day outdoors at drill, sports, or hunting. He wore his beard clipped short and his hair in the traditional manner, neatly braided from his brow to the back of his head in eight strands that hung halfway down his back, each bound at the ends by tarred twine covered by a bronze clip.

As a youth and young man he had been considered less attractive than his friend Alkander, whose fine blond hair, blue eyes, and classic features reminded everyone of images of Apollo, but Leonidas had aged well. He was now thirty-six, and his rough brown hair was as thick as ever and peppered with gold rather than gray hairs. His hazel eyes were set well apart under a high brow, flanking a straight if somewhat long nose. The lines on his face had been made more by smiles than by frowns.

Nikostratos had witnessed the making of those lines. He had watched Leonidas grow up and take over his responsibilities. He had applauded Leonidas' advancements in the agoge and the army, and comforted him in his private disappointments and tragedies. Recently he had come to rely on him as one of the most sensible citizens in Sparta. Leonidas was, in Nikostratos' opinion, quite simply the best man of his entire generation.

"You've heard the news?" he asked.

"Technarchos sent a runner. He caught up with me on maneuvers. My lochos is still halfway to Gytheon, but I borrowed a horse and rode back as fast as I could. What truth is there in these accusations?"

Nikostratos sank down on a bench by the door, prompting Leonidas to grab a more comfortable chair with arms and a leather seat and back and bring it to Nikostratos. The councilman transferred wordlessly to the new chair and then looked up at Leonidas with an expression of deep concern. "More truth than is good for Sparta," he admitted unhappily.

"How can that be?" Leonidas protested at once. "Surely these are just machinations of my brothers and Leotychidas?"

"I wish," Nikostratos admitted with a deep sigh. "But the witness Leotychidas dug up is exactly who he says he is: Diophithes, son of Paidaretos. Furthermore, he was ephor the year of Demaratus' birth; we've checked the records. Third, the story he tells is not new. I heard it as a young man—and so did several other councilmen, including Eukomos and Polypeithes." The opinion of these latter men mattered, because they were the oldest men in the Gerousia.

"In that case, what has changed? If no one took the accusations seriously before, why take them seriously now?"

"Because when Demaratus was born, your father had not yet produced an heir, either. There was genuine fear that both houses were on the brink of extinction. More important, Demaratus was a newborn infant who seemed full of promise."

"And now he is a mature man of proven ability and considerable intelligence."

Nikostratos nodded. "I thought you would come to his defense. Which is to your credit, of course. But don't forget, Demaratus is also the man who humiliated us in front of our allies and cost us our position of preeminence in the Peloponnesian League."

"You supported him!" Leonidas protested. "You said we were stronger to have allies that followed us freely, rather than vassals who followed us out of compulsion."

"Indeed. And so we are. I know that. Kyranios knows that. Epidydes knows that, and very likely a majority of the councilmen and citizens know that. But that is not the opinion of either of your brothers—or that faction that rages against the humiliation and dreams of glory far beyond our real means. That faction of irrational but bigoted citizens has been seeking Demaratus' downfall for the last four Olympiads."

"And they prefer Leotychidas?" Leonidas asked, incredulous.

"Leotychidas is a tool, nothing more. Because he is a weak, selfish man with no thought for Lacedaemon, only his own power, they believe they can manipulate and control him."

"And such a man might replace Demaratus as the Eurypontid king?" Leonidas did not want to believe this was possible.

"Not if I can help it, but I am here to tell you the truth, Leo. The Gerousia is bitterly divided, and your brother played the outraged traditionalist, shocked beyond measure to think that some man not entitled to the honors of kingship had shared power with him for a quarter century. He may not have been credible in himself, but his words were welcome grist for the conservatives. The Assembly might be more favorably disposed to Demaratus, but they will not have any say in this. An accusation against a king is tried by the Gerousia together with the ephors. Leotychidas timed his attack well. Except for Technarchos, this year's ephors are not men of strong character. They will cave in to pressure, if it is great enough. If your wife has any influence with her father, she would be advised to use it now. She must try to talk him out of this madness."

Leonidas said nothing. Gorgo's relationship to her father was volatile at best, and was particularly strained since she had sided with him rather than her father in the aftermath of the campaign in Argos. Furthermore, Leonidas increasingly questioned whether Cleomenes was accessible to reason at all.

Nikostratos understood his silence and took a deep breath. "No matter. We are referring the issue to Delphi. We will ask the oracle what we are to do. Not—note—whether Demaratus is legitimate or not, since that is not so much the issue as whether at this stage, and given the alternatives, it would be right to depose him in favor of Leotychidas, regardless of his bloodlines."

Leonidas still said nothing. He supposed it was the best solution. Sparta had always turned to Delphi in times of crisis. Lycurgus had taken their radical new Constitution to Delphi fifty Olympiads ago. They had consulted Delphi during the Second Messenian War, and at the oracle's advice they had welcomed Tyrtaios, whose music had restored morale. It made sense to consult Delphi—if only he didn't have this horrible suspicion that his brother Cleomenes could manipulate the oracle. For years now, the oracle at Delphi had delivered judgments that conformed uncannily to Cleomenes' wishes. And Cleomenes wanted Demaratus humiliated and destroyed.

"Do not confuse the oracles you've paid for with the will of the Gods," Asteropus, the Agiad permanent representative at Delphi, warned King Cleomenes of Sparta. Asteropus was approaching forty years of age, and for more than a decade he had been serving Cleomenes at Delphi. The years away from Sparta had left their mark. Asteropus, who had never been a particularly handsome or athletic man, now had sagging shoulders and a paunch. The hours spent in libraries rather than on drill fields had left his acne-scarred skin pale and had given him a permanent squint. "You may be able to frighten the ephors and manipulate the Spartan Assembly with the forgeries I give you, but the Gods have not been bought!"

"Well," Cleomenes snapped back, "don't forget that *you* have been bought, and by whom!"

Asteropus caught his breath and straightened his shoulders. "I am entirely in your service, my lord," he protested. "Have you ever had cause to complain of me?"

"No. So don't give me grounds for complaint *now*," Cleomenes retorted, downing the contents of a large kylix of red wine without stopping for breath.

"Think of the consequences of this, my lord!" Asteropus tried again. "Demaratus has been king for decades—"

"And all he's ever done is get in my way and weaken Sparta. Now he's interfering with my policies in Aegina, and I won't have it!" Cleomenes declared, pounding his fist on the table before his couch and making the empty kylix jump.

"But Leotychidas—"

"Is a greedy little weasel who can be controlled with gold," retorted Cleomenes, dismissing the Eurypontid challenger. Then he looked hard at Asteropus. "You never had any scruples about the other hoax oracles, why now?"

Why now, indeed? Asteropus asked himself, but he couldn't shake the sense of impending catastrophe.

"I want a very clear statement," Cleomenes continued in a tone that brooked no further argument, while he reached down to tie his sandals. "Something like: Demaratus has not a drop of Eurypontid blood, is not a descendant of Herakles, and has absolutely no right to rule in Sparta. Nothing ambiguous. Nothing that can be interpreted to his benefit. The oracle must *order* us to depose him."

"But, my lord—"

"Asteropus! You deliver this oracle just the way I want it, or you are dismissed. Do you understand? It's as simple as that. There are plenty of other ambitious young men who can write silly rhymes that sound like oracles." Cleomenes stood, swung the end of his himation over his shoulder, and went out into the windy night, leaving Asteropus alone with the flickering lamps and a cold sweat.

There was nothing that Asteropus feared more than returning to Sparta. If he returned to Sparta, he would be compelled to live by Spartan law: to attend his syssitia every night and eat the dreary communal meals, to drink only watered wine, to give up all gold and silver, and to drill regularly with his reserve unit. The social pressure to pretend interest in the athletic contests and the boys of the agoge would be almost as oppressive. Worst of all, he would be subjected to ridicule and abuse for not being married—because the woman who kept his house and had given him children was a local Phocian girl, not a Spartan citizen. He couldn't bear the thought of returning to Sparta.

But that meant faking an oracle—again.

Why was that so terrible? He'd done it before. Why did his stomach tie itself in knots at the mere thought of it this time?

Asteropus realized with terror that he had a real premonition. It was these rare flashes of second sight that had attracted Cleomenes' attention to him in the first place. Asteropus had spontaneously predicted the demise of Cleomenes' elder brother Dorieus months before it happened, and had forecast a disastrous storm shortly afterward. Throughout his life ever since, the Gods had sporadically revealed fragments of the future to him. But they did it when it suited *them*, and always just like this: without his asking, without his reading entrails, and without even sending birds or snakes that behaved strangely.

Yet when he had one of these flashes of insight, there was no room for interpretation. Today's divine message was absolute and immutable: Deposing Demaratus would be disastrous for Sparta.

As if to underline the message, the door of the room, which Cleomenes had not closed properly, blew open with a loud crack, and a gust of wind extinguished every lamp in the room. Asteropus leaped to his feet in alarm, his heart beating wildly. A cold sweat chilled him to the marrow of his bones. He was certain: Deposing Demaratus would set in motion a series of events that would not only harm Sparta, but tear all of Greece apart.

Chapter 2

AN EXCESS OF HEIRS

"A male child, my lord!" Laodice announced timidly to Nikostratos. Laodice was the wife of Leonidas's chief tenant, Pelopidas. Although she had been told to bring the councilman the news at once, she was awed by his age and status, and so was hesitant to wake him.

Nikostratos had been dozing in the afternoon sun on the back terrace of Leonidas's kleros. He sat on one of the wooden benches, leaning against the plastered façade with his hands resting on the cane between his knees. Laodice's words brought him instantly to his full senses. He looked sharply at the helot woman, noting the sweat that dripped down the side of her face and the blood smeared thinly on her hands, suggesting that she had rubbed them on a cloth but not yet washed them in water.

"A male child?" he anxiously asked the aging helot housekeeper. "Healthy and whole?"

"Yes, my lord. He is smaller than his sister was at birth, but he is whole and fair."

At that moment a loud wail went up from the side wing where Gorgo had endured the ordeal. With far more relief than joy, Nikostratos exclaimed, "May all the Gods be praised! I have promised Zeus a ram for this, and I will go fulfill my promise at once." After the Delphic oracle had pronounced Demaratus a bastard and the Gerousia and ephors had felt compelled to set him aside, Sparta was ruled by a madman and an unscrupulous charlatan. This boy, however, was a direct male descendant of the ruling Agiad king, Cleomenes, and as such he had the potential to change everything. Leonidas *might* have claimed the Agiad throne by right of his wife, but he *certainly* could by right of his son. This was very good news indeed!

Nikostratos paused and asked next, "And Gorgo?"

"She is exhausted but well so far," Laodice assured him cautiously. Too many women died after childbirth from bleeding or milk fever. Laodice did not want to presume all was well just yet.

"I will offer an amphora of milk to Eileithyia in thanks for that. Your son is waiting to bring the news to Leonidas?" This being the Chalkioika, the annual feast in honor of Sparta's patron goddess, Athena, Leonidas was taking part in the festivities.

"Yes, my lord," Laodice assured the councilman. "He is waiting in the helot hall."

"Send him to Leonidas at once!" Nikostratos urged. "This is very good news, good woman. Very good news indeed!"

Crius, Laodice's youngest son, was twenty-one. Since childhood he had suffered from a strange weakness in his hands that prevented him from doing manual labor, but he was exceptionally fleet, and so he had become a messenger for the Spartan army. The work could be hard: he had to be available day and night in all weather, and any message entrusted to him was urgent by definition. Yet like a healthy hound or horse, he loved feeling the strength of his own young body and loved being out in the open countryside. Furthermore, Crius' work took him to every corner of Lacedaemon and even beyond to Tegea, Mycenae, Elis, and Corinth. Crius knew how to use this freedom to his advantage. He was conscientious about delivering his messages, whether verbal or written (the latter completely mysterious to him, as he could neither read nor write), but there was rarely a return message of equal urgency, and there was always dead time when his services were not needed. He knew the best places for a good, cheap meal, knew the taverns with the best wine, and had many girlfriends scattered far enough apart not to know about one another.

But today he had only a short sprint into the city to tell the master that he was now father of a son. Crius was happy for him. Leonidas was a good man. Almost two decades earlier, he had brought Crius' whole family from one of his estates in Messenia to run the kleros on the Eurotas. He allowed Crius' mother, Laodice, to earn extra money selling her sweets and baked goods, and he had let Crius' elder brother, Pantes, set up in his own carpentry shop, where he made good money. Leonidas treated them well, and Crius knew that couldn't be said of all Spartiates. Many helots, especially those still in Messenia, were subject to arbitrary and harsh treatment.

Crius reached the end of the drive flanked by cypress trees and turned north onto the sunny road coming down out of the Parnon range from Epidauros Limera. To his right and a little behind him, crowning a small hill, was the Menelaion, built to honor Menelaus and Helen and constructed, some claimed, on the foundation of their ancient palace. At the foot of the hill was a more recent shrine to the Dioskouroi. Crius knew that Leonidas frequently brought offerings here because, as a twin himself, he honored the Divine Twins particularly. Now that he had a firm, dry road under his feet, Crius picked up the pace despite the intense summer heat.

Within a quarter-hour he had reached the junction with the road to Tegea. From here on into the city, the road was paved. Crius continued, loping lightly past the wide drill fields on which units of the Spartan army and classes of the agoge drilled almost daily. Today, however, was the fourth day of the Chalkioika, so the drill fields stood lonely and deserted under the hazy summer sky. As on all major holidays of the Spartan calendar, the agoge was closed, and the army, except for a small watch from each regiment or lochos, was furloughed.

Crius crossed the bridge across the Eurotas, still at an easy lope. Although he breathed audibly and glistened with sweat, he was in his stride and could run like this for hours. Beyond the bridge, the city started with an imposing temple to Poseidon Earth-Holder. According to legend, it had been built during the Great Troubles after a particularly destructive earthquake, which had destroyed most of the temples of the time. It was very solid, with squat Doric columns that had once been painted red but were now naked stone. This temple was not as popular as the newer temple to the Horse-Breeding Poseidon,

Crius thought, because no one alive today could remember an earthquake. Horse breeding, on the other hand, was increasingly popular.

In addition to the temple there were a variety of civic buildings, including the barracks, warehouses, and stables of the Limnate Lochos near the bridge. Then came one of several gymnasiums, a couple of monuments to long-dead heroes, and a stoa often used for practice by the choruses. Beyond this, the city started to spread away from the road. In the side streets were the workshops, stalls, and apartments of craftsmen serving the city's daily needs. Houses hid behind high walls that enclosed courtyards, and fountain houses on small squares broke up the maze of alleys.

By continuing down the broad main road, flanked by leafy plane trees, Crius would pass the Canopy, and beyond that reach the main city square on which the Council House and Ephorate faced each other. At this time of day on a holiday, however, the square would be deserted, because everyone would be over at the racecourse to watch the youths and maidens competing for the festival prizes. Crius turned into one of the side streets to cut across the city.

Crius knew the back streets of Sparta well, and he ran surely, his naked feet all but soundless on the paving stones, until he came around a corner and almost collided with a body of men. Crius drew up sharply, initially registering only that the men were Spartiates in standard-issue red himations. A moment later, however, he realized that three men were brutally beating up a fourth. The victim was already on his knees, vomiting from the blows and kicks to his stomach, while his assailants hissed insults along with their abuse: "Helot lover!" "Traitor!" "Blood putrefier!"

Crius wanted to turn around and run in the other direction, but just beyond the three men beating up their fellow citizen, a fourth man held Crius' sister Chryse. The man had her so firmly in his grasp that she could not break free, although she was struggling, and he had a hand over her mouth so she could not cry out.

Crius understood instantly. Chryse had a Spartiate lover, Temenos. Of course, a lot of helot girls had boyfriends among the youth of the agoge, but once the youths became citizens they were supposed to turn their attention to Spartiate maidens and think about marriage. Chryse's lover hadn't done that. Instead he remained single, recognized the two sons he had sired on Chryse, and visited her and the boys whenever he could. He was more devoted and considerate of her wishes than most helot husbands, so Crius' parents had accepted the situation. Even Leonidas had given up trying to end the relationship, although he disapproved.

Whatever Leonidas thought of the relationship, Crius was certain he would not approve of what these young men were doing to Temenos. Crius took a step back, on the brink of turning and continuing his run to Leonidas with a second, urgent message about what was happening here, but then he saw the way the man holding his sister was mishandling her. What would these brutes, who did not shrink from attacking one of their own, do to Chryse when they had finished off Temenos? Crius imagined them raping her, one after another. Crius couldn't just leave her here in their hands.

But he couldn't attack four Spartans, either. They were Spartiates and he was a helot. They were trained soldiers in bronze armor, and he had crippled hands, weak arms, and was wearing nothing but a short chiton. He could do nothing alone. He had to get help.

He spun about and headed for the next major street, looking desperately for a Spartiate, any Spartiate. The first people he ran into, however, were two youths of the agoge. Crius' desperation was such that he addressed them. "Sirs! Please, help me! Around the corner! Please!"

The youngsters looked at each other.

"Please! My sister!" Crius begged.

Again they looked at each other, then shrugged and followed Crius.

By now Temenos was trying to crawl to safety, while his assailants kicked and spat at him.

Crius heard one of the youths behind him gasp, "That's Temenos!" Then the youth raised his voice and called out: "Stop!" But his voice quavered as he spoke. He was just eighteen and the assailants were citizens. He had no right to give them orders.

Still, his call caused the attackers to pause in their assault long enough to look over. Then the leader made a dismissive gesture. "Keep out of this, boy! Or I'll report you to the Paidonomos."

"And I will tell *him* what I saw!" the youth countered with surprising courage. His companion, however, hissed: "We'd better keep out of this!"

The first youth shook his head doggedly and started forward, dragging his obviously reluctant companion in his wake. Crius couldn't let them go alone. If the three of them distracted the Spartiates, maybe Chryse could get away.

Simonidas was eight. He had been in the agoge more than a year now, and he was not happy. He did not like having to be with a dozen other boys all the time. It wasn't that he was in any way inferior to them. He was fleet, agile, literate, and had a lovely singing voice, but he liked being on his own and free to follow his own whims. As soon as his herd joined the large crowd around the ball field to watch a match between two teams of eirenes including their own, Simonidas slipped away. They wouldn't notice he was gone for a long time, he figured, and then they would just think he had gotten lost in the crowd.

As he ducked down one of the side alleys heading for the river, hoping to get clear out of town to be by himself for a bit, he collided with a horrible brawl. It looked to him like two youths of the agoge were being set upon by a whole pack of citizens. Simonidas turned to run.

"Simonidas!" A voice pierced the air and made the hair on the back of his neck stand up. He continued running, but the voice followed him. "Fetch Leonidas!"

Simonidas didn't stop, but his destination had changed. He recognized the voice of Crius, and Crius served his father's best friend. Crius often came to his kleros with messages from Leonidas or Gorgo. Furthermore, Simonidas knew exactly where Leonidas was, because he'd seen him talking to the ex-king Demaratus on a corner.

Leonidas had not actually witnessed the incident that had occurred in the theater on the first night of the Chalkioika, because he'd been with the rest of his chorus preparing to perform. However, he had heard about it from various reliable witnesses, including his good friends Sperchias and Euryleon. Both friends had claimed that the ex-king had done nothing to provoke the new king's insult. Demaratus, they conceded, might have been a little slow to get to his feet as Leotychidas took his seat on the Eurypontid throne, but he *had* stood. It was understandable, they said, that a man who had been king all his adult life found it difficult to treat his hated rival with the respect due a king, but Demaratus had done nothing to provoke Leotychidas.

"It was vindictive!" Sperchias insisted. "Purely vindictive. Leotychidas sneered at Demaratus in a tone that wasn't fit for a grown man, much less a former king. He was trying to provoke Demaratus into some truly disrespectful act. Just as he did during the Gymnopaedia."

Leonidas could well believe that. Leotychidas had been insufferable ever since the Delphic oracle declared Demaratus was not Ariston's son and the Council and ephors had set him aside. Leonidas had never liked Leotychidas, but even he had been surprised by the extravagance of the new king's household and his arrogance in dealing with citizens and perioikoi alike.

Demaratus, meanwhile, had been elected magistrate, and the majority of the citizens were sympathetic to his awkward position. After all, he had been raised to believe he was the rightful king. No one (except Leotychidas himself) accused Demaratus of knowingly usurping the throne. Yet during the Gymnopaedia, which had occurred shortly after Demaratus' deposition, Leotychidas had actually sent a man to ask "how it felt to be a mere magistrate after having been king." Demaratus had responded cleverly by saying that he at least knew what it was to be in *both* positions—a pointed reminder that Leotychidas had never been elected to any office. Then, with great dignity, Demaratus had pulled his himation up over his head and walked away in silence. In the more recent incident, Leonidas' friends reported, Demaratus had not answered at all, just repeated the gesture of covering his head.

That was what the public saw, but Leonidas knew that within hours of both incidents Demaratus' wife had been on her brother's doorstep pouring out her woe. She claimed Demaratus had returned home fuming and vowing to leave Sparta forever. She claimed he was threatening to go to the Persian court, presumably to request that the Persians restore him to his throne by force.

This news alarmed Leonidas enough for him to feel he must speak to Demaratus alone, but it wasn't until today that he had found an opportunity. During the games marking the Chalkioika, Leonidas noticed that the ex-king turned his back on the ball field the moment he spotted Leotychidas approaching. Leonidas had extricated himself from the crowd to follow him, catching up with him halfway to the agora.

"Demaratus!" Leonidas called out to stop him.

"Well, if it isn't Little Leo!" Demaratus sneered, turning to face Leonidas.

Leonidas drew a deep breath to curb his own anger. "I understand your bitterness."

"Good, then I hope you also understand your own cowardice! You could have prevented this!"

"How could I have prevented this?" Despite his best intentions not to get into a discussion on this point, Leonidas found himself unable to ignore such an absurd accusation.

"Don't play dumb with me!" Demaratus snapped back. "You may lack backbone and ambition, but you're not stupid. This oracle is no more genuine than any of the others your brother has bought in the last five Olympiads! It was forged by that weasel Asteropus! If you had taken up my offer to work together, we would both be kings, and Sparta would be in good hands instead of having the choice between a madman and a usurper to command her army."

"And because you are not king, you would betray Lacedaemon to the Persians?" Leonidas wanted to know.

"Where did you hear that?" Demaratus snapped—much too defensively for Leonidas' comfort. Then before he could answer, Demaratus added, "If you've been listening to that foolish woman you and your friend Alkander foisted upon me, you can forget it. She has the brains of a hare—if that. Percalus can go to Hades! She's brought me no heirs, just endless cares. I will divorce her. Tell your bosom friend, the stutterer, that!"

Leonidas held his tongue for fear that if he opened his mouth he would not be able to control his anger. Percalus had never been accused of being bright, and she *was* barren, but Demaratus had wanted her for her beauty and he had forced the marriage on Alkander, insisting on taking her despite her official betrothal to Leotychidas and her lack of dowry. Still, what really made Leonidas furious was the slur to Alkander. Alkander had indeed stuttered as a boy, and people had insulted him and imputed cowardice to him because of it. Leonidas had learned at a very young age, however, that Alkander was no coward and that what he had to say made sense. Few things angered Leonidas so much as blind prejudice.

Demaratus turned on his heel and walked away. Leonidas could only gaze after him, angry and concerned that Demaratus might indeed intend to go to Darius to request Persian troops to invade Lacedaemon and put him back on the throne.

Before Leonidas could resolve what he should do, however, a small, soft hand clasped his. "Father!" Simonidas whispered, using the form of address required of boys for all full citizens. "Father! Come quick!" Simonidas tugged at his hand as he had often done in the past, before he was sent to the agoge and taught his manners. "Crius is in trouble!"

Leonidas felt as if he'd been hit by lightning. Gorgo's water had broken in the night, and the women had collected to help her through this birth, while the men were banished from the house except for Nikostratos and Crius. The latter had remained with the sole purpose of bringing him news of the birth. Simonidas' words, that *Crius* was in trouble, made no sense to Leonidas, who instantly concluded that something terrible had happened to Gorgo. The fear made Leonidas lengthen his stride until Simonidas had to run.

As they rounded the corner, the fight was almost over. One youth was still on his feet, but he was bleeding from his nose and mouth as he faced one of the citizens. The other youth was curled up in a ball, trying to protect his head from the fists of one of the citizens. A third citizen held Crius against the wall with his knee as he punched him with both fists. Temenos had collapsed against the side of a building in a pool of blood, while Chryse was still held by the fourth youth. Her face was swollen, her hair hung in disarray, and her peplos was half off; it looked as if she had been briefly engaged in the fight.

"Let go of my helots!" Leonidas bellowed.

Startled, the four assailants turned to stare. For the first time, they were at a disadvantage. All young men were on active service and so subject to Leonidas' authority as a regimental commander. Hesitantly at first, but then more rapidly as the full extent of the potential danger dawned on them, they ceased their violence.

"Fall in!" Leonidas ordered, and the four men fell into line.

Chryse at once rushed to Temenos, pulling her torn peplos together modestly over her breasts, while the youth that was still standing went to his friend. Crius dropped to the ground and started vomiting into the gutter.

Leonidas was looking the four assailants in the face, one after the other. They kept their eyes straight ahead, focused over his left shoulder. He knew only one by name—Bulis son of Nicoles, a scion of one of Sparta's richest families—and, like the others whose names he could not remember, a member of the Guard. They were also all protégés of his brother Brotus.

"If you think my brother can stop you from being thrown out of the Guard after what you've done today, you are mistaken," he said slowly and deliberately.

That startled them. "But, sir, you haven't heard our side of it. Your helot and these youths *attacked* us!"

"Only to save Temenos!" Chryse screeched hysterically. "They've killed him, master! They've killed him, just because he loved me!"

Leonidas glanced over at her. Tears were streaming down her face and her whole body was trembling. One of the youths staggered over to her and went down on his knees to place the flat of his hand on Temenos' neck and feel for a pulse. Leonidas did not recognize the youth.

Leonidas turned back to the four guardsmen. "If he's dead, you'll not only lose your place in the Guard, you'll be tried before the kings and Council for *murder*." Leonidas was furious. How dare these brutal men call themselves Spartiates!

"He's alive, sir," the youth who had gone to Temenos declared, adding cautiously, "at least for the moment."

"Then I suggest the four of you go to Asclepius' temple and offer up urgent prayers for his life," Leonidas suggested. "If he dies, I promise you, I will see you *hang*. Dismissed!"

"But, sir! Your helot and these youths attacked us!"

"If they did anything inappropriate, they will be suitably punished, but in your skin I would be more worried about my own. Get out of my sight!"

As soon as they had disappeared, Leonidas went down on his

knee beside Temenos and checked for his pulse himself. Temenos was indeed still hanging on to life, but Leonidas shared the youth's concern that it might not be for long. He turned to the youth. "Who are you and how did you come to the assistance of Temenos?"

The youth had to reach up with the back of his arm to wipe away the blood dripping down from his nose before he answered. "Don't you remember me, sir? I'm Eurytus, son of Lysimachos. You helped me during my Phouxir when Temenos would have turned me in for stealing from your pantry."

"And you risked so much to help him now?" Leonidas asked, amazed.

"He was an eirene then, sir, and only doing his job. I know that."

Leonidas looked toward the other youth, who had staggered to his feet. It was Aristodemos, his attendant Meander's younger brother. Meander had been forced to drop out of the agoge because his father was too poor to pay the agoge fees for two sons and had favored the younger boy. When, after their father hanged himself and Aristodemos too was on the brink of being thrown out of the agoge, Meander had come to Leonidas, offering to sell himself into slavery if Leonidas would pay his younger brother's agoge fees. Leonidas had hired Meander as his attendant and duly paid Aristodemos' agoge fees, but he felt strongly that Meander was the better of the two boys—even if Aristodemos would one day be a citizen. He was surprised to find the spoiled Aristodemos here. "And you, Aristodemos?" he asked simply.

Aristodemos shrugged and didn't meet his eye. "It was four to one," he mumbled unconvincingly.

Leonidas guessed that Eurytus had led him into this, but he had to give Aristodemos credit for following. "Well done," he told the youth, and Aristodemos looked up, startled. He had waited a long time for Leonidas' praise.

At last Leonidas turned to Crius. He guessed at once that Crius had several cracked ribs, just from the look of the bruises that were already spreading across his naked chest. There was no telling what injuries he had sustained to his internal organs, but he did not look like he was going to die. "We'll get you fixed up," he told the helot, and then asked the question that was burning on his lips. "You were bringing me word from my wife?"

"A boy, master. A healthy boy, and the mistress is fine."

For a moment Leonidas could hardly believe it. After steeling himself for bad news, after pretending for two years that he didn't mind having only a daughter, it was almost too good to be true. "Truly?"

Crius managed a crooked smile. "Yes, master. You have a son."

It took Leonidas a half-hour to organize a stretcher to take Temenos to a military infirmary and to ensure that Crius and the youths were attended by one of the agoge surgeons. Then, at last, he took one of the horses he kept at the lochos stables and galloped home.

By the time he arrived, the women had washed and changed, wine had been distributed liberally, and a feast was in preparation, smoke billowing up from a crackling fire in the outside pit. The sound of laughter wafted over the roof from the terrace and greeted him as he swung down from his horse.

"Congratulations!" Hilaira called as Leonidas emerged from the stables. Then Chilonis, his stepmother and Nikostratos' wife, came to give him a kiss on both cheeks, announcing with warmth, "He's beautiful, Leonidas, perfect! Absolutely perfect!"

"And Gorgo?"

"She's so proud of herself. She's been asking for you every two minutes."

"Where is she?"

"Still in bed. Go to her, so she can get some sleep," Chilonis advised.

Leonidas did not need to be told twice. He started up the outside steps two at a time, but at the top of the stairs he nearly tripped over his daughter. "Daddy! Daddy!" Agiatis cried, holding up her arms to him.

Leonidas swept her up into his arms without stopping, and she clung to him, ducking from experience as he went through the bedroom door.

Gorgo had been sponge-bathed by the other women, dressed in a fresh linen chiton, and propped up in bed with her hand on the cradle beside her. "Leo!" she called out with a radiant smile. "Come see him!"

Leonidas swung Agiatis down but firmly held her hand as he bent to kiss his wife. Then he looked into the cradle.

"Daddy! Daddy!" Agiatis stamped her foot and held up her hands to be lifted up again.

Leonidas laughed and took her on his hip as he gazed into the cradle. His son slept blissfully, with his bright red hands balled into two fists on either side of his bald head.

"He's ugly!" Agiatis declared emphatically, eliciting a laugh from her parents. "I didn't look like that, did I?" she demanded, and got only laughs for answers. Then her father showered her with kisses of sheer joy and assured her. "No, princess, you were much, much prettier!"

Leonidas could not contain his joy: This boy changed everything. He was the direct descendant of the ruling king, and both parents were Agiads. Whether the Assembly voted to depose Cleomenes for madness or whether he just died of natural causes, this boy now stood in the way of Brotus' ambitions. Brotus might *claim* the Agiad throne, but Leonidas had a valid, legitimate means of opposing him. Leonidas would not let Brotus seize the Agiad throne without a fight.

Leonidas looked at Gorgo again. She was gazing up at him, smiling, but her eyelids were half falling over her eyes. He bent and kissed her again without letting go of Agiatis. "Get some rest. I'm not going anywhere."

"Where's Chryse?" Gorgo asked drowsily. "Her mother was angry that she wasn't here to help."

"She—Temenos—don't worry. It wasn't her fault. Get some rest." He kissed her on the forehead and then withdrew, closing the door behind him.

"Daddy?" Agiatis was thoughtfully picking at the brooch holding his red himation to his chiton. "Why is everyone so happy it's a boy?"

"Because, precious, only a boy can be king."

"But you aren't king," Agiatis pointed out.

"That's because your grandfather is still alive. When he dies, your brother will become king."

"But why won't you become king?"

"Because I have a twin brother, your uncle Brotus," Leonidas answered, hoping she wouldn't press him to explain how this barred him, but not her brother, from the throne. Leonidas started back down the stairs to the terrace.

Fortunately, Agiatis had lost interest in a throne she couldn't have, and asked instead, "Were you as happy when I was born?"

"Yes, of course," Leonidas lied. "And I'm happy now because your brother, when he grows up, will be able to look after you and your mother, even if something happens to me."

At the bottom of the steps to the main entrance of the Agiad royal palace, Gorgo paused to inspect her son. He was barely a week old and still very tiny, very red, and very sleepy. Gorgo adored him, but she was not blind to the fact that he was still a squirming infant; his character lay inchoate inside him, not yet apparent even to her. He was definitely different from Agiatis. He was gentler, less demanding, more easily satisfied. She wondered if those were traits he would have all his life, or if he would grow out of them. What had she been like as an infant? She had never thought to ask her mother. Maybe this would be a good opportunity.

But first she had to face her father. She took a deep breath and started up the stairs to the main portico facing Herakles Square. This portico was supported by a battery of six kouroi dating back to the age before Lycurgus. Once they had been painted, as was still the custom in other Greek cities, but during the last ten to fifteen Olympiads such decoration had become unpopular in Sparta and was increasingly scorned as extravagant. Newer buildings had plain white kouroi and pillars, but the royal palaces were not only ancient, they also represented the kings' divine ancestry. The ancient decoration had been left intact, except that wind and weather had dulled the colors over time.

At the massive, ten-foot double door, studded with bronze rosettes, the meleirenes on duty came to attention and opened both wings for the king's daughter without hesitation. That wasn't entirely correct, Gorgo reflected. She didn't live here anymore, and maybe her father didn't want to see her. His moods were increasingly fickle, and he was as likely to throw her out as welcome her.

Beyond the door she found herself in the large, formal reception hall. This had a high painted ceiling, frescoes recording the labors of Herakles, and a mosaic floor. The mosaics were uneven from age, and over the centuries some of the stones had been replaced for one reason or another so that the coloring was uneven, too. Surrounding the mosaic center were a shallow gutter and benches. Gorgo had been told that when the palace was built it had been customary for visitors to sit here while slaves washed the dust from their feet before they entered the palace itself.

Gorgo passed through the opposite door to an interior peristyle with a central fountain. Although Gorgo had rarely entered the palace this way, she moved confidently around the peristyle, avoiding the oppressive, ancient core of the palace with its fat, painted pillars and murals of legendary battles, and headed for the more modern courtyard around which the private apartments of the king were grouped in two-story buildings. Here she had the good fortune to encounter her father's personal secretary.

"Mistress Gorgo!" the man exclaimed, breaking into a smile. Before she could even answer he asked, "And is that the little one? What did you name him? Pleist—? Pleist—?"

"Pleistarchos."

"Yes. Pleistarchos. Isn't he a fine little man!" the old secretary declared as she held out the infant for his inspection. He smiled at the infant, offering a finger for him to hold in his fist. "You must be very pleased with yourself and that husband of yours."

"Yes. We are very happy."

"Come to show him to his grandparents, eh?"

"Yes—but it is a surprise," Gorgo admitted.

"Your mother is lying down, but your father is in the library."

Gorgo thanked him. To get to the library, she had to pass through the private courtyard. Here she kept in the shadows under the roof of the peristyle to avoid attracting her mother's attention. She would visit her later; she wanted to face her father first. The sight of the nursery window, however, reminded her that her mother had given birth to no fewer than four sons—and not one of them had lived to adulthood. Three of the boys had died as infants before they could walk or speak. The eldest, Agis, had died in an accident at the age of ten. She cast a frightened glance at Pleistarchos, sleeping as if exhausted in the crook of her arm. He was so very vulnerable!

She mounted the stairs to the gallery along the back of the library, and entered the library by the first door. Here she paused. King Cleomenes sat halfway down the room on a throne adorned with bronze griffins and swans. He sat at a table, peering intently at a scroll rolled out before him. The sound of someone entering distracted him, and he looked up and straight at her. He stared at her for a long time, almost as if he did not recognize her.

"Father."

Cleomenes just continued to gaze at her.

Gorgo started forward cautiously, her eyes on her father's. He looked older than she remembered him, older and more strained. He was only twelve years older than Leonidas, she reminded herself, amazed, but he looked twice that. His shoulders were starting to bend and his belly to expand. He did not exercise as much as citizens his age because he was not required to drill with a reserve unit, and in recent years he'd lost his passion for the hunt.

Only when she was right before him did she draw attention to her son. "I've brought your grandson to see you, father," Gorgo explained, holding Pleistarchos out for her father to see.

Cleomenes turned his eyes to the infant, and Gorgo held her breath. She could see the bandage on her father's arm from an incident shortly before Pleistarchos' birth. The palace servants had come to her in distress because, they said, he had tried to tear open his own veins, claiming someone had tried to poison him. What if he reached out a hand to do violence to Pleistarchos?

The king did reach out a hand, or rather a finger, but not in violence. Very gently he stroked the back of his grandson's hand. A smile spread across his face. His finger went up his grandson's arm, and then touched his forehead. Then Cleomenes pulled back his hand, straightened, and looked up at his daughter. "Your husband didn't have the courage to come face me?" he asked.

"My husband does not believe in coming uninvited."

"But he had no objection to you coming?" Cleomenes asked with raised eyebrows.

"My husband would not come between me and my own parents," Gorgo replied steadily. While this was true, it was also true that Leonidas had been opposed to her coming. He argued that if her father was interested in his grandson, he would either send for him or come to see him. He had been uneasy about exposing Pleistarchos to the unpredictable moods of a madman—and apprehensive about exposing Gorgo to the vituperative tongue of her father.

Cleomenes guessed the truth. "Ah, from being an unruly daughter you have turned into a disobedient wife," he summarized.

"If that is what you want to call it."

"What do you call it?"

"A plea for reconciliation, acceptance, a new beginning. You are my father, and I your only surviving child. I adored you once, and I thought you loved me."

"Loved you?" Cleomenes sounded surprised, but then he shook his head. "To say I loved you would not do justice to what I felt." His eyes went through her, seeing beyond the present to the past. He saw Gorgo as she had been: a bright-eyed, impertinent, but always observant child. Her older brother had never been able to focus on anything for long—his mind wandered and his attention was easily distracted—but Gorgo had tagged around behind her father whenever she could, taking an interest in whatever he did and said. She had been like a faithful dog, always in his shadow with adoring eyes.

"What have I done to so disappoint you, father?" Gorgo asked softly.

"You grew up," Cleomenes told her simply, and Gorgo caught her breath. She could not have stopped that even if she had wanted to, nor could she reverse it. If only being a little girl again would please him, then there was no hope for reconciliation.

Cleomenes reached out his hand and patted her arm. "Don't be distressed, child. I did not mean to suggest that you should have died like your brothers. I was simply noting that the changes were indeed inevitable. It was unreasonable to expect you to remain an adoring child. It was only natural you grew up, developed your own opinions and fell in love with a young man. You could have done worse than my brother Leo." That was the closest he had ever come to a compliment about Leonidas. Gorgo started to hope her gamble had paid off.

"Will you trust me to hold my grandson?" he asked her next.

Gorgo immediately handed over Pleistarchos, who stirred and frowned in his sleep but did not wake up.

Cleomenes inspected the boy very carefully, even unwrapping the blanket to inspect his chest, legs, and genitals. "He seems very healthy," he concluded. "Let us hope I live long enough for him to survive the agoge."

"I will do everything in my power to ensure that he is healthy and ready for the agoge."

"You will have to do more than that," her father warned, handing the baby back and looking hard into her eyes. "You must never, ever leave him alone without an armed man in attendance."

"Father, what are you talking about? We live practically in the heart of Lacedaemon. No enemy has come within—"

"That boy's enemy lives not more than five miles away. He will kill him, if he gets a chance, and women helots will not stop him. Surely your husband has one or two army helots he could spare for the protection of his son?" The insulting tone Cleomenes usually used when speaking to or about Leonidas tinged his voice again.

"Leonidas will not let any harm come to his son," Gorgo replied firmly.

Cleomenes narrowed his eyes as he considered her. "You and your son would be safer if you moved back into the palace."

"Me and Mother under the same roof?" Gorgo quipped back, and to her relief her father burst out laughing.

But when he was finished laughing, Cleomenes leveled his eyes at her and said: "I could send your mother away."

"Could you really?" Gorgo asked back. "After all she has suffered? The dead children and your infidelities? Could you throw her out, when she has done no wrong?"

"Are you my child or my conscience?" Cleomenes retorted, exasperated.

"I am your child, father—but if you can confuse me with your conscience, then that is only because I say out loud what *it* has already whispered to you softly."

"Why weren't you born a boy?" Cleomenes asked, wistfully and bitterly at the same time.

"So I could marry Leonidas and reunite the family."

"You do love him, don't you?" Cleomenes observed, not entirely pleased.

"Yes, I love him. More than I imagined possible."

"And I love you, Gorgo. Don't ever doubt that, no matter what happens."

Gorgo leaned forward and kissed his forehead. Cleomenes responded with a kiss to her cheek. Their eyes met at close range and Gorgo could see love in them—but also fear.

"What are you afraid of, father?" she asked very softly.

"I—am—not always—sure—of what is real," he whispered, his eyes clinging to hers for understanding.

"My love for you is real, father. And so is Leonidas' loyalty. And Mother's despair and need for you."

"But what about the snakes, Gorgo?"

"What snakes?"

"The snakes that have infested this palace!" her father answered, annoyed by her evasiveness. "They are everywhere! Not a room is free of them. Look at those shelves!" He pointed angrily at the honeycomb of shelves lining the library wall and designed for scrolls. "There must be hundreds of them nesting in there! They coil in the shadows and as soon as you sit still even for a moment, they slither over your feet, and at night they slip between the sheets and coil themselves around my ankles!"

Gorgo was speechless.

"Go! Take my grandson away before one of them worms its way into his blanket. They aren't poisonous, but I don't think it would be good for them to coil themselves around him as they do me. They might choke him by mistake. Take him to his grandmother, but don't put him down anywhere where the snakes can get to him."

"Yes, father," Gorgo answered, her stomach knotting itself with fear as she kissed him again on the forehead and then withdrew to seek out her mother.

Dienekes was an ambitious man. He always had been. But he did not come from a "good" family, and his father had made things worse with a bad temper that led him one day to kill a man in a rage. Dienekes had always felt he had to work twice as hard as his comrades to gain recognition, and he sometimes went out of his way to draw attention to himself. For example, rather than just braiding his hair from forehead to neck, he braided it at an angle from right eyebrow to left ear. It looked rakish, and not a few of the younger men were following his fashion. He had also taken to wearing chitons with red, white, and blue stripes. Combined with a red himation, these gave him a striking look. Thus he had gained a reputation as a dandy, which distracted people from the fact that he could not afford fine armor, and even after he went off active duty he carried a standard-issue shield with the lambda on it. It was a measure of his popularity among the younger men that others had started to do the same.

He was, therefore, extremely keen to succeed when given orders to bring ex-king Demaratus back to Sparta. Demaratus had made good his promise to abandon Sparta, leaving his wife behind. Demaratus claimed to be heading for Delphi, but there were too many rumors circulating about his intent to go to the Persian king for the ephors to be comfortable. After consulting with the Gerousia, they ordered a pentekostus to bring Demaratus back to Sparta. Dienekes' pentekostus was entrusted with the task.

By the time the decision had been made, Demaratus had a three-day lead—but a Spartan king, even a former Spartan king, attracted attention wherever he went. Every village he had passed through, even shepherds with their flocks, could readily confirm his passage and point in the direction he was headed. Furthermore, he had not traveled light, taking an ox-cart of personal effects and provisions as well as his chariot and no less than ten horses, four dogs, and a score of servants. This large entourage and convoy forced him to keep to the main roads.

By the afternoon of the second day, Dienekes' pentekostus was just hours behind him, and at nightfall Dienekes ordered the company to make camp while he went forward with just one other man to the next city, Zacynthus. After assuring himself that Demaratus was spending the night there, Dienekes returned, awoke his men, and brought them to the walls of Zacynthus, ready to enter the city as soon as the gates opened the next morning.

Shortly after sunrise the following day, they surrounded Demaratus' wagons and chariot as the servants were hitching up the teams and reloading the items used during the night. When Demaratus emerged from the large house where he had spent the night, he saw only a sea of scarlet and bronze completely surrounding and overwhelming his little convoy. He turned on his heel and retreated into the house.

Dienekes bounded up the steps and tried to follow him, but Demaratus' Zacynthian host blocked the way. "Demaratus, son of Ariston, is my guest. I will not allow you to violate my hospitality by seizing him!" the man told Dienekes indignantly. He was white-haired, tall, and elegant. He spoke with authority—and with a touch of contempt for the brash young Spartan officer.

"Let me speak to Demaratus!" Dienekes demanded.

"I will see if he *wants* to speak with *you*," the Zacynthian replied haughtily. "Who should I say begs audience?"

"Dienekes, son of Polybius, on orders of the ephors of Sparta!" Dienekes replied proudly—but he was still left standing before a closed door.

Dienekes had plenty of time to notice how foolish he looked with a hundred armed men surrounding an ox-cart and an empty chariot. Meanwhile, the whole town of Zacynthus collected to gape, point, and stare—or so it seemed to Dienekes.

Eventually the Zacynthian gentleman returned. "You may come in unarmed," he announced.

"Unarmed?"

"Yes. It is quite a simple procedure. You remove that baldric and sword and leave it, along with your spear, with your attendant," he explained patronizingly.

Dienekes had no choice but to comply, seething inwardly. Unarmed, he was at last admitted into the dark and richly decorated home. He was led down a corridor to a small atrium where he found Demaratus pacing back and forth under a low tile roof supported by slender pillars.

Demaratus was a half-century old. He was stocky, bowlegged, and scarred. His face was dominated by a large nose, and his hair was coarse and graying. Even as king he had not placed much emphasis on the trappings of royalty (unlike Cleomenes), and had usually dressed simply. Now he was wearing only a pale blue chiton under leather armor and practical, sturdy boots that came halfway to his knee. When he spun about and faced Dienekes, his eyes flashed like a caged lion. Dienekes instinctively came to attention.

"You!" Demaratus snarled. "Who do you think you are? How dare you stand in my way? I have every right to travel wherever I please!"

"No, sir. As a Spartan citizen under the age of sixty, you require the permission of your commanding officer to leave Lacedaemon." The ephors had provided Dienekes with this little speech.

Demaratus snapped helplessly for a retort. He had forgotten that every Spartan citizen serving in either an active or a reserve unit of the army needed the permission of his commanding officer to leave Lacedaemon; as king, he had never needed such permission and had traveled at whim. Furthermore, since he had been deposed, no one had seen fit to assign him to any particular unit in the army, as it would have been embarrassing for everyone involved. Since the reserves were not called up and there was no immediate prospect of that happening, the oversight seemed inconsequential. Now, however, Demaratus realized that he had no one from whom he could even ask for permission. He decided not to address the issue. "I am going to Delphi to consult the oracle. What on earth could be the objection to that?"

"I don't know, sir. I did not make the decision to come after you. I am only following the orders of the ephors."

"The *ephors*." Demaratus said the word as if it left a bad taste in his mouth. "Well, I suggest then that you go back to the *ephors* and find out what their objections are. I do not intend to return to Sparta just because the *ephors*—without explanation or apparent reason—order me to do so."

Dienekes opened his mouth twice, but he could not think of a suitable reply. He was abruptly confronted with the unexpected fact that he would have to use force to make Demaratus return with him. He realized that he was not prepared to do that. He tried a bluff. "I have a hundred men outside. It would be child's play for us to force our way into this house and seize you. Sir."

"Then do it, Dienekes," Demaratus called his bluff with a grim smile.

"Do you wish to see the innocent servants of your host, not to mention this noble gentleman," Dienekes nodded to the Zacynthian, still standing in the shadows listening to the entire exchange, "harmed?" Dienekes tried again.

"Not at all," Demaratus retorted. "Do you?"

"No, sir. But if you will not come willingly, I will *have* to use force. No one will be harmed if there is no resistance." Dienekes said this with a glance at the Zacynthian host.

The old man, whoever he was, drew himself to his full height and announced: "I will not allow my hospitality to be violated without defending it! If you use force against me and my household, you will have committed your city to war, because my neighbors, friends, and family will not allow me to be cut down in my own home. If I die, my death will be avenged. We may be a small and insignificant city in *your* eyes, but we are a proud people, Spartan. If you kill me and my servants just to arrest your former king, you will find we are a vicious and tenacious opponent that will take more than one of your red-cloaked warriors to a premature grave before you crush us."

"I doubt you were given the power to make war and peace, young man," Demaratus scoffed at him.

"No, sir," Dienekes admitted, and then looked at Demaratus a second time with a rush of unexpected respect. The former king was not mocking him, just showing him the bridge on which to retreat. "I will inform the ephors, sir!"

Yet in the moment of his victory, when it was clear Dienekes was going to let him proceed, Demaratus no longer looked fierce or even angry, only sad. Endlessly sad.

Dienekes turned to go, but something about Demaratus' countenance stopped him. For the first time since the oracle had delivered Apollo's judgment against Demaratus, Dienekes found himself wondering if it had been right to depose him. He reflected on the fact that Demaratus had always been a competent commander, and recently a good magistrate. Dienekes turned back to the deposed king.

"Sir, think about it once more. Being king isn't everything. There is nothing disgraceful in being a Spartan Peer."

"No disgrace, perhaps, but I cannot bow to the likes of Leotychidas and Cleomenes."

"Then don't! Come back and help us to keep them in check," Dienekes countered.

Demaratus flinched, and the sadness in his eyes deepened. "You're good, Dienekes," he murmured. "I wish we had a thousand of your caliber...."

"Don't we, sir?"

Demaratus shook his head. "No. We don't. That's what I've discovered in the last six months. Under the façade of equality and equal justice for all, we are riddled with intrigue and jealousy and hatred. If you thought the spectacle of Leotychidas humiliating me was demeaning, wait and see what awaits Cleomenes when Brotus makes his move."

"Come back and stop it from happening, sir!"

Demaratus shook his head slowly. "I am too bitter. Too full of hate. Go now, Dienekes." He waved with his hand, not in dismissal but in farewell.

Dienekes still hesitated. He felt he ought to have some argument that would persuade Demaratus to return. He wanted to find the right words not only because he did not want to return empty-handed, but also for the sake of bringing this seasoned and reasonable man back to Sparta. Half the Gerousia was senile, the ephors were mediocre men elected for not offending anyone, Leotychidas was interested only in his personal gain, Cleomenes was mad, and Brotus was dim-witted, brutal, and self-serving. Dienekes turned back one last time with the word "please" on the tip of his tongue, but Demaratus forestalled him with a shake of his head.

"Do not beg me, Dienekes. I do not want to see a Spartan officer beg."

"Then come of your free will, sir."

"You're persuasive, young man. You will go far. But I did not depart on a whim. My mind is made up. Now go, and don't look back."

As he watched Dienekes turn and walk away, however, Demaratus felt as if his heart were being slowly pulled out of his breast. It had cost him far less to say goodbye to his wife than to this young man, a virtual stranger, because Dienekes incarnated for the deposed king all the manly virtues of Sparta. Demaratus wondered if he would ever again have the privilege to see Spartan soldiers. Part of him hoped so, and part of him knew that the sight of them would tear him apart with regret.

CHAPTER 3

WAGES OF CORRUPTION

"THE FOUR GUARDSMEN HAVE SOME VERY powerful friends," Oliantus told his lochagos cautiously, his face drawn and worry hovering around his eyes. Oliantus had served as Leonidas' quartermaster for a decade, moving up the ranks in Leonidas' wake. Oliantus knew that on his own, he would have ended in obscurity—an intelligent, well-meaning man, conscientious and hard-working, but always overlooked, always second best. His whole life seemed a repeat of the long-distance race at Olympia more than a decade ago, when he had performed better than anyone expected, leaving a score or runners in his wake, but still had come in third behind two brilliant runners. His only comfort was that Leonidas, a truly exceptional man, trusted him, relied on him, and sometimes took his advice.

"Ex-guardsmen," Leonidas corrected, "and they are being protected by no one but my brother Brotus."

"Yes, your brother Brotus—and Bulis' father Nicoles—"

"Nicoles should be ashamed of raising such a youth! Nicoles is a magistrate, and his son tramples on the law with both feet by brawling in the streets like a Syracusan sailor!"

"Nicoles refuses to believe his son could do anything wrong, and your insistence on punishing his son is turning a man who once supported you into a bitter enemy."

"Temenos almost died, Oli. He cannot yet walk. The surgeon says he will have damage for life; the only question is how severe it will be. If we let these four thugs get away with what they did to him, we are barbarians. They broke the law, and in Sparta the law applies to all of us—including the kings, much less guardsmen."

"Nicoles argues that Temenos also broke the law through his liaison with your helot girl—what's her name?"

"Chryse. And if sleeping with helot girls is a crime, we are all criminals. Every Spartiate youth has a helot girl when he's growing up. It's how we learn about sex."

Oliantus smiled faintly. Leonidas was talking to him as if he didn't know. But he had had a helot girl, too, and he sometimes thought back to her wistfully. She had been kinder to him than his well-born wife. He sometimes wished ... But he did not have Temenos' courage. "Brotus and these young men have the support of a significant portion of the population, Leo. There are quite a few citizens who think the helots are getting 'above themselves' and need to be put down. They want to make an example of Temenos that will remind everyone that helots are inferiors and enemies. They say Temenos is undermining the foundations of our society and deserves to lose his citizenship—while his assailants, they argue, deserve to be rewarded, not punished."

"And they are wrong," Leonidas told his quartermaster flatly.

"They are many."

"How many?"

Oliantus shrugged to indicate he was not certain, then estimated, "Maybe a thousand two hundred, a thousand five hundred."

"That's at most 20 per cent of the population."

"A loud and angry 20 per cent."

"I will fight them, Oli," Leonidas insisted. "This is about who we are. Either we are civilized men who respect our laws and one another, or we are beasts and thugs who respect nothing but brute force."

"Leonidas, you know I support you. I only ask you to consider whether this is the *right* fight. And: is it a fight you can *win*? Might you not do more damage to your position and long-term goals by fighting this battle, than by letting it go, so you are stronger for the next fight?"

Leonidas stopped pacing and stared hard at his faithful quartermaster. Oliantus knew Leonidas intended to claim the regency at an appropriate moment. Oliantus was warning him that pressing charges against the guardsmen who had assaulted Temenos might jeopardize that move. He had to respect Oliantus enough to consider this possibility seriously.

Before he could answer, however, they were interrupted by a knock on the door, followed by the meleirene on duty entering to report. "Sir. Your wife has sent for you. She says you must come to the Agiad palace at once."

Leonidas stared at the meleirene for a stunned moment, and then grabbed his baldric off the wall and pulled it over his head as he started down the corridor at a run. In four years of marriage, Gorgo had never sent for him. Only an emergency could have induced her to send for him now. His first thought was that something had happened to Pleistarchos. Infants were terribly vulnerable, and Brotus wanted nothing more intensely than to see "something happen" to the boy that threatened his succession to the throne. But the summons to the palace suggested this had to do with Gorgo's father rather than her son.

On the front porch of the barracks Leonidas hesitated, unsure whether it would be faster to go to the stables and tack up one of his horses or just run. It was late afternoon. The pipes would soon wail out the call to dinner. If he took a horse, it would be easier to get to his syssitia from the palace, but it would delay him. The Agiad palace was not far away, and, by taking the back streets, he could avoid crowds that might slow him down. He started running.

The meleirenes on duty at the palace had left their posts beside the front door and were peering curiously around the side of the palace. When they caught sight of Leonidas, they pointed vigorously and called out, "The kitchen door! Your wife is waiting at the kitchen door!"

One of his own chariots and the pair of matched gray mares that Gorgo liked to drive were blocking the alley. As he ducked under the necks of the horses he could hear shouting and crashes coming from inside the palace. Gorgo was standing with her back to the door. Her himation had fallen off her head, and her hair was exposed; she looked stunned and helpless. Relief flooded her face when she saw Leonidas. "It's my father! He's trying to kill the cook!"

Leonidas took her arm in a gesture of reassurance. "He's doing what?"

"My father's trying to kill the cook. The staff sent for me, but when I went in he chased me out again. He's got his sword, and he's trying to hack his way through the door to the pantry where the cook has taken refuge."

Leonidas met her eyes, shook his head in momentary disbelief, and then nodded to indicate he was resolved. He turned, opened the door to the delivery entrance, and stepped inside with his hand on the hilt of his sword. Gorgo followed in his wake, clutching her himation around her shoulders.

They were greeted by crates of fresh vegetables that had been knocked over and cabbage heads that had rolled in every direction across the courtyard. Amphorae lay shattered on the paving tiles, spilling oil across the floor, while chickens fluttered about, screeching in panic. Leonidas slipped on the oil and fell, landing so hard on his elbow that numbness shot up his arm. Gorgo was splattered with blood from a headless chicken that was still twitching on a bench. Toppled chairs, heaps of broken pottery, and an overturned table greeted them next. From the room beyond, they could hear shouting. Cleomenes was hewing at a door with his sword and screaming at the top of his lungs: "Assassin! Assassin!"

The kitchen staff had evidently scattered or taken cover.

Leonidas gestured for Gorgo to stand back and advanced to just a few feet behind his father-in-law before asking in a firm, commanding voice, "What is this about, brother?"

Cleomenes spun about to look at Leonidas, apparently only moderately surprised by his sudden appearance. He then pointed with his left hand at the closed pantry door. "That man is an assassin! He put vile poison in my wine!"

"It's not true, my lord Leonidas! I swear on my mother's grave. It's not true!" The protest came from the far side of the door.

"That's old Prothous," Gorgo recognized and identified the voice.

"Assassin!" Cleomenes screamed, swinging his sword into the

door again. The blade sliced into the surface and stuck for a moment before Cleomenes yanked it free.

"Why in the name of the Twins would Prothous try to kill you, brother?" Leonidas asked, stepping cautiously closer to Cleomenes.

Cleomenes spun about and pointed his sword directly at Leonidas' heart. Leonidas was wearing a linen corselet that would not protect him from a direct thrust, and Gorgo called out sharply, "Father! Stop it!"

Cleomenes eyes shifted. "Gorgo!" This time he recognized her. "Get away! Get away! We aren't safe here anymore. Take Pleistarchos to safety! Go to Arcadia! To the springs!"

"Not without you, father," Gorgo answered, getting a grip on her own terror and moving steadily forward. Leonidas glanced at her and back at her father, uncertain if this was safe. Cleomenes was confused. He looked from Leonidas to Gorgo, then over his shoulder at the door. "Brotus! Brotus is trying to kill me," he declared.

"Now *that* I can believe," Leonidas conceded in such a normal tone of voice that Gorgo almost laughed, and Cleomenes was instantly disarmed. He let the point of his sword sink so that it no longer threatened Leonidas' chest. "You know about Brotus?" he asked in astonishment.

"Believe me, I *know* about Brotus. He has more than one murder on his hands already. He would like to murder both of us—and I don't doubt he has his designs on Pleistarchos. But poor old Prothous is not in his pay," Leonidas added, reaching out and taking Cleomenes' sword from his limp hand.

"You're sure?" Cleomenes asked, glancing again at the door.

"I swear, my lord. I swear!" Prothous raised his voice emphatically and hopefully.

"The wine tasted funny," Cleomenes felt compelled to justify himself.

"It was from Sicily, my lord. Maybe it was a bit off, but there was no poison."

"Let me taste it," Leonidas ordered generally, and Gorgo blanched.

"I threw it out the window," Cleomenes admitted with a giggle.

Gorgo reached her father's side and stroked his arm. "That was very wise, father. Whether it was poisoned or just off, it deserved to be thrown out the window."

Cleomenes stroked her cheek and looked at her as if she were his long-lost bride. "My child. Have you come home?"

"Only to see that you are safe, father."

"But you won't leave me alone tonight?" Already Cleomenes' look was wild again, and he looked around the shattered kitchen in alarm, as if expecting assassins to spring up from the corners.

Gorgo glanced at Leonidas, who answered for her, "No, we'll both stay with you tonight. Come, let Gorgo take you back into the house and we'll have some *good* wine together. I'll send word to your syssitia that you are ill, and to mine that I am looking after you."

Cleomenes docilely allowed Gorgo to lead him out of the kitchen. As soon as he was gone, Leonidas crossed to the pantry door and knocked once. "You can come out."

The door opened at once and a half-dozen terrified helots spilled out into the kitchen, while from outside came the wailing of the pipes calling the men to dinner.

"Fetch good wine—make it neat and put poppy seed in it," Leonidas ordered.

Prothous, however, was kissing his hand in gratitude. "You saved my life. You saved all our lives. He surely would have butchered us!"

The images of the wood by Argos were too vivid in his mind for Leonidas to dismiss the thought altogether, but he tried to reassure the terrified old cook. "It's over now. Put together a tray with things my brother likes to eat, especially fruit or nuts, foods hard to poison, and serve up a familiar wine laced with poppy seed. Gorgo and I will stay the night with him and see that he stays calm."

"Thank you, my lord," they murmured in unison around him.

"Don't call me 'my lord,'" Leonidas corrected them. "I'm just an ordinary Peer."

"Yes, my lord—I mean, sir."

At the door into the courtyard he glanced back at the chaos left behind by his father-in-law and the anxious faces of the kitchen staff, and he knew this could not be allowed to go on much longer.

The old man had his himation up over his head in a gesture of grief, and he shuffled more than walked. He had hitched his chiton up through his belt, exposing his scrawny, scarred legs, which were dusty to the knees. His feet were bare. Most people passing him on the road took him for little more than a beggar, at best a pilgrim. Agiatis, seeing him coming up the drive toward her father's house, ran home frightened.

Agiatis' agitated arrival warned Gorgo a visitor was on the way. She stopped weaving, pulled a himation over her peplos, and covered her head with a snood. If a stranger was coming unannounced, she did not want to look slovenly.

The old man reached the front porch and rang the bell. The helot Melissa opened for him and invited him inside, leading him to a bench in the hall, before she excused herself to fetch the mistress. Gorgo left the children on the terrace in the care of Laodice with orders to keep them quiet, then went to greet the stranger.

The old man was waiting for her with his walking stick between his knees. He looked up at her as she entered, with large, milky eyes covered with cataracts. Yet he knew her without seeing. "Lady Gorgo?"

"Hekataios!" she exclaimed, astonished. The old man had been a priest and royal seer as long as she could remember. He had assisted at almost every sacrifice of her childhood and had his own apartment in the royal palace. "What a surprise! Wait just one moment, and I'll bring wine and a snack."

"No need. I do not drink wine anymore," Hekataios answered, his voice flat and hollow as if he were already dead.

Gorgo felt a chill go through her and she clutched her himation closer. "Is something wrong, sir?" she asked. "Can I help you in any way?"

"All my life I have served your family," the old man answered, staring not so much *at* her as *past* her.

"Yes. I know. We have always valued you—"

"Valued me? Valued me? Is this how you pay someone you value?" he demanded in return.

"What do you mean? Has my father dismissed you?"

"No. He has killed me."

Gorgo stared at the man, so obviously alive, and knew no answer. She shivered again and wanted to flee as Agiatis had done.

"My son is dead," Hekataios declared woodenly.

"Your son? Asteropus?" Gorgo had heard that news, brought from Delphi by a runner weeks ago.

"Asteropus," Hekataios confirmed.

Gorgo held her breath. She had heard that Asteropus had been found at the foot of a cliff near Delphi. People had speculated about whether he had fallen by accident or whether someone had pushed him. The Agiad representative to Delphi had enemies, it was rumored. He lived an extravagant lifestyle and cohabitated with a Phocian woman, who had given him several children. The conservatives in Sparta were outraged by Asteropus' lifestyle, and even Leonidas did not like him, if for more personal reasons. No, Asteropus did not have many friends in Sparta, but he was said to have powerful friends in Delphi and even Athens.

"I went to Delphi," Hekataios told her in his dull, lifeless voice. "He had a woman." Hekataios dismissed his son's foreign concubine with a contemptuous wave of his hand and a sneer. "An illiterate goose. She did not understand the importance of things written down. She sold my son's papers to another man."

Gorgo still did not know what to make of this bizarre interview.

The old man focused his eyes on her. "The papers made everything clear. Your father—" He stopped.

Gorgo held her himation closer around her shoulders. "What about my father?"

"He—he bribed the Pythia. He bribed the *Pythia*! He corrupted the most sacred voice of Apollo—turning a servant of the Gods into a vile, self-interested creature who defiled her office with falsehoods!"

Gorgo drew a deep breath. Leonidas had long claimed that Asteropus' oracles were fraudulent. He refused to trust any of them. "You mean your son—"

"No! That's just it!" Hekataios all but shouted at her. "My son may have produced documents that he claimed came from the Pythia, but he never corrupted *her*. When he refused to condemn Demaratus, however, your father went to the Pythia *herself*! He paid her gold through a man called Cobon, and in exchange she lied. *She lied.* She pretended to speak the words of Pure Apollo when she was spewing sewage put into her mouth by your sick and selfish father! And now, because of my son's suicide and his stupid illiterate concubine, it has all come to light. The whole world will soon speak of nothing else! The vile woman who was honored with the most sacred office of Pythia has been disgraced and sent from the sacred city forever, and Cobon will be killed—if they can catch him."

"That sounds most just from what you say, Hekataios," Gorgo assured the old man cautiously, still bewildered.

He stared at her. "You still don't understand what I have said, do you? Clever as you are, you still don't understand."

"No. I don't," Gorgo confessed.

"The oracle about Demaratus was purchased with your father's gold, and the whole world knows it! Demaratus is the rightful king of Sparta and Leotychidas is a usurper, while your father is the most corrupt, vile, putrid, evil—" The old priest could not find words strong enough to express his hatred, and as he raised his voice, saliva splattered from his mouth with his bad breath and his anger. "Your father is—is the man who bribed the Pythia at Delphi!"

"Brotus wants Cleomenes deposed, not just exiled," warned Sperchias, one of Leonidas' oldest friends. It was the middle of the night, but he felt Leonidas had to be warned. "He's cobbled together a majority in the Gerousia, and they will put forward a proposal at the extraordinary Assembly tomorrow to depose Cleomenes—and with him Gorgo and Pleistarchos—as illegitimate bastards of an illegal marriage. The Assembly will then have no choice but to declare Brotus the rightful Agiad king."

Leonidas was wrapped only in his himation, having answered the knocking at the door from his bed. He was not yet fully awake, but he felt as if he'd gone through this all before. "I'm not surprised," he told his friend, clutching the himation around his shoulders from the inside, his bare feet sticking out below the uneven edge. "It's been Brotus' position for as long as I can remember. We were raised to see Cleomenes as 'that bastard.' There's hardly anything new about the claim."

"Everything is new! Cleomenes isn't a young prince with Chilon's blood in his veins. He is an aging man, who over the last quarter-century has slowly but surely squandered the support and respect of even the most conservative citizens. He turned Athens from a friend into a dangerous rival. He lost us the support of our allies in the League. He sullied our reputation as the saviors of Greece by failing to support the Ionian revolt, and he failed to subdue Argos—even when we had a chance. And now, as the final straw, he has earned us the disdain of the entire civilized world by corrupting the Pythia."

"He is mad, Chi," Leonidas answered simply and sadly.

"That's not the point, Leo!" insisted Sperchias, frustrated by Leonidas' apparent refusal to see the danger he was in. "The mood is ugly. People feel they were duped into deposing Demaratus, and they fear Apollo's vengeance for the insult to his oracle. An angry mob is one easily swayed by those who shout loudest."

"But it is less than a year since we—wrongly, it now seems—declared Demaratus illegitimate. Surely the Assembly is not going to be so foolish as to make the same mistake again."

"The Assembly can be manipulated," Sperchias argued. He knew. For years he had tried to get elected to public office, only to lose again and again because, he felt, Leonidas' rivals and enemies had manipulated the Assembly to stop him. And all the while, Leonidas had been focused on his family and his duties, keeping aloof from politics because he claimed not to be ambitious.

Leonidas nodded and put a hand on Sperchias' shoulder. "Thank you for warning me, Chi. Now try to get some rest."

"What are you going to do?"

"Sleep and collect my strength."

"Leo! Don't you understand? Brotus is going to come to Assembly tomorrow with a large body of men prepared to shout down any common sense. They are determined to win any vote, if not with numbers then simply by shouting louder."

"Then I will demand a head count," Leonidas countered.

Sperchias sighed in frustration. As so often in his life, he had brought forward good arguments and he had presented them cogently and clearly, but no one, not even his best friend, seemed prepared to heed him. He felt like Cassandra, warning of impending catastrophe and condemned to watch his vision come true. Discouraged and exhausted, he descended the stairs from Leonidas' front porch to walk down the long cypress-lined drive as the moon rose above Parnon.

Leonidas started up the stairs to his bedroom, but collided with his wife. She was sitting on the stairs, clutching her himation around her just as he was. She had been eavesdropping, but he could hardly blame her. What happened at Assembly tomorrow would affect her father, her husband, and her son. "What are you going to do, Leo?" she asked him earnestly.

"What *can* I do, my love?" Leonidas answered as he dropped down beside her and put his arm over her shoulders. "Your father is not fit to be king. You know that as well as I do. It is time he was set aside."

"But Brotus—"

He silenced her with a finger to her lips. "Brotus is more dangerous when he lurks around in the dark than when he makes a frontal assault in Assembly. You will see: just because people recognize your father is mad does not mean they think he is illegitimate."

Gorgo was far from comforted. Then she had a thought. "Leo?"

"Yes."

"Would you do me a favor?"

"What?" he asked cautiously.

"Tomorrow, when you go to Assembly, wear your father's armor."

Leonidas didn't answer for a moment. His father's armor was ancient because it had been inherited from his father King Leon—and it had been left to his eldest son, Cleomenes. Leonidas only had access to it because the palace staff treated Gorgo as their mistress, turning to her rather than her mother with their problems. If Gorgo asked them to bring this armor that had belonged to Leonidas' grandfather and father before it belonged to Gorgo's, they would do it.

The breastplate was too small for Leonidas across the shoulders and it cut in under his arms uncomfortably. He would not have thought to wear it for any military purpose, but it had been worn by Sparta's Agiad kings for fifteen Olympiads, and it was very showy and distinctive, with relief spirals on the breasts. If he wore it, everyone would know exactly what he was wearing, and it would send a clear nonverbal message.

He drew a breath and then nodded. "Yes. I'll wear it, if you can get hold of it in time."

Spartan Assemblies were held in the Canopy, a large stoa with a hundred columns in five rows, built some twenty-five Olympiads earlier by Theodorus of Samos. It was located on the street leading from the Market Square, beside a rotunda dedicated to the Olympians Zeus and Aphrodite, and the Temples to Athena of the Council and Zeus of the Council. It was also not far from Kastor's tomb, and Leonidas rode into the city early so he could go first to Kastor's tomb before proceeding to the Assembly.

Leonidas had viewed Kastor as his special protector ever since he had been a child. It was logical for him to look to the Dioskouroi—since they, like he, were Spartan princes and twins. His particular affinity for Kastor came from the fact that Kastor was the mortal twin. Because Brotus had always been bigger and stronger and more successful when they were boys, Leonidas thought of him as like the demigod Polydeukes, while he identified with Kastor. The association with Kastor was reinforced by the fact that Polydeukes was a boxer like Brotus, while Kastor was the master of horses, a role Leonidas was happy to play.

It was chilly this early on a winter morning, and the Eurotas River was shrouded in mist; the entire valley still lay in the shadow of the Parnon range. Leonidas dismounted and tied his horse behind the temple. He took olive oil, honey, and cheese, produce from his kleros, from a canvas satchel he carried over one shoulder, and set them upon the altar of the ancient Doric temple that marked Kastor's tomb. The offerings were modest because Leonidas despised gifts that had the appearance of bribery. He unloaded the goods in silence and then stood back and considered the ancient statue, which depicted Kastor smiling enigmatically.

Kastor and Polydeukes had been inseparable, and Polydeukes' grief for his mortal brother had been so great that he had been prepared to spend half his time in hell so that his brother could escape the grave every other day. In contrast, Leonidas reflected, if *his* twin got the chance he would kill him or his son for the sake of worldly power. Leonidas wondered if he had come to the wrong shrine after all. But just as he turned to leave, the sun abruptly cleared the Parnon range, and light flooded into the temple to light up the face of the mortal who had become immortal through the love of his brother. Even though Leonidas knew it was a perfectly natural phenomenon, he smiled and was encouraged nevertheless.

Leaving the empty satchel with his horse, he started for the Canopy. The street before the stoa was starting to fill up. The army did not drill when there was Assembly, and the young men came over in hordes from their barracks, while the older men were flooding in from the surrounding countryside on horseback and chariot. Under the roof of the Canopy, men were congregating in spontaneous groups that then drifted apart and reformed in new constellations. The faces, tone, and mood were earnest.

As Leonidas made his way through the crowd, his armor attracted attention. Some men even turned to follow him with their eyes, but he ignored the looks and focused on what his ears collected as he passed. He heard many angry and indignant remarks about Cleomenes coming from the clusters of citizens. Sperchias was right; sentiment was very much against his father-in-law. But that in itself was not a problem. He was as keen as anyone to see his father-in-law declared incompetent.

"Leonidas!" Leonidas halted and looked in the direction of the caller. Alkander, with Euryleon beside him, signaled for him to wait. Leonidas halted for his friends to catch up with him. A moment later Oliantus and then Sperchias joined him. Each noted his armor without comment—but Sperchias looked relieved, Alkander smiled, and Oliantus nodded his approval.

It was starting to get crowded in the Canopy as more and more citizens arrived, but there was still no sign of Brotus. Sperchias kept looking anxiously for him, muttering about how he was bound to be collecting his faction.

Finally Brotus appeared, just as Sperchias had predicted, surrounded by his hangers-on including Orthryades, Talthybiades, Lysimachos, and the four ex-guardsmen who had nearly killed Temenos. The older citizens ignored Leonidas as if he did not exist, but Bulis smiled as he went past and asked in a low, malicious voice, "How's that helot-lover friend of yours?"

"Better than you," Leonidas retorted, eliciting a puzzled look, but Bulis had to keep moving to stay with Brotus.

"How *is* Temenos?" Alkander asked.

"He's recovering, but that ass hasn't seen the end of this incident yet."

Alkander nodded absently, because his attention was drawn toward the front where the councilmen were arriving, including Leotychidas but not Cleomenes.

"Where's Cleomenes?" Leonidas asked in alarm. He had expected his father-in-law to put in an appearance at this critical Assembly. Indeed, he had counted on Cleomenes defending his legitimacy—and revealing his madness at the same time.

"I don't know," Sperchias answered.

There were seats for the Gerousia, because some of the men were very old. Leonidas turned to Alkander. "See if you can find out from Nikostratos where Cleomenes is." Nikostratos had taken his seat just one from the end beside Epidydes, the only member of the Gerousia who had been elected more recently than he. Alkander nodded and started to gently excuse himself through the press of citizens.

The ephors filed in, led by Technarchos. Leonidas thought the poor man looked ten years older than he had when he took office ten months ago. The deposing of Demaratus had been a crisis for him, and to now discover it had been predicated on a lie—that the momentous dismissal of a man who had ruled for a quarter-century had been wrong—had shaken the honest, true-hearted Technarchos to the core. As if that weren't enough, now voices were calling for the deposing of Sparta's other king. Leonidas thought Technarchos would be greatly relieved when his term as ephor ended and he could turn the burden of office over to someone else.

But today he had a duty to perform. He called the Assembly to order, and the traditional ode was sung to Athena. One of the priests from the Temple to the Bronze-House Athena performed the sacrifice of a cock and announced that they could proceed. Finally the Assembly moved to the agenda. Technarchos laid out the facts: irrefutable evidence had come to light proving that King Cleomenes had bribed the Pythia in Delphi to obtain the judgment against Demaratus.

"That only means we have no valid judgment," Leotychidas pointed out, in a loud voice that carried to the back of the Canopy. "It doesn't mean that the opposite is true!"

Technarchos looked uneasily at Leotychidas, while a ripple of comment swept through the Assembly. Like it or not, most people felt compelled to admit, Leotychidas was right. *Apollo* had not given any judgment in the issue at all. They were back to where they had been nine months ago—except that Demaratus had fled the country and Leotychidas was sitting on his throne.

Technarchos continued. "In light of this scandalous abuse of his office, the Gerousia finds King Cleomenes unworthy of his high office. He has broken his covenant with Fair Apollo and besmirched the reputation of our city. The Gerousia proposes that the Assembly find King Cleomenes of the Agiad House guilty of sacrilege and that he be set aside in favor of his rightful heir."

Technarchos fell silent. The entire Assembly appeared gripped by the seriousness of the charges and the decision they were about to make, and then Brotus shouted out: "Cowards! You—" Orthryades grabbed Brotus and said something directly in his ear. Brotus shook off the other man and continued in a loud voice: "The world is laughing at us, and we can only imagine what punishment Apollo plans." There was a general murmur of agreement at this. The citizens were acutely aware of both their humiliation and their vulnerability. "King Cleomenes should never have been king!" Brotus continued. "He is a bastard no less than Demaratus."

"We don't know Demaratus was a bastard!" someone called from the crowd.

"But we *do* know Cleomenes was a bastard! Until we throw the bastard out, we cannot prosper. The Gods abhor bastards. We must restore our honor and placate the just anger of Fair Apollo by repudiating this charlatan who calls himself a king!" Brotus' words succeeded in eliciting a rumble of assent from the Assembly. A quick glance around the crowd revealed that most men were nodding. The success encouraged Brotus. He repeated in a low, confident bellow, "Cleomenes should never have been king!" and added, "My heroic brother Dorieus was the rightful king of Sparta!"

Calling to mind this paragon of youthful virtue, who had

died heroically in Sicily, was clearly a better ploy to win popular support than claiming the throne outright, Leonidas conceded. He wondered who had advised Brotus, and suspected the wily Talthybiades.

But when Brotus tried to continue with "My brother Dorieus—" a shout of "Dorieus is dead!" cut him off. Leonidas turned to see who had made this salient point, but could not locate the speaker in the crowd.

Meanwhile, Brotus' faction ignored the objection and started to chant: "Out with the bastard! Out with the bastard!" The chant rapidly mutated into the simple: "Out, out, out!" as it spread across the Assembly.

Leonidas' friends were starting to look alarmed, and stirred uneasily. They glanced repeatedly at Leonidas, until the latter at last raised his voice: "I have a question."

Relieved, Technarchos signaled, then shouted, for silence. Gradually the chant died away and a semblance of order returned. Technarchos nodded to Leonidas to speak.

Leonidas leaned forward and spoke directly to his twin rather than to the Council, ephors, or Assembly. "Just who are you proposing as the rightful Agiad king, Brotus?"

"Me, of course, you bone-headed dolt! I'm next in line to the true heir to the throne. A bastard's brat's babe and a bastard's wishes mean nothing! I am the oldest surviving son of King Anaxandridas by his legal wife."

A cacophonous uproar followed until from the back of the Assembly someone shouted, "Prove you were the firstborn twin, Brotus!"

"Who said that?" Leonidas asked his companions, surprised, but they didn't know.

The ephors were consulting anxiously among themselves, and the eldest member of the Council, Hetoimokles, kept demanding from his fellows an explanation of what was going on.

Desperate to regain control of the situation, Brotus blustered furiously, "Everyone knows I'm the firstborn twin. Everyone! Leonidas was a little runt!"

This remark brought guffaws of laughter, particularly from the younger age cohorts, who could not remember when Leonidas had indeed been smaller than his twin brother.

But Brotus' followers countered by taking up the chant of "Brotus! Brotus!"

Technarchos raised his voice above the chant to announce: "We will vote on the motion to depose King Cleomenes for blasphemy!"

"Not until we know who his rightful heir is!" a voice shouted back from the crowd.

"I am his rightful heir!" Brotus insisted, and his entourage of young men, led by Bulis, chanted again, "Brotus, Brotus!"

Leonidas raised his voice and shouted, "Pleistarchos is Cleomenes' heir!" But no one took up a chant of "Pleistarchos! Pleistarchos!"

"I told you this would happen," Sperchias said in a low voice to Leonidas. "Spartans don't want an infant for their king."

"He's right, Leo," Euryleon agreed. "No one knows your son is even going to survive to adulthood, much less what sort of man he'll turn out to be."

"They'd be getting me as regent."

"We haven't had a regent since Lycurgus."

"Not a bad precedent."

Alkander was back. Leonidas turned to him desperately. "Where is he? Where's my other brother?"

"Nobody knows. He did not attend the Council meeting. When they sent for him, they were told he did not want to be disturbed."

The chants for Brotus were growing louder and stronger, while the rest of the Assembly appeared to be arguing among themselves.

Leonidas tried again. "My son Pleistarchos is Cleomenes' heir! Cleomenes has recognized him. He is Agiad on both his mother's and his father's side. We should depose Cleomenes in favor of Pleistarchos!"

This only caused the debate to become more heated still. Men argued with the men beside them, while the chant for Brotus became an incessant drumbeat that was only gradually overpowered by a new chant calling for "Vote! Vote! Vote!"

"Do something, Leo!" Sperchias urged desperately.

Technarchos shouted for silence, and amazingly both chants died away and the Assembly fell into a restless silence. "Those in favor of deposing King Cleomenes, say 'Aye!'"

Brotus' faction shouted wildly, but the rest of the Assembly was remarkably still.

"Those opposed?" asked Technarchos, apparently as startled as Leonidas.

"Nay! Nay!" The shouts erupted from all around them, and Leonidas joined in, baffled by the turn of events. It amounted to little more than a vote for a familiar evil over the unknown, but in the face of what Cleomenes had done, it surprised him nevertheless. It was also a clear vote against Brotus, but Leonidas took little comfort from this in the face of the obvious lack of support for Pleistarchos.

The Assembly started to disperse, but Leonidas found himself surrounded not just by his friends, but by virtual strangers as well. They were saying to him what they had said to their fellows only moments earlier. "The boy's too young, Leonidas! We can't afford an infant king in times like these!"

"I would be regent," Leonidas again tried to make the point, but the men shook their heads.

Alkander caught sight of Dienekes toward the back of the crowd. He slipped out of the circle immediately around Leonidas and caught up with the debonair officer. "Dienekes!"

Surprised, the officer looked over with a raised eyebrow that gave him a haughty look.

"Were you the one who questioned whether Brotus is really the older twin?"

Dienekes shrugged and retorted, with a touch of defensiveness disguised as self-assurance, "It's a fair question, don't you think?" But then he seemed to remember that Alkander was Leonidas' closest friend and dropped his voice to add, "Cleomenes may be mad, but Brotus is a man without scruples or honor. I can hardly imagine a worse king."

Nodding, Alkander drew Dienekes even farther from the dispersing crowd and dropped his voice. "When Leonidas and Brotus were born, their mother was over forty. She knew she could not nurse them both, so she brought two helot girls to the palace, one for each of the twins. They were present at the birth."

Dienekes was listening very attentively, but he said nothing.

"It would be wise," Alkander said very softly, "to find those girls before Brotus does. . . ."

Dienekes looked hard at Alkander. Up to now he had not taken much note of him, a man known to have been a stutterer as a boy, an unremarkable soldier, and now the assistant deputy headmaster for the *little* boys—a position that Dienekes did not think important. But Dienekes was rapidly reassessing his opinion. He nodded slowly. "Yes. I think that is a very good idea. Can you tell me any more about these girls? Where are they? What are their names?"

"Seek me out in five or six days, and I will have all the information you need by then—but say nothing about this to Leonidas."

Both men looked back toward Leonidas, who was still surrounded by a crowd. "Does he have any idea of how much depends on him?" Dienekes asked.

Alkander nodded. "He knows. But he is very stubborn and he likes to do things his way. He does not want to lower himself to Brotus' level, and he does not want to break the law."

Dienekes nodded, then smiled, a smile that women generally found irresistible. "Then let's be sure he doesn't have to break the law, shall we?"

Chapter 4

A SPARTAN EDUCATION

By the Feast of Alexandra word had reached Sparta that Cleomenes was in Thessaly. While the Assembly had debated his fate, he had slipped out of Sparta, allegedly to go hunting, and had never returned. Cleverer than Demaratus, Cleomenes had traveled light and in disguise. Only weeks later were the Spartans able to trace his trail east to Argos, where Cleomenes had taken to the sea. Ships left no tracks that dogs could follow and no string of witnesses with memories of a passing stranger. Thus it was not until word filtered back to Sparta that their king had been seen, indeed received with great hospitality, in Thessaly that they knew where he had gone.

Most Spartans were not entirely displeased with the development. Cleomenes' disappearance removed the madman from their midst and postponed the need to face the thorny issue of determining his successor. Brotus raged and Sperchias worried, but the majority of Sparta's citizens hoped the problem would somehow just go away.

Leonidas put his hopes in Pleistarchos growing up. He reasoned that if Pleistarchos was not just an infant but a boy in the agoge, a boy already showing himself mentally agile and physically fit, a boy with obvious promise (as his father was certain he would be), then the majority of Sparta's citizens would take a chance on him. Gorgo, on the other hand, worried that her father, mad as he was and cut off from his familiar surroundings, would come to harm. Yet there was nothing she could do. Thessaly was hundreds of miles to the north, and she had two small children and a husband in Sparta....

On the whole, the Spartans were more distressed by the news that Demaratus had been seen in Sardis. Demaratus, like Hippias before him, had evidently sought out the hospitality of the Persian satrap and, according to Ionian traders, he too had been received graciously. Demaratus, the rumors suggested, had asked to be taken to the court of the Great King. Demaratus wanted revenge on those who had deposed him—and that was the entire Assembly. Among themselves the Spartans asked anxiously, "And what if he *was* the rightful king after all?"

Leotychidas countered by pointing out that Demaratus was a traitor. Anyone, he argued, who could befriend a despot like Darius was at heart also a tyrant. Darius, after all, had murdered his predecessor and then slaughtered every Mede in the city just to cover his own tracks.

Even Leonidas, whose feelings toward Demaratus were ambivalent, found his feelings hardening against the Eurypontid. Leonidas understood that Demaratus wanted revenge on Leotychidas and Cleomenes for their unscrupulous plot against him. He even understood Demaratus' resentment of his loss of status. Leonidas could have forgiven Demaratus for going to Thessaly as Cleomenes had done, or to Macedonia or Thrace—but not to Persia. Going to Persia was, literally, going too far.

Leonidas was not alone in feeling this, and it was because Demaratus had gone to Persia that no one suggested, much less undertook, a second attempt to get the opinion of Delphi on Demaratus' legitimacy. People doubted Leotychidas' right to the throne, but they were not prepared to beg Demaratus to come back. So they lived with the situation, some more uneasily than others, and trusted in the Gods to keep Sparta from some catastrophe.

Late one afternoon shortly after the Achilia, the meleirene on duty at the entrance to the Mesoan headquarters reported to Leonidas, "There's a boy outside asking for you, sir."

"A boy?"

The meleirene shrugged. "He looks about eight—at the most, nine."

"Asking for me?" Leonidas pressed the meleirene, amazed. Boys of the agoge did not usually seek out contact with full citizens, much less officers or officials.

"Yes, sir."

"Well, let him in," Leonidas agreed with a shrug.

"He didn't want to come in, sir. He's out on the front porch."

Leonidas frowned, vaguely alarmed. It was really *very* rare for a boy to want adult attention. Leonidas remembered spending the better part of his childhood trying to avoid it. "I'll be right back," Leonidas told Oliantus, and went out to the front porch of the lochos headquarters.

It was a beautiful early spring day and the air was pleasantly warm. The barracks looked out on one of the smaller squares of the city and faced the main temple to Asclepius. The square was as empty as the porch of the barracks. Leonidas frowned and turned to return inside. Then he spotted, crouched behind one of the pillars and clutching his knees to his chest, a boy with his himation pulled completely over his head and shielding his face. One of the hands hidden in the folds of the coarse woolen garment was trembling.

Leonidas went down on his heels before the boy. His sword tip scraped the pavement as he asked softly, "You asked for me, boy?"

A sob answered him, and then a hand was thrust out of the himation. It was swollen twice its normal size and covered with blisters, some of which were putrid.

Leonidas didn't need to see any more. In a single motion, he swept the boy up into his arms and carried him inside the barracks. The boy dropped his head onto Leonidas' leather corselet and sobbed miserably, the himation still covering his face.

As he passed his office, Leonidas called into Oliantus. "We'll talk later. I have to take care of this first."

He almost collided with one of his enomotarchs. "Sir—"

"Later!"

Leonidas cut across the atrium to the divisional infirmary, calling out to the helot orderlies lounging around in the sunshine, "Get the surgeon!"

They looked astonished, but hastened to obey.

Leonidas reached the infirmary. It was empty of patients. He set the boy down on the nearest bed, which was made up with fresh, clean linens. He pulled the himation from the boy's head. As he'd suspected, it was Simonidas. "I—I only—came—because—" Simonidas was trying to get hold of himself, wiping at the tears with his good hand. "I—I—can't move—my fingers—and—"

"Shhh!" Leonidas ordered, pressing him back onto the little pillow and holding his hand on the boy's forehead. He wasn't good at these things, but he thought Simonidas had a fever.

"You sent for me, sir?" the divisional surgeon started, but then he caught sight of the boy. He crossed the room in two quick strides, took one look at the hand, and started calling for his orderlies.

"Can you save it?"

"I don't know. Who is he? How did it happen?"

"Simonidas son of Alkander, and I wager it was done *to* him." Leonidas kept his eyes on Simonidas as he said this. Simonidas said nothing, but he didn't protest, either.

The surgeon raised his eyebrows, but he said nothing—just set about preparing his instruments and getting the plants, powders, ointments, and pastes he wanted. Leonidas stood beside Simonidas with a hand on the little boy's bony shoulder. Simonidas closed his eyes. The tears had stopped. He took a deep breath.

"Give him that!" the surgeon ordered, handing Leonidas a kothon with a sticky, unpleasant-smelling liquid in it. Leonidas looked skeptical. "Give it to him *now*," the surgeon ordered. Leonidas slipped one hand under Simonidas' head and held the kothon to the boy's lips with the other. He didn't have to say anything to encourage the boy to drink.

Although he unconsciously made a face, Simonidas was at the end of his nine-year-old strength. He had turned himself over to the adults and surrendered all personal will in doing so. He would do whatever they asked of him, even kill himself if that was what they wanted. He'd tried for more than two years to survive on his own, and he had failed. It was that simple. But the thought of failure enclosed him as he started to drift off to sleep, and for a brief moment he wanted to cry out again from the sheer agony of realizing he had failed his father, his mother, his big brother, and everyone! And then he heard Leonidas say over his head, "Relax, Simonidas. Everything will be all right."

The first thing he heard as he came to again was his mother's voice. He heard it as if it was far away, and yet it was very clear and emphatic. "I knew he was going to have trouble from the very start. He is not a herd animal. He can't be put in a herd and chased around like he's a boneheaded calf!"

"That's the way the agoge is organized, and it works for most of us," Leonidas answered reasonably.

"But not for all of you!" Hilaira retorted sharply. "There has to be some way of making exceptions for boys who aren't suited to the agoge."

"If we start making exceptions, the whole system will break down."

"Well, maybe it is *time* to let it break down," Alkander answered softly but firmly.

Hearing his father say something as heretical as this made Simonidas sit bolt upright. At first he couldn't figure out where he was. The room was completely dark, but a gentle, indirect light was coming in through an open door. Slowly he made out the silhouette of a handrail, and, after a moment, he realized he was in the upstairs bedroom of his parents' town house. The voices had to be coming from the hall and hearth room on the floor below. He flung back the soft covers and paused to look at his hand. It was still there. That was a good start. It was bandaged, and now that he looked at it, he decided it was throbbing and uncomfortable, but it didn't really hurt. He made a tentative attempt at moving his fingers, but gave up; the bandages were too tight. He stood up, looked around for his himation, didn't see it, and so continued on to the gallery naked. It was chilly but not really cold. He could see shadows moving, and he could hear the adults better.

Leonidas was pacing back and forth and saying, "... The rich will pay for exemptions for their sons and raise them to be pampered sissies just like the Athenian dandies I saw! The next thing you know, they'll be buying places in the Guard, and officer's berths in the army—just like in Corinth and Athens, where wealth alone determines a man's rank. In the end, there will be nothing left of what makes us who we are!"

There was a moment of silence, and then Alkander said, "Leo, I know you feel very strongly about this, but you saw the condition Simonidas was in. What if he had waited another day or two? Not every boy in the agoge would have had the courage to demand to see a lochagos—nor have the good fortune to be given a hearing if they did."

"No, most boys would have gone to their fathers," Hilaira pointed out, making the others—including Simonidas—catch their breath.

"What is that supposed to mean?" Alkander asked defensively. "Are you saying I've failed him in some way?"

"Not failed him," Hilaira equivocated, "but I think it is a very sad commentary when a boy in such straits went to a practical stranger."

"I'm hardly a stranger!" Leonidas protested, and Simonidas leaned over the railing and called down: "Mom, you don't understand!"

The adults instantly stepped out into the courtyard and looked up at him, all four of them—his parents, Leonidas, and Gorgo.

Simonidas ran down the wooden stairs into the courtyard to fling himself into his father's arms. Alkander clung to him for a moment, and then Simonidas freed himself and turned to his mother. "It's only because of who Dad is. Because he's a deputy headmaster. If I went to him it would be ratting."

"And going to one of the most powerful men in the city isn't?" Hilaira asked in disbelief.

Simonidas had not looked at it that way. Leonidas was just his father's best friend, a man he had known all his life, a man he trusted. He tried to explain, "But, Mom, he can't do anything to them. He has to go to the Paidonomos, but if I'd gone to Dad, then—then it would have been ratting."

The nine-year-old's logic escaped the adults, but they were not inclined to argue with the little boy. Hilaira, noting he was naked, was more worried about him catching cold and wound him in her own shawl, while Gorgo suggested they go back to the fire.

Simonidas took shameless advantage of the obvious concern of the two women to declare that he was starving. He asked his mother if they didn't have "real" (meaning white) bread and asked Gorgo if she'd brought any sweets. The women shooed him indulgently toward the hearth, leaving the two men behind, arguing. "Leo, we've been through this before: we aren't equals, and no amount of making us wear the same clothes and suffer the same indignities as children will change that."

"It's not just about being equals," Leonidas countered. "The agoge is about giving every boy the same start in life. It is the best means to teach all boys about our history and our laws, to teach the songs we sing, the way we honor the Gods—our ethos. And it is a *good* education, Alkander! Have you never talked to Ibanolis? He spent twenty years in Athens and swears that what we teach here is far more valuable. He says we make philosophers, not sophists. We value truth over argument, and prefer silence to specious discourse, whereas in Athens it is the reverse. In Athens they mocked him for being old-fashioned and provincial. They laughed at him for his accent and his clothes because, there, everything must be in the latest fashion. Athenian youth have no respect for age or wisdom."

"And you think our youth does?" Alkander asked incredulously. "You should hear what the boys say about Ibanolis behind his back! They are only polite to him to his face."

"Well, at least they *are* that. In other cities they are impudent and rude."

"At what price do we buy that hypocritical politeness? Simonidas almost lost his hand. Other boys are ruining their backs or their feet because they carry too much and walk too far—all out of *fear*. Fear of ridicule, fear of scorn, fear of not being accepted."

"Then someone isn't doing their job! The eirenes are supposed to ensure that no serious harm comes to the boys."

"Not all eirenes are up to the job, and you know it! What if Brotus had been given a class of defenseless seven-year-olds?"

"That's what you and the other agoge officials are there to prevent."

"How in the name of Almighty Zeus can we do that when we have a power-hungry sadist as headmaster!" Alkander exploded. There was so much passion in his voice that the others, even the two women and Simonidas, turned to stare at him.

Alkander broke away, ashamed of what he'd said in front of his son, crossed the courtyard, and went out into the street, the door clacking shut behind him.

Leonidas looked at the shocked women, focusing on Hilaira.

She shook her head. "You have no idea what it has been like since Alcidas took over, Leo. He's to blame for this!" She indicated her son's hand. "Technically, maybe, it was two other boys in the herd, but *they* only risked doing it because they were certain that their eirene would let them get away with it. And their eirene let *them* get away with it because he was too afraid of Alcidas to face him down!"

"That can't be!" Leonidas protested, and followed Alkander outside.

He found him standing in the narrow alley staring at the stars.

Alkander did not turn as the door behind him creaked open and clacked shut. He knew it was his best friend. He just started speaking, while still gazing up at the stars. "Just last year at the Gymnopaedia I found myself talking to a stranger who, like most, was avidly interested in our agoge. I told him how free the boys were and how we teach them not to judge a man by what he wears. I explained how every citizen takes equal responsibility for all the boys, and how the boys share among themselves. Although I did not lie, it was not the truth either—because, in the end, education consists of teachers and pupils. It is all about individuals."

"Yes, of course," Leonidas agreed, adding, "and institutions. Eirenes come and go, and so do instructors and headmasters, but the agoge itself is stronger than that."

Alkander turned on him and asked explosively, "Do you know what Alcidas did to the two youths who came to Temenos' rescue? He had them flogged for attacking citizens. Four respected citizens all but killed one of their fellow citizens just because they don't like the woman he's sleeping with, but two youths who came to the aid of the victim were taken down to the pits and flogged as if they'd neglected their duties or committed sacrilege! Aristodemos dropped early, of course, not willing to suffer for something he'd been led into, but Eurytus had to be carried off unconscious. He was furious about a punishment that he felt was unjust."

The silence was tense. Then Leonidas asked, "Why didn't you tell me?"

"What good would it have done? Alcidas has the right to order them flogged, and it is *their* right to decide how they will stand up to it. The problem isn't one flogging or another, it is the cumulative impact of too many floggings, insults, and downright *indifference* to the welfare of the boys themselves. Yet another youth tried to run away this week. That's three this year. I don't remember anyone in our time even contemplating it, do you?"

Leonidas shook his head.

Alkander continued, "When we were growing up, we were told that we would never be punished without telling our side of it. Even when charges were brought against you by the Eurypontid king, you were given a chance to tell your side of the story."

"It would have done me no good if you hadn't spoken up for me," Leonidas reminded Alkander. He would never forget that this was the start of their friendship.

"That's the point, Leo! We were just two—what were we? Ten-year-olds?—and me a notorious stutterer always in the place of dishonor, but when I said you were telling the truth and a priest and king were lying, Epidydes believed *us*. He dismissed the charges. Alcidas lets the boys tell their version of things, but he doesn't *listen* to them. They might as well be speaking to a stone wall. Formal protections that are not *lived* are worthless. Most boys, and particularly the eirenes, have given up expecting any kind of fairness. They think the system is stacked against them, and they believe they are just expected to *endure* everything."

Leonidas was inwardly shaken. "A sense of justice is fundamental to respect for the law. If youth think they will be punished regardless of whether they are right or wrong, then they will grow up without any sense of right and wrong at all—only self-interest."

"Exactly," Alkander agreed, gratified that Leonidas at least grasped the significance of what he'd said.

Leonidas shook his head. "The agoge is the foundation of Spartan society. If it is in the wrong hands, future generations will be ruined."

"Yes," Alkander agreed again, meeting his eye.

"Come back inside. We can't discuss this out here in the street."

Alkander turned and they went together back into the house, but they stopped in the courtyard just inside the door so they would not be heard by the others. The cheerful sound of the women and Simonidas chattering together filtered out of the hearth room with the soft light of the fire. Leonidas came to the only possible conclusion. "If Alcidas is that bad—"

"He is!"

"Then he has to be removed. The Gerousia must propose his dismissal and the Assembly must approve it."

Alkander nodded tensely. To seek the removal of his immediate superior smacked of insubordination, if not outright rebellion. It made Alkander suddenly nervous when he realized what he had done. He was a little afraid of his own courage, and his hands started sweating.

"We will have to have concrete evidence of his misuse of power."

"Oh, Leo!" Alkander cried out in exasperation. "That's just what we don't have! Alcidas *appears* to do everything 'by the book.' He fulfills all the formal requirements, from inspecting barracks to daily eirene briefings—he just doesn't give anyone a chance to disagree with him. You should hear the tone of voice he uses with the eirenes! Or the way he talks about them behind their backs! He has nothing but contempt for his charges, and they can sense that—but he doesn't do anything you could charge him with in front of the full Assembly."

Leonidas thought about this for several seconds, and then decided. "Then we must go to Epidydes. If we can convince him that Alcidas is as bad as you say, and he introduces a motion against Alcidas, his word will be enough to sway virtually everyone who went through the agoge under his aegis. If Epidydes sticks by Alcidas, it will be impossible to find a majority, even in the Gerousia."

Alkander sighed. He hated politics precisely because it was always about "finding a majority" for things that ought to be simple common sense. And he hated politics because negotiations and building majorities were slow, uncertain processes. Politics took time, and he didn't know how much longer he could endure Alcidas' leadership. If it hadn't been for his sons, he would have quit months ago.

But what good was he doing his sons? Or any of them? No one under Alcidas' control could do anything. Help had to come from outside, from the Gerousia. "Even if Epidydes were to turn against

Alcidas, do you think you can find a majority in the Gerousia with Leotychidas presiding?" he asked his friend.

"Leotychidas is planning to go to Aegina. The Athenians have talked him into going—or rather, made it worth his while. He'll get no regulars, but will take volunteers. That means there will be no kings in Lacedaemon. Epidydes will only have to convince the other elected members—assuming we can convince him to take the lead on this."

Alkander nodded unhappily. It seemed such a frail hope in face of a situation he considered increasingly acute, but there seemed nothing more to say. He changed the subject, "What of these rumors that your brother has left Thessaly and is now making trouble in Arkadia?"

It was Leonidas' turn to sigh. "They are true."

Alkander was silent. If the mad king was in Arkadia stirring up trouble, then the question of his rightful successor would surface again soon. Too soon. Pleistarchos was still an infant. Alkander felt a chill run down his spine. If Brotus seized the Agiad throne, there would be no hope of replacing Alcidas, and the entire city would be in the hands of two utterly unscrupulous kings.

"Who is going to lead the paeans, make the sacrifice, and crown the victor?" Gorgo asked her husband as she finished her toilette for the feast of Artemis Orthia.

From the Sanctuary of Artemis of the Goats high up in the Taygetos, the procession of maidens, with their escort of troops carrying torches, would have started. The maidens were selected for their grace, beauty, and voices (Gorgo had never been among them), while escort duty was an accolade awarded the pentekostus that had most distinguished itself in the course of the previous year. The procession was by now winding its way down the lower flanks of the mountains toward the valley and the Temple of Artemis Orthia, where the annual ritual commemorating an ancient battle, in the form of mock combat between the sixteen- and seventeen-year-olds, would be staged.

Conducting religious rituals such as this was traditionally the duty of the kings, not the elected officials. The kings were the high priests and the protectors of tradition, the symbols of continuity with the past, and the living link to the Gods through their divine ancestry. Traditionally, both kings sat on the thrones provided and together opened and closed the ritual—making the sacrifices, leading the opening and closing paeans, and most important, crowning the victor. Traditionally, the Agiad king opened and the Eurypontid king closed the ceremonies. When one king was absent, the other performed both the opening and closing rituals.

But Cleomenes was still in self-imposed exile and Leotychidas was in Aegina with an all-volunteer force, "restoring order" against the will of the population. Thus, although Sparta had three kings (if one counted the deposed but possibly legitimate Demaratus), there was none in Sparta to perform the ritual duties.

"I'm sure the ephors will have come up with a solution," Leonidas answered his wife, gesturing to Meander, who had just appeared at the door. Addressing the young man a little impatiently, he ordered, "Help me with my hair. We're running late."

Meander was already dressed in leather armor and greaves over a fresh, clean sleeveless chiton. He promptly took Leonidas' bone comb from the dresser and set to work combing out his shoulder-length hair, asking as he did so, "Do you mind if I join my brother for the festival, sir?"

Meander's brother Aristodemos was now a meleirene, but for years Aristodemos had scorned Meander's company, ashamed to be seen with a non-citizen, a mere attendant. It was because of his thanklessness to his elder brother that Leonidas had long held a low opinion of Aristodemos. Leonidas turned to look questioningly at Meander.

"He asked me to, sir," Meander said, not without a mix of pride and embarrassment.

"If that's what you want," Leonidas agreed in a tone that suggested skepticism, before adding, "Now, better hurry with my braids, or we'll be late."

"Do you want them straight or diagonal?"

"Straight, of course. I'm not one of Dienekes' rakes."

Gorgo had been waiting patiently throughout this exchange, but now she remarked as if casually, "I wouldn't trust this crop of ephors to make any decision that is very sensible."

Leonidas could not turn his head because Meander was working on his hair, but his eyes shifted. "They were the lowest common denominator—the only way to stop Brotus from getting his candidates elected."

"I understand," Gorgo agreed. "I just think... maybe you should wear my father's armor again."

"*My* father's armor," Leonidas corrected.

It was both: it had been Leonidas' father's armor before it had been Gorgo's father's armor. Gorgo laughed, but she repeated, "Wear it, Leo."

"You have no idea how uncomfortable it is!" he protested with a frown.

"Not as uncomfortable as Brotus' rule would be," she answered.

While Meander hitched up the horses to the light chariot, Leonidas peered across the river toward Taygetos for some sign of how far the procession had progressed on its way down the mountainside. By now, he thought, it ought to be swelling with families, the matrons with their cheeses, men in armor, and helots and perioikoi in their festival finery, not to mention the children frolicking in excitement. Apparently, however, there were too many trees blocking his view, because he saw nothing.

Once they joined the main road, they were in traffic. Many other citizens with kleros this side of the Eurotas were riding or driving with their families to the temple of Artemis Orthia. By the time they reached the city, the streets were congested. They caught up with the end of the crowd in Lycurgus Square and could see the torches of the escort several blocks ahead, giving off more smoke than light as dawn broke. They turned down the next alley, following the progress of the procession by ear. The singing sounded clearly through the morning air. People joining the procession took up the song the maidens were singing, so the chorus was constantly increasing. At the divisional barracks they turned the horses over to a helot groom, and Meander went in search of his brother Aristodemos.

Leonidas and Gorgo followed after the crowd on foot. Although the procession was a good half-mile ahead of them, they were confident of overtaking it because the procession moved slowly.

Suddenly, Alkander joined them. "I was waiting for you on the porch of the barracks, but you didn't see me."

"Alkander! Aren't you supposed to be at the temple with the rest of the agoge officials?"

"Leo ..." he started, glanced briefly at Gorgo, and then took a deep breath and announced, "I couldn't take it any longer. I quit."

Leonidas stopped dead in his tracks and turned to face his friend. Alkander looked down, ashamed.

"Why?" Leonidas demanded.

"Alcidas has won."

"What do you mean?"

"He's broken me."

"I don't believe you."

"Leo, last night one of the eirenes came to me and said one of the sixteen-year-olds was too ill with fever to take part in the ritual today. He begged me to go to Alcidas and explain the situation, to get the youth excused—"

"Why hadn't he gone himself?"

Alkander shook his head. "Leo, listen to me! The boy's eirene *had* gone to Alcidas, but the answer had been no. So the boy's brother, also an eirene, came to me for help. And I *turned him down*. I refused to go to Alcidas on behalf of a sick sixteen-year-old youth. I had a lot of excuses. I said that since the boy's eirene had already tried and failed, I didn't have a chance of success. I said, bitterly, that taking the side of the youth would only turn Alcidas against him even more. I said—it doesn't matter what I said. It was all sewage! The fact is: I was too scared to face him. Scared, Leo. So, you see, I've become the trembler everyone always accused me of being."

The sound of singing was growing fainter, while the sun brightened the sky behind the Parnon range, and birds were singing jubilantly at the promise of a warm, sunny day. It was as if they were utterly alone in an abandoned city.

Leonidas stared at his friend. Alkander looked as if he had not gone to bed, certainly as if he had not slept. The skin of his face hung upon the fine bones that had made him such a classically handsome youth. His eyes were bloodshot and sunken, underlined by dark circles. His chiton looked as if he'd slept in it, and over it he wore leather training armor rather than the bronze the rest of the city was wearing today in honor of Artemis.

Leonidas had a thousand questions and didn't know where to start. He decided on, "What are you afraid of?"

"He reduced me to stuttering the other day," Alkander admitted, looking away, not meeting Leonidas' eyes. "In front of everyone."

Leonidas felt himself returned to his childhood, when Alkander had been incompetent at everything, a time when he had stuttered whenever he opened his mouth in front of others, causing them to mock and belittle him. It had taken years for him to overcome that handicap, but it was now two decades since he had stopped stuttering.

Leonidas understood, but Gorgo didn't share those memories. She was a mother of a boy who would one day have to go through the agoge. She couldn't stop herself from asking, "What about your sons?"

"If I thought there was anything I could do to protect my boys, I would." Alkander's eyes burned almost feverishly at Gorgo as he said this. "But I *can't*. I can't help *any* of them. If I even try, it will do them more harm than good."

"What happened last night exactly?" Leonidas asked.

"One of the eirenes, Maron, came to me and said his younger brother, Alpheus, had a fever and stomach cramps and could hardly stand up. I asked why he was coming to me, and he said because his brother's eirene had already reported the situation to the Paidonomos, but Alcidas' answer was that if Alpheus wasn't fit to compete, he could just sit in the safe zones all day."

"That's absurd!" Leonidas protested. "He'd be utterly disgraced for the rest of his life."

"But the eirene, not unnaturally, felt he'd done his duty, and told Alpheus what the Paidonomos had said, but he also told his fellow eirene, Maron. Do you know him? Orsiphantus' son?"

"Wasn't Orsiphantus the man who died in the fires the year I lost Eirana and the twins?"

"Yes, exactly. His barn caught fire with the bull inside. He went in to free it, but the roof collapsed and he was trapped under the main beam, pinned down but not dead. Maron saw it happen, and the helots had to drag him away screaming. I have no idea if he was hurt in some way during the incident, but since I've known him he has been—well, not really slow-witted, but not the brightest. Still, he's very conscientious and kind. I wanted to give him a class of seven-year-olds because I thought he'd be protective of them and ease them into the agoge, but of course, because I suggested it, Alcidas overrode me—"

"You say, 'of course.' Does he always override your suggestions?"

"Leo, haven't you listened to anything I've said in the past year?"

Leonidas took a deep breath and started walking in the direction of the temple of Artemis Orthia, his thoughts so focused that he lengthened his stride and Gorgo had a hard time keeping up with him.

Alkander fell in beside them. He did not know what Leonidas was thinking, and he would have liked to. He almost wished Leonidas were asking all those cruel questions he'd been asking himself throughout the night; if he'd been forced to defend himself out loud, maybe he would have convinced himself instead of simply hating himself.

They reached the temple precinct around the shrine of Artemis Orthia. As usual the crowd was large, spilling out of the actual precinct, and to Leonidas' astonishment they were already singing the initial paean. Since the sun had not yet cleared Parnon and latecomers were still trickling in, the ceremony appeared to have started prematurely. Then again, he supposed, the ephors were not used to managing these things.

As lochagos, Leonidas was entitled to a position near the front of the crowd, so with Gorgo clinging to his elbow and Alkander trailing, he started to worm his way through the crowd. As he neared the front he got a glimpse of the two thrones set up opposite the entrance to the temple. They should have been empty. Instead, Brotus was occupying the Agiad throne. Leonidas cursed himself under his breath, and glanced back at his wife.

Brotus stood to make the offerings to the Gods with a great deal of unnecessary theatrical show (as far as Leonidas was concerned). He was wearing his flashy armor over a red chiton with a gold border that glinted as the sun burst over the peaks of Parnon on the other side of the valley. He had also stiffened the crest of his helmet with gold wires, and these too caught the sunlight. Someone was giving Brotus good advice, Leonidas noted with inner fury, and he looked fleetingly for Sperchias with a twinge of guilt. Sperchias had been warning him about this for months....

The sacrifice done, Brotus turned demonstratively to the defending youths, waiting eagerly with their canes cut and ready in their hands, and signaled for them to take up their positions flanking the entrance to the temple. He then waved to the sixteen-year-olds to start stripping down and oiling in preparation for the ritual attack.

Leonidas pulled Alkander closer and asked urgently under his breath, "Which one is Alpheus?"

Alkander pointed out the youth. He looked flushed, but several of the youths were flushed from sheer excitement, and the oil made them all shine. Leonidas nodded. "Stay here," he ordered Alkander, while taking Gorgo's elbow again. He pushed the rest of the way through the crowd toward his brother.

Brotus turned and watched as Leonidas approached, with a smug expression on his face. Only at the last minute did he realize Leonidas' goal, and by then it was too late. Leonidas laid his hand on the Eurypontid throne. Brotus looked about at the crowd with a gesture of outraged astonishment, as if asking them to protest. A ripple of undefined excitement spread through the crowd, but no one voiced a protest.

Brotus set his jaw, then leaned over to mutter in Leonidas' ear, "You're superfluous, as always. You could have stayed home. I doubt anyone would have missed you."

"You miscalculated," Leonidas retorted, seating himself on the Eurypontid throne with a degree of inner unease that he hoped was not visible. Although he did not feel comfortable occupying a throne that did not belong to him, he could not afford to leave Brotus unchallenged, and the looks Nikostratos, Kyranios, Sperchias, and, indeed, virtual strangers in the crowd cast him were more than approving—they were relieved. Gorgo, meanwhile, moved to stand between the two thrones, her head held high and a reassuring hand on her husband's shoulder.

Brotus' eyes shifted resentfully to Leonidas' armor, but any further exchange between the brothers was cut off by a shout signaling the start of the mock battle. Public attention was drawn away from the Agiad twins, both impersonating kings, to the sixteen-year-olds, who rushed forward to storm the little temple.

As usual, the first assault swept virtually everyone inside without much trouble, but because the youths trickled out in ones and twos rather than collecting and charging out as a group, they gave the seventeen-year-olds good targets. Since the sixteen-year-olds were still fresh, little damage could be done at the speed they were moving. They turned over their cheeses to their eirenes at the tables in the shade of the plane trees by the river, and then, rather than collecting into a pack again, they turned to rush the temple in an even more disjointed, strung-out fashion. This gave the defenders all the advantages, and the spectators could hear some of the blows hitting home. Leonidas couldn't remember seeing a class of youths perform so poorly. There seemed to be no cohesion, teamwork, or élan.

Alpheus had made it in and out once, but he was trailing behind the others. The leaders were already emerging with their second cheeses when he turned to make his second attempt. Because Leonidas was watching him so closely, he saw the youth stagger a little, as if dizzy, but he couldn't be sure. Alpheus went up the steps not at a run but at a walk, his arms crossed over his head to protect it from the blows of the defenders' canes. Stoically, he accepted blows to his naked shoulders, arms, and back. He got inside the safety of the temple. The last of those who had gone before him ran out again, and the leaders were on their third assault—still strung out and competing individually against one another rather than working in teams.

Alpheus emerged from the temple with his second cheese. He bent over, holding the cheese to his belly, and started down the stairs. He was not running, just taking one step at a time as if it were an effort. The seventeen-year-olds lashed out at him, but their attention was distracted by the youths coming the other way. Alpheus, however, missed his footing or his balance and suddenly fell headlong down the stairs. He dropped his cheese, and it rolled away to the edge of the crowd.

The crowd let out a collective cry at the sight of Alpheus falling, but when he continued to lie there, apparently stunned, voices called out to him—some rude, some concerned—to get up. Leonidas, from his front-row seat, could see that Alpheus was still conscious. He moved. He got his hands under his chest and tried to push himself up, but by now some of the seventeen-year-olds had come off the steps of the temple and were all over him with their canes. As the blows rained down on him, Alpheus sank under them rather than trying to get up and away.

It was when one of the seventeen-year-olds threw an alarmed look over at the Paidonomos, clearly longing for orders to desist, that Leonidas knew Alpheus was really sick. He sat up straighter and looked sharply at Alcidas.

Alcidas took no notice of what was happening at the foot of the temple steps. He was watching the temple entrance intensely; then he looked toward the tables as if to get a count. There was some sort of scuffle going on among the eirenes. Two were obviously trying to hold a third back, who was flailing at them furiously. A third and fourth eirene jumped on the struggling youth, and the Paidonomos didn't stop that either.

Leonidas looked back at Alpheus. Now several of the seventeen-year-olds were looking to the school officials for guidance, and their blows had become more perfunctory than serious. They wanted permission to stop. But the school officials were all studiously looking somewhere else. The crowd was shouting—some for the seventeen-year-olds to stop, others for them to 'do their duty,' some for Alpheus to get up, others for the Paidonomos to intervene.

Leonidas stood up and walked over to Alpheus.

At the sight of a citizen in bronze approaching, the seventeen-year-olds drew back, even before they recognized him. Once they realized a regimental commander and Agiad prince was approaching, they retreated even further. Leonidas heard Brotus screaming, "Come back here, Leo! You have no right to interfere! Come back!"

Leonidas ignored his twin and the crowd. He wasn't even sure what the crowd was screaming. He went down on his heels beside Alpheus. The youth was vomiting and drenched in sweat. He was much too big and heavy for Leonidas to pick him up as he had Simonidas, so he threw his cloak over him instead and shouted to the orderlies, "Stretcher!"

The orderlies responded with alacrity. They had watched the spectacle, half-expecting the summons—although, as helots, they were never really sure when their Spartiate masters would ask for assistance.

Meanwhile the rest of the boys, defenders and attackers alike, had fallen into confusion. The mock battle had ceased while everyone stared at Leonidas. The eirene who had been overpowered by his fellows took advantage of the stunned reaction of his assailants to break free and run up beside Leonidas. "He fell sick yesterday, sir! I tried to warn—"

"You must be Maron." Leonidas stopped his flood of words.

"Yes, sir." The eirene came automatically to attention.

"We'll talk later. Return to your post."

"Yes, sir."

As soon as the still-vomiting youth was lifted face down onto the stretcher, Leonidas started back to his throne and, with a wave of his hand, indicated that the ritual should continue. And it did. He found that remarkable. He had just walked out there, done what he had no right to do, and the entire city accepted it—except Brotus and his minions, of course. The latter were howling "unfair" and "coward" and demanding that Brotus call his brother to order.

"How dare you do that?" Brotus demanded. "You understand nothing of this ritual! *I* was the Victor of Artemis Orthia in our time!" He said this loudly, to remind as many people as possible.

Leonidas leaned over and whispered in his brother's ear, "Victor of Artemis Orthia? Do you think I don't know you *murdered* your way to that title?"

Brotus caught his breath and turned his head sharply. Their eyes met. Leonidas could see the alarm in Brotus' eyes. He must have truly believed that he had gotten away with murder. He appeared genuinely amazed that his brother knew what he had done.

Leonidas seated himself, and from behind him Gorgo whispered, "Well done!"

Although the sixteen-year-olds were still competing, the attention of the crowd had disintegrated. Some people were watching the agoge surgeon, who had gone to meet the stretcher bearers and was now looking at Alpheus, checking his eyes, his pulse, and other vital signs. Others were watching the eirenes and the school officials, who appeared agitated. Others were focused on the kings and Council. Only a few were still watching the boys.

Under the circumstances, the boys, not surprisingly, gave up. Most sought the shelter of the safe zones; all waited to see what would happen next.

"You've ruined everything!" Brotus declared angrily. "This is a disgrace! Half the cheeses are still on the altar."

Leonidas looked over at the tables where the eirenes, school officials, and Paidonomos were together in a group. "Do we have a victor?" Leonidas called out.

Alcidas looked back at him with open hatred in his eyes, but he had control of his voice. "No, there is a three-way tie."

"This is disgusting!" Brotus barked, turning on Leonidas to assert aggressively: "This is all your fault!"

"Is it?" Leonidas asked back, then stood and approached the school officials while the crowd chattered excitedly in his wake. "Who are the three youths?"

They were pointed out to him.

He called them over to him. They formed a line in front of him. One had a bad welt across his upper left arm, the second had ugly scrapes on his knees, and the third was nursing a swelling lip. Leonidas walked around them to see their backs, which inevitably took the worst blows. He could see welts starting, but none of the youths looked like they were near the end of their strength.

As he walked back around to the front of the youths, Brotus joined him, but Leonidas forestalled his brother, asking, "So, how many cheeses do you have?"

"Four, sir," they replied in a ragged chorus.

Brotus snorted, and even Leonidas found the number paltry. He'd collected five in his time without being among the top contenders. He'd been in the temple snatching his sixth when he'd discovered his classmate Timon in a coma. In their distress for their comrade, he and his friends had forgotten all about the cheeses and rushed out to tell their elders—only to discover that no one had been interested in what they had to say. Meanwhile, Brotus had continued competing, had collected eight cheeses, and had been declared the winner. Timon died three days later without ever regaining consciousness. After that, Leonidas had never much liked this ritual.

Now he looked at Brotus and announced, "I don't think any of them deserve to be declared a victor, do you?"

Brotus spluttered in indignation; Leonidas had just stolen his line. He had expected Leonidas to favor ending the competition—which would have given him the opportunity to heap insults on him.

"I think," Leonidas continued, speaking to Brotus, but around them everyone was listening so intently that the crowd was gradually falling silent. "I think either they should agree to compete until one of them is the winner, or we declare this a year without a winner. What do you think?"

Brotus was cooking with anger, but he could hardly disagree. "I agree," he croaked out.

Leonidas turned back to the three youths with an expression of inquiry. They looked at the seventeen-year-olds, who were standing about uncertainly in front of the temple, and then at the agoge officials. Someone in the crowd called out: "What are you waiting for? Go for it!"

After that, many people started giving the same advice, some calling to the youths by name. With an exchanged look, the three contenders made a ragged dash for the temple, catching the defenders off guard. Ten minutes later a victor was finally declared with seven cheeses.

The moment had come when traditionally the Eurypontid king crowned the victor. Brotus got to his feet with a belligerent look toward Leonidas, warning him to stay out of the way, but he had not reckoned with Gorgo. Before anyone grasped what was happening, she snatched the prepared wreath of yew from the cushion it had been waiting on between the thrones and handed it to Leonidas. While Brotus choked on his indignation, Leonidas stepped forward and crowned the youth; then he stepped back and struck up the paean to Apollo.

"I'll kill you!" Brotus threatened in Leonidas' ear, his words drowned out by the singing crowd. "I'll kill you and your son!"

"You can try," Leonidas answered.

As the paean ended the crowd started to disperse, with everyone talking at once. Leonidas was certain there would be repercussions. There was no way of predicting what the majority would think of the shabby performance Brotus and he had put on today, but he also knew there was now no retreat. He immediately turned upon the Council before they could get away, and announced in a loud voice that carried far: "I want an inquiry into why a boy with a severe fever was participating. I want a *full* inquiry."

"You have no right to demand anything, Leonidas son of Anaxandridas!" one of the oldest Council members told him in a breathy voice, trying to dismiss him with a wave of his gnarled hand.

"I have as much right as any citizen."

"If anything was amiss, let the boy's father—"

"The boy's father is *dead*—and aren't we all supposed to be fathers to our youths? I want an inquiry—"

"I'm sure the Paidonomos just didn't know—" Eukomos, another elderly councilman, started.

"He knew, and I have three witnesses who can testify that he knew." As he spoke, Leonidas focused his eyes on Epidydes. He had approached him after the incident with Simonidas, but Epidydes had been reluctant to believe what Leonidas told him and insisted he would conduct his own discreet inquiries. Leonidas was relieved to see Epidydes nod slowly and finally speak up in a low voice: "I think we should at least ask Alcidas to explain himself."

Alcidas was already there. "Leonidas is quite correct," he announced in his precise voice. "I was informed that the youth had a fever. I found it highly suspicious—not to say convenient—that he had developed a fever the very night before this important test of his courage, and I pointed out that he was perfectly free to seek out the safe zones if he didn't feel up to competing."

Several of the Council members reacted indignantly, but others nodded as if this were perfectly reasonable.

Alcidas was continuing, "Of course, once I saw that Alpheus was really ill, I was about to intercede, but the Agiad forestalled me." He smiled at Leonidas with his lips, while his eyes wished him a shameful death and an unmarked grave.

Around him most of the Council members were docilely nodding their heads, but Epidydes was frowning. The former Paidonomos asked his successor, "Why didn't you send the agoge surgeon to at least check on the youth last night?"

"It seemed such an obvious excuse," Alcidas dismissed the suggestion. "I would have treated my own son no differently."

Leonidas found this a facile answer, since Alcidas had no son, but the moment for discussion was past. Several of the councilmen started saying this wasn't the time or place for a discussion. It was a holiday, and time for everyone to go home. After all, everything had turned out all right in the end....

Leonidas was left with a bitter taste in his mouth as the sanctuary grounds emptied around him. He looked for Alkander, but could not find him.

"He will have gone on ahead," Gorgo read his thoughts. "We can talk at his kleros." The two families always spent the afternoon following Artemis Orthia together. Leonidas' chief helot tenant, Pelopidas, and his family had been told to take the children to Alkander's kleros by cart while the Spartiates were at the temple.

"You can start walking, and I'll go fetch the chariot," Leonidas offered.

Gorgo did not protest. It was a pleasant, warm spring day.

As Leonidas passed through the line of poplars that marked the edge of the sanctuary, a form separated itself from the trees. It was an eirene, who came to stand respectfully before Leonidas with his eyes down and his hands at his sides.

"Maron," said Leonidas, recognizing him.

"Yes, sir. You said we would talk later, sir."

"Yes. Walk with me back to the city, would you?"

"Yes, sir."

Leonidas glanced sideways at the youth. He was exceptionally tall, with a broad, flat face and straight black hair. He was not a handsome youth. His features were too rough for that, his lips too thick. The words 'gentle giant' came to mind, prompted by Alkander's report of wanting to put him in charge of seven-year-olds.

"Tell me about yourself, Maron."

"Sir?"

"What age boys do you have charge of?"

"Thirteen-year-olds, sir."

"That's a challenge. You need to prepare them for the Phouxir."

"Yes, sir."

Leonidas stopped and looked at the youth again. He just stood with his eyes down.

"Are you afraid of me, Maron?"

That got a response. He glanced up, flushing. "No, sir!"

"Then talk to me."

The youth swallowed visibly. "I—want to thank you, sir. For interceding on behalf of my little brother."

Leonidas noted that when Maron said "little brother," it was not derogatory, not like when his elder brothers had used the term to describe him: it was simply protective.

"He's not a coward, sir. He wanted to compete as much as any of his fellows—"

"Which was notably *not* very much!" Leonidas pointed out, starting forward again. "I've never seen such a disgraceful performance by an entire age cohort." The eirene looked down, ashamed, as if he were at fault. But he wasn't; they hadn't been his boys. "Why do you think that was?" Leonidas persisted.

Maron swallowed again. "Alpheus said…"

"Yes?"

"Alpheus said that none of them cared about winning."

"Didn't *you* care? When you were sixteen?"

"Yes, sir! But…"

"But what?"

"Things have changed."

"What do you mean?"

The youth shrugged.

Leonidas stopped. "That was an order, eirene. Tell me what has changed in the agoge."

"We just want to get it over with, sir. The other eirenes and I. We just want to get it over with. We count the days, even the hours."

Leonidas thought back. Of course he had wanted to get it over with. They all did. They wanted to come of age, become citizens, be part of society and the army, to have rights, a mess, and a kleros. They wanted to start doing great deeds, and be free to marry. But obviously this was different.

"Being an eirene is the most rewarding job you will ever have. I say that as a lochagos, which is usually considered a prize position. But the satisfaction of command in the army is less than the satisfaction of being a good eirene. As an eirene you have a chance to impact young lives in a dramatic way. You can make a huge difference to the development and character of a dozen boys. At a minimum, you have the pleasure of watching your charges learn to trust you, and then start to protect you. At a maximum, you may have the privilege to help a boy be better than before, to grow beyond his own expectations. It's a rare and wonderful opportunity."

Maron looked down, and Leonidas noticed his knee was jerking spasmodically. "The boys are good, sir. I know that. I want to help them survive the Phouxir, if there's any way I can, but..."

"What?"

"I don't know how, sir."

That seemed a bald confession, and Leonidas thought it was better not to probe too deeply at the moment. Instead he asked, "What about the others? Why do the others just 'want it to be over'?"

Maron looked down and was silent. Leonidas sighed and started walking again. The eirenes were the most important link in the entire chain. The eirenes made the agoge work—or not. If the eirenes were demoralized, the system wouldn't work. One bad eirene could be punished—as Brotus had been. One or another timid eirene could be encouraged, mediocre eirenes assisted, but the bulk of the eirenes had to be trying their damnedest—or the whole system broke down.

Leonidas suspected that this was exactly what had happened, but suspicions were not going to be enough to get Alcidas removed. Epidydes had immediately cast doubt on Alkander's testimony, suggesting that he identified too strongly with weak and incompetent youth. What Leonidas needed, if he was going to talk Epidydes into spearheading a motion to remove Alcidas, was irrefutable evidence.

"Leo! Leo!"

The call came from behind them and it was Hilaira, driving one of her father's chariots. Leonidas waited for her. She had both her sons in the chariot with her. "We've been looking all over for you," she explained as she drew up. "Alkander was sure you'd know where we always tie up the chariot, but when you didn't come he went on ahead to see if you'd started walking, and sent me to see if you were fetching your own chariot. Do you want to come with us, or should I give you a lift back into the city?"

Leonidas didn't answer, but turned to Maron instead. "Where are you spending the holiday?"

"In barracks, sir—especially now that Alpheus is in the infirmary."

"I think I could persuade Hilaira to invite you to dinner today, if you want. Your brother won't be in much shape to see you until tomorrow—even if the surgeon lets you see him, which he won't."

Hilaira smiled at the eirene. "It's a family tradition to welcome youth with nowhere else to go." Her father had welcomed Leonidas and Alkander when they had been growing orphans. "Would you like to join us?"

Maron looked from her to Leonidas and then at Simonidas and Thersander. "You're sure you don't mind, ma'am?"

Hilaira just moved over to make room. At a gesture from Leonidas, Maron stepped on to the chariot cart and Leonidas followed him. Hilaira turned the team around, and they started back past the temple of Artemis, heading beyond Amyclae toward Alkander's kleros.

"Maron's got thirteen-year-olds, and he was just telling me he wanted to help them survive but didn't know how; isn't that right?"

"Yes, sir," Maron mumbled, full of shame.

"Hilaira, tell him about your brother."

Hilaira cast Leonidas a questioning look, but he nodded and she laughed. "My brother stashed stuff away in a cave he found—food, water, firewood, even wine. He built himself a bed from reeds and had blankets to make it comfortable. I wonder how he managed to steal all that stuff from my mother without her ever noticing. Then again, she was probably helping him," she reflected with a laugh.

"Do you know where the cave is?" Thersander asked eagerly. He was thirteen this year and would soon—in just five months—be facing the fox time himself.

Hilaira glanced at Leonidas.

He shook his head. "I've forgotten." Although he knew roughly where it was, he was not certain he could find the entrance after a quarter-century. It was better not to give Thersander false expectations. "How did *you* survive, Maron?" Leonidas asked next, taking the eirene by surprise.

Maron swallowed hard, looked down, and then admitted, "I—I—almost died, sir. In fact, I collapsed from hunger. I would have died, but a shepherd found me and took me in. He kept me hidden in his hut, and fed me on his gruel for almost a week. He managed to get me strong enough to walk back to Sparta just in time for muster. I almost died, sir. If that helot hadn't been willing to risk his neck for me..."

There was an awkward silence as the others sympathized with Maron. Then Leonidas announced simply, "We can talk about this later."

They had reached the drive of Alkander's kleros, and Hilaira quickly noted that more than her husband had gotten here before her. "Who are all those people?" she asked uncomfortably. "One orphaned eirene is one thing, but that looks like the entire age cohort!"

She was not entirely wrong. There were a least a score of eirenes collected in front of the house—and as they got closer, Leonidas noted two of Alkander's fellow deputy headmasters. In addition there were Oliantus, Sperchias, Euryleon, Kyranios, Nikostratos, and Chilonis.

"I don't think this is about a holiday meal," Leonidas concluded, and Hilaira looked at him tensely.

When Hilaira stopped the chariot, Leonidas stepped down. Suddenly the collected men fell silent. He found himself facing Nikostratos and Kyranios. Nikostratos was leaning heavily on his walking stick, and Kyranios was accompanied by the helot youth who looked after him since his stroke.

"That was well done, Leo," Nikostratos opened, nodding with satisfaction. "Especially since Alkander tells us you didn't know about Alpheus until this morning."

"That's correct." Leonidas found Alkander in the crowd and met his eyes; Alkander was looking much better. Although he still looked exhausted and unkempt, the defeated look was gone.

"These young men," Kyranios announced, "have been filling our ears with their complaints, and they want you to take the case to the Council."

"Is that correct?" Leonidas looked around at the twenty-year-olds.

"Yes, sir," they said almost in unison, nodding.

Leonidas turned to look at Maron. Maron nodded vigorously.

"Sir," one of the other eirenes spoke up. "You can't imagine what he's like to us." Suddenly they were all talking at once. "We can't do anything right, sir." "He humiliates us in front of our charges." "He corrects everything we do." "He has favorites." "No matter what we do, it's wrong."

Leonidas held up his hands for silence, and they were instantly still.

Leonidas looked at the two other deputies standing beside Alkander. One, Ephorus, was the deputy for eirenes and had been his herd leader as a boy. "Do you agree with these charges?" he asked pointedly.

Ephorus should have been the man the eirenes turned to, and Ephorus should have taken the lead in protesting Alcidas' mismanagement, but all he managed was a weak, "Oh, yes, of course."

"Then why didn't you protest what is going on, Ephorus?"

Ephorus shrugged. "Because it's pointless. He won't listen to reason, and if we resign he'll just appoint worse men."

Leonidas smiled cynically to himself, thinking how everything had always been so easy for Ephorus. Ephorus was an only son of wealthy parents, gifted with speed and strength and intelligence. Ephorus had been elected herd leader year after year, and had won an Olympic crown at twenty-four. Ephorus had never had to fight for anything—not like Alkander, Maron, Meander, Temenos.... Leonidas nodded understanding. He looked at Euryleon, Sperchias, and Oliantus. "And why are you here?"

"In case you need us for something," Oliantus answered for all of them.

"Why should I need you on a holiday? Go home to your wives and families." He paused and then added to the eirenes, "All of you. Just be sure you stop by my kleros when the holiday is over and give me specific examples of Alcidas' behavior."

"Yes, sir," they said again in a ragged chorus, and then took their leave of him, nodding and sometimes grinning, and once or twice adding a remark from "Thanks!" to a more intense, "Next year we can vote—and we'll be with you!"

Kyranios left, but Nikostratos stayed behind with his wife Chilonis, Cleomenes' mother. Having come this far, he was happy to stay the rest of the day, and he settled himself down on a bench in the sun with his walking stick between his knees, looking contentedly at Leonidas. "You did me proud today, young man. Particularly the way you stole Brotus' thunder by making the contestants continue. You're as much a fox as a lion, when you have to be." He nodded approvingly, adding with a special smile for Gorgo, "And you, my dear, were quick-witted as ever. I wanted to chortle with delight when you snatched the yew wreath before Brotus could lay a hand on it."

Chilonis sat beside her husband and he gave her one of his hands, which she took in both of hers. It was she who said, "You're going to have to move soon, Leo. Brotus left in a bad temper, surrounded by his faction. He looked like he was intent on murder."

"I know—but that is hardly anything new," Leonidas dismissed her concerns.

"Unless my son returns very shortly, Brotus will make his move," Chilonis warned. "Polypeithes is going to introduce a motion to depose my son for abandoning his post."

"That won't wash," Leonidas assured her. "The kings are not enrolled in the army and do not need permission to leave Lacedaemon. If they move against Cleomenes, they'll have to move against Leotychidas and Demaratus, too."

"Don't be so sure they won't," Nikostratos warned, a slight frown drawing his brows together. "You should have heard what was being said in the crowd today. More than one person pointed out that the original kings were descended from twins, and that since both Eurypontids have discredited themselves, it might be wise to elect both you and Brotus king."

"Me and Brotus—permanently at each others' throats?"

"Your hostility is hardly worse than that between Cleomenes and Demaratus," Nikostratos pointed out.

"It would stop Brotus from having an interest in killing our son," Gorgo reasoned.

"Come! Sit down with us," Nikostratos ordered Leonidas and Gorgo.

Gorgo willingly sat beside her grandmother, but Leonidas complained, "I need to get out of this armor first. It's doesn't fit and it chafes under my arms." Maron, who had been standing in the background feeling out of place and lost, at once sprang forward. "Can I help, sir?"

Leonidas nodded with relief and lifted his arms so Maron could unlatch the casing. Before Maron could finish, however, Agiatis came running around the corner of the house and flung herself into her father's arms.

"Daddy, Daddy! Did you hear us singing? Aunt Hilaira says we can have a bonfire tonight. Why were you so late?"

Leonidas ignored her questions, which were unending and never seemed to need answers anyway, and admonished her to wait for him to get out of his breastplate. This drew her attention to Maron. "Who are you?" she asked.

"That is Maron, son of Orsiphantus."

"What's he doing here?"

"I invited him. His father was killed when he was a little boy."

"Doesn't he have any sisters or brothers?" Agiatis asked, looking up at Maron with big eyes.

"He has a younger brother, who is very sick and in the infirmary, so I asked him to join us. If that is all right with you, madam?"

"Oh, yes, that's fine. I better introduce you to the others," Agiatis decided, taking Maron by the hand. Maron cast Leonidas a questioning look, and Leonidas nodded for him to go. Then he turned to Chilonis as he sank down on the bench and asked, "Was Gorgo like that?"

"Sometimes. Gorgo listened more than that one does."

They all watched the odd pair as Agiatis solemnly introduced the shy Maron to one person after another. Then Nikostratos stamped with his cane on the earth and asked Leonidas: "So, young man, what is your next move?"

"I'm going to bring charges against Alcidas, whether Epidydes backs me or not, and I am going to bring him down."

"You'll make enemies," Nikostratos warned. "Just like you did by attacking Bulis and the other guardsmen who beat up Temenos."

"Not really," Gorgo declared, with so much conviction that the others turned to look at her expectantly. "Never underestimate the power of Spartan mothers, especially when they are protecting their young. They know what has been going on, and they have long been frustrated by the reluctance of their husbands to act. Leonidas has more to win than to lose in this fight."

"Have you been talking to other women?" Leonidas asked, astonished.

"Of course. Ever since the incident with Simonidas, Hilaira and I have both been talking to the mothers of other boys in the agoge. They know what has been going on, and they are angry—not least at their husbands, who are afraid to speak up."

"Don't be so harsh on them, child," Nikostratos urged. "A man who got up in Assembly and complained that his son was being treated too harshly would only harvest scorn. No one would give him time to explain himself. And much as I hate to say this, the situation is only aggravated by Alkander being Alcidas' opponent. People remember he had a terrible time in the agoge himself and don't want to side with a former stutterer."

"Which is all the more reason that Leonidas can profit from the situation," Gorgo insisted unabashedly. "He thrived in the agoge, and his own son is years away from enrollment. If Leonidas puts himself at the head of the movement against the hated Alcidas, he will win support from people who up to now have been completely disinterested or neutral in his rivalry with Brotus."

CHAPTER 5

THE LIMITS OF DIPLOMACY

"AND THIS IS IT?" THE PERSIAN interpreter Zopyrus asked incredulously. "This is Sparta?" He looked around, baffled, as his chariot drew up in front of a modest whitewashed building with a sober portico on a pleasant, but far from grandiose, square.

Zopyrus was the official translator of a Persian diplomatic mission sent to Lacedaemon by the Great King. His mother had been the daughter of Aristagoras, who had been married by her father to a Persian satrap in the years when he was still currying favor with the Persians. Zopyrus had learned Greek from her and the nanny she brought with her.

But Zopyrus was also one of Persia's most successful cavalry commanders. He had risen high and fast in the Great King's service after saving the life of his commander, the Great King's son Masistius, during the dreadful storm that destroyed so many troop transports during the last expedition against Greece. Masistius had arranged Zopyrus' current assignment with the ulterior motive of giving a trusted cavalry commander the opportunity to get a closer look at the Spartan army.

"King Demaratus is making all sorts of wild claims about the Spartans," Masistius had scoffed. "He says the Spartans are more disciplined than the Immortals and can outmarch and outmaneuver any army in the world. I'm no fool," Masistius had remarked. "They have no cavalry, and even if their foot soldiers are exceptionally good, they are no match for us. After all, they were defeated by Samos and humiliated by Athens. But I want a soldier—not just diplomats—to take a closer look at them."

Zopyrus had not been disinclined to take on the task. This was an opportunity to increase his reputation and standing. Furthermore, it was clear the Great King had no intention of abandoning his plans to teach the mainland Greeks a lesson just because he'd lost three hundred ships and ten thousand men during his last expedition against Athens and Euboea. The ships were already being replaced in the countless shipyards of the Levant, while conscripts were being called up from all corners of the Empire. Zopyrus believed there would be war with the Greeks sooner rather than later, and it could only help to have seen the enemy up close.

Besides, traveling with a diplomatic mission meant traveling in comfort. Altogether they had a convoy of over twenty wagons and fifteen camels packed with their wardrobes, bedding, furnishings, cooking utensils, games, hunting dogs, horses, slaves, and women.

Traveling in easy stages, it had taken four months to reach their destination, and Zopyrus had been looking forward to staying in one place for a month or more. Now that he was here, however, he found Sparta so disappointing that he was no longer certain he wanted to stay for long.

There was no denying that the capital of Lacedaemon lay in beautiful surroundings. It sat cupped in the hands of a fertile valley enclosed on three sides by mountains. The majestic peaks of Taygetos rose up to the west, and the Parnon range provided protection to the east. The two ranges met in the north so that as the Persian convoy worked its way up from the port of Gytheon on the Gulf of Laconia toward the city, the valley narrowed more and more.

But Sparta itself made no sense to Zopyrus. Throughout the rest of the known world, cities were surrounded by massive walls. In the more primitive countries, these might be little more than mounds of earth surrounded by ditches, but in the more civilized parts of the world, the walls were of quarried stone and fired brick. Major cities often had walls twenty yards thick and fifty yards high, strengthened with towers that stood even higher, and many walls nowadays were faced with polished stone or glazed tiles. While more prosperous cities often spread beyond their walls, so that dwellings, stalls, shops, and other semi-urban structures cluttered the surrounding countryside in ever greater density, all the important civic buildings and palaces of every metropolis Zopyrus had seen up to now lay behind defensible walls with ramparts and fortified gates manned by soldiers.

Sparta was different. It had hundreds of temples, shrines, monuments, and public buildings. It had fountains, broad avenues, gymnasiums and palaestra, stoas and baths, and an amphitheater below the acropolis. It was undoubtedly urban, but because it had no walls, it seemed to sprawl across the plain as if some giant had spilled a basket full of buildings. It was haphazard. There was no urban planning. There was no gridwork of streets running at right angles to one another, and there was no logical organization into quarters for administration, trade, worship, finance, and dwelling. There wasn't even any separation of rich and poor.

Furthermore, the royal palaces were primitive. Rather than sitting above the city surrounded by gardens fed by streams and encased in high, glistening walls, they were located right in the heart of the city, crowded by other buildings that had grown up around them over time. They were too cramped to be comfortable or have pretty grounds, and they were completely indefensible. From what Zopyrus could see during their initial drive through the city to the official guest house, the royal palaces were not significantly bigger or grander than his own house. Kings such as these hardly deserved the title at all, Zopyrus concluded, and his opinion of Demaratus fell even further.

It was now three days since the Persian emissaries had been officially received in Gytheon by a representative of the Spartan kings. (Zopyrus had not been able to comprehend which one exactly, because the emissary kept referring to "the Spartans," as if the people and not the kings controlled affairs.) They had taken two days to travel up from the coast, and on arrival in this curious city had been escorted to an official guest house. There the Persian party had unpacked, settled in, and refreshed themselves from their journey for a day before now, at the appointed time, two officials arrived to escort them to the kings for the presentation of their credentials.

Meticulously observing protocol, Zopyrus waited for the two ambassadors, dressed in magnificent silk robes embroidered with gold and silver thread and studded with precious stones, to dismount from their state chariots and start up the stairs to a rather squat old building with a portico, before following in their wake.

The Persians proceeded through the columns fronting the broad porch of the modest building and passed two young soldiers in black chitons under leather armor (who looked smart but not exceptional to Zopyrus) into the inner room. Here they found themselves in the center of a chamber with four tiers of stone steps (or seats) on three sides and five throne-like chairs carved in stone in front of them. Two other similar chairs stood several meters inside and on either side of the entryway, facing the line of five chairs. These two chairs were empty, while the five seats facing the entryway were occupied.

The five men in the five seats rose as the ambassadors approached. They were dressed very similarly, in short red chitons under white linen corselets with a border composed of repeating lambdas. They had red himations draped around their torsos or hanging down their backs. They had cropped beards that barely covered their faces and were not long enough to curl, braid, or otherwise decorate. Their head hair, in contrast, was braided in rows from the forehead to the back of the head, where it hung down in several braids tied at the ends with bronze or ivory clips or silver wires. The men all wore swords, but no greaves or helmets.

The ambassadors bowed graciously to these curious-looking men and announced that they had come with a message from the Great King, listing his various titles, for the Kings of Sparta. Zopyrus duly translated the message into Greek.

The man in the middle welcomed the ambassadors, announced that he and his four colleagues were the officials of the city tasked with receiving ambassadors, and invited the Persians to deliver their credentials and their message. Zopyrus translated this astonishing reply.

The two ambassadors were more than astonished—they were insulted. They told Zopyrus in no uncertain terms that they were *personal* emissaries of the Great King, and as such they expected to deliver their message *personally*. It was impossible to give a *personal* message from the Great King himself to minor officials!

Zopyrus tried to convey both the message and the outrage of the ambassadors, but the Spartans considered him as if they were five fish, without a trace of emotion or understanding. When he finished, they stubbornly insisted that they were responsible for receiving ambassadors.

Offended, the Persian ambassadors replied that they would not talk to mere "slaves" and again demanded an audience with the Spartan kings. When the Spartan officials again refused, the Persian ambassadors withdrew in dignified haste.

Back at the guesthouse, Zopyrus requested permission to explore the town and see what he could see on his own, but the senior ambassador, Tisibazus, forbade him. "It would be inappropriate," Tisibazus admonished the impatient cavalry officer, "for any of us to be seen walking about until we have presented our credentials to the Spartan kings."

This ritual repeated itself three days in a row, but on the fourth day the Spartans agreed that the two kings could be *present* at the meeting the following day. So on the fifth day, when the Persians returned again at the appointed time, they found not only the five men who had received them before, but two men seated in the other two chairs as well.

The men in the two chairs facing the five officials were not crowned in any way, but they wore armor. One was stocky and dark, his hair already flecked with gray, and his armor embossed with elaborate battle scenes. The other was taller, fairer, and wore ancient armor decorated with coils on the breasts. They both wore heavy bronze bracelets on their forearms, and the darker man had a sword hilt set with stones. Although neither could be compared to even lesser noblemen at the Great King's court, there seemed little doubt that these were Sparta's (pitiful) kings.

The Persians bowed to them, and Zopyrus was urged to inquire their identity.

"We are the descendants of Herakles," the lighter of the two answered, and Tisibazus nodded knowingly, noting in Persian to the ambassadors that the Spartan kings claimed their descent from this legendary hero. He then, at last, pulled his credentials from his long, flowing sleeves and handed them to Zopyrus to hand to the Spartan kings. For a moment Zopyrus was disconcerted because, with two kings, he did not know which took precedence. He decided to give the credentials to the man who looked older. Although this man snatched the scrolls eagerly and unrolled them, he then seemed confused, frowned, and shoved them at his companion. The fairer man accepted the scrolls, scanned them with his eyes, and then handed them back to Zopyrus with a nod before urging, "Deliver your message to the ephors. We are here at your request, but only as witnesses."

The Persians consulted and agreed to proceed. They carefully positioned themselves between the ephors and the kings so they could deliver their message without having their backs to either.

Tisibazus was an eloquent man. Zopyrus felt his own Greek was not always up to the level necessary for a good translation. He found himself using some words over and over again, and he was frustrated that he could not seem to convey the message adequately. The Spartans listened, utterly expressionless.

Tisibazus reminded the Spartans of the Great King's many conquests, stressing both his great generosity to those who submitted to his justice and his wrath with those who defied him. He spoke of the utter obliteration of the defiant Samians, and described vividly the crushing of the Ionian revolt. Three of the ephors appeared to have fallen asleep with their eyes open. Tisibazus realized he might have talked too long. He shortened his prepared speech slightly, coming to the point. "Athens and Eretrea—without cause or provocation—chose to attack the Great King. They burned and sacked his city of Sardis. They killed his soldiers and captured his ships. Yet the Great King has not punished them. He has—with infinite and truly sovereign restraint—sent ambassadors to these cities, just as he has sent us to you. All with a single purpose: to secure peace and end this senseless bloodshed unworthy of two civilized peoples. He begs you to come to your senses, to use reason rather than passion, as civilized peoples do. He begs you to accept his offer of peace, to bask in the sun of mutual prosperity—rather than call down the horrors of war upon your innocent wives and children."

Tisibazus paused. The Spartans sat, blinking like sun-bathing lizards. Tisibazus looked to Zopyrus in exasperation.

Finally one of the Spartan officials, apparently more quick-witted than the rest, seemed to sense that the Persians were finished with their appeal. He asked, "The Great King is offering peace?"

"Yes, exactly," Tisibazus responded, as soon as Zopyrus had translated. He was relieved that at least one of these apparent idiots had grasped what he was saying.

"But that's what we already have," the shorter, darker king burst out, scowling. "We are not at war with Persia."

"Not yet, perhaps," Tisibazus responded as soon as Zopyrus had translated, "and war is what the Great King, in his divinely inspired mercy, is anxious to avoid. He wishes nothing more earnestly than peace for both our peoples."

"Well, he can have it. We aren't going to attack him," the short, dark king declared decisively, glaring at his fellows as if daring them to contradict him. Zopyrus was relieved that at least one of the kings had the backbone to act like a king, while his co-regent raised his eyebrows but said nothing.

"That is wonderful news!" Tisibazus declared when he heard Zopyrus' translation. He laid a closed fist on his chest and bowed first to the king who had spoken, then to the other king, and finally to the ephors. He then asked via Zopyrus, "Then you will send the tokens of submission back with us?"

"What tokens of submission?" the dark king demanded.

"Earth and water—a jar of each—mere symbols," Zopyrus explained without waiting for Tisibazus' answer.

"Symbols of *submission*, did you say?" the taller king asked.

Zopyrus repeated the word, confident he had made no error of translation here, embellishing on his own, "Yes, yes, a mere gesture to show that you wish the Great King no harm and accept him as your overlord."

What happened next was confusing. As if the five ephors had indeed fallen asleep during the bulk of the speech, they now all came to life, looking at one another and repeating the word "Overlord?"

"What is the matter?" Tisibazus asked Zopyrus irritably.

"They seem unhappy with the word 'overlord'—or, indeed, with the idea of submitting earth and water."

"Nonsense!" Tisibazus exclaimed. "Tell them it is a small price to pay for peace." Zopyrus passed on the message.

"Small?" the taller king asked in a voice that silenced the room. "You call it small?"

"Yes, of course," Zopyrus answered even before translating.

Tisibazus elaborated on the answer. "Most subjects of the Great King are compelled to send tribute of all kinds and worth thousands of gold pieces. Yet, in his infinite mercy and generosity, Darius the Great has chosen to ask for only tokens from you: a jar of earth and a jar of water, mere acknowledgment of the objective facts."

"What facts?" the stocky king demanded, frowning.

Zopyrus began to suspect that the man was thick in the head. "The plain facts that you are weak and Persia is strong," he replied without first seeking Tisibazus' answer. "You cannot hope to defend yourselves against the might of the Great King," Zopyrus replied in Greek. Tisibazus added in Persian for Zopyrus to translate: "By submitting freely to Darius the Almighty, accepting his sovereignty over you, you do no more than bow to the inevitable, to what is reasonable and what is right."

"How dare you tell us what is right!" the stocky king growled belligerently.

This latter remark Zopyrus translated with some trepidation. However, Tisibazus was an experienced diplomat and took the insult in his stride. He bowed with mock respect to the petty king, with a smile on his lips that betrayed his contempt. "Forgive me. Perhaps it is presumptuous for us to tell you what is right, but you must concede—whether it is right or not—that the Great King commands armies of millions and fleets of thousands. Your pitiable army would be crushed like ants beneath the heel of a giant if it dared to defy us—just as your brothers in Ionia learned."

Everyone in the room seemed to hold their breath while Zopyrus translated this reply. When he finished, it was the taller, fairer king who answered: "That, sir, is tantamount to saying that the prospect of defeat is grounds for surrender."

"Isn't it?" Tisibazus asked, opening his arms in a gesture of absolute innocence, and his answer seemed to need no translation. He continued, "Is it not the *duty* of reasonable men to bow to the inevitable? Is it not the *privilege* of intelligent men to avoid foreseeable disaster? You look like an intelligent man to me," Tisibazus admitted generously, gesturing for Zopyrus to do his part. Once his message was delivered by the translator, the ambassador added, "Surely you can see that it is sometimes wiser to bend with the wind than to fight a storm you cannot beat?"

"You have misjudged me," the tall man snapped, rudely (or so it seemed to Zopyrus) rejecting the compliment the Persian had paid him.

Baffled, Tisibazus cast his colleague a look of incomprehension. They had expected the Athenians to be emotional and foolish, but the picture they had been given of Sparta was of a single-minded, disciplined people, well suited to life within the Persian Empire. These men were so docile and obedient, they had been told, that the sons of even their noblemen allowed themselves to be publicly flogged!

Tisibazus' companion took over, speaking in shorter sentences to ensure the translation went faster. "My colleague has been too oblique, perhaps," the second ambassador said. "The Great King is making you an offer. It is a simple and fair offer. Surrender your sovereignty to him and enjoy his benign reign, or face his wrath."

"Surrender? Without a fight? To some stranger on the other end of the earth?" the stocky king demanded in a loud voice, his face turning red. "You're out of your minds!"

Zopyrus did not dare translate that verbatim, but he didn't need to. Tisibazus, who understood some Greek, had understood the gist of it without translation, and answered immediately. "No. Rather, *you* are mad not to accept this generous offer. The Great King could simply have come with his armies and wiped you out. He could have obliterated your entire insignificant city!" He gestured with his hand as if he were shooing away a fly. "Instead, His Magnificence has shown the kindness of a father toward a wayward son. He has given you the chance to be taken under his care. He has given you an opportunity to become part of his great empire. You should be grateful."

The two kings looked at each other, and then both stood and

walked out of the chamber together without another word. One of the five officials hastily announced, "We will have to take this to the Assembly. We will put it to the Assembly. You will have your answer in three days."

The twins looked at each other. They hated each other. They were rivals. They did not trust the other farther than they could spit. And they had never been so utterly in agreement. They would not surrender. They would not give the "Great King" so much as a single pebble or a drop of water. They would rather die.

They did not speak. They turned their backs on each other and went their separate ways—which was the same way: to tell their friends and followers what was at stake and where they stood.

Even after five days in Sparta, Danei hated going out in public.

Danei was a harem eunuch serving Zopyrus' newest wife, Phaidime, the only wife the Persian interpreter had brought on this voyage. Danei had been captured at the age of thirteen, and castrated because he was one of those beautiful, golden youths that the Greeks occasionally produced. Persian noblemen liked to surround themselves with things of beauty, both animate and inanimate, and Danei fit that category. So for five years Danei had looked after Phaidime, going as part of her dowry to Zopyrus' household when she married at the age of twelve. Phaidime's dependence on Danei had compensated him a little for his fate.

But Danei had never expected to find himself back in Greece. When he was ordered to prepare his mistress for a long voyage, no one bothered to tell him where they were headed. The Persian Empire was so vast that a "long voyage" need not take one beyond its borders. Even when slave gossip suggested Zopyrus had been given an important "diplomatic mission," there was no reason to assume the mission was to the Greeks. It could just as well have been to the Egyptians or the Nubians or the wild peoples to the east.

It was only after their ship put in at a Greek port after a frightful voyage that Danei learned where he had landed. The realization that he was in Lacedaemon had filled him with amazement—but not joy.

Rather, he felt confused and ashamed. In fact, he wanted to hide, but slaves soon learn to accept everything....

The ambassadors traveled with almost sixty slaves altogether, and while the ambassadors kept inside the guest house to underline their displeasure with the reception they had received from the Spartans, the slaves were expected to purchase fresh goods for their masters' kitchen, to replace broken pottery, to find workshops to repair damaged tack and equipment, to find and use wash houses to clean their masters' clothing, and to do all the other things necessary to ensure their masters' lives were comfortable.

Because Danei could speak Greek, the other slaves insisted he accompany them on their errands. At first Danei was terrified that someone would realize he was Greek and recognize that he was a slave and a eunuch. In Persia there were tens of thousands of eunuchs, many in powerful positions, so it didn't seem so bad. Here, among his own people, Danei felt mutilated and unnatural. So far, however, no one appeared to have taken particular note of him at all.

And today he was alone. He was dressed in the clothes of a Persian slave: unbleached raw linen trousers bound at the waist with a drawstring, and a long-sleeved shirt. He wore a floppy cotton hat to cover his blond hair, and straw sandals that rasped (rather than clicked) on the paving stones. He hobbled around the edge of the agora, clinging to the shadows as best he could, with his head down to avoid catching anyone's eye. As he moved, he cast furtive glances in the direction of the produce stands being set up.

Phaidime had one of her headaches. She got them for no apparent reason and they drove her almost mad with pain. She claimed that crushed poppy seeds helped to ease them, and she had begged Danei to find some for her, pressing into his palm silver coins of far too great a value. Phaidime was illiterate and innumerate and had absolutely no concept of the value of things. But her generosity was of little use to Danei. He could not run away because he could hardly walk. Nor did he have any place to run to. His family was dead or enslaved. His island was occupied. His farm was tilled by strangers.

Danei thought he saw a stand selling nuts and other dried goods in small canvas bags standing open side by side. He approached cautiously, his eyes down so that he saw the goods but not the man behind the stand. Walnuts, cashews, pistachios, chestnuts, sesame and caraway seeds, nutmeg, and black pepper—but no poppy seeds.

Danei risked a glance up at the shopkeeper. He seemed a humble man, with a bushy, graying beard, naked scalp, and weathered skin. Certainly he was not one of the terrifying Spartiates that Danei had glimpsed from a distance on his hurried excursions. "Excuse me, sir," he muttered.

The man did not hear him, and concentrated on opening a bag of something on the cart behind him.

"Excuse me, sir," Danei spoke up louder.

"Huh?" The man looked over at Danei.

"Poppy seeds."

"What about 'em?"

"Do you have any?"

"Can't you see for yourself? If I had 'em, I'd have 'em out, wouldn't I?"

"Where might I find them, sir?" Danei persisted.

"Try over there," the man replied, gesturing vaguely toward some stalls that spilled out of the agora and down a side street. Danei noted with relief that these were manned by women. Danei was more comfortable with women. He hobbled over to the women's stands.

The first was laden with baked goods: flaky crusts oozing honey, tarts with raisins and crushed walnuts, sweet bread pockets stuffed with apples, and other delicacies that made Danei's mouth water. What a wonderful surprise for Phaidime, he thought at once, his eyes widening.

The woman at the next stall burst out laughing. "Looks like you've got a new customer, Laodice!"

The woman behind the sweets stand smiled at Danei with an expression that reminded him so sharply of his mother, it made his heart miss a beat. When the Persians came, he and his mother had been separated almost at once. He had never seen her again. She was not young even then, and she had raised four children almost to adulthood. Danei hoped they had spared her the indignity of rape. There had been so many young girls to satisfy their lust.... He preferred to think of his mother like the slaves in the harem, looking after the children of Persian wives and concubines, cooking and cleaning for the privileged women of the rich. But sometimes, when he saw a slave woman bent under a load of firewood, or struggling with an amphora of water, he pictured his mother's face—lined and worn and hopeless.

"What can I sell you today, young sir?" said the woman behind the sweets stand, bringing him back to the present.

"Oh, I'm just a slave," he hastened to correct her, ever conscious of his status. "But—but I do have money to buy—for my mistress. I'm sure she'd like some of these." He pointed to the honey squares.

"*Only* those?" the saleswoman asked, astonished. "What about some of the raisin and walnut tarts? Or my lemon squares? Do you want to test my wares to be sure they are good enough?" she suggested with a little wink.

Danei understood her gesture as one of kindness from a woman showing sympathy for a boy in bondage. Her kindness lured a smile from him as he glanced up and asked, "May I try the lemon squares and the almond tarts, please?"

She smiled back and bent to retrieve a knife from under the counter to start cutting into her wares. His eyes focused hungrily on the sweets, Danei did not realize someone had come up behind him until a deep male voice asked, "Where are you from, young man?"

Danei nearly jumped out of his skin. He turned to look over his shoulder at the owner of the voice and felt his heart in his throat. It was one of the Spartiates—tall, muscular, tanned, and wearing bronze armor including a helmet tipped on the back of his neck, the nosepiece resting on his forehead. Danei wanted to flee. He started to shrink back, away from this man who smelled of sweat and bronze and freedom. "I—I'm—no one," Danei told him. "I'm sorry." He turned to run, but the woman stopped him.

"There's nothing to be afraid of, young sir. That's just the master come to snatch a slice of cheesecake for himself. Here."

Still poised to flee, Danei turned to look at her. She was smiling at him, an almond tart on the palm of her hand. "You need it more than he does," she noted with a little nod in the direction of her master—who, incomprehensibly, laughed at her impudence. Danei gaped. No Persian's slave would risk using such a tone of voice with his master, and if they did, they would probably have their tongue torn out. "It's all right," she assured him gently, "the master won't hurt you."

"She's right. I won't."

Danei still hesitated, but now it was in shame rather than fear. The man was the embodiment of masculinity, and Danei felt the scar between his legs as if he were naked. He looked down at the pavement beneath his feet, rooted to it from sheer humiliation. He was remembering how they had been lined up and castrated on a bloody block, one after the other, without so much as a glass of wine. Two men held the boys down backward over the block. The surgeon made a few expert cuts with his knife. The removed genitals landed in a bucket that had to be emptied several times before the day was over, and then each new eunuch was pushed off the block to make room for the next victim.

Danei had struggled too much at the wrong moment. The surgeon's knife slipped and the man cursed in professional annoyance. Another man grabbed Danei and crushed a cloth down into his wound with all his might, ignoring Danei's screams. Danei passed out. When he came to again, a crude bandage was made fast to his crotch with tarred twine and the bleeding had slowed to a trickle, but he would never again walk without a limp.

He was yanked from his memories by the saleswoman. She reached out and took his hand, pressing her pastry into it. As he looked up and met her eyes, he saw only his mother looking back at him, not just pitying him but encouraging him, too. He closed his eyes, unable to bear it.

"You speak with the accent of the islands," the terrifying Spartan hoplite insisted. "Which island are you from?"

Danei looked up at him and mouthed the word. When was the last time he'd dared utter it? "Chios, master," he whispered, and then he dropped his eyelids over his eyes to hide his tears. The word, said at last, instantly conjured up images: the sun coming up over the Aegean, the smell of the soil when his father turned it with a plow, the humming of the bees in their little orchard, his mother singing....

"Chios?" the Spartan inquired, unsure if he had read the youth's lips correctly.

Danei nodded, his eyes still down and staring, unintentionally, at the Spartan's sandaled feet while his free hand tugged unconsciously at the hem of his shirt, pulling it down to cover his crotch more completely.

There was a pause. Then the deep voice said softly, "A man's heart—not his extremities—make him a man. My life was once saved by a squadron of Chian triremes. I know the Chians did not go crawling on their bellies to the Persians, but died upright, as free men. I believe the sons of such men have the hearts of lions—no matter what the Persians have done to their bodies."

Danei gasped and looked up. Their eyes met only for an instant, and then the Spartan turned and was gone. Danei stood rooted to the pavement and watched the Spartan continue down the street. He was filled with a strange sensation of lightness.

Danei's father had been boatswain on one of Chios' proud triremes, and he had been killed at sea in the great sea battle. More than half of Chios' ships had been crushed and sunk in that battle, but the remainder, with shattered rams and crushed sides, limping and listing, had been dragged to Chios by the triumphant Persians. There the captive men had been hog-tied and run up the halyards of their own ships like bunting. There they had been left to die slowly of thirst as the sun burned them like rotting grapes. Danei had recognized some of the men, the fathers and brothers of friends, his cousins, a maternal uncle. While the men died overhead, the Persians had herded the boys onto the open decks and divided them into categories: the galleys, the mines, whores, eunuchs....

Danei stared after the Spartan until he turned a corner and was lost from sight, and still he stared after him, trying to remember with every nerve of his body what he had said. A man's heart, not his extremities.... The image of his father, dressed as he had been the day he sailed away for the last time.... His father had died a free man.... The sons of such men.... He turned and looked at the saleswoman in wonder.

She was no longer alone. The exchange had attracted two other Spartiates. They were younger than the man who had spoken to Danei. The first, wearing a striped chiton and hair braided at a rakish angle, remarked, "You can take his word for it, young man. He knows what he's talking about."

"But—who was he, master?"

"That was Leonidas, the man who *should* be king of Sparta."

Danei looked again in the direction in which the Spartan had disappeared, as if hoping he might re-emerge, but he did not. When Danei turned back, the other Spartiates, too, had faded into the crowd. Only the woman selling sweets was still there. "How many do you want?" she asked.

It was the filthy boys with their bare feet and shaved heads that Zopyrus found most repulsive. They were everywhere, and always in swarms—like locusts. Since they did no work, they could not be slaves, but they dressed too poorly to be the sons of noblemen. They were, he supposed, street urchins of some sort, although the numbers of them were quite astonishing. Zopyrus kept a hand on his purse whenever they came near him.

As for the women, also much in evidence, Zopyrus had been warned about them before his departure. He knew that many were the wives of citizens, and while he found it odd that men of standing allowed other men to see their wives, he soon realized it was not particularly risky. These women were strikingly unattractive—brown and muscular and direct. They would literally look a strange man straight in the eye on the open street! His youngest bride, in contrast, was so well brought up that she was still too shy to look him in the eye even in the privacy of their bedroom after almost a year in his harem. The mere thought of having one of these man-like women in his bed turned Zopyrus' stomach. He was certain he would be impotent if forced into naked proximity with the creatures. He could not imagine how the Spartans procreated.

But Zopyrus had not come to Sparta to see either the children or the women, but the men. It frustrated him that except for the sentries guarding certain public buildings, he saw almost no soldiers. For a city in which allegedly every citizen was a soldier, this seemed very odd. In any provincial capital of Persia, let alone in Susa, soldiers of the Great King were prominently in evidence.

No sooner had the thought formed, however, than Zopyrus caught sight of a man leading a large dark-gray stallion. In the next instant he recognized him as one of the two kings. Zopyrus spurred forward to catch up with the man and jumped down from his stallion to bow politely. "Your Excellency and Magnificence! Accept my most humble greetings!"

The man stopped and looked at Zopyrus in astonishment and then remarked, "There is no need to address me like that."

"Are you not one of Sparta's kings?" Zopyrus asked, bewildered, looking up from his deep bow.

"No, I am his younger brother."

"But you look—I could swear—" Zopyrus was certain he had made no mistake: this was the taller and fairer of the two kings.

"I am the younger of twins," the man explained.

That explained everything, Zopyrus thought with relief. Although the man looked identical to one of the kings, he was dressed in simple but modern armor and wore no jewelry. That gave Zopyrus an idea. He measured the man in front of him only a second longer, and then with the instincts of a cavalry commander, plunged into the attack. "My lord, I have traveled almost half a year to come to Lacedaemon, and for hours now I have wandered the streets of your city, yet I cannot find what I am looking for."

"What are you looking for?"

"The Spartan army."

The king's brother did not seem surprised. He nodded as if to himself and then offered, "If you come with me, I will show you the Spartan army, but you will be disappointed."

"My lord, why do you say that?" Zopyrus asked, surprised.

"Because it is better than it looks."

Zopyrus thought that was the excuse of everyone with something shoddy for sale, and his respect for this man—and the Spartan army—dropped correspondingly, but his curiosity was heightened nevertheless.

Meanwhile, the king's brother had flung himself onto the back of his colt and indicated that Zopyrus should remount and come with him. Zopyrus was riding a fine-boned, high-strung black stallion that pranced and shied as he made his way through the city. Zopyrus' bodyguard, a tall Nubian wearing a leopard-skin skirt and a necklace of shells on his naked torso, trailed them silently on foot. As Zopyrus fell in beside his Spartan guide, he took advantage of the situation. "Who are all these boys I see everywhere?"

"The sons of citizens in our public school," the king's brother answered.

"Sons of poor citizens, then?"

"Rich and poor."

"Rich men let their sons run around like that?" Zopyrus asked, pointing in horror at a troop of boys just back from some outing that had left them muddy and sweaty.

"They are on their way to the river to clean up," the king's brother answered apologetically.

"But they are shaved and barefoot!"

"It does them no harm."

"It demeans them."

"No. A boy dressed like that cannot hide his fat, his wounds, or his bad character—like a rich boy can hide behind bright cloth."

Zopyrus stared at the boys a moment more, but then shook his head and returned his attention to his guide. A closer look revealed that although his armor was not highly decorated it was of excellent workmanship, and the sleeves and skirt of the man's chiton were beautifully woven flax with a fine border. His sandals were sturdy, his horse blanket thick and soft. All of these little things signaled wealth, but as a connoisseur of horseflesh, Zopyrus could not understand why a king's brother rode an ugly, big-boned colt with oversized hooves.

They crossed a wide bridge, crowded this time of day with wagons coming and going, and reached the drill fields, where the king's brother led them to a hillock that provided a relatively good view of the flat area used for training. Here he jumped down, and Zopyrus followed his example, handing the reins of his stallion to the black slave. The Spartan, in contrast, left his reins on the horse's neck and let go. The cavalryman raised his eyebrows, because, as a horseman, he considered that foolish. As expected, the horse walked away in search of grazing material, but his master took no notice; he was pointing to the troops on the drill field.

"What you see at the moment are the Amyclaeon and Pitanate lochos. The Amyclaeons are practicing a relief maneuver, when a fresh unit replaces an exhausted front line, enabling the tired unit to pull back to tend wounds and refresh themselves. The Pitanates are the enemy—There! Did you see that?"

Zopyrus didn't have a clue what he was talking about.

"On the far right! Don't you see? The line's bending backward. The Amyclaeons didn't get the wing reinforced fast enough, and the 'enemy' is turning the line. If they're any good, the Pitanate will rapidly reinforce there and start rolling the defenders back. See! They've increased the depth to ten. Good."

Zopyrus looked at the mass of men pressing against one another in a cloud of white dust and didn't understand anything. This heaving mass of men pushing and shoving had nothing to do with war as he knew it. This was a war of ants, not men. Men rode into battle with their armor glinting and banners flying. They galloped forward with their bows raised, firing at the gallop as they circled their enemies. They clashed with their equals and fought like dancers, pirouetting around one another while their horses whinnied, mad with the smell of blood. Sabers flashed in the sunlight and turbans fluttered in the wind as they fought, man to man, in duels of courage and skill that could be seen and sung about for generations. No man of courage and breeding cowered behind a shield or hid himself in anonymity. Zopyrus shook his head in disgust and looked away.

The king's brother smiled faintly before remarking, "I warned you. Shall we get out of the heat? Have you visited the Menelaion yet?"

Zopyrus agreed to the suggestion, asking as he snapped his fingers at his slave to bring up his horse, "Have you no cavalry?"

"The perioikoi provide mounted reconnaissance in the field," the king's brother answered, looking about for his horse, which had (predictably) wandered twenty yards away to nibble at the leaves of a tree.

"Do you have no chariot or mounted *fighting* troops?" Zopyrus persisted as he settled himself comfortably on the back of his stallion, feeling better as soon as he was remounted. He rarely walked when out of doors.

Rather than answering the question, the king's brother put his fingers to his lips and whistled once. The errant horse stopped eating and looked over at him. He seemed to think for a moment before trotting back to his master, shaking his head low to the ground as if in protest. That was a neat trick, Zopyrus admitted mentally.

While waiting for the horse to arrive, the king's brother pointed again to the drill field. "Look at that phalanx, sir. The one coming toward you. Do you have horses that could ride it down?"

Zopyrus looked at the phalanx. It was ten men deep and twenty men wide. The shields overlapped and the men had lowered their heads so that only their eyes and the crests of their helmets showed above the wall of bronze. The black crests of the helmets shivered in the breeze, but otherwise the line was as solid as a rock—a rock that advanced at a slow but steady pace. His stallion was already nervously swinging his haunches back and forth, unnerved by the advancing wall of bronze, which caught the sunlight and flashed irregularly.

"You're welcome to try riding it down," the king's brother suggested.

Zopyrus glanced over at him hard. The Spartan's gray colt was snuffling around his master's shoulders, taking the Spartan's long braids in his lips in affectionate playfulness—while the Spartan stood looking out at the drill fields, ignoring the horse altogether.

Zopyrus looked at the advancing phalanx again and tried to imagine riding against it. The Spartan was right. It would not be easy. Horses would shy, and even if a man got within range, it would be hard to do damage to men so well protected by heavy shields and bronze helmets. Certainly it would be difficult unless one had overwhelming superiority of numbers and could loosen the line with a barrage of arrows and javelins before pressing in for hand-to-hand combat. Still, Zopyrus thought, if they got in close enough, they would be able to wreak havoc. Men so cowardly that they had to crouch close together for comfort would be thrown into complete disarray as soon as their line was breached.

The king's son flung himself up on the back of his horse, took up the reins, and smiled at Zopyrus. "Shall we charge it together and see who comes closer?"

Zopyrus already knew the answer. His nervous young stallion clearly wanted to flee in the opposite direction. He sweated and swung his haunches back and forth, searching for an opportunity to bolt. In contrast, the big gray the king's brother rode seemed oblivious to the phalanx. Clearly he had been trained in proximity to the bronze men and knew better than to fear them. That said it all. The famous Spartan line could indeed be breached by cavalry—you just had to be sure you had the right horses and men.

Zopyrus smiled graciously and bowed his head to the king's brother. "No, my lord. I know you would win, because your horse is familiar with a Spartan phalanx and mine is not. What price do you want for him?"

"For who?"

"Your horse, my lord," Zopyrus replied with a smile.

The king's brother smiled but shook his head. "He is not for sale."

"I'll give you ten gold pieces," Zopyrus offered extravagantly. No horse was worth that much, but he wanted to both show that he could afford it and indicate he was not about to haggle. He wanted the horse.

"He's not for sale," the king's brother repeated more firmly. He was no longer smiling.

"Twenty," Zopyrus retorted. He hated being thwarted in anything, and he wanted to show he would have his way at any price.

"Sir, you could offer me the entire Persian treasury, and the answer would be the same. He is not for sale."

"No horse is priceless," Zopyrus scoffed.

"I did not say he was priceless; I said he was not for sale. I do not sell the things I love for any price."

Zopyrus laughed. "You are a strange man. What did you say your name was?"

"Leonidas."

"The Lion's son. Do you not resent that your brother, your twin, is a king and you are given no honors? In Persia, the twin brother of the king would be the second greatest nobleman in the realm, with vast powers and riches."

Leonidas smiled but replied earnestly, "In Persia, I do not believe the twin brother of the king would be allowed to live at all."

Zopyrus was caught off guard by this perceptive remark. Although he had given it no thought until now, he realized that no king with absolute power could risk having a living twin.

Zopyrus' curiosity was aroused. "Do you have many sons, Leonidas?"

"I have one son and one daughter."

"Is that all?" Zopyrus was flabbergasted. Leonidas looked about forty years old, an age at which a Persian nobleman usually had scores of children.

"I lost two children in a fire," Leonidas conceded, his face closed, and he quickly asked back, "And you?"

"I have seven sons by my wives and another nine by concubines."

"And daughters?"

"I don't keep track of them," Zopyrus replied, dismissing the nuisances. Each female child was a wasted pregnancy and an added expense.

"You are a poor man." Leonidas turned his horse around and started riding down from the hillock, his big horse on a loose rein.

"Poor?" Zopyrus' temper flared, and he put his heels to his stallion so that with a leap he was beside Leonidas again. "You dare to call me poor when you ride around on a plow horse and have only one son?"

Leonidas pulled up and stared at the Persian. "Tell me, what was the first word your eldest son said?"

"How should I know?" Zopyrus dismissed the question irritably. "Nursery talk is for women and eunuchs. What matters is that I have *seven* legitimate sons who will carry on my line, and *nine* more that carry my blood. Furthermore, my newest wife will give sons of the Great King's own blood! They will grow up to be great warriors!"

"I have a thousand boys who call me 'father,'" Leonidas countered, "and each of them is being forged into a splendid soldier, but my son—and my daughter—have enriched me beyond measure with their smiles and temper tantrums and the trust in their eyes when I take them in my arms. You are a poor man, Persian, who has never known the joy of a little girl's laugh or the peace of holding a sleeping infant in your arms."

Zopyrus had no answer to this speech. It was incomprehensible to him. They were both speaking Greek, but they clearly did not understand each other.

"I have shown you what you came for. Is there anything more?"

"No," Zopyrus told him irritably. "I've seen quite enough."

"Good. Can you find your own way back?"

"Easily."

The Spartan king's brother bowed his head, turned his horse on his haunches, and was gone. The "plow" horse showed a burst of speed that left Zopyrus more annoyed than ever that he had not talked the Spartan into selling him. A good lesson, he told himself: the horse might be ugly, but it had strength and speed and uncanny intelligence.

For several minutes Zopyrus simmered with discontent, provoked by the man and his arrogance, but as his temper cooled, Zopyrus realized the encounter had been productive. He now knew that the Spartan army, because of its equipment and discipline, was a formidable force, but—he was certain—when attacked by well-trained and well-led heavy cavalry it would collapse quickly. More important, he had learned just how proud—arrogant, really—these Spartans were. They vastly overestimated both their prowess and their importance. They needed to be taught a lesson, he concluded, and Zopyrus found himself hoping they would be foolish enough to reject the Great King's generous offer of peace. He looked forward to leading the cavalry that would shatter their line and trample these arrogant barbarians under the hooves of Persian horsemen.

Tisibazus sat absolutely still while the slaves fluttered around him like moths around a lantern. One slave was carefully outlining his eyes with a tiny pointed brush full of black ink, another was kneading oil into his long black curls in preparation for binding them at the back of his head, a third slave was finishing his pedicure, and a fourth stood ready with his ivory-and-gold decorated sandals.

Meanwhile, Zopyrus, already fully coifed and dressed, paced fractiously back and forth.

"You will never make a diplomat," the older man observed, his eyes closed and his hands relaxed on the arms of his chair (which had been brought with them in the baggage train rather than risk his having to sit uncomfortably while visiting primitive countries such as Greece).

"Frankly, my lord, I do not want to be a diplomat, but a soldier. I'm the best rider in Persia—"

"Hush! Bragging is unbecoming," the diplomat rebuked. Zopyrus, recognizing his error, bowed deeply to the older man. They had been told the Spartan Assembly was in session and to expect a decision by noon, but the sun was already past the apex now. Although the ambassadors remained confident that they would receive the tokens of submission, Zopyrus was beginning to hope that the Spartans really did so overestimate themselves that they would actually refuse to submit.

"What if the Spartans turn the Great King's offer down?" Zopyrus asked.

"Tush!" Tisibazus dismissed the thought without moving, adding, "The preparations for war have not stopped even for a moment. If the Spartans refuse, they will be crushed. It is as simple as that."

The slave with the eyeliner was finished and stepped back, bowing low. Tisibazus opened his eyes and snapped his fingers. At once a mirror was placed in his hand. He examined the work of his slave critically and smudged the eye shadow upward at the end of his eyebrows with his baby finger before telling the slave working on his hair, "Enough. Bind it up." While the slave complied, with another snap of his fingers Tisibazus summoned a jewel box. He selected several rings, and then he gestured for his sandals.

Standing, he was a tall man, over six feet but slender, and he had impressive, thick black hair, brows, and beard. Naked, he could have been taken for a soldier, but he was dressed now in turquoise silk robes over purple silk trousers, all embroidered with peacocks. Beside him, Zopyrus looked almost dowdy in his gray silk trimmed with gold filigree.

"If, on the other hand, they prove reasonable—as I expect—and surrender earth and water, then I will present them with the documents naming me Satrap of the Peloponnese and will assume office at once. Why do you think I brought such a large baggage train and three wives? I expect I'll be here until the Great King captures Athens. Then I hope to be able to go home. After they've seen what our armies can do, they will be more submissive."

"But you could be in great danger until then!" Zopyrus warned in genuine alarm. He did not think the Spartans would make docile subjects even if they, contrary to his expectations, were reasonable enough to offer up tokens of submission in the form of earth and water.

"I don't think so," Tisibazus answered, inspecting his manicure carefully. "The Argives are only awaiting my signal. They will come to provide me with a bodyguard."

That sounded better, and Zopyrus relaxed a little.

A slave entered, bowing low. "The Spartans have sent for you, my lords."

"Excellent," Tisibazus responded, signaling to his colleagues.

"The Spartans request that you go to their place of Assembly, to the Canopy," the slave told them. "You are to put your case to the citizens directly."

Tisibazus raised his eyebrows and remarked, "I'm not sure we should lower ourselves to talking to rabble."

"These so-called kings are singularly powerless. They cannot even tell their Assembly what to decide!" his colleague answered.

"Go back and tell the Greeks that Persian ambassadors do not talk to riffraff," Tisibazus ordered.

The slave bowed deeply and backed out.

"You know, there is something very fishy about these kings," Tisibazus admitted. "My body slave claims that your wife's eunuch overheard talk that the Spartan kings are both away. Allegedly one of the kings is in Arkadia and the other in Aegina."

Zopyrus thought about that for a moment and started to put two and two together. He became excited by what he deduced. "Maybe they are! Do you remember? When we asked who they were, they said they were the descendants of Herakles, but any member of the royal family could claim that. Maybe they weren't the kings at all! Maybe they are no more than younger brothers; that would explain why they have no real authority here."

"Didn't you say you'd met the younger brother of one of the kings?"

"Exactly. I recognized the man as one of the two men who had been at our meeting, but he said he was the king's younger twin—"

The slave was back, bowing low again. "My lords, the Spartans say you must come to the Assembly or return to Susa."

"What did you say?" Tisibazus demanded, thinking he had misunderstood something.

The slave bowed deeper and pleaded in a whine, "My lord, forgive me if my words displease. I am only a messenger."

"Send the man in here!" Tisibazus snapped, with a dismissive gesture.

The slave scuttled out, leaving the three Persian emissaries staring at one another.

"They are surely mad."

A Spartiate was in the doorway. He was dressed in armor over a red and black chiton with a red himation over his shoulders. He had a high forehead formed by receding blond hair over a round face. He bowed his head. "You wished to speak to me?" he asked in Greek, and Tisibazus waved at Zopyrus to reply.

"We do not understand this request to come to your Assembly," Zopyrus explained. "We appreciate that you have your own peculiar customs, but ambassadors of the Great King are here with a personal message for your kings and have no business with your commoners."

The man swallowed and was obviously uncomfortable. Apparently he had enough breeding to be embarrassed by the obstinacy of his compatriots. "My lords," he replied, bowing his head to the ambassadors, "there is no one in Sparta willing to present your case to the Assembly. The ephors say the request is improper and they will not voice it."

"And your so-called kings?" Zopyrus said the word "kings" in a way that suggested he had not been fooled.

"Our kings are not in Sparta," the man admitted. "Their representatives likewise refuse to put your proposal to the Assembly. Either return to your own king with a negative answer, or come and argue the case yourselves."

Zopyrus translated the message, gratified that his suspicion had been confirmed. Tisibazus frowned in annoyance at having been tricked earlier, but it was too late to change that. He decided, "We will go and talk with this rabble, since their cowardly officials will not. Come!"

They took two chariots, their guide in the first with Tisibazus and Zopyrus with the other ambassador in the second. They found what looked like six to seven thousand men standing about in the shade of a large stoa and apparently arguing among themselves like a bunch of craftsmen bickering in a market. At the front of the stoa was a row of chairs filled with old men facing the rabble. In front of them stood the five men who had received the ambassadors, but there was no sign of the two pretenders who had hoodwinked the ambassadors three days earlier by impersonating Sparta's kings.

Zopyrus could tell by the way Tisibazus moved, in long strides that made his robes flutter about him revealing his ankles, that he was very angry. He gestured irritably for Zopyrus to join him. "Ask them where they want me!" he ordered.

But already the chairman of the five officials was making gestures and calling for order. Across the stoa, conversations died and eyes turned toward the front. Tisibazus strode to the center of the open area, the sun glinting off the gold embroidery that edged the peacocks on his robes.

Tisibazus raised his voice. "Men of Sparta! The Great King, King of Kings, Lord of Persia, Master of the Medes, Conqueror of Armenia, Cilicia, Lydia, Babylon, Phoenicia, Syria, Assyria, Egypt, Nubia Arabia. Subjugator of Cyprus, Rhodes, Samos, Chios, Lesbos, and all the islands of the Aegean; Sovereign of Parthia, Bactria, Caspia, Susiana, and Paphlagonia; his Magnificence, Darius the Great—sends you his greetings and reaches out his gracious, God-touched hand to you in friendship. All praises to the Great Ahuramazda! His Awesomeness has sent me and my colleague on a journey lasting half a year just to bring you his munificent offer of peace, and to assure you of his benevolence toward you. Although he has never seen your valley or city, still he is prepared to embrace you, to enfold your homeland and hold it to his bosom, making it an integral part of his vast and eternal empire."

There was a growing restlessness among the audience. Tisibazus concluded that the Spartans, like young children, had short attention spans. They were too dull to follow lengthy discourse, it seemed, and needed to have things worded succinctly. "His Majesty, Great King Darius, is prepared to accept you into his service and extend his peace and protection to you without demanding the usual—and seemly—tribute that he has every right to demand. He does not ask you to send him a thousand tetradrachma to compensate him for his troubles, nor even five hundred horses for his stables, nor a hundred virgins for his—" At this point in Zopyrus' translation of the ambassador's speech, he was interrupted.

The uproar was so loud and hostile that Tisibazus found himself shouting just to be heard above the uproar. "All he asks are tokens! Mere tokens! Nothing but earth and water!"

Zopyrus shouted out the translation, only to be answered by an unmistakable roar of: "We'll give you earth and water!"

Several men lunged out of the crowd and grabbed the Persian emissaries roughly, shoving them backward as the entire crowd surged forward. Zopyrus could hear the frail voices of the old men calling out for order, and here and there other alarmed voices were raised in protest, but the mob was out of control. Young men were manhandling them so roughly that Tisibazus lost his footing, yet even that did not slow them down. The Spartans were dragging, pushing, and carrying the Persian emissaries out of the stoa. They could not see where they were being dragged. All they could see were the square-faced young men in red and bronze. The stink of sweat choked the ambassadors' nostrils, and the shouts of the assailants in their barbarian tongue were deafening.

Tisibazus had never been so frightened in his life. As a young man he had had his share of battles, but this was different. He had no weapon but his diplomatic immunity, and these barbarians seemed to have forgotten that.

Zopyrus didn't give diplomatic immunity a thought. He was a soldier and he was in danger. He struggled so violently that more men grabbed him. They lifted him clear off his feet and clung to his legs even as he kicked out, twisting his whole body left and right.

"Don't harm them! They have diplomatic immunity! Let them go!" a voice shouted frantically. "Let the Persians go!" a second voice ordered. But these voices of reason were far away, and the men who had hold of Zopyrus and the ambassadors paid no attention.

Zopyrus' struggle had succeeded in separating him from his companions. He saw Tisibazus and the other ambassador being heaved upward. He heard the dignitary cry out once in pain, and then again not so much from pain as from sheer terror. Zopyrus caught a glimpse through the crowd of the ambassador being held upside down by his ankles, his robes falling over his face. It was an image of only an instant, but it would stay with Zopyrus for a lifetime.

The stocky, dark man with the gray-flecked beard who had impersonated one of the two kings was screaming, "You'll find all the water and earth you need right there!"

Still Tisibazus struggled. Although he could see nothing and was nearly suffocating under his robes, he tried with the desperation of panic to twist free of the men holding him by his feet. His arms were no longer held by anyone and he tried to grab hold of something. But each time his fingers caught something—a person, a piece of clothing, the edge of something hard—someone pried his fingers away.

Then they let go of him.

Tisibazus fell headfirst into darkness. He screamed, and his scream echoed on the stone around him. It was a terrifying howl that multiplied and grew louder and lingered, fading slowly, even after he was gone.

The brutal murder of an unarmed ambassador gave Zopyrus new strength. He lashed out with his teeth, clamping them into any flesh he could reach, and yanked his head back and forth. He drew blood that drenched his face and beard, and someone loosened his grip enough for Zopyrus to tear one arm free and throw a punch at someone's throat. The man staggered backward, and another man lost his hold on one of his legs. Zopyrus drew his knee up and kicked out with all his force into a man's belly. He drew in his knee for a second kick, and took a brutal punch in the face instead. The men who had been carrying him toward the well dropped him and started hammering him with their fists and feet.

Muffled through the press of men surrounding and assaulting him, Zopyrus heard the second scream. It was another high-pitched shriek of terror that slid down the scale to whimpering silence.

Suddenly the men around him were being yanked back, shoved aside, flung backward. "Barbarians! Thugs! These men are under the protection of the Gods!" The man shouting this was already hoarse from trying to make himself heard. He was frantic. His round face was bright red and sweating as he struggled against men younger and stronger than himself.

Zopyrus was seized again, but this time he was pulled upright. Someone strong had him around the waist. Another man pulled his arm over broad, bronze-clad shoulders. He found himself surrounded again, but this time the men around him had their backs to him and were facing outward. One or two of them seemed to have shields on their arms; others were armed with swords. The men who had been assaulting him drew back, and the men who had hold of him started to withdraw. He was being pulled away from the fateful well, away from the screaming and shouting and madness.

Zopyrus was too dazed to offer any kind of resistance. He let his rescuers set the pace and direction. He was dizzy from the blow to his head, and he stumbled more than once. The men around him held him up.

He could not grasp it. Could it be true? Had the Spartans, before his very eyes, murdered two Persian ambassadors? It was impossible. Ambassadors could not be touched—not imprisoned or harmed—not even during war. Persia was not at war with Sparta. How could they have killed two unarmed ambassadors?

"Here," a voice said at his ear. Dazed, Zopyrus realized he was at the entrance to the guesthouse. Persian slaves were spilling out the front door, chattering stupidly. His slave bodyguard let out a roar and rushed down the steps. The Spartans parted and let the man come to his master.

"Get inside," someone ordered, and Zopyrus turned to see who it was. He did not recognize the man, but he had a distinctive hawk-like face and braids that cut diagonally across his skull. The man beside him, however, was the very man who had come with that treacherous message that they must come to the Assembly. It had been a trap! For an instant, Zopyrus wanted to fling himself at this man and silence him forever. Then he noticed that this man's hair was torn free of his braids and his lip was swelling. Zopyrus registered that he must have been one of the men who had finally driven the assailants off, bringing the other soldiers. The part of his brain that was not numbed by shock registered that the assault had come as a surprise to at least some of the Spartan citizens.

The first man was ordering again: "Get inside. We'll mount a guard, but until things have quieted down, you should stay out of sight."

More troops, fully armed and armored, were coming down the street at a brisk pace. Not knowing what side they might be on, Zopyrus darted for the house, slammed the door shut behind him, and ordered slaves to barricade it.

Half the slaves started fluttering about to obey, but a handful of others clustered around him asking what had happened. His body slave was wailing out that he had been wounded. One of Tisibazus' slaves kept asking, "Where is my master? Where is my master?"

"Shut up! All of you!" Zopyrus shoved them away furiously. "The ambassadors are dead! Murdered! We are among barbarians!" Only when he said it out loud did it truly sink in.

Danei was in pain as he hobbled out to the courtyard with yet another load of his mistress' things for the wagons. He was not used to either walking this much or carrying heavy loads. The damaged ligaments at the top of his thigh were overstrained by so much movement, and his arms and shoulders ached from the unusual exercise. But Zopyrus had ordered them to load ten of the wagons with their most valuable goods and prepare to depart before dawn. They had been working for hours, and it was now the middle of the night.

"Hurry! Hurry!" the self-important Nubian ordered Danei contemptuously, landing a kick in his backside for good measure. The black despised eunuchs and liked making fun of them in his free time; sometimes he masturbated in front of them to remind them of their inadequacies. Danei hated him.

"Where's your mistress?" Zopyrus came out of the darkness and addressed Danei directly.

"She's inside, master."

"Is she dressed and ready?"

"Yes, master, but—" Danei had never dared to say "but" to the master before, and he bit his own tongue and cringed in anticipation of a blow.

"But what?" Zopyrus demanded in a searing tone, his eyes smoldering with anger in the dark.

"She is very frightened and crying."

"Well, she has every right to be frightened," Zopyrus admitted, his tone softening a fraction, "but tell her she must pull herself together. She is a Persian princess." He turned to go, stopped, and added, "Tell her we have an escort of one hundred Spartiate guardsmen."

Danei gazed after Zopyrus as he continued to the next wagon, ordering some boxes to be removed and left behind to make room for other things he thought more important. Danei had no thoughts for the chaos in front of him anymore. One hundred Spartiate guardsmen? Even on Chios, Spartiate guardsmen had an awesome reputation. The elite of the elite. An escort of Spartiate guardsmen. Danei thought he remembered hearing that only the Spartan kings could command Spartiate guardsmen ....

Zopyrus was back. "What are you standing around gawking at? Get your mistress! Get her inside that covered wagon."

"Yes, master."

Phaidime was sitting on the bed, numbed with fear. She was wrapped in three veils because she could not decide which to leave behind, and her hands were heavy with all the rings she owned, all the gold armbands and bracelets Zopyrus had ever given her.

"It's time to go out to the wagon," Danei told her gently.

Phaidime got to her feet without a word. She wrapped one of her veils across her face so that only her eyes showed, and tucked it under the end of the others to keep it there. Danei took her trembling little hand and led her out into the courtyard.

The master's dogs had been let out and were circling around, sniffing everything in confusion. Horses were being hitched up. Cursing broke out somewhere on the far side of the courtyard, but was quickly silenced by a barked order.

Danei helped Phaidime up and into the canvas-covered wagon. Inside behind the driver's box, a nest of silk cushions had been prepared for her and the five wives—now widows—of the two ambassadors. It was not large enough for the women to stretch out, but they could sit or lie curled up. Danei urged Phaidime to lie down, but she shook her head and insisted on sitting with her back against the side of the wagon, clutching her knees. Danei seated himself on the driver's seat and waited. After a few moments the older eunuchs brought the other five women, and then the driver emerged out of the darkness, hauled himself up, and plopped himself down beside Danei.

Zopyrus, mounted on one of his stallions, rode up to take his place directly beside them and ordered the gates opened. They drove out into the night.

Danei heard a short, low shout and then an indefinable sound like many people stamping in unison. Peering into the darkness he saw them, and his heart missed a beat. Spartiates in full battle kit! It was too dark to distinguish colors, but their himations and the crests on their helmets were dark, and their shields gleamed even in the dull light of the moon.

A man separated himself from the others and came to stand at Zopyrus' stirrup. "The city is under curfew and quiet. I expect no trouble."

It was Leonidas! Danei's heart was fluttering in his chest and Leonidas' words echoed in his skull. "... They did not go crawling on their bellies ... the sons of free men."

"My wife is a niece of the Great King by his most important wife. If any harm comes to her, he will see you skinned alive and then burn your entrails in front of you before he does the same to your wives and children."

Leonidas shrugged. "If fear motivated me, I would have already killed you." Then he stepped back, leaving Zopyrus no option but to spur away in a showy but futile display of horsemanship.

Danei twisted in his seat to keep his eye on Leonidas as long as he could. Abruptly Leonidas seemed to feel his gaze and looked over. Their eyes met.

The streets were deserted in the moonlight. The temples gleamed white, the barracks were dark, the public buildings brooded. Here and there a fountain gurgled gently, catching the moonlight, and the plane trees lining the wide avenue whispered in a light wind. Gradually the density of the buildings thinned. Proud public buildings and monuments to heroes, statues and stoas gave way to humble workshops, dwellings, warehouses, and lumberyards. They passed a whole series of low buildings with similar porticos that looked like the treasuries Danei had seen when he went to Olympia with his father ....

They came to an urban cluster of taverns and inns, but even here most of the lights had burned out and the voices were silenced by sleep. Beyond, the countryside opened up. The road followed the wide river of the Eurotas, while the flanks of Taygetos loomed to their right. The escort relaxed enough to start singing, led by Leonidas himself. Danei held his breath. It was the "Song of Troy," a song he had learned as a boy. Once or twice Danei mouthed the words with the men beside him, but he dared not sing. His voice would never have the timbre of a man; it was frozen in its high, childish octaves by the knife that deprived him of his manhood.

When the sky was graying to the east, setting the Parnon range into dark silhouette, they came to an inn. Zopyrus ordered a halt and announced his intention to spend what was left of the night here. They turned into the courtyard and the drivers climbed down to unhitch the horses as the innkeeper stumbled out, rubbing sleep from his eyes in amazement.

Zopyrus ordered the eunuchs to get the women inside, indicating that they should follow the innkeeper's wife. Danei and Phaidime were shown to a room that was little more than a closet. It was windowless and dank. There was nothing but filthy straw pallets on the floor. Phaidime sucked in her breath in horror and clutched her rich robes about her to keep them from getting dirty.

"I'll fetch cushions," Danei promised and went back out into the courtyard, doubled over with pain and moving like a man with a false leg. Grimacing, he hauled himself up onto the wagon again and collected as many cushions as he could carry, then took them back to spread them about the little room for Phaidime. At once she sank down with a sigh of relief and ordered, "Bring me something to drink and a snack. I've had nothing to eat since midday."

Danei had not had anything to eat, either. And while Phaidime had sat waiting, he had worked through the night. He was in pain. Didn't she realize that? Didn't she notice he could hardly stand, much less walk? Didn't she see that his limp was worse than ever? Didn't she care?

With cold clarity, Danei realized that Phaidime was happy enough to let him comfort her when she was in distress, but he was still just a slave to her, a eunuch. And as he stared at her in this new light, he noticed for the first time that she was growing up. He confronted something he had tried to ignore: that Phaidime no longer feared Zopyrus' visits as she had at the start of her marriage. Nor was she frightened of the other women, because she was Zopyrus' favorite wife—and *proud* to be his favorite.

Suddenly Danei knew he had to run away. Tonight. He could not crawl on his belly to the Persians any longer. He would rather die standing upright as his father had.... "I'll see what I can find," Danei promised her, thinking only of the immaculate Spartan Guard. If they were still outside....

He hobbled around the peristyle past the other slaves unloading this or that, or simply rolling themselves in blankets to try to catch some sleep. He hobbled to the front of the inn and put his hand on the door.

"Where are you going, gelding?" It was the sneering voice of the black man, standing with his arms crossed on his chest and his legs wide apart, guarding the exit.

Danei felt his knees go weak. His resolve collapsed. He had witnessed what this man's fists could do, and he knew he could not endure it. "I need to pee," he told the Nubian, doubled over as if trying not to wet himself.

The Nubian laughed. "Use that corner over there with the other mules." He pointed toward the stables.

Danei hobbled toward the stables and slipped inside. The horses and mules stirred, but at the far end of the room was a square of gray light. It was a door. It stood wide open. Danei stood straighter and walked toward it, disbelieving. There was no one guarding it. He looked around, over both shoulders. There was not another person in the stables. He walked out the door. The Eurotas valley was starting to awake. Birds were singing in the orchards, goat bells tinkled from the hillside behind him, and somewhere men were singing a round, a song to Hyacinthos and the dawn of a new day....

Zopyrus woke from his drugged sleep with a groan. Every muscle in his body ached. His shoulders had been wrenched and his knee and hip bruised in the horrible scuffle the day before. He had numerous bruises and cuts, which his slaves had diligently cleaned and salved before giving him a heavy date wine, brought all the way from home. Zopyrus had been too dazed to do anything but let them minister to his body the night before. Now, even by the light of a new day, he could not fathom what had transpired.

The Spartans had murdered two Persian ambassadors. He could not yet decide which aspect of the crime was worse: that they were so disrespectful and foolhardy as to lay hands on men representing the Great King, or that they were so barbaric as to violate diplomatic immunity. Any way one looked at it, the Spartans were madmen, and despite his immediate escape from harm, Zopyrus felt anything but safe.

His head ached as much as his body. Indeed, his head throbbed and felt swollen. He needed something cool. Without opening his eyes, he snapped his fingers.

There was no response.

Frowning more darkly, he snapped his fingers again, but still no one answered. He could not even hear anyone moving. He opened his eyes and turned his head from side to side.

Sunlight was stretching its greedy fingers between the slats of the shutters on the windows. His golden goblet lay on its side, spilling its sticky contents onto the floor. Ants and flies were swarming over the drying liquid. Otherwise, the room was empty.

Zopyrus sat up with a groan, but anger overpowered discomfort. He clapped his hands loudly. "Come here! I need to dress! Hurry!"

No one answered.

Furious, he stood sharply, and then had to catch his breath and stop as the room spun around him. He yanked open the door and stared into an empty hallway.

Only at the far end of the corridor did anything move. A little crowd of slaves was standing about, chattering in agitation.

"What is the matter with you?" Zopyrus called at them. "What are you all gaping at?"

An old slave came running, shaking his head helplessly as he came. "I was asleep—like you. But they—they killed the Nubian. Cut him into little pieces and—left. They took most of the horses and they plundered the wagons."

"Who did? The Spartans?" Zopyrus couldn't believe it, but then again he could. They were barbaric cutthroats and thieves!

"The drivers and some of the other slaves."

Zopyrus stared at the man in disbelief. "What did you say? *My* slaves ran away?"

"Some of them," the man answered, wincing in anticipation of the blow, "including that Greek eunuch."

"Danei? Where's my wife?"

No sooner had he asked the question, however, than he registered that someone was sobbing miserably. His gaze followed the sound, and he strode into the little closet that housed his wife. She was sitting on the floor amidst her silk cushions, crying miserably.

Zopyrus went down on his heels beside her and stroked her shoulder. "Hush. There's nothing to fear."

"Danei! Danei abandoned me!" Phaidime wailed in heartfelt misery.

Zopyrus pulled his little bride into his arms. "Hush, little bird. I will buy you two new eunuchs to replace that worthless wretch. He will pay for his treason, I promise you. He and all Sparta will pay. We will return with the army. We will turn this fertile valley into a desert and crush and burn the pathetic heap of stones they call a city. We'll cut Danei's hamstrings when we catch him, so he'll have to crawl for the rest of his life. As for the others, we will seize every man, woman, and child and parade them naked through the streets of Susa before we turn every male into a mule and put every woman into the brothels that service the lowliest and filthiest of our subject soldiers. Sparta will not just regret what they did yesterday. Sparta will be obliterated so completely that no one will ever know it existed."

CHAPTER 6

FOXES LARGE AND SMALL

THE SCREAM WAS FALLING, FALLING, FALLING . . . and then with a horrible crash it ended and Sperchias sat bolt upright in bed, screaming. He was drenched with sweat and his breath came in gasps.

"Good heavens!" his wife complained from the bed beside him. "Quiet down! You'll wake the children."

Sperchias could only stare into the darkness, his breath ragged and his eyes wide. Tisibazus was staring back at him—bloated and bloodless as he had been when they retrieved his body from the well, but with alert, glittering eyes alive with reproach and threat. He did not need to say anything. Revenge was already winging toward them from the four corners of the heavens. The Furies were undoubtedly plaguing the Great King. They would drive him mad with rage. The priests had read it in the entrails of every beast sacrificed since the day the ambassadors were murdered. The Gerousia and ephors had consulted the heavens, and the stars hissed back in the silence of the night: doom.

Worse. From the Temple of Talthybius, the herald of Agamemnon and ancestor of all Spartan heralds, noises had been heard on each successive night since the murders. The sounds were unclear, and yet the terrified meleirenes patrolling the streets and the residents of nearby dwellings reported it was like the crashing of shields against one another, the moan of wind in canyons, and the cry of vultures. One didn't have to be a seer to understand that war and death were the herald's message.

"Come, lie down and go back to sleep!" Sperchias' wife patted the bed invitingly, but Sperchias knew it would be no use. The nightmare would only return. He shook his head and threw the covers off his legs. Grabbing a chiton from where he'd left it on a chest, he pulled it over his head and went out of the bedroom, closing the door behind him.

On bare feet, he tiptoed past his widowed mother's chamber. He could hear her snoring. He went to the ladder leading to the spacious loft where the children slept. The wood of the ladder creaked under his weight, so he moved very slowly. When he reached the top, he had to bend over to move under the slope of the roof. Just beyond the small dormer he came to the bed of his two daughters. They lay on their sides, the older girl holding the younger in her arms; their bright curls framed their soft, round faces. The sight of them always filled Sperchias with a sense of overwhelming protectiveness, and the dark, inchoate threats that were gathering made him shiver. There was nothing he could do to protect them from the wrath of the Gods.

He continued to the other bed. His only son, Aneristus, lay on his belly, a naked leg falling off the bed. How he loved the boy! And at the next winter solstice he would be admitted into the agoge, Sperchias thought with a tightening around his heart. He would leave home, and they would see him only at holidays thereafter. His laughter would be missing from the kitchen and his shouts of excitement gone from the fields. He would no longer come home bedraggled from a day of adventure to tell them breathlessly of the birds he'd almost caught and the fish that somehow slipped away. The thought of the kleros without him made Sperchias sad, but even worse was the thought of him at the mercy of Alcidas.

At Leonidas' insistence, an inquiry into Alcidas' policies had been initiated, but the process was long and Alcidas was fighting back, supported by Brotus and the other conservatives. Meanwhile, a boy had died from an adder bite simply because he had been afraid to seek help in time. Sperchias hoped Aneristus knew he could always—

always—come to him, but he was afraid just the same. Peer pressure could be brutal.

Sperchias went backwards down the ladder and continued down the flight of wooden stairs into the hall. The room was getting lighter, and the sound of birds calling to one another came through the open windows. Sperchias went on to the front porch of the house, enjoying the feel of the cool flagstones under his bare feet. He gazed across the Eurotas toward the pale yellow of the sky beyond the Parnon range. It was going to be another hot, sunny summer day. It was all so deceptively beautiful: the calm before the storm.

With a sigh Sperchias returned inside, found a pair of sandals and tied a leather thong around his waist, then slipped outside again. The helots were coming out of their cottage on the far side of the farmyard, scythes over their shoulders and little bags of food around their necks. They were evidently heading out to cut the hay. They nodded to him wordlessly and he nodded back. Sperchias found no fault with the helot family of six that efficiently worked his estate, but his wife complained that they filched little things—leftover food, eggs, cheese, and the like—and she said she did not trust them. Sperchias sighed; his wife was not a happy woman, and his mother complained about her being lazy.

Sperchias owned several horses, but he left them in the stables and struck off on foot. Riding might get him someplace faster, but walking was more calming to his nerves. Besides, he was in no hurry, because he needed time to think. He was convinced that things couldn't be allowed to continue the way they were, but he wasn't sure exactly what to propose.

Sperchias headed downstream to where an enterprising helot kept a flat-bottomed boat tied among the reeds. For an obol he would ferry anyone across the Eurotas, and for two he'd take a man and a beast of burden. It was so early in the morning, however, that the ferryman was still in his thatched hut, and Sperchias had to rouse him.

He came out readily, since customers were rare. Sperchias settled in the bow of the wooden boat, while the ferryman untied the boat from the pole. He waded into the water thigh deep, pushing the boat deeper into the lazy, brown river, then clambered aboard and rowed easily to the far shore.

Sperchias paid him and started up the road along the eastern shore of the river, heading north as the sun cleared the Parnon range and the day started to get warm. About an hour later, he passed below the Temple to Helen on its steep hill and reached Leonidas' kleros. He turned off the main road to walk down the long, stately drive, flanked by cypress trees. To the right of the drive a half-dozen horses grazed contentedly in a broad paddock, while to the left the field was thick with growing wheat—a reminder of how rich this kleros was. Not every kleros had soil that could support wheat. Sperchias was reminded of when he'd first become friends with Leonidas, the year after they gained citizenship and were serving together in the same enomotia of the army. This kleros had been derelict then, ruined five Olympiads earlier by a devastating fire. There had been no cypress trees lining the overgrown drive, and the fields had been fallow and lost in weeds.

It was a mark of Leonidas' increasing importance that even at this early hour of the morning, Sperchias was not Leonidas' first visitor. A heavy chariot waited in front of the colonnaded porch. He paused uncertainly. What he had to say to Leonidas was not for everyone's ears.

Suddenly two little boys came tearing around the side of the house, shouting. They screeched to a halt, stared at him for a moment, and then ran back the other way, shouting even louder than before. A moment later Temenos came around the corner of the house and looked at him solemnly. "Can I help you, sir?"

"I was looking for Leonidas, but I see he has visitors already."

"Nikostratos is here, with Kyranios."

Important visitors indeed, Sperchias noted. "Then I won't disturb them. I'll just wait here." He gestured toward the front porch of the house, flooded with sunshine.

"Come around to the back terrace, sir," Temenos urged, "and I'll have Chryse bring you some refreshments."

Sperchias didn't really want that—it would be rather like accepting Temenos' relationship with the helot woman—but it seemed rude to say no, so he followed Temenos around to the back, thinking that he liked the young man. Indeed, he felt badly about what had happened to him last year, and agreed with Leonidas that the four assailants deserved disgrace and punishment. He asked, "How are you doing these days? I heard you were back on duty. No permanent damage after all, it seems?"

Temenos shrugged. There was permanent damage—to his psyche, if nothing else. He was bitter and he was angry, but he preferred not to talk about it. "Nothing serious, but I can't do long marches yet, which is why I'm here. My enomotia is on maneuvers in Messenia."

Sperchias accepted the explanation up to a point. Temenos was just twenty-five. He would be on active service for another five years, and meanwhile he had to live in barracks and serve with his unit. He could not be away from his unit at this time of day without permission from his commander, so there could be little doubt that his physical condition was less than perfect. Nevertheless, Temenos could have chosen to go to a gymnasium, or he could have visited his parents or done any of a number of other things. He did not have to spend his free time with a helot girl and her two bastards. "Were those your boys?" Sperchias asked, indicating the two little boys that had come around the corner a moment earlier.

At last a smile split Temenos' serious face, and his eyes followed the boys as they rushed out into the nearby orchards, playing some game of tag only they understood. They were trailed by a half-grown puppy from Leonidas' famous kennels. "Yes," Temenos said at last. "Pelops and Kinadon."

Sperchias considered the two little boys, who he guessed were four and five. They were brown and healthy, dressed only in short chitons cut down from something else, but neatly sewn and trimmed in bright thread by a loving mother. Sperchias felt sorry for the boys. Today they were happy, basking in the love of parents and grandparents, growing up on a large, prosperous estate with lots of horses and dogs to play with, good food (their grandmother Laodice was one of the best bakers of sweets in all Lacedaemon!), and apparent freedom. They did not yet understand that they owned none of the wealth they enjoyed, or that they could not grow up to be like their father. Bastards of a liaison frowned upon by the Spartan government, they would never be more than helots, and Sperchias doubted if Temenos—or the boys themselves—would be happy with that.

Certainly they would not be happy when Temenos was forced to take a Spartiate wife, as he eventually would be.

Sperchias' thoughts were distracted by the arrival of Chryse herself. She was dressed modestly in a long-sleeved striped peplos bound at the waist. She had a snood over her head, and she bowed humbly to Sperchias as she set a kothon of cool water and a plate of flat bread, fresh goat's cheese, and olives on the bench beside him.

From the house came voices, and a moment later Leonidas emerged, holding up the lame Kyranios on his arm and followed by the nearly blind Nikostratos on Gorgo's arm. Kyranios had been Sparta's best lochagos until he was struck down by a stroke during the Battle of Sepeia. For several months he had lain paralyzed on one side, but his fierce will had eventually triumphed. He could now walk with the help of a cane and had limited, if awkward, use of his left arm. Sperchias knew he intended to run for the Gerousia at the next vacancy.

At the sight of Sperchias, Leonidas' face lit up. "Chi! Why didn't you tell us you were here? Or did you just come to see what Laodice had in the kitchen? Come join us at the table." Leonidas gestured with his head while guiding Kyranios to the table under an awning of grape leaves. Sperchias brought his plate and mug and sat opposite the older man, while Nikostratos sat down at the far end facing Leonidas. Gorgo settled herself beside her husband.

"I want your opinion," Leonidas addressed his friend. "We were just discussing if there might be some way to get word to Persia that we regretted the murder of the ambassadors, without appearing to submit to their demands."

"Send me, Leonidas!" Sperchias burst out. He knew instantly that this was his destiny.

Leonidas looked stunned, and Kyranios barked, "Don't be ridiculous! They'd kill you."

"Yes. Better me than the whole city. If we don't do *something* to appease them, they'll descend upon us all—with the Gods on their side. Let them kill me, if it will sate their anger."

"Which it won't," Nikostratos countered firmly. "They sent the ambassadors here with the message that we were to submit to them or they would conquer us. Since we're not going to submit without a fight, nothing will stop them from coming. Your death would serve nothing."

"It might appease the Gods," Sperchias insisted, his eyes only on his friend.

Leonidas was shaking his head, his expression worried. "You tried to stop the murders, Chi! You were the one who managed to save the interpreter. Dienekes and I were too far away and couldn't have gotten there in time. If you hadn't intervened, it would have been too late." Chi unconsciously felt the scab over his lip, where he'd been injured in the scuffle to get the interpreter out of the hands of the mob. "The Gods don't want your blood, Chi, they want Brotus'—and that of his thugs!"

"I must admit, sending Brotus to the Great King's court to apologize for what he did does have a certain charm," Nikostratos remarked with a chuckle.

The others looked at the aging councilman for a moment, but Leonidas brought them back to reality. "He won't go."

"Might he be convinced to send a pair of his followers? Bulis, for example? He first disgraced himself in the affair with Temenos, and he was one of the men who upended the senior ambassador over the well," Kyranios reminded them.

"You think Bulis is so loyal to Brotus, he'd be willing to die for him?" Leonidas asked back, alarmed.

"Good question."

"We could at least suggest it," Nikostratos persisted. "I'll put it to the ephors."

"Speaking of ephors," Kyranios started, "this lot ought to be hanged! They mismanaged the whole affair. They should have admitted we had no kings, rather than coming up with that masquerade! And you shouldn't have been part of it," Kyranios told Leonidas pointedly before returning to his topic. "We need to ensure that better men stand for election this year."

"Chi?" Leonidas turned to his friend.

"What?"

"Will you stand for ephor at the next election?"

"Leo! I'm not yet forty, and everyone knows I'm your protégé."

"Exactly," Kyranios remarked dryly.

Sperchias looked from one to the other and finally to Nikostratos. "This city is afraid of what it's done, Chi," the old man explained. "It's afraid of the omens, and it knows you were one of the few voices of reason in that mob—you and Leonidas and Dienekes. We need to exploit those sentiments while we can, because we need a strong government."

"Is that what you think, too, Leo?" Sperchias looked at his friend. Sperchias had wanted to be elected to public office ever since they'd gone off active service. He'd run for one office after another, and had only a string of electoral defeats to show for it. The prospect of being elected to the most powerful and prestigious of all offices was at once immeasurably tempting and overwhelmingly intimidating. For a second, he was filled with the ambitions of his youth and visions of all that he could do, but then the weight of a decade of defeats settled upon him again. "You know I'll do whatever you ask of me, but what makes you think I'll win this time?"

"You'll win," Kyranios told him simply. "And so will Dienekes. It's the other three candidates I'm worried about. Alkander—"

"No." Leonidas cut his former commander short. "I won't subject him to what they'd put him through—all the slanders about his stutter as a boy and questions about whether a mothake qualifies for public office. Besides, I want him appointed Paidonomos as soon as Alcidas is finally dismissed. Furthermore, I'd rather have Dienekes appointed hippagretai than ephor—he's the ideal man to appoint guardsmen and he's the kind of commander we need."

"Granted," Kyranios conceded at once. "But that means we need four reliable candidates besides Sperchias here."

"Why don't you run yourself?" Nikostratos suggested, adding before Kyranios could protest, "It won't disqualify you from running for the Gerousia, if a position becomes vacant, but we have no way of knowing when one of the current councilmen might die. Better to have you elected ephor *now*. When the Persians get wind of what happened here, we will face the greatest threat in our history, and the army will be leaderless without kings. Unless we can get the Assembly to accept Pleistarchos and name Leonidas regent, we will be facing the Persians under the command of a venial usurper."

"What about my father?" Gorgo broke into the conversation,

amazed that Nikostratos could talk like this, as if her father were already dead.

Nikostratos at once looked contrite and assured her, “Child, you know your father cannot be entrusted with command—not after what he did in Argos.”

“I’m not suggesting he should be given command, but the last we heard he was making trouble in Arkadia. He is said to be trying to stir up our allies against us. Don’t you see he will use this incident with the Persian ambassadors? He will tell the Arkadians that it proves we cannot govern ourselves, and that he must be restored to his throne or the Persians will come and destroy us all. If he talks them into taking up arms against us, we could find ourselves facing an army led *by* him. We’ve got to find a way to bring him home,” Gorgo insisted, all her fears for her father bubbling up. The men stared at her with looks that betrayed they had not thought of this.

Then Nikostratos patted her shoulder. “Don’t worry, child. When we get our slate of ephors elected we will send an embassy to your father, assuring him he has been forgiven and urging him to come home.”

Gorgo looked skeptical.

“We’ll do better than that, love,” Leonidas added, pulling Gorgo into his arms and kissing the top of her head. “We’ll send you! Your father will come home if you ask him to.”

The crowds were noticeably larger at the Orestes gymnasium, where Brotus coached both boxers and competitors for the pankration. Brotus took it as an indication that support for him and his claim to the Agiad throne were growing. He noted, too, that ever since he and his followers had thrown the Persian ambassadors down a well, people took him more seriously. He’d shown leadership and decisiveness, and the Spartans admired that. They admired strength. The way his brother and his followers had run about like a bunch of old women, whimpering about “diplomatic immunity” and fretting about offending the Gods, had completely discredited them. Brotus felt stronger than ever.

That strength encouraged him and buoyed him up. Here among his admirers, he could always be sure of harvesting laughter whenever he made jokes at the expense of his twin. As he encouraged Philocyon, his favorite protégé and hope for an Olympic crown in the pankrantion, Brotus called out, "Squeeze his balls till he peeps like my brother's little eunuch friend!" Everyone standing about in the shade of the peristyle roared with laughter, while the antagonists continued their brutal, no-holds-barred struggle, twisting, gouging, and kicking.

"Isn't it amazing how my brother's menagerie is growing?" Brotus asked, basking in the obvious approval of the crowd. "First he adopted that stutterer Alkander, then he brought back from Athens a dithering old Thespian schoolmaster, next he appointed that loser Oliantus his deputy, and soon he started sheltering that helot-lover Temenos. Now he's as good as adopted that moron Maron, and most recently gave refuge to a Chian eunuch! If he keeps on collecting human rubbish, he's going to need a special place to put them all." Brotus laughed so hard at his own joke that he didn't notice the others weren't laughing.

The struggle between the two eirenes had ended with a victory for Brotus' protégé, Philocyon. Brotus ignored the loser and gave his hand to help the victor to his feet. He offered the youth his critique as they walked to the spacious dressing room, where athletes scraped sweat and sand from their bodies and oiled themselves down.

Brotus snapped his fingers at one of the helots, growling: "Can't you see we need water?" Then he addressed the young athlete in a low voice, "So, is Pausanias ready for the Phouxir?" In only two months' time his eldest son would face the demanding test of living outside society for forty days. Brotus worried that the boy might disgrace him.

"Don't worry about Pausanias," Philocyon retorted with a grin at his trainer. "I've got everything set up for him." Brotus had ensured that Alcidas appointed Philocyon as Pausanias' eirene.

Brotus clapped the young man on his shoulder and nodded contentedly before saying in a louder voice, "Yes, you should be up to competing at Delphi next year, if you keep up your training." Then Brotus left the dressing room by the far door, stepping on to the back porch facing the open grassy field where athletes practiced running, discus, javelin, and long jump. A line of plane trees marked the border of the gymnasium property some fifteen yards away, and the shrine to Orestes stretched between the palaestra porch and the trees at one end, while a simple stoa closed off the fourth side.

There were only a handful of youth practicing javelin at the moment, but a group of men were clustered in earnest discussion in the shade of the stoa. Brotus went to join them. Orthryades was leaning against a column, looking calmly superior as always, but Lysimachos was clearly agitated.

"What's the matter?" Brotus asked.

"Your brother and his wife!" Lysimachos spat out. "First he let her go to her father, and now we've had word she's talked him into coming home. The last thing we need is for that wily old fox to come back here and dump his fat ass firmly on the Agiad throne again. Things were going our way!"

Brotus frowned, but then he shrugged. "When he gets back, he'll remind people of just how crazy he really is! Besides, the way I heard it, for some reason he refused to return before the solstice. Meanwhile, with Gorgo away, little Leo is weaker." Brotus would never forget or forgive the way Gorgo had snatched the victor's crown right out from under his fingers and handed it to his brother at the festival to Artemis Orthia. "There must be some way to use her absence to our advantage," he suggested, looking hopefully at Orthryades.

The older man nodded with a faint smile. Brotus was learning, he thought to himself. "It's time we took the offensive against Leonidas' pack of self-pitying dogs! His case against Alcidas is based almost entirely on the testimony of that stutterer Alkander—who everyone knows was a coward—and a half-dozen sniveling eirenes who don't deserve citizenship. Alcidas, surely you can discredit the lot of them?" he asked, turning to the embattled schoolmaster.

Alcidas' face was expressionless as usual, but he raised an eyebrow. "Alkander has discredited himself by quitting his post last spring." He made a dismissive gesture with his hand. "In addition, I think we can be confident that his eldest son will fail the Phouxir." He added this with a twitch of his lips that suggested he was pleased with the arrangements he had made to ensure it. "As for the eirenes, I think we need only make a lesson of one of them: Maron. The others have fathers, whom we need not alienate. But Maron is an orphan—and he's turned into Leonidas' lap dog. If we expose him as a liar and a cheat, Leonidas' whole case against me will collapse."

Maron and his brother Alpheus had been invited to spend the ten-day festival of Herakles at Leonidas' kleros, but Maron had been summoned to report to Alcidas at noon on the second day of the holiday. As the afternoon wore on and he still hadn't returned, Alpheus started to get nervous. By the end of the afternoon watch, he could stand the waiting no longer. He approached Leonidas, who was discussing various aspects of farm management with Pelopidas in the shade of the front colonnade, and announced, "Sir, I think I should go into the city and find out what's happened to Maron."

Leonidas looked at the youth and considered him. Alpheus was the brighter and better-looking of the two boys, and usually the more cheerful. Maron was shy and withdrawn, often acting as if he were ashamed to speak up for fear of ridicule. He was also slow to smile, like a man nursing an inner grief. Alpheus and Agiatis seemed to be the only ones able to overcome Maron's reticence and get him to talk and laugh. But it was rare to see Alpheus nervous and brooding. "What is it?" Leonidas asked him.

"The Paidonomos hates my brother, sir. Ever since the Feast of Artemis Orthia."

"No," Leonidas corrected, "Alcidas hates *me*, and he is attacking me by attacking your brother. But what is bothering you so much right now?"

"I don't know," Alpheus admitted uncomfortably. "I just have a bad feeling. Maron has been so miserable lately. The Paidonomos has made him feel worthless. He told me the other day that he didn't deserve his citizenship because he wasn't smart enough to become a citizen, and that it would be better for me if he just 'disappeared.'"

Leonidas unconsciously straightened and his voice was taut. "When did he say that?"

"Shortly before the Herakleia. I—I brushed him off and said he was just tired, and a holiday would do him good...." Alpheus admitted guiltily. "Now I'm afraid—"

"Pelopidas, ask one of your boys to tack up two of the horses. We'll go into town at once, Alpheus."

With school out, the agoge was deserted, but Alcidas was in his office, and that was where Leonidas found him, leaving Alpheus out in front. As always, the two enemies were exceedingly polite to each other. "I'm sorry to disturb you, Alcidas," Leonidas opened.

"Not at all, not at all. Please sit down. What brings you into the city in the middle of the holiday? I thought you would have been enjoying the time off duty on your kleros or even in Messenia."

"It seems the same duty brought me here as you."

"Me? But I am just going through the school accounts. What has that to do with you?"

"You sent for Maron."

"Indeed, I did, as it was my duty to do as soon as I discovered that he has been embezzling state funds. Since the courts are closed, I cannot officially file charges against him until after the Herakleia, but I thought it only fair to warn him."

"Embezzling?"

"Yes, do you need to see the proof? It is right here." He patted the accounts. "On more than one occasion, he has drawn more supplies than he is entitled to for his unit."

"How much more?"

"Oh, it varies. Here, for example." Alcidas had the evidence at his fingertips, marked for easy reference. He was very sure of himself, and he couldn't resist showing Leonidas just how solid his evidence was. "The boys are entitled to an ounce and a half of oil a day. Maron has sixteen boys and because of a holiday he was drawing for a period of seventeen days rather than the usual twenty, but instead of drawing 407 ounces he drew 429."

"That's hardly going to break the treasury."

"I should have known you'd take that kind of indulgent attitude," Alcidas sneered, "but I do not believe in indulging theft, no matter how petty it may *seem* to someone of *your* wealth. It is the principle that matters. Stealing from the state treasury is stealing from all of us, most particularly from the poorer members of our society." This was the argument that was going to hold water in Assembly, Alcidas thought to himself.

Leonidas noted mentally that Alkander had endured under this pompous ass longer than he would have done; the man was dangerously self-righteous. He answered, "You put Maron under arrest?"

"No. I saw no need for that. If he runs away, he not only admits his guilt but proves himself a coward as well. Besides, there are not enough meleirenes on duty during the holiday to keep watch on the punishment cell."

"So where is he?"

"How should I know? I told him I had discovered his systematic theft of state property and that I would take the matter up with the proper authorities as soon as the Herakleia is over. Then I dismissed him."

"When was that?"

"Hours ago. Why?"

Leonidas stood. "It is not important to you. Good day." He walked out calmly to disguise his agitation, but once he'd left the agoge building he signaled urgently to Alpheus. "He left hours ago, after being told he was under suspicion of embezzling public funds—"

"That's absurd! Maron wouldn't know how—"

"Shhh! I know. We've got to find him. Where would he go after hearing something like that? One of the temples? A close friend?"

Alpheus was shaking his head vigorously. "It's not that he doesn't have friends. I mean he gets along with everyone, but he doesn't feel like he fits in with the others. That's why he's been so pleased to spend holidays with you."

"What about a girl?" Leonidas was thinking of how Temenos had turned to Chryse at the same age, finding in her the comfort and reassurance he had not received from his family or peers.

But Alpheus shook his head again.

"Where could he have gone?" Leonidas persisted.

Alpheus thought a moment and then decided, "Our mother's grave. It's in an orchard, and when we were children he used to go there to talk to her sometimes when things were really bad. He remembered her, you see."

"Take me there."

It was a mixed orchard and some of the trees were heavy with green fruit. A light breeze stirred the long grass between the trunks. A small herd of goats was straying through the far edge, their bells clanging. Everything seemed peaceful.

Then Alpheus spotted him. Maron was stretched out lifelessly on the grass. Only as they came nearer, leaving the horses behind, did they see the noose still around his neck and the broken branch beside him.

Alpheus ran forward and flung himself on the ground beside his brother, turning him over, calling his name. Leonidas went down on one knee and took the limp wrist in his hand to feel for a pulse. His own distress blotted it out at first, but then he felt it. "He's alive. Stay with him. I'll fetch water."

Alpheus pulled the noose off over his brother's head and talked to his unconscious brother in a stream of angry insults. "You idiot! What did you think you were doing? How could you do such a stupid thing? Don't you give a damn about me?" The flood of curses almost disguised the fact that he was crying. Leonidas paused to lay a hand on his shoulder. Only after Alpheus had calmed down and was just holding his brother in his arms did Leonidas go back to the horses and take one to ride to the nearest fountain.

By the time he returned, Maron had come to. As Leonidas approached, he heard the brothers speaking.

"...But it doesn't matter if it was a mistake," Maron was saying earnestly. His rasping voice betrayed the violence done to his windpipe by the noose before the branch broke.

"Of course it matters! You're not a thief, Maron. All you did was multiply wrong!"

"I know, but that's the point! I'm too stupid to become a citizen. Sparta doesn't need idiots."

"Just because you aren't particularly good with numbers doesn't make you an idiot!" Alpheus protested, in the exasperated tone of someone who has said the same thing many times and is tired of repeating himself.

Leonidas stepped into the circle and handed the goatskin to Maron. "I brought some water."

"How did—?" Maron looked at Alpheus.

"He went to the Paidonomos."

"But then he must have told you, sir? About the money." Maron looked down miserably.

Leonidas went down on his heels, pressing the ignored goatskin on Maron. "Drink slowly. It will help your throat."

Maron glanced up and met Leonidas' eyes. "Aren't you angry with me, sir?"

"Why in the name of the Twins should I be angry with you?"

"For—for stealing."

"Were you stealing?"

Maron lifted his shoulders and took a deep breath. "Not intentionally, but in effect."

"He's just not very good with numbers," Alpheus tried to explain. "He'd memorized the quantities for each item, but whenever there was a holiday or something varied, he—"

Leonidas waved Alpheus silent. "Maron, do you think I am a good Spartan?"

"Yes, sir! One of the best!" Maron told him, so earnestly that Leonidas would have laughed if the circumstances had been different.

"Do you think I know what is good for Lacedaemon?"

"Yes, sir!" Maron assured him.

"Then I want you to listen to what I am going to say very carefully, and I want you to remember it and remind yourself of it whenever you doubt yourself. Are you listening?"

Maron looked at him with wide, dark eyes under a forehead creased with concentration—anticipating that what Leonidas was about to say would be hard to understand and memorize.

"Sparta needs good men. It needs clever men." Leonidas heard Alpheus suck in his breath in outrage, but Maron just stared at him like a calf looking at the butcher. "And it needs men who are *not* so clever." Alpheus let out his breath in relief, but Maron still looked like a steer awaiting slaughter.

Leonidas took a deep breath and dropped on to the ground to make himself more comfortable. He looked up at the branches overhead and had an inspiration. "Maron, what kind of trees are in this orchard?"

"Plums, pears, apples, apricots, and almonds."

Leonidas nodded. "And which is the best fruit?"

"Do you mean, which do I like most?"

"No, which is most important for Lacedaemon?"

Maron frowned harder and glanced at Alpheus, but his younger brother lifted his shoulders and shook his head to indicate he didn't know the answer, either. After a moment he gave up and admitted, "I don't know, sir. I can't work out which is most important." As he spoke, he hung his head in despair over his own stupidity.

"That's because they are all *equally* important," Leonidas told him. He waited. "Do you understand what I am saying? We are *all* equally important. Lacedaemon needs us all." Then he couldn't control himself and added a little flippantly, "With some rare exceptions like Alcidas and my brother Brotus." Alpheus laughed, but Maron was confused and looked back and forth between them. Leonidas grew serious again. "That was just a joke—about my brother, I mean. I am very serious about Sparta needing *you*, Orsiphantus' son Maron—"

"But I'm not good at anything!" Maron protested. "If you knew—"

Leonidas cut him short. "I know a great deal more about you, Maron, than you think. I know you are more dependable than most of the so-called 'clever' boys—including your own brother here." Leonidas said this with a quick grin at Alpheus, who understood him and smiled back. "I know you are conscientious—far more so than I was at your age." He paused and then asked, "Did you know I had a son by my first wife?"

Maron shook his head.

"Well, I did. He was killed in the same fires that killed your father. But if he had lived, he would be old enough for the agoge now, and there is no other youth in your entire age cohort that I would rather have had for his eirene."

That took Maron by surprise, and he looked at Leonidas with wide, questioning eyes. "Really, sir?"

"Yes," Leonidas assured him and waited. Although it surprised him that this was what seemed to reassure Maron the most, there was no doubt that for the first time, the eirene's brow cleared and he sat up a little straighter.

"I'm not going to let Alcidas bring charges against you, Maron. I am going to bring charges against him first—for driving you to attempt suicide, and so risking the loss of a valuable future citizen after fourteen years of painstaking and expensive education."

Both youths gasped. "But, sir," Alpheus protested, gesturing toward the noose and broken branch, "then we'll have to admit what happened."

"Why shouldn't we admit what happened?"

"Won't people see it as an admission of guilt?"

"I cannot control what some people say or think. Some people are fools. However, I don't think most people are fools, and I think the facts will speak for you, Maron. But you must be prepared to tell the truth." He turned his attention to the elder youth again. "You must admit that you miscalculated without becoming ashamed."

Maron bit his lower lip and then asked, "Sir? Did you really mean what you said about me being the eirene you would want for your own son?"

"Yes, I did."

"Why?"

"Because you sincerely care about the welfare of your charges. You are more concerned about helping them than about your own advancement. Most of your peers have those priorities reversed."

"But I make mistakes—"

"We *all* make mistakes, Maron. I have made more than my share. Now, I think your throat could use some milk and honey." Leonidas pushed himself to his feet and offered his hand to Maron.

Maron took it self-consciously and then looked up at him again. "And you meant what you said about Sparta needing even men like me, who aren't particularly clever?"

"Yes, I did."

Pausanias had never been so hungry in his whole life. Even worse, his bowels weren't working properly. He had constant diarrhea and stomach cramps. That frightened him. Every boy in the agoge had heard about how some of the boys *died* during the Phouxir. Pausanias was starting to think he was going to be one of them. He was starving, and there were still twelve days to go.

This wasn't supposed to be happening! Not to him. He was an Agiad prince, second in line to the throne after his father. If his father were king (as he should be), Pausanias reasoned, he wouldn't have had to go through the agoge at all! He didn't think he ought to be subjected to these risks, and his eirene had promised him that everything had been arranged. He only had to check under a certain stone every couple of days and he would find instructions on a shard of broken pottery telling him where to find food. It had all sounded so easy.

But after just four days, the shards with the instructions stopped appearing in the designated spot. Pausanias hadn't been too worried at first. He'd done some trapping and scavenged a bit, thinking that the messages would resume. But they hadn't.

Then his traps had been cut to pieces, evidently by one of the other boys. Pausanias wasn't sure who it was because he didn't see it happen, but he had his suspicions. There were several boys in his herd who were weaklings and pricks! He'd let them know it more than once, and Philocyon had laughed at them and told them to eat shit when they protested. Pausanias was certain one of them had destroyed his traps. Inwardly he vowed revenge, solemnly closing his eyes and invoking Orestes, his favorite hero. But first he had to survive the Phouxir.

He had lurked around his Dad's kleros for several days, watching for an opportunity to snatch something edible from barns or sheds. He knew his Mom would never intentionally leave anything out for him, and she kept most things bolted inside because the helots were untrustworthy. But Pausanias figured that since the dogs knew him, he ought to be able to get in and milk one of the cows at least, or take some of the eggs.

To his dismay, however, he soon realized that that bonehead Maron and some of the other eirenes were patrolling around his Dad's kleros as if they expected him. That could only be because his Dad's friend Alcidas had been dismissed by the Assembly for driving Maron to attempt suicide. The old Paidonomos had temporarily taken over the agoge again. Pausanias concluded they were out to get him, too, just to shame his father.

Pausanias gave up trying to take anything from his own kleros, and decided to steal from some poor helots instead. He figured they wouldn't have the courage to report him even if they caught him. But he hadn't reckoned with their geese. The geese attacked him viciously, leaving him covered with horrible bruises on his calves where they had bitten him with their beaks. That would have been bad enough, but then he heard laughter from the hillside as he fled from the geese. The treacherous little shitheads who had cut up his traps were apparently following him and watching his every disaster.

It was after this incident that Pausanias started heading downriver. In part he thought to feed himself by fishing, but another part of him just wanted to get away from everyone: away from Philocyon, who had broken his word about helping; away from Maron and the other eirenes, who had it in for him, and away from the turds in his herd, who were tormenting him.

Pausanias wanted to get beyond the reach of eirenes and citizens. They would all stay within a day's walk of Sparta. If he went beyond that, he figured, he would find it easier to steal. What he hadn't reckoned with was the fact that the perioikoi *always* vigilantly protected their homes and farms from thieves.

So Pausanias had come to this. He was starving. He was going to die. He sat down on the beach and, clutching his knees to his chest, stared out to sea feeling sorry for himself.

There was a cold wind whipping up whitecaps on the Gulf and a little fishing smack smashed through the waves, flinging up great sheets of spray and spume. The boat seemed to be heading straight toward him, and Pausanias started to contemplate begging. It was not a Spartan thing to do. Spartans weren't supposed to beg. But who would ever find out?

Were fishermen helots or perioikoi? It would be horrible to lower himself to begging from a helot, but it wouldn't be so bad to ask a perioikoi for help, he told himself. Or maybe he could just order the helots to give him their catch. Maybe they were so dumb down here that they didn't know about the Phouxir and how the boys were supposed to survive on their own. Maybe if he just went up to them and demanded that they give him their fish, they would be so intimidated they would give him everything.

The fishing smack was close now, and Pausanias could see there were two people on board, a thin youth and a boy about his own age. The youth was at the tiller and the boy was standing ready to drop the sail. The smack swung up into the wind. The youth gestured and the boy loosened the halyard. The youth went forward to help hand sail and then ran out the oars, while the boy went back to the tiller. They were rowing right toward Pausanias, and he couldn't believe his eyes.

The boy was Thersander! The son of that stutterer, the former deputy headmaster. What was he doing here?

With a last pull at the oars, the little fishing boat crunched on to the beach. The oarsman shipped the oars, then turned and climbed into the bows, removed a bowline, and jumped on to the beach.

Pausanias' jaw dropped. It was the Chian eunuch!

"That's cheating!" Pausanias shouted, jumping to his feet. "You're cheating!" he shouted at Thersander in outrage.

Thersander had been busy collecting the nets in the bottom of the boat, which were full of fish. Astonished, he looked up at Pausanias standing on the beach, shouting at him in rage, and laughed.

Pausanias ran up to the edge of the boat, shouting furiously. "You're cheating!"

"And what do you call letting your eirene feed you?" Thersander threw back at him with a sneer.

"How do you know about that?"

"Everybody knows about it!" Thersander retorted. "Are you going to help me with these fish or not?"

"Will you share them with me if I do?" Pausanias wanted to know.

Thersander shrugged. He didn't like Pausanias much, but he didn't want him ratting, either. It would be a lot safer making him an accomplice. Pausanias reached in and grabbed hold of one of the nets.

They got the nets ashore and hauled them up to a little shed filled with fishing gear. On the back side of this was a stone hearth, and Danei sent the boys to collect firewood while he cleaned a fish apiece. At last they had enough wood, and Danei got the fire started while the boys sat down to watch the fish grill. Thersander handed Pausanias a goatskin of water with a trace of wine in it.

"Things are going to be different from now on," Thersander announced, without even looking at Brutus' son. "Wait and see. My dad is going to be made Paidonomos."

"*Your* dad?" Pausanias exclaimed in horror, then laughed. "Your dad's a stutterer! A trembler!"

Thersander hit Pausanias so hard it took his breath away, and the next thing he knew Thersander had pinned him to the earth and was holding his head down with a hand on his throat. "My dad is braver than anyone! He stood up to Alcidas, when the rest of them just crawled on their cowardly bellies. And *your* dad is nothing but a brute! A *dumb* brute!"

Pausanias didn't have the option of protesting. Thersander was cutting off his air, slowly but surely.

Thersander's eyes bore into Pausanias. "Cleomenes is so crazy they're going to have to lock him up, and Leonidas is going to become regent, and my dad is going to be Paidonomos."

Pausanias managed to get out a choking sound, and Thersander let him go. Pausanias grabbed his throat in both hands, gasping open-mouthed for breath. Dazed, he stared at Thersander. Was it really possible that everything was going to be turned upside down? That his uncle Leonidas would dare usurp the throne? It didn't seem possible. All his uncle's friends were like this eunuch—misfits and foreigners and inferiors! But Pausanias felt uneasy, too, because he was here eating Thersander and Danei's catch, and he realized that Thersander was right: nothing was going to be the same again.

Chapter 7

INVASION

It was the fourth day of the Karneia, and nine tents had been set up along the Eurotas. The herds of sacrificial cattle were grazing in an enclosure just beyond the ball field, and the athletic contests were in full swing around the racecourse to the west. As always during a religious festival, the army was furloughed and the drill fields empty. The runner coming down the Tegean road did not, therefore, encounter anyone until he reached the bridge across the Eurotas itself. Even here, the first man he saw was evidently a somewhat senile old helot, who only gaped at the lone runner.

Pheidippidas had no choice but to continue. He was beyond pain or breathlessness. His whole body was numb to itself and its surroundings. Only his heart, and to a lesser extent his head, were still consciously functioning. His feet pounded heavily on the paving stones, all elasticity long since consumed by the miles behind him. His eyes could hardly focus as they swept the eerily empty city, looking for someone who could direct him.

At last he came upon some young men with sweat-soaked hair and towels hung over their shoulders. They were chattering among themselves, apparently arguing good-naturedly. Pheidippidas tried to call out to them, but he didn't have the breath. All he managed to do was marginally correct his course in order to intercept them.

They drew up and gaped at the apparition. Then one lifted his head sharply and said, "Isn't that the Owl of Athena? Are you from Athens?"

"I—must—speak—" Sweat started to seep from every pore. It made Pheidippidas glisten in the afternoon sun. "—to—to—" He was so tired he couldn't remember the curious name the Spartans used for their archons, so he said, "archons. I have—a message."

"He must mean the ephors," one of the youths translated for his fellows, and then told the Athenian, "I'll lead you." He pulled the towel from his around his neck and tossed it to one of the other youths, then with a signal to the Athenian to follow him, started jogging.

The ephors were judging the races, and so Pheidippidas found himself being led through crowds of spectators. He could hear voices exclaiming, "Athens! A runner from Athens!" Soon the entire crowd was watching him anxiously. The Spartans could tell just by looking at him that he was nearly finished—and good news is never urgent.

The youth indicated five middle-aged men with long Spartan braids in robes with purple trim. With relief, Pheidippidas realized he had reached his destination. There seemed no reason not to blurt out his embassy; certainly there was no secret about it. So he gasped out: "The Persians. The Persians have landed at Marathon."

The five ephors immediately withdrew to the Ephorate to hear the full text of the Athenian plea for help. The Athenians were nothing if not eloquent, and Pheidippidas, by then refreshed with some water laced with wine, was not just a long-distance runner, he was also a good messenger. He conveyed the full pathos of the situation. Six hundred triremes, two hundred horse transports, thousands of horses, and tens of thousands of archers had landed just twenty-six miles north of Athens on the plain of Marathon. Athens would fight with every man she had. Athens would fight to the death. But against these numbers! Against the invincible Persians....

"Men of Sparta," he urged, "do not stand by while the most ancient city of Greece is crushed and enslaved by a foreign invader."

The ephors heard him out, and then solicitously told him to rest. They would give him their answer before sunset. Pheidippidas was escorted out, and then the five men faced one another.

Kyranios was the oldest of them, a year short of being eligible for the Gerousia. He had been elected by a large majority. Sperchias, in contrast, had only just squeaked through, helped along by Leonidas' emphatic support. But then, having elected two of Leonidas' closest associates, the Spartans showed their reluctance to commit themselves to one or the other of the increasingly hostile factions by electing two of Brotus' followers as well, Lysimachos and Euragoras. The fifth man was Polymedes—a sober, withdrawn widower who had distinguished himself as an administrator of public works, particularly a tricky drainage system. His election had taken both Leonidas and Brotus by surprise. No one knew exactly where he stood on most issues—which seemed to be exactly what the majority of Sparta's citizens wanted when they elected him.

Kyranios sat stiffly in one of the five chairs in the center of the chamber, with Sperchias nervously beside him. Polymedes preferred to sit on one of the benches circling the room and Euragoras leaned against one of the thrones, while Lysimachos paced the room like a caged lion. "The Persians have never—never—been defeated in battle."

"The Scythians didn't exactly get crushed," Euragoras noted.

"Only because they had no cities, no crops, no orchards—nothing but their herds and women to defend. They withdrew before the Persians into the endless spaces of their country, but they never met the Persians face to face. They never fought them, much less defeated them." No one contradicted Lysimachos; everything he said was true. "And twenty thousand fighting men! Just how many men can the Athenians field?" Lysimachos directed the question to the two former officers.

Kyranios shrugged and answered, "Ten thousand hoplites."

"And maybe another ten thousand archers," Euragoras added.

"Then they can match the Persians one to one?" Lysimachos stopped pacing and looked at his fellows in amazement. He hadn't realized Athens was *that* populous.

Kyranios made a face and a dismissive gesture. Euragoras answered for him, "Only if you call potters and fishmongers soldiers! What the Athenians can field is a hodgepodge force composed of farmers and craftsmen. Such men at best know how to put on the breastplate their granddad left them, and at worst don't even own one! They're no match for a Persian army of this size."

"Then you think the situation is hopeless?" Polymedes asked in a sharp, almost reproachful tone.

"No. Fifteen to twenty thousand Athenians stiffened by two to three thousand Lacedaemonians should be sufficient to stop a Persian force of this size; after all, the bulk of the troops landed at Marathon won't be Persians, but conscripts from their subject peoples. There's no way of knowing the exact mix, but many of Persia's subject peoples have only second-rate troops. We can presume that many of the men under Persian command at Marathon are resentful and nearly worthless. There are probably no more than three to five thousand Persians in this invasion force, and maybe that many Medes as well. These are the men we need to beat," Kyranios judged.

"So. We agree," Lysimachos concluded, astonished. So often in the last nine months the ephors had been divided: Kyranios and Sperchias on one side and Lysimachos and Euragoras on the other. Again and again, Polymedes had either broken the stalemate or abstained and forced decisions to be postponed.

Kyranios was relieved to discover that for once there would be no bitter fight with Lysimachos and Euragoras. He nodded. "We must support the Athenians with our standing army immediately," Kyranios declared firmly.

"Exactly," Euragoras concurred, glancing at Sperchias to see if the man who had been so keen to save Persian lives a year ago when the ambassadors were here would now find some objection.

But no matter how hard his enemies tried to portray him as a Persian toady, Sperchias was not pro-Persian, he simply believed in civilized behavior—which did not include killing ambassadors. He nodded now, although he was frowning in anticipation of the next problem.

"And who will command the army?" Polymedes asked.

Stunned silence answered him.

When a Spartan army left Lacedaemon, it was always commanded by one of the kings. Indeed, until Cleomenes and Demaratus had fought publicly during the campaign against Athens more than a decade earlier, *both* Spartan kings had led her armies in the field. But the man occupying the Eurypontid throne was viewed as a usurper by at least half the citizens (and that meant half the troops), and the Agiad king was obviously insane. Not one of the five men in the room was willing to entrust Sparta's army to either of these men in a confrontation with the most powerful military force on earth: the Persians.

Kyranios took the initiative. "Leonidas," he declared firmly.

"No!" Euragoras responded instantly and emphatically.

The other four men, however, gazed at him so intently that he felt embarrassed by his own transparently knee-jerk reaction. He tried to make himself sound reasonable. "He's only thirty-eight. And he's the most junior of the lochagoi. Why not one of the others? Hyllus is senior."

Kyranios snorted. "And he's a boneheaded old mule. Leonidas is the best of the lot."

"That is *your* opinion!" Euragoras snapped back. "Not shared by everyone."

"Not everyone has to," Polymedes reminded them. "Leonidas is an Agiad prince and husband to the ruling Agiad king's only surviving child."

"If he is to be appointed for his bloodlines, then Cleombrotus—"

"—would never be accepted by the army. He was never so much as an enomotarch!" Kyranios cut Lysimachos off before he could finish.

"We have to put this to the Assembly—both the deployment outside of Lacedaemon and the command." Polymedes put an end to the threatening altercation.

"Assembly?" Lysimachos protested. "It's the middle of the Karneia! We can't hold an Assembly during the Karneia. Besides, Sparta's citizens are scattered to the corners of Lacedaemon. Men are as far away as Kythera and Pylos. It will take us at least two days to get word to all of them, and another two days before they can get back here."

"Whether in their capacity as citizens or as soldiers, it will take that long to recall them anyway," Polymedes argued. "After they are assembled, it is only a matter of one extra day to get the approval of the Assembly before deploying."

"But time is critical!" Kyranios protested. "One day could make all the difference between victory and defeat. The Persians have *already* landed. For all we know, the Athenians are fighting for the freedom of Greece at this very moment!"

"In which case we will come too late in any case," Polymedes retorted, unimpressed. "We cannot commit the Spartan state and Spartan army in a matter as important as this without the approval of the Assembly."

"What is there to debate? We chose war with Persia the day we murdered Darius' ambassadors, rejecting his peace offer," Sperchias reminded them bitterly.

"After we rejected Persia's *demand for submission*," Kyranios corrected his younger protégé sharply, adding, "What is left for the Assembly to decide?"

"The number of age cohorts to call up and the commander," Polymedes insisted. "We can go to the Gerousia with our proposals, and they can prepare to bring a petition before the Assembly five days from today. Meanwhile, we can issue orders for the perioikoi to muster their forces and set in motion all other necessary preparations for a deployment, including sending the perioikoi with arms and supplies to the Isthmus. The Assembly can be held on the first day after the end of the Karneia, when everyone is sure to be back in Sparta. The army can march the following day, fully sanctioned by the Assembly and with a commander supported by the majority of citizens."

"That's almost a week away!" Kyranios protested. "If we wait that long, our troops will not reach Athens for ten days. Is that what you're going to tell the Athenian runner? That we'll come—but not for another ten days?"

"Yes. That's exactly what we must tell him."

"I don't know if it is wise to let the Athenians—or anyone else—know that we have no king capable of taking the army to war—or that it takes us five days to mobilize during a religious holiday," Sperchias remarked.

"For once Sperchias is right," Euragoras admitted grudgingly. "Cleomenes seems to have sparked latent resentment among some of the Arcadian cities. He invited them to attack us. It would not be good for them to hear that we are leaderless."

"We need not tell the Athenian our reasons," Polymedes observed.

"All he needs to know is that we will come—but not before the full moon."

"Calm down, Euragoras," Talthybiades urged the younger man, handing him a glazed, cream-colored mug decorated with a black horse and containing more wine than water. "I'm not sure it is such a bad thing for Leonidas to be sent north to support Athens."

"Not a bad thing?" Euragoras asked incredulously. "It's practically like appointing him king—or at least heir to the throne!" Euragoras' words were chosen to enrage Cleombrotus, but he had miscalculated.

Brotus, frowning, turned to Talthybiades to ask: "Do you really think my brother might be dumb enough to accept this command?"

Talthybiades smiled. "Yes. I do. He's like our friend Euragoras here. All he sees is the potential for military glory. What he doesn't see is that he will probably arrive too late and find himself facing the Persians alone. Even if the Persian forces take some casualties in their fight with the Athenians, the Persians are still bound to outnumber the two thousand men we are sending north. If Leonidas leads the army north to fight the Persians, I think it will be the last we ever see of him."

"It sounds too good to be true," Brotus concluded.

"It won't be the last you *hear* of him, of course," Talthybiades noted. "He will earn eternal glory. A new Achilles—dying away from home against an enemy that hasn't done us any harm. No doubt poems will be written about him and songs sung in his honor. You might even have to build a monument to him."

"As long as he stays dead and doesn't rise from the grave like Kastor! Brotus exclaimed, raising a laugh from the others.

"I believe Polydeukes had to beg Zeus for the favor—and be prepared to sleep in his grave every other night—which I gather you don't plan to do," Talthybiades remarked with a smile.

"You're damned right! Let Leo have his hero's grave—as long as I am king."

"Who can stand in your way? His infant son, perhaps, or his sharp-tongued wife?"

They laughed again. Then Talthybiades turned deadly serious.

"This is your chance, Brotus. This is the moment you have been waiting for. You need to seize the opportunity and act decisively the moment Leonidas crosses out of Lacedaemon."

Gorgo couldn't sleep. Leonidas had drifted off, his steady breathing almost a snore, his hands—so powerful and fractious when conscious—lying limp and harmless on the white sheets of the bed. He needed his sleep. He was determined to reach Athens as soon as possible, and had already announced his intention to march twelve hours a day. Twelve hours of marching with breaks every two hours would leave them less than eight hours to sleep at night by the time the camp was made and food cooked.

And what would he find when he reached Marathon?

Gorgo slipped gently from her marriage bed so as not to disturb her sleeping husband. She pulled a peplos over her naked body, dispensing with breast-bind and chiton at this time of night. She moved out onto the exterior stairs, avoiding the nursery, where her children might not be sleeping as soundly as she hoped.

The moon was high and only a sliver short of full. It lit up the night so brightly that the potted plants cast sharp shadows onto the terra cotta of the terrace, and turned the leaves of the apple trees silver as they shivered and swayed in a light breeze. Farther away, Taygetos stood out sharply against the bright sky.

Gorgo could see her footing clearly as she descended the stone stairs to the courtyard. The limestone steps were rough but still warm under her bare feet. At the foot of the stairs she was met by one of the cats, who trotted out to rub herself against Gorgo's legs. Gorgo leaned down to pet her without thinking.

Everything seemed so normal, so peaceful, but it wasn't. Somewhere roughly 150 miles to the north, tens of thousands of barbarians threatened Athens, and if Athens fell, Lacedaemon would be next. Darius had defeated one nation after another. He had put down every revolt against him—and there had been many! He did not suffer insubordination. He did not tolerate diversity or dissent. Darius saw himself, as Danei explained it, as the representative of the one true God, Ahuramazda. He believed that he, Darius, had been sent to bring order out of chaos. Darius despised the Greeks precisely because they were organized in hundreds of squabbling cities, always at war with one another. He believed it was his duty to civilize the Greeks. He had offered to do so without bloodshed or oppression when he gave them the opportunity to submit without warfare. Instead they had killed his ambassadors, confirming all his prejudices against them.

Now Persia came not just to civilize them, but to punish them for their impudence. It would be far better for Sparta to face the inevitable at the side of Greece's most populous city than to do it alone. It would have been better for Sparta to have responded at once to the plea for help. Gorgo understood all that. She understood her husband's urgency to march north—and she knew, too, that she would have been insulted if the ephors and Assembly had chosen anyone other than her husband to command the army.

But she couldn't shake the unease that filled her, either. She knew her role as a Spartan wife was to smile and wave as her husband marched off to war. She knew it would be unforgivable to voice any regret or concern. Leonidas was only doing his duty, and he would be accompanied by two thousand other citizen-soldiers—the entire active army. Furthermore, Leonidas had confided in her that his orders were to join the Athenians and fight with them, but to return without engaging the Persians if he found Athens already defeated. He was not being sent out to fight a hopeless battle against all odds. If Athens was still defiant, his troops would form part of a much larger force; if Athens had caved in, he would not be asked to fight at all, but to return to Lacedaemon with his entire force intact so they could prepare to defend Lacedaemon with their Peloponnesian allies closer to home. Either way there was a risk, but no certainty, of death. She ought to be able to face this with more fortitude than she felt.

But the demons she faced were all the more unbearable because she could not confess them to anyone—least of all to Leonidas himself. Gorgo did not want Leonidas to go. She could not explain it. It was not rational. But she could not shake the feeling that something terrible was about to happen.

Chapter 8

DEATH OF A KING

Nikostratos liked his midday nap. It was, of course, a self-indulgence, one he would not have granted himself if he were younger. But at seventy-four, he thought a body that had served him so prodigiously long deserved to be treated with respect.

Since it was late summer and the days were blisteringly hot, he decided to take his nap on the rooftop terrace that opened off the bedroom on his wife's estate. The property had been a gift of King Cleomenes to his mother on her marriage to Nikostratos. It lay on the east bank of the Eurotas almost opposite Amyclae, but not on the river itself. Instead, it backed up against the Parnon range. It consisted almost entirely of terraced orchards and vineyards. The house was small and simple, but it had a covered roof terrace with a magnificent view north toward Sparta. It was one of Nikostratos' favorite spots on earth.

Nikostratos settled himself on a couch placed strategically in the shade and cooled by breezes. He stretched himself out with a contented sigh. The crickets chirped in the pine trees, and a calico cat sat primly, washing her face with a white paw.

Chilonis was off somewhere. Nikostratos didn't remember what she'd said, exactly, but he suspected she was visiting her granddaughter Gorgo. Their relationship was close, and Gorgo needed a little extra support today after seeing her husband march off yesterday to face the Persians.

She'd played her role very well, Nikostratos thought. She had stood prominently beside her bewildered father as the army marched past, smiling and waving not only to Leonidas but to family friends as well: Oliantus, Temenos, and Maron were all on active service and left with Leonidas, while Sperchias had been one of the two ephors sent with the army, the other being Euragoras. Gorgo had looked lovely, Nikostratos thought, completely biased and unashamed of it.

The sound of galloping hooves brought Nikostratos from his shallow doze with a start. The road here was too steep and too rough for that pace, he thought with irritation. If some youth of the agoge were riding a horse like that, he deserved to have his hide taken off! And then the hoofbeats broke into a clatter, and Nikostratos realized the rider had turned in at the gate. From below he heard the helot housekeeper exclaim in surprise, "Can I help you, sir?"

"I need to see Nikostratos at once!"

With a grunt and a wince (because his back increasingly gave him pain), Nikostratos sat up and swung his feet down. With another inward groan, he pulled himself to his feet and went to the railing to look down at the unexpected visitor.

The housekeeper had moved inside and was calling up the interior stairs, but Nikostratos leaned over the railing and called directly down to the young man, who wore leather training armor. His eyesight was no longer the best, and he could not make out the young man's features, but he thought the braids of dark-blond hair raked across his skull at an angle; if so, it was probably Dienekes.

Dienekes had been appointed one of the three hippagretai this past spring, and the Guard had not deployed with the rest of the army because it always remained with the kings; no ruling king had marched to Marathon.

"I'm up here, young man!" Nikostratos called down. "Is something amiss?"

Dienekes took a step back to get a better look at Nikostratos. "Sir!" he shouted back. "You must come to the city at once. The ephors have ordered the arrest of King Cleomenes."

"What? On what charge?"

"To prevent him from doing harm to himself and others, sir."

"That's ridiculous," Nikostratos retorted.

"Not entirely, sir. He attacked Talthybiades with his staff, breaking his nose and knocking one of his teeth loose."

"Talthybiades?" Nikostratos asked, instantly smelling a rat. Talthybiades was one of Brotus' cronies. No doubt he had provoked the attack. "And Lysimachos, as ephor, demanded Cleomenes' arrest," he concluded out loud.

"Sir. It is worse than that. Please come."

"I'm coming, I'm coming." Nikostratos stopped only to slip his feet into sandals, and made his way down the stairs and out the front door in his chiton without bothering about a himation in this heat.

As he came out of the house, the look of worry on Dienekes' face set off every internal alarm. Dienekes had a reputation for nerves of stone. He was the kind of young man who joked even in the worst situations, and it was this—more than his jaunty braids or flashy striped chitons—that had won him the admiration of the younger men. "What is it?" Nikostratos demanded at once.

"Sir. They ordered King Cleomenes put in the stocks."

Nikostratos' first reaction was, "They can't do that!" Then he thought to ask, "Who do you mean by 'they'? Kyranios and Polymedes would never condone such an insult to a son of Herakles!"

"Lysimachos signed the order, sir, but it was Cleombrotus who gave it."

"In the name of Zeus himself! By what authority? Brotus has no right to arrest *anyone*—let alone a ruling king!"

"He is King Cleomenes' closest male kinsman, and he gave Lysimachos permission to do this."

"And the Guard let it happen?"

"The company on duty was commanded by Pieros son of Aekesilos, and he is one of Orthryades' men."

Nikostratos felt as if his head were spinning. "You're saying that Talthybiades provoked the king into hitting him, Lysimachos used it as an excuse to arrest him, and Brotus then authorized putting his own brother in the stocks? This is preposterous! How could Brotus dare such a thing?" he asked again, incredulous, yet increasingly convinced that this was a plot.

"Brotus argued that Cleomenes is dangerous, sir. What he did to Talthybiades is harmless compared to his other acts of violence.

Brotus claims the palace staff lives in terror of his sudden und unpredictable outbursts. There has been more than one instance since his return from Arkadia in which servants have been injured. In one case, Brotus claims, the king took a knife to a man and tried to flay him alive, saying he would do what the Persian king did to his enemies."

Nikostratos paled in horror. In Thessaly, Cleomenes had learned that Darius punished rebel leaders by first flaying them alive and stuffing straw into their skin like scarecrows and then impaling the skinless, but still living, victims on stakes to starve and bleed to death before the eyes of their followers. Gorgo claimed she had heard her father say: "I am more a king than Darius! Darius is a usurper! But Darius cuts out the tongue of anyone who tells the truth about how he came to power on the pretext that he is telling a lie. If a usurper can turn lies into truth and truth into lies just by skinning people alive, why shouldn't the son of Herakles teach impudent Spartans respect by the same device?" Until now, Nikostratos had not realized that he'd actually tried....

Cleomenes had periods when he appeared simply confused and harmless rather than wild. Yesterday had been such a day. Chilonis and Gorgo had cajoled him into carrying out the sacrifice always performed by Spartan kings before an army left Lacedaemon. Cleomenes had readily agreed without even protesting that he wasn't leading the army anywhere (as they had half expected). Furthermore, he spent a great deal of time earnestly turning over the entrails and inspecting the liver and heart of the calf before declaring with astonishing sobriety (in marked contrast to his usually flippant tone when speaking of the Gods) that the signs were exceptionally good. "Really," he announced as if amazed, "I've never seen anything quite like this before. A triumph beyond all measure. A victory to be sung as often as the Song of Troy. And all the glory will go to you, little brother." He had then flung his arms around Leonidas and started to cry, babbling about how much he loved him and wished he could go with him, and then that he envied him the fame he would earn. "People will remember you forever," he declared, his mood already shifting as he started to sound jealous.

"He threatened to skin Brotus alive," Dienekes continued, bringing Nikostratos back to the present. "He drew his sword, and it took several guardsmen to hold him back and wrench the sword out of his hand."

Nikostratos met Dienekes' eyes, and now he shared the alarm in them. Cleomenes had delivered himself into the hands of his enemies. He had given them the grounds they needed to move against him, and Nikostratos felt lamed by a sense of destiny. He would go with Dienekes into the city, and he would see what he could do to get the mad king released from the stocks. But Cleomenes' throne was no longer salvageable. The Gods were taking their revenge for a lifetime of blasphemy.

Yes, Nikostratos thought mournfully as he let Dienekes help him up onto a horse, Cleomenes was lost—but what was to become of Sparta? Leonidas was by now halfway to Athens, and to call him back was unthinkable. Sparta's safety depended no less on his ability to deflect the Persian invasion than on deflecting Brotus' bid for power.

Only slowly did Nikostratos grasp the full magnitude of the threat. Not only was Leonidas gone, so were most of the men who supported him: Sperchias, Oliantus, Temenos, and last year's eirenes who were devoted to him for his intervention against Alcidas—Maron most of all, but a score of others as well. They were now all citizens, and so had marched away with the army. Nikostratos knew he could count on Kyranios and Alkander, and Gorgo and Chilonis too, of course, but he feared that would not be enough.

He gripped Dienekes' strong arm. "Young man," he said, "I am going to need your help in the days ahead."

"You will have it," Dienekes assured him simply.

To make use of the cool part of the day before the unbearable heat of noon, Phormio had risen early. He left his wife sleeping and dragged himself up the outside stairs to his office. Here, with the doors to the balcony open to the cool breeze and the twittering of birds, he worked carefully through the receipts from the day before, checking the entries of his clerks. He did this routinely to keep them honest, but his thoughts were not really on the neat figures entered on the rosters. His thoughts were in the north.

Phormio calculated that the Spartan army was by now in

Corinth, heading for the Isthmus. There they would surely get word of whether the Athenians had managed to hold the Persians at Marathon or had been pushed back toward the city itself. Phormio was moderately optimistic that Athens had not yet suffered a decisive defeat, because he had agents in the east-coast ports where news from Athens would first go ashore. His agents had orders to send runners with any important intelligence. By tomorrow night the Spartan army could reach Athens, and the day after that they could be in Marathon. If the Athenians could hold the Persians just three more days, they would be reinforced by the full Spartan army, two thousand strong, supported by an equal force of perioikoi infantry. Phormio was confident that this force would make the difference between defeat and victory.

A strange rhythmic pounding penetrated his consciousness. It was a dull but resonant sound, not the metallic ring of a smith, but the higher-pitched crack of an axe on wood. It sounded like a drumbeat, but that made little sense early on a working day.

With a grunt, Phormio heaved himself off his chair and moved on to his balcony, frowning with unease. He planted his fleshy hands on the railing and looked down into the street. It was empty at this time in the morning, except for a stray dog sniffing along the edge of the house opposite and a slave boy dawdling in obvious reluctance to do whatever task he'd been assigned.

Then from the top of the street—from Sparta—a rider appeared. The man was swathed entirely in black and riding a black horse. Drums hung on either side of the horse's withers, and with steady, merciless regularity the rider pounded the head of one and then the other. Phormio caught his breath. This could mean only one thing: one of Sparta's kings had died. He leaned over the balcony and called down to the rider, alarmed and shocked. "Which king? Which king is dead?"

"The Agiad Cleomenes," the rider answered and continued down the street, as more and more people came out onto the balconies to stare in dread.

As she drew up to the back entrance of the Agiad royal palace,

Gorgo could hear the hysterical screaming of her mother, even above the clamor of the women banging cauldrons. While the black-robed, mounted drummers brought the news of a king's death to the scattered perioikoi cities and towns of Lacedaemon, within Sparta itself the death of a king was traditionally announced by a procession of women beating cauldrons. The procession had formed and was starting to weave its way through the streets. The residents of the houses it passed were required to drape their doors in black cloth and dress in mourning.

One of the palace grooms caught sight of Gorgo and ran out to take her horses. "Mistress Gorgo! Go in at once. I'll see to the horses."

Gorgo nodded and entered through the door he had left open, wishing her mother could be more dignified. Apparently she was going to have to calm and comfort her mother when she was feeling weak and vulnerable and desperately in need of comfort herself. If only Leonidas were here!

But she did not make it to the private apartments. As she tried to cross the kitchen courtyard, the palace staff blocked her way. "Mistress Gorgo! It wasn't Prothous' fault. Truly, he had nothing to do with it!"

"I swear, Mistress, he never left his bed all night!"

"You've got to save him, Mistress!"

"What are you talking about?" Gorgo countered, confused and resentful. Didn't they realize her father was dead? Did they have to assault her with their pleas for favor and intercession even at a time like this?

"Your uncle! He is threatening all of us with punishment. He says we can be charged with murder!"

"I only just learned of my father's death. Let me go to him and my mother!" Gorgo replied stubbornly; she did not want to even hear their problems right now.

"But, Mistress, Cleombrotus might arrest us all! Order our death! He says he is king now, and that he can have us killed."

"Don't be hysterical. Brotus isn't king, and he can't just kill you anyway. Why would he want to?"

"For giving your father the knife!"

"And we didn't, Mistress! We were all asleep in our beds."

"Your father asked for wine, and we gave him that," one of the younger staff admitted, "but not the knife, Mistress. You've got to believe us!"

"I don't know what you are talking about," Gorgo insisted irritably. "I must go to my mother and tend to my father's corpse. This is no time for other matters. Let me go to my father!"

"But, Mistress—"

Suddenly they were all silent and staring at her.

Finally someone asked, "Didn't they tell you how he died?"

"No. Why? How did he die?"

Dead silence answered her; her mother's screaming seemed all the louder. A shudder ran down her spine and she shivered in the heat. "How did he die?" she asked again, more insistently.

Now they looked away, embarrassed and ashamed.

Gorgo pushed past them. She moved rapidly until she reached the atrium of the private apartments. Here she paused to lift her head and listen to the sound of her mother's screams. At last her mother sounded less hysterical; she seemed to be sobbing now rather than screaming. Gorgo crossed the courtyard and reached the shade on the far side. Her mother had gone silent, but the silence was eerie. She ascended the stairs and started down the hall toward the double doors that gave access to the king's bedchamber. She had gone only halfway when the doors opened and a figure draped in black emerged. It was a moment before she realized she was standing face to face with her grandmother.

Chilonis took a step forward and took Gorgo into her arms, but her grip was not soft. This was not the comforting embrace of a loving grandmother. Chilonis' arms were fierce and imprisoning.

"What is going on?" Gorgo demanded, instinctively pulling free of a hold that seemed to arrest rather than support. "How did my father die?"

"You do not want to see him," Chilonis answered obliquely, turning Gorgo around in her arms and pushing her back toward the stairs.

Gorgo resisted, raising her voice to demand almost hysterically, "What is going on here?"

Chilonis took Gorgo by the shoulders, and her fingers dug into Gorgo's flesh like claws. "Listen to me!" she hissed harshly.

Gorgo went deadly still. She could not remember her grandmother ever talking to her like this, not even when she'd been a disobedient child. When she met her grandmother's eyes, her heart missed a beat. This was not the woman who had been more a mother to her than her own. This was a gray-haired, sharp-featured crone, whose eyes blazed with an intensity that was almost evil.

"Someone has systematically sliced the skin off your father from his feet to his belly."

Gorgo stared at her grandmother, disbelieving.

Chilonis dropped her voice even further. She was almost inaudible. "According to your uncle Brotus, your father did it to himself."

Gorgo stared at her grandmother in horror. Cleomenes had taken knives to himself before, and once he'd tried to tear his skin off with his fingernails. His boasts about imitating Darius and flaying "insubordinate" Spartans alive echoed in her skull. Instinctively, she knew he was capable of this. But then she remembered. "But he was in the stocks .... His hands were bound ...."

"He was *not* in the stocks. They brought him here for the night, but you are right, his hands were bound. According to Brotus, he used threats to convince one of the helots to bring him a kitchen knife."

"But the staff knows how dangerous he is—" Suddenly Gorgo understood what the staff had been babbling about.

"They know how dangerous he *can* be—and so does Brotus," Chilonis whispered. She could see the understanding widen Gorgo's eyes. Chilonis dropped her voice further. In fact, she did not speak the words at all, not even in a whisper. Instead, she mouthed them precisely and clearly. "Go—home. Get—Pleistarchos—to safety. Send—word—and this—" she pressed Cleomenes' ring, the ring of the Agiads, into Gorgo's hand, "to—Leonidas. Now!"

For a moment Gorgo felt so weak she thought she was going to faint. This was the nightmare scenario Leonidas had always warned her about. Her father was dead. Brotus needed to eliminate Pleistarchos to clear the way to the throne—and Leonidas was a hundred miles away with every citizen of the active army!

Laodice, who had not been in Laconia when Cleomenes' father died, was worried about conforming to the letter of the law with respect to honoring a Spartan king at his death. "We must all wear mourning for ten days after the funeral, and a male and a female member of each household must attend the funeral and keen loudly. Does it have to be the head of the household and his wife? Or do you think Polychares and Melissa could go?" she asked her husband anxiously, thinking she didn't have time to go to a funeral. There was bound to be an endless stream of visitors coming to pay their respects to Gorgo, and she needed to have snacks for them. Or should they slaughter a calf?

"The funeral will not be until tomorrow at the earliest," Pelopidas declared practically. "And meanwhile, we've got chores to do. Polychares," he signaled to his eldest son, suggesting by his look that they had lingered too long with the women already, "it is time to get to work."

"We're going to have to dye some old things black so we can cover the door and have enough to wear. Where are the girls?" Melissa demanded irritably, getting to her feet and going to the kitchen window. "They ought to set up a vat for dyeing in the back yard." She peered out, searching for her errant daughters.

"Pelopidas!" Laodice stopped her husband as he was going out the door. "We must slaughter a calf, or at least a kid."

"Did the mistress order it?"

"No, but we can't expect her to think of everything herself at a time like this. She just saw her husband off to war, and now her father is dead."

"I don't think we should slaughter anything without the mistress' express permission—"

"Agiatis!" his daughter-in-law cut him off as she called urgently out the window. "Come down this instant!" Turning to Chryse, Melissa ordered, "Run outside and get Agiatis out of that tree before she does herself harm. You shouldn't let her play with your boys!"

Before Chryse could protest that she could hardly stop it, her mother added, "And bring some fresh fennel and mint from the garden for dinner."

Chryse slipped out the back door and hastened to the orchard.

Her oldest boy, six-year-old Pelops, and Leonidas' four-year-old daughter Agiatis were clambering about on an apple tree, while her youngest son Kinadon complained about being left behind. His elder brother scoffed, "Even girls can do it!"

The sun-warmed tiles of the terrace felt good under her bare feet, but between the trees of the orchard the soil was dry and littered with sharp little stones. She moved more slowly, but called, "Pelops, Agiatis! Come down at once!"

"Watch me!" Agiatis responded and let go of the branch over her head altogether. She started to fall backwards, and Chryse's heart missed a beat. A second later Agiatis giggled delightedly as she hung upside down by her knees, her hair reaching for the earth in a bright cascade. Chryse crossed the distance in four long strides, unceremoniously grabbed her master's daughter, and pulled her down off the branch, ignoring her howls of protest and pain as the little girl scraped the back of her calves on the bark. "If you don't do as you're told, I will tell your father you were a *bad* girl when he gets back. He will make you stand naked with your face to the wall and take a cane to your saucy backside!" Chryse threatened, with enough conviction to make Agiatis uncertain.

Pelops meanwhile decided it was time to beat a fast retreat. He jumped down from the tree and ran as fast he could in the direction of the river Eurotas.

Chryse took Agiatis firmly by the hand and suggested, "Come help me pick fennel and mint for dinner."

Agiatis, who had been looking over her shoulder at her disappearing playmate, looked up curiously at Chryse and consented with a single nod. Chryse led her around to the far side of the house with four-year-old Kinadon trailing them.

The kitchen garden was neatly enclosed in a low limestone wall to keep out straying animals. Here beans, peas, asparagus, leeks, onions, cabbage, cucumber, fennel, coriander, cumin, sesame, mint, oregano, parsley, thyme, and rosemary were raised in neatly cultivated rows and harvested as they ripened.

Chryse turned to Agiatis. "Can you find the fennel?" she asked.

Agiatis bit her lower lip as she surveyed the plants stretching out before her, and then started wandering down a lane looking intently, but Chryse's own attention was distracted by horsemen galloping along the road beyond the adjoining pasture.

Chryse had been born on a horse farm in Messenia and spent the first years of her life there. Even after coming here with her parents as a child, she was familiar with horses because Leonidas had a large stable. The approaching horses were galloping like racehorses, which was crazy on a hot day like this—unless they were bringing news. Chryse's heart froze in her chest. The army! Her lover and the father of her two sons had marched north with the army. If the army had engaged the Persians, who was to know if he were still alive?

But messages were usually sent by runner—and if by rider, then not by men in armor like these two men.

Worse! The riders now plunged down off the road and rode full tilt toward the outer pasture wall. Chryse could only gape as the horses lifted up their front feet and sprang over the fence without breaking stride. To Chryse's amazement, the riders were still with them as they landed on the far side and charged diagonally across Leonidas' pasture, scattering the grazing mares, heading straight for Chryse.

A new fear paralyzed Chryse. Two years ago four men had set upon Temenos, nearly killing him. They had threatened to rape her until she bled and to kill her "putrid" sons. With Temenos and Leonidas away with the army, Chryse was suddenly afraid these men had come to carry out their threat.

Chryse looked desperately for a place to hide, but the thundering hooves were coming closer by the second. In a panic, she turned to run back to the house, but already one of the horses was beside her. "Where's your mistress?" a voice demanded as the horse was hauled to a sudden stop, reared up, and sidled in agitation. Sweat dripped from its belly and foam splattered from its mouth as it flung its head around.

Chryse glanced up in wide-eyed terror, only to recognize not one of her assailants but Eurytus, one of her rescuers. "Your mistress," the youth repeated. "We need to speak to Lady Gorgo."

"But she went to the palace this morning. Her father died in the night, and she went to help her mother with the corpse," Chryse stammered out.

"Where's Leonidas' son?" the young man's companion asked,

pulling up beside him. It was Aristodemos, the younger brother of Leonidas' attendant, Meander, and the other rescuer on the day Temenos was assaulted.

"Pleistarchos is upstairs in the main house sleeping. He—" Chryse started.

"You've got to hide him!"

"Hide him?" Chryse asked, uncomprehending.

Fortunately the riders had drawn the attention of Chryse's father. Pelopidas arrived at a run from the stables, calling out to the two meleirenes, "Is the young master in danger?"

"My father, Lysimachos, is an ephor, and I overheard him give orders to seize Pleistarchos," Eurytus explained. "Members of the Guard will be here any minute!" He looked anxiously over his shoulder.

Leonidas had warned Pelopidas from the day Pleistarchos was born that Brotus wanted his son dead. Leonidas had told Pelopidas that the time might come when the boy's life depended on him.

Pelopidas did not hesitate now. "Go fetch Pleistarchos," he ordered his daughter. "Wrap him up and take water and bread from the kitchen!"

"You'll see that he's safe?" Eurytus asked anxiously.

"We will protect him with our lives!" Pelopidas replied.

"We'd better disappear! If your Dad finds out—" Aristodemos urged, looking over his shoulder.

"Yes, go!" Pelopidas urged; then he turned and ran for the kitchen to tell his wife what was happening.

Crius had settled into the running. He had reached the phase where as long as nothing unexpected happened, he could run indefinitely. His lungs and legs had found a rhythm that required no conscious will to keep going, while his brain wandered.

The events of the last days had been exciting. His parents were old worry-warts! They feared that Leonidas might get killed and never return. They feared that Leonidas' enemies would find Pleistarchos and kill him. They even feared that harm might come to Gorgo. Typical helots! he thought with a touch of contempt.

Crius didn't see things like that at all. When the men had come looking for Pleistarchos they found nothing, and just when they started to threaten and become violent, Lady Gorgo had arrived with Dienekes and an enomotia of guardsmen. Now his parents and Gorgo had protection day and night.

Meanwhile, he was on his way to take the news of King Cleomenes' death to Leonidas. Lady Gorgo had confided all the details of how the old king had been found, and ordered him to tell Leonidas *everything*. Crius could read between the lines. Gorgo thought her father had been murdered, and the murderer was her uncle and Leonidas' twin brother Cleombrotus, who was trying to take the throne away from little Pleistarchos. Crius found the whole situation thrilling—particularly his role in it.

He was confident that he would find Leonidas and deliver Cleomenes' lapis lazuli ring as proof of the king's death, and that Leonidas would return to put an end to Cleombrotus' ambitions. But first Leonidas had to beat the Persians, so Crius' main question was whether or not he'd get a chance to see the Persians. If he was lucky, the Spartan army would already have crossed the Isthmus, and he would have to go all the way to Marathon to catch up with Leonidas.

Crius pictured himself finding Leonidas in the Greek camp facing the Persians. Leonidas would nod and point to his unfinished business with the enemy, saying he could not return until the Persians had been sent back where they came from. Then, while Crius was still there, the Persians would attack and the Spartans would rush out to fight. Crius would see it all.

It didn't occur to Crius that the Greeks might lose. He knew that theoretically it was possible, but he did not believe it. The Greeks would win, and he would see it all from some vantage point high on a hill overlooking the battlefield. Then he would run back to Sparta, and he would be the first to reach the city with news that the Greeks had won a great victory—and that Leonidas was on his way back with the army. He would bring the news to Gorgo—no, with news like that he would go directly to the ephors.

The sound of hooves behind him reached his ears and, delayed, his brain. By the time he registered there was a horseman behind him, the horse was not far away. Without slackening his pace, Crius moved to the side of the road to let the horse and rider pass. The hoofbeat altered from the three-quarter tack of a canter to the steady click-clack of a trot. The shadow of horse and rider fell over him. Crius just kept running.

The horse passed him and then swerved and stopped, cutting him off. Baffled, Crius stopped and looked up at the rider uncomprehendingly.

The face that grinned down at him was familiar and triumphant: it was Bulis, one of the four men who had tried to kill Temenos. "You!" the man exclaimed with obvious satisfaction as he recognized Crius. "You arrogant little asshole! You thought you could get away with thumbing your nose at us forever, didn't you? You and your whore of a sister—sleeping with Spartiates and thinking she's special. We'll show her how *special* she is, one after another—just as soon as we take care of you!"

Crius had just a split second to register that the horseman was drawing his sword. He ducked and flung himself to the side in a single motion. But his body was numb from running for almost ten miles already, and the mounted man was a trained soldier. Crius succeeded only in prolonging his agony. Because he'd moved, the first thrust did not completely gut him. Instead it sliced between his ribs and penetrated partway into his rib cage. The ex-guardsman used his foot against the gushing wound in Crius' side to brace himself as he yanked out his sword. Crius reeled and staggered away, trying to run. His assailant urged his mount forward, and this time rammed the sword between Crius' shoulder blades with more force than before. The tip came clear out the other side below the rib cage. When his murderer again braced himself with his foot to remove the sword, Crius was pushed down onto his knees, spewing dark blood and other liquids from his mouth.

Bulis tried to ride over Crius, but his horse refused, rearing up and pivoting away; so Bulis jumped down. He went over to where the young helot lay bleeding and kicked him in the side. A twitch and groan revealed that Crius wasn't dead yet. Bulis reached down, wrapped the fingers of his left hand in Crius' hair, and yanked the young man's blood-soaked upper body off the ground. With a single stroke of his sword, he hacked off his head. As the head came free, he used the momentum to fling it as far from the road as possible. It landed in the scrub-brush-covered field and rolled against the foot of a gorse bush. Then he kicked the body off the road, wiped the blood off his sword with a rag from his pouch, and tossed the rag into the gorse bushes before remounting and riding back to Sparta.

Euryleon rose to get more wine for the men collected in his andron. He took the pottery pitcher with him and stepped out into the paved courtyard of his house. Here he paused to look up at the clear night sky. The stars were bright overhead, the constellations easily identifiable because the moon had not yet risen. More than a hundred miles north of here, Leonidas might also be looking at the same sky, the same stars, Euryleon thought, and he poured the last remnants of wine out onto the earth with a prayer to Kastor to bring Leonidas home—in time.

The men behind him in his cozy andron, with the mosaic floor and frescoed walls, were all Leonidas' friends. They were collected here to work out how best to ensure that Brotus did not steal the Agiad throne in his absence. For the others this was largely about what was good for Sparta—at least it was for Kyranios, Nikostratos, and Dienekes. For Euryleon, however, much more was at stake. For him, the danger from Brotus was personal.

When Euryleon had been a child, he had fallen ill with a fever that left him partially blind and asthmatic. Because of his poor eyesight he was useless with bow and javelin, moved only uncertainly at night, and generally lost confidence in his own body. His shortness of breath meant he was bad at running, jumping, and indeed every sport. Sometimes he even had trouble on marches or during drill. At first the other boys made fun of him, but over time he had carved out his own place in the herd. Since he could not hunt, he stayed in the camp, kept the fire going, and gradually became a good cook. He had a good singing voice and an ear for melody. More unusually, he could imitate accents and inflections with uncanny accuracy. Noting how this delighted his fellows, he cultivated this skill, and soon he had become a gifted storyteller who could keep his audience breathless with anticipation—or move even callow youths to tears.

He had been progressing steadily toward citizenship in his own unorthodox way when, in his eighteenth year, Brotus became his eirene. Brotus did not value any of his skills. Brotus not only ridiculed him, he started to systematically torture him by demanding that he do things he could not do. Because he failed, he was punished. When he dropped his shield on the way back from drill, he was made to clean everyone's equipment. When he tripped during a march, he was forced to crawl the remainder of the distance, with Brotus himself standing over him to make sure he didn't cheat. The punishments seemed to get worse with each incident until, because he spilled wine on Brotus when serving him, he was forced to lie on his back while Brotus urinated on him. At first the others protested Brotus' treatment of their fellow herd member, but Brotus soon silenced them with his fists. By the time it came to the urinating incident, they had not said a word, as if they didn't care. That had hurt most of all. But that night, after Brotus had gone to sleep, the others threw a himation over Brotus' head, dragged him out to the barrack latrines, and beat him brutally before rolling him into the filth.

The next day Brotus had reported this unprecedented insubordination and demanded that all his charges—since he had not seen or heard who had actually committed the outrage—be flogged "until they whimpered like newborn kittens." Technarchos, the school official in charge of the eirenes at the time, responded by saying no eirene had ever before provoked such collective rebellion. He noted further that the unit did not have a reputation as difficult. He suspended Brotus from his position and personally took temporary command.

That had not been a pleasant week, but better than under Brotus. Technarchos had been an enomotarch in the army. He pushed them to their limits, but without the vindictive streak so characteristic of Brotus.

Still, the Paidonomos remained reluctant to disgrace a youth who had been the victor at Artemis Orthia four years earlier. Furthermore, to permanently remove Brotus from his position as eirene would have denied him, an Agiad prince, his citizenship. So rather than humiliate Brotus outright, the Paidonomos ordered the Agiad twins to swap units. Leonidas became Euryleon's eirene.

At first Euryleon and the others in his unit assumed that the twins would be similar and feared Leonidas. Euryleon still remembered vividly the way Leonidas had walked in and announced that he wasn't his brother and didn't want to be treated like him—and then suggested lunch at a perioikoi tavern down in Amyclae.

But this incident of provoking unprecedented insubordination had ruined Brotus' army career before it even started, and he had always blamed Euryleon for that. Over the years, Brotus had hinted more than once that he would take his revenge on Euryleon when he became king....

Euryleon was a full citizen and a popular choral master. He knew a king did not enjoy the same kind of power over a citizen that an eirene had over his charges. Still, Euryleon did not fool himself that Brotus was inhibited by the law any more than he was by conscience. Brotus was a man who believed that the stronger was always in the right and should do whatever he could get away with. Furthermore, Euryleon no longer had only himself to worry about; he had a son and a daughter. He did not want them at the mercy of a king like Brotus.

With a start, Euryleon realized he had lingered too long with his thoughts. The others would start to wonder where he was. He hastened to the hall, where his wife Mania was at her loom with the cradle beside her. She looked up anxiously, and before she could ask a question Euryleon explained himself. "I've just come for a lamp so I can get more wine from the cellar."

Mania shoved back her stool and stood. "I'll take care of that. You go back to your friends."

Euryleon gratefully turned over the pitcher with a smile and a quick kiss. Euryleon had married very late, at age twenty-eight, and Mania was ten years younger than he, a plump girl who, like himself, had been a bit of an outcast. She was not particularly clever, certainly not like Gorgo, but she was fiercely loyal to Euryleon, protective of her children, and proud of her household.

Euryleon returned to the andron. As he entered, Nikostratos was reminding the collected company, "The law prohibits Council and Assembly meetings until ten days after the interment of a king. Meanwhile, assuming Crius reaches Leonidas by tomorrow night, which is reasonable, Leonidas can be back in Sparta in four days' time."

"Can—but won't," Kyranios countered. "No matter what is at stake, Leonidas will not abandon his post as commander of the army until the Persians have been engaged for better or for worse. Furthermore, we must face the fact that he could be killed or seriously wounded in that engagement."

The others stared at the former lochagos for a moment; then Alkander answered for all of them. "What you say is true, but if Leonidas dies at Marathon, then we are all in Brotus' hands regardless. The Assembly, as we have seen before, is not going to accept a child as king, and even if it did, Brotus would be named regent in the absence of Leonidas. Our duty is to ensure Brotus does not seize power as long as there is even a ghost of a chance that Leonidas will return."

"Agreed."

"So what is the mood in the Council?" Dienekes asked, his eyes directed at Nikostratos.

"Divided. Leotychidas supports Brotus—which has done the latter more harm than good, pushing some of the men who were undecided before to look more favorably on Leonidas. If you asked me to add up the votes today, I'd say there are ten men solidly for Leonidas, nine men solidly for Brotus, including Leotychidas, and nine men who are undecided."

"Where does Epidydes stand?" Alkander asked about the former—and acting—headmaster.

"A critical question!" Nikostratos noted with a quick look of approval at Alkander. "Epidydes thinks highly of Leonidas and has no illusions about Brotus, but he is a conservative through and through. He believes in legitimacy more than expediency. He will not cast his vote for Leonidas unless he is convinced he is the legitimate heir. This is even more true of Polypeithes and Hetoimokles. The issue of legitimacy, not character or capability, is our greatest problem. If you were to ask the Council today who would make the *better* king, we would easily have a majority of two to one for Leonidas. But if you ask them who is the *rightful* king, the majority dissolves."

"The Council is made up of old men," Dienekes growled back, "men who still remember Leonidas as 'Little Leo'—the runt of the litter, the last born and least loved of Queen Taygete's brood. In the

Assembly—and it is the Assembly that will have the final say—the young men have a voice, and they are overwhelmingly in favor of Leonidas."

"One man, one vote," Kyranios agreed. "But add it up: there are not enough young men to outweigh the older age cohorts, and not all the young men are necessarily in Leonidas' camp. A critical faction in the Assembly, as on the Council, is undecided—or worse, simply afraid to make a decision that might be in violation of the law."

"Is there *no* way to make them see sense?" Euryleon asked, anxiously.

"I think there might be," Dienekes answered, narrowing his eyes.

"Better still would be to convince them that Leonidas is the elder twin," Alkander suggested softly.

For a moment there was stunned silence in the room. Nikostratos and Kyranios both looked shocked, while Euryleon was simply baffled. Everyone knew Leonidas was the youngest of the Agiads. But Dienekes understood instantly. He sat bolt upright. "Of course! We don't have a moment to lose—or Brotus might forestall us." Dienekes swung his legs down and reached for his sandals.

Euryleon, like a good host, got to his feet with him, asking a little plaintively, "You're sure you don't want to wait until morning?" Euryleon did not like doing anything in the dark if he could help it.

"By then it might be too late!" Dienekes answered, annoyed with the dithering Euryleon. He did not understand Leonidas' affection for the choral master. He started across the courtyard, ignoring the weaker man.

Euryleon trailed him to the door, bringing him his himation, which had fallen unnoticed to the floor as Dienekes left the andron. "Dienekes!" He stopped the Guard commander as he went to open the door out to the street.

Dienekes looked over impatiently, his face betraying his contempt for this man who shared none of his virtues.

Euryleon was used to seeing disdain in other people's eyes. It did not particularly surprise him. He ignored Dienekes' expression and appealed to him from the depth of his heart: "Don't dismiss me! I want to help. There must be something I can do!"

Dienekes was taken aback, abruptly ashamed of himself. He

looked Euryleon in the eye, all his arrogance of a moment ago gone, and recognized that strength of character was indeed more important than strength of body. "Yes. There is something you can do," he concluded. "Go to Phormio, Leonidas' steward and the spokesman of the perioikoi. Tell him he must bring Kleta to Sparta."

"Kleta?" Euryleon asked uncomprehendingly.

"He'll know who I'm talking about. Be sure he brings her disguised and keeps her hidden until we send for her."

Chapter 9

MARATHON

Panic had seized Athens. As he rode through the city, Kimon noted that in the poorer quarters families were hastily loading their movable chattels on handcarts and donkeys, while their howling children and frantic women got in the way. In the richer districts, wagons stood in front of more than one house, and although the slaves loading them worked more discreetly and efficiently, the intention was the same: flight.

It infuriated Kimon. Just yesterday, word had reached Athens that at Marathon the Athenians had attacked and defeated the Persians. This was an astounding victory, more than anyone had expected ten days ago when the Persians first landed. The combined forces of Athens and Plataea had been greatly outnumbered, after all, and although the Spartans had promised aid, they had not yet arrived.

Yet yesterday, the famous runner Eukles arrived on the outskirts of Athens, having run all the way from Marathon. Gasping for air and coughing up blood, the athlete struggled to deliver his message. "Victory," he gasped out. "Victory… half… Persians… defeated… defenseless… traitors…"

Except for the first word, it was not entirely clear what Eukles meant to say, but by evening reports were flooding in from the southeast coast of Attica that a Persian fleet was sailing toward Piraeus. The best that people could figure out was that the Persians had divided their forces. The Athenian army at Marathon had apparently defeated only half the Persian force, and the rest—possibly the larger force—was approaching defenseless Athens.

Furthermore, people believed that Eukles' reference to "traitors" meant that the Persians had allies inside Athens itself. People concluded, full of alarm, that Hippias' friends and supporters were going to betray the city. In panic, men claimed that the landing at Marathon had from the start been a ruse to lure the army away from Athens. Hysterically they declared that the city was lost.

Kimon refused to believe that. He couldn't afford to. His father, once a Persian vassal when he ruled the Chersonese, had burned his bridges behind him by joining the Ionian revolt. If he fell into Persian hands, they would flay him alive and stuff his skin with straw as they had the other rebel leaders.

But it would not come to that, Kimon told himself firmly. His father would bring the Athenian army back to Athens in time to defend it. All that was needed was for those who had remained in the city to prevent the Persians from landing until the army returned. It was just twenty-six miles to Marathon, a seven-hour march, maybe eight or nine since the men were exhausted from the battle yesterday. But they *would* come, Kimon was certain. It was just a matter of time....

Kimon's colt stumbled on the rough cobbles, and Kimon pulled up, steadying the young horse. He slowed to a walk and patted the colt's neck reassuringly. There was no point in endangering the colt or himself. Two minutes more or less were not going to make any difference to the fate of Athens, but the number of people streaming away from the port angered Kimon. Damn them all! Didn't they see what was at stake? Did they want to become Persian slaves?

For half his young life Kimon had been, through his father, vicariously at war with Persia. The Persians had taken away the home of his birth and childhood, the Chersonese. His family had been forced to flee, packing their movable goods onto five ships, but leaving behind immeasurable treasure—and his mother's heart. She had never adjusted to life in Athens—or to the loss of her firstborn son.

The Persian fleet was already blocking their escape when they set off in five ships from the Chersonese. Kimon's older brother Metiochos had been nineteen, the same age Kimon was now. Their father

Miltiades had allowed him to command one of the five ships. Kimon, who had been fifteen at the time, had been jealous and begged his father for a command of his own. He had been furious when his father ordered him to travel with his mother and sisters, as if he were a child. They had set out in convoy, with his father aboard their escorting trireme—but Metiochos, always a little rebellious and daring, put on more sail than the other four ships and soon disappeared from sight. At first Kimon was filled only with envy for his brother's freedom, but soon they learned that Metiochos' ship had been intercepted by the Persians. Metiochos had paid dearly for his independent command and impudent disregard of his father's orders: he had been sent to Darius in chains.

Kimon sometimes still had nightmares about his brother's capture, and his mother was convinced that her son had been betrayed by his faithless and greedy crew. Certainly the ransom Darius had offered for Miltiades and his family had been enormous. No doubt it still was, Kimon reflected nervously....

Kimon reached the waterfront. He was encouraged to find that barricades were being erected with anything that came to hand. Men were frantically rolling barrels over and even breaking up furniture. But then loud quarreling broke out and brought work to a halt. Apparently no one was in charge, and Kimon felt a new flash of frustration. Even now, when their very existence depended on it, the Athenians could not unite behind a single leader. They couldn't just take orders. Everyone not only had an opinion, they had to express it!

"Kimon! Over here!" From the next quay someone was waving and shouting.

Kimon passed the men arguing about the best place to erect the barricade, and joined the other youths of his ephebe unit. They had been summoned here by their commander. As Kimon joined them, the old man growled, "What news?"

"There's no sign of the army yet, but I'm sure—"

"I'm not interested in your opinion! I want facts. And that *is* one!" He stabbed his stubby finger in the direction of the harbor entrance. Persian ships were clogging the narrows at the mouth of the harbor. "And something is going on out there, too! A trireme arrived from the east, and now there is activity aboard every ship. They are preparing something. Look!" Kimon's commander pointed to the coastline to the west. "Do you see?"

Kimon shook his head.

"Something's moving along the coastal road. Either the Persians have landed troops to our west—or the Spartans are coming."

"It's too soon for the Spartans," Kimon protested.

"Well, I sure the hell don't like the alternative!" the old man snapped back. "Instead of just sitting pretty on that fancy horse of yours, why don't you take your ass over there and find out?"

Kimon drew a deep breath to protest such language, but the man had already turned away. Kimon swallowed his protest and turned his colt around to start working his way through the maze of streets toward the western road.

Finding his way occupied so much of his attention that it was only after he had left the congested part of the port that Kimon could focus on his task. Since there was no way the Spartans could be here in less than three days, he was preoccupied with the idea of riding to warn his father that Persians had landed to the west.

He drew up and looked along the coast, squinting in an effort to see better. He could see nothing—except the sunlight glittering on the blue waters of the bay, heat waves shimmering upward from the nearest fields, and dust drifting off to the north. The dust must have been stirred up by men on the road. He'd better find out more before he reported to his father, he decided, and kept riding. After another quarter-hour, he was convinced that a large body of troops was indeed approaching. Wasn't that enough information? How much further should he go?

With a shock, Kimon recognized that he was afraid. He did not want to go any closer. He wanted to gallop in the opposite direction, and it was precisely this realization that made him urge his colt forward, his lips pressed together unconsciously. He kept his eyes on the coastal road until they watered from the strain. Then he blinked and wiped sweat from his eyes with the back of his naked arm. Keep riding, he ordered himself, reminding himself that his colt was the direct descendant of one of the four mares with which his grandfather won the Olympic chariot race three times. The colt would bring him to safety.

But what if the colt stumbled? Or was killed by an arrow?

Or could it really be the Spartans?

It penetrated Kimon's terrified brain that there were no mounted officers with the approaching troops. Persian noblemen never walked. These troops could be neither Persian nor Mede. Ionian allies of the Persians? But how could the Persians trust them not to join forces with the Athenians? Certainly if they were Ionians, it would be worth appealing to their patriotism. Kimon urged his horse forward a little more hopefully.

Abruptly he caught a wisp of what sounded like singing. He pulled up and held his breath, his ear cocked. When the wind fell away, it came again: men's voices raised in song. The approaching troops were singing as they marched.

Spartans! Only Spartans sang as they marched!

He started cantering forward in relief.

The troops came to a sharp halt in response to a command, and the column stood still and silent. Kimon could see the faces of the men at the front of the column. One of them was dressed in a white linen corselet over a red chiton, and he said something to the man behind him. A helmet was handed forward, which he put on before he stepped forward to meet Kimon.

Kimon flung himself down from his horse and crossed the last few yards on foot to ask breathlessly for confirmation: "Sir? Are you . . . from Sparta?"

"We are. And Athens? Is it still free?" the Spartan inquired with a gesture toward the bay. Kimon looked over his shoulder and realized that from here, the harbor appeared clogged with Persian ships. From here it looked like Piraeus was already in Persian hands.

Kimon turned back to the Spartan, grinning. "Athens is more than free! We defeated half the Persian forces at Marathon yesterday. It is the other half that is—as you can see—threatening Piraeus. The army is returning even now to face them. Although it has not yet arrived, you'll be able to hold off the Persians until my father brings the Athenian army back!" Kimon's relief had turned into excitement.

Miltiades could hardly move. He doubted if there were any

muscle in his aging body that had not been stretched out of shape and strained beyond endurance. The stiffness reached from his toes, which had pushed for relentless hours against the dirt of Marathon to keep him upright, to his fingers, which he had hardly been able to uncurl when he finally put up his sword. Yet it was unthinkable that Spartan officers be escorted to Marathon by anyone other than himself.

Kimon seemed to recognize his father's state, because he stepped forward with a smile to help him mount. Kimon was a good boy, Miltiades reflected. Boy? Miltiades looked at his younger son again. He was still slender and had always been darker than Miltiades himself, but there was no question he was almost a man. He had grown up fast these last years.

And Metiochos? The thought of his eldest son sent a stab through his chest, worse than the pain of his tortured muscles. Miltiades wondered what he looked like now, but the image that came to mind was brutal: he pictured him in Persian clothes. Miltiades could not shake the suspicion that his son had consciously defied him and sailed intentionally into the Phoenician fleet. Metiochos thought the advantages of being a wealthy vassal to the greatest power on earth outweighed the dubious benefits of freedom. He had told his father he preferred to pay homage to the Great King rather than be a "slave to the mob" in Athens. Miltiades' suspicions about his son's intentions had been fueled by rumors that, when his son was laid a prisoner at Darius' feet, he had been graciously freed by the Great King. Indeed, some claimed he had been given land, income, and even a Persian wife, so that he lived at the Persian court like other exiles rejected by their own people.

Meanwhile, Miltiades had good reason to remember his son's refusal to submit to the Athenian Assembly when it put him on trial for tyranny. After he had lost everything because he sided with the democracies, the Athenians had labeled him tyrant. The memory filled him with bitterness.

"It's all right, father," Kimon's voice brought him back to the present. "I've got him." He meant the fidgeting stallion.

Miltiades nodded once, forcing himself to ignore the pain and stiffness of his body as he swung himself onto the horse's back. In the end, the majority had voted in his favor, Miltiades reminded himself. And the majority had elected him general. After the victory he had given them at Marathon, maybe they would even start to respect him.... More likely, they would not. The mob was made up of mediocre men, and such men hated leaders. They especially hated successful leaders. No doubt the mob would feel compelled to cut him down to size *precisely* because he had saved them from slavery. The mob devoured leaders the way wild dogs tear apart a lone stag.

Lost in these thoughts, Miltiades did not speak to his younger son as they rode to the arranged rendezvous with the Spartan officers. The latter had expressed interest in visiting the battlefield at Marathon, and Aristides, who was hosting them, provided them with mounts to cover the distance more rapidly.

It was only a small party. Most of the Spartans remained behind to rest from their forced march. The group consisted of four senior officers and one of their archons, or ephors as the Spartans called them, a certain Euragoras.

Miltiades' life had been spent in the Aegean and he had never taken any interest in the Peloponnese. He knew almost nothing about Sparta, and these men did little to arouse his interest. They were dressed the same, wore their hair in quaint braids and their beards trimmed close to their chins. The oldest was completely gray-haired and made a rather dull impression, while the youngest had warm brown hair and lively intelligent eyes but was otherwise unremarkable. The others fell somewhere in between. If he had been more interested, Miltiades might have noticed more about them, but he was in too much pain and too depressed to make an effort, and the Spartans were suitably laconic. So they rode in silence, following the longer but easier coastal road with the sea to their right, sparkling in the morning sun. Around them the farmland lay parched and bleached between the olive trees, and a deceptive peace lay in the hot air. Ahead of them the sky was thick with swirling clouds of vultures.

After several hours they reached what had been the Greek camp, still scarred by campfires and trampled bare. When they caught sight of the mound being prepared to bury the Greek dead, Miltiades unexpectedly started to speak. "There," he announced, lifting his arm and pointing. "That was where the Persian host camped. All the way from there to there. And there, to the left, near Makaria Spring, is where they grazed their horses. And their ships were beached not just here, but there as well."

"What did you say your casualties were?" a Spartan asked in evident disbelief as he gazed across the field, still strewn with Persian corpses. Some were already collected into heaps in preparation for burial; others still lay scattered. Everywhere, the corpses were set upon and the flesh torn away by rapacious crows and vultures amid swarms of flies. Many corpses were feeding stray dogs as well as the birds. The air was increasingly hard to breathe.

"192 Athenians, and, I believe, 19 Plataeans."

The Spartan looked again at the field, then back at Miltiades. "There must be five to six thousand barbarian dead out here. How did you do it?"

Miltiades took a deep breath and glanced at his son. Kimon looked as if he were holding his breath with anticipation. "It wasn't easy," Miltiades started, and suddenly the words started flowing. It was good to talk in this company, free of naysayers, rivals, and jealous little men. Here he could talk, knowing that no one was hanging on his every word in the hope of finding fault. No one here wanted to drag him down just because he was better than they.

"You know that Athens elected ten generals to command our army?" he asked the Spartans.

They gaped at him, dumbfounded.

"Yes. My sentiments exactly. But, you see, the Athenians fear the rule of one man more than they fear defeat itself. They would rather be defeated as free individuals than be victorious under the command of a strong leader. On the one hand, of course, this is what makes them hate the Persians so much. They will never accept the rule of a king, any king—much less a Persian usurper who calls himself a "Great King" simply because he has conquered other tyrants and kings. On the other hand, they fear that one of their *own* may rise up and become even a little more powerful than the rest.

"So there were ten generals, and five of them thought we should stay on the defensive and do nothing beyond block the road to Athens and make the Persians fight their way through us. Such an attitude invited what happened: the Persians sent half their forces around our flank by sea, to attack Athens behind our backs. I knew we had to attack, but I hoped that you would be with me." He looked reproachfully at the Spartans.

"We had no choice," one of the men answered defensively. "We cannot march to war before the full moon."

Miltiades did not deign to answer. He simply continued, "So I waited. Maybe I would still have been waiting until today if the Persians had not embarked half their army and most of the cavalry. We saw it happen, and we managed to capture a slave who revealed all he knew. He could not give us exact numbers, but he said he had heard officers saying that Athens would be betrayed to them. He knew the ships were sailing to Piraeus, and he believed Athens would be seized without a fight.

"That left me no choice. I knew we could not afford to wait for you any longer. We had to defeat the Persian forces still at Marathon, and then return to defend Athens from the rest.

"Although there seemed to be less cavalry in evidence, they still had many archers. When we started to form up in battle order, the Persians responded, and their line stretched from there to there." He pointed.

"We could only prevent our flanks from being turned by weakening the center. Furthermore, they had so many archers that a barrage was like a hailstorm. To reduce exposure to that storm, we broke into a run as soon as we came in range and ran all the way to their line.

"When the lines crashed, it was terrible. While some Persian conscripts and subject peoples can only be forced to fight by whip-wielding officers, the Persians and Medes themselves are brave men and fierce fighters. They are proud of being warriors, and they were holding the Persian center, exactly where we were weakest.

"When I realized that our wings were gradually overpowering the weaker troops of Persia's subject states but that we were making no progress in the center, I let the center give ground. Very slowly—as if we did not *want* to give up a single foot, but simply *could* not hold out any longer. I let that happen until we had lured the Persians halfway back toward our starting line. To about here." He stopped abruptly and looked about.

The Spartans looked at the ground. The sun had baked it hard again, but to a practiced eye it was clear that not so long ago it had been a morass of mud—artificial mud created by sweat, blood, and urine.

Miltiades continued. "I gave the prearranged signal; the Plataeans turned right from the left wing and Kallimachos turned left from the right wing, and our two wings started crushing the Persians from both sides as the center stopped giving ground.

"The Persians did not realize at first what was happening. When they did, they tried to pull back toward their ships in an orderly fashion. But panic seized some of the allied troops and that, as you know, is infectious. Some troops broke and ran for the ships; then others did as well, fearing that if they did not, the ships would be launched without them. The battle turned into a slaughter as we chased the fleeing, panicked men all the way to the beach. In the end we captured seven ships, although most got away."

The Spartans surveyed the field again in light of this information. The way the dead were strewn substantiated Miltiades' account; many more were heaped on the beach in untidy piles than lay here on the tortured, cluttered field itself. Here were broken weapons, and the earth bristled with arrow shafts, but on the beach the dead were bunched together, reaching out toward the sea.

"As you can see," continued Miltiades, gesturing toward a heap of corpses—on which crows hopped about, cawing and fighting over strips of bloody flesh—"most of the dead are not Persians or even Medes."

"How can you tell?" asked one of the Spartans.

"Their clothes," Miltiades responded simply, and the Spartans were reminded that this man had been a Persian vassal until he joined the Ionian revolt.

"Their armor has been stripped away," a Spartan observed.

"No. They wear none, or rather, nothing like ours. The Immortals wear suits made of metal scales, but most troops in the Great King's army have nothing but cloth, wicker, and leather to protect them."

"Ah! Then that is how you managed to kill so many of them."

"Do not make the mistake of underestimating them!" Miltiades warned sharply. "The battle lasted half the day before we finally managed to turn their flanks and crush their center." There was no triumph in his voice; he sounded only weary. Kimon looked at him anxiously, suddenly fearing that his father, like Eukles, had some wound he was ignoring or disguising.

The Spartan commander spoke for the first time. "How many casualties did you have from arrows?"

"Not more than a dozen. The bulk of our men died in hand-to-hand fighting."

"You believe advancing at a run reduced casualties? I would have worried about the line becoming porous."

"Look at this field: it widens in the space between the two camps. If I'd maintained cohesion and advanced slowly, the Persians would, with their greater numbers, have been able to outflank us—or deploy the cavalry they still had. If I'd stretched the line to prevent that, it would have been porous anyway, with a gap two or three feet wide between each hoplite. The advance at a run took the enemy by surprise, and we crossed the widest part of the plain before they could respond. Then the territory itself compressed the files again."

The Spartan commander nodded, but then he glanced back the way they'd come, distracted by a horse and rider coming after them at a dangerous pace. The others followed his gaze.

"That's Sperchias," Euragoras announced, recognizing his fellow ephor.

Leonidas had already recognized him, but he said nothing. He was trying to imagine what would have brought Sperchias chasing after them. What news could not have waited until tonight? Or had Chi just changed his mind and decided to join them? That wasn't like Chi. He was not at heart a military man.

Sperchias was not the best rider, either, and his face was red when he pulled up beside the waiting party. "Leo—nidas!" He took a deep breath. "Polymedes sent a message to Euragoras and me." As he spoke he handed the scroll to Euragoras, but his eyes remained fixed on Leonidas.

Euragoras opened the scroll to read the official message from the chairman of the ephors, but Sperchias told Leonidas the contents verbally. "Your brother Cleomenes is dead."

"Dead?" The exclamation came not just from Leonidas, but from the other lochagoi as well.

"How?" Leonidas asked.

"Suicide. He took a knife to himself—"

"What? When?"

"Two days after we marched out. The law requires he be interred within three days. That is tomorrow."

All Leonidas could see was Brotus' face as he voted for Leonidas to be given command of the army. At the time he had been thankful that Brotus had let their rivalry rest for the sake of Greece; now he knew his motives had been very different.

Euragoras finished reading the official message and announced: "Sperchias and I must return to Sparta at once!"

Miltiades asked, "What has happened?"

"One of our kings is dead," Euragoras answered.

Miltiades looked sharply at Leonidas, only now registering that he was someone of importance.

"Which one?" Miltiades asked.

"The Agiad, Cleomenes."

"Didn't Cleomenes' son die? Who is his heir?"

"His brother Cleombrotus," Euragoras answered before Leonidas could open his mouth, but Leonidas did not let him have the last word. "Or his grandson Pleistarchos," he added.

"I see." Miltiades understood instantly that Sparta was divided over the issue. "And you," he addressed Leonidas, "are brother to both the dead king and this Cleombrotus?"

"And father to Pleistarchos."

Miltiades cursed his own weariness. Why hadn't he taken greater notice of this Spartan? Why hadn't he paid him more attention? He glanced at Kimon. Perhaps the boy had learned more about him? But there was no time for regrets. Leonidas was asking politely but urgently, "I know this is a terrible imposition, but could you spare horses for me and the two ephors," he nodded toward Euragoras and Sperchias, "so we can return to Sparta at once?"

"You don't want to take the whole army?" Diodoros questioned.

"No. There's no time—or need—for that."

"They make up the better part of the Assembly," Diodoros reminded him with an expression of concern on his face.

"And no Assembly can be held until ten days after the funeral.

Hyllus?" Leonidas turned to the gray-haired lochagos. "I herewith turn command over to you. Bring the army back in reasonable stages so they are in Sparta no later than eight days from now."

"They'll be back a damn sight sooner than that!" the older man replied gruffly. "We'll march tomorrow."

Leonidas bit his tongue. He had just turned over command. He looked questioningly at Miltiades.

"You will be given fleet horses—I only ask you to return them as healthy as you receive them."

"I personally guarantee their good treatment and prompt and safe return—with interest. I understand from Kimon that you admire Kastorian hounds. I will send you two of my best."

Miltiades nodded, satisfied. This was definitely a man worth befriending. "Then let us return to Athens at once."

Chapter 10

THE ELDER TWIN

Agiatis was throwing one of her temper tantrums, but Gorgo had no nerves left to deal with it. It was six days since her husband had marched away to war, and four days since her father's gruesome and unexpected death. Twice since then, guardsmen had come to the kleros demanding that she surrender Pleistarchos to "safekeeping." She had had no word from her husband, and could not even be sure he was still alive. Indeed, she was beginning to believe he was dead, because he had not answered the message she'd sent via Crius. She had known from the start that he might not be able to abandon the army and *return* to Sparta, but she had trusted him to *respond.* She had counted on his advice, encouragement, and promises.

Instead, there was nothing—absolute silence—while Brotus grew bolder from day to day. Today, she was sure, Brotus would follow directly behind the funeral bier, in the place traditionally reserved for a king's heir and ahead of Gorgo, her mother, and her grandmother. Gorgo's mother wanted her to bring Pleistarchos with her, to remind the city that she had a son, but Gorgo was afraid of bringing the boy out of hiding. She feared that Brotus would use the opportunity to get his hands on him.

At all events, she had to attend the funeral as a reminder of both Pleistarchos and Leonidas, and it was getting late. The road was already clogged with thousands of mourners flooding in from the surrounding countryside. They would slow progress into the city. Pelopidas had a matched team of black mares, draped in black feathers, waiting out front. The last thing she needed was for Agiatis to throw a tantrum and insist she would *not* stay home.

"I'm better than Pleistarchos!" Agiatis screamed at her mother, stamping her foot. "I'm granddad's favorite! I want to come!"

"The answer is *no*!" Gorgo shouted back, looking around for Laodice or Chryse or Melissa. Why weren't they here to take Agiatis off her hands at a time like this? "Go to your room and wait there—"

"No!" Agiatis refused.

Chryse emerged in the doorway. "Mistress, Phormio is downstairs asking for you."

"Phormio?" Gorgo's heart lurched in her chest. She had sent Pleistarchos to Phormio's keeping, believing Brotus would never think to look for an Agiad prince with a perioikoi family. Now she feared something had happened to him after all. She rushed out of the room.

Agiatis grabbed her as she went by, screaming, "I'm coming, too!"

"You'll do as you're told!" Gorgo answered, and for the first time in her life she slapped her daughter.

Chryse jumped in at once, sweeping the now howling Agiatis up into her arms. "It's all right, Mistress. I'll take care of her."

"What's been keeping you up to now?" Gorgo answered, without awaiting or expecting an answer. Instead she ran down the stairs to the hall and out onto the front porch, leaving Agiatis screaming and kicking in Chryse's arms.

At the sight of Phormio, Gorgo's panic dissolved. The plump perioikoi did not look like a man bearing bad news. He had come in his chariot, evidently to take part in the funeral procession, and his wife was beside him, dressed in a glamorous black himation studded with pearls and silver beads.

The perioikoi steward was smiling broadly. "I thought I should drop by and assure you that all is well," he explained, letting himself down from the chariot with an unconscious grunt and coming forward to take both of Gorgo's hands. "The boy's no trouble at all," he murmured in a low voice, as if he didn't want even his wife to hear. "My daughter-in-law assures me he is a very good boy."

"Which is more than I can say for his sister," Gorgo admitted, with a sigh of relief and a glance over her shoulder at the upstairs windows of the house, from which Agiatis' enraged protests could still be heard.

Phormio looked intently at Gorgo and could see worry and sleeplessness written all over her face. He had come to remind her of perioikoi interests, but at the sight of her he could not bring himself to voice them. The poor girl, he thought, had enough worries—although he'd expected her to look better now that the Persian threat was banished. Then he had another thought. "You *have* heard the news of Marathon, haven't you?"

"What news?" Gorgo asked, instantly alarmed again.

Phormio calmed her with a wide smile. "The Athenians routed the Persians completely! My sources said something—probably greatly exaggerated—about six thousand Persian dead for just two hundred Greeks. But regardless of details, there can be no doubt that the Persians have withdrawn. Their fleet was last seen heading for Mykonos. Your husband may already be on his way home with the whole army at his back."

Gorgo caught her breath and looked up at him hopefully. "Is that true? You're sure of it?"

"Not a doubt. The battle took place four days ago. Did no one tell you this?" Phormio asked anxiously, realizing that something was very wrong if this important information had not been delivered to Gorgo.

"No," she answered simply, instantly understanding that Brotus must have withheld the information. She felt as if she could hardly breathe. She was suffocating under her black himation, which seemed to absorb and magnify the almost unbearable heat of the summer sun. She could feel sweat trickling down between her breasts and under her arms. She ought to be overjoyed that Leonidas was out of danger, but she could not afford the luxury of joy: if Brotus knew Leonidas was alive and was returning, he would be compelled to act sooner and more forcefully. Brotus didn't have any choice but to lay claim to the throne today. He had to seize power at once, and confront Leonidas with a fait accompli. Gorgo could see that, but she couldn't see how she could stop him.

"Are you all right?" Phormio asked solicitously.

"I must go to Sparta," Gorgo answered, turning to mount her own waiting chariot, but she had moved too abruptly in the heat. The world started to sway unnaturally.

Phormio caught her. "Steady. Sit down for a moment. Catch your breath."

Gorgo got hold of herself again and shook her head. "I must get to Sparta," she repeated.

The road was so crowded that they moved at walking pace, and things only got worse in the city itself. It was much more congested here even than during the major holidays. Gorgo remembered hearing that almost ten thousand people had attended her grandfather's funeral, and that was thirty years ago; the population of Lacedaemon had grown since.

As they approached the Agiad royal palace, not only did the crowd become denser, but many of the women were keening and hitting their foreheads as well, in the prescribed gestures of grief. The drummers that had carried the word of the king's death to the borders of Lacedaemon now flanked Herakles Square, beating in slow unison. Their deep, resonant pounding provided a counterpoint to the keening of the mourners.

Yet it was the sight of the boys and youths of the agoge that struck Gorgo most forcefully. They were all in black and collected by unit along the processional route. Despite the obvious excitement of the younger boys, a surprising solemnity and dignity had gripped the youths. Even the little boys knew they were witnessing history. It was a generation since Sparta had last buried a king, and only full citizens were old enough to remember that event.

On the front steps of the royal palace, the Guard was drawn up three hundred strong. They too wore black chitons under their blackened armor, and their helmets were pulled down over their faces. Gorgo looked for Dienekes but could not find him. They all looked the same, and she shuddered; she knew that at least one company sided with Brotus.

The funeral procession was forming up in the alley beside the palace. Gorgo joined her mother and grandmother, turning the chariot over to the palace grooms. Her mother wore her veil completely over her face. She grabbed Gorgo's arm and hissed, "So! You have just given up. Abandoned everything to Brotus! I should have known!" But then she clung to Gorgo's arm as if she could not stand up without it.

Gorgo glanced at her grandmother. Chilonis just nodded briefly. She looked even worse than Gorgo felt. She looked like a living corpse, and Gorgo felt a flash of guilt for leaving her here to deal alone with the mutilated body of her only son and his hysterical wife.

The palace steward approached Gorgo. "My lady? May we proceed?"

"Yes, of course," Gorgo assured him.

He disappeared again. The drums started beating faster and faster until they sounded like galloping cavalry. From the front door of the royal palace, between the rows of guards, the bier emerged. Her father's body had been skillfully wrapped in a purple shroud that exposed his face and torso, encased in armor, but hid the hideous, self-inflicted wounds. Gorgo got only a glimpse of her father's face, but it appeared remarkably relaxed and peaceful in death. The bier was carried by the six youngest Council members. The rest of the Gerousia and three ephors followed in two files.

Then came Brotus.

Gorgo had expected it, but it still made her blood boil. He was dressed, like everyone else, in black, but it was black accented with gold. Gold framed his greaves and his breastplate, the latter evidently purchased for this occasion. Gorgo didn't get a good enough look to be sure, but she thought the gold figures on the black background showed a man strangling a lion. This scene ostensibly depicted Herakles killing the Nemean lion, but it was, she thought, intended to symbolize Brotus defeating Leonidas. Yet by far the worst aspect of his attire was that he was wearing a cross-crested helmet. Such a helmet was reserved for Sparta's kings, and it was the most prestigious of all royal symbols because it was the symbol a Spartan king wore in his most important function: as commander of Sparta's army.

Gorgo heard her mother suck in her breath and then spit out, "What did I tell you?"

The funeral procession started forward at a solemn pace set by the drums, which had slowed again to a solemn march. Behind the family came the Guard and then the Spartiates, followed by the perioikoi, and finally the helots, who formed the long tail of the procession.

The procession wound its way through the city past the most important temples—the Bronze-House Athena, Poseidon of the Family, Zeus and Athena of Counsel, the Argive Hera, Helen's Sanctuary, Alkman's Grave, the Horse-Breeding Poseidon, Kassandra's Sanctuary, Kastor's Grave, the Olympian Aphrodite, Zeus of the Trophy, and more—every one, it seemed, but the Menelaion and Apollo at Amyclae. It took almost two hours to complete the route, with the keening and the drumming never letting up for a moment. Gorgo had a headache and her mother was limping by the time they finally arrived at the Theomelida, the tombs of the Agiad kings.

The priests were waiting here with a pure white steer, heavily tethered and held by two burly helots. The steer sensed danger and was not about to submit docilely. Gorgo's first thought was that this did not bode well, but on second thought she wondered who had selected this bull. If Brotus stepped forward to make the sacrifice reserved for the new king, and the bull resisted....

The paean to Hades was struck up and sung by the assembled crowd. Silence fell. The bier was carried inside the mausoleum. The Council and ephors followed it inside. Brotus, then Cleomenes' widow, mother, and daughter, followed the ephors. The corpse was set upon a marble slab and everyone filed past, taking their last leave before filing out again in the same order. Gorgo's mother let go of her arm and stood staring at her husband's corpse. The Council, ephors, and Brotus were already out the door. Gorgo gently began to urge her mother to move on.

She was gripped from behind by a powerful arm. She opened her mouth to scream, but a hand was clamped over her mouth, silencing her. She made a desperate attempt to break free, but hot breath and a familiar voice spoke into her ear. "Relax. It's me."

She twisted around to stare into her husband's face. He removed his hand and replaced it with his lips. Then he took her hand and led her out of the mausoleum, right past her mother, who was still communing with her husband's corpse.

They emerged just as Brotus stepped forward to dispatch the still struggling bull. Leonidas dropped Gorgo's hand and reached out to grasp Brotus' arm before he could raise it. An exclamation of excitement and amazement ran through the crowd like a sudden squall of wind. "Don't you think we should do this together, twin?" Leonidas asked, in a voice that carried far out into the crowd.

Brotus looked as if he were seeing a ghost. He could only stare at Leonidas as if it couldn't be true. His surprise was so complete that his strength temporarily failed him. Leonidas put his hand over Brotus' and led it to the sacrificial kill.

"And nobody knows what the Council is going to propose today?" Leonidas pressed Alkander. His friend had come to collect him for the extraordinary Assembly marking the end of the ten days of official mourning for King Cleomenes.

Alkander shook his head. "They were still in session when I drove through the city on the way here."

"They sat through the night?"

"Yes."

Leonidas drew a deep breath and turned to help Gorgo into the chariot. They exchanged a glance. Then Leonidas glanced over his shoulder and up at the balcony over the front porch where his children were: Pleistarchos in Laodice's arms and Agiatis holding Chryse's hand. It crossed his mind that his children would be safer if Brotus were declared king; as king, Brotus would have no reason to fear them. But this wasn't about what was good for him and his family; it was about Sparta and Lacedaemon....

The sight of the two helot women, however, reminded Alkander of Crius. "Did you ever find out what happened to Crius?" he asked Leonidas, as he took up the reins of the chariot to drive his friend into the city.

"Didn't I tell you?" Leonidas asked back. "We found the body—but not the head."

"Murdered?"

"Obviously—and not by common thieves. The Agiad ring was still on him, along with the five drachma Gorgo had given him to cover his expenses. The murderer was so intent on silencing him that he didn't even bother to look for valuables." As he spoke, Leonidas unconsciously stroked the lapis lazuli ring, set in heavy gold, that had been a symbol of the Agiad kings for a century or more. He wore it on his own right hand. "It was Brotus' work, we can be sure, but as with his other murders, I have no evidence." Leonidas' expression was grim, almost defeated.

Alkander felt compelled to point out, "Support for Brotus has been crumbling ever since your return. The story that he dropped his sword and shield in the middle of the assault on the Argive camp during the recapture of Kythera hurt him badly, too. Even Euragoras, a staunch supporter of Brotus up to now, couldn't stomach the thought of taking orders from a man who would put his lust ahead of his military duty. Many men feel like that."

Leonidas glanced sidelong at Alkander. "Funny, isn't it, that Kleta turned up in Sparta for the first time in sixteen years just when the issue of the succession was being debated?"

"She came to pay her respects to your brother, as the head of her household."

"Of course ... and then just happened to start talking about something that she has been ashamed to tell all her life."

"Not exactly," Alkander admitted.

"Do tell me more," Leonidas urged.

"Dienekes was the one who came upon Brotus in the tent. He interrupted the rape and booted Brotus out. That's the main reason Dienekes has opposed Brotus for decades. But for all his other virtues, Dienekes is not the most eloquent of speakers. Besides, he's been so hostile to Brotus in recent years that some people questioned his motives, claiming he had made up the whole story just to discredit Brotus."

"And Kleta was viewed as less biased?" Leonidas asked skeptically.

"Not less biased, perhaps, but her testimony was too vivid to be discounted."

"So Nikostratos and Sperchias told me ...." Leonidas hesitated and with a glance at his wife added, "She arrived looking like a modest matron, humble and shy, and then bared her breasts to the entire Council, showing the alpha carved into her flesh by the Argives. She described the attempted rape, including lurid details that shook the Council, Nikostratos claims."

"Including a vivid description of Brotus," Alkander added.

"Yes," Leonidas agreed with a glance at Alkander. "Just where did Kleta stay, by the way, when she came to Sparta?"

"At our kleros, of course," Alkander admitted readily. "After all, Hilaira was instrumental in convincing you to get her released after Brotus had her arrested for soliciting. She was happy to host Kleta, and Kleta felt safe and comfortable with us."

"I can imagine," Leonidas agreed with a knowing nod.

Gorgo looked from her husband to his best friend and back again. She didn't quite understand the tension between them.

"And nobody mentioned that Brotus never removed his helmet during the attempted rape?" Leonidas wanted to know.

"How do you know that?" Alkander asked, astonished.

"That's what Kleta told Laodice—that she didn't know and couldn't identify the Spartan who had tried to rape her."

"But Dienekes recognized him—and Kleta could describe him because of the later encounter."

Leonidas nodded again. "Is there anything else I should know?"

Alkander decided it was time to confess. "We located your wet nurse."

"Dido?" Leonidas looked over sharply. He had been paying her a pension for years, but she was old and ill. He did not want her dragged into this. After all, all she could possibly do was confirm that Brotus was the elder twin.

Alkander hesitated and then admitted, "Unfortunately, Dido is dead. She died several years ago."

"But I've been paying a pension—"

"To her cousin Polyxo, so it wouldn't fall into the hands of Dido's unscrupulous sons. Polyxo didn't see any reason to put an end to that welcome stream of income just because its intended recipient was gone...."

Leonidas thought about that a moment. He couldn't particularly blame the old helot woman for pocketing Dido's pension. After all, Brotus had never thought to send her anything. But it also meant that the only witness to his birth was inexorably biased in favor of Brotus. The hopes he'd surreptitiously harbored about claiming the throne for himself were fading fast.

When they reached the bridge over the Eurotas, the streets were full of citizens dressed for Assembly. Leonidas asked Alkander to see to the chariot and then to take Gorgo to the Canopy, while Leo went to Kastor's tomb.

Leonidas had brought a special offering this time, rather than the usual produce from his kleros. Stopping just inside the entrance, he fished in the leather pouch that hung at his right hip and removed a beautiful brooch of jade and coral. It had belonged to one of the Persians who fought at Marathon. Miltiades had handed it over to Leonidas when they parted, "as a remembrance." Leonidas approached the altar and laid the brooch upon it. Then he stood in front of the smiling figure of the young demigod and took a deep breath. "Kastor, help me today, and I will dedicate the rest of my life to Lacedaemon." Was that enough? Shouldn't he be doing that anyway? He added, "The Persians will be back. We cannot fight them alone. Lacedaemon has to act in concert with Athens and our allies. We need the support of perioikoi and helot both. We need a fleet. We need all the men who have lost their citizenship because their land is marginal and they cannot pay their syssitia fees, and we need their sons, too. Lacedaemon cannot afford a king like Brotus—selfish, brutal, bigoted, and blind. Whatever the Council proposes, give me the words to sway the Assembly today so that Brotus does not become our next king." He stopped there, short of asking for the crown himself. He still could not overcome his reluctance to ask for something that wasn't his.

The Canopy was packed to overflowing. From the look of things, every citizen who was not absolutely bedridden had obeyed the summons—and that meant close to eight thousand men, many of whom had brought their wives with them. Sparta's citizens were standing nearly as close together as in a phalanx, as the men at the back pushed forward as far as they could to ensure they could hear when the proceedings started.

Brotus and his wife Sinope stood at the very front with a large body of supporters around them. Brotus was wearing his new armor, which depicted Herakles slaying a lion. Don't count on it, Leonidas thought to himself belligerently, but he noted that Brotus looked very self-assured and relaxed, while his wife looked outright haughty.

Although she scorned jewelry, she was wearing a peplos in vivid purple with crisp white trim that was ostentatiously regal. Gorgo looked modest by comparison, although she was wearing a jade necklace and earrings as well as bronze bracelets her father had once given her. She, too, was standing in the front row, beside Alkander. She took Leonidas' hand as he joined her, her face strained. She was afraid, and her fear gave him new determination.

The Council and ephors took their places facing the Assembly. Leonidas tried to read Nikostratos' face, but his mentor only looked tired. Kyranios looked even worse, while Sperchias looked nervous. Not good. A glance at Leotychidas and Lysimachos, however, revealed that his enemies looked hardly any better. Leotychidas looked dazed, and Lysimachos was frowning furiously.

Polymedes called for order. The paean was sung, the sacrifice made, a priest read the entrails and declared all was in order: the Assembly could proceed.

Polymedes cleared his throat. "King Cleomenes died without a direct male heir. Since women cannot inherit, the Agiad throne passes by right to Cleomenes' closest male relative, his eldest half-brother on his father's side—"

A cheer went up from Brotus' faction, dissolving into a chant of "Brotus!"

Brotus, with a look of triumph in Leonidas' direction, started forward to join the Council.

Polymedes raised his hand and shouted: "Wait!"

Although Polymedes could hardly be heard above the enthusiastic cheers of Brotus' friends, his gesture was unmistakable. Meanwhile, from the back of the Assembly, a counterchant of "Vote! Vote! We demand a vote!" went up.

Brotus turned to his followers and gestured for them to calm down. "We will, of course, await the vote of this sacred Assembly. According to the law, the Assembly has the *final* say!" He said this pointedly to Leonidas.

"Of course," Leonidas agreed, speaking to be heard even on the outer fringes of the large crowd. "The Assembly's vote is final—which is why the proposal needs to be debated. The Council has ruled that no woman can be king of Sparta and that my brother Cleomenes should be followed by his closest male relative. The question is who that is."

"The Council ruled that it is his *eldest half brother*," Brotus corrected him smugly.

"But who is that?" Alkander asked, looking—to Leonidas' bafflement—no less smug that Brotus.

"Everyone knows I am the elder twin!" Brotus snapped back, with a dismissive gesture to Alkander.

"I demand to hear the testimony of the wet nurse!" Euryleon shouted.

"Wet nurse?" Brotus looked around, bewildered.

"Your wet nurse." Euryleon faced Brotus, looking him straight in the eye, confronting him defiantly with obvious pleasure.

"If you've dredged up Dido out of a slum someplace to lie on Leo's behalf, don't think it will work!" Brotus flung his remark at Leo to show his utter contempt for Euryleon. To the rest of the Assembly he announced, "Dido was Leonidas' wet nurse. Of course she'll lie for him. Her word is worthless."

"And Polyxo's?" Euryleon asked with obvious amusement.

"She nursed me. She knows the truth!"

Euryleon turned and beckoned to Aristodemos and Eurytus. The two meleirenes had been standing in the doorway to the Temple of Athena of Counsel as if on guard duty. Now, however, they disappeared inside the temple to re-emerge on either side of a fat, frightened helot woman. Leonidas would not have recognized her as Brotus' old nurse. Her round face was flabby, her white hair thin. Her eyes, half lost in the folds of skin around them, darted nervously without fixing on anything, while her shallow, gasping breath was audible. Not a terribly credible witness, Leonidas noted, wondering why Euryleon had insisted on her testimony and what Aristodemos and Eurytus, who had helped save Pleistarchos, had to do with it.

The woman was brought to the front of the Canopy, while the men at the back craned their necks to get a look at her and asked one another what was going on. Polymedes asked her name, her patronymic, her profession, and then if she had anything to say that was relevant to the debate. "I—I—" she started, in a breathy voice no one could hear. Polymedes ordered her to speak up.

"I was there—at the birth of the twins!" she squealed in a high-pitched voice that now reached even the back of the crowd.

"Tell us what happened," Polymedes urged.

"I was standing beside the midwife. The queen was having a terrible time and the first baby, when it came, seemed lifeless. The midwife cut the cord in haste and handed it to me because she could see the second baby was already on the way. I thought the first baby was dead, so I handed it off to my cousin Dido in order to help with the second baby. The second baby was much bigger and stronger than the first, and he screamed lustily when we cut the cord. I put him to my breast at once and cherished him like he was my own little boy." Tears were by now streaming down her face. Although her account was by no means audible at the back, it was very audible to the Council, the ephors, and those in the first rows, including Brotus and Leonidas.

Brotus leaped forward as if he would strike the old woman, roaring out: "Traitor! Liar! Filthy helot slut!"

Leonidas only stared at the woman, stunned. Then he looked from Alkander to Euryleon and back at Polyxo. The old woman was blubbering, holding out her hands to Brotus, and calling him baby names. "My little puppy! My baby bull! I loved you! I loved you!" she wailed.

"I'll kill you!" Brotus screamed, and had to be held back by his own supporters.

Polymedes was calling for order, while the gist of Polyxo's message was relayed to the back of the Assembly by those in front. When the citizens at the back realized what Polyxo had said, the commotion in the Canopy grew louder and louder. Leonidas couldn't hear what was being said by everyone, but the exclamations sounded more amazed than outraged. Here and there someone whooped as if in triumph. That would be one of the young men, most likely one of last year's eirenes; they had become his staunchest admirers.

Orthryades had a grip on Brotus. He was not just holding him back from attacking Polyxo, but facing him down. He was saying something straight into Brotus' face from just inches away. Leonidas couldn't hear him, but his stance was unmistakable. Meanwhile, the smooth Talthybiades was asking for the floor.

Polymedes demanded order, and eventually an uneasy, anticipatory silence spread across the floor of the Canopy. He nodded to Talthybiades.

"The testimony of this woman, who *claims* to be Cleombrotus' wet nurse, is very dramatic. My compliments to my fellow citizens," Talthybiades bowed to Alkander and Euryleon with a supercilious smile on his thin lips, "for dredging her up and for—shall we say?—*persuading* her to tell such a—how should I word it?—*plausible* but transparently partisan tale."

There were grunts and nods of assent from Brotus' faction, but farther away a young man shouted: "Just because it doesn't suit *you*, Talthybiades, doesn't make it false!" This remark also won an audible share of approving comments.

Talthybiades ignored them and continued in his precise magistrate's voice, "Has Leonidas no *credible* witness to bring forward? Does no one other than a Kytheran whore and a blubbering helot woman speak on his behalf?"

"Do you consider me a credible witness, Talthybiades?" The question came from Epidydes, the youngest councilman and former headmaster.

Talthybiades was genuinely astonished by the question. He agreed instantly, "No one can doubt your credibility and integrity, Epidydes—but with all due respect, you were not in the birthing chamber when the Agiad twins were born."

"No, but I was present when King Anaxandridas brought his twin sons to the agoge for enrollment." Epidydes got to his feet and moved front and center. Polymedes instantly and instinctively took a step back to make way for him.

Epidydes raised his voice and his eyes swept the crowd. He had been headmaster of the agoge for more than thirty years, and in that time most of the citizens now assembled had passed through his upbringing. Some, like Leonidas and Brotus, had known no other headmaster and would never be entirely free of their awe of him. The elder men, in contrast, respected him precisely because they had known his infamous predecessor, while the youngest citizens had suffered under his successor and remembered Epidydes with nostalgia. There could be no question that if one man had influence in this Assembly, it was Epidydes.

The silence that gripped the Assembly was correspondingly profound. The sound of some helot workman hammering in the distance could be heard distinctly. A light breeze from the invisible Eurotas was a breath of sweetness among the sweating men. No one dared move or even breathe as they waited for Epidydes to continue.

"King Anaxandridas came to me, flanked by his boys," Epidydes continued. "Brotus was noticeably bigger and stronger, making him look a year or more older than Leonidas." Leonidas remembered that, too, and Brotus was grinning again—or rather, leering at Leonidas with malicious satisfaction. But the old headmaster wasn't finished. He added, "Leonidas was on the king's right."

The Assembly erupted. Brotus was shouting again, first "Liar!" and then, after Orthryades rebuked him, "It was just chance. Chance! It meant nothing!" Meanwhile, from the back, other men started cheering, calling, and chanting: "Leonidas! Leonidas! Leonidas!"

For the second time this morning, Leonidas was stunned. He could picture the scene from more than thirty years ago as if it were yesterday: his own anxiety, the way the instructors had fawned over Brotus because he was so big and strong, and then the way Epidydes came around his desk to approach him, saying, "Then *you* must be Leonidas." But because, at the time, he did not know the significance of standing on the right, he had taken no notice of the fact—until now.

With a sense of amazement, he realized he *had* indeed been on his father's right. And no Spartan *king* was unaware of the significance of such a position: his father had given him the place of honor.

Leonidas looked around for Polyxo. Could her story also be true? Not merely a fabrication forced upon her by his friends? Had he really been born first, but half dead? Dido had always claimed she'd saved his life; he'd assumed she meant afterwards, through a dozen childhood illnesses, accidents, and fights with Brotus. Now he wondered if she had, in fact, forced the first breath from an infant dismissed as dead, superfluous, while the others focused on Brotus.

Polymedes moved for a vote. Brotus was furiously protesting, denying that Leonidas was the firstborn, but the roar of "ayes" for the motion was deafening, and the "nays" came out like embarrassed whimpers from men too tied to Brotus to risk abandoning him despite the evidence.

Part II

KING LEONIDAS

CHAPTER 11

I, LEONIDAS

FOR TWO YEARS LEONIDAS HAD PLANNED what he would do if he became regent for Pleistarchos, but he was not prepared to become king. Suddenly he found himself seated beside Leotychidas as Polymedes adjourned the Assembly, and when he stood, still distracted by the turn of events, the men around him hastened to get to their feet—even the ancient Councilmen Polypeithes and Hetoimokles, his mentor Nikostratos, and Epidydes, the man to whom he owed his sudden elevation. Leonidas paused, thinking how Demaratus had preferred exile in a foreign land to showing this simple courtesy to a lesser man.

Leonidas looked at Leotychidas, but his co-monarch avoided his eye.

"You must go to the Agiad palace, Leonidas," Nikostratos urged. "Everything has been in limbo for weeks."

Leonidas looked at him blankly.

"For a start, you need to appoint a bodyguard of one hundred men, and also two Pythians to Delphi—remember Sperchias when you do that. It is also customary to forgive all debts, and there are various other matters you need to know: for example, the number and age of heiresses in your care, whether any adoptions are pending, the status of public road projects.... I can't remember everything, but Eukomos, the Agiad steward, will have drawn up a list. *I* am going home to get some needed sleep, but I will see you at dinner.

Remember you are now chairman of the syssitia and must open and close all meals."

Leonidas nodded absently.

Kyranios was beside him, leaning heavily on his cane, his twisted face gray with exhaustion. "I'm going to bed, too, but I'd advise you to immediately appoint Dienekes and his one hundred men as your bodyguard. You can select another bodyguard later, if you like, but for now Dienekes will ensure you have the ceremonial protection prescribed. You must also send royal messengers out to every perioikoi town declaring yourself king. They will probably hear of it before the messengers arrive, but it's better to make an official statement."

Leonidas nodded again, glancing toward Gorgo and his friends waiting for him in the street. His friends were jubilant and looked it, while around them an ever larger crowd of well-wishers was collecting. Among these Leonidas recognized many of the young men who had been eirenes last year, as well as the officers of his lochos and all four of his fellow lochagoi, but some of the men gathering were virtual strangers. Were they men seeking advantage already, or simply the men who had elected him? Men who had been neutral in the past, yet cast their vote for him today at the critical juncture? Leonidas believed that his reputation and popularity, as much as the technicalities of his birth, had played a role in the final vote.

As he reached the little crowd, men surrounded him—grinning, congratulating, even clapping him on the back. Leonidas thanked them absently, his eyes on Gorgo. She looked more relieved than radiant, even a little dazed. "Is it permitted to kiss a king in public?" she teased as he reached her.

"Under the circumstances, it is mandatory."

She went on tiptoe and touched her lips to his, but it was a fleeting kiss, too conscious of the audience.

Leonidas took her hand and announced that they must go to the royal palace. They started walking together, the little crowd opening for them but then keeping pace with them as they moved along the street. The crowd grew as they advanced deeper into the city.

By now the news had reached the boys of the agoge. More and more of them flooded the street and joined the back of the moving crowd, loud and excited. Here and there women came out on balconies and waved; some even called out congratulations to Leonidas or Gorgo by name.

In the agora, the helot vendors raised a loud cheer at the sight of Leonidas and his amorphous escort of well-wishers. Leonidas acknowledged the cheer with some embarrassment, telling himself it was impersonal and little more than good business, but three-quarters of the way across the agora an old man blocked his way. "Little Leo," the old man addressed him, squinting up at the much taller man, his wizened face twisted into a half-toothless smile. "Don't you recognize me?"

Leonidas tried to place him. By his dress he was a helot, but Leonidas did not recognize him. Two middle-aged men were beside the old man, frantically offering Leonidas their apologies and trying to drag their father out of his way. Suddenly Leonidas remembered: "You used to sell meat pies, and you gave me one for free after my brother Dorieus dressed me down as a seven-year-old."

The man's face split into a wider smile.

"And I promised to always buy from you," Leonidas continued, more for the crowd than for the old vendor.

"I said you would one day make me a purveyor of the Agiad royal house, didn't I?" the man insisted, to the mortification of his sons.

Leonidas laughed. "So be it."

It was now the man's grown sons who looked stunned.

At the palace itself, an enomotia of the Guard was on duty. They snapped to attention at the sight of Leonidas. As he started up the stairs, Alkander and Euryleon excused themselves, saying they would see him at dinner, while the others took leave with a last congratulation. By the time they reached the top of the steps, Leonidas and Gorgo were alone. The meleirenes saluted smartly and opened the massive brass-studded wings of the ten-foot door to let the king and queen inside.

In the shade of the entry hall the palace staff was drawn up. The chief steward had evidently marshaled them here, and this elegant perioikoi, usually so cool and emotionless, was actually smiling. Some of the staff were weeping, notably the cook Prothous, while several of the women tried to kiss Leonidas' hand as he greeted them.

Eukomos suggested Leonidas accompany him to the library where the royal accounts were awaiting his inspection, and Gorgo agreed to follow Prothous to the kitchen to go over the household accounts and address pressing issues of the immediate household. "Sinope has been threatening us ever since your father died," Leonidas heard one of the laundresses complain. "She said the days of sloth would end. Sloth! And she…."

Eukomos led Leonidas through one of the interior courtyards and up the outside stairs to the long, second-story library of the Agiads. They passed through one of the column-flanked doors into a room completely lined with shelves divided into sections like a honeycomb. These contained all the oracles ever delivered by Delphi to the Spartan kings, as well as discourses by Pythagoras, transcripts of the *Iliad* and the *Odyssey*, Aesop's fables, the poems of Tyrtaios, Terpander, and Alkman, and various other works valued by the Spartans. The library had been off limits to Leonidas as a little boy, but forbidden fruit tastes sweetest. Leonidas remembered sneaking up here shortly before he went to the agoge. At the time, Brotus and he were learning to read. Brotus hated the tedious hours spent tracing letters on wax tablets and had often thrown his to the ground in frustration. Leonidas, in contrast, had been fascinated by the fact that letters lined up in different formations could tell whole stories. He had slipped in here, determined to get a look at a whole document, but his timing had been poor, and his father had been in the library.

As a boy, Leonidas had had almost no contact with his father. His father was "the king," and he never came to the nursery or took any particular interest in his youngest sons, or so it seemed to Leonidas. When he realized his father was in the library, Leonidas had tried to run away, but the old man had seen him and called out, "Stop!" Leonidas did not dare disobey this awesome personage, and had frozen in his tracks. "What are you doing here, boy?" the old king asked.

"Want to see a page of writing," Leonidas remembered mumbling in terror.

"Come here, boy," said the old king, snapping his fingers at Leonidas, and Leonidas dutifully went to him, trembling internally.

King Anaxandridas had been sitting on a beautiful throne with bronze lion's paws for feet, bronze griffins adorning the sides that enclosed the deep seat, and a back formed by bronze swans whose heads met in the middle. It was the very chair in which Eukomos now indicated Leonidas should sit.

Leonidas approached the empty throne, seeing in his memory his father, hunched over the writing table with his thinning white hair revealing a scalp covered with age spots. He had put an arm around Leonidas' frail shoulders and pulled him close. At the time Leonidas had been very uncomfortable: his father was a stranger to him, and he seemed as ancient as the Gods themselves. "Here is a page of writing," his father had said, showing him the document he was then reading. Leonidas had nodded quickly, by then only interested in a hasty retreat. "And here is your name," his father had said, pointing to a row of letters. Leonidas had peered at the paper with new interest. His father had ruffled his hair, which had annoyed him, and he'd squirmed in his father's arm, trying to break free.

The adult Leonidas wished he hadn't done that. In retrospect, it was the only time in their lives that they had been alone together. Otherwise, one of his brothers or his mother or the nurses had always been present when he encountered his father.

"Is something the matter, my lord?" Eukomos asked, baffled that Leonidas was just standing and staring at the throne.

Leonidas shook the memories away, mentally promising to offer a prayer for his father's shade when he made his first sacrifice to Apollo as king. He had never prayed for his father before. He had never particularly thought about him at all. But his father had put him in the place of honor. No one would ever know if it was because he was the firstborn—or simply because the dying Anaxandridas had secretly liked Leonidas better.

"My lord?" Eukomos prompted again.

Leonidas sat down on his father's throne. Eukomos spread out a stack of papyrus and weighted it at both ends. The first page was covered with columns of tiny, regular, neat writing. "This is an inventory of arable properties, acres of timber," he pointed to the appropriate column for each item, "livestock by breed, houses, factories, and so on—right to this last column, which is the inventory of your treasury in gold and silver objects, with the total weight by precious metal noted here."

Leonidas' eyes worked their way slowly across the tiny columns of figures. He did not try to add up everything mentally, but he was no longer as unfamiliar with bookkeeping as he had been when he first came into his inheritance. Gorgo might have day-to-day responsibility for his finances, but he retained an overview of his possessions and a rough understanding of what things were worth. He looked up and straight at the elegant perioikoi manager. "This is—scandalous."

Eukomos was taken completely by surprise. He had, until an hour earlier, expected to be facing Brotus. Brotus, he was certain, would have been impatient with the details, but pleased with the bottom line. Leonidas responded exactly the reverse, and it startled him. "My lord?"

Leonidas leaned back against the swans and looked at the old steward. He could remember vividly the day, shortly before he attained citizenship, when Eukomos had summoned him to the palace to reveal his inheritance. Brotus had been summoned, too, of course, because their father had ordained that the twins receive equal portions, but left it to his trustees to make the actual allocation. Brotus had not wanted any of the shares in factories, quarries, and the like, dismissing them as beneath his dignity. Brotus saw himself as a landowner and soldier only; he viewed trade and manufacturing as demeaning. Brotus had insisted on swapping these holdings for estates from Leonidas' share. Leonidas had agreed because he thought shares of things managed by perioikoi would be less trouble to him, but Eukomos thought it was because he knew the shares were more valuable than the land.

Eukomos, Leonidas calculated, must be over sixty now. He was almost completely bald, with only a thin fringe of hair at the base of his skull. His aquiline nose seemed sharper than ever, and he was dressed in beautifully patterned, loosely flowing linen. He wore several rings on each hand and was nervously twisting one, despite an expression of perfect calm.

"This inventory suggests that the Agiad royal house is obscenely rich. If the Eurypontids are as rich, it is no wonder hundreds of citizens are living on marginal estates and that many are unable to pay their syssitia fees. This is in blatant contradiction of Lycurgus' laws."

"No, my lord," Eukomos answered in a crisp yet defensive tone. "Lycurgus' laws never applied to the kings, and never to Messenia."

Leonidas sensed that the steward felt personally attacked. That would get him nowhere. Eukomos was a proud man, a man who had been a devoted servant of the Agiads all his working life. He had served the dying Anaxandridas and the immature Cleomenes, helped finance Dorieus, and husbanded Leonidas' inheritance through the years of his immaturity. He had recommended Phormio to Leonidas when Leonidas came of age and needed someone to look after his affairs full time. Leonidas owed him a great deal, and he was a skilled administrator. He was a man to cultivate, not alienate. "Eukomos, you are to be highly commended for preserving the Agiad estate in such abundance despite my brother's often irrational and extravagant tendencies."

Eukomos gently let out his breath and smiled faintly, but he was still twisting the ring.

"I am deeply indebted to you for that—and for recommending Phormio."

Eukomos nodded his thanks, but he was still on his guard after Leonidas' startling opening attack.

"Please, sit down. Can we send for refreshments? I was standing all morning at Assembly and, I confess, I was too nervous to face breakfast." Leonidas offered the last comment with a smile meant to disarm.

Eukomos jumped to his feet, mortified with embarrassment. "My lord! Why didn't you say something sooner? I beg your forgiveness. At once!" He was gone before Leonidas could stop him, plunging out onto the long gallery and calling down in an imperative tone to someone below. Leonidas leaned forward to look more closely at the documents prepared for him.

The second papyrus showed income (in black ink) and outlays (in red). Most entries were quite understandable, but there were two enormous outlays that were unlabeled. As soon as Eukomos re-entered, promising a tray of food and wine "in a moment or two," Leonidas asked about these two entries.

Eukomos nodded. "Yes. They jump out at you, don't they?" Leonidas wondered if Brotus would have noticed, but said nothing.

"Officially, I don't know what they were for. After all, your brother did not have to explain himself to me. The other outlays were paid by the household treasury with my approval, of course. Those two were payments directly to your brother at his insistence."

"You said that 'officially' you did not know what they were. What about *un*officially?"

"That," the steward put his finger on the papyrus, "was drawn when your brother fled Lacedaemon, the sum he felt he needed to finance himself while he was away—and that," he moved his finger up the page, "was to bribe the oracle at Delphi."

Leonidas caught his breath to hear this sacrilege referred to so casually. But how else should the steward speak of it? It wasn't a secret anymore. He nodded. "What else have you prepared for me?"

"This is the list of debtors and the sums owed. Whatever else one can say about your brother, he was not prone to lending. You can cancel these debts without a second thought."

"Most of these men are foreigners," Leonidas noted.

"Yes, that's true," Eukomos admitted without further comment.

"Why?"

Eukomos shrugged. "Your brother sometimes played with the notion of inviting foreign 'friends' to eliminate his domestic 'enemies.'"

Leonidas caught his breath, then let it out and said no more. He let Eukomos turn to the next papyrus. "And this is the list of heiresses in your guardianship."

"Heiresses?"

"Girls whose fathers died before they were betrothed. The kings act as surrogate fathers and must approve a marriage."

"Jointly?" Leonidas asked, instantly alarmed.

Eukomos almost laughed. "No. That may have been the original practice, but it proved untenable long ago. Nowadays, heiresses are assigned to one king or the other, based on a complicated formula."

"And how many do I have to look after?" Leonidas sounded distinctly alarmed.

"Fourteen at the moment, none yet of marriageable age. The eldest is, I believe, thirteen. If I may make a suggestion, my lord, I think it would be best if you asked your wife to call on all the girls as soon as possible. Fatherless girls can be quite difficult sometimes." Eukomos did not meet his eye as he said this, but then he risked a glance at Leonidas and suddenly they were both laughing. The ice was finally broken.

By the time the snack arrived, Eukomos and Leonidas were deep in a congenial conversation, but they were soon interrupted by one of the servants. He came to the door of the library and reported, "My lord, there is a young man outside demanding admittance. The meleirenes stopped him and he's getting very loud."

Leonidas looked at Eukomos, who shrugged and remarked, "I'm sure he'll calm down when the watch arrests him."

"I want no one arrested because they seek to speak to me."

"Not everyone has pleasant things to say," Eukomos noted dryly.

Leonidas laughed. "My brothers taught me that long ago. I'll see who it is and what he wants. Then I'll be back."

From the front entry hall he could hear shouting coming from the street. He recognized the voice that was shouting insults at the meleirenes in a raw fury, calling them bastards and curs and sons of whores: it was Meander.

Leonidas thrust the doors open and stepped out onto the porch, making the meleirenes jump and look over in alarm. "What the hell do you think you are doing denying access to my attendant?" he demanded of the youths.

"But he's a helot, sir! Helots—"

Meander roared in pain, "I'm no more a helot that you are, you bastards! I'm just as good as you are! I'll—"

"That's enough, Meander," Leonidas told him sharply. "Stop making a scene. Come inside."

Meander did not wait to be told twice, pausing only long enough to spit at one of the meleirenes in passing before darting inside the palace and asking Leonidas, "Did you hear what they said, sir?—I mean, my lord!"

The meleirene on duty protested, "We were only following orders, my lord. Helots have no right to enter the palace by this door. They have to go around to the stables or the kitchen."

"Tell me, meleirene, did you never see Meander with me in the past?"

"Of course, sir—my lord—but that doesn't change the fact that he's a helot."

"He may not be a Spartiate, but he is no helot!"

"I don't understand, my lord."

Leonidas resisted the temptation to admit he didn't, either, and said instead, "I am king to helots as well as Spartiates and perioikoi, and I will see any man who comes in peace." Then he closed the door behind him and growled at Meander, "I should have your hide for making a scene like that!"

"But, sir, I just found out you are king. I came—I mean—isn't it my place to be with you?" Meander couldn't decide if he should be belligerent, apologetic, or jubilant.

"Come with me," Leonidas ordered, and started back for the library with a still confused Meander in his wake.

For almost a decade, Meander had served as Leonidas' attendant, but he preferred to live in the lochos barracks, where the camaraderie among the attendants made him feel his loss of status less acutely. As he trailed in Leonidas' wake through the ancient halls of the royal palace, he started feeling more and more intimidated. To serve the wealthy, respected officer Leonidas was an honor that helped compensate him for the fact that he would never be a citizen, but serving a *king* was very different. "Sir?"

Leonidas glanced over.

"If—if you are king, then you can't be lochagos anymore, can you?"

Leonidas hadn't thought that far himself yet, but it was true. He nodded.

"But then, we'll—I'll—have to move out of your quarters there...."

"Yes... unless my successor wishes to hire you."

"Who is your successor, sir?"

"It is too soon to know. I only became king a few hours ago. There's no rush about moving out. Come up these stairs."

When Leonidas re-entered the library, he was surprised to find that Eukomos was no longer alone; Phormio had joined him. Phormio broke into a broad smile and pulled his heavy body up at the sight of Leonidas. "Congratulations, my lord! Congratulations. You have no idea how delighted I was to hear the news! No idea! I hoped, of course, I did what I could to help things along, but who can predict what will come out of a Spartan Assembly? A pride of Spartiates is more unpredictable than the Gods themselves."

Leonidas waved him to sit down again and checked the pitchers on the table. They were almost empty. "Meander, fetch us more water and wine," Leonidas ordered, handing the vessels to his attendant.

"I don't know my way around—"

"Then ask someone," Leonidas ordered. "You'll have to learn fast—if you want to remain in my service."

"Yes, sir!"

Only after Meander was out of hearing did Leonidas himself sit down and announce, with a gesture in the direction of the door by which Meander had exited: "It's because of young men like that that we, the three of us, need to consider a new land reform."

"Zeus help us all!" Phormio exclaimed, only half in jest. "He's been in power less than five hours and he's already trying to compete with the reformer king, Polydorus."

Leonidas ignored his own steward to focus on Eukomos. "That young man's parents were both Spartiates and he attended the agoge until his fifteenth year, but then his father couldn't afford the agoge fees anymore and yanked him out. At the next bad harvest, his father wasn't able to afford his syssitia fees, either, and he hanged himself. We have barely eight thousand citizens. Corinth has twenty thousand, Athens thirty thousand, Thebes fifteen thousand. We Spartans can't afford to lose men, and their sons, just because they can't pay their syssitia fees. That is exactly what Lycurgus' land reform was intended to prevent!"

"The figures you cited are misleading, my lord," Eukomos remarked in a calming tone. "In other cities, whether in Athens or Corinth, citizens too poor to fight as hoplites are still counted among the citizen ranks. In Lacedaemon, in contrast, you don't count even the perioikoi hoplites. If you compare Lacedaemon, including the perioikoi, to other cities, the imbalance is not significant."

"Agreed," Leonidas conceded. "But that doesn't address the problem."

"What problem?" Eukomos asked, confused.

"Inequitable distribution of wealth!" Leonidas replied impatiently.

"My lord! Wealth is *never* equitably distributed. It is always concentrated in the hands of the rulers and elites—from Persia and Babylon to Egypt and Macedonia. To my knowledge, Sparta is the only place on earth where anyone ever tried to redistribute it and where every citizen is at least *entitled* to an estate. But no one ever said that all citizens' estates must be equal!"

"Of course the estates are supposed to be equal!" Leonidas countered. "That's why we call ourselves 'Peers'—equals. The land reform that made all citizens equal is the basis of our entire constitution. Furthermore, it was approved by Apollo himself. Regardless of how others live, we have a sacred duty to respect the Laws of Lycurgus—and those Laws entitle each legitimate son of Spartan parents to a landholding large enough to support him and his family. Instead of that, hundreds of citizens live on land that is marginal and are at risk of losing their citizenship. It is an intolerable situation—doubly so when I see that I, one man, must own almost 20 per cent of Lacedaemon!"

Eukomos looked at his new master as if he were sprouting a second head.

"I tried to tell you he was not your ordinary prince," Phormio remarked, with a chuckle at the expression on Eukomos' face.

"And while we're on the subject of reforms," Leonidas continued, as the reality of his power started to sink into his consciousness, "we have to find a solution for the illegitimate offspring of Spartiate youth by helot girls. I watch Temenos' boys growing up each day, and it tears me apart that they cannot follow in their father's footsteps, that they will be denied an education and a chance to serve Lacedaemon."

"There are many more ways to serve Lacedaemon, my lord, than in the Spartan phalanx," Eukomos pointed out. "Every man has his place. Some are born to work the fields and others to tend the flocks, some to sit behind the spinning disk of the potter's wheel, and others to hammer at the forge. Why, even heralds, flute players, and cooks are hereditary professions."

"But that's the point: Temenos is Spartiate. His sons should be, too."

"Leonidas," Phormio started in a warning voice, "if you start making every bastard child a citizen, there will be no reason for marriage anymore, and all your maidens will go husbandless to their graves."

Leonidas laughed. "Take another look at our maidens, Phormio! But I didn't mean every bastard, only those a man acknowledges and sponsors."

"There are much more serious and pressing issues than this," Phormio retorted, provoking raised eyebrows from Eukomos, who found the tone disrespectful. He glanced at Leonidas to see his reaction. Leonidas appeared more curious than offended. He asked back, "Such as?"

Meander returned with two large pitchers, and while the young man set about filling the cups on the table, Phormio began. "Seventy per cent of Lacedaemon's population is made up of helots. Some of them live in conditions far worse than that of your marginalized citizens. Although the law says a helot has the right to retain 50 per cent of the yield of his labor, helots tend to have larger families, and their share often does not stretch far enough. Children put out to service earn almost nothing—particularly the girls in household service, who are frequently treated no better than chattel slaves. Some helots sell their children outright."

Leonidas stared at Phormio. He could not imagine any circumstance in which he would sell Agiatis or Pleistarchos. He would literally sell himself first. "What are you saying?"

"Desperation leads to discontent, and discontent can lead to revolt."

Leonidas shook his head, not because he disagreed but because he thought the problem insoluble. "Our economy depends on helot labor. We can't free the Messenians and retain our position in the world."

"Who said anything about freeing Messenia? The point is not to take wholesale measures, but to provide other legitimate routes for impoverished helots to get ahead in the world—to make money or to emigrate."

"They can do that now, can't they?"

"Emigrate? No, helots are not allowed to set foot outside of Lacedaemon except in the company or in the service of their masters."

"They can certainly make money! Last I heard, my helot Pantes had built himself a ten-room house with two atriums, and his little boys run about dressed much better than the boys of the agoge!"

"Which, of course, is not saying much, but you are only making my point for me, my lord. Pantes is very successful and has far too great a stake in Lacedaemon to want anything to change. That comes from you letting him set up his own shop. But there are many Spartiates who deny their helots that right. Many Spartiates insist that their helots not only remain in Lacedaemon, as the law requires, but on the estate to which they were born. These Spartiates stifle initiative and foster discontent, because too many helots on one estate leads inevitably to impoverishment, rivalries, jealousy—and all the while we perioikoi are suffering from a profound labor shortage."

"Ah," Leonidas observed, raising his mug to Phormio. "Now we are at the crux of the matter."

"My lord," Phormio stated diffidently, "I am here in my capacity as spokesman of the Council of Forty." This was the governing body of the perioikoi community, made up of representatives from the most important perioikoi towns. "Of *course* I represent perioikoi interests."

"Of course," Leonidas agreed with a smile. "Go on."

"My lord, without the perioikoi, Lacedaemon would be an agricultural society dependent on imports for everything from the weapons and armor your army needs to the marble facings on your temples. Perioikoi turn Lacedaemon's forests into furniture and ships. Perioikoi quarries produce the paving stones for your roads and public buildings. Perioikoi—"

Leonidas held up his hand. "I know all that, Phormio. Get to the point."

"We're only 20 per cent of the population, and everywhere I go I hear the same story: we could expand production, if only we had more workers. Recently I was in a pottery factory where the owner was so desperate he had hired some women! They were sitting right there in his workshop—only segregated from the men by a flimsy cloth curtain."

Leonidas nodded. "I understand. Was there anything else you were burning to convey?"

"Yes, I wanted to talk to you about taxation."

"Taxation?"

"Yes. Lacedaemonian laws are not always designed to encourage manufacturing and trade. The right way to go about it is to tax profit, not production. Taxing a man for what he produces, rather than what he sells, only encourages him to produce less."

"The kings do not set taxes; the Assembly does."

"I understand, but the Council makes recommendations, and the kings chair the Council. And then there is the issue of ships."

"Again?"

"Now that you control the entire Agiad fortune—except Brotus' share, of course—how many more keels do you plan to lay down?"

Eukomos looked shocked, but Leonidas laughed and remarked, "You just told me you don't have enough men to man your factories. How can you man ships?"

"That's different. Going to sea—"

A servant was in the doorway again. "My lord, your wife asks you to see this man. He came to the back and would have gone away again, but she says you will want to see him."

Leonidas looked curiously past the servant to the man behind him. The untidy flaming-red hair of the burly artisan gave him away; it was Arion the bronze worker. Leonidas signaled at once for the man to enter. Arion was carrying a large krater in his arms. The bronze vessel was so heavy that the artisan was red-faced from carrying it up the stairs. He was also clearly embarrassed to be facing the king himself. In the past, Phormio had communicated between them. Phormio beamed and gestured vigorously for the Thespian craftsman to come deeper into the room.

"It's a gift, my lord," Arion explained, setting the krater down inside the door and stepping back from it so the others could see.

Leonidas stood to get a better look at it. As with everything from Arion's workshop, this was a product of superb craftsmanship. Two upright lions with curling tails formed the handles, their faces turned sideways. Around the long neck, a hoplite, with his helmet tipped back to expose his face, drove a four-horse chariot, while Kastorian hounds chased boars around the base. On the broad body of the krater a lion attacked a boar. The animals were so lifelike, they looked as if they would move at any moment. Leonidas glanced at the burly artist, who stood tongue-tied near the door, as if ready to flee. "This is beautiful!" Leonidas assured him.

"Thank you, my lord," the man managed. Then his pride in his work overcame his natural diffidence, and he leaned forward to point out the details. "This tall horse represents the big gray you like to ride, and these are the twin dogs that you hunt with, and this, of course, represents you killing the boar in Corinth."

"You made this specially for me?" Leonidas was touched.

"Of course, my lord!"

"But how could you know I would become king?"

"I didn't, my lord," Arion replied a little sheepishly. "I made one for your brother as well."

"Hopefully it didn't show Herakles *killing* the lion!" Leonidas quipped, harvesting laughter from Phormio, but Arion didn't get the joke.

"No, no. I chose boxers as the motif."

"Very good. Have some wine. Meander, fetch more cups and more wine and water."

Meander again withdrew, while Arion shifted from one foot to the other, stammering. "I just wanted to deliver this to you, my lord. I didn't mean to disturb you."

"I understand, but I have a question for you."

"Yes, my lord?"

"Can you find enough workers for your factory?"

"Good heavens, no! I could do far more work if I could find some more skilled craftsmen. I've thought of going home to Thespiae to see if I could recruit more workers, but the news from home is not good," he added, looking sorry. "There have been more clashes with Thebes, and some families have lost their land entirely." He fell silent, apparently thinking of his home city.

Leonidas waited a moment and then suggested, "Why don't you go home? I will pay the expenses of your trip—provided you promise to come back to Lacedaemon."

The artisan looked up again sharply. "I can pay my own way!"

"I meant no offense."

"Of course not, my lord. I—I will think about it. Now if you will excuse me..."

"Don't you want to wait for your wine?"

"No, thank you, my lord. Just—just remember Thespiae in your prayers. Now that you are chief priest to Zeus Lacedaemon, I'm sure your prayers will be more powerful."

"I will remember you and Thespiae in my prayers."

The man backed out of the library. They could hear his footsteps on the stairs, but also someone in the courtyard saying, "The king is in the library with the royal steward and the Chairman of the Forty."

Phormio got to his feet, remarking, "It is going to be like this all day, my lord. We'll have time to talk later—at least, I hope we will. Eukomos." He nodded farewell to his fellow steward, while the latter started to roll the papyrus sheets together. The information on them was not for everyone's eyes, and if Leonidas was going to receive one guest after another, even craftsmen, then the scrolls needed to be put away.

Leonidas' thoughts had drifted to the priesthood of Zeus. He felt utterly unprepared for it. He did not understand the mysteries of divination and felt uncomfortable with the duties of a priest. Not that his brother had ever taken it overly seriously, he reflected—but he was not his brother.

A figure darkened the door, and Leonidas stood up automatically without even thinking about it. It was Epidydes.

"Sit down, my lord," Epidydes ordered.

"When you do," Leonidas answered, indicating the chair Phormio had vacated. "Can I get you—"

"No. Sit down. I wish to speak to you alone."

Eukomos bowed deeply and withdrew silently, his scrolls of confidential information under his arm.

The library was still. A breeze blew the long gauze curtains in along one wall and out along the other. From somewhere came the sound of women laughing. Ah, Gorgo, Leonidas thought with a rush of affection; she had everyone laughing already.

"Leonidas," Epidydes began, looking at him hard. "I hope I have not done you a disservice."

"Meaning?"

"It would have been so easy to say nothing."

"Yes. I know."

"But it was true. You *were* on your father's right."

"I know. I remember."

"Then you have known you were the firstborn all along?" Epidydes was astonished. "All these decades? When others, including Brotus—"

Leonidas shook his head. "No, because, at the time, I didn't know the significance of being on my father's right. Like Brotus, I thought it was just chance. By the time I learned about the importance of standing on the right, I had other things to worry about. I never once thought back.... But you knew. You knew all along. Why didn't you say something earlier?"

"A fair question. But at the time, it seemed unimportant which of you was the elder twin. You had two older brothers, and the struggle for the throne was between *them*. You and Brotus were just two little boys—boys of good family, but no more than that. Only after Dorieus was dead and Cleomenes went mad did it start to matter again, and by then I had forgotten all about that day. Make of this what you will, but it came to me like a vision. We had debated so long and so hard and all the arguments had been brought forward, everything had been said a hundred times—and still we were deadlocked, lamed by the belief that Brotus was the rightful heir but you would make the better king. I was prepared to let the Assembly decide—to see if the Assembly would find the old woman credible enough. And then, after we'd adjourned, I dozed a bit in the Council chamber while waiting until it was time to go to Assembly. Suddenly I had this image of you and your father coming toward me. It tore me from my sleep, and still the image was before my eyes. You, your father, and Brotus—and you were on your father's right."

"So the Council had not heard your testimony—until the Assembly."

"Exactly."

"And you wanted me to know that?"

"Yes, but that is not why I came."

Leonidas just waited.

"I came because I am very tired. The duties of Paidonomos are too heavy for me. I wish to resign."

"I can understand."

"Good. I will announce my resignation tomorrow. Call for an election immediately and put Ephorus' name forward." He held up his hand to stop an expected protest from Leonidas. "I know Alkander is the better man. I have come to see that. And what he wants to do is right. It would make the agoge more what it was when I was growing up. But too many people remember his stutter and think of him as a 'mothake.' To put his name forward for Paidonomos would arouse instant opposition. Even if, out of respect for you, he were to win election, the men who look down on him would only make his job impossible. If you propose Ephorus, who is an Olympic victor, no one will object, not even Alcidas. Ephorus and Alkander can work together. Alkander will have his way, and Ephorus will get the credit. It is a solution they both can live with, and one that will be good for the boys. Use your current popularity to strike at once."

Leonidas nodded.

"The agoge, Leonidas—the agoge is the most important institution in Sparta. We cannot afford to have it in the wrong hands. I was hesitant about Alkander's reforms, but after seeing the damage Alcidas did, I know he is right. We need to redress the balance between intellectual and physical training in favor of intellectual training. We need thinking citizens, not automatons, and we need soldiers who can act independently without orders and take the initiative when opportunities arise—like a good hunter." He paused and then resumed. "Do you know? I find myself thinking more and more often of your friend Prokles. Wondering if we could have done more to tame his rebelliousness without alienating him. His exile is over in two years. Do you think he will return?"

"No."

Epidydes was surprised by Leonidas' tone. "You are certain?"

"He told me so."

"Then you have seen him since he was exiled?"

"He sailed with me to the Hellespont and back—as a marine."

"I didn't know."

"He asked me not to tell anyone."

"But when he hears you're king…"

"It will make no difference. He is ashamed of what he has become. My being king will only make it harder for him to return."

"I see." Epidydes sighed and pulled himself to his feet. "I fear I may have done you a disservice, Leonidas, but I will sleep easier knowing that you—rather than your brother Brotus—are in that chair." He indicated the swan-backed throne.

The last visitor of the day was Leotychidas. The Eurypontid king arrived in a state chariot escorted by an enomotia of guards. He waited in the cart while a herald was sent to inquire if the Agiad king would receive him.

Leonidas went to the ancient throne room with its heavy columns and fading frescoes. He waited, standing in front of his throne, instinctively avoiding a situation where he had to either stand for the other king or insult him by remaining seated.

Leotychidas was dressed in glittering purple. His long chiton had a foot-high border of woven gold. His himation was striped with gold. His sandals were studded with pearls. Mentally, Leonidas noted that if he started dressing like this, he'd soon consume the hoard of precious objects left him by his brother.

"My dear brother," Leotychidas opened.

Leotychidas had brought no one with him into the palace, and Leonidas' servants had discreetly withdrawn from sight—though, he suspected, not from hearing. "Dear brother," Leonidas answered without feeling, and indicated the visitors' couch.

Leotychidas reclined on it. Refreshments were already waiting beside the couch on a table with slender silver feet on tiny wheels. Leonidas gestured for Leotychidas to help himself.

Leotychidas looked over the offering of nuts, dried fruits, white rolls, cheese balls, slices of sausages, and grapes, and picked at this or that as if he had nothing better to do. Leonidas waited.

"Talkative, aren't you?" Leotychidas commented.

"You requested this interview."

"I did, didn't I?" Leotychidas looked up and met his eyes.

"Why?"

Leotychidas shrugged. "I was very annoyed with you for giving Percalus to Demaratus, you know."

"I didn't. Alkander did."

Leotychidas dismissed the answer with an irritated wave of his hand. "You could have stopped him."

"Demaratus was a ruling king. Besides, he took Percalus without awaiting formalities."

"Well, in retrospect, good riddance. She was barren."

"Oh? I thought Demaratus was sterile."

"One or the other," Leotychidas dismissed his hated rival. "Probably both," he added maliciously.

Leonidas waited. He was sure Leotychidas had not come here to discuss the woman he hadn't married or the man he had deposed.

"I didn't bribe the oracle, you know," Leotychidas snapped. "Your brother did that."

Leonidas had never doubted that, and this morning he'd seen the evidence in the accounts. He nodded.

"I am the rightful Eurypontid king," Leotychidas insisted.

"Maybe."

"Why do you prefer Demaratus?" Leotychidas demanded, sounding petulant.

Leonidas sighed, sorry that Demaratus had burned his bridges and made it impossible for Sparta to ever take him back. "It is irrelevant now."

"We could work together, you know," Leotychidas pointed out, in a tone that was almost pleading.

Leonidas stared at him. This man had first worked with Cleomenes to bring down Demaratus, then with Brotus to bring down Cleomenes, and recently had done all he could to stop Leonidas himself from becoming king. As king, Leotychidas had consistently discredited himself, most recently by transferring a group of Aeginan hostages, who had surrendered in good faith to his safekeeping, to the Athenians. This act of betrayal had so outraged Sparta's citizens that Leotychidas had been condemned by the Assembly. He was venal, corrupt, self-serving, sly rather than intelligent, and very likely a usurper. "Work together on what?" Leonidas asked. "What on earth do we have in common?"

"All right," Leotychidas conceded with a shrug, "not together, but we don't have to be enemies, do we?"

"Then don't get in my way!" Leonidas warned.

By the time he could get away from his syssitia, it was very late. The syssitia had been brought the carcass of the sacrificial bull offered to Apollo to mark the occasion of the ascension of a king. The head cook, his sons, and two assistants had spent the entire afternoon carving it up and preparing a huge feast with contributions from all the syssitia members, right down to Maron, their newest and youngest member. Maron's estates were in bad shape and he had little extra, but he had harvested by hand from his mother's orchard the first of the ripening pears. A little sour still, they had been cooked in milk and honey and then sprinkled with powdered nutmeg. There were many other contributions as well, from wine to wheat bread, and the mood among his mess-mates was so high that Leonidas didn't have the heart to call an end to the meal until it was very late.

Despite liberal watering of the wine, they were all a little tipsy by the time they broke up, and Leonidas was grateful that Meander, contrary to his usual practice, had waited for him. He had two horses with him and helped Leonidas mount, then rode with him through the city, past the royal palace and beyond. Leonidas had talked enough at dinner and was silent.

The kleros appeared to glow in the darkness as they approached. Leonidas realized that torches had been set up and lit all across the front, but they were now burning very low. Oh dear, he thought: Pelopidas and his whole family had probably wanted to give him a royal welcome, and he had failed to turn up....

Sure enough, as he reached the front of the house it was clear that the helots, who would have to rise early the next morning, had retired. In fact, except for the spluttering torches, the house was dark and still.

"I'll see to the horses, sir," Meander offered, and Leonidas turned over his reins without a word. He walked into the darkened hall and cocked an ear.

"I'm out here," Gorgo called from the back terrace.

Leonidas went to her at once, an excuse on his lips. "I'm sorry I'm late. Everyone was—what's the matter? Gorgo? What's happened?"

Gorgo was sitting on the bench with her back against the house, and tears streamed down her face in such a flood that they glittered even in the darkness.

In answer to Leonidas' question, all she managed was a ragged sob and a shake of her head.

Gorgo could be very snippy and sarcastic when she was annoyed or felt slighted. Leonidas had been prepared for that. He was not prepared for this picture of sheer misery. He was seized with panic. Something terrible must have happened in his absence!

"Gorgo! The children? Has something—"

"No!" She put her hand to his lips and then pulled him down beside her on the bench. "Hold me!"

Leonidas gladly took her into his arms, thinking of all she meant to him. She leaned her head on his shoulder and he felt her tears on his naked arm. He felt and heard her hiccup. He heard Meander say something in the distance and Pelopidas answer. A breeze rustled the leaves of the orchard.

"Leo?"

"Yes?"

"I don't want to go."

"Go? Go where?"

"To the palace."

He didn't answer. The kings lived in the royal palace. When Cleomenes had become king, he had given his stepmother, with all her brood, just hours to get out. When Leotychidas had become king, he had been nearly as ruthless to Demaratus and Percalus. And Gorgo had grown up in the palace. It was her home more than it had ever been his....

Gorgo was speaking again. "The happiest times of my life were spent right *here*. I don't want to move back into the palace—with all its ghosts and memories. I don't want to sleep in the room where my parents fought and tore each other apart. I don't want to put Pleistarchos to bed in the room where my brothers died, one after another. I don't want to walk every day across the courtyard where my father cut himself to pieces. I don't want to go."

Leonidas took a deep breath and looked across the terrace toward Taygetos. He could understand her feelings, but they didn't have a choice. He had been elected king, and all that came with that title was now his sacred duty.

Chapter 12

LACEDAEMON RISING

The wind blew out of the north at gale force, and the Athenian merchantman had been forced to shorten sail. With the mainsail reefed, however, the little freighter could hardly make headway. The yard was braced hard to starboard, but still the vessel could claw only a few hundred yards to windward with each tack. The waves, whipped up until they were crested with whitecaps, broke over the bows of the ship. The two lookouts clinging to the forward rail could hardly keep their footing on the corkscrewing foredeck, while aft two helmsmen struggled to hold the little vessel on course as it soared and plunged.

The Athenian captain looked nervously over his shoulder at the ominous coast of Kythera. A high promontory of land hid the port of Skandia from view, and the coast here was inhospitable, steep, and barren. The only sign of habitation was a herd of goats grazing haphazardly among the gorse bushes. A little to starboard, low against the higher cliffs of the island, were the Dragoniden, two tiny islands that jutted out from the end of the high promontory. On the larger of these, the temple to Poseidon gleamed white in the summer sun.

The captain cursed. He had been in too great a hurry with his cargo of Sicilian wheat to stop and make an offering to Poseidon. His vessel was small, and he counted on earning a higher margin by beating the rest of the fleet into Athens. He had not reckoned with this wind springing up suddenly—much less with the ominous black penteconter that was lurking off the tip of Maleas.

The captain turned his nervous gaze back toward the penteconter on his port bow. He didn't like the looks of her. She was pitch black—as if fresh from the dockyard—with evil eyes flanking her prow. He could not make out any nationality. In these waters she ought to be Lacedaemonian, but he didn't like the way she just prowled offshore with no apparent goal. Or was she getting closer?

He braced himself against the moving deck and squinted into the wind. It was hard to tell, but she seemed to have turned away from the shore and to be rowing eastwards. He didn't like that, and ordered the helmsmen to fall off the wind a fraction. No harm in going a little farther eastward for the moment. Let the penteconter be on her way....

Not that he wanted to hold this course for long. There were currents out there that carried a ship southwards. Against wind and current, he didn't have a chance. Maybe it would be better to come about and try to pass astern of the penteconter? But that would make it more difficult to clear Maleas. Better to hold course for the moment.

He looked over his shoulder at the helmsmen. Usually one man could steer his handy little craft. He'd owned her for nearly twenty years now, and rarely had he seen her struggle so hard. She was heavily laden, of course. Maybe they should set the foresail again?

He squinted forward, trying to gauge the wind, and caught his breath as he realized the penteconter had changed course again and was plunging straight down at him. She had her sail set and all fifty oars were pushing off from the water in frightful unison, making the penteconter all but fly. Too late, the Athenian captain recognized the danger: painted proudly on the bellying canvas sail was the sea turtle of Aegina.

There could be no more question about the ship's evil intentions. For more than a decade Athens and Aegina had been entangled in an undeclared war. After Athens refused to release the hostages the Spartan king Leotychidas had taken and treacherously turned over to them, Aeginan ships had raided coastal towns in southern Attica, burning, looting and raping the girls just like common pirates. This spring Aeginan ships had captured an Athenian ship carrying priests and sacrifices bound for the Sanctuary of Poseidon at Sunium, and

Aegina still held the passengers captive. The Athenian captain knew he could expect no mercy from an Aeginan penteconter.

In panic, he ordered the helmsmen to fall off the wind more, and screamed forward to the deckhands to set the foresail and shake the reef out of the main. His only hope was to outrun the oared ship.

The ship responded to the helm and started to fall off the wind, wallowing briefly as it lay broadside to the waves. The Athenian captain shaded his eyes and peered toward his adversary. Sunlight glinted on bronze. The penteconter had marines on board!

In his heart he knew it was hopeless. He couldn't possibly outrun a penteconter, not a well-manned one like this. The oars rose and fell in perfect unison. Were those archers moving on to the foredeck? Ares! This isn't fair! I'm not a man of war! My daughter isn't married yet! I'm in debt to half the chandlers in Piraeus!

Panic had gripped the Athenian captain so completely that he didn't hear the helmsmen call out in alarm. In any case, it was too late.

With a horrible thud the ship came to a sudden stop. Every man aboard was knocked off his feet, and then the mainmast came crashing down on them. The planks of the ship started screaming as they were wrenched and twisted. The bow was stuck fast on an underwater ledge, while the stern was grasped inexorably in the waves and flung forward. Men started screaming as within seconds, with a horrible crunching and cracking of wood, the wreck was torn in two. The merchantman started to bleed its cargo into the sea. The sacks of grain sank silently into the shallow water, while barrels of oil and wine bobbed like corks on the blue and aquamarine waters of the bay.

The penteconter sheered off to the east, turned into the wind to hand sail, and then started rowing toward the wreck at a leisurely pace. Like a living thing, it circled its stranded prey as if gloating, apparently oblivious to the trireme that was bearing down on it from the west.

An expert might have detected imperfection in the slant or pull of some of the oars on the trireme, but her crew was more than adequate for the current task. All three banks of oars thrashed up the deep at a rate that closed the distance to the penteconter in a matter of minutes. The bronze-sheathed ram sliced through the sea, sending water upward in great curving sheets that shattered and fell back to the sea in glittering showers of water diamonds. The high, curving tail of the great warship left a wake of turbulence visible from the heights of Maleas and Kythera.

Abruptly the penteconter noticed the trireme, and with amazing agility pivoted dramatically to avoid going on the rocks. But the trireme had cut off any escape. "Surrender or we ram!" a voice shouted across the water.

It took the commander of the penteconter only a split second to decide to signal capitulation. Oars were shipped, and the trireme came alongside with a crunch and squeak of wood. A dozen armed men poured over the side of the trireme to take control of the penteconter. Within minutes the penteconter's officers, their hands tied behind their backs, were being transferred to the trireme. In less than a quarter-hour, the penteconter had been taken and was being towed.

The handful of Athenians from the wrecked freighter who managed to make it to shore alive found the consolation cold. No matter what the fate of the attacking penteconter, they had lost everything. The captain collapsed on the sand; all he could see in his mind's eye were the bills of his creditors in Piraeus, and the face of his daughter when he told her she was penniless and her marriage was off....

On the afterdeck of the trireme, Leonidas turned to the perioikoi captain to remark, "Well done."

Leonidas had come down to Boiai to witness the launch of his latest trireme. Since becoming king two years earlier, he had persuaded the Spartan Assembly to finance the building of no less than six triremes, and had added two from his own resources. This building program had more than doubled Lacedaemon's fleet to eighteen vessels—hardly large enough to challenge Corinth or Aegina, but no longer insignificant, either. With eighteen triremes and twenty-seven penteconters, Lacedaemon was gaining the capability to protect her merchant fleet and project power.

While the latest trireme was now bobbing peacefully at anchor in the harbor at Boiai, awaiting outfitting, Leonidas had snatched the opportunity to go aboard one of the commissioned triremes when a lookout reported an unidentified penteconter lurking off Maleas.

For months the waters around Kythera and Antikythera had been plagued by a series of attacks on merchant ships. At first people had thought it was pure coincidence, but soon it became clear that pirates were operating from somewhere within Laconia. Although no Lacedaemonian ships had been victims yet, everyone presumed it was only a matter of time before this happened. Orders had gone out for Lacedaemon's nascent fleet to start a systematic search along the coastline for the pirate's lair. The sighting of the strange penteconter during Leonidas' visit to Boiai seemed like a remarkable stroke of luck—one quickly attributed by the ever-superstitious sailors to the presence of their king.

"Hmm," the captain answered his king's praise, torn between pleasure and honesty. "At least we got her, but the launch took much too long, and half the men aren't putting their backs into it properly. Didn't you hear the clatter of oars colliding as we made the final run in? This crew needs much more practice before *I'll* be satisfied, but what can you expect from a bunch of farmers?" the captain added rhetorically, half under his breath.

Leonidas had recently passed a measure through the Assembly that granted freedom to helots who manned Lacedaemon's fleet for a minimum of ten years, provided they were not the oldest tenant on an estate. The law gave younger sons and other impoverished helots an opportunity to better themselves, and it had produced more volunteers than Lacedaemon's fledgling fleet could absorb. It also caused considerable outrage among Leonidas' enemies. But they were far away at the moment, and Leonidas was thoroughly enjoying himself.

"The crew of that penteconter is first rate," the captain continued, "but then, that's what I'd expect of Aeginans. It's no wonder their symbol is the sea turtle. No sooner is an Aeginan born than he waddles down to the sea and starts to swim. They can row and sail before they can talk."

Leonidas glanced back at their prize, and then forward to where two perioikoi marines were escorting the Aeginan officers to him.

"But they failed to capture their prize," Leonidas pointed out.

"Pah! They never intended to capture her. They drove her onto the rocks intentionally."

"Why would they do that?" Leonidas wanted to know. "There's no booty from a wrecked grain carrier."

The captain shrugged. "We'll have to ask them." He nodded toward the two prisoners. One was a grizzled veteran with shoulder-length hair, more gray than brown, and wearing the breastplate, greaves, and helmet of a marine. His face and arms were burned a dark brown from decades on decks in the blaze of the Mediterranean sun, and the lines around his eyes were cut deep into his skin. The other man looked much younger by contrast, although he was no youth. His almost-black hair was cut short at the back and his beard was neatly trimmed.

Leonidas started violently. The elder man was none other than his childhood friend Prokles, who had been exiled for dereliction of duty just before reaching citizenship. Almost as astonishing, he was accompanied by a young Spartiate, whose name escaped Leonidas at this moment.

"Prokles! What are you doing preying on innocent ships—and under the turtle of Aegina?"

Prokles, who had been fussing at the guard and not focused on the men on the afterdeck, broke into a grin. "Well, I'll be damned! I never expected a landlubber like you to catch me off guard like that." He glanced at the perioikoi captain and nodded once in respect, giving credit where he thought it was due.

"You didn't answer my question," Leonidas pointed out and turned to the younger man, who at least had the decency to look worried, to add, "and you need to explain yourself, young man!"

"I went off active service at the winter solstice, my lord," he spoke up at once, "and I'm on leave from my syssitia."

"With what possible excuse?" Leonidas wanted to know.

"To look after my affairs, my lord. My estates are on Kythera."

"Since when did looking after your affairs include attacking innocent merchant ships?"

"That's the second time you've used the adjective 'innocent,'" Prokles pointed out. "But you are using the term inadvisably. The Aeginans provided our ship and are paying us. The Aeginans do not view Athenian ships as 'innocent,' while Eurybiades here has a grudge against the Argives, whose ships have been our principal target."

"The Argives burned my kleros to the ground and murdered every man, woman, and child on it," Eurybiades explained at once.

Leonidas well remembered the damage wrought by the Argives on Kythera, but he still did not approve of someone taking the law into his own hands. "In my waters, I'll decide who can be attacked and who can go free," Leonidas countered.

"Your waters be damned!" Prokles spat in the direction of the side of the ship, and the perioikoi marines stiffened in alarm, looking to Leonidas for orders to put the impudent man in his place. Leonidas signaled for them to relax, even as Prokles continued. "Power has gone to your head, Leo. We didn't break any law. Can we help it if an Athenian captain puts his own ship on the rocks?"

Leonidas addressed himself to the baffled perioikoi marines, who appeared ready to slit Prokles' throat for his impudence. "Untie them. They will do us no harm." The perioikoi obeyed with obvious reluctance, and then moved only a short distance away, both curious and suspicious.

Prokles demonstratively stretched and wriggled his shoulders, while Leonidas asked, "Just what are the terms of your commission from Aegina?"

Prokles shrugged. "Ask Eurybiades. He's the captain. I'm just commander of the marines."

Leonidas looked at the younger Spartiate, even more amazed. "How did you come by an Aeginan commission? And where did you learn seamanship?"

Eurybiades, his hands now free, gestured vaguely around them. "Here, my lord. I spent my holidays here, not just on Kythera, but on the waters around it."

"Who is your father?"

"Eurykleides, my lord."

The name was familiar. Eurykleides had a distinguished career behind him and had served once as ephor. He stood a good chance of election to the Gerousia when a vacancy came up. Generally seen as a conservative, he had nevertheless, Leonidas now remembered, spoken forcefully in favor of the building of a fleet, and he also supported the law to allow helots to improve their status through service on Lacedaemonian ships.

"My mother killed herself when she realized the Argives had breached the wall of the courtyard," Eurybiades continued, breaking in on his thoughts. "My father remarried and has two younger sons by his second wife. I inherited my mother's property here."

"Where did you recruit the crew of your penteconter?" Leonidas asked next.

"Oh, mostly in Skandia."

"They're Kytheran, not Aeginan?" the perioikoi captain asked, astonished.

"For the most part," Eurybiades agreed, "maybe a third are Aeginan."

"And where do you come in, Prokles?" Leonidas redirected attention to his old friend.

"Eurybiades and I met on that convoy to Byzantion and back."

"You were with me on that?" Leonidas turned again to Eurybiades, shocked that he had not recognized someone who served with him on that fateful expedition.

"I was assigned to the *Harmony*. We hardly saw each other."

"I showed Eurybiades Byzantion while you were with that Corinthian cripple," Prokles added.

"Lychos," Leonidas rebuked Prokles, "attacked a Phoenician trireme with his merchant ship."

"Brave," Prokles agreed with a nod, "but a cripple all the same—and too rich for my liking. He smelled of gold as bad as Croesus!"

"Eurybiades is not exactly poor," Leonidas reflected, with a glance at the younger man.

Prokles shrugged, "But *he* smells of salt water and pitch."

While they had been talking, the trireme had rounded the Dragoniden and was making for Skandia. The Kytheran port crouched along the shoreline, a jumble of whitewashed structures with pale tile roofs. Many of the buildings, particularly along the shorefront, were new; most of the town had been burned down by the Argives twenty years ago.

The high headland started to provide protection from the north wind, and the seas were beginning to calm. The trireme steadied, but below deck the rowing master prowled the gangway between the oar banks, calling out insults more than encouragement.

"Just how many helots do you think are going to last ten years on a trireme?" Prokles scoffed. "They'll desert before half their time has run."

"If they desert, they remain helots."

"So what? If they jump ship in Memphis or Syracuse, who's going to care what status they have here in Lacedaemon?"

"I'll worry about that when Lacedaemonian triremes regularly call at Memphis and Syracuse," Leonidas retorted, turning to Eurybiades. "And what do you think of the law, young man?"

"I agree with Prokles."

That surprised Leonidas, because Eurybiades' father had supported the law. He asked somewhat defensively, "Where else are we to get crews? There aren't enough perioikoi."

"I know. I meant we should free them sooner—not after ten years."

"But then there will be no incentive to serve at all!" Leonidas protested.

Eurybiades shrugged. "Other cities man their ships with citizens. How can we expect equal service from men with only second-class rights?"

"The men who man Aegina's oars don't have the same rights as the men who command the ships, either," Leonidas reminded him. Aegina's oligarchy was small, even by Peloponnesian standards, and poorer citizens had fewer rights and status than perioikoi. "And Athenian thetes can't even run for office!" Leonidas scoffed.

Eurybiades considered this a moment, but then he nodded. "True, but ten years is a long time to pull an oar...."

"No longer than we are on active service," Leonidas pointed out.

That made Eurybiades break into a smile as he answered provocatively, "And that seemed like *forever*!"

They laughed together, the two Spartiates who had served in the Spartan army, unconsciously excluding Prokles and the perioikoi around them. When their laughter faded, however, Leonidas turned to the perioikoi captain to ask, "What do you think?"

"About the helots, my lord?"

"Yes."

The captain weighed his head from side to side, more cautious than the Spartiates about disagreeing with a king. "I said earlier today that it is hard to turn a farmer into a sailor. Half of them will never get the hang of it, really—they'll be seasick every time we put to sea, and terrified in every gale. A man's got to have the sea in him...."

That was a different issue, so Leonidas let the topic drop. He turned instead to Prokles. "So, when are you coming home to Sparta to get your cloak and shield? Your exile ended at the winter solstice."

"I've told you before, Leo. I'm not coming."

Leonidas had not expected any other answer, but it still saddened him. "May I tell your family I saw you here?"

"Would you hide the fact if I asked you to?"

Leonidas thought about it and realized he would not. "No."

"Then why ask?"

"Your mother is very ill. It would comfort her to see you alive."

"Don't try to pressure me, Leo," Prokles warned, while the men around him stirred uneasily, angered by Prokles' insolence to their king.

Leonidas again signaled for them to relax, and turned his attention to Eurybiades. "I regret that you are in Aeginan pay; I would rather have you serving Lacedaemon."

Eurybiades did not hesitate for an instant. "Give me a ship, my lord, and you'll find I can serve Lacedaemon very well—far better at sea than on land."

Leonidas glanced at the perioikoi captain and then remarked, "I'll keep that in mind."

Alkander caught a glimpse of himself in the face of a shield, and drew up short to look again. He looked middle-aged. His hairline was receding, his nose sharp, his throat creased with lines. If he stopped to count the years, it was only natural; he was forty-one. But how was it possible that he was forty-one? He didn't feel forty-one. He didn't feel like a man who had been out of the agoge longer than he had been in it. He still identified with the boys more than the "adults."

He turned away from the shield and sank down on the heavy, throne-like chair that served as his seat of office. Alkander was deputy headmaster of the agoge with responsibility for the "little boys," the boys aged seven to thirteen. In this austere office, furnished only with the chair, a table, a chest, and a bench against the wall, he directed the fate of roughly 350 boys. Here he worked out the lesson plans, gave instructions to instructors, listened to complaints from citizens, eirenes, and boys, and meted out punishment....

Alkander knew that many people, particularly Brotus and his cronies, believed he had been defeated and humiliated when Ephorus had been elected Paidonomos shortly after Leonidas became king. Indeed, he had felt humiliated when the votes were shouted out and so few had acclaimed his name compared to the loud roar in favor of Ephorus. Sperchias, so often defeated in his own ambition for public office, had met his eye with an unspoken "See how it feels?" But Alkander had long since come to terms with his defeat.

Hilaira had been the first to point out the advantages of his situation. As Paidonomos, she reminded him, he would have been an elected official, subject to public censure. As the deputy headmaster appointed by Ephorus, he answered to Ephorus alone. Ephorus was a sensible man, one who did not feel compelled to say no to sensible ideas just because they originated from a subordinate or because they differed from the way things had been when he was a boy. Furthermore, he'd been Alkander's herd leader when they were boys, and he'd won Olympic laurels as a young man. As a result, he felt himself so inherently superior to Alkander, the former stutterer, that he did not feel threatened by him—certainly not after Alkander's resounding electoral defeat. In short, Ephorus patronized Alkander, generously giving him a free hand—and taking credit for his successes.

Leonidas had argued the advantages of Ephorus' election differently; he told Alkander that Ephorus was his "shield." Noting that Ephorus was widely seen as independent of Leonidas but popular for his own tangible successes, Leonidas claimed that Ephorus deflected criticism from Alkander. "Let them think they have defeated us, and that by holding fast to Ephorus they are keeping us down," Leonidas reasoned.

Alkander, however, had come to see the advantages of his non-election in the fact that Ephorus was biased in favor of the eirenes and meleirenes. He left the "little boys" entirely in Alkander's care largely because he didn't care about them. He did not have any particular ideas of his own about how they should be raised or what they should learn. He approved Alkander's changes because he didn't have any ideas of his own on the subject.

Alkander smiled to himself. That was a mistake many men made: to dismiss little boys as uninteresting and unimportant. Alkander believed, in contrast, that it was easier to influence a boy at ten than at twenty. By the time a boy was an eirene, his personality was already formed for the most part. It was because he believed his influence was greatest with the little boys that Alkander liked working with them.

But there were times when he was forcefully reminded of the limits of his influence. Today had been one of those days. A pair of eight-year-olds had been caught throwing stones at helots harvesting hay. Their eirene had locked them in a pen and let the other boys throw stones at them—which was as appropriate a punishment as any—but it bothered Alkander that these boys would even think of stoning helots. Their excuse from the start had been, "But they're just *helots*." Alkander had heard that contempt too often in his lifetime. For hours he had been trying to think of some way to impress upon the boys the importance of helots.

A knock interrupted his thoughts. To his astonishment, neither an eirene nor a boy from the agoge entered. Instead, a middle-aged man in a long, elegant chiton stepped into the room. The man was obviously a stranger. He wore his hair cut short, and his dark green chiton had a broad border of lotus blossoms the color of ripe wheat. His himation reversed the color scheme and was wrapped with an elegance rare in Sparta. He had armbands on his wrists and his shoes were decorated with bronze.

It was only a few days before the start of the Gymnopaedia, and Sparta was overrun with visitors at this time of year. More seemed to come from year to year, with a veritable explosion of interest, ever since Leonidas had became king. This was in part because the tradesmen and craftsmen, who had flooded into Lacedaemon in response to Leonidas' incentives, told their friends and relatives not only about the opportunities opening up in Lacedaemon, but about the Spartan festivals as well. They encouraged people to visit them during the major holidays. It was also due to the fact that word was spreading that a new wind was blowing in Lacedaemon.

Alkander politely rose to his feet and asked courteously, "Can I help you, stranger?"

"I am looking for a man called Alkander, the son of Demarmenus."

Astonished, Alkander admitted, "I am he."

The stranger smiled and continued into the room. He moved awkwardly, a little twisted and tilted to one side, and he seemed to drag one of his feet. Alkander started to guess who he was even before the stranger announced, "And I am Lychos, son of Archilochos. Twenty years ago you saved my life."

Alkander came around the table to meet the man halfway, dismissing the praise. "Leonidas killed the boar. I only—"

Lychos cut him off. "Two men came to my rescue, and two men felled the wild boar. It makes little difference who delivered the coup de grâce. I owe you *both* my life, but while I have had several opportunities to thank Leonidas, today is the first chance I've had to thank you."

This was true. Leonidas had met Lychos at Olympia more than a decade ago and traveled with him to Athens. They met again when Leonidas commanded the Spartan marines that escorted a Corinthian grain convoy during the Ionian revolt. Lychos and Leonidas had become friends.

Lychos opened his arms and Alkander embraced him. Then they drew back to look at each other again.

Although Lychos was younger than Alkander, pain had carved his face, and he looked ten years older. Alkander knew, too, that Lychos owed his tan to years at sea, because despite being an extremely wealthy man, Lychos regularly sailed with one or another of his nearly one hundred merchant ships. For nearly twenty years Leonidas had pleaded with Lychos to visit Sparta, but Lychos had always refused, claiming that overland travel was too strenuous. "What finally brought you to Sparta?" Alkander asked candidly.

Lychos nodded. "A good question. Shall we sit?"

Alkander indicated the bench lining the room and sat beside him.

"Leonidas," Lychos started with a faint smile, "has always praised your public school, your agoge."

Alkander laughed. "He would! He loved it."

"And you did not." It was a statement, not a question. Leonidas had clearly told the Corinthian about their childhood.

"No. It was hell for me."

"But you and your sons are here."

"My sons have no choice. As for me, I am here to try to make it as good as Leonidas thinks it is."

Lychos laughed, but then grew serious. "I, too, have two sons. The elder is seventeen, almost the age I was when we met so fatefully. He has turned into exactly what I was then: a spoiled dandy interested only in fashion, fast horses, and theater. He is rude and disrespectful, self-indulgent and lazy. I do not want my younger boy to turn out like him, so I was thinking of enrolling him in the agoge."

"How old is he?"

"He is fourteen."

Alkander thought about that. It was not a bad age for a visitor to enter the agoge, because it was the first year of "youth," when much was new for the Spartan boys, too. It was also after passing the "fox time," when the boys had to live outside society for forty days—something the gentle sons of aristocrats from other parts of Greece could not be expected to endure, much less survive. It had another advantage as well, as Alkander admitted: "That is the age of my son Simonidas. We should introduce them to each other and see if they get along." Alkander was thinking that Simonidas was still too much of a loner, and having responsibility for a stranger might be integrative. At the same time, Simonidas could be trusted to teach the Corinthian the rules.

Lychos agreed enthusiastically. "That's an excellent idea. I will not tell Kallias what I plan—just let him see for himself that the agoge is not as bad as people say it is."

Alkander nodded, but he did not look convinced. "You can use the time to observe and think this through again. After all, there are many things he will *not* learn here."

"Leonidas assured me that a Spartan education trains the intellect as well as the body."

"Yes, of course," Alkander agreed. "But—"

There was another knock on the door, and Alkander called, "Come in."

An eirene in the distinctive short haircut of his position, wearing an unbleached chiton under a leather corselet, pushed two boys with shaved heads, bare feet, and ragged chitons into the office. "You sent for us, sir," the eirene explained, coming to attention with his hands at his sides and looking respectfully over Alkander's shoulder.

Alkander excused himself to Lychos and went to stand in front of the boys. While the eirene stood very straight and still, the miscreants were eight-year-olds, and they had not yet absorbed the agoge discipline to the same degree. They kept squirming and sneaking glances at Alkander.

"Do you know why you are here?" Alkander opened the interrogation.

"Alpheus says it is just for throwing stones at some stupid helots," one of the boys announced in a defiant tone, with an angry look at his eirene.

"And you do not think that is reason enough to have to face me?" Alkander answered the boy's tone rather than his words.

The boys continued to look sullen, and one of them asked, "What's wrong with throwing rocks at helots?"

"Well, tell me this: Can the Spartan army fight without food?" Alkander asked.

They shook their heads vigorously.

"Do you produce food for the Spartan army?"

They shook their heads even more vigorously.

"Does your father produce food for the army?"

"Of course not! He's Spartiate," the bolder boy countered indignantly, and then dropped his eyes before his eirene could cuff him.

"But Spartiates have to eat," Alkander told him reasonably. "If you don't produce food and your father doesn't produce food, who does? Does your mother plow and plant the grain?"

"Of course not!" The talkative boy sounded very angry.

"Who does?" Alkander insisted.

"Helots!" he spat out.

"Exactly. So you, your father, and the Spartan army all depend on helots to survive, don't you?"

Sullen silence answered him.

"Don't you?" Alkander insisted.

"But farming is slave work, helot work! It's for stupid beasts!" the other boy insisted.

"Do you know a beast that can plow and plant and harvest?"

Silence.

"The character of your actions was fundamentally hostile to the Spartan state, because no matter how small or minor your actions may seem, they were directed against a pillar of our society: the freedom of Spartiates to focus on their duties as citizens." Alkander looked from one boy to the other. They were both frowning, but he hoped it was now more from puzzlement than from resentment. "Without helots to work our estates and grow our food, we would be like the other Greeks, who have to earn a living first and are soldiers second." Again he paused to let this sink in before asking, "For sabotaging the Spartan state, your punishment has been very mild, hasn't it?"

The boys started squirming in anticipation of the cane.

"Eirene." Alkander turned to Alpheus. "I think these boys should go without bread, cheese, sausage, honey, or any other farm produce until they learn to appreciate the importance of agricultural labor. They are to be allowed to eat only those things they can gather, trap, or hunt from the wild."

"Yes, sir," the eirene answered dutifully, looking uneasy. At eight, the boys could not yet hunt, had barely learned the fundamentals of trapping, and had not yet learned how to distinguish edible from poisonous plants.

"I want to see these boys again in a week."

"Yes, sir," the eirene swallowed nervously, recognizing that his obedience to these orders would be assessed by the state of the boys in the next interview.

"Dismissed," Alkander ordered, and the eirene shooed the boys back out into the hall.

Alkander turned to Lychos and opened his hands in a gesture of helplessness. "You see the limits of our discipline."

"I see that you demand understanding as well as obedience."

"That is the objective, but those boys learned contempt for helots from their parents—evidence that my predecessors failed to impress upon earlier generations our interdependence and respect for each man, free or unfree."

Lychos raised his eyebrows at that. "Would you teach the boys respect for slaves?"

Alkander tilted his head. "Why not? A man's status has little to do with his character. After all, a slave can be set free, or a freeman can be captured. There is a young man here, a Chian, who was born free but taken captive by the Persians when he was still a boy. The Persians cut off his genitals so brutally that he was lamed. Yet he freed himself by running away. Didn't he show his greatest courage when—as a slave—he ran away?"

Lychos bowed his head in concession. Alkander continued, "I try to teach the boys that a man's character—not his status, his clothes, or his looks—is what makes him valuable. I try to point out that a helot who is hard-working and honest is better than even a king who is deceitful, corrupt, or profligate."

"Using, I presume, Leotychidas and not Leonidas as your example of a profligate king," Lychos quipped.

Alkander laughed briefly, but then grew serious. "The Spartan agoge teaches paradigms for living rather than facts."

"And what is the most important paradigm of all?" Lychos asked.

"Consciousness of our mortality."

Lychos started, but then nodded knowingly, "Yes, of course. You want to prepare the boys to die for Sparta."

"No, not at all!" Alkander countered emphatically. "We make our sons confront death when trapping, hunting, and sacrificing so that they learn to appreciate the sheer beauty of *life*." He paused and then tried to explain. "Look at it this way: A Spartan youth does not need a fancy new himation to make him feel good; just being warm will satisfy him. Nor does he need exotic fish rushed into the city on ice and doused in spicy sauces in order to feel well fed; just filling his belly will do that. Just as deprivation makes a man satisfied with very little, consciousness of his mortality makes a man treasure each and every day. At its best, consciousness of the shortness of life makes a man use each day the way a miser spends gold. Does this make sense to you?" Alkander stopped himself to ask the Corinthian.

Lychos nodded slowly. "I think for the first time I am beginning to understand Leonidas."

Demophilus, like so many other strangers, had come to Sparta for the Gymnopaedia. Thespiae honored the Muses more than any other city in Greece, and Demophilus, as one of Thespiae's wealthiest citizens, had sponsored a young composer in the traditional composers' competition. Unfortunately, the Thespian had lost to a refugee from Potidaea, who (Demophilus thought) had captured the favor of the jury more with his story than with his music. The Potidaean refugee had written a ballad describing Darius' murder of Cyrus' rightful heir and his massacre of the Magi to clear his way to the throne. Not surprisingly, the Persian king had ordered the presumptuous tongue of the Potidaean poet torn out of his mouth for "lying." The poet had escaped the Persian authorities by the skin of his teeth, literally flinging himself into the sea when they cornered him. He managed to swim to an outbound Corinthian vessel before the Persians could launch a boat to pursue him. Such a story had captured the imagination of the Spartan judges, and the Potidaean poet had been crowned with a laurel wreath and given a stipend for a full year in order to train the choruses for next year's Gymnopaedia.

The selection of next year's composer was the final event of this year's holiday, however, and many visitors hadn't bothered to stay for it. The roads out of Sparta were thus already crowded with departing guests, some on carts or horses but most striding along under broad-brimmed sun hats, their walking sticks in their hands. The other Thespians were preparing to return, too, disappointed by the defeat of their countryman and discouraged by a growing sense of divine disfavor.

Other peoples might not take an artistic defeat so seriously, but Thespiae wasn't like other cities. Furthermore, the disfavor of the Gods had been plaguing them for a long time. It was with a sense of desperation that Demophilus resolved to seek assistance from King Leonidas.

Demophilus had duly reported to the Agiad royal palace to request an interview, and had been surprised to hear that the king had already left the city and gone to his "kleros." The palace officials had, however, encouraged him to follow the king, and had provided him with instructions. So, just beyond the Temple to the Twins, he turned up a cypress-lined drive leading to a simple two-story house.

Here Demophilus dismounted, confused by both the simplicity of the structure and the stillness around him. Here were no bustling slaves, no bodyguards, no supplicants or court officials. Horses grazed peacefully in the sunny paddock, swatting lazily at flies with their long, well-combed tails. A calico cat was licking herself on the steps up to the house. Birds called, and from somewhere came the high-pitched voices of children.

A young man emerged around the side of the house. He was muscular, tanned, and barefoot, and wore his chiton pinned on only one shoulder: evidently one of Sparta's state slaves, a helot. "Can I help you, sir?" he asked politely.

"I'm here to see King Leonidas. Where might I find him?"

"The master? I think he's in the orchard." The young man pointed to the far side of the house.

Demophilus set off in this direction, feeling disoriented by the lack of ceremony. Up to now he had seen Leonidas only from a distance, and the king seemed a very regal figure, always flanked by four impressive guardsmen in gleaming bronze. Leonidas, unlike his co-monarch, had cut a magnificent figure: tall, straight, and attractive, his chiton and himation pristine and trimmed with gold, while the massive signet ring and the heavy bracelets on his forearms had evoked images from the Age of Heroes.

As he rounded the end of the house, Demophilus was distracted by two children jumping up and down excitedly on either side of a man with the broad shoulders and powerful thighs of a hoplite. He was dressed in a short white chiton with a broad blue border, and the wind fluttered the skirts and sleeves as he raised his arms to throw a rope over the limb of a mighty plane tree. A moment later the second rope went up; Demophilus realized that a wooden plank between the ropes formed a swing. A little girl was crying shrilly, "Me first! Me first! I'm the eldest!" The man, presumably her father, lifted her onto the seat of the swing, and at once she started pumping so vigorously that her father warned, "Not so hard or you'll break the branch!"

"No, I won't!" the little girl answered defiantly, with a toss of her fair curls, and pumped even harder.

Her younger brother clung to his father's hand as he watched his sister, his whole head swinging from side to side.

At last the man realized he was being watched, and turned to look over his shoulder. When his eyes rested on Demophilus, he smiled and turned around to offer the stranger an outstretched hand, although his son clung to the other one. "Welcome, stranger. What can I do for you?"

Demophilus felt an absolute fool. He wasn't at all sure that this gentle-looking man with the rich brown beard and alert hazel eyes was the same man he had seen performing the sacrifices and leading the ceremonies, the man for whom everyone sprang to their feet, parted, and fell silent. He was suddenly afraid he was in the wrong place. "Forgive me for intruding, sir. I am looking for King Leonidas."

"And you can't imagine him making a swing for his daughter?" Leonidas asked with a smile. "But, you see, when I am here I am not King Leonidas, just the father of my children and husband to my wife. So you will either have to wait for me to return to the palace to meet the king, or take me as I am here. The choice is yours." He let this sink in only a fraction of a second and then offered, "While you think about it, why don't you join me for some light refreshment?" Leonidas indicated the back terrace of his house.

Demophilus recovered from his amazement and thanked the Spartan king. "Yes, thank you, of course."

"Come." Leonidas led him around the nearest wing of the house, pausing to plunge his hands into the basin of a small fountain and splash water onto his face. He dried his face on the back of his arm like a soldier and continued to the back terrace, indicating that Demophilus should sit on one of the benches beside a large wooden table, while he continued to the low tract of buildings. He spoke to someone inside, saying something about "visitors," before returning to sit opposite Demophilus, pulling his son into his lap.

"So who are you, stranger, and why do you want to speak with a Spartan king?"

"My name is Demophilus, son of Diadromes, of Thespiae, my lord—"

"Thespiae?" Leonidas interrupted, leaning forward with interest. "I have never been to your city, but I have met two of your compatriots—and both impressed me with their intelligence, common sense, and skill. Not to mention that your poet this year was the best, even if he didn't win. You aren't here to complain about that, are you? I must disappoint you if you are. A Spartan king cannot override the decision of the artistic committee."

"No, we respect that. I'm here about something much more important...." Demophilus broke off. All his prepared speeches had been designed for an aloof, purple-robed king on a throne or a hard-nosed Spartan general in bronze, not for a man sitting astride a wooden bench with his young son on his knee. Demophilus threw his prepared speeches to the winds, took a deep breath, and asked instead, "My lord—sir—do you know what is happening to Thespiae?"

"Not a clue. It is beyond Sparta's sphere of influence."

That was not a good start. "Please hear me out."

Leonidas smiled and gestured to the peaceful scene around them—the bees collecting pollen from the blooming oleander, the screeching of the crickets in the pine trees beyond the stables, the calico cat nursing three kittens in the shade of a potted palm. "Take as long as you want—but first, let me introduce my wife." Leonidas had caught sight of Gorgo coming from the helot quarters, flanked by two young Kastorian hounds.

Demophilus got awkwardly to his feet. Even after a fortnight in Sparta, he was still embarrassed by the way Spartan women walked around unveiled in public. In Thespiae, respectable women rarely left their homes at all, and then only furtively. But he had seen Leonidas' queen at all the major events of the Gymnopaedia—always standing at his shoulder, her head upright and her himation at best lightly laid over the back of her head, so you could still see her whole face and neck.

"Am I interrupting?" Gorgo asked, a smile flirting with her lips.

"No," Leonidas answered untruthfully (Demophilus thought) before continuing, "Demophilus, son of Diadromes of Thespiae, was just about to explain his purpose. You'll join us?"

Demophilus opened his mouth to protest. The story he had to tell was not for a lady's ears, but something in the way Leonidas gestured for Gorgo to sit beside him made him bite his tongue. Gorgo did not hesitate, and at once her son changed from his father's lap to hers without a word. Gorgo put an arm around him and adjusted her seating to make them both comfortable, but her eyes and attention remained fixed on Demophilus.

Demophilus took a deep breath. "Thespiae is a small but ancient city. And we are a peaceful city. We revere no God greater than the God of Love. We have never sought to expand, nor have we practiced the art of war. On the contrary, in addition to our cult to Eros and Aphrodite, we revere Asclepius and Hygieia above the other Gods. They passed through Thespiae after learning their craft from Chiron, you see, and Asclepius planted the arbutus trees on Mount Helicon in thanks for the kindness our ancestors showed him when he was burned by Hades' lightning bolt. These trees have great healing power, so great that even the water in which their leaves are boiled can cure fever, and a poultice from the leaves will draw the poison from the bite of any viper.

"It was because of the healing power of these trees that Pieros of Macedon came to Thespiae and brought us the Muses. There are nine Muses, not just three as some people think, and they inhabit the valley below Mount Helicon. Many scholars and artists come to the Valley of the Muses to pay tribute to them in a little grove near a spring. Our maidens show their respect for the Muses by making sacrifices to them, particularly before a wedding. A bride-to-be, accompanied by her female relatives, goes there to sacrifice her dolls, and the women sing and dance together." Demophilus risked a short glance at the Spartan queen. She was listening very intently and he said a short prayer to Aphrodite, realizing that although awkward and unusual, her presence might be a blessing after all.

He focused again on Leonidas and spoke with greater intensity. "We have lived in peace for so long, following our customs without intending or enduring harm, that we were utterly unprepared when one day word came that hundreds of Thebans were on the slopes of Mount Helicon, hacking down the sacred trees.

"Outraged, my father grabbed his armor and called on the fighting men of Thespiae—such as they are—to follow him. Although just seventeen, I grabbed a sword and swung myself onto my fastest horse.

"Thespiae is a city of roughly twenty-four hundred citizens. About five hundred men can afford panoply, but we are not trained fighters—not like you Spartans. Our hoplites and cavalry are more for adorning our festivals than for fighting. When my father rushed to the defense of our sacred trees, he did so in indignation, confident that the Gods would be with us.

"The bulk of the Thebans hacking our sacred trees were slaves and workmen, sent to collect branches and carry them back to Thebes to fight a raging fever. My father and the other Thespian fighting men easily drove these workmen away from the trees, but the Thebans had sent a company of hoplites to escort the workmen. These attacked first with javelins that killed or wounded many of our horses, and frightened many more. Then they formed a phalanx and attacked the confused and partially injured men around my father. My horse had reared up and taken a javelin in his belly. It fell over backwards, pinning me to the earth. I could do nothing, even when the Thebans overwhelmed my father and killed him before my eyes." Demophilus kept his eyes fixed firmly on Leonidas, embarrassed to look at the woman.

"You would like us to help avenge his death?" Leonidas surmised.

Demophilus shook his head. "No. I was not raised to seek blood for blood. Instead, we sent priests to Thebes asking reparation for the loss of twenty-eight men and the damage to the sacred trees, but the Thebans refused, saying that we had attacked them and that Mount Helicon belonged to them anyway. We then sent to Delphi for a judgment, and the oracle ordered Thebes to pay us one hundred head of cattle in reparation for the damage done. But they sent sick cattle that all died and infected our own herds, leaving us poorer than before. Meanwhile they closed their market to us, and when we send goods to Athens, they attack us on the road and steal our goods and slaves, leaving many honest tradesmen to die in their own blood.

"My countrymen have been slow to understand, but it is clear to me that the Thebans want to subjugate us. Just as they tried to dominate Plataea until Athens offered Plataea protection five Olympiads ago, they want to turn us into their subjects and slaves.

"We may be peace-loving men, more devoted to the Muses and Eros than to war, but we are lovers of freedom, too. More and more Thespians are willing, ready, and eager to fight. Especially since this most recent episode." He paused dramatically and turned to Gorgo.

"I told you how our young maidens prepare for their weddings, how they go out into the Valley of the Muses to the sacred grove with their gifts of dolls and other childhood treasures. I am sure you, Madam, understand such things, as Sparta must have similar customs."

Gorgo considered enlightening him, but decided against it because it was irrelevant. She smiled and nodded for him to go on.

"You will understand, too, that at such a time the women want no male relatives looking on. They go without men because this is when the married women tell a maiden what to expect on her wedding night. Men never take part in these rituals."

Gorgo nodded again, less in agreement than in anticipation. She could sense what was coming.

"Then you will understand how devastating it was when a young bride and her female escort were surprised by a party of Theban youth. The Thebans stalked the women from hiding in the high grass, then burst out of hiding and took as many of the girls as they could, ravishing some right there and carrying two away."

Demophilus was disappointed that Gorgo did not cry out in shock, but Leonidas made a sharp noise. Looking back toward the Spartan king, Demophilus found him frowning. "And what satisfaction has Thebes given you for this outrage?" Leonidas wanted to know.

"None," Demophilus answered. "Absolutely none. They claim the assailants were not Theban, suggesting they were passing strangers. But how would strangers know our customs? How would they know where to lurk, as these youth did?"

"What do the two girls who were captured say?" Gorgo asked. "Surely they know where they were taken?"

"But they have not been recovered," Demophilus told her solemnly. "We fear the worst: that they were killed or killed themselves in shame. One was the bride-to-be."

"What do you want Sparta to do?" Leonidas asked bluntly.

"We want you to guarantee our safety—as Athens does Plataea's."

"A defensive alliance?"

"Yes, exactly!" Demophilus agreed enthusiastically, relieved that the Spartan king understood their need so quickly.

Leonidas shook his head. "It won't pass the Council, much less the Assembly. Thespiae is even farther away than Plataea. Have you gone to Athens?"

"Athens!" Demophilus spat out in disgust. "Marathon has gone to their heads! They drove Miltiades to his grave, did you know? They refused to recognize his preeminent role at Marathon, and then put him on trial for not capturing Paros. He was not only found guilty, he was fined so heavily in punishment that he would have died in poverty had he not first died from his wounds! Now they are at war with Aegina, raiding the coastline and seizing ships on the high seas—all without even sending heralds to declare war first. Athens told us bluntly that they have no interest in our 'petty' problems. They told us to 'come to terms with reality and submit to Thebes!'" The mere memory of his reception in Athens made Demophilus shake with indignation.

"I was distressed to hear what had happened to Miltiades," Leonidas answered solemnly, adding, "and I am equally sorry to hear Athens will not aid Thespiae as they did Plataea."

"Sparta is our last hope! Our *best* hope. The mere mention of a Spartan alliance would make Thebes stop these acts of aggression! You need not actually come north," Demophilus pleaded.

Leonidas frowned. "I'm not so sure. Besides, it makes no difference whether or not the treaty is nominal—the proposal will find no majority in the Council or Assembly. You may think from watching the Gymnopaedia that Sparta's kings are still as powerful as in the age of Menelaos, but that is not the case. Our role is largely ceremonial—until the army crosses out of Lacedaemon. And, believe me, getting the Council, ephors, and Assembly to agree to a Spartan army leaving Lacedaemon is almost as difficult as getting Poseidon to stop shaking the earth. Let's look for other solutions." Leonidas' tone was so earnest and yet friendly that Demophilus did not have time to feel the full weight of his disappointment.

"You said you had five hundred citizens capable of bearing arms?" Leonidas asked.

"More," Demophilus corrected him. "Since the abduction of the maidens, many men of lesser means have come to me saying they want to fight. The abducted bride was betrothed to a stone mason, and he and all the masons are furious with the inaction of 'the rich.'

Other craftsmen have rallied to me as well. But I must be honest with you, Leonidas: many of the prominent citizens, particularly the old men, are afraid of Thebes. They say we cannot win and that it is better to come to some arrangement. The poorer citizens fear that they will be the losers in any 'arrangement.' They fear the rich will look after their own interests and leave them with heavier taxes and fewer freedoms. I could field a thousand men eager to fight Thebes, but most of them have no panoply. And even the other rich men who would like to defend our freedom have no training or experience in war."

"How many men willing to defend their freedom have panoply?" Leonidas asked.

"Three hundred eighty-eight."

"How many hoplites can Thebes field?" The question, to Demophilus' amazement, came from Gorgo.

"More than ten times that," her husband answered before Demophilus had recovered from his surprise. "But numbers are not important. You are not about to declare war on Thebes, and Thebes has no need to declare war on you—because they can get what they want without it. What you need is not a hoplite army that can face down the full force of Thebes on a battlefield, but troops capable of standing up to individual acts of Theban aggression. You need to teach Thebes respect for your independence."

"Yes! Exactly!" Demophilus was excited that Leonidas both grasped the situation and spoke as if it were possible. "Could you teach us how to do that?" he asked, torn between hope and disbelief.

Leonidas looked at Gorgo.

"You don't need the approval of the Council or Assembly to take the Guard to Thespiae and train volunteers," Gorgo answered his look.

Demophilus looked from one to the other.

Leonidas nodded. "My wife is right. If you have young men willing to learn the art of war, then I am prepared to take Spartiates to Thespiae to train them. But your young men must be willing to learn from us. It takes a lifetime to make a Spartiate hoplite; you cannot expect to turn farmers or masons into hoplites overnight. And it will not happen without very hard work."

"You will find Thespians exceptional pupils, King Leonidas!" Demophilus assured him with a rush of inner excitement. His imagination was on fire already. It was much more honorable to defend their own freedom than to depend on the promises of others.

CHAPTER 13

WARRIORS FOR THE WORKING DAY

OLIANTUS HAD NOT WANTED TO COME with Leonidas on the training expedition to Thespiae. Leonidas might like seeing new places and visiting other cities, but Oliantus was content to stay at home looking after his own affairs. He was forty-three and he had three sons, the eldest of whom was almost eighteen. But, as so often in the past, Leonidas had proved irresistible; Oliantus always caved in when Leonidas said: "But I need you, Oli! No one else is as good as you."

Oliantus didn't flatter himself that other people valued him the way Leonidas did. On the contrary, most people didn't take any particular note of him at all. And it was that which made him so vulnerable to Leonidas' appeals.

Now he found himself stranded in a little hilltop town on the edge of the Boiotian plain, sweltering under a blistering sun hotter (Oliantus swore) than two suns in Lacedaemon. There were plagues of flies here as well, because in contrast to Sparta with its wide avenues and sprawling suburbs, here the dwellings, workshops, and public buildings were all piled up on top of one another inside the perimeter walls. Nor was there a broad river like the Eurotas sweeping through the city, flushing out the refuse and cleansing the air. Instead, everything just stagnated under the merciless heat.

Oliantus sighed and longed for home, but he did not delude himself that Leonidas was going anytime soon. He knew Leonidas too well, and Leonidas was fascinated by the challenge of training Thespiae's eager but amateur soldiers. Oliantus suspected Leonidas was also secretly enjoying the fact that he was thumbing his nose at both Athens and Thebes at the same time. A Spartan *alliance* might have been a provocation he was unwilling to risk, but the presence of a company of Spartan guardsmen led by a ruling king was a political statement nevertheless: Lacedaemon was taking an interest in Boiotian affairs.

Otherwise, things were not going well. On the first day the troops had mustered, almost half had no hoplons. Some had shown up with kitchen knives in self-made sheaths, and half the "spears" had been crooked, cracked, or just too damn short. Even Leonidas had been unable to disguise his chagrin. "We can't train men to use arms they don't have," he'd told Demophilus in an exasperated voice, and the Thespian aristocrat had made embarrassed promises to find arms for those who couldn't afford them.

Ever since, Demophilus had been trying to persuade his fellow aristocrats to finance arms and armor for the poor, but he had not been entirely successful. The money was trickling in, to be sure, but as the man tasked with actually purchasing the required equipment, Oliantus knew just how far they were from their goal.

Meanwhile, Leonidas and his guardsmen attempted to teach the Thespians the basics of marching and maneuvering. It wasn't until they tried to teach the eager but seemingly left-footed Thespians how to form up, reverse direction, and shorten and extend their lines that the Spartiates realized just *how* difficult it all was. They had learned step by step over decades, but the Thespians needed to learn all at once. The result had been sheer chaos, robbing even Leonidas of his patience.

Oliantus sighed and scratched his scraggly beard, wondering if they were on a fool's errand. Not that his opinion mattered....

A knock on the door jerked him from his thoughts, and a moment later the door frame was filled by the broad, stocky figure of Dithyrambus. The man was a mason, and it had been the abduction of his bride and another maiden some four months ago that had brought the anger of Thespiae's working-class citizens to the boiling point. Dithyrambus and the other masons had gone to the city council demanding action. Instead, nothing but weak protests had been sent to Thebes, which (as expected) yielded absolutely nothing. Dithyrambus and his friends were convinced that the old men—the "aristos," as the tradesmen called them derisively—were too timid to do anything, and saw in Demophilus the only rich man with backbone. Dithyrambus and the others were prepared to follow Demophilus almost anywhere, and no one had worked harder to learn from the Spartans than Dithyrambus.

Dithyrambus appeared to have come from some exertion—whether from the drill fields or his labor, Oliantus did not know. He was gleaming with sweat, and his fair hair was drenched with it. He had twisted a rag into a cord and tied it around his head below the hairline to catch as much sweat as possible, and still sweat glistened on his cheeks and dripped from his chin. "Sir?" he addressed Oliantus. "Can you spare me a minute, please?"

"Of course." Oliantus was happy for the interruption. Being good at organization and numbers did not make him enjoy the tedium of bookkeeping. He indicated the somewhat rickety bench opposite his table.

Dithyrambus dropped down on the bench, causing it to creak in protest, but the mason ignored the furniture. He leaned forward to rest his elbows on his knees, breathing heavily. He clenched his hands into fists, then stretched his fingers, before forming fists again in an unconscious nervous gesture. "Sir, I hope you won't find this impertinent," the big man stammered, "but, but, you seemed the most approachable of the Spartans...."

Oliantus smiled faintly and nodded. Yes, an ugly, aging logistician must indeed seem less intimidating than the hardened guardsmen in their prime, much less the Spartan king.

"You see, we know your king is very disappointed in us...."

Oliantus was torn between the instinct to comfort and his personal code of honesty. He opted for compromise. "A little, yes, but no doubt we expected too much."

Dithyrambus dropped his head in his hands and seemed to want to crush it between his powerful fists.

"There's no need for despair," Oliantus assured him. "It just takes time. Meanwhile we've collected enough money to arm almost a hundred poor men."

Dithyrambus shook his head without daring to look at Oliantus. "You don't understand, sir. It's—it's—I—you see—I need your help!" He lifted his head to look straight at straight at Oliantus. "I know what your king will say!" he burst out angrily. "I know he will say it is foolish and not worth his time. A woman soiled and hardly better than a whore! I know. Even Demophilus only shook his head and said how *sorry* he was. But, but, you have to understand! It's not because she was to be my bride. I could never marry her after what's happened. It's not that. But she was my mother's sister's only child. We grew up together! If she had been a boy—I mean if a boy had been abducted—who would hesitate to try to get him back?" The mason stopped to look at Oliantus expectantly.

"But we don't know where they are—the abducted women, I mean," Oliantus pointed out.

"Oh! Didn't you hear? A traveling knife grinder! He was in Thebes yesterday. He overheard men talking about a Thespian captive in a tavern. I'm sure it's my cousin!"

"Talk in taverns is rarely good evidence of anything," Oliantus pointed out cautiously.

"This was!" Dithyrambus insisted. "The men were quarreling, and so their voices grew louder and louder. A working man was demanding more money from a young aristocrat for the upkeep of the 'Thespian bitches.' When the young man brushed him off, he threatened to go to the young man's father. That got the young man very agitated, and after insulting the working man for extortion and calling him many names, he promised more money. The first man said he'd heard that before, and wanted his money now. The young man promised to bring it the next time he visited. The poor man said he'd give him three more days, but after that he'd tell the young man's father and start renting out the girls to make some money off them. So we have to move fast! Today or tomorrow!"

"The story sounds reasonably credible," Oliantus admitted, although still dubious, "and suggests that at least the girls are still alive, but we don't know where."

"But we do! The knife grinder knew what happened to me, and as soon as the men had left the tavern he asked the landlord about them. The landlord said the old man was a miller with a windmill *outside* of Thebes. In fact, it's between Thebes and Thespiae. It all makes sense, you see. The Thebans abducted the girls from the Valley of the Muses and only dragged them as far as this mill. Then, to disguise their misdeeds from their elders, they left the girls there. When we demanded the return of the girls, the Theban magistrates denied all responsibility, you see, because they *honestly* knew nothing about the abductions!"

This, too, sounded plausible enough to Oliantus, but he still wasn't entirely convinced. "But for four months? You think they could keep two captive girls quiet and hidden for four whole months?"

"Apparently," the mason answered with a shrug of his massive shoulders, while continuing to stare expectantly at Oliantus.

"What is it you want us to do?" Oliantus asked cautiously, scratching pensively at the thin hairs under his chin.

"To help us attack the mill and take the girls back!" Dithyrambus declared, clenching and releasing his fists faster than before. "Please! I thought our cavalry could do it, but Demophilus said he would not risk it. He said it would be too provocative. He said the Thebans would declare war on us, and that we cannot win a war. He said he was very, very sorry, but it was too late to help the girls. They are lost to us, he said, and we must focus on learning how to defend ourselves so it never happens again to other girls. But it wasn't his cousin who was abducted...." Dithyrambus fell silent, his eyes boring into Oliantus.

"I will talk to Leonidas," Oliantus promised.

Dithyrambus reared up in protest, "Do you have to? Is there no way you can help us *without* going to him?" Then, giving Oliantus no chance to answer, he cried out, "The king will never understand!" In despair the mason pressed his head with his hands again and muttered, "A disgraced basket weaver's daughter. Why would a king, a son of Herakles, care about the likes of that?"

"Let me talk to him," Oliantus insisted calmly.

"Couldn't you at least give us the arms you've collected?" Dithyrambus asked plaintively, looking up and gazing at Oliantus with burning eyes. "I have two score men prepared to go with me—if only we had arms."

"I will bring you an answer within the hour. Where can I find you?"

The Thespians were very nervous: Dithyrambus because the day was almost over and time was wasting, and the others because they had never done anything like this before. Now, with the sun close to the horizon, Oliantus was issuing arms and armor, while the Lacedaemonian helots helped the inexperienced Thespians equip themselves. Oliantus overheard a helot patiently explain, "Not so tight; you need room to breathe," while another man tried on the third pair of greaves, still not satisfied.

Dithyrambus, meanwhile, kept glancing at the horizon. "The sun will be down in less than two hours!" he complained. "We have only three hours of daylight and over an hour's walk. Couldn't we do all this adjusting and fitting later?"

"No." The answer came unexpectedly from Leonidas, who had just come around the corner into the little square. He was accompanied by Dienekes, Maron, and six other guardsmen in battle kit and accompanied by their attendants. The latter were wearing open-faced pilos helmets and carrying slingshots, bows, or javelins, an indication that they came in their capacity as light auxiliaries rather than as mere servants to their heavy-infantry masters.

When they realized the Spartan king was among them, the Thespians first froze and then tried to come to attention as they had been taught. The effect was quite comic in their half-dressed state, and Oliantus had to suppress a laugh. He caught Dienekes looking toward the heavens as if praying for patience. Meanwhile, several of the Thespians cast furtive and admonishing glances at Dithyrambus, because he had not warned them to expect the Spartan king. But no one was more dumbfounded than Dithyrambus himself. He licked his lips nervously and looked at Oliantus, feeling betrayed.

"Relax," Leonidas ordered. "We won't depart until after dark. We'll stage well short of the mill and send scouts forward." As he spoke he indicated the Spartan attendants, resting his hand on Meander's shoulder. "I asked you to assemble now so we can get in a couple hours of drill with your new panoply by daylight before setting out."

"We're going to conduct this raid in the dark?" one of the Thespians asked, incredulous.

"Yes, that's when the Thebans least expect us, and surprise makes a good ally."

"Are—are you—coming *with* us, my lord?" Dithyrambus asked Leonidas, amazed.

"Of course," Leonidas responded. Then, in answer to the incredulous looks of the Thespians, he added, "It's my first opportunity to see how you fight."

Meander was more nervous than he let on. He had served Leonidas for a dozen years, and in that time Leonidas had given him many opportunities to develop his fighting skills. Although Meander was barred by his status from standing in the line of battle as he wished, he'd nevertheless taken part in annual maneuvers as a skirmisher, and he was good with a bow and could throw a javelin as well as most. Furthermore, he had attended Leonidas at the Battle of Sepeia. He'd taken part in the subsequent campaign in the Argolid, and more recently he'd marched with Leonidas to Marathon and had seen the aftermath of battle there. Most relevant for tonight's mission, however, he was familiar with the essence of reconnaissance and was comfortable moving about in the dark, something the Thespians evidently found difficult.

But even if Meander had regularly practiced reconnaissance of this kind on maneuvers, lives had never been at stake before, and the task of going forward to the windmill to reconnoiter *alone* was daunting. For a few seconds Meander even found himself wishing Leonidas had chosen someone else, but then he kicked himself mentally.

Leonidas was giving him a special chance to prove himself because he had been born a Spartiate, and Leonidas had promised him more than once that he would do everything in his power to see that his status was restored—if not for his sake, then for his sons. Meander planned to marry at the winter equinox, and his bride-to-be was, like him, the daughter of a former Spartiate too poor to pay his mess fees.

Meander drew a deep breath and unnecessarily tightened the strap of his quiver. Leonidas was reminding him, "If there's any way to get the girls out without bloodshed, so much the better. Your job is just to find out where they are and if they are guarded. If we're lucky, the girls will be kept in a separate room and everyone will be asleep."

Meander nodded, took off his pilos, readjusted the felt cap under it, and then put the helmet back on. He didn't dare meet Leonidas' eye for fear the king would read his inner doubts. He set off.

The windmill stood on a low hill, its sails turning slowly and creaking slightly in the gentle breeze. Meander approached from the back, crossing first a flat, fertile plain with long, soft grass, then up a more barren incline, to climb over a low, dilapidated stone wall that enclosed a handful of sheep. The sheep stared at him without even getting to their feet, their jaws working slowly. Meander eased himself over the far wall of the paddock into the courtyard behind the mill itself. This was home to a score of chickens, and they were more excitable than the sheep. Almost at once they started clucking in alarm, and an instant later a dog barked close at hand.

Meander froze, his heart pounding in his ears. He had screwed up! He was about to be attacked and torn to pieces!

The dog came trotting into the yard to see what was going on. He spotted Meander and lowered his head, growling.

Meander stopped breathing. Then slowly, slowly he reached over his shoulder and brought his bow to the ready.

The dog raised his head and barked twice. He took a step closer, growling more ominously than before.

Meander fitted an arrow.

The dog raised his head and barked twice more—loud enough to wake the dead, or so Meander felt.

The arrow slammed into the dog. It went right through his chest and out again behind his right shoulder, knocking him down. He let out a wail of anguish unlike any bark and writhed in agony, trying to rise up again. Meander leaped forward to silence him with his knife, cursing his bad luck. The howl was sure to warn the whole household that this was no passing fox or stray!

But no one raised the alarm. No one came crashing out of the house. Meander waited tensely, his bow at the ready, for another thirty seconds. Only gradually did he let the bow fall. After another thirty seconds, he returned it to his back and started cautiously forward again.

He searched the outbuildings first. These were filled only with supplies, farm tools, firewood, and junk; there was no sign of any captive women.

Meander had no choice but to approach the house itself. This was a one-story stone structure with a crude chimney that backed up almost to the windmill. It had two windows facing this direction, and both were shuttered. Meander crept up to the first and looked between the slats. Inside it was very dark, but some light seeped from the adjacent hearth room, and he could just make out a man and a woman lying on a low bed, one of whom was snoring loudly. The next window opened to the hearth room itself, and he could see the interior of this room better because the hearth was still aglow with embers. Two men and two children were lying on mats before the fire. There was not a trace of any young women.

This is ridiculous, Meander thought. Maybe they were at the wrong mill, or the knife grinder had misinterpreted what he heard? He couldn't return from his reconnaissance until he'd at least looked in the mill, however, so Meander crept around the side of the house and crossed to the mill. He pushed the door open and stood in the low room with the grinding stone. The sails had been disconnected for the night so that although they turned, the grindstone was still. The room smelled good: of fresh ground flour and wood. Meander drew a deep breath and turned to leave.

Something clunked and then scraped on the wooden ceiling over his head. He froze, and his heart beat loudly as he listened. From overhead came a soft, scraping sound and then a moan, a voice.

Meander looked around the room again, only now noticing the stones that jutted out of the wall spiraling upward. He started up them cautiously, one hand on the rough interior wall to steady himself.

As he ascended, the ceiling came down to eye level, and he was looking across it from the perspective of a mouse. There were heaps of straw and something white on them. Something that moved. With horror he realized it was a girl, completely naked, and beside her another girl. They were dirty and unkempt, and one had vivid, dark bruises on her buttocks as if she'd been given a horrible thrashing. The other was covered with a variety of cuts and scratches—some almost healed, some still swollen and scabbed. There was little doubt that these were the captive girls.

Meander looked down at the empty room below and considered the open door, the sleeping family, the dead dog. Leonidas had said his job was just reconnaissance, but why risk bringing a lot of men here and waking everyone up, if he could just take the girls back with him? If he rescued the girls single-handedly, maybe they would even reward him, give him back his citizenship.... He continued up the stairs.

One of the girls sat up abruptly and looked right at him. Her eyes widened in horror, and Meander hastened to put his finger to his lips. "Shhh! Silence!"

The girl answered by shaking her companion awake and pulling herself into a ball, clutching her knees to her chest, in a gesture so piteously pointless and so childish that it melted Meander's heart. The second girl groaned slightly as she was torn from her sleep, but seeing her friend's pose she gasped, looked toward the stairs, and likewise took up a defensive position.

"There's nothing to be afraid of," Meander told the frightened girls. "We've come to set you free."

"Who are you?"

"I'm not important. King Leonidas is here."

That obviously made no sense to the girls—who, Meander supposed, might never have heard of him. "Dithyrambus brought us."

The girl with the horrible bruises gasped and lifted her head slightly. "Truly? Dithyrambus? He has not forgotten and rejected me?"

"No, we just didn't know where you were until yesterday. Come with me; I'll lead you out."

"But—" the girl cut herself off. "But—"

"What?"

"We have no clothes! They tore away our clothes when they seized us, and will not give us even a rug or a blanket or a rag to hide our shame."

"We have plenty of himations," Meander answered practically, regretting he was not wearing one himself at the moment.

"But—but—there are men."

"Half a hundred altogether," Meander admitted. "We thought there might be guards here, or anyway, more men."

The girls were shaking their heads. The girl who had been Dithyrambus' bride was biting her lower lip and starting to cry. The other begged Meander, "Can't you bring us something to hide our shame? Please! We can't go out like this! Please!"

Meander didn't understand. Girls of marriageable age in Lacedaemon were not in the habit of going around naked, either, but they did as girls. In a situation like this, where it was a matter of freedom or slavery, he felt certain they would have followed him without another word. He looked down at his own chiton, but couldn't bring himself to give it to one of the girls and thereby leave the other alone. He tried to reason again. "Don't worry about being naked. We're only about a mile away. Just out the back and across the meadow to the trees. We'll be there in just a few minutes."

The girls were shaking their heads. Dithyrambus' bride was weeping. "But we're *naked*," her companion wailed. "Completely naked! Please! Please help us! Just an old blanket would do. Anything at all! Oh, please! Don't dishonor us in front of our own brothers and cousins!"

"All right," Meander capitulated, not prepared for this situation. "I'll see what I can find." He descended the stairs backwards, slipped out of the mill, and stood looking around the little complex in feverish confusion. On the one hand, he had orders to do reconnaissance only. On the other, it would take so much longer to return and report, and by then maybe the miller and his family would have woken. If he could just find a sheet, a himation, a chiton....

But there was nothing lying around outside. He crept back toward the house and peered through the window again. There were hooks along one wall on which the inhabitants had hung their own clothes, and there were blankets, too, but even as he watched, one of the men woke enough to sit up, scratching his crotch, and then lay down again, trying to make himself more comfortable on his straw pallet. There was no way Meander could slip inside without arousing attention.

Cursing, he started running, past the dead dog, through the cackling barnfowl, leaping over the stone walls, and jumping the little gullies in the field below the mill. He was panting when he arrived among the band of men who loomed up among the darkness of the trees, surprising him, even though he knew they were there.

"I found them!" he announced breathlessly. "They're up in the loft of the mill itself. No one's guarding them—I killed the dog, and the miller and his family are sound asleep. I tried to talk them into coming back with me, but they haven't any clothes. The miller won't give them any, to keep them from running away."

Exclamations of outrage and bitter cursing erupted from the Thespians until Leonidas hushed them. "Dithyrambus and Kleandor" (that was the brother of the other girl), "take a couple of himations apiece, go into the mill, and bring the girls out. The rest of us will surround the house and make sure the miller and his family don't interfere. Let's go."

The Thespians rushed forward, chattering in excitement.

"Halt! Silence!" Leonidas ordered.

The Thespians fell silent in embarrassment and waited anxiously, but in his eagerness to carry out the rescue at last, Dithyrambus could not keep still; he stood shifting from foot to foot, his expression tortured because he did not dare contradict a king. "Come!" Leonidas clapped him on the arm. "But silently!"

They started forward again, the Spartans leading this time. They easily covered the field below the mill. Just as they started up the incline, the sound of hooves on the road brought them to a halt. "Drop!" Leonidas ordered.

The Spartans hit the ground almost instantly to lie flat and still, invisible in the darkness. The Thespians, less well drilled, went down more slowly and more raggedly, one knee at a time.

Fortunately, the rider was not looking toward the field. He rode past at a good clip, and Leonidas was on the brink of giving the order to rise again when they heard the canter break into a trot, then a walk, and the man pulled up—at the mill.

Dithyrambus started cursing. "That's the bastard who abducted her! He's come to visit her while the miller is asleep to avoid paying what he promised!"

Meander and Leonidas both stared at him, amazed by how rapidly he put things together. There was little doubt that the horseman had come to visit the girls, however, because he had tied the horse by the mill and they saw him disappear inside.

There was no holding Dithyrambus now. He sprang to his feet and started running with all his might, his arms pumping like an Olympic athlete. There was nothing to do but follow.

Dithyrambus was easily a hundred yards ahead of them by the time they reached the first wall. High-pitched screams were coming from the mill, and as they came abreast of the house, the door crashed open and men started stumbling out. They were dressed in unbelted chitons and one had grabbed an axe, another a poker. The sight of men in armor with crested helmets and hoplons spilling into the narrow space between mill and house stopped them in their tracks. Leonidas nodded to Dienekes, who drew his sword and pointed it at the man closest to him. "Get back inside!" Dienekes ordered, while Leonidas turned his attention to the struggle taking place behind him in the mill.

As he approached, he could hear men cursing and hurling insults at one another. When he reached the door, he realized Dithyrambus was standing just inside, blocking the exit. The desperate young Theban clearly cared only about escape. "Come on! Come on!" Dithyrambus mocked. "Show me how brave you are, Theban!"

"What's the point of killing me now? Your bride's a little whore! We all had her more than once, front and back!" the Theban mocked.

In answer, Dithyrambus roared and rushed the man, who stepped aside nimbly and made a dash for the door. Instead he ended on Leonidas' sword. He had not even noticed that another man had entered, and the look of amazement on his face suggested that his last thought was one of sheer surprise. Dithyrambus brought his own sword down with all his might and rammed it into his neck to make sure he was dead.

Leonidas heard gasps and glanced toward the stairway, but the girls had already disappeared. He could hear their footfalls overhead as they ran about in apparent confusion. Leonidas removed his own cloak and handed it to Dithyrambus. "Hurry! Bring them out before someone else comes."

"I'll never forget this," Dithyrambus answered.

Chapter 14

WRATH OF THE GODS

"The ephors require your attendance, my lord," the herald announced, delivering the traditional summons with a bow to the king.

It was the new moon—that day of the month on which the ephors and kings exchanged their monthly vows, the kings to rule in accordance with the constitution of Lycurgus and the ephors to support the kings as long as they so ruled. But since this was also the first new moon after the winter solstice, it was also the date on which the new ephors, elected at the last equinox, met together for the first time as a ruling body. Furthermore, as chance would have it, it was the ninth year since the last time the ephors had conducted the ritual star-gazing.

Nine years ago, two shooting stars had been sighted. In retrospect, everyone understood that these had foretold the deposing of Demaratus and the untimely demise of Cleomenes. At the time, however, the interpretation of the shooting stars had been quite different. In any case, Leonidas had not been privy to the earlier interpretation, because he was not yet king. This was the first time since his ascent to the throne that this particular ritual had been carried out. Leonidas was correspondingly wary.

It was traditional for a king to refuse any summons from the ephors at least twice before, with great dignity, going slowly to the Ephorate. So Leonidas sent the herald back and turned to Sperchias, who he had appointed one of his two representatives to Delphi. "You, too, were up all night, and you look like death warmed over. Is it really as bad as all that?"

Sperchias looked older than his almost forty-three years. His hair had receded to the middle of his skull, his eyes were sunken in their sockets, and the skin on his neck and around his eyes was marred by a complex network of tiny wrinkles.

"The heavens foretell disaster. More I cannot say for sure, but I'm not talking of one or two stars falling from the heavens: it was a shower of stars. More than I could count. I am frightened. You heard about the Egyptian?"

"I heard only that an Egyptian sought audience with me and was referred to the ephors."

"Yes. He may be there now."

"Do you know what he wants?"

Sperchias sighed. "What they all want: help against Persia."

"The Egyptian revolt was crushed."

"Mercilessly."

"And this man?"

"He appears to be nothing but an old scribe."

"Have you spoken with him?"

"Briefly. He speaks Greek well."

The herald returned. "My lord, the ephors request that you meet with them."

Leonidas nodded and waved the herald away impatiently. He was as anxious to meet with the new ephors as they were to meet with him. "Traditions can be irritating," Leonidas remarked to his friend.

"Be careful, Leo," Sperchias warned. "The Spartan Assembly is more fickle than a spring breeze. The majority is still with you, but the younger cohorts have little interest in trade, crafts, and the arts. They sense Lacedaemon's rising status in the world, but that only makes them impatient to prove themselves. They are spoiling for a fight."

"Will they never grow up?"

"Every year—and every year there is a new cohort hungry for glory."

Leonidas made a face because he knew Sperchias was right; it was the nature of young men to be aggressive. He changed the subject. "Will the ephors make a stink about Pleistarchos entering the agoge?"

"I think not, provided Ephorus is willing to accept him."

"Ephorus will accept him."

Sperchias changed the subject. "You must not try to protect Temenos," he warned.

"Why should I want to? He has broken the law willfully and provocatively. He must pay the price."

Sperchias frowned, unsure if Leonidas were being honest or only putting on this face because he knew he had no choice.

The herald was back. "The ephors beg you to sacrifice together with them to Athena Protectress."

"Then I will come," Leonidas agreed at last, and with Sperchias at his heels he left the Agiad palace and strode purposefully through the still darkened streets to the Ephorate. Although the stars had faded, the dawn had not yet broken, and it was bitterly cold. Leonidas could see his breath and was grateful for his thick wool himation and his high leather boots. For a moment he felt guilty about sending Pleistarchos to the agoge next week. He remembered vividly the day his father had taken him to the agoge, and how cold it had been. There had been snow on the ground that year. But that day had been his first step on a path that had made him who he was: not just a king, but a Spartan Peer.

A hound started yelping somewhere, and Leonidas automatically turned in the direction of the sound. "What's that light?" he asked, startled.

"What light?"

"There!" Leonidas pointed to an eerie greenish light that lurked low on the horizon below the Parnon range, as if on the road to Tegea.

Sperchias stopped and followed his finger. At length he said, "That is what people have been talking about."

Leonidas stopped and stared at him. "What do you mean?"

"Has no one told you?" Sperchias sounded both surprised and weary. "It shines many nights, from the Temple of Talthybius."

"But what causes it?"

"Have you forgotten that we murdered two Persian ambassadors?" Sperchias asked, adding, "Talthybius has not forgotten."

"The Persian king appears to have forgotten!" Leonidas snapped back, irritated by Sperchias' reproachful tone, "He has never demanded reparation of any sort."

"No. He simply vowed to obliterate us."

"He is dead."

"He has a son."

"A man many say does not half fill his father's shoes."

"Ask the Egyptian."

They had reached the steps of the Ephorate and went up them together. On the porch the two meleirenes saluted. Leonidas recognized Alkander's elder boy and paused. "Thersander. How are you?"

"Well, my lord," Thersander answered, with a self-conscious smile and a glance at his comrade, before adding, "I rather like being a meleirene—so far."

Leonidas laughed. "You will never have so much freedom ever again. Enjoy it. Has Leotychidas arrived yet?"

"No, my lord."

"Maybe you should wait," Sperchias suggested.

Leonidas shook his head. "I don't give a damn about Leotychidas." They passed through the door into the antechamber, and Leonidas continued through double doors into the actual chamber.

The ephors were not expecting him yet. They had not taken their seats, but were speaking earnestly in a cluster. Leonidas waved the herald silent and descended the steps to join them unannounced.

"There can be no question the omen is bad!" one of the newly elected ephors declared in an agitated tone.

"But it was not in the right quadrant of the sky. It did not pertain to the kings."

"But so many stars! What can it possibly mean?"

"Good evening," Leonidas interrupted them. The ephors spun about, startled. Leonidas shook hands with each, offering congratulations on their election one after another. Before he could engage them in earnest conversation, however, Leotychidas arrived. They retreated to their assigned seats.

Leotychidas nodded curtly to Leonidas and then announced: "Let's keep it short; I'm in a hurry." He raised his hand. "I solemnly swear that I, Leotychidas—What's the matter, Leo?"

Leonidas shrugged. "I am not in a hurry," he answered, but then he raised his hand and took the traditional oath.

"The omens?" Leotychidas demanded impatiently.

The ephors looked at one another, and the chairman answered. "They portend terrible things, but—so far as we can tell—not for the Spartan kings."

"Good. Anything else?"

"There is an Egyptian scribe—"

"A man of no importance. A refugee with nothing left but the rags on his back!" Leotychidas dismissed him.

Leonidas nodded, "Quite. Don't let us keep you." Leotychidas was already on his feet and halfway up the steps out of the chamber before he had second thoughts. "What about you, Leonidas?"

"I wish to meet the Egyptian."

Leotychidas' eyes narrowed. He returned to his throne. "I will, too."

The ephors signaled to the meleirenes to bring in the Egyptian, and shortly afterward a man entered and descended the steps. He was frail and wore long cotton robes with wide sleeves. His head was covered in a neat striped headdress that hung to his shoulders. He was flanked by two black men, one burly yet aging and the other small, wiry, and young. The Egyptian turned a worried face to Leotychidas and seemed to dismiss him. He turned to Leonidas, paused, and seemed to straighten before asking with great dignity in heavily accented Greek, "Are *you* the Lion's Son?"

"That is what I am called."

"Ah." The Egyptian fell onto his knees and bent his head to the floor at Leonidas' feet.

"He's no more important than the rest of us," Leotychidas protested irritably and ineffectually.

The Egyptian ignored Leotychidas. "Great King! I have come a long distance and suffered many hardships to tell you of the people who have destroyed my homeland. I beg you to hear my testimony."

"I am listening, but first stand and look me in the eye."

The Egyptian raised his upper body and sat upon his heels. His lined face looked up at Leonidas. "Great King, I have been told that you defeated the Persians in a great battle to the north." Leonidas wanted to correct him, but the chairman of the ephors caught his eye and shook his head sharply. Leonidas said nothing and the Egyptian continued. "But the army you defeated was only a small force, a tiny token army. It was commanded by a Mede—not the Persian emperor.

"I, on the other hand, have seen the Persian emperor himself: the man Xerxes, who calls himself the King of Kings, although he is the mortal son of a mortal man. Xerxes came to my homeland, and he brought with him his whole host. He came because we dared to want to live as our ancestors lived. He came not to conquer us, but to crush us. He came not to secure submission and tribute, but to eradicate our very essence.

"Xerxes is like no conqueror that has gone before—not even like his father. He is not content to rule over his subjects. He demands that they accept his god and his language and his way of life.

"Xerxes has not only killed the living, but destroyed the graves of the dead. He has taken not only our independence but our pride, our dignity, and our identity as well.

"Great King, I am here to warn you that if you do not want to fight the Persians in the temples of your Gods and over the bodies of your forefathers, then you will have to fight the Persians before they get here."

The Egyptian folded his body again, banged his forehead on the floor and concluded, "That is the message I have traveled longer than the length of the Nile to deliver, Great King. I have nothing left to gain or lose. The graves of my ancestors and my beloved wife have been destroyed, their bodies disinterred and allowed to rot like the carcasses of vermin. My son was killed and his body left exposed, so that his soul will wander homelessly for all eternity. My soul has nowhere to go, but what is the use of living in eternity when all those I loved are lost in nothingness? I beg only one favor of you, as you are a Great King: take my slaves, Kaschta and Taiwo, and treat them with kindness out of respect for an old man, who can no longer look after them."

Leonidas glanced at the two black men, who appeared astonished by this plea. They looked at one another with what Leonidas interpreted as alarm.

Leonidas stood and stepped forward. He reached down and took hold of the Egyptian's arm to raise him up. "Thank you for bringing me this warning. I will consult with my advisers about what is to be done. Meanwhile, you and your two slaves will be my guests."

The Egyptian looked up and straight into his eye. His look pierced Leonidas to the quick. In his eyes were terror and desperation. "Great King, believe me! You *must* fight them. If they come too close, you—and all you love—will be doomed."

"Brotus!" Sinope called irritably. "What's keeping you?" Sinope was standing in front of their kleros dressed for going into the city, and she was in a hurry. Today the full citizens who were still bachelors would be submitted to public humiliation. It was a day she always looked forward to, but today more than ever—because her brother-in-law's protégé, Temenos, was finally going to get his due for preferring a helot slut to a Spartiate bride.

There had been frost overnight and the sun rose through the winter haze, pale and weak. Sinope wore sturdy leather shoes and a thick peplos folded double, fastened by heavy fibulae decorated with silver snakes. Over this she had draped a large purple himation that advertised her royal status. As always she wore no jewelry, and she combed her graying hair severely away from her face.

Pausanias, lounging against the front of the house, thought she looked rather like a vulture, and made a mental note not to marry a girl who would age like this.

"Pausanias!" His mother turned on him, making him jump guiltily and come to attention.

"Ma'am?" he asked dutifully.

"Go and find what's keeping your father! We don't want to be late, or we won't have a good view. I want to see your uncle's face while his little protégé parades around showing his limp dick to all the maidens."

Pausanias couldn't understand why his mother got so agitated about Temenos. If the fool didn't want to have legitimate sons, that was his problem. It wasn't as if Sparta were short of young men. Even his ugly sister Megisto was bound to find a husband sooner or later—especially given the dowry his father was willing to dump on her,

Pausanias thought resentfully. He glanced at her before heading back into the house.

Megisto took after their mother. She was thin and flat with overly prominent teeth. She had a terrible temper, too. Pausanias didn't envy the man whose greed for her dowry led him to take her to wife.

"Dad?" Pausanias stopped in the center of the hearth room and shouted, "Mom's in a hurry!"

There was no response.

Pausanias frowned and looked around. He took a few steps up the stairs and shouted again, "Dad?"

Still no response.

He moved toward the back of the house, to the bath and latrine. "Dad?"

A grunt answered him from the direction of the latrine.

Pausanias continued to the door. "Dad? Are you in there?"

"Help!" his father grunted back.

Pausanias grabbed the door and yanked it open. His father fell forward onto Pausanias' feet. He was ghastly pale and was clutching his stomach with one hand.

"What is it, Dad?" Pausanias asked, alarmed.

"It hurts!" Brotus croaked back. "Help me up."

"Mom wants to go—"

"Tell her to go on her own. Help me!"

Pausanias bent and tried to help his father to his feet. He was nineteen and in good physical condition, but his father was very heavy. Too heavy, Pausanias noted to himself. His father's once massive muscles were slowly turning soft. In armor he still looked like a fiercely powerful man, but up close and naked Pausanias could see he was turning downright fat.

"My arm," Brotus complained. "I can't move it. It's numb."

Pausanias stared at his father's limp arm, then took it over his shoulder, and with his arm around his father's waist he got him onto his feet. They staggered together toward the hearth room, where Brotus croaked, "Lay me down!" indicating a wide couch by the hearth, covered with thick cushions.

Pausanias guided his father to this couch, and Brotus dropped down on it with a grunt. "Lift my feet!" he ordered, and Pausanias obeyed.

Megisto burst in complaining, "What is the matter with you two? Mom's furious—"

"Dad's not feeling well. Go on ahead of us," Pausanias answered.

Megisto stared at her father for a moment and then asked, "What is it?"

"Probably just something I ate. Go on! Tell your mother to go ahead," Brotus barked at her, scowling darkly.

Megisto darted out before he could add a cuff of his hand to his words. Brotus was always quick to lend his orders a little physical urgency.

"You go, too!" Brotus ordered his eldest son. "I don't want your sister wandering around without some protection."

Pausanias refrained from remarking that Megisto was one of the last maidens in Sparta who was going to attract amorous male attention, and asked instead, "Are you sure you're going to be all right?"

"Of course! It was just a dizzy spell. Go on!"

Pausanias retreated warily, his eyes on his father. Brotus lay on his back with his eyes closed. He was still very pale, and the lines on his face were pronounced. He was swallowing and sweating. This isn't the first time this has happened to him, Pausanias thought. His father was sick, he realized, not just aging and softening, but sick.

Pausanias reached the door to the hearth room and stopped. He turned and stared at his father again for several seconds, trying to come to terms with the situation. He wasn't sure of all the consequences, but he knew this changed a lot of things. Then, with a faint smile, he turned and started running to catch up with his mother and sister.

"Shhh!" Pelops hissed furiously at his younger brother Kinadon, twisting the younger boy's arm to lend his words weight.

Kinadon let out a closed-mouth grunt of protest and kicked out at his older brother's shins. The abrupt attack was enough to make his brother loosen his hold on his arm, and Kinadon yanked his arm free but stood staring up at his brother defiantly, his eyes blazing with fury.

Pelops was unimpressed. "Keep your clap closed, or I'll leave you behind!" he threatened.

Kinadon stuck out his tongue in answer, but emitted not another sound as he followed his brother.

Pelops' courage this day was awe-inspiring. He had stolen one of the master's horses, ridden it into town, and boldly walked into one of the army stables, where he glibly lied: "The king wants to leave this horse here for a few hours."

From the stables, Pelops led his brother to the back of the agoge barracks and walked straight in as if he belonged there. Of course, the boys of the agoge were all collected on the square to witness the humiliation of the bachelors, and Pelops had taken advantage of this fact to lead his little brother up into attic of the barracks. It was when Kinadon had tried to ask him how he knew about this that he'd been so severely reprimanded. The only thing Kinadon could think of was that Agiatis, who had been enrolled in the agoge for two years now, had shown Pelops around. Agiatis seemed to know her way around everywhere, and she and Pelops were friends.

The attic had a musty smell, and there were dead flies all over the place. Kinadon didn't like the sound they made when he stepped on them, and he minced his way across the roof, doubled over because the ceiling seemed so low, although he could have walked upright.

Ahead of him, Pelops stopped and crouched down. He craned his head this way and that, trying to see through a ventilation duct to the street below. Pelops dropped to his knees and then onto his belly and thrust his head out of the opening. "What are you looking at?" Kinadon demanded.

His elder brother didn't answer.

Kinadon nudged him with a foot. "Pelops! What is it? What are you looking at?"

In irritation Pelops kicked out with a foot. Kinadon easily evaded the kick and demanded again, "What is it?"

From the street came the sound of a crowd hooting and whistling derisively, the way Spartan crowds ridiculed boys who collapsed too quickly during a flogging or booed bad losers in games and contests. It was common to hear such hissing and catcalling down at the pits, at the ball field, or at the racecourse, but rare to hear it in the heart of the city, on the steps of the Council House and Ephorate.

"Has somebody done something bad?" Kinadon asked his big brother.

Pelops didn't answer. He just lay on his belly, as tense as a cat waiting to spring on a mouse.

From the street came the sound of voices singing—not the harmonious singing of a chorus, or the sound of young men belting out a marching song, or the solemn sound of a crowd singing a paean to the Gods. This was a ragged song of mismatched voices singing out of tune and stumbling over the words. "... I'm just a worthless weasel with the weenie of a mouse ..."

Kinadon giggled at the crude text. Before he knew what was happening, his brother had pulled back and yanked Kinadon's feet out from under him. He crashed down onto the wooden floor so hard he burst out crying, but his brother slapped him across the face. "Shut up! Shut up!"

"Stop it!" Kinadon protested, thrashing with his feet as he tried to get free of his brother.

"Shut up or I'll strangle you!"

"Why?"

"You don't understand anything, baby!"

"Because you won't let me see!" Kinadon countered.

"Look then! Look for yourself!" Pelops shoved Kinadon under the rafters, toward the hole that looked down at the street. His hands were rough and his face bright red.

It took Kinadon several seconds to get his bearings, and then he saw something horrible. His father was standing in a line with a half-dozen other naked men. Each wore a dead mouse around his neck, and they were all singing this silly song, while the crowd around them hissed and jeered.

Kinadon pulled back inside and stared at his brother with wide, horrified eyes. "But why? What has Dad done?"

"It's because of us," Pelops told him. "It's because he won't give up Mom and marry one of *them*!" His anger had turned him the color of a cooked crab, and his little, bony chest was heaving with indignation.

Kinadon gaped at him, and in his chest the first flame of hatred ignited.

Hilaira let herself into her townhouse, the wooden door creaking on its rusty hinges as she pushed in and moved, more by instinct than sight, down the dark corridor to the courtyard. As she emerged into the light again she drew up, shocked by how rundown things looked. The flower beds were sprouting nothing but the dead stems of last year's weeds. Dried leaves lay about in heaps. One of the kitchen shutters hung askew, a hinge broken, and a dead bird lay in the gutter below the roof.

For a moment she let her memories run away with her. She remembered the day Alkander had brought her here for the first time: she a bride of not yet twenty and he still a young man on active service. He had taken her without her father's permission, and they had spent their wedding night in the ruins of Leonidas' not-yet-renovated kleros, giving free rein to their pent-up desires in the safety of a house without so much as a helot tenant to disturb or inhibit them. But Alkander had had to return to his barracks before morning roll call, and she to her father's home and recriminations. Fortunately, her father had proved understanding and had forgiven Alkander for eloping with her, but neither of them felt comfortable trysting under her parental roof. Alkander had consequently been in a hurry to find rooms to rent in the city.

This tiny craftsman's house, squeezed into a row of such houses behind one of the city bakeries, had been available very cheap. Alkander had shown it to her eagerly, blind to all its many shortfalls in his eagerness to have her near his barracks. Hilaira had not been particularly enthusiastic about the cramped house, but she shared Alkander's impatience for a place of their own, so she had agreed to take it. She'd then set to work trying to turn it into a home, with the help of just one helot girl and the occasional assistance (for heavy and carpentry work) of Leonidas' tenant Pantes. With each year the house had become more comfortable, and by the time Alkander went off active service and they moved to his kleros, it had become home. There had been climbing flowers tumbling off the balcony and potted flowers marking each stair. There had been bright home-woven hangings on the walls, and cheerful homemade cushions offering comfort in every room.

It was here that both her sons had been conceived, she noted, with a glance up the wooden steps to the gallery giving access to the upstairs bedroom. Here that she had comforted that poor perioikoi girl that Brotus had put in the stocks. Here, too, that Simonidas had recovered from the damage done to his hand, and—oh, there were so many memories! It would be hard to part with this house, but what was the point of keeping it any longer?

Thersander was already a meleirene, and even Simonidas appeared to have no need for his mother's care and cooking any longer. He had adjusted to the agoge after all, and now spent all his time with his Corinthian friend. Hilaira sighed, knowing it was for the best, and yet at some level sad, too. Soon it will be just the two of us again, she thought, Alkander and me, an aging couple.... But Alkander was so busy. Rather than two sons, he had 350. He hardly noticed his own sons were almost grown.

Nor did he have to put up with his sister all day, Hilaira thought with a sigh. After Demaratus fled Lacedaemon, Percalus had moved in with them. She was not an easy house guest, because she was used to being a queen. She never tired of talking about her former life—when she wasn't heaping recriminations on Demaratus or speculating about how many concubines he kept in the Persian court....

Maybe she should fix up this house after all, Hilaira thought, and use it as a refuge from Percalus. Or Thersander might marry young, as Alkander had done. They suspected he had a sweetheart already, and Hilaira lifted her head suddenly, noticing that there were ashes on the house altar. Maybe he had been trysting here with his girl already?

With these thoughts in mind, she righted one of the overturned flowerpots and went into the kitchen for a broom to clear away the dead bird. As she came out again, something crashed in the back of the house. Hilaira nearly jumped out of her skin. There was someone here!

"Thersander? Is that you?" she called out, fear that it was someone else evident in her voice. What if it was a thief or a runaway helot?

There was another crash and a scraping sound, followed by a grunt that could only be human. Hilaira's hair stood up on the back of her neck, and she started to back toward the exit. Her son would have answered her properly. Whoever it was, he meant her harm.

As she backed up, her eyes were fixed on the hearth room beyond the interior porch. She saw something move in the darkness, and then a bent-over figure was in the doorway. He was naked, but glistening with sweat and covered with a horrible red, pustulate rash. "Mom!" he gasped out.

Hilaira screamed, not from fear but from horror. It was Simonidas.

Within a week a quarter of the boys in the agoge had come down with whatever it was. Within two weeks more than half were ill. The agoge was closed and the boys sent to their own homes. But it didn't stop. The first boy died on the eighth day of the epidemic. By the end of the second week, the death count was already twenty-two.

In the Assembly Alcidas blamed Alkander, saying that his methods had made the boys "soft" and "vulnerable." He was shouted down, but Alkander resigned anyway. A week later the death toll had risen to forty-nine, and the epidemic had spread to helots and adults.

An extraordinary Assembly resolved to consult Delphi. A runner set off before sunset and ran without pause, just as Pheidippidas had done from Athens to Sparta to bring word of the Persian landing at Marathon. The Spartan runner reached the coast in less than twenty-four hours and paid a boatman to take him across the Gulf of Corinth by the light of the stars.

Sperchias, resident in Delphi as one of Leonidas' two permanent representatives, was shaken awake by his attendant before the light of dawn. "Sir, a messenger from Sparta."

Unlike his predecessor Asteropus, Sperchias did not live in a large, elegant house with a concubine and many slaves. He had only a rented flat above a local shop. He clattered down from the loft room where he slept, dazed by the unexpected summons. The messenger had slept and regained some strength during the boat crossing. As Sperchias dressed, he explained the desperate situation in Sparta. "No one is safe. Priests and women have been infected no less than the boys of the agoge. Whole households have been stricken, and even those who recover are often left horribly scarred—utterly disfigured for life."

Sperchias hardly dared ask, "Do you have word about my family? My children?"

The messenger shook his head mutely. "I was not given time to inquire."

Sperchias nodded. What right had he to worry about his kin when the whole city was struck like this? "And the king? Leonidas and his family?"

"When I left they were well. His bodyguard will let no one in or out of the Agiad palace except the king himself. King Leonidas has ordered Queen Gorgo to remain at home, although he himself is everywhere. He is not at risk," the messenger declared confidently. "He is a true son of Herakles and so has the protection of Asclepius. But Leotychidas caught the fever, proving he is a usurper."

"Leotychidas is dead?" Sperchias could hardly believe it.

"No, no. He recovered, as most adults do, and is hardly scarred at all—just here and there—but his son Zeuxidamus was very ill when I left Sparta. We must find out how to appease the Gods, sir. Will the Pythia see you?" the messenger asked anxiously. "It is not the new moon."

"She will see me," Sperchias assured the runner. It was a privilege of the Spartan kings that their representatives had access to the Pythia at any time during the nine months of the year when Apollo was present in Delphi. "But we must make a sacrifice first, and cleanse ourselves."

It wasn't Sperchias who told the Spartans they had to send two men to Persia to atone for the murdered ambassadors. It was Megistias. Megistias, an Acarnanian, had an international reputation as a great seer. Sperchias had been so intimidated by the disaster that had struck Sparta that even after receiving the oracle delivered by the Pythia, he had sought the advice of the more experienced seer. Megistias, however, had only confirmed his own interpretation, adding greater urgency and authority. "At once!" he had told Sperchias. "You Spartans must send two defenseless men, not slaves but citizens, to the Persian court to offer their lives in atonement for the outrage committed by the Spartans against the Persian ambassadors."

Sperchias had nodded. He had known it would come to this ever since the murders, but precisely because he had said this before and been ignored by his fellow citizens, he feared he would not be believed now. So he had begged Megistias to come with him to Sparta.

Megistias had not hesitated. On the contrary, he had set out at once with Sperchias, his son Adeas, and a couple of slaves. They hired a boat to cross the Gulf of Corinth, and then horses on the far side. They reached Sparta just five days after receiving the oracle and delivered it to the ephors. An extraordinary Assembly was called at once in which the oracle was read out loud, and Megistias interpreted it for the assembled citizens. The Assembly was noticeably smaller than usual; many citizens did not attend because they were either sick or caring for wives or children who were.

As soon as the Assembly adjourned, Leonidas asked both Sperchias and Megistias to join him. He took them into one of the smaller, more intimate and recently renovated androns and ordered refreshments. Until the helots had withdrawn, they talked only about the journey, but once they were alone, Leonidas bluntly confessed to Sperchias: "You warned me about this when the murders took place. I did wrong not to listen to you."

"It wasn't just you, Leo. No one listened."

"I should have made them," Leonidas insisted.

"Will you be able to find volunteers?" Megistias asked earnestly, his dark eyes bright under bushy white brows.

"We will have more than enough volunteers," Leonidas assured him confidently. "The problem will be choosing between them. The men who ought to go are the men responsible. It was Brotus and his minions who were responsible for this catastrophe, and they are the ones who should pay for it."

"They won't, Leo, and you know it. They don't think they did anything wrong. To this day they brag about their role in 'teaching Persia a lesson.'"

"Is this true?" Megistias asked, looking to Leonidas in horror.

Leonidas sighed. "It is true."

A helot arrived at the door. "My lord, Dienekes wishes to speak with you."

Because Dienekes commanded his guard, Leonidas ordered him admitted at once, expecting there had been some incident he needed to know about. The debonair Guard commander stepped smartly into the little room and nodded his head to the others in greeting before reporting, "My lord, I have two volunteers to go to Persia."

"Who?" Leonidas demanded warily.

"Myself and Maron."

"You see?" Leonidas addressed Megistias. "Just as I told you." To Dienekes he said, "Out of the question. I will not give any member of my Guard permission to go on this suicide mission. In fact, I will give no member of the active army permission to go, and no man who does not have living sons," Leonidas added as he thought the situation through. "The ambassadors were noblemen and high court officials. Nothing will satisfy the Persians—or the Gods—but sacrifices of equal rank, standing, and importance."

Megistias nodded his approval vigorously. "That is very wise," he said out loud, cutting off Dienekes' protest before it could even be voiced.

"And preferably the men directly implicated in the murders," Leonidas added as Dienekes withdrew.

Sperchias sighed and shook his head. "I doubt that is going to happen, Leo. Wouldn't it be better—for Sparta's sake and the sake of our children—to just let two volunteers go?"

"You heard the good Megistias," Leonidas countered. "We must send men of equal rank and status to the men killed."

"Then who better than me? I am your ambassador to Delphi—the closest thing we have to permanent ambassadors—and my family is one of the best in Sparta."

"But you tried to stop the murders, Chi! No one tried harder than you."

"But I failed."

"We all failed."

"I want to go, Leo. This is my destiny. I'm sure of it."

They stared at each other, and Leonidas remembered the last time Sperchias had asked this of him. He had refused, and they were paying a terrible price. He took a deep breath. "If you are certain this is what you want, I will not stand in your way. But the other man—the other man must be one of the murderers!"

It was the third extraordinary Assembly since Megistias had told the Spartans what they must do to appease the Gods, and still Sperchias was the only volunteer that met the Council's (Leonidas') criteria. Meanwhile, no less than sixty-eight children, thirty-nine (mostly elderly) citizens, and unknown numbers of women and helots had died. There was no sign of the epidemic abating, and the urgency was making men angry. Bitter recriminations were traded, men volunteered their enemies, and in the midst of it all two councilmen and one of the ephors fell victim to the fever. The vacancies needed to be filled at once, and the maneuvering for election mixed with the calls for a second volunteer willing to serve as a sacrificial animal at the Persian court. The pressure on Leonidas was growing to give up his insistence that one of the men be directly implicated in the murders.

Alkander came to Leonidas and insisted he should be allowed to go with Sperchias. "I have held high office, and my sister was once a queen," he pointed out. "Indeed, Demaratus is reputed to be at the Great King's court; he can identify me as his brother-in-law, and that should impress the Persians."

"No."

"Why not?"

Leonidas did not have a good reason, so he did something he did not often do. He said: "I am king of Sparta. I do not have to explain myself."

"You do to me, Leo," Alkander stared him down.

"Then I will tell you the truth: because I do not want to lose you. Because I do not want to be hated by Hilaira. Because I could not bear to take from Philippos the son-in-law he loves more than the son he lost to this fever." Leonidas referred to Hilaira's younger brother.

"And because I could never look your sons in the eye again if I let you go."

Alkander thought about this answer and nodded. "Then that is the end of it."

"Yes. It is."

"Who else has volunteered?"

"Don't ask."

"Euryleon?"

"No, his wife won't let him."

"Oliantus?"

"Yes—but he was relieved when I said no. He does not like the idea of just being butchered. He would die fighting, but this idea of just submitting...."

"That bothers many men, Leo. It takes a very different kind of courage than going into battle. We have all spent too much of our lives learning that it is the greatest honor to die fighting—no matter whether in victory or defeat. All that matters is that we *fight*, that we sell our lives dearly. And suddenly we are asking a man to walk, intentionally defenseless, into the enemy's hands. We are asking a man to surrender and accept death like a sacrificial lamb. That is not very Spartan."

"Not to mention the risk of torture. I know."

Alkander had not wanted to raise the issue of torture, but the Great King's reputation for mutilating, flaying, tearing out tongues, and generally tormenting his victims before he allowed them to die in agony was well known.

"Leo, if you weren't king, would you volunteer?" Alkander asked him.

Leonidas caught his breath and their eyes met. They were alone together, and after a long moment, Leonidas shook his head and admitted, "No. I love life—and Gorgo—far too much."

Alkander nodded. "Then I think I know whom we should ask."

Leonidas stared at him.

"Bulis, Nicoles' son. He was one of the four men who nearly killed Temenos."

"And one of the ringleaders who laid hands on the ambassadors," Leonidas remembered, nodding.

"He gained full citizenship this past winter, and is not on active duty," Alkander continued. "I know he has not held high office, but he comes from a very prominent family, and his father has been a magistrate for many years."

"Yes, he fits the criteria, but what makes you think he could be persuaded to volunteer? He certainly hasn't come forward up to now!"

"He wasn't at the earlier Assemblies."

"Why not?"

"He was ill—and nursing his family."

"I see. And now?"

"And now they are all dead. His wife, his two sons, and his daughter."

Leonidas said nothing. He hated Bulis. And yet he felt sorry for him in this tragedy. He, too, had lost a wife and two children in a single blow, more than a decade ago.

"I will ask Epidydes to approach him," Alkander suggested, and Leonidas nodded mutely. Someone had to go, and they had to go soon.

CHAPTER 15

MISSION TO THE GREAT KING

THE HARDEST PART HAD BEEN TAKING leave of his daughters. His son Aneristus was already twelve, and he had made a manly effort to show no emotion beyond pride and awe of his father's courage. But the girls had not lived up to the Spartan ideal, despite their mother's scolding. "What is to become of us?" the little one had asked her father, tears streaming down her face; while the elder worried, "Who will find me a husband if you aren't here to talk to my suitors?"

At least he had an answer to that. "King Leonidas will be your guardian and see that you both find good husbands," Sperchias assured her, holding her soft, sweet-smelling body in his arms a last time.

His daughters' tears, and the unexpected number of men who had come to thank him for his singular courage, had made it very hard to leave Sparta. Sperchias found himself thinking that if all the men who came to express admiration for his courage had only listened to him when the Persian ambassadors were being attacked....

It would also have been easier to leave if only the weather had been gloomy. Or if the orchards hadn't been in bloom, or the snow on Taygetos not so white and pristine, or the foals in the pastures less playful... But then, Sperchias realized, he would have found Lacedaemon beautiful even in streaming rain or scorched brown, and he let his eyes caress each familiar contour and landmark as he passed them for the last time.

The party was composed not just of Sperchias and Bulis with their respective attendants, but also the Egyptian scribe, who had volunteered to be their interpreter, and his two African slaves. The younger of the two Africans drove the chariot, which Leonidas insisted on sending because Susa lay a long way inland from the Levant, where they were expected to disembark. It was important, Leonidas insisted, that Sperchias and Bulis arrive at the Persian court looking like men of means and status.

The little party came around a bend, and the road started to decline sharply. Ahead they had a view to the harbor of Epidauros Limera. Taiwo leaned back to slow the horses, nodded toward the harbor, and remarked with a grin, "Good fighting ship!"

"Yes," Sperchias agreed, following the African's gaze to a slender penteconter lying offshore. "That will be the ship Leonidas promised."

The ephors had refused to detail one of Lacedaemon's small fleet for this mission, arguing that, given what they'd done to the Persian ambassadors, it might be seized and confiscated, crew and all, as soon as it was identified as Lacedaemonian. The concern was not groundless and Leonidas conceded the point, but insisted that if they weren't willing to send one of their own ships, then they had to hire a foreign vessel to transport their emissaries to the Persian Empire.

Bulis had exchanged not a word with Sperchias since remarking as they set out: "Just because we are on the same mission doesn't mean I like you any more than before." Now he roused himself to look at the ship and spat out in evident shock, "That's a pirate!"

Sperchias looked again. The ship was painted black, as pirates often were, and there was something ominous about the slant of her masts, but Sperchias doubted the ephors would engage a pirate ship for such an important mission. After all, Bulis and he were accredited ambassadors of the Lacedaemonian state.

Meanwhile, a lookout on the penteconter had spotted the chariot, and a flurry of activity broke out on deck. Men ran to the oar banks, and the anchor was hauled in hand over hand. The chariot, however, had reached the foot of the hill and entered the port town, losing sight of the ship as it clattered, creaked, and bounced its way over the cobblestones. Behind it came the cart with their luggage, the other African, and their attendants.

The walls of the city seemed to crowd them, and the driver called to the horses in his own tongue to steady them as they slowed to a crawl. Sperchias had the feeling that everyone in the whole port was staring at him with a mixture of awe and aversion. They must be wondering what sort of men volunteered to be slaughtered like sacrificial beasts. He glanced at the man beside him, still baffled to find himself paired on this mission with the arrogant ex-guardsman. Whenever he looked at his companion, he was reminded of the way Bulis had held the struggling Tisibazus over the well by his ankles while Brotus screamed, "You'll find all the earth and water you need down there!"

Bulis was a good four inches taller than Sperchias, ten years younger, and had been a star on the ball field in his youth. He'd set upon Temenos in the street, too, some years ago, nearly killing him, Sperchias remembered. He was a bigoted man, full of hatred for everyone who didn't share his viewpoint.

No, Bulis was certainly not the man he would have expected to volunteer for this mission, nor was he the man Sperchias would have chosen as a companion for a long journey to anywhere. He was glad, therefore, that the Egyptian and the Nubians were with them. The Egyptian seemed a very learned and wise man, while the Nubians even now were laughing at some joke, and the younger man flashed a smile at a bold maiden as they passed.

When they reached the quay, they found that the penteconter had already gone alongside and a gangway had been run out. The hatch was open, giving access to the narrow boxes, built under the afterdeck, in which the horses would be transported. The chariot would be dismantled and stowed in the forepeak. The men themselves traveled on deck with the crew. They would stop for water and food each night and camp ashore, so there was no need for accommodations or to carry provisions for the men.

As the team halted beside the dark penteconter, a grizzled old marine barked an order and a white pennant was run sharply up the mast, showing the coiled hydra of Argos.

Bulis recoiled instantly. "Worse than a pirate! It's Argive!"

"Argos is an ally of Persia," Sperchias pointed out, annoyed by Bulis' knee-jerk hostility. "This way we'll have access to Persian ports, as we would not in one of our own ships."

"An Ionian would have done just as well. This stinks of treachery!" Bulis insisted.

Meanwhile the company of ten marines came to attention on the afterdeck of the vessel, while a lithe, black-haired young man sprang lightly ashore. He was darkly tanned, so that his white chiton stood out crisp and clean against his skin. Incongruously for an Argive, his beard was cropped and his hair braided like a Spartiate—at the diagonal just as Dienekes did it.

"Eurybiades!" Bulis gasped. "What the hell are you doing here?"

The dark-haired man bowed mockingly to Bulis. "Captain, to you, Bulis. I am captain of this fine, private penteconter. Take no note of the pennant—we fly whatever suits us. Argos just happens to be what we prefer for this voyage."

"Private, my ass!" Bulis growled. "That's just another word for pirate!"

"We serve whoever pays—in this case, King Leonidas of Sparta," Eurybiades corrected him, and turned to smile at the dumbfounded Sperchias.

They were both Kytherans, and Sperchias' deep-seated aversion to war dated from the Argive raid on Kythera. He remembered hearing that Eurybiades' mother hanged herself when the Argives broke into her estate. Eurybiades had been a little boy of twelve or thirteen, and the news of his mother's violent death had reached him in the agoge. His father had gone at once to try to find and bury the body of his wife, only to return with word that the house was completely gutted and uninhabitable, the helots and livestock slaughtered. Sperchias understood that such an experience might have turned Eurybiades into a rebel, and yet he was not entirely comfortable with someone as irreverent toward the law and the Gods as Eurybiades was reputed to be.

Eurybiades gestured for the emissaries to board his vessel and turned to give instructions about the horses, while the helots started to offload the luggage from the cart. Sperchias was reminded that they had no time to waste. Children were still sick and dying at home.

He followed a still-smoldering Bulis across the gangway, and his eyes fell on the captain of marines. The man looked vaguely familiar, although he wore his hair short and his beard long like other Greeks. Sperchias thought maybe he'd seen him in Delphi, a supplicant to the oracle perhaps?

But then the man introduced himself: "Prokles," he growled, "Prokles, son of Philippos."

"Of course! You were Leonidas' boyhood friend."

"Was, yes. Now I'm just a mercenary like my men—the scum of the earth with nothing to lose. We hire our skins out for pay. King Leonidas pays well, I might add. Better than most."

"But you're Hilaira's brother," Sperchias protested. "Your term of exile expired three years ago. You could—"

"Don't start that! I'm not coming back!" Prokles snarled, and then, sensing he had overreacted, he asked in an almost normal tone of voice, "Is Hilaira still well, and Alkander? This sickness has not struck them, I hope?"

"They are both well, but your nephew Simonidas nearly died. He has been scarred for life."

Prokles nodded emotionlessly. Why should he care about a boy he had never met? On the quay they had started to dismantle the chariot. Prokles stepped back. "We'll have plenty of time to talk later. I have orders to take you all the way to Susa."

They stopped on Crete, Rhodes, and then Cyprus. They rounded the Karpasian peninsula from the north and put in at Salamis to take on water and rest one last time before striking out for the Levant. Although Cyprus technically belonged to the Persian Empire, the culture and language were Greek. Indeed, Cyprus had briefly joined the Ionian Revolt. From Sperchias' point of view, Salamis was the last port of call in friendly territory. The next stop would be Sidon, and there the two emissaries would enter an alien world commanded by the world's most powerful despot—a man who had vowed to destroy their homeland.

Still, they were accredited ambassadors of the Lacedaemonian state with an embassy to the Great King. If all went according to plan, their diplomatic immunity would enable them to travel all the way to the Great King's court, where they would reveal their mission and make their sacrifice to him directly. Sperchias was acutely aware, however, that the Great King might have long since issued standing orders to treat any Spartan ambassadors as the Spartans had treated his own. Even if such orders had not been issued, there was no assurance that the local satrap, Hydarnes, would not prefer to dispatch them on his own initiative, in order to send their heads to Xerxes as a means of currying favor.

Under the circumstances, Sperchias found he could not sleep. Clutching his himation around his naked body, he left the carpet of crewmen and marines stretched out and snoring on the afterdeck to walk forward between the oar banks to the prow of the ship. Here he leaned on the port railing and gazed at the stars, brilliant in a cloudless sky.

He still did not fully understand how it had come to this. He accepted that it was his destiny, and part of him was secretly pleased that a even a mediocre man might yet find his way into history. Leonidas had promised him the Spartans would raise a monument to him just as if he had died in battle, and he knew the boys of the agoge would be taught that Bulis and he embodied Sparta's spirit of self-sacrifice for the common good. And yet, how was it that a man of only average talent and understanding was the only one who had foreseen this?

"It's your last chance to jump ship," remarked a dry, cracked voice in the darkness, making Sperchias start. He turned and looked over his shoulder at Prokles.

"I have no intention of jumping ship," Sperchias told him.

Prokles shrugged. "Xerxes is a spoiled princeling—not as ruthless as his father, but more dangerous, because he is fickle and unpredictable. Darius was rational. Darius knew perfectly well he stole the throne from Cyrus' rightful heirs. He knew he slaughtered and cheated his way into power—and that he had to put down revolts with merciless brutality or risk falling victim to the next Darius. But he also knew flattery when he heard it. Xerxes, on the other hand, confuses it with the truth. He actually believes he is all the things his father's relentless bureaucracy tells him he is—Godhead of all Wisdom, Source of all Civilization—all that kind of crap."

"Have you met him?" Sperchias asked.

Prokles shrugged and answered evasively, "Near enough," and then, apparently insulted by the mere question, withdrew.

Sperchias was left to his own thoughts, and was soon so lost in them he did not even notice that Bulis had joined him until Bulis remarked, "The stars are fading."

Sperchias shook himself out of his reverie and looked at his companion. Bulis looked at the horizon, his head held high, his expression haughty. Sperchias waited.

"Since I may never have another chance to ask this question, I want to know before we die together just why you, an inveterate Persia-lover and compromiser, volunteered for this mission?"

Sperchias almost protested angrily that he was not, and never had been, a Persia-lover, but then he realized it would do no good. He'd tried to explain a hundred times already, but Bulis wasn't listening, so he kept his answer to the minimum. "I volunteered for this the day after the murders—foreseeing the wrath of the Gods, although not what form it would take."

"There was no call for volunteers back then!" Bulis scoffed.

"No, and Leonidas dismissed my offer out of hand, saying it would serve no useful purpose. He was only thinking of the Persians, you see, not the Gods. Our sacrifice will not stop the Persians from bringing war to Lacedaemon, but before that war comes, I want the Gods to be appeased. I would not want Sparta to go to war with Persia while the Gods are set against us."

Bulis was still staring at the horizon and gave no indication of having heard, much less being impressed by, Sperchias' answer. Sperchias sighed and asked, "And why did you volunteer?"

"To prove to Leonidas that I am a better man than he thinks I am," Bulis snapped back.

That sounded petty to Sperchias, and he unconsciously raised his eyebrows.

Bulis didn't notice; he was still staring eastward, where a sliver of golden sun was peeping over the horizon, turning the sea purple. "It is no great sacrifice I make," he added in a murmur without turning his head, "because I am already dead. The moment she died in my arms, proving all my strength and skills and prayers worthless...."

Hydarnes was in his prime, and a successful man by any standard. He was currently in command of the seaports of the Levant, a notoriously lucrative post. For the two Spartan emissaries en route to the Great King in Susa, he ordered a banquet that would manifest his wealth and power. The kitchen was tasked with producing a variety of dishes using exotic ingredients—from ostrich eggs and pineapples to the meat of crocodiles, swans, and piglets of wild boar. These and other dishes were to be prepared with spices from the farthest corners of the Empire: white and black peppers, saffron, cinnamon, nutmeg, cumin, tarragon, sesame, and more. To drink, the guests would have a choice of date wine, wine from red or white grapes, honey mead, or Assyrian barley beer. For entertainment, Hydarnes ordered Egyptian dancers, Indian gymnasts, and a juggler from Armenia, but held fighting cocks in reserve in case these primitive visitors could not appreciate his more refined offerings. Music was to be provided by Babylonian and Ionian musicians, as well as a Nubian slave with an amazing voice.

At the appointed time, the visitors were admitted to Hydarnes' palace and escorted to the banqueting hall by one of the assistant stewards. The steward wore soft shoes of doeskin and flowing robes in bright patterns. Compared to this mid-ranking official, the Spartan ambassadors looked like a pair of sentries in their near-matching red chitons and cloaks and their bronze and leather armor.

As ambassadors, Sperchias and Bulis had a status equivalent to that of their host, and protocol was finessed with a herald announcing them at the entrance to the banquet hall and their host rising to meet them halfway. The steward bowed to his master and withdrew to the side. Hydarnes bowed his head first to Bulis and then to Sperchias; they returned the gesture with dignity. Hydarnes led them to the seats flanking him.

For men from a country that murdered ambassadors, Hydarnes was impressed by their good manners. Both men behaved like civilized men, washing their hands, making offerings to the Gods, politely awaiting their host's invitation to each course, and then taking small portions of everything. They took only small bites and chewed with their mouths closed. Nothing about their behavior suggested they were barbarians, Hydarnes thought with surprise.

Because Hydarnes' Greek was good, the Egyptian interpreter was all but superfluous, and he withdrew self-effacingly into the background. Hydarnes inquired after his guests' voyage, narrated the dishes laid out for them, drew attention to the music, and related anecdotes about the musicians or other guests, generally playing the good host. Bulis acted as if they were speaking Persian, nodding politely now and again but stubbornly keeping silent, leaving it to Sperchias to be gracious and respond to Hydarnes' questions.

As he did so, Sperchias found himself thinking how useful all his observations would have been to Leonidas. From the moment they docked, he had been noting things—for example the shipyards, where no less than nine triremes were being built, but also the abject poverty of the people crushed into the sector of the city beyond the harbor. Sperchias noted, too, that there were many public buildings in shabby condition, and the roads were in poor repair. He guessed that tax money was being siphoned off to maintain a military establishment stretched to the limits, at the price of other state expenditures. He suspected that there was more unrest in this vast empire than outsiders realized. Darius, after all, had to subdue nineteen revolts in his first years on the throne. Might it be that Xerxes, too, was being challenged—and running scared? True, he had crushed the Egyptian revolt, but the Egyptian scribe Teti claimed there were uprisings in places he had never even heard of.

Sperchias longed to report these observations to Leonidas, but he would have no chance—unless he wrote them down and entrusted them to Teti. He glanced over his shoulder at the Egyptian; the old man met his eye, then looked down humbly. Sperchias had the uncanny feeling the Egyptian saw a great deal more than he did—and his hatred of Persia was insatiable. That calmed him a little. A report on the state of Persia would get back to Leonidas even without his own commentary.

"Has Sparta at last seen the wisdom of becoming friends with the Great King?" Hydarnes' words broke into his thoughts. Before Sperchias could even draw a breath to answer politely, however, Bulis barked out, "On the contrary. We are here to reaffirm our position."

Hydarnes looked shocked, and Sperchias hastened to soften the impact of Bulis' outburst. "We are here to make amends for the violence done to the Great King's ambassadors. We recognize the grievous nature of our transgression and have come to make reparation," Sperchias assured him.

Hydarnes raised his eyebrows, an expression of skepticism on his face, but he refrained from saying what he thought.

Sperchias continued. "As my colleague noted, however, Sparta has not changed its fundamental decision to remain independent."

"But why?" Hydarnes asked. "You have only to look at me and the position I enjoy to see that the Great King knows how to reward merit. From what I have heard, Lacedaemon has many men of merit. Indeed, you seem to me to be such men yourselves. I can see that you are men of good breeding, education, and distinction. If you go to the Great King in friendship and submit to his generosity, I am sure he would reward you for this. Indeed, you might find yourselves endowed with vast authority over lands in Greece, which he will certainly give to those who embrace his friendship of their free will."*

"He has to take those lands first," Bulis growled, but fortunately into his cup and under his breath, so that Hydarnes appeared not to hear.

Sperchias spoke louder and held his host's attention. "Hydarnes, your advice is good as far as it goes, but it is based on only half the facts. You understand well what slavery is, but you have never known freedom. If you had but tasted freedom as we know it, you would advise us not to submit, but to fight—and not just with our spears, but with axes and swords and, indeed, our naked hands."

The answer left not only Hydarnes dumbfounded, but Bulis as well.

They had been traveling together for almost four months, the first month by sea and since then by land. They had left Eurybiades and his black ship in Sidon in order to follow the Imperial Highway,

* This speech is recorded in Herodotus, as is Sperchias' answer.

paved with massive square stones, to Damas. Damas was a bustling, rather chaotic city, where hundred-camel caravans coming up from Arabia with spices met the equally long caravans from Egypt with Nubian gold. The squares and taverns of the city were clogged with pack animals, their drivers, and merchants speaking every known tongue under the sun. Bedouins, all but lost in their fluttering robes and elaborate turbans, mixed with near-naked Nubians, whose skin gleamed with sweat as they labored under the lash of their masters. Elegant Egyptians with naked torsos and striped headgear moved with upright dignity among the lively, bird-like natives in their striped kaftans. Ionian Greeks and Cypriots in brightly dyed chitons mingled with the peoples of the Orient. Here the Spartans and their tiny escort were lost in the melting pot.

From Damas, the King's Highway cut across the arid plain to Babylon. A caravansary located every twenty or so miles along the road provided water, shade, and shelter for the night. At each, a horde of local craftsmen and farmers descended on the travelers like vultures, selling everything the local economy could produce—from dates, milk, and trinkets to "virgins." Travelers usually rested at the caravansary during the hours of darkness and set off after dawn the following morning.

While some fast-moving travelers, particularly messengers or soldiers on well-bred horses, rushed ahead and the slowest fell behind, the bulk of the travelers moved along the paved road in a loose clump, forming impromptu convoys.

The Spartan emissaries generally found themselves moving along in this disorganized horde, but as soon as word of their nationality spread, they were isolated even in the midst of many others. Spartans? Weren't they that barbaric race of godless warriors who had dared murder two ambassadors of the Great King? Merchants, tax collectors, messengers, and slaves carefully kept their distance from the men in red, while casting surreptitious glances filled with awe and horror. They *looked* quite normal, but they were evidently untrustworthy, like captive wild beasts.

Teti, his two African slaves Kaschta and Taiwo, and the helot attendants, Geranor and Samias, had an easier time mingling and socializing. Teti spoke five languages, including Persian, and Taiwo and

Kaschta each spoke their native African tongue as well as Egyptian, rudimentary Greek, and Arabic. The two helots were at the greatest disadvantage, speaking only Doric Greek, but the other travelers on this great east-west highway generally knew enough Greek for them to communicate.

By the time the little party reached Babylon, the four servants were a good team. Taiwo had a natural gift with animals, and he looked after the two teams of chariot horses with an attentiveness born of affection. Kaschta was the consummate bargainer and could not only find everything their hearts desired, he could usually get it at a price they could afford. Geranor, Bulis' attendant, was the brawniest among them, and he handled any heavy lifting, pushing, or hauling with a swagger and pride in his own strength. Samias was their cook. He was the younger son of a syssitia cook, who had taken service with Sperchias after a fight with his father.

Babylon impressed all of them—the Spartans included. Only Teti seemed unimpressed by a city of such gigantic dimensions, populated with so many different peoples and animal species and overflowing with what seemed like hundreds of palaces. They found time to visit the hanging gardens, which were now open to the public, and shopped in bazaars larger than any they had ever seen.

From Babylon they took the road to Susa. Although this paved road was wider than any they had traveled before, it was still congested. More and more tribute convoys were converging on the Persian capital, and these were slow-moving assemblages of laden wagons and beasts of burden mixed with herds of animals—goats, sheep, cattle, horses, and pigs. They moved at the pace of the bleating sheep or lowing cattle, herded by barefoot slave boys who were tanned almost as black as the Africans.

There were also increasing numbers of soldiers on the roads. Some, of course, were escorts for the tribute convoys; others were sorry and reluctant bands of conscripts reporting for duty under the angry and disgusted leadership of Persian recruiters. But there were also troops of smartly outfitted fighters apparently deploying from one place to the next. They wore a wide variety of uniforms, depending on their nation of origin, and Teti kept a careful record of them all, just as he wrote down in his copious notes everything else of possible interest to Leonidas.

The slaves and helots reported to Teti, too, telling him anything that seemed noteworthy and leaving it to the Egyptian scribe to decide what was important. Eventually even Prokles, who on Leonidas' orders was escorting Sperchias and Bulis all the way to Susa, started to tell the Egyptian things he thought odd or exceptional. Prokles knew a great deal about the Persian army and could distinguish among the various troops, which was particularly useful.

In Susa, the Spartans were dismayed to learn that Xerxes was yet farther away. They were told he was currently at his newly finished palace in Persepolis—a place they had never even heard of. The court officials in Susa refused to guess when the Great King might return to Susa; to speculate on the Great King's intentions and plans would have been "presumptuous," they insisted haughtily, suggesting it could be many months.

Although in this strange continental climate they had no real sense of changing seasons, Sperchias and Bulis were nevertheless aware that time was passing. They thought of the fever raging at home and counted the passing days in dead children. They felt they had to press on to Persepolis despite their weariness.

Travel had lost its appeal. New landscapes, buildings, costumes, languages, and customs no longer aroused particular curiosity, much less fascination. They were tired of new impressions—tired of dusty roads, strange beds, food, and beer. Even Samias lamented that he would give anything for a bowl of his Dad's black broth and a cup of Laconian white wine. And they were tired of being stared at, too—at least Sperchias and Bulis were.

Despite all this, Persepolis could not fail to impress them. It was not just another bustling, trading city; in fact, it was hardly a trading city at all. It lacked the cacophonic hum of too many people crowded into too-narrow streets. It lacked the smell of spices and dung, cook shops and workshops, and the smoke of cooking fires, forges, and pottery furnaces.

Persepolis was striking for the very absence of all that had made the other Oriental cities so vibrant. Here the streets were quiet and wide—almost as wide as in Sparta—and they were empty. More important, the poor had been banned, or so a fellow traveler told Kaschta. Cook shops and workshops of any kind were prohibited, while street vendors and beggars were chased away by the Great King's guard if they dared to set their dirty feet inside his pristine new capital. There was not even a bazaar. Rather than the smell of goods for sale, massed humanity, and domesticated animals, the air in Persepolis was dominated by the smell of jasmine and juniper.

Persepolis was an administrative capital with ancillary military barracks, royal stables, and chariot house. Above all, it housed the royal treasury, in which the accounts of tribute (but not the stinking, bleating, bleeding beasts, slaves, and goods) were kept by an army of royal scribes and auditors. The city was, of course, dominated by the palace complex, a structure started by Darius shortly after he came to power and still not completed. The palace compound of marble buildings consisted of the Great King's own Apadana palace as well as a number of secondary palaces for Xerxes' brothers. Each of these had exquisite bas-reliefs depicting the conquests of Darius, the wealth of the Empire, and its nations. The royal compound sat high above the rest of the city on a terrace partially carved out of the mountain behind. Two broad but shallow staircases gave access to the terrace. As a local explained to Taiwo, the stairs were shallow enough to enable horses to go easily up and down, so that the Great King and his nobles did not have to dismount until they were on the same level as the entrance to the royal palace. The terrace was constructed from limestone joined by polished bronze clips, which caught the sunlight like gold scattered regularly across the floor.

The Spartan ambassadors were graciously taken to an elegant tract of guest quarters that lay in the middle of a garden only slightly lower than the royal compound. These limestone buildings backed up against the gigantic reservoir that served the city. They had a smaller terrace and an interior courtyard with a fountain. The official who led them to their quarters promised to present their credentials to the Great King "at the earliest opportunity," and begged them to consider themselves guests of "his master the Great King" until such time as they were summoned. They were shown the baths and the dining hall and told to request anything they desired.

The two Spartan emissaries retired to separate rooms, understandably taciturn now that their journey was almost at an end. Prokles disappeared, presumably in search of a drink or a whore. Teti took out his rolls of papyrus, his brushes, and ink, and began to record recent impressions with single-minded concentration, bending over the writing tablet balanced on his crossed legs. So the two slaves and the two helots withdrew to the outermost chamber of the guest apartment and sat around on the cool marble floor, eating fresh oranges that Kaschta had bought.

"It will be strange returning without the masters," Taiwo remarked—as so often on this trip, putting into words what the others were thinking.

"I won't be coming with you—at least not all the way," Geranor announced, causing the other men to gape at him.

"What do you mean?" Kaschta asked, sitting up straighter and pausing in his orange-peeling. "You think the Great King might kill us, too?"

"No, no," the burly helot assured the aging African, "I just mean I have no intention of going back to Lacedaemon. Why should I?"

"But I thought Spartan slaves were the property of the Spartan state," Kaschta protested.

"Yes, well, let them come and find me!" Geranor scoffed. "I see no reason to return to Lacedaemon when I can live in Babylon."

"You want to find a new master?" Taiwo asked, puzzled.

"Master? What do I need a master for? From the moment the last breath leaves Bulis' body, I intend to be my own master!" Geranor declared emphatically.

"But who will look after you if you get hurt, or sick, or old?" Taiwo asked, alarmed. He had been sold by his parents to slave traders when he was little more than a toddler. He had never in his life had to look after himself.

"I can take care of myself," Geranor answered with a stubborn set of his jaw—adding, "Maybe I'll find a wife and start a family."

"You think you can just live here as if you were a free man?" Kaschta countered with raised eyebrows.

"Why not? How would the Persians know I'm not a free man?"

Kaschta weighed his head from side to side. "It is not so easy. The Persians keep long, long lists of everybody living in their territories—"

"All these millions of people?" Geranor asked, disbelieving.

Kaschta nodded. "Yes, that is why they have so many scribes. They keep track of every single person, and for each person there is a tax. The head of each household pays for his wives and children and slaves. Don't you remember all the guards at the gates of the cities? All the toll booths along the roads? And the inspectors in the caravansaries? Every time we entered or exited a city, or passed a checkpoint, or stopped for the night, we had to show the ambassadors' credentials. If you were alone, you would be arrested at once. You have no stamp that proves you have a right to move freely and have paid your taxes." Kaschta pressed his right fist into the palm of his left hand to imitate the sound of a stamp. "The Persians are very strict about collecting taxes. They even have standardized weights and measures and test all metals for their purity, so that no one can pay less by using a different measure or by offering impure silver, tin, or gold."

"I will tell them I am a traveling salesman," Geranor insisted, frowning.

"You cannot just travel around the Persian Empire without permission," Kaschta countered. "You need a document that gives you permission to pass the ports, use the highways, and enter the cities."

Geranor frowned more darkly and protested, "There has to be a way! There are so many different peoples here—I can't even remember the names of them all—Parthians and Scythians and Elamites and the like. Surely one lone helot can disappear among the hordes of them?"

Kaschta shook his head slowly. "I don't know how you could do it. You need a paper sealed with a stamp to stay in one place, and another to travel. You need documents to come and to go. Besides, a strong man like you will be a prime candidate for conscription. The Great King's officers are always looking for men to serve in the army or with the fleet. If a recruiter sees you and you cannot show him you are exempt from conscription, he will have you in uniform and locked in a barracks before you know what is happening to you."

Geranor was starting to look uneasy, but he resisted giving up his dream of freedom, so he growled belligerently, "Let 'em try!"

"If you must run away, then it would be better to wait until we are back in Sidon," Kaschta suggested. "Most galley captains don't ask a lot of questions. If they're short of rowers and a man offers himself for hire, they'll take him."

Geranor grunted. Working the oars of a merchant galley wasn't his idea of freedom.

"You do not want be arrested by the Persian authorities as a deserter or a runaway," Kaschta continued, helping himself to a second orange. "The kindest thing they would do to you is put you in their army, but they might instead send you to the mines or the quarries. The slaves in such places are not treated like men at all. They are treated even worse than animals. They are kept chained together at all times, even when they relieve themselves or lie down to sleep at night. They are not allowed to even look at women, much less lie with them. In the mines you never see the light of day, but crawl in the darkness until you go blind and your knee bones wear away. Then they roll you aside and leave you to die down there in the underworld. In the quarries you go blind, too, not from the darkness but because the fine dust of the stone scratches away the surface of your eyeballs, just as it fills your lungs until there is no room for air to go into them. No one lives more than a few years in the mines or the quarries."

By now both helots were gaping at Kaschta in horror. Taiwo broke the tension with a bright smile and the observation, "It is much better you travel with us back to the sea!"

Geranor was inwardly convinced, but reluctant to admit it, so he grunted ambiguously, and Taiwo turned to Samias. "And you will come back with us to Sparta, won't you?"

Samias nodded vigorously. "I can't wait to get home, and when I do I'm never going to travel again!"

The others laughed briefly, but Geranor frowned and wanted to know, "But why? In Lacedaemon you will be just a helot again."

Samias shrugged. "What's so bad about being a helot? It's a lot better than the slaves Kaschta just told us about, and better than being a beggar, too."

"You spent the first half of this trip bitching about Sperchias' wife and how she made your life hell on the estate!" Geranor protested.

Samias shrugged. "I know, but I've learned better; besides, I won't go back to there. I'll make it up with my father and work at the syssitia."

"You can just do that?" Taiwo asked, amazed. "*Choose* where you want to work?"

"Within limits," Samias explained. "Being a cook is a hereditary profession, so only the sons of cooks can become cooks. But Geranor could seek employment with a different hoplite, or hire himself out in one of the factories or shipyards or on a farm."

"For fixed wages!" Geranor scoffed. "Starvation wages!"

Samias shrugged and admitted, "There's a girl I want to marry . . . ."

"Ah!" Kaschta exclaimed with a knowing grin. "Women make a man do crazy things."

Taiwo, however, asked, astonished, "Marry? You are allowed to marry?"

"Yes—if I can convince the girl's father I can look after her. Which, if I make it up with my Dad, shouldn't be that hard. You see, if I go back to working with him, my wife and I could live over the syssitia—in a stone house heated by the syssitia ovens." Samias was clearly taken with this idea.

"I thought you said she was a slave?" Taiwo asked, confused.

"A helot like me, the daughter of Pantes the carpenter."

"Pantes is stinking rich!" Geranor protested. "He'll never have you!"

Samias just smiled slyly and remarked, "He might not have a choice."

The Africans at once threw back their heads in approving laughter, and Taiwo clapped Samias on the back in congratulation.

But in the next instant Teti stood in the doorway, looking reproachfully at his slaves. "Have you no sense of propriety?" he asked sadly. "The good Spartan ambassadors are on the brink of death. They may be tortured or horribly humiliated. And you sit here laughing like heartless children!"

"What did you say?" Xerxes sprang up from his throne in anger and stared at his uncle Artaphernes. Then, not giving the older man a chance to answer, he exclaimed in a tone of outrage, "*Spartans*? Is that what you said? *Spartan* ambassadors dare to come here, all the way to Persepolis, to seek audience with me?"

"Yes." Artaphernes was not in the least intimidated by his nephew. He did not think Xerxes was particularly gifted, brilliant, or competent—but Artaphernes had no interest in civil war, either, and was content to let his nephew be the "Great King."

"How dare they?" Xerxes demanded.

"Oh, they are nothing if not impudent," Artaphernes observed. "Have you forgotten that they 'warned' Cyrus to keep out of Greece? No one here had even heard of them at the time. An insignificant city, but a singularly self-important one."

"Self-important? You call a people that could murder two ambassadors carrying an offer of peace and friendship 'self-important'? A strange choice of words, uncle! I call such men *barbarians*. Did you not hear the account Zopyrus made of their brutality?"

"Zopyrus was badly shaken."

"As I think we *all* would have been, uncle, under the circumstances," Xerxes told him primly.

Artaphernes raised his shoulders and conceded, "No doubt you are right, but I would advise you to hear these men out nevertheless."

"Why?" Xerxes asked sharply. "I have half a mind to —"

"I know what you have a mind to do, and understandable as it is, I still advise you to hear them out."

"Give me one reason why I should."

"Curiosity, your magnificence, curiosity."

At first Demaratus did not credit the rumors that two Spartans had come to Persepolis, but then his own attendant returned with too many details for Demaratus to dismiss them. He reported which guesthouse they were in and that they were traveling with their attendants: two black men, an Egyptian, and a marine.

"Did you see them yourself?" Demaratus wanted to know.

"I caught a glimpse of them."

"And?"

"They wore their hair long and their beards short and had red cloaks."

"Brilliant. Tell me something I don't know!" Demaratus scoffed. "Do you know who they are?"

"No."

"No one mentioned any names?"

"No."

"The second house, you said?"

"Yes."

Demaratus dismissed his man, but the thought of two countrymen less than a mile away was too much for him. He could not sit still; he started pacing around his own quarters speculating on whether they had come to submit earth and water after all. It was the only sensible thing to do, of course, but in his heart he hoped that his former subjects would not cave in after their display of defiance.

Of course, they should never have murdered the ambassadors. Demaratus had been deeply embarrassed by that, especially since Darius had sent for him and demanded an explanation. Indeed, Darius had required him—a king!—to kneel for over an hour while he insulted and abused Demaratus for his former subjects' behavior. Demaratus had been forced to repeat over and over that this could only have come about because the Spartans were kingless at the time. They were like wayward children, he told the Great King—like willful, disobedient children. Eventually Darius had accepted this argument and allowed Demaratus to withdraw without further consequences. But it had been a near thing....

No, the Spartans should not have murdered the ambassadors, but nor should they submit earth and water. If these men were here to do that now, Demaratus reasoned, then he would be ashamed of his homeland yet again. It was bad enough to kill ambassadors in the name of freedom, but worse to commit the crime and *then* barter away their freedom anyway!

And why else would they be here? It must be obvious to even an idiot like Leotychidas that nothing less than abject submission would avert the rage of Xerxes. Xerxes was more determined than his father had been to crush Greek defiance and bring Hellas under Persian hegemony. Xerxes would have moved against Greece two years ago if the Egyptian revolt hadn't forced him to divert troops and ships to Egypt.

Maybe he should go to these men and tell them to return home. He should at least find out who they were, Demaratus convinced himself, and without another thought he strode out of his apartments.

No one was guarding the apartment assigned the Spartan ambassadors, and no one was there to announce him, either. Demaratus plunged into the inner courtyard and there drew up, looking about uncertainly. A man came to the doorway of one of the chambers, expecting a messenger from the Great King. "Demaratus!" he exclaimed in shock.

"Son of Nicoles?" Demaratus answered uncertainly. He recognized the face, but was uncertain of the name.

"Damn you!" Bulis barked back, coming out of the chamber. "Damn you!" Bulis was taller than Demaratus, and he came to stand very close so that he towered over the former king. "Isn't it bad enough that you abandoned your duties and your city? Do you have to crawl up Persian asses—"

"How dare you talk to me like that?" Demaratus cut him off with a roar of injured pride. "I am your rightful king!"

"You might once have been my king, but you're an ass-licking bugger now!"

"You gave me no choice!" Demaratus protested, his face red with outrage. "You voted for that piece of slime Leotychidas! You let him humiliate me!"

"Nothing humiliates you so much as eating Persian shit!" Bulis countered. "And the stink of it on your breath makes me sick to my stomach!" Bulis opened his mouth as if he were literally going to vomit on Demaratus, but instead delivered a ball of spittle directly into his face. Then he turned on his heel and stormed out.

Demaratus was left cooking in his own rage. With revulsion he wiped the spittle off his face with a corner of his himation, his head filled with inarticulate insults and excuses and counterarguments. It was several moments before he realized a second man was in the little courtyard. This man was sitting on the edge of the fountain, looking as if he had been there for some time. Demaratus pulled himself up straighter and stared at him, his brain again searching furiously for a name.

"Sperchias, son of Aneristus," the man helped him out.

"Of course. Sperchias. You are one of Leonidas' friends."

"I am privileged to count myself among his friends, yes."

"A singularly dishonest man!" Demaratus declared, with a flash of temper that lit up his eyes.

"Leonidas? Dishonest?" Sperchias was taken aback by the accusation. There were many men in Sparta who disliked Leonidas for various reasons—mostly because they did not like his policies, especially those with respect to the perioikoi and helots, but he could think of no one who would deny Leonidas' integrity.

"What do *you* call it? Telling me to my face that he did not want his brother's throne, only to turn around and murder for it!"

"Murder?" Sperchias was flabbergasted. "Have you gone mad? Or is that the way the Persians tell the story?"

"You don't expect me to believe Cleomenes truly tried to flay himself alive!"

"You, of all people, ought to know just how mad Cleomenes was."

"Mad, perhaps, but someone put a knife in his hand, and we know who profited...."

"Leonidas was more than a hundred miles away the day his brother died. If you're looking for a murderer, look no farther than Brotus."

Demaratus grunted, unable to deny the logic of what Sperchias said, despite his fury with Leonidas. Instead, he tried to justify himself yet again. "It need never have come to this. If Leonidas had only listened to me. If he had made the first move, we could have been kings together. We would have made a good team."

Sperchias sighed and nodded, conceding to an astonished Demaratus, "I know, but you know as well as I do that Leo can't be pushed into things. He has to find his own way in his own time."

"All very well for you to say! You haven't been robbed of your rightful inheritance, humiliated, and driven out of your city. You are the confidant of a ruling king, an ambassador! You can go home to Sparta!"

Sperchias smiled bitterly and remarked in a soft voice, "Actually, I can't."

"What do you mean? Why not?"

"I have come here to die—to make reparation with my life for the murdered Persian ambassadors."

Demaratus could only gape at him. He had never thought of Sperchias as in any way heroic—until this very minute.

Samias and Taiwo helped Sperchias prepare for his audience with Xerxes. They came unbidden and with a certain sheepishness, ashamed that they had forgotten themselves the day before and had laughed so heartily. But Sperchias made no mention of the incident and seemed hardly to notice the two servants. While Samias polished his bronze armor a final time, Taiwo oiled Sperchias himself, rubbing the oil deep into his skin with strong yet gentle fingers. Taiwo clipped and filed Sperchias' fingernails and toenails as well, while Samias clipped his beard and then solemnly combed out his hair. Finally, Taiwo ran his oily fingers through Sperchias' hair, divided it into sections and, with great concentration, set about braiding it very tightly in neat, straight rows. Samias, meanwhile, pressed Sperchias' chiton and himation. Together they helped him dress, Samias kneeling before his master to snap the greaves in place. As he stood to hand his master his helmet, tears were welling up in his eyes.

"I've asked Leonidas to emancipate you, Samias, as soon as you return."

"Master!" Samias gasped.

"It was the least I could do," Sperchias told him.

For a second they stood awkwardly, staring at each other. Then Sperchias turned and strode out into the courtyard, where Bulis was already waiting.

The two Spartiates mounted the grand steps to the royal terrace together. At the top of the stairs, hundreds of Persian courtiers milled about awaiting a summons, but at the sight of the two Spartans they parted and drew back with a rustle of whispers. From the back of the crowd erupted a few catcalls of "murderers" and "barbarians," but the royal steward, who was leading them, ignored the calls. With great dignity he led the Spartans to the central of three wide, wooden doors. Without a word, these swung open to admit them.

They found themselves in a vast hall filled with wooden pillars that soared upward for a hundred feet. The pillars were set in stone bases on which were depicted scenes from palace life: the Great King receiving tribute, the Great King sitting in judgment, the Great King reviewing his troops, the Great King reviewing his fleet, the Great King sacrificing to Ahuramazda . . . .

Ahead of them was another building, so that the entire hall was nothing but a covered forecourt. This second building had towers at the corners, and a company of Immortals was lined up across the front of the façade. Sperchias already knew a great deal about the Immortals from conversations with various people they had encountered during the long voyage. He knew that the total strength of the elite unit was ten thousand, but that nine thousand of these were archers and only one thousand were spear bearers, or more accurately, "shielded spear bearers," as his interlocutors had stressed. The shielded spear bearers, he had been told, were all sons of noblemen, so that this unit was the elite of the elite—rather like the Spartan Guard.

Unsurprisingly, the Immortals guarding the audience chamber of the Great King were from this unit, and they were splendid young men—tall, tanned, broad-shouldered, and straight. Somewhat more difficult to appreciate was their dress, from their crocus-yellow leather shoes to their turbans of the same color. In between they wore tight trousers under a thin, tight gown that reached almost to the ground in the rear but was caught up in a broad belt in front, providing more freedom of movement. The upper body was encased in a tight-fitting shirt with sleeves snug to the elbow and then long, full, and hanging. Their clothes were cut from a shiny pale-blue material covered with bright yellow sunbursts. Wicker shields hung from their left shoulders onto their backs, and they stood with the orb-like silver butts of their spears resting on their left feet. They held their spears extended at arms' length, with both hands, one over the other, grasping the shaft as they stared straight ahead.

They stood wonderfully still when on parade like this, Sperchias thought as he passed between them, but would they show as much fortitude facing a Spartan phalanx? It was an idle thought, a flash of foolish bravado, designed to give himself courage. Certainly he would not live to see such an encounter—unless they let the shades out of Hades now and again to drink the blood of battlefields....

The royal audience chamber was lined with columns topped with animal heads, while the plaster walls were decorated with frescoes depicting lions, bulls, and flowers. What an eclectic combination, Sperchias had time to think, before one of the Immortals, who had turned and entered the room with them, put a heavy hand on his shoulder and tried to force him to the ground. On his right, a second Immortal was doing the same thing to Bulis.

Only then did Sperchias register that, at the far end of the hall on a raised platform, a man sat on a throne. The throne was so far away that he had not immediately registered the fact that he was in the royal presence. Both Sperchias and Bulis responded instinctively to the heavy hands on their shoulders. Like wrestlers, they twisted away and stiffened their backs in resistance.

"Bow down!" came the order, barked from a man in the same uniform as the guards but with an even larger turban, evidently some kind of officer.

"No!" Bulis retorted.

"It is not our custom," Sperchias tried to explain.

"You are in the presence of the Great King!" the officer insisted. "Bow down!"

The guards lent force to his words: one pushed down on Bulis' shoulders and the other on Sperchias'.

"He is not our king!" Bulis insisted, trying to pry the guard's fingers off his shoulders.

"We do not bow even to our own kings," Sperchias explained. "Spartans worship no man like a god."

"You are in Persia now!" the officer retorted, and with a gesture, two more guards joined in the effort to force Sperchias and Bulis onto their knees. Bulis was struggling so violently he had no breath to speak, but Sperchias raised his voice as his legs gave way. He called down the length of the hall. "King of the Medes! Your men can force my head to the floor with their greater strength, but such a bow is meaningless! What matters is only what a man does freely!"

Sperchias and Bulis were on their knees now, but still struggling against the guards. The latter were indeed trying to force Bulis to touch his forehead to the floor. Sperchias' guards, on the other hand, seemed stunned by the fact that he dared address the Great King. A glance at the officer, however, suggested that the latter had seen some signal from Xerxes at the far end of the hall.

"Speak!" the officer hissed in Greek to Sperchias. "Why are you here?"

"We are here to make reparation for the ambassadors we Spartans murdered."

"How can you make reparation for dead men?" Xerxes' voice reverberated down the length of the great audience chamber. The voice was not as deep as Leonidas', Sperchias found himself noting, and it had a hint of contempt in it—which only made Sperchias sit up straighter and look directly at the man on the distant throne.

"With our lives!" Sperchias answered. This time it was his voice that echoed down the length of the hall, and even the guards went still.

Bulis used the moment of shock to shake off the guards and, like Sperchias, sit on his heels looking down the length of the hall at Xerxes.

Xerxes was not alone on the raised platform. He was flanked by two other men in elaborate court robes with long, carefully coifed beards. One of these leaned forward and whispered something in Xerxes' ear. Xerxes did not look at his adviser, but he raised his right hand and snapped his fingers.

Abruptly their guards were pulling them up. They were marched up the length of the hall and brought to the foot of the stairs leading to the throne platform. Sperchias felt his heart beating in his chest and found it hard to breathe. He was terrified of what would happen next.

Opposite him was a young man, too young to be a full citizen in Sparta. He was handsome, with a high brow, a fine straight nose, dark brown eyes, and rich brown hair. He smelled of yew oil and incense. His eyes were outlined in black to make them larger; his lips were painted red. He wore a golden diadem, much heavier than Greek victory wreaths, which sat heavily on his brow. He also wore a gold collar made of multiple strands of gold woven together, alternating with strands of coral and lapis lazuli beads. Multiple gold bangles clattered on his wrists, and rings adorned every finger. His robes were of brightly dyed silk studded with golden bangles that shimmered and trembled when he moved.

"What is your name and station?" the young man asked Sperchias in a haughty voice.

Sperchias bowed his head respectfully and announced, "I am Sperchias, son of Aneristus, and my colleague is Bulis, son of Nicoles. We are full Spartan citizens, as our former king Demaratus can verify."

"Are you noblemen? Men of property?" Xerxes wanted to know.

"We are both," Sperchias assured him.

"Why did your king pick you to be slaughtered? Why you and not someone else?"

"Our king did not pick us or send us here," Sperchias answered.

"And could not have made us come if he had wanted to," Bulis added gruffly. "We are here of our own free will."

Xerxes' eyes shifted briefly to Bulis and then settled again on Sperchias. "If your king did not send you, why are you here?"

"As I said before: we are here to make reparation for the murder of your emissaries. To offer up our lives in payment."

"We do not understand. Who sent you, if not your king?"

"Sparta has two kings, but the kings do not make policy. Sparta's citizens in Assembly make policy. It was the Spartans that killed your ambassadors, and the Spartans who make reparations, not our kings."

"The Spartans—collectively." Xerxes sounded skeptical, or was it contemptuous?

"Yes."

"And why did they *collectively* choose you?"

"They did not; we chose ourselves," Sperchias insisted, but, because Xerxes looked as if he did not understand, Bulis added, "Have you never heard of volunteers? Does no one in your Empire ever do anything of his own free will?"

Xerxes raised his eyebrows and his expression lifted somewhat, as if he were intrigued, even pleased. "You volunteered to come here and offer yourself as sacrifices?"

"Yes," Sperchias and Bulis said in unison.

"Ah." Xerxes leaned back in his throne, and his eyes shifted from one to the other. Then he looked up at the older man behind his throne and smiled slightly. "Very interesting. So you will accept any sentence we decree?"

"Our lives are yours to do with as you please."

"You are either very brave men, or very stupid. Do you not know the punishment for crimes against the Great King?"

"King of the Medes," Sperchias began, "we have heard that your father instituted many very wise laws, one of which was that no man should be put to death for only one crime, but always given a second chance—" Xerxes drew a breath to answer, but Sperchias kept talking, "but we know this does not apply to us, because what the Spartans did was not a crime but an offense against the Gods. Also, we have heard that men who speak against you have their tongues twisted out of their mouths, and men who give false witness have their eyes burned out with hot pokers. We know that men caught spying have their ears cut off and then spikes are pushed into their ears until their eardrums bleed out of their heads, while those who rise up in rebellion against you have their skin cut off from their living bodies and are then hung up to feed the flies. We have not heard the specific punishment for men who kill the personal representatives of the Great King, but we presume," Sperchias glanced once at Bulis and continued, "that it is terrible."

Xerxes considered the men before him, his eyes again shifting from one to the other. Then he nodded once and spoke in a loud voice, pitched at the chronicle of history rather than the men in the room. "Then hear the sentence of the Great King. The King of the Persians and the Medes, of the Parthians, Babylonians, Elamites, Scythians, Indians, Egyptians, Armenians, Arabians, Nubians, Ionians, Cretans, and many other peoples, Xerxes son of Darius, will not sink to the level of beasts who murder ambassadors in violation of the laws of civilized men. The Great King will *not* do that very thing for which he holds your countrymen in abject contempt. Nor will he"—Xerxes' voice was getting louder, whether for greater effect or because he was genuinely agitated—"nor will he, by taking reprisals on two brave yet insignificant sacrificial lambs, absolve the Spartans of the blood guilt for their crime. You *cannot* make reparation—brave and noble as your gesture may be—you *cannot* save your fellow citizens from the punishment they deserve—and will reap!

"So, remain as long as you wish in my capital. My servants and treasury are at your disposal. You will want for nothing as long as you wish to remain my guests, and when you wish to return, you will be escorted by a company of cavalry who will see to your safety and comfort.

"But take this message back to Sparta—her kings and her citizens alike: Sparta is *not* yet absolved of its barbarous crime, and has *yet* to pay the price of offending the law of civilized nations."†

† Herodotus records that this was the fate of the Spartans Sperchias and Bulis, who were sent to Xerxes to atone for the murder of the Persian ambassadors.

Chapter 16

DEFENDERS OF SPARTA

The Feast of the Dioskouria, in honor of the Divine Twins, was one of Sparta's most sacred holidays. However, because it fell after the autumn equinox, when travel was uncertain, it was not well known outside of Lacedaemon and was rarely attended by strangers. In consequence, it was a more domestic festival than the Hyacinthia, Karneia, and Gymnopaedia, but no less important in Spartan eyes.

The Dioskouria traditionally followed the end of the Phouxir, and was an opportunity to celebrate the successful graduation of a class of little boys to the status of youths. It also anticipated the winter solstice, when a class of eirenes would graduate to citizen status. The five-day holiday celebrated the most important deeds of the Divine Twins and culminated in a torchlight sacrifice at Kastor's Tomb, conducted by the reigning kings. Events included singing and dancing to mark the birth of the twins and their sister Helen, equestrian events in honor of Kastor, boxing to honor Polydeukes, and a day-long boar hunt culminating in an outdoor feast on the banks of the Eurotas. Throughout the holiday, special pear pastries and a pear cider were consumed in large quantities. All in all, the Dioskouria was one of Sparta's most pleasant festivals.

The atmosphere this year was mixed. The summer festivals had been celebrated hardly at all. Word of the fever had spread and the foreign visitors stayed away, while the Lacedaemonians themselves were either mourning the dead, tending the ill, recovering from the fever, or terrified of catching it. The summer sporting events had been canceled for lack of competitors, and the choruses' singing and dancing were decimated by losses.

But by late summer, about the time when Sperchias and Bulis should have reached Susa, the fever stopped claiming new victims. After that only a handful of deaths occurred among those already infected. By the fall equinox, everyone who had survived had recovered. Sparta had lost almost 12 per cent of all school-aged children and 4 per cent of the adult population, but the wrath of the Gods appeared to have abated.

The agoge reopened, and all active army units returned to barracks. Even the Phouxir went ahead, albeit somewhat shortened. Elections were held for next year's ephors and to replace three Council members who had died of the fever, including Leonidas' mentor and old friend Nikostratos.

By the time the Dioskouria arrived, some people felt a need to celebrate lavishly, while a minority, particularly the parents of the dead children, still mourned. A majority argued that it was only appropriate to honor the Divine Twins wholeheartedly, because they had again proved their affection for their homeland—as demonstrated by the fact that the Agiad twins, Leonidas and Cleombrotus, had come through the ordeal unscathed, while Leotychidas had been touched and scarred by the illness.

This had the effect of increasing the standing of both Agiads, while diminishing Leotychidas' already weak position even further. People started to say openly that Demaratus must have been the rightful king, while Leotychidas had merely benefited from—and possibly instigated—the sacrilegious bribing of the oracle at Delphi. Some of Brotus' followers—particularly Talthybiades, who had been elected to one of the vacant seats on the Council—hinted that Leotychidas ought to be deposed and exiled *not* so that Demaratus could return, but in order to give his place to Brotus. This faction argued that no one could be *certain* Leonidas was the elder twin, and that before Sparta's fate was left to two usurpers, it would be better to put Brotus on the "vacant" Eurypontid throne.

"You'd better win the boxing today," Brotus warned his firstborn son bluntly, as the pair set out from their kleros on the second day of the Dioskouria. The first day of the Dioskouria had been marked by sacrifices and women's choral singing to celebrate the birth of the twins and Helen, but the second day celebrated the voyage of the Argo and was marked by boxing contests in honor of Polydeukes. "It looks like I'll be king soon, and that makes you the heir apparent, but you don't act like one! You haven't won a damn thing since Artemis Orthia," Brotus complained. "You're lazy, that's what you are! And you lack ambition, too—just like my jackass brother, Leo."

Pausanias glanced resentfully at his father, noting with inner relish the little rolls of excess flesh that pushed their way out at the armholes and along the lower rim of his father's breastplate. His father had somehow managed to squeeze himself into the bronze, but the excess flesh had to find somewhere to go, and formed a pudgy, fleshy rim to the sleek-looking metal case. In answer to his father's words, Pausanias remarked as if surprised, "For such an unambitious man, Uncle Leo has gone far. As for the boxing, you know it isn't my sport. I don't have the—ah—head for it."

"If you don't want your head hurt, then use your fists better!"

"Oh, is that how you got a broken jaw at Olympia?"

"Don't be impudent!" Brotus barked. "Or I'll give you a lesson in manners."

"Ah, yes, of course. That'll be what was missing up to now," Pausanias answered sweetly.

"You're trying my patience, boy!" Brotus grabbed his son's upper arm and spun him about to make him stand face to face with his father. Brotus' face was red with agitation and his eyes glinted in fury.

But Pausanias was half a head taller now, and he stared his father down. "Just what exactly do you plan to do, father?" Pausanias asked, his lips curling in more of a snarl than a smile.

"Why, you—" Brotus cocked his balled fist to strike his son, as he had so often in the past, but Pausanias was faster. He caught his father's forearm in midair and held it arrested there. For a moment they were frozen in this pose, Brotus struggling with all his might to complete the blow, and Pausanias warding it off. Then Brotus tried an underhanded punch at Pausanias' stomach, but again Pausanias anticipated the blow, stepped lightly aside, and then spun about, twisting his father's arm behind his back.

"I've had enough of your lessons, old man!" Pausanias told him in a low, ominous voice. "Do *you* get the message, or do I have to underline it?" As he asked this, he twisted Brotus' arm ever harder.

Brotus clamped his jaw shut and gritted his teeth. His eyes met his son's with a look between hatred and defiance. The blood was flooding his face, and his veins seemed close to bursting, but his eyes said he would not back down. Father and son confronted each other for another couple of seconds, and then Pausanias realized he wasn't willing to risk doing his father serious injury. He wasn't a citizen yet. There might be consequences. He slowly released his father and stepped back warily, out of range. Brotus drew a deep breath, their eyes locked.

"Do we understand each other better?" Pausanias ventured to ask at last, trying to cover his capitulation with bravado.

"I see you're not the son I wanted!" Brotus countered.

"Perhaps," Pausanias shrugged, a twisted smile on his face. "But whatever I am, you made me that!"

The third day of the Dioskouria commemorated the participation of the Dioskouroi in Herakles' hunt of the dangerous Kalydonian boar. The central event was a boar hunt led by the kings and guard, in which theoretically every able-boded Spartan male participated. As citizen numbers had grown over the years, however, such a hunting party became unwieldy. Nowadays, many citizens, particularly the older men who felt they couldn't keep up with the Guard, went off in small groups to hunt on their own. The objective was to bring in as much game as possible to lay on the altar of the Twins. After the hearts and livers of the game had been given to the Divine Twins, what was left of the carcasses was taken down to the Eurotas and the meat roasted over open fires for a collective feast.

Preparations began almost as soon as the hunting parties departed. Under the direction of the syssitia cooks, the helots brought, chopped, and stacked firewood in long trenches beside the Eurotas north of Amyclae. When, shortly after midday, the trophies of the day's hunting started to arrive, the syssitia cooks hung the carcasses up to bleed, while other preparations for a collective feast continued energetically. Barrels of onions, carrots, and cabbage were collected near the roasting trenches, where the first fires were lit under massive cauldrons. Freshly baked bread and pear pastries were brought on carts from bakeries in the city. Amphorae of wine and pear cider were brought from Amyclae, and spring water was carted down from the springs of Taygetos. In addition, hundreds of tables and benches were hastily constructed. These would be dismantled and the wood used for other purposes as soon as the feast was over, but for one night they needed enough tables and benches for almost ten thousand people.

As a skilled carpenter, Pantes did not usually waste his time with this kind of work, but there was money in it. Since his workshop now employed seven trained and three apprentice carpenters, he didn't need to do the work himself in order to profit from it.

Pantes allowed his nephews Pelops and Kinadon to come along as water boys for the carpenters. Their mother was trying to convince him to let Pelops apprentice with him, but Pantes preferred the sons of strangers, knowing he could never treat his nephew the same way he did the others. Still, Chryse could be persuasive, pointing out that her sons had no future on the kleros as long as Polychares and Melissa had living sons, and noting (correctly) that other helot craftsmen were reluctant to give apprenticeships to the sons of a Spartiate father. The boys enjoyed being in the midst of the excitement, so much so that they forgot their duties more than once and had to be forcefully reminded of it by Pantes or one of his men.

By late afternoon most of the tables and benches were finished, and the air smelled of the stew bubbling in the cauldrons. The first deer, wild goats, and hares were spitted and turning over the trench to roast. The hunters themselves, having delivered the game, went to wash, change, and collect their families before returning, but well before dusk the men who had been out at dawn and had brought in the first trophies were gathering. They arrived with their wives, their children, and sometimes an aging parent. Since the agoge was closed for the holiday, even school-aged boys were with their families.

By dusk people were streaming in. Matrons carried smaller children on their hips, grandparents held young children by the hand, youths and maidens flirted openly, and the men were exuberantly exchanging accounts of the day's hunt as the scent of roasting kid, pig, venison, and hare mingled with that of smoke, hot oil, and cooked onions.

Pelops sat astride one of the benches his uncle's men had made earlier in the day and explained to his wide-eyed younger brother Kinadon, "... and it was on a night just like this that Aristomenes and a companion slipped across Taygetos from Messenia. They were dressed all in white with golden headbands with bright stars on them, and they rode pure white horses!" Pelops narrated. "It was getting dark, just like this, but a moon was rising," he continued, pointing unnecessarily to the far side of the Eurotas. "And the light of the moon made Aristomenes and his companion on their white horses stand out in the darkness. Aristomenes was tall with long, golden hair," Pelops explained to his awestruck younger brother. "And his companion looked just the same—like twins, you see?"

"Leonidas doesn't look like Brotus," Kinadon protested.

"That's different!" Pelops retorted, dismissing the annoying interruption. "The Divine Twins looked so much alike that mortals couldn't tell them apart. And from a distance, Aristomenes and his friend looked just the same. When the Spartans saw these two beautiful youths on white horses riding along the side of Taygetos, they thought they were the Divine Twins come back to life!" Pelops started giggling. "The Spartans threw themselves down on their knees, and started worshiping Aristomenes of Messenia as if he were a god! And so he and his companion rode closer and closer, and the Spartans were so dumb they still didn't see through his disguise. So he rode right in among them and then jumped down and started—"

Pelops was cuffed so hard on the back of his head that he nearly fell off the bench. Reeling, he turned to see who had delivered the blow, and came face to face with his father. "Since when do you tell tales of Aristomenes of Messenia?" Temenos demanded. Then, without giving his son a chance to answer, he added, "Aristomenes was a coward! A man who preferred to attack unarmed women and children. A man who attacked by night and in disguise. A man who impersonated Gods and raped priestesses! Where did you learn to admire such a creature? If Pelopidas has been telling such tales—"

"Temenos!" Chryse hissed, coming up beside him. "Not so loud! You're attracting attention. Of course my father didn't tell them about Aristomenes. They hear it from their friends."

"What friends? Laconian helots don't idolize Aristomenes."

"There are plenty of Messenians here, Temenos, working as attendants, or in the workshops and stores and factories. Aristomenes appeals to some Laconian helots, too—"

"You mean because he fought us?"

"Yes, it's only natural—"

"Natural? Natural to admire a man who kidnapped girls, raped priestesses, and impersonated the Dioskouroi? Why do you think he lost the war despite all his tricks?" he demanded of his sons, but he did not give them a chance to answer. Instead, he declared himself, "Because the Gods were offended by his impious behavior!"

"Yes, Temenos," Chryse tried to calm him. "Of course. Come along, boys. It's time to go home."

The boys had long since gotten to their feet, expecting this, and yet something got into Kinadon and he burst out angrily: "Why can't we stay? Why do we have to hide? Everybody knows about us! What more can they do to you after making you walk around naked with a dead—" It was his mother who hit him to shut him up, but his father's face was enough to make him wish she had killed him. His father hadn't known they knew....

The equestrian events on the fourth day of the Dioskouria included horse and chariot racing. One of the favorite events was a two-horse chariot race in which Spartan maidens drove light chariots in competition. Over the years it had become customary for the sweethearts of the maiden charioteers to gallop alongside their favorite's team, cheering and urging on the horses. Gorgo had hated the event as a maiden because she didn't have a sweetheart, and though she was sure she could have won the race itself, she was ashamed to advertise her lack of popularity by competing.

Agiatis, however, was so excited by the event that she immediately rushed to the barn calling, "Pelops! Pelops! You've got to cheer me on this afternoon!" Agiatis was entered in the junior races for girls under the age of fourteen, which entailed driving a pony in front of a two-wheeled cart from the Menelaion to Kastor's tomb.

When Agiatis burst into her father's stables, Pelops was in Elephant's stall, brushing the last traces of stable stains from the gray's hocks. (Leonidas was racing the horse himself in the last event of the day.) Pelops paused to look over the stall door at Agiatis, perplexed. "Of course I'll cheer you—even if you won't see me behind all the crowds of *Spartiates*." He spat out the last word as if it tasted foul in his mouth.

Agiatis was too fixated on her race to notice his tone of voice and insisted, "I mean on horseback. You can ride Red!" she decided. "He's fast enough to keep up and—"

"I can't ride Red in competition!" Pelops interrupted her. "I'm just a *helot*—"

"Not in competition!" Agiatis corrected, annoyed by how dense he was being. "Just to cheer me on, in my race."

Pelops was starting to understand. "You mean, as if I were your sweetheart?"

"Well, you are, in a way," Agiatis rationalized. "I'm not old enough to have a sweetheart, and you're my best friend."

"No, I'm not. I'm one of your Dad's *helots*!" Pelops told her bitterly. Agiatis just stared at him, baffled. For her, nothing had changed. Pelops was compelled to add cruelly, "I'm not your *friend*. Helots and Spartiates can't be *friends*."

"But we always have been!" Agiatis protested. "And what about your parents?"

"They're stupid! Stupid idiots!" Pelops shouted at her, all his anger and frustration exploding out of him.

One of Pelops' cousins, a son of Melissa and Polychares, looked over the edge of the loft where he was stacking hay and rebuked Pelops sharply. "Don't talk like that!"

"Why not?" Pelops called back furiously. "It's a lot nicer than what your Mom calls mine!"

"What the hell's got into you?" his cousin asked, and Pelops threw the curry comb down and stormed out of the stables.

Agiatis went to her mother. "Mom? Why is Pelops so angry at me?"

Gorgo was preparing to watch the afternoon events, and she was surprised to see Agiatis in the house rather than down in the stables getting her pony ready. "Agiatis! Is your pony ready? And the cart?"

Agiatis frowned. "I don't care about them or the race! Why is Pelops so angry?"

Gorgo took a deep breath. Although used to Agiatis' sudden shifts of mood, she was annoyed by her lack of constancy. Then, on second thought, Pelops *was* more important than a race, and she had to applaud her daughter's instinctive priorities. She let out her breath and said slowly, "Pelops got in trouble with his father yesterday for telling a story about the Messenian rebel Aristomenes as if he admired him. I expect that is what has upset him."

"But what does that have to do with *us*?" Agiatis wanted to know. "Why can't we be friends anymore, just because he told a stupid story?"

"It's not about a story, Agiatis. Aristomenes is the national hero of the Messenians. By identifying with them, he was declaring himself an enemy of Sparta," Gorgo tried to explain.

"But that's silly. How can he be an enemy of Sparta when he *is* Spartan?"

"But he's not. That is, he's not Spartiate. He's a helot."

"But what's wrong with being a helot?"

"A helot isn't free, Agiatis. A helot belongs to the Lacedaemonian state."

"I thought we all did," Agiatis countered.

Gorgo had to stifle the desire to laugh as she heard her husband speaking through her daughter. "We all *serve* Lacedaemon," she corrected, "but we are free and the helots are state slaves."

"So what?"

"Well, they have to work, and aren't allowed to leave Lacedaemon except when accompanying a Spartiate. They cannot be soldiers or priests or hold office or—"

"Gorgo!" It was Leonidas. He was standing at the door. "What's taking you so long? Agiatis, what are you doing here? Are your pony and cart ready?"

"I'm not going to race," Agiatis told her father, frowning.

"Why not?" he asked, astonished. She had been talking about this race for weeks, practicing each day with a dogged determination that bordered on fanaticism.

"Because Pelops says he won't cheer me because we can't be friends anymore because he's a helot and I'm Spartiate." Agiatis sounded indignant.

Leonidas glanced at his wife and their eyes met. He forgot his hurry and went down on his heels before his daughter. "That is a very hard lesson, I know, sweetheart." Agiatis looked infinitely beautiful to him in that moment. She had the soft, unblemished skin of a child. Her golden eyes were bright and wide-set. Her hair was fine and silky, her red lips soft and moist.

"But why can't we be friends?" Agiatis wanted to know.

"Only equals can be friends," Leonidas answered simply.

Agiatis frowned at him. "But that's not fair! We've been friends up to now. What's changed?"

"Pelops has learned his place in the world—and he doesn't like it."

"Why not?"

"Because he is bright and strong and thinks he could be more than he will be allowed to be."

"Why can't he be what he wants to be?"

Leonidas drew a deep breath and glanced again at his wife. She could only lift her hands in helplessness. "Agiatis, it is just like you and your mother not being able to become king. You are women and can't be soldiers and kings, and Pelops is a helot and can't become a soldier either. Are you really sure you don't want to compete? If I come help you with your pony, would you change your mind?"

Leonidas had said the right thing. "Oh! Would you? Let's hurry!" Agiatis was off before Leonidas could even get to his feet again. He looked at his wife and she just shook her head, then reached for her himation to wrap around her head and shoulders.

Out in the stables, Agiatis had already taken her pony out of his stall and tied him up in the middle of the aisle so she could pick out his feet. She worked with sudden, frantic urgency, and Leonidas wordlessly helped her, but he was wrong if he thought she had forgotten Pelops. As soon as she finished with the hooves and was brushing straw from the pony's tail, she started again. "The kings aren't equals with anyone, either. Does that mean you can have no friends?"

"In a way, yes. The kings have to uphold the law. So, you see, even though I like Temenos very much, and Chryse and their boys, because he broke the law by not marrying before the age of thirty, I had to let him get punished."

"Isn't Uncle Alkander a friend?"

Leonidas drew a deep breath. "We have been friends ever since we were little boys. Before I was king. But if he broke the law, then I would have to treat him like any other criminal, no matter how much it hurt me inside."

Agiatis burst out angrily, "I would rather *not* be king than have to betray my friends!"

The choral performance that evening struck a chord with the audience in a rare way. Somehow Euryleon had put together a program that acknowledged and honored the dead, but at the same time focused on new life. The story of Kastor was well suited to that, of course, and yet not every choral master could have pulled it off. The audience was given a chance to mourn, and Leonidas heard more than one person sobbing in the darkness behind him. Even Gorgo clutched his hand more tightly and dabbed at her eyes with her other. But then the maiden chorus came down the aisles of the amphitheater, singing lyrics about Helen guided home from Troy by the stars of her brothers in the night sky. Each girl was carrying an oil lamp and when they met in the center, they joined their lamps together to light a larger fire. They formed a circle and started to dance around it, soon joined by young men. The song was joyous, and the dancers, followed by the audience, started to clap in time. At the end, the audience broke out into thunderous applause.

Gorgo leaned to her husband to shout in his ear over the cheering, "Do you really think they have anything in Athens that can beat this?"

"It would be interesting to see, wouldn't it?" Leonidas answered, clapping vigorously and getting to his feet, taking the rest of the audience (obligatorily) with him.

Eventually, after Euryleon had taken many extra bows, the applause died away and the audience started to disperse for home. Leonidas and Gorgo lingered, waiting for a chance to talk to Euryleon, who was still surrounded by other well-wishers. They took no note of a minor commotion at the edge of the amphitheater.

Several men were moving the wrong way, pushing against the crowd toward the theater. Because of the darkness, people didn't always recognize them, but then someone exclaimed in a loud voice, "Bulis? Is that you?" Followed by: "Sperchias! The ambassadors! The ambassadors are back *alive*!"

Leonidas snapped his head around and saw Sperchias and Bulis break free of the stunned crowd, which had stopped dispersing to stare at the apparitions of two men they had thought dead. Had they been resurrected like Kastor himself?

Sperchias reached Leonidas first, and the words freed themselves of his lips as he sank down on his knees before his friend. "We failed!"

Leonidas stared at his friend in horror. Sperchias looked ten years older. His hair had gone white and had receded farther from his forehead. Beside him, Bulis looked powerful and young. Leonidas' gaze fell on the younger man with the unspoken question.

"He's right. We failed."

Around them the people who had been dispersing started whispering among themselves. Oliantus worked his way through the crowd to stand at Leonidas' elbow, conscientiously putting himself in a position to take any orders Leonidas gave. Dienekes approached from the other side with a handful of guardsmen, as if Sperchias and Bulis were foreigners and threats.

"What happened?" Leonidas demanded. "Didn't you reach Xerxes?"

"We reached him! That's the worst of it. We reached him, but he refused to accept our sacrifice!" Sperchias explained.

"He said he would not commit the same crime!" Bulis added bitterly. "And he sent us back to tell you that the crime has *not* been atoned for."

"But the fever has burned itself out!" someone in the surrounding crowd protested.

"Yes, the fever is gone!" another agreed nervously.

But fear was hovering tangibly in the air again.

Sperchias was gazing up at Leonidas with burning eyes. "We failed," he repeated.

Leonidas felt compelled to say, "You did *not* fail!" He reached down to pull Sperchias back to his feet, adding, "What does Xerxes know of the will of *our* Gods? Apollo was appeased by the gesture alone. He did not require your lives! He values you precisely because you were *willing* to die for our sakes. How else explain that the fever is gone?"

Sperchias let Leonidas lift him off his sore knees, but he shook his head. "It's not that simple," he exclaimed. "Remember the thousands of stars that fell from the sky? I'm convinced that the epidemic was only one of many calamities we will face."

"You're exhausted from a long trip," Leonidas countered. "Come back with me and tell me about everything."

"Teti," Sperchias drew attention to the patient Egyptian, "has kept a record of all we saw and heard, but I was also given these." As he spoke he dropped his leather satchel from his shoulder, reached inside, and removed a wooden writing tablet folded together. "From Demaratus," he declared, provoking a rustle of exclamations.

"You talked to a traitor?" Lysimachos asked indignantly, echoed by others.

Leonidas simply took the tablet and opened it warily. The face of the tablet was blank. "There's no message," he exclaimed, perplexed, holding it up for all to see.

Sperchias took a deep breath and explained, "I know. I don't understand. But that's what he gave me." He glanced at Bulis and Teti for support, and both nodded confirmation, while Bulis added gratuitously, "Ass-licking bastard!"

Teti spoke up at last to explain: "The former king brought the tablet to us personally just as we were preparing to depart. One of the Immortals tried to stop him from passing it to us, but seeing it was blank, he allowed it."

"Ah." The exclamation came from Gorgo.

Leonidas turned to look at her.

"I think," she ventured, "that if you scrape the wax *off* the tablet, you will find a message scratched into the wood underneath."

Leonidas hesitated only a second and then, drawing his knife, started scratching the wax away from the surface of the tablet. Oliantus, Bulis, and Sperchias looked over his shoulder as he worked. Bulis grunted first and Oliantus exclaimed more articulately, "The queen is right! There is a message underneath!"

Leonidas scraped at the wax more urgently, yet taking care not to scratch the message underneath. He frowned as he worked, and then held up the tablet toward the nearest torch, irritated by the poor lighting.

"What is it? What does he say?" the voices came from the back of the crowd—yet Gorgo, too, seemed to be holding her breath. Sperchias and Bulis stared at Leonidas' face, watching for the first indication of what he'd found.

"A warning," Leonidas finally announced. "A very blunt warning of Persian intentions." He snapped the tablet shut. "We will have to discuss this in Council and with the ephors—not here in the middle of the night or during the Dioskouria. Come!" He held the tablet firmly in his left hand, and with his right he took Gorgo's elbow. "Sperchias, Bulis, Teti, you are all welcome to join us." With his eyes he included Oliantus and Dienekes.

As he moved forward, the crowd fell back before him. Only Gorgo could feel his tension. She looked up at him, worried. Whatever had been in that warning, it had not been good.

Throughout the last day of the Dioskouria, Leonidas maintained a façade of cheerfulness and confidence. He went out of his way to honor and shower praise on Sperchias and Bulis, telling everyone that they had achieved their mission simply by their willingness to die. Apollo had been appeased, he insisted, and no one contradicted him. He was a descendant of Herakles. He was a priest to Zeus. Besides, everyone wanted to believe him. They wanted to believe that that the epidemic was over, never to return, that the Gods had forgiven them, that life could return to normal. Only Gorgo knew that Leonidas had not slept.

He had, of course, let her read the message Demaratus had scratched on the back of the tablet with his own hand. It was a promise of cataclysm—of destruction without hope of survival. Demaratus warned that the full might of Persia—not a single army under a Mede commander as at Marathon, not even an army under Xerxes himself, but a horde of armies (or should that be a pride of armies?), was collecting and preparing to descend upon Greece. Xerxes planned, Demaratus warned, not to punish but to obliterate, not to conquer but to enslave—just as Teti, too, had warned.

Gorgo had spent much of the night trying to convince herself that Demaratus was intentionally exaggerating. After all, he had every reason to hate the Spartans. Yet if things were as bad as he said, why should he warn them? Surely he would have been more interested in disguising the true state of affairs and gloating from the sidelines as Sparta was crushed.

But Gorgo could not convince herself of that. She had not known Demaratus well, but her grandmother had. Chilonis called him vain and overly proud, had deplored his temper and his inability to compromise, but had refused to believe he was a traitor. Meanwhile, Leonidas had considered it dishonorable for a Spartiate, let alone a former king, to sulk at the Persian court. But sulking was not the same thing as wanting to see Lacedaemon defeated, occupied, and enslaved. In short, Demaratus had many weaknesses, but he loved Lacedaemon and Sparta.

And that left only one interpretation of his message: that Demaratus sincerely believed the threat was as bad as he painted it, and he wanted to warn Sparta.

Maybe he thought if he warned Sparta, the Spartans would ask him back. Maybe he hoped the Spartans would offer him back his throne on the assumption he knew how to deal with the Persians.

If that had been his intention, he had miscalculated. They would not ask him back, Gorgo was sure of that. They would not ask him back, but they would ask Delphi what to do. Leonidas had already told Sperchias he must rest and prepare for the trip to Delphi. "There's no rush," he'd told the exhausted ambassador, "but we will have to see what Delphi says about this message before too long."

Sperchias nodded wearily, that look of already knowing that worse was to come settling on his prematurely aged face.

Now the crowd was gathering for the traditional end of the

Dioskouria, when the kings jointly offered a final sacrifice of a pure white bull to the Divine Twins. There were various theories on what the white bull symbolized, the most popular being that it represented the Minotaur, a sacrifice by Theseus of his greatest trophy to the Dioskouroi to placate their anger over his abduction of their sister Helen. Earlier in the day, wrestling matches had been held and the victors crowned by maidens dressed to represent Helen. These, too, commemorated the brothers' rescue of Helen from the rapacious Athenian king.

In ceremonies where Leotychidas had to make a joint appearance with Leonidas, the Eurypontid was always in a hurry to get things over with. Leonidas had learned to let him take the lead rather than fight him for primacy. Usually, Leotychidas sprinkled water on the bull's face and all but tossed the entrails on the flames, while Leonidas stood back and let him perform the rites in careless haste. Then, when he was done, Leonidas calmly and carefully performed his own rites, reassuring the populace by his composure and dignity.

On this occasion, too, Leotychidas flung the water at the bull so recklessly that the bull shied, rearing up his head and then shaking it so obviously that the crowd gasped. Leonidas waited for the helots to calm the bull, and then gently let water from the sacred spring at Delphi drip on to the thick white hair of the bull's brow as he made soothing sounds under his breath. The bull relaxed, then nodded his head in obvious consent. Leonidas was handed a knife, and he opened the jugular so rapidly that the bull hardly had a moment to even look surprised.

The experts stepped in to remove the heart and lungs of the powerful beast, and Leonidas and Leotychidas offered these to the Dioskouroi with prayers and an ode sung by the collected citizens. No sooner had the last notes of the ode died on the air than Leotychidas disappeared as usual, but Leonidas lingered by the altar as the crowd started to disperse.

Brotus couldn't stand the way his twin brother stood alone before the altar. Light from the two torches at the entrance to Kastor's tomb reflected off his bronze armor, making him look almost golden against the darkness. Most infuriating was the way the torchlight caught on his cross-crested helmet, the helmet reserved for Spartan kings. Brotus had worn such a helmet only for a single day, the day Leonidas returned so unexpectedly from Marathon to snatch it away from him. Brotus felt an almost physical craving to have the heavy helmet, with its white horsehair crest, on his own head again. He was so close—but now this message from Demaratus had sparked talk of recalling the deposed king and restoring him. It was crazy. Unfair.

And little Leo strutting about so pompously, as if he didn't know he was a usurper!

Brotus couldn't stand it a moment longer. He stepped up beside his twin brother and growled, "Except for being king, you're no better than the rest of us!"

Leonidas, startled out of his thoughts, turned and answered without pausing to think, "If I weren't better than you, I wouldn't be king."*

Brotus snarled back, "Piss off!" and ducked away into the darkness.

Gorgo watched him go warily. She knew Brotus' hate was undiminished, and she knew he would kill Pleistarchos if he could find a way to do it without being discovered. She also knew that there was no way to eliminate this threat short of killing Brotus, which was something neither she nor Leonidas was prepared to do—or to order. She stepped beside her husband. They were now almost alone. "Shouldn't we go home?" she asked softly.

"Not yet. Give me a moment," Leonidas answered, and slipped past the altar into Kastor's tomb.

The tomb was unlit except by the torches on the outside of the entrance. Leonidas had to stop just inside the door to let his eyes adjust. He sensed, more than saw, the statue of the mortal brother of Divine Helen and Divine Polydeukes in the darkness.

Brotus' words were ringing in his ears: "You are no better than the rest of us."

"But you can choose to be," a voice said very distinctly in the darkness.

Leonidas looked around. Had someone said that? No. It had just been a thought. It was also nonsense. Choose what?

"Choose to earn the highest privilege of all: immortality."

---

* Plutarch records this exchange without identifying by name the man who challenged Leonidas, saying he was "no better."

Leonidas held his breath, and every fiber of his body strained to see or hear the presence that was speaking. His eyes had adjusted to the darkness. He could clearly see even into the corners of the little temple. He was certain that no other living creature was here with him. Yet he was not alone. The Kouros smiled at him, his long curls hanging down his back and his hands raised in welcome. It was just a statue made by man, Leonidas knew that. But the Gods were known to inhabit inanimate objects when it suited them....

Leonidas answered the God mentally, afraid to speak: "My twin won't retrieve me from the underworld as yours did."

"He does not need to retrieve you," the Other insisted. "He is irrelevant. You alone decide your destiny."

"How?" Leonidas asked, incapable of imagining what he could do to gain the ultimate honor of life after death. He was acutely aware of his mortality, and if mortals could simply choose immortality, they *all* would.

"Earning immortality is harder than you think," the alien voice corrected his unspoken thoughts with a touch of amusement, before adding, "It requires selflessness rather than vanity, self-sacrifice rather than greed."

Leonidas shook his head doggedly in answer to the voice he did not dare contradict. He knew many humble men, good men, selfless men, and countless self-sacrificing wives and mothers, all of whom lay dead and buried now.

"Immortality lies beyond the grave," the disembodied voice continued patiently, "but only if you make the right choice."

Leonidas felt certain that he was encountering Kastor himself, the God to whom he had so often spoken in one-way conversations in the past. The God he had begged, promised, bargained with.... "What choice?" he asked cautiously.

"You must live to improve the condition of those in your care."

Leonidas nodded; he could—would—strive to do that.

But then the voice came again. "And die for a good purpose."

"What purpose?"

"You will know when the time comes."

"But—" Leonidas started, but he broke off his thought. The temple was abruptly cold. A gust of wind rushed in and swirled around inside, knocking over a tripod and temporarily dimming the torches at the door.

"Leo?" Gorgo called anxiously. "Are you all right?"

Leonidas knew Kastor was gone. He turned and went back outside. He put his arm around Gorgo and pulled her closer to him, kissing the top of her head, in need of her warmth and softness.

"Is everything all right?" she asked again.

"Fine. I have decided I must speak with our allies about a common defense against Persia. I think I will start with Corinth."

"May I come with you?" Gorgo asked, motivated by an irrational desire not to be separated from Leonidas for even a single month.

"Why not?" Leonidas answered. "We'll take Kallias home and bring Simonidas along—to cheer him up and show him a little of the world."

Chapter 17

A SPARTAN ABROAD

It was almost a quarter-century since Leonidas had first visited Corinth, and he could still vividly recall how fascinated and alienated he had been by the opulence, the noise, the gaudy colors.... Nor had he forgotten how intimidated he had been by the Corinthian polemarch Archilochos. On this first visit Leonidas had found him arrogant and ungrateful, though he had been a gracious host four years later.

Now he was a testy and aging man. His hair was completely white and thinning, his skin splotched and sagging. His finger joints were disfigured with knobs of excess calcium that made them claw-like. "I have resigned all my offices," Archilochos informed his guest irritably. "I've had enough of all the bickering! I'm fed up with it!"

Leonidas glanced at Lychos, inwardly alarmed. He needed Corinth, and he had always counted on his friendship with Corinth's leading citizen to help him get what he wanted. He asked anxiously, "Has Lychos succeeded you, then?"

"No, no," father and son spoke at the same time. Lychos added, "I have no political ambitions," while his father protested indignantly, "Damned fools don't think a cripple can be a polemarch—though you witnessed with your own eyes what a fighter the boy is!"

"I owe my life to your son, sir," Leonidas agreed earnestly.

"But they treat him like he was worthless! They—"

"Calm down, father! We can't blame them for wanting a more vigorous polemarch."

"But they could at least have elected you archon!" Archilochos countered indignantly.

"Could have, but the craftsmen complain we landowning merchants do not represent their interests. They say we favor agriculture over manufacturing, and that we ship owners make as much money carrying Athenian goods as Corinthian ones." Turning to Leonidas, he explained, "The manufacturers feel the landowning merchant class has not done enough to keep Athenian products out of the Peloponnese—and they are now powerful."

"We should never have given them the vote!" Archilochos fumed.

"Then they would have killed us all," Lychos countered, with a sad smile and a glance at Leonidas.

"Some of these new citizens can't even read or write!" Archilochos ranted.

"But they can calculate fast enough," Lychos pointed out. "They know what's happened to their profit margins in the last two decades."

"But isn't that attributable to Persian dominance in the Aegean?" Leonidas asked hopefully. He needed allies against Persia, not men angry with their own leaders.

"Not really," Lychos answered for his father. "Persian dominance in the Aegean has forced us to shift our trade to the west—above all, to Sicily. There are good profits to be made there, too, but our manufacturers are facing increasing competition from Athenian pottery and from Lacedaemonian bronze work." He ended with a smile and a bow of his head to Leonidas.

"What if I told you the Persian emperor plans to invade the Peloponnese?" Leonidas asked.

Archilochos snorted and snapped, "Let him try!" but Lychos met Leonidas' eyes and nodded. "I've heard similar rumors. They say he has built a fleet of a thousand ships."

"A figure of speech!" Archilochos scoffed. "Comes from Homer."

"He crushed the Egyptians," Leonidas pointed out.

"They were never fighters," Archilochos dismissed the Egyptians.

"You need to talk to Adeimantus, son of Ocytus," Lychos answered Leonidas. "We can invite him to a symposium tomorrow or the next day."

"I don't like the man!" Archilochos told his son, frowning. "A petty man. A man whose hands smell of wet clay!"

"He made his money with tiles—virtually all the painted, glazed tiles you see on temples and houses in the city came from his factory. But he has the ear of the ordinary citizens."

"He only has property because he divorced his wife to marry his cousin's heiress," Archilochos reminded his son.

"His means of obtaining property is not important. He has property and he was elected archon."

"The man doesn't know the bow from the stern on a trireme," Archilochos scoffed.

"But he knows how to convince other men to man our triremes. You need to talk to him, Leo."

Later, after his father had gone to bed and the youths had slipped out for a night on the town, Lychos suggested to Leonidas that they drink a last cup together. Leonidas knew Lychos was a moderate drinker and that this had nothing to do with more wine. He waited.

Lychos craned to watch his father's progress from the door of the andron. Only after his father disappeared from the landing on the next floor did he turn his attention back to Leonidas and urge, "Go to Athens, Leo."

"Athens? We've been at war with them four times in my lifetime."

"Yes, but they will fight Persia, and they have forty thousand citizens. That's more than Lacedaemon and Corinth together."

"But only ten thousand hoplites," Leonidas demurred.

"That's still twice what Sparta or Corinth can field separately. Furthermore, Aegina's aggression has provoked Athens into building more triremes. Last I heard, the Athenians had nearly sixty. That's slightly more than Corinth has nowadays. Last but not least, they've struck silver—a huge amount of it. My elder boy, Agathon, wrote me about it. He says there's more silver than anyone thought possible in a single lode. All Athens is arguing about what to do with it. There's a risk they will simply divvy it up among themselves, squander it to make the hoi polloi happy. It would be far better spent to complete the walls they started to build around Piraeus before Marathon. Or to outfit hoplites at city expense, as Sparta does. If you tell them what you have told us, maybe they will wake up to the danger and stop thinking everything was decided seven years ago at Marathon."

Leonidas did not have positive memories of Athens. He remembered it as crowded, chaotic, filthy, and unjust. He thought of how the Thespian scholar Ibanolis had been reduced to slavery simply for not paying his taxes, and he thought of the shabby treatment Miltiades had received from the Athenian assembly.

"You could stay with Aristides," Lychos coaxed. "He is a good and honest man."

"With Gorgo?" Leonidas questioned provocatively.

Lychos was taken aback. He would not dream of taking his wife out of the safety of her house, much less traveling with her to another city. It was one thing for Leonidas to bring her here; she had met him during his visit to Sparta, and Leonidas and he were old friends. Taking her to Athens would be entirely different. Cautiously he asked, "Are you sure you want to expose her to the risks and hazards of such a journey? Besides, Gorgo must be anxious to return to her children."

"The children are in the agoge. Gorgo is curious about the rest of the world. If I go to Athens, she will accompany me, but I question the utility of such a trip. The Athenians are notorious for not listening to anyone. They do not even listen to their *own* leaders for very long. Someone once described them to me as a school of fish that changes direction in a split second for no apparent reason."

Lychos laughed at the apt image, but then grew serious and urged, "Leo, Athens is the most important power in Hellas—after Lacedaemon, of course. If we want to have a chance against the might of Persia, we must fight together."

Leonidas sighed. Whether he liked it or not, Lychos was right. "All right, I'll go—eventually."

Lychos shook his head. "You must reach Athens before the end of the Lenaia. That's when they will hold an Assembly to vote on the silver. Right now the Athenians can think of nothing but theater, but thirty days from now they will start thinking about that silver, and everyone will want to get their hands on it. If you wait until next year or even next spring, it could be too late. I could put a ship at your disposal if you want."

"No offense, but a Spartan king cannot travel to Athens aboard a Corinthian ship. It would make me look dependent at best, and ridiculous at worst. I'll send for one of my own."

When word reached the Spartan fleet at its home base of Gytheon that King Leonidas required a trireme in Corinth, the duty vessel was launched at once. Although this was not the sailing season and merchant vessels kept to the safety of their harbors (if they weren't pulled up on the beach for repairs and maintenance), triremes were built to take any weather, and the trip along the coastline to Corinth entailed little danger. Because of a heavy east-northeast wind, however, the trireme turned west and set all sail, with the obvious intention of sailing westward around the Peloponnese.

Eurybiades watched it until it was out of sight, and then called his crew together. His crew now numbered two hundred men; for taking Sperchias and Bulis safely to Persia and back, Eurybiades had been rewarded with command of Sparta's newest trireme, the *Minotaur*. In fact, he had been charged with overseeing the construction and with recruiting the crew, at Leonidas' personal orders and expense. Eurybiades had chosen to use the shipyard at Skandia, and the keel had been laid down only six months earlier. The launch had taken place barely a fortnight ago, and the *Minotaur* had not yet completed her sea trials.

But Eurybiades was an ambitious and impatient man. He had already hired the bulk of his penteconter crew, and many of the other oarsmen were local men from Kythera. He was willing to take a chance. With the wind whipping his long black braids and trying to drag his himation right out of his hands, he put his proposal to the crew collected in a curious group around him.

"King Leonidas requires a trireme in Corinth. The duty vessel has departed, heading west. It will take two days by that route. If we can row through the Malean Straits, we can beat them by as much as a day and be the first ship to respond to the king's summons." Eurybiades did not need to say that rowing against the northeasterly gale would be exhausting; even the least experienced among them knew that. He chose not to stress that it would also be extremely dangerous.

They would have a mountainous lee shore licking its chops the whole voyage north, and they would also be crossing the Gulf of Argos, the lair of Sparta's most tenacious foe. While it was not likely that Argive warships would be prowling around at this time of year, they could not exclude the possibility. A prudent man would not suggest this voyage, not with an untried ship and crew.

Eurybiades was not prudent; he was driven by the desire to prove what he could do. It was the kind of competitive instinct that drove other men to athletic feats or to climb mountains or explore the unknown. But Eurybiades also knew that he could achieve nothing with an unwilling or frightened crew. He knew that he had to sweep them up in his own enthusiasm. With his old crew, that would have been no problem. Even now, his helmsman of nearly a decade was asking rhetorically with a deep growl, "Why are we wasting time? Let's launch the bloody boat."

But Eurybiades wasn't worried about the men from his penteconter, nor about the perioikoi deck hands and marines. They would not bear the brunt of the hardships. It was the 170 men who manned the oars who had to be willing to fight a running gale. And more than half these men were helots.

Eurybiades had initially concentrated his recruiting on Kythera, talking to the sons of fishermen, men often too poor (after surrendering half their catch to their masters) to support a family. But he had not found nearly enough men to man a trireme, so the remaining oar-banks had been filled with country lads who streamed down to Boiai, where he put in with a ship still smelling like a lumberyard and nearly one hundred vacancies at the oars.

Eurybiades focused on Hierox, his bosun or rowing master, the *keleustes*. Hierox was a burly man with a full black beard that looked permanently salt-soaked. He too was a Kytheran, a perioikoi who had kicked around on foreign ships for half a lifetime before attaching himself to Eurybiades like a barnacle. They had been inseparable ever since, a team that could make even a half-rotten penteconter a dangerous pirate with the help of marines like Prokles.

To this man had fallen the main responsibility for sorting the wheat from the chaff as the country bumpkins, still stinking of the barnyard and literally unable to tell stem from stern, streamed in looking for a berth. To him had fallen the even more difficult task of trying to make seamen of these farm lads. Eurybiades knew that this man would sail into Hades itself with him—but only if he thought the crew was up to it. Eurybiades found himself regretting his own impulsiveness. He should have consulted Hierox first.

Hierox seemed to be thinking the proposition through carefully. He looked up, sniffed the wind, and squinted at the breakers, which were rolling into the bay in stately rows to dissolve with a roar and hiss on the long beach. Then at last he asked dubiously, "What happens once we reach Corinth?"

Eurybiades understood his concerns. Taking such a green crew on this voyage was only half the danger. The other risk was that these eager farm lads, who had never before set foot outside their villages, would find themselves overwhelmed by the charms of a city like Corinth. They might desert (or get kidnapped by unscrupulous foreign captains) and leave the *Minotaur* short-handed in a foreign port.

"King Leonidas will board almost straight away and we will take him to his next destination, wherever that might be," Eurybiades answered. He opened his mouth to add that there would be no shore leave, but he didn't get the words out.

From the crowd of men standing in the blustering wind, a young voice asked, "The king himself will sail with us? King Leonidas?"

"Yes," Eurybiades confirmed, "so there'll be no—"

"Then let's go!" the voice called eagerly.

To Eurybiades' and Hierox's surprise, this suggestion was met with a cheer and the shout, "For Leonidas!"

Without awaiting further orders, the men turned and ran to the trireme, which crouched on the sand with her snout pointed toward the white-capped bay. Eurybiades looked at Hierox, baffled, and Hierox looked at the men crowding around the trireme, only partially organized by the more experienced oarsmen. He shrugged. "For the first time in thirty Olympiads, they see prospects of a better future. To them, Leonidas isn't just a Spartan king—he's a liberator."

Eurybiades shrugged and turned his thoughts to more immediate concerns, but Prokles stood watching the launching of the trireme, his perpetual frown masking his thoughts.

Eurybiades and his helmsmen knew these waters intimately, and they made the most of prevailing currents to sail as far as possible until the moment came to turn right into the teeth of the gale and run out the oars. Eurybiades took the storm head-on, to avoid the corkscrewing that came from angling into the waves. The trireme, built for ramming, was heavily reinforced at the bow and shaped to send anything she pierced off to her sides. Her timbers were less likely to be strained by a frontal assault on the seas than by the twisting that came from slanting through them. Furthermore, by going dead into the wind, Eurybiades reduced the risk of shipping water through the open sides of the upper oar-decks, while hide coverings with a hole only for the oar kept the lowest oar-ports reasonably dry.

When they started rowing, the crew at first sang, something Hierox had taught them to do to help keep them synchronized, but the wind proved too strong. Within minutes they needed all the air they could suck into their lungs just to breathe. The aulos alone kept time.

The bronze-sheathed ram smashed through the waves, flinging great plumes of water twenty feet into the air. The water fell back on the foredeck like violent rain showers, driving sailors and marines aft. The timbers of the vessel shuddered and trembled, frightening the inexperienced crewmen, but the veterans were not concerned. They had watched like brooding hens as the keel of the *Minotaur* was laid down and day for day as the ship had taken shape in the yard at Skandia. They knew the men who had fashioned her out of wood and the priests who had blessed her at her launch. Her prow had been soaked in the blood of a sacrifice to Poseidon at Dragonara, and she had been dedicated to him. They trusted her.

By midafternoon some of the crew were nearing the end of their strength. From the deck, their increasingly unsynchronized rowing betrayed their waning energy. Eurybiades looked anxiously over the sides, noting that now and then the oars clattered against one another. Some of the rowers on the lowest deck seemed hardly able to lift their oars out of the water anymore, and each time an oar hit a wave on the back-stroke it acted like a brake on forward progress. If he had been a nervous man, Eurybiades would have started to look anxiously at the shoreline or started praying.

Instead, Eurybiades turned command of the deck over to his mate and descended into the bowels of the ship, to the lowest tier of oars. Here, light and air filtered down from the decks above only through the gangways at bow and stern. The air was rank with the smell of sweat and urine and hung like a heavy cloud over the straining men. Eurybiades let his eyes adjust to the darkness, then swept his gaze along the two rows of men separated by the narrow walkway, thirty men per side. Their faces were strained. Some bit their lips, some gritted their teeth. Some grunted. Some blew out like long-distance runners at the end of a race. They all shone with sweat.

"You're all wishing you were back on the farm by now, no doubt," Eurybiades remarked with a laugh.

One or two of the men glanced up. Most didn't risk it.

Eurybiades started down the aisle between the men, his head swinging from side to side. He put a hand on a shoulder. "Take a break," he ordered. The youth looked up at him, disoriented. "Just ship your oar and catch your breath."

Eurybiades moved on, his head swinging back and forth until he found the next culprit. Again he put his hand on the man's shoulder and ordered him to rest. At the bow, he turned and started back down the aisle. Now they had their backs to him, but he could see even better who was having difficulty holding the rhythm and pace. Again he ordered the weakest to take a break.

Hierox appeared at the foot of the gangway in the stern. "Sir?"

"Just giving some of our landlubbers a rest."

Hierox nodded and handed a flask of water to the first man with a nod. "We need to bandage some hands as well," he told his captain, nodding toward a youth. Several of the unfortunate beginners had burst blisters on their hands that left streaks of blood on the oars. Eurybiades nodded and disappeared back up the ladder to the main deck to get bandages.

Meanwhile, even the experienced men on the upper tiers of oars had growling stomachs and were starting to glance out the open sides to judge their position. Others glanced at the deck over their heads, wondering when the order would come to stop pulling. Hierox had less tolerance for this and called out to them sharply, before returning to the lowest deck to tend to the youngsters with bloody hands.

"How much longer?" one youth dared to ask as Hierox bandaged his hands. Hierox thought it was the same helot who had been so naively enthusiastic about embarking on this dash into the teeth of a gale. He considered making a snide remark about being more cautious next time, but thought better of it. Did he want crewmen who shied away from a challenge? Instead he said gruffly, "That's for the captain to decide!" Then, relenting, he added, "But we've made good progress. Maleas is off our port quarter."

Sure enough, within the hour Eurybiades ordered the helm over and all sail set. The oars were shipped, and the oarsmen from the lowest, breathless tier were allowed on deck for fresh air and a meal. A meal of hard sausage and bread was also distributed to the other oarsmen while they sat at their benches. Quickly the mood turned positive, and soon the men started singing as they flew northward on close-hauled sails.

No one objected when Eurybiades asked for the men to take turns manning the upper tiers to add an extra knot or two to progress. As dusk fell, they had cleared the Kokoreli, and the wind was on their starboard quarter. It would have been more prudent to put ashore either at Troizen or at Aegina, but the crew had caught their captain's competitive fever, so they pressed onward through the night, relying on the following wind. A nearly full moon provided enough visibility to distinguish shore from sea. Late in the night they made out Epidauros, by the concentration of fires and torches that merged together in a large orange blur on the darkened coast. When the morning star rose over the high-curving stern-post, they glided with a dying wind into the harbor of Kenchrea, Corinth's port to the Aegean.

The crew was sent ashore to get a hot meal and rest on the sandy shore, while the marines kept watch over the vessel and crew. Eurybiades, however, combed out his hair and rebraided it. Then he changed into a red chiton and pulled on his armor before going ashore in search of Leonidas.

In the courtyard of Archilochos' residence, Leonidas was mounting in preparation for an excursion to Acrocorinth. The appearance of the dark sea captain in Spartan scarlet brought him up short. "Eurybiades! What are you doing here? I thought you were putting the *Minotaur* through her sea trials in the Gulf of Laconia."

"We put her through her paces rounding Maleas in the teeth of a nor'easter. She's awaiting your pleasure at Kenchrea."

"She's where?" Leonidas asked, astonished.

"Kenchrea."

The two men stared at each other. Eurybiades was cocky and obviously pleased with himself. But then again, he had a right to be. Leonidas overcame his disapproval of the impudent attitude and conceded, "Well done." Then he thought to ask skeptically, "You did that with a Lacedaemonian crew?"

"A half-helot crew, to be precise. They may not have salt water in their veins, but a whiff of freedom seems to have been sufficient to enable them to overcome even seasickness."

"But what does he *want* here?" Nicodemus, Athens' archon for the year, asked somewhat plaintively into the symposium.

"And with his wife! Whoever heard of such a thing?" Xanthippos added with a disapproving frown. "Why, she even attended a play yesterday!"

"Other women attend the tragedies," Kimon pointed out. "Even my mother likes to go."

"Maybe he's afraid that if he leaves her behind like Menelaos did, she might run away from him like a modern Helen!" This suggestion came with a laugh from Kallixenos, who could remember the youthful Leonidas from his last trip to Athens. "He's not much of a lover, I'm sure. More of a dry stick, I tell you. A prude and a man of ponderous intellect."

"And she's no modern Helen, either!" one of the younger men pointed out. "I hear she's quite plain, in fact. Brown like a slave and red-haired like a barbarian."

"I wouldn't say that!" another man protested at once. "I caught a glimpse of them going into the theater, and she was anything but ugly. Not even dowdy. She's as slim as a youth, with these long, shapely legs and a long neck and these *huge* eyes that look openly at the world. I'd give a tetradrachma to get her on my couch!"

That brought a roar of laughter from the others. "I can just see you, Pheidon!" someone declared, and Kallixenos teased with, "And what will Agido say when she hears that?"

"Agido is an expensive whore," Pheidon retorted, dismissing the object of last week's passion and provoking a new round of laughter. Agido was a professional courtesan, the former property of Kallixenos (who still took a cut of all her earnings). Pheidon had been infatuated with her for some time, and had recently been involved in an unseemly brawl because he wanted her "loyalty," but couldn't afford to pay for it.

"I'll tell her you said so," Kallixenos told Pheidon with a grin.

"Well, it's not as if it were something she didn't know!" Pheidon defended himself. "But the Spartan queen—"

"The Spartan king, not his immodest wife, is what should concern us!" replied Xanthippos, cutting short the conversation of the younger men. "Nicodemus is right to ask why he's come, and why now?"

"And why did he come by trireme, I wonder?" Kallixenos added. "The world knows the Spartans have some of the finest horses in the world—easy matches for the Persian stables. Leonidas himself was a halfway passable horseman," he admitted patronizingly. (As the commander of Athens' cavalry, Kallixenos thought Athenian horsemanship superior to any on earth.) "I've heard that Leonidas himself has a reputable stud, though it was Demaratus who won at Olympia—"

"We know all that!" Xanthippos cut him short, annoyed by the cavalryman's obsession with horses. "How he got here is of no importance. The question is why?"

"Maybe he just wanted to see our tragedies?" Pheidon suggested, harvesting laughter again. No one took Pheidon seriously.

"Well, we'll know more tomorrow," Nicodemus declared. "Aristides has invited *some* of us to an intimate symposium which, I presume, the Spartan king will attend."

"What about his wife?" Pheidon asked anxiously. "If she'll be there, I'll crash the party!"

"Don't be ludicrous. Of course she won't attend a symposium! She's a queen and Aristides' guest, not a flute girl!"

"And as Dionysus is my witness," Kallixenos groaned, "Aristides' symposiums are the driest, dullest affairs one can imagine. He's so boringly sober all of the time! What was the topic of the last one?" Kallixenos asked the room at large. "Cosmic influences on the life cycle of the grasshopper—or something like that."

They laughed, and the conversation turned to other things.

They had been in Athens five days, and Gorgo had been out in the city only twice: once in the company of her hostess to attend a ceremony on the acropolis with other women from the neighborhood, and once to attend the theater with Leonidas and their host. Their hostess, Eukoline, had emphatically refused to go to the theater, noting that too many "lewd women" lurked about and that one was never safe from "lecherous looks" even if completely veiled. Gorgo had been far too curious to let her hostess' warnings or her hosts' disapproval dissuade her, but the experience had been sobering. Despite Leonidas' presence, not to mention his escort of four guardsmen, she had attracted more attention than she enjoyed. In fact, the looks and her sense of being talked about had made it hard for her to concentrate on the play itself. In the end, she was glad to return home.

But that had been three days ago. After three days cooped up in the bowels of Aristides' house, where hardly a drop of sunlight penetrated, she'd had enough. By now, however, she knew it would be quite pointless to tell her hostess she was interested in seeing more of Athens. Eukoline was, like her husband, a very self-righteous person who believed that she knew exactly what was right and proper and had no tolerance for diverging opinions. According to her, a "good woman" never left her house except for weddings, funerals, or to honor the Gods. Working and shopping was for slaves, and everything else—from talking to fighting—was the exclusive preserve of men.

Not that Eukoline was stupid. She ran her household with an eagle eye for possible waste or theft. She locked the storerooms, the pantry, and the slaves up at night (to be sure the latter couldn't get up to any "hanky-panky"). She was the first to rise each day to let the slaves out again so they could go about their work. She was illiterate and innumerate, so she did not keep any books as such, but she seemed to have a sixth sense for possible malfeasance. Her sharp tongue discouraged the disobedience of slaves, children, and her husband alike. She was not a pleasant companion.

Gorgo had no intention of even mentioning to this formidable female dragon her desire to see more of Athens. Nor did she mention the matter to Leonidas. Leonidas would have felt compelled to accompany her or detail one of his guardsmen to escort her. But today he was going with the four of them to one of the famous gymnasiums outside the city walls for some sports event. It was important for him to go, to be seen, and to compete. It was almost as important for him to have the guardsmen with him, since they were young and could uphold the reputation of Lacedaemon in the event Leonidas, at forty-five, was no longer competitive.

Gorgo saw him off cheerfully, assuring him that she understood perfectly why she was not allowed to come along. "It would embarrass the Athenians that I'm so familiar with the naked male body—at least when I started making unkind comparisons to our own incomparable youth." Leonidas had laughed, kissed her, and then hesitated at the door to ask if she'd be all right. "I'll be bored to death—but I'll think of something," she answered. From the courtyard they heard Aristides asking what was keeping Leonidas, so he ducked out the door, leaving her behind without another word.

Gorgo was on her own to implement her plan. Or almost. She was not so foolish as to venture out into the maze of dirty, crowded, chaotic streets without a guide or a disguise. Her plan was dependent on the cooperation of the slave who had been put at her disposal. Eukoline had been shocked to find that Gorgo had traveled at all, of course, but doubly so to find she had come without a personal slave. She had then, hospitably, delegated one of the housemaids to see to Gorgo's needs, admonishing the girl to do absolutely everything the guest requested, before saying to Gorgo in the girl's presence: "She's a lazy slut, so you'll have to chase after her half the time, but it's the best I can do."

Gorgo had not yet found it necessary to chase after Uche. On the contrary, the black girl seemed fascinated by her and followed her about on silent feet, gazing at her in wide-eyed expectation of some order. At first Gorgo had found this unnerving, and she suggested that it was unnecessary. Uche's reply had disarmed her. "But you are a pharaoh! Taiwo told me so." (Leonidas had brought Taiwo along with them because of his gift with languages.)

Now Gorgo turned to the African and explained her desire to go out into the city of Athens. Uche's eyes widened. "Just the two of us," Gorgo insisted. "Not as a queen. I want to dress just like you, and go out as if we were two slaves on an errand."

"But, my lady, that would be humiliating!"

"No, Uche, it would be liberating. I'm not used to living inside in the dark. I'm used to walking in the open, even driving chariots. Taiwo tells me the African and Egyptian women are the same way."

Uche seemed to think about that for a moment, and then she nodded.

"You'll help me?" Gorgo asked uncertainly.

Uche nodded again and broke into a wide smile. With evident enthusiasm, she started helping Gorgo change out of her fine peplos into a simple striped chiton. Gorgo's woven gold belt with lion-head ends was replaced with braided twine. Her hair was combed back into a pony tail and clipped up on the back of her head with a wooden barrette. "What about your feet?" Uche asked as the rest of Gorgo's transformation was complete. "I don't own any sandals," the slave-girl admitted.

"I'll go barefoot."

Uche's eyes widened in shock.

"I went barefoot most of my childhood," Gorgo assured her, "and I go barefoot at home all the time. I'll be fine."

As they crossed the kitchen courtyard, Gorgo saw Prokles sitting on a bench sharpening his sword. She greeted him, asking, "Didn't you want to go to the gymnasium?"

"Why? To watch a bunch of lecherous old men ogle the white-skinned little boys of their neighbors? I've got more important things to do with my time!" Gorgo did not ask what, but simply bade him good day and followed Uche into the street.

Aristides' house stood in a narrow, unpaved alley lined by high walls. No windows opened onto the street, not even where the second story of a house crushed up against the wall to the street. Only the painted doorways, roof tiles, and trees that peered over the walls suggested that these were the homes of the affluent.

Uche led at an easy, long-legged pace, used to walking long distances, but Gorgo had little trouble keeping up. "What is it you want to see?" Uche asked as they approached a broader, paved thoroughfare that appeared to be an important artery of the city.

"The agora, for a start, and the bouleuterion, the library..."

Uche nodded and started to the left, admonishing Gorgo, who seemed inclined to walk in the middle of the street: "Keep to the side. Horsemen and charioteers would rather trample a slave than slow down!"

Gorgo dutifully moved to the gutter, although this was littered with refuse and made for unpleasant walking. In fact, she was so busy looking where to put her feet that she hardly had eyes for the changing character of the city around her. Gradually the purely residential buildings gave way to structures with commercial and public functions. A fountain house was followed by a little square crowded with fruit and nut vendors. An old woman was milking a goat at a street corner and selling the fresh milk to passers-by in a chipped pottery cup. Here and there schoolboys trailed along behind household slaves with the unenviable task of bringing their reluctant charges to their lessons. Gorgo was distracted by a pouting boy who was arguing in a loud voice with an elderly slave about how he "would *not* go there, ever again!" The slave tried to reason in an exasperated whine, "But, young master, your father wants you to...."

The next thing she knew, she almost tripped over a basket containing a whimpering infant.

Gasping, she pulled up and looked around, bewildered. The infant was very tiny, not more than a few days old, with a red face and clenched fists. "Good heavens! Where's the mother?" Gorgo asked, horrified.

Uche was already several paces ahead of her and looked back, surprised. "The mother? Who knows?"

"But how could any woman leave such a tiny baby just lying around?" Gorgo asked, outraged, still expecting to see a woman buying something or gossiping near by.

"The mother has nothing to say about it," Uche told her with a shrug. "The father or master will have left it there."

Gorgo stared at Uche, speechless, but a chill ran down her spine.

Meanwhile, Uche returned the two steps and looked down at the infant squirming in the shabby basket. She noticed the lack of clothes, the misshapen basket with broken edges, and shrugged. "Probably just a slave girl's. Or a poor man's child."

"Just left here?" Gorgo asked, still unwilling to accept this. "On a public street? In broad daylight? As if there were nothing shameful about it?"

"What's shameful?" Uche asked. "If they don't want it, they'll kill it one way or another. This way, there is at least a chance someone else will take it. Not likely, though," she added realistically, "since it's a girl. Sometimes exposed boys find new parents, since a man without a son will sometimes adopt an orphan. But who wants the burden of another girl?"

"Burden?" Gorgo asked. Had she been a burden to her father? Was Agiatis a burden? "We need women as much as we need men!" Gorgo answered indignantly.

Uche shrugged again. "But daughters require dowries, and who wants the cost and trouble of raising a slave baby for four or five years before it can be any use? It's cheaper to buy slave girls already old enough to work."

"But where do the girls in the markets come from, if no one bothers to nurture baby girls?" Gorgo wanted to know, noting with a degree of embarrassment her complete ignorance of how slave markets worked; Sparta didn't have any.

"Oh, they're mostly captured, like I was," Uche answered, continuing down the street and drawing Gorgo away from the discarded infant.

Gorgo looked back uneasily over her shoulder. The infant had been perfectly healthy....

Uche distracted her, explaining matter-of-factly, "I was out collecting cattle dung for the fire when some youths from the neighboring tribe saw me. I tried to run away, but I was very little and they were already half grown. They caught me and took me back to their village. Their elders kept me in a cage until the next slave trader came, and he bought me from them for, I think, a whole cow," Uche added educationally to the obviously ignorant visitor. "Lots of tribes in Africa make extra money that way, by selling off their extra children or the children they capture." She had Gorgo's attention again. Gorgo stared at her and asked, "What happened next?"

Uche shrugged. "I was sold down the Nile—just like Taiwo."

The two Africans had evidently been talking quite a bit, Gorgo noted, mentally amused by the thought that Eukoline's locking up the slaves at night was probably quite futile.

"I was bought by a carpet maker because I was so small my hands were good for making knots, but he was very poor," Uche explained. "We had hardly anything to eat and I was supposed to sleep on the naked floor—though I would try to climb on the carpets. He chased me off if he caught me, but I was very good at waking up just before he came, and he rarely caught me." She smiled at the memory.

"How old were you?"

Uche shrugged. "Four or five. Maybe six or seven. I had not yet learned to tell the seasons. I remember the first time the Nile flooded; I thought it was the end of the world. I was very frightened, and the Egyptians laughed at me."

"How did you come to Athens?"

Uche shrugged. "My master was very poor, and he couldn't afford to keep me. One day he took me down to the market and sold me."

"There must be a slave market here in Athens, isn't there?"

"Of course. It's just over there." Uche pointed to the left and bent her long-fingered hand back to indicate around the corner. "Do you want to go?"

Gorgo hesitated. She wasn't sure she wanted to see this, but at the same time she felt a certain curiosity. She had come out to see Athens, and this was evidently very much a part of Athens. There were more slaves in Athens than helots in Sparta, since most helots lived on the land. Leonidas claimed there were as many as a hundred thousand slaves in Athens. Certainly they dominated the streets. Gorgo nodded assent to Uche.

They came to a square surrounded on all sides by stoas. The slaves huddled in the shade of the stoas, grouped by trader. Most sat on the floor, although some lounged against the walls or pillars, or stretched out as if to sleep. Some of the men were chained together, but females outnumbered men by two to one, and what immediately struck Gorgo was that most were children. After thinking about it, however, she supposed that slaves either grew old with one master or changed hands directly without going via market. A man who no longer needed a tutor for his sons recommended him to a friend with younger sons; a young man who tired of his concubine sold her to a fellow who had expressed interest....

A large, noisy crowd of men bunched before one particular trader, Gorgo noted. "What's that all about?" she asked.

Uche shrugged, then turned to ask the trader nearest her.

"They're selling an Athenian girl," came the surprising answer.

"What?" Gorgo thought she had misheard the man.

The man shrugged. "When she was married, her husband found she was not a virgin, so he returned her and her dowry to her father."

Gorgo stared at the man, still not comprehending. "Why didn't her father find out who had dishonored her and make *him* marry her?"

"Oh! She claims her uncle slept with her." The trader related this as if it were obviously a stupid lie, concluding, "What else could her father do but conclude she was a hopeless slut and invoke the law?"

"What law?"

"Where are you from?" the trader asked back, frowning and looking at Gorgo more closely than was comfortable.

"She's just come from Lacedaemon," Uche told the trader, adding hastily as she pulled Gorgo away, "I'll explain everything."

Gorgo went willingly, gladly moving into the shadows to avoid the man's piercing look. Uche explained in a low voice, "An Athenian citizen can sell his daughter into slavery if she allows herself to be seduced."

"*Allows* herself to be seduced?" Gorgo echoed, staring at Uche in disbelief. From what Gorgo had seen, Athenian girls almost never set foot outside the women's quarters of their own houses, let alone out of the house—and then, only surrounded by their male relatives. The man's words about the girl blaming her uncle rang in her ears, and it sounded completely plausible to Gorgo. Who else but a male relative would have had a chance to seduce one of Athens' shy fawns? Or was there a side of Athenian society she had not yet seen? Gorgo looked again toward the crowd, trying to get a glimpse of the object of curiosity.

Uche hissed at her and signaled with her elegant hand, "This way." She led Gorgo behind the slaves of other merchants and around the back of the stoa, until they were very close to the trader with the Athenian girl. She had been made to stand on an upturned crate, so that she was raised enough above the other human wares to make her more visible. She was at most thirteen or fourteen. Frail and white, like most girls of the rich, she stood with her head bent so far forward that her chin almost touched her chest. Her shoulders curved inward in evident shame and humiliation. Her hair had been cut short like a slave's, crudely with rough scissors that left tufts at odd places and bleeding cuts in others. Her knees were trembling so violently beneath her skirts that her skirts shivered.

Gorgo couldn't bear to look at her. She turned and stormed away, stepping over other slaves and attracting momentary attention from the crowd. Someone called something at her, but she kept her head down and did not stop until she was a block away.

Uche caught up with her. "What's the matter, mistress?"

"That little girl! She doesn't deserve to be treated like that!"

"But she wasn't a virgin when she married," Uche insisted.

"And whose fault was that? Anyone can see that that timid little thing was the *victim*! Why, she couldn't have been more than ten or eleven when some man—very likely her own uncle—raped her! How could her own father not see that? How could he take his brother's side? Leo would kill any man—*especially* his brother!—who laid a hand on Agiatis, and my father would have done the same for me. It's that girl's uncle who deserves punishment!"

"But he's a man. Men are never to blame for anything. Women are the cause of all evil in the world," Uche answered.

"You can't believe that!" Gorgo challenged.

Uche shrugged. "That's what they say here. It's written down in their books, and they say it in the plays, too. Didn't you go to the play? I've seen one or two. Athenians say women are worse than poisonous snakes." Then she flashed a mischievous smile at Gorgo and added, "But Taiwo says that is not what they think in Egypt—or Lacedaemon."

"It is most certainly *not* what we think in Lacedaemon. In Sparta, a man who violates a child—male or female—can be castrated or killed!" Gorgo answered. "Is there nothing nice in Athens? Nothing beautiful? Nothing uplifting?"

"You've been to the acropolis?"

"Yes. It is beautiful, but it's up there!" she pointed. "It is as if the Gods themselves have fled the filth, chaos, and moral perversion of Athens in order to float above it all."

"The potters!" Uche suggested. "I'll take you there!" Enthusiastically she plunged down the street, and Gorgo had to hurry to catch up. "I know an old slave," Uche told Gorgo eagerly, "who can paint so well you know exactly what and who it is! His name is Menekles. He's the overseer of a whole shop! But first we'll go to the agora, like you wanted."

Athens' famous commercial center, the agora, was undoubtedly impressive. Even the smaller of the two stoas was as large as Sparta's great Canopy where the Assembly met, and the other was two stories tall, something Gorgo had never seen before. It was also striking that the agora was dominated by two large temples, rather than several smaller temples as in Sparta. As Gorgo was starting to comprehend, the Athenians were very devoted to the Olympians, but at the cost of neglecting lesser deities. Particularly confusing to a daughter of the Eurotas was the fact that the temples here, in the heart of Athens' commercial district, were dedicated to Hephaestus and Ares, respectively. Gorgo could not understand why Ares, a violent, destructive God, should have a temple in the commercial heart of a city.

The other odd thing about the Athenian agora was that it was filled with men. Not men engaged in trade, but men simply standing around talking. Here and there, men appeared to be holding forth at great length about one topic or another, from ethics to cosmetics, while other men stood around listening. Other groups were more chaotic, with many men talking at once. From what Gorgo heard as they passed by, the men were talking about law and lawsuits, about taxes and tolls, but also about plays and actors and the best way to spend silver....

The two "slave" women attracted frowns and even hissing as they wound their way past the clusters of men. Their looks and remarks made Uche uncomfortable and anxious to hurry away, but Gorgo ignored the animosity, immune to it because she returned the sentiments whole-heartedly. All these men just standing around talking struck the Spartan queen as vain. Had these men nothing better to do? From the fine cloth and elaborate embroidery on their chitons, not to mention the sturdy shoes or boots on their feet, it was evident that most of these men were affluent. The poor were no doubt laboring in their workshops, but here the elite loitered in idle conversation. They appeared more interested in impressing their fellows with their clothes and their words than in resolving any particular issue. A bunch of chatterboxes, Gorgo concluded with contempt.

On the far side of the agora, Uche led her down a side street lined by jewelers' shops. Gorgo would have liked to stop and look more closely, particularly at some of the gold filigree work and glass beads, but the shopkeepers shooed them away. "Don't block the view for customers!" one ordered sharply, while another advised them not to fill their "empty heads" with things meant for their "betters."

Uche giggled and looked sidelong at Gorgo. "If he knew—"

"Hush!"

The potters' quarter was near the eastern gate. The clay was brought in on heavy wagons from the surrounding countryside. The wagons lined the main road in from the east, and a maze of factories stretched away from the road like a rabbit warren. The low dividing walls of the different shops did not block the view of men working at their wheels, with baskets of clay and amphorae of water set up on either side of them. Customers liked to watch a lump of clay being coaxed into a krater or a kylix by the shimmering hands of the potters. The less experienced potters, usually still young boys, rolled the coils that were used to conceal the joints of composite vases, and specialists, often older men, created handles and covers in the shapes of snakes, bulls, lions, horses, and humans.

Smaller potteries sold raw wares to painters, who added decoration in their own shops before firing, but the larger establishments had potters, painters, kilns, and sales rooms all under one roof. It was to one of these larger factories that Uche took Gorgo.

In the outer yard a wagon was being loaded with sawdust-filled crates into which the finished products, individually wrapped, were carefully placed. Display shelves crowded the kiln itself, and wood stacked to feed the kiln created a barrier between the shop and the workroom. Uche squeezed past the display tables and stepped over some logs that had fallen off the end of the woodpile to reach the open-air factory. Here long tables flanked by benches clogged the courtyard.

"Uche! What brings you here?" a jovial voice called out from the far side of the yard, and a moment later a grotesque figure emerged, hobbling toward them on uneven legs. Gorgo was reminded instantly of Hephaestus himself. The man had a hunchback, which shocked Gorgo, but Uche smiled broadly and introduced him. "This is Menekles, a great artist!"

"And Uche is my muse!" the potter answered, patting Uche affectionately, while looking at Gorgo with curious, almost suspicious eyes.

"Menekles, this is the Spartan queen, Gorgo!" Uche introduced her guest before Gorgo could stop her. "She wanted to see Athens. That's why she is disguised as a slave."

Menekles looked at her again, and his expression was more amused than shocked. He nodded. "Spartan queens have always been curious. Why else would Helen have run off with a nonentity like Paris? Then again, maybe she had her eye on Hektor, eh?" He laughed at his own joke, and then bowed his head to Gorgo and asked, "How may I be of service to you today, my lady?"

"Uche has praised your wares."

He smiled at Uche and beckoned to Gorgo. "Judge for yourself."

Despite Uche's praise, Gorgo was impressed by the creativity, grace, and realism that this master—though unfree—artisan commanded. The pottery of Lacedaemon suddenly seemed pedestrian and uninspired, although until this moment Gorgo had loyally liked it. Yet this Athenian craftsman offered no conventional images of sphinx and hawks, of the Dioskouroi and Herakles, nor simple patterns that repeated themselves. All his works recreated lifelike scenes in which motion and emotion were captured. Two boxers stood off against one another in the bowl of a kylix, and determined runners circled a large, fat jug. On another kylix a hunter returned holding the legs of a frail-legged doe in his hands, her delicate head hanging down his back while his hounds danced about him with upright tails. Gorgo was particularly fascinated by pottery showing workmen at their daily tasks: a carpenter sanding, a smith at his anvil, even a sculptor in his workshop. Menekles tried to interest her in his "women's wares": the amphora with a wedding scene in which a youthful groom led his heavily shrouded bride away from her mother, a woman weaving, even a woman playing a lyre. Gorgo disliked the way all these women stood or sat with their heads bowed—just like the girl being sold in the market after being raped by her own uncle—and turned pointedly away from these images. She moved to the part of the shop with the larger, more official pieces.

A large, two-handled pelike with a cover immediately caught her attention. Chariots chased one another across the shoulder, but on the body hoplites fought. Strikingly, in the center on one side stood a remarkably lifelike image of a bearded man with raised spear—and he wore a cross-crested helmet, the symbol of a Spartan king.

"A Spartan king?" Gorgo asked, astonished.

Menekles smiled. "Of course! Menelaos—and here is Paris taking flight." He pointed at a thin, beardless figure in hoplite armor and an open-faced helmet with raised crest. The youth looked fearfully over his shoulder as he dropped his sword. "Would you like the pelike, my lady? It would be an honor for me to think it adorns Menelaos' home." The slave-artisan bowed deeply.

"I would be delighted to make a gift of it to my husband, but I would not risk taking it with me in my current state. I will send a servant with Uche for it later," Gorgo assured him, thinking she would send Taiwo with some money as well. Taiwo would know the value of the pelike and persuade the potter to take at least some compensation.

Hunger, more than anything, reminded Gorgo and Uche that they had been out for hours now and it was time to return before they were missed. They thanked Menekles, left the potters' quarter, and soon came to an intersection where the avenue from the east crossed the broad road up from Piraeus.

Ahead of them a trio of sailors was sauntering, stopping to look at the cheap goods offered for sale. They were in no hurry, and from the excited way they pointed at this or that, they were clearly strangers to Athens. Uche suggested to Gorgo that they pass them when the sailors stopped at a street-side stand to buy bread stuffed with spinach and cheese. Gorgo nodded and extended her stride, but she glanced sideways as they passed. Her eyes met one of the sailors, and he recognized her at once. "My lady!" he exclaimed, and then to his mates he added, "It's the queen!"

Gorgo looked again. All three sailors were looking over at her, smiling and bobbing their heads. She realized they must be crewmen from the *Minotaur*, so she smiled and paused to ask, "Are you enjoying Athens?"

"Yes, my lady!"

"But the prices are crazy!"

"And people talk funny!"

Gorgo laughed, and they laughed with her.

"They don't know about helots. They think we're slaves!" one complained.

"Will we be here much longer?" his friend asked.

"A few more days," Gorgo guessed. "Have you been to the theater?"

"Yes, my lady. But the chorus was paltry! We have much better music!"

"And better dancers!" his colleague added, nodding vigorously.

Gorgo laughed again, but then told them, "I must go. I'm late already. Enjoy your shore leave—but try not to get hoodwinked into staying. We need you to take us home."

"Of course, my lady!" "Not a chance!" "The sooner the better!" they answered in a cacophonous chorus.

Gorgo waved to them as she stepped out to continue up the street, but she did not get far. Suddenly a young man on a prancing, fine-boned horse cut in front of her and blocked her way. "What's your price, then?" he asked, leering down at her from his superior vantage, a broad-brimmed hat on his head and gold glinting from his rings as he held the fretting stallion.

"I don't have a price!" Gorgo told him indignantly.

"Don't play with me," the man answered, nudging his horse closer, effectively pinning Gorgo and Uche against the wall of a factory that backed up against the street. "I saw you talking to sailors. If you sleep with scum like that, you can't be worth much. Half a drachma?"

Uche tried to pull Gorgo back, calling up to the young man, "We're not whores! Leave us alone!"

The horseman ignored Uche, his eyes fixed on Gorgo as he leaned lower. "Come on, name a price! I'm feeling generous today. Even if you do it with sailors for less, I'll pay a whole drachma. And you'll enjoy it more. I don't smell." He reached out with one hand to run a finger along the side of her face.

Gorgo could smell his perfume, and she noticed, too, the delicate embroidery that dusted his chiton with bright bursts of blue iris and yellow lotus. "Go away!" Gorgo ordered, making a face and drawing back sharply. "You can't even play a female role!"*

The young man laughed and grabbed hold of Gorgo's upper arm, pulling her to him, as he urged his horse closer to the wall so she would have no escape as he bent to kiss her. Gorgo reacted by lifting her knee into the belly of the horse with such sudden force that the horse reared up. Her assailant was nearly thrown, and had to let go of her to grab the reins and cling to the mane. Gorgo darted past the horse and ran up the street, with Uche several strides behind her.

As soon as the horseman recovered his seat and control of his horse, however, he cantered after them, cursing. "Forget about payment! I'll f**k you for free for that!"

Gorgo spun about and darted back the other way, knowing that he could not reverse so quickly on horseback. She almost collided with a marine in full armor, who pushed her aside to reach up and drag the young dandy off his horse. The horse whinnied and spun away, while Prokles pounded the impudent young Athenian with his right fist as he held him fast with his left. Blood gushed from the Athenian's nose and mouth as his knees crumbled under him. Still Prokles continued hitting and kicking him at the same time, preventing him from escape by holding him fast and knocking his feet out from under him when he tried to run.

"Stop it!" Gorgo ordered. "That's enough!"

A crowd was gathering. The three sailors had run up behind Prokles, and from across the street other men rushed over. A heavily laden wagon stopped in the middle of the street.

"Enough! That's enough!" men echoed Gorgo.

"What's this all about?" the teamster asked in a deep voice.

---

* Plutarch attributes this rebuttal to Gorgo when "a stranger in a finely embroidered robe was making advances to her."

"Just some whore," a man in the crowd answered with a nod toward Gorgo. Instantly the three sailors of the *Minotaur* flung themselves at the man who had dared to call their queen a whore, knocking him off his feet. Prokles abruptly let go of the dandy and dealt him a final kick that sent him staggering into the collected crowd. He grabbed Gorgo by her arm and hustled her up the street, with a frightened Uche trailing them.

"Where did you come from?" Gorgo asked.

"You don't think I'd let you wander around in this piss-pot on your own, do you?"

"You've been following me all morning?"

"I knew it would come to this sooner or later. The Athenians are all—" he swallowed the word he'd been about to use.

"Did Leonidas tell you—"

"I don't take orders from Leo—unless he's paying me."

Gorgo thought about that. "Then there's no reason that he has to find out about this, is there?"

"Not that I know of." They looked at each other—and slowly, a little timidly, they both smiled before continuing up the street in comfortable silence.

Only now, when it was over, did Gorgo realize how much danger she had been in and how badly shaken she was by the encounter. For the first time this day she was frightened, and she kept close to Prokles, taking comfort in the familiar smell of sweat-stained leather.

Prokles was acutely aware of Gorgo's presence. He noticed her dirty bare feet and slowed down to accommodate her shorter strides, noting that she had not asked it of him. He glanced at her sidelong. "Are there any maidens like you left in Sparta?"

"Dozens," she assured him with a nervous laugh.

"Willing to take a grizzled old salt with a stinking past?"

"One or two," she assured him.

Prokles snorted and pointedly looked away.

Again they continued in silence for a dozen paces. Then Prokles cleared his throat and asked, "Is Leo serious about taking me back? Would he make the ephors give me a kleros, cloak, and shield?"

"Prokles! Of course he would! You know he would. He has wanted you to return from the day you left! Alkander and Hilaira, too."

"And you think I could really find a bride—one who wouldn't hate me?"

Gorgo thought about that a minute and then declared, "I think I know exactly who would suit you. She's an orphaned heiress whom Leonidas will give in marriage."

"Don't say a word about this to Leo!" Prokles warned gruffly, and then added apologetically, "Forgive my rude tone. Old habits die hard. But let me think about this before I talk to Leo myself."

"As you wish, but you can count on my support."

He smiled at her and nodded.

Preparations for the symposium were well under way by the time Leonidas and the four guardsmen returned. They were in exceedingly good spirits and feeling proud of themselves. The Spartans had won at every sport that mattered to them. Who cared about discus and boxing when they could beat the youth of Athens in javelin and wrestling and broad jump? And while they had to concede pride of place to a truly magnificent Athenian sprinter, as soon as the runners put on armor, the Spartan guardsmen had left the competition gasping in their dust. Even Leonidas was feeling very proud of himself for having outperformed if not the best, then at least the bulk, of the competitors, who were much younger than he. Indeed, there had been hardly any Athenian men of his generation who did more than jog a little or toss a javelin or two. Mostly they were there to watch the young men and boys rather than to exercise themselves.

"They spend more time eating than exercising," one of the four guardsmen scoffed as they turned their horses over to the grooms, his nose already catching the scents wafting out of Aristides' kitchen.

"These meals go on all night!" his colleague complained. "And then you're so befuddled in the morning that you couldn't keep a straight line to save your life."

Leonidas raised an eyebrow at him and remarked, "You can only get drunk from the wine you drink yourself."

The others laughed, but the young man defended himself. "True enough, but it's hard to lie around for hours without drinking."

"Since when do Spartan guardsmen only do what is easy?" Leonidas countered.

While his fellows laughed again, the target of Leonidas' remark swore passionately, "I swear by the Twins I will not touch another drop of wine as long as we are here! You are my witnesses!" he admonished his grinning comrades.

Leonidas simply nodded and took his leave of them to go in search of his wife. He called out her name as he entered the darkened corridor that led to the women's quarters beyond the andron. She answered from the long hearth room to the left, and as he approached he could hear the rhythmic thumping of the loom. Entering, he saw Eukoline at the large loom, surrounded by half a dozen women carding and spinning and coiling wool. Gorgo sat there with the others as if she were a handmaiden to Eukoline. Leonidas frowned, but made no comment.

Gorgo looked up from her work to ask, "How did it go?"

He tried to act casual. "Lakrates outdid himself. He's got Olympic potential. What was also interesting—"

Taiwo was in the doorway, evidently having spotted Leonidas, and followed him anxiously. "My lord, Eurybiades is here. He needs to talk to you urgently."

"Let him in!" Leonidas answered without thinking, turning toward the door, so that he didn't even notice the shocked way Eukoline straightened and sucked in her breath. She then made a show of snapping her fingers at one of her slaves, who hastened to bring her a veil. This she draped over her head and wrapped around her shoulders so that, hunched over the loom, she was invisible to the strange man Leonidas had so rudely invited into the presence of a respectable woman.

To make things worse, Eurybiades was not alone. Hierox was with him, and both men looked grave. Leonidas asked at once, "What's the matter? Has something happened to the *Minotaur*?"

"Not directly. But some of the crew were involved in a terrible brawl, sir," Eurybiades answered. "Aside from more than one broken bone that will make them useless at the oars, they've been arrested, and the Athenians want a drachma a head for their release."

"How many men were involved? What was it all about?" Leonidas was frowning.

Hierox glanced once at Gorgo, but said nothing, while Eurybiades answered smoothly, "There's no knowing what it was about, sir. These things happen in port. A sailor is insulted or notices he's been cheated—as sailors always are—and demands his money back. The locals always gang up sailors, and a sailor in trouble calls out the name of his ship. His shipmates come to his aid without question. That's the way it's always been and always will be."

"So how many men are in jail?"

"Seventeen."

"You want me to choke up seventeen drachma for crewmen who have disgraced Lacedaemon abroad?"

"No, sir," Eurybiades answered steadily, although Hierox moved uneasily from one foot to the other. "I could find seventeen drachma. The problem is that the Athenians want us to pay damages for the destruction of furnishings in a tavern and an overturned cart loaded with what they claim was the finest Attic pottery."

"How much are they asking?" Leonidas asked, horrified.

"Three hundred drachma."

"That's ridiculous. They're trying to take advantage of us! I'm not paying an obol for rowdy sailors. We'll sail seventeen short if we have to."

"That's not fair, Leo," Gorgo spoke up, drawing the attention of the three Lacedaemonians and a gasp from Eukoline. Leonidas waited for his wife to continue, and she nodded toward Eurybiades. "You heard the captain. Our men were very likely provoked. Athenians don't understand that helots aren't slaves. They might have been refused service or the like. Even if they *were* to blame, we brought them here, knowing they had no experience of any place but Lacedaemon. We have no right to abandon them here. We don't know what might happen to them if we did. They might be enslaved as Ibanolis was."

"No one's arguing about seventeen drachma to get them out of jail, but this bill for damages is bogus."

"Very likely," Gorgo agreed. "I'm not suggesting you should just pay it outright or without question. Make the Athenians list each object allegedly destroyed and provide an itemized estimate of fair market value. Better still, insist on an *independent* assessment of value—but first apologize profusely and make fulsome promises of fair restitution, to get them off their guard."

Hierox laughed outright, while Eurybiades nodded his head approvingly in Gorgo's direction. Leonidas simply agreed, "Good idea. I'll fetch my purse." The three men departed together, Leonidas asking for more details as they went.

Eukoline shoved her veil off her head and turned on Gorgo, asking in a tone that mixed disapproval with amazement: "Why are you Spartan women the only ones who *rule* your men?" She did not mean it as a compliment.

"Because we are the only women who give birth to men!"† Gorgo snapped back.

"As if I hadn't given birth to two sons?" Eukoline retorted indignantly. "Athens has five times the number of citizens Sparta has!" she added proudly.

"Athens has forty thousand *males* who think that making clever speeches is the pinnacle of manliness." All Gorgo's pent-up anger at what she had seen since her arrival boiled over. "That's why they're afraid to educate their daughters and why they keep their women in the dark—physically and mentally!" Gorgo could not resist adding, "Sparta's men prove their manhood with their spears, and need not dismiss good advice just because it comes from the mouths of women!" She threw down the wool she had been working and stormed out of the chamber, leaving the other women stunned in her wake.

Rain, driven by a strong wind, swept in from the east. The sky darkened dramatically and the clouds hung low, reaching out ephemeral yet ominous hands toward the rooftops. The temperature dropped abruptly and men clutched capes and cloaks more tightly around their shoulders, even before the first heavy drops of rain fell from the hostile sky. The torrent that followed pelted the open

† This is Gorgo's most famous line, attributed to her by Plutarch and others. Plutarch specifically identifies her questioner as "a woman from Attica."

squares so violently that the drops jumped up again like millions of tiny fountains, while the rooftops reverberated. The rush of water overwhelmed the gutters and fell in sheets from the roofs, to join the rivulets cascading over the paving stones and sweeping refuse down the alleyways.

Leonidas and his companions dived for cover under the nearest roof and found themselves in the shop front of a shoemaker. Belts hung from hooks hammered into the plaster wall, and pairs of sandals were lined up in neat rows. The man and his two apprentice sons looked up astonished from their workbenches as four armored men suddenly burst into the humble shop.

One of the boys gaped with an open mouth, but the older man, sitting astride his workbench and pushing a thick needle with thread through the sole of a sandal, got to his feet and came forward, bobbing his head. "My lord, what an honor!" His words were directed not to the Spartan king, whom he did not recognize, but to young Kimon, who had offered to help Leonidas negotiate with the outraged landlord about the damages allegedly done by the *Minotaur's* crew.

"Ah—" Kimon took a moment to remember the name, and then it came to him. "Demeas! What a surprise! How are you?" Before the man could answer, he added, "This is King Leonidas of Sparta." The shoemaker dutifully bobbed his head to Leonidas, while Kimon continued with the introductions. "Demeas fought with my father at Marathon."

"Indeed! What a day that was! Look!" the shoemaker ordered the Spartan king, "I got this wound there!" He turned slightly sideways and lifted his short, rough chiton to reveal an ugly scar that ran down the side of his thigh. "And there hangs my hoplon!" He pointed deeper into the darkness of the shop, where a battered hoplon hung beside a sword in its baldric.

"Are you well, Demeas?" Kimon asked the shoemaker with apparent interest. "I heard you were ill."

"No, not really, but business is bad." He shook his head. "Too many cheap wares flooding the market from Thessaly these days. They have cheap leather up there because they have room for huge herds of cattle. The workmanship is crap, but people aren't willing to pay for quality anymore. All they care about is the price! If it's cheap, they'll buy it even if the straps break in a fortnight. Then they run back and buy another pair of cheap sandals, rather than investing in good wares like these!" He grabbed a pair and held them out to Kimon, as if he expected him to inspect them.

Kimon nodded politely and remarked, "I'm sorry I have not sent my steward around to buy for the household as my father used to do. I just can't afford it."

"I know, my lord—not after the fines the Assembly leveled on your good father. I voted against it! You can be sure many of us did."

"I know, Demeas," Kimon assured him. "I was there, even if I wasn't old enough to vote."

"They drove your father to his grave, they did—Xanthippos and the others."

Kimon drew a deep breath but answered with restraint, sad rather than angry: "My father was seriously wounded, Demeas. There was little hope for his recovery."

"But these ungrateful wretches! If you'd but seen him at Marathon. No one fought better than he did—but they would not even let him put up a monument to himself!"

"But it is true, Demeas, that he could not have won the battle without the others—without you."

"Well said," Leonidas remarked, prompting Kimon to add, "In Sparta no living man is allowed a monument—isn't that right, Leonidas?"

"Yes. Not even Olympic victors," Leonidas agreed.

Demeas looked surprised, but not particularly taken with the idea. "But why not? If a man has done something noteworthy, why should he have to die before it is commemorated?"

"Perhaps because too much praise can go to a man's head—and a man who is top-heavy tends to fall down," Leonidas explained.

Demeas liked that and laughed heartily, but then he turned to Kimon again and asked, "Is it true, my lord, that we're all to get ten drachma apiece from the silver mines?"

"That's the proposal of the Council," Kimon assured him.

"I could use ten drachma!" Demeas admitted. "There's a break somewhere in the drainage pipe from our latrine, and I need to have the whole thing dug up and replaced. Besides, my daughter's almost twelve, and I'll need a dowry for her soon."

"Ten drachma won't last for long, though, will it?" a deep voice growled as another man entered the little shop. The newcomer was stocky with a burly chest and a thick, short neck. His short-cropped curly beard and short hair were wet with rain. His chiton came to mid-calf, an awkward length that had neither the elegance of the long robes worn by the rich nor the practicality of the knee-length clothes of workmen and slaves. His nose was rather flat in his broad face, but his eyes were sharp and seemed to glint even in the poor light. They focused directly and pointedly on Leonidas. "King Leonidas, if I'm not mistaken?"

"You are not mistaken, and with whom do I have the honor?"

"Themistocles, son of Neocles."

"Ah!" Leonidas recognized the name. He had heard much about this man already. But to be sure he was not mistaken, he added, "The man who wanted to build a wall around Piraeus?"

"Yes, that's me," Themistocles agreed, his eyes still inspecting Leonidas intently. Abruptly he broke eye contact with Leonidas and turned on the poor shoemaker. "So, Master Shoemaker, you could use ten drachma, but what happens after the ten drachma are used up?"

Demeas shrugged, "At least I'll have a fixed drainage pipe."

The others laughed, but not unkindly. Themistocles clapped him on the shoulder and declared, "Indeed, so you would. But what would you say to money that comes in year after year? Not just once, but with every summer?"

"Is there that much silver in the mines?"

"No. That's the point. The silver won't go on forever. But if we *invest* the silver in something that makes Athens strong—really strong—we could multiply the benefits many-fold and keep the money coming in for years into the future."

"How?" the shoemaker wanted to know.

"You'll hear about it at the Assembly tomorrow," Themistocles promised. "But remember what I said. My proposal will put money in the hands of Athens' poor for generations to come." Then, without even drawing a new breath, he pointed to a pair of sandals and declared, "Those look about my size."

Demeas hastened to hand them to him.

Themistocles inspected the sandals closely, pulling expertly at the places where they were most likely to come apart, then sat down on the nearest bench, removed the muddy sandals from his feet, and tried on the new pair. Meanwhile Kimon, noting that the rain had let up, suggested to Leonidas that they continue.

They bade Demeas goodbye, but Themistocles stopped them with a "Wait for me!" He turned to the shoemaker to ask, "What do you want for these?"—pointing to the sandals now on his feet.

"Four obols."

"Done!" Themistocles fished in his purse, removed the coins and put them in Demeas' hands, then took Leonidas by the arm and held him fast as they went outside.

The rain had indeed let up and so had the wind, but it was still drizzling and the streets were deserted. Themistocles spoke in a low voice. "So, Leonidas of Sparta, you think the Persians are coming back."

"I have proof of it. An Egyptian scribe spent almost a year inside the Persian Empire taking meticulous notes, and—"

"You don't have to convince me—any more than young Kimon here." He nodded toward the younger man, who raised an eyebrow but held his tongue politely. "*I* know the Persians are coming, but Athens"—he gestured grandly with his arm to include not only the workshops, factories, and taverns around them, but also the acropolis visible in the distance—"does not want to believe it. They close their eyes to the threat. Besides, fear makes men small-minded and selfish. If you want the masses to forgo their ten drachma, you have to offer them something more than threats. You have to give them a vision. I learned *that* from your father," he added to Kimon almost reproachfully.

"What sort of vision?" Leonidas asked warily.

Themistocles shrugged. "A vision of glory—with very real material benefits in the short term."

"Meaning?"

"I will ask the Athenian Assembly to build a hundred triremes with the silver," Themistocles declared, his eyes fixed on Leonidas.

Kimon gasped. "A hundred triremes? We'd need seventeen thousand men to man them!"

"We would, wouldn't we?" Themistocles agreed.

Kimon said no more. Leonidas nodded, understanding: oarsmen had to be paid year after year....

Themistocles continued, "With the seventy triremes we already have and some more private contributions, Athens should be able to launch a fleet of two hundred triremes in the next couple of years—twice what Chios ever had. Together with Corinth and Megara, and Lacedaemon, of course, we would be a formidable force. Don't you agree, my lord?"

"Two hundred triremes?" Leonidas asked, unable to imagine it. He had struggled to find the means and the men for just twenty. "With citizen crews?"

"With citizen crews," Themistocles confirmed.

"It would alter the power equation in the Aegean altogether," Leonidas concluded, not entirely comfortable with the proposition. Such a fleet would be an asset in the fight against the Persians, of course, but what then?

"It would, wouldn't it?" Themistocles agreed. Then he bowed his head to the others and turned to stride away in his new sandals. They watched him go until he was long out of hearing, and then Leonidas turned to young Kimon to ask: "What am I to think of all that?"

"Themistocles is a brilliant man. My father mistrusted him, yet warned me never to underestimate him. Themistocles seems to have an uncanny ability to anticipate developments. Certainly if Themistocles' walls had been finished in time, we would have had no need to fear the Persians during the last invasion. Can a navy replace walls? Can it defeat an enemy like Persia before it lands? I don't know. But I certainly doubt whether even Themistocles can convince the Athenian Assembly—men like Demeas—to give up their ten drachma for the sake of a navy."

"But the navy would put money in their pockets, too. That was his point," Eurybiades entered the conversation. "He's trusting that men much poorer than Demeas will see the advantages of a standing fleet that needs more than seventeen thousand oarsmen—year after year."

"Yes, that's what he's counting on," Kimon agreed. "But triremes don't last forever. They ream from beaching too often, or grow barnacles from being too long at sea. And once they start taking on water or can't keep up with the others, they will be discarded like a pair of old shoes. Who will pay then for the new ships? Go down to Piraeus and count the number of hulks rotting on the shore—all once-proud triremes."

"Athens discards her heroes when they no longer serve her," Leonidas reflected sadly, adding softly, "Like your father."

Kimon sighed and looked away, not meeting Leonidas' eyes.

"Why do you stay? With the money you paid to an ungrateful Assembly, you could have founded a colony somewhere else. My brother did."

"I can't leave," Kimon admitted, helplessly gesturing to the city around him. "Athens isn't Aristides and Xanthippos—much less Kallixenos or Pheidon! It's not even Themistocles or my father. It's Demeas and all the men like him: men without any particular politics or vision, yet a dogged determination to be themselves. Demeas can't afford his panoply, and he is certainly no trained soldier like you Spartans, but when the Persians landed at Marathon, he was there with that battered hoplon and his cheap sword, and he stood for six hours with blood gushing from his thigh against the onslaught of an army twice our size." Kimon shrugged. "I can't explain it, but it has to do with something in the air here. Freedom—despite the stink of broken latrines." He paused and turned to look at Leonidas. "And, I promise you, they will fight for it as they did at Marathon. They will fight when the Persians come, by land or by sea. They will die fighting rather than surrender their freedom. You can count on that, Leonidas. On us."

Part III

THERMOPYLAE

Chapter 18

CONFEDERACY FOR FREEDOM

"Three years ago they refused to believe there was any kind of threat at all, and now they are like chickens with their heads cut off!" Sperchias complained to Leonidas. They had come yet again to the Isthmus for a meeting of the Greek cities determined to oppose the Persian invasion.

The loose confederation had first met more than a year earlier. At that time, still not wholly convinced of the threat, they had agreed to send spies to the Persian court. These, however, had only confirmed what Teti had recorded and Demaratus had warned in his secret message to Sparta. Ever since then, the Confederation had been in almost permanent session, and appeals for help had been sent to Syracuse, Crete, and Corcyra. Indeed, over Spartan objections, a delegation had been sent to Argos to try to convince this powerful city to give up its neutrality and join the coalition against Persia.

Meanwhile, at a leisurely, confident pace, Xerxes had collected a massive army and then moved it up the Asian coast of the Aegean. All along the projected march route, his quartermasters had hoarded grain and other foodstuffs in massive warehouses. Herds of livestock were corralled to provide meat, while the fields were shorn of grass to provide fodder for both his meat on the hoof and the Persian cavalry. At the Hellespont, a bridge was created out of ships tied side by side.

Across the ships a wooden walkway with handrails was constructed. It was so wide and steady that even chariots could roll over it, their drivers and archers upright in the carts, and the cavalry did not bother to dismount.

Meanwhile, to ensure a safe passage for his ships, a canal was dug through the Athos peninsula. This ensured there would be no repeat of the disaster that struck Darius' fleet more than a decade earlier.

The Thessalians, steadfast opponents of the Persians, demanded immediate aid from their allies, and so ten thousand hoplites from the coalition had been sent north to the pass at Tempe by Mount Olympus to protect Thessaly. The Athenians had provided the largest contingent of troops under the command of Themistocles, but Leonidas had been unable to convince the Spartan Assembly to approve deployment of even the active army so far from home. Instead, the Spartan Assembly voted to send a force of perioikoi hoplites under the command of a single Spartiate, Euanetus, son of Karenus.

Euanetus was a conscientious commander, the very man who had replaced Leonidas as lochagos when Leonidas became king, but Leonidas was not surprised he'd fallen under Themistocles' spell. The Athenian effectively seized control of the operation, and heeding warnings from a friend in Macedonia that Tempe could easily be outflanked, Themistocles ordered a retreat.

While this saved ten thousand hoplites from death or captivity, it also meant the effective abandonment of Thessaly. The Thessalians understandably felt betrayed, and promptly offered earth and water to Xerxes. The Persian army was now deep inside Greece, advancing slowly and steadily, and apparently as irrevocably and unstoppably as lava from a volcano.

Leonidas nodded to Sperchias, his eyes on the agitated plenum meeting below the Temple to Poseidon in the amphitheater at Isthmia. The Confederation meetings had started here when the Greeks were gathered for the Isthmian Games, but this was an Olympic year, and normally the cult site would have been abandoned. Instead, despite the absence of athletes and trainers, the guesthouses were filled to overflowing with the representatives of the Confederation, their scribes, and their slaves. The locals catering to their needs for refreshment and entertainment moved in and out in a constant hubbub.

The Athenians had imposed their rules for debate upon the Confederation Assembly. This meant that as long as a man did not slander another representative, attack the president of the Assembly, or speak to a topic not on the agenda, he could talk as long as he wanted. Leonidas had the impression that there was an inverse relationship between the size and importance of a city and the long-windedness of its representatives. In any case, even men from the most obscure of cities—cities with only a pair of penteconters or a couple of hundred hoplites—were capable of talking for what seemed like hours.

Leonidas had heard nothing new for a long time. City after city had sent to Delphi for advice, only to be told the same thing: surrender or flee. Leonidas turned to Sperchias and remarked, "When Leotychidas' representative returned with the latest oracle saying that Sparta would lose a king in battle or be destroyed, I wondered if Leotychidas had bribed the oracle, but now I'm beginning to wonder if it was Xerxes!"

Sperchias nodded glumly. "Very likely. The Persians, you know, believe Apollo is simply another name and manifestation of their god Ahuramazda. Xerxes has sent many embassies to the priests at Delphi assuring them of his respect and promising them his protection—once he has control of all Greece. We can be sure he sent them tokens of his admiration as well. No doubt those gifts were linked to services—or threats."

Leonidas considered his friend for a moment, flabbergasted by this conclusion. On second thought, now that Sperchias had put it into words, it seemed obvious. Of course the Persians would try to bribe the oracle. After all, his own brother Cleomenes had proved it *was* corruptible. The actors might have changed, but ultimately the Pythia herself, and the priests who interpreted her messages, were just human beings. Why should anyone think they would be impervious to Persian gold? "Why didn't you report this earlier—to the ephors and Council?" Leonidas asked his friend.

"Would it have made a difference? Or rather, would it have helped *you*?" He paused to let Leonidas consider the consequences before putting his thoughts into words. "Because of the oracle, all Sparta agrees we have to fight in order to save the city. Without the oracle, you might not be here with a mandate to form a coalition that can fight at Thermopylae and Artemisium. The message to Athens was much worse, by the way. They were told: *Why sit you, doomed ones? Fly to the ends of the earth, leaving home and the heights your city circles like a wheel. The head shall not remain in place, nor the body... but all is ruined, for fire and the headlong god of war, speeding in a Syrian chariot, shall bring you low,*" Sperchias quoted.

"That's not what Themistocles told me. He said their oracle predicted his fleet would save Athens."

"That's Themistocles' interpretation of the second oracle."

"What second oracle?"

"Well, what I quoted was the first oracle Athens received. The men sent to Delphi were, understandably, devastated—until a prominent Delphian suggested they return again with olive branches and beg Apollo to reconsider. They duly received a second oracle, which warned: *Await not the host of horse and foot coming from Asia, nor be still, but turn your back and withdraw from the foe.* But it also included the phrase: *Though all else shall be taken... and the fastness of the holy mountain of Kithairon, yet Zeus the all-seeing grants to Athena's prayer that the wooden wall only shall not fail, but help you and your children.* Themistocles believes—and I tend to agree—that the 'wooden wall' is the Athenian fleet, and that it will not 'fail.' But whether it fails or not, Athens will be lost."

"Correct!" Themistocles growled, dropping beside Leonidas on the marble bench of the theater. "That is the reason some fools think that what is meant by the wooden wall helping us is that our fleet should be used to transport all our citizens and their households to the ends of the earth, where we must found a new city. That, however, would leave the rest of you without a fleet."

"Indeed," Leonidas agreed cautiously, wondering where Themistocles' agile Athenian mind was leading now.

"I, on the other hand, believe that triremes are built to fight, not flee. They certainly weren't built to carry goats and women! They will help us best by destroying the Persian fleet."

"Indeed," Leonidas agreed again, still unsure what goal Themistocles was pursuing.

"For that small service, I expect Sparta to be willing to forfeit any claims to command at sea; am I right?" Themistocles' eyes bored into Leonidas.

Leonidas shook his head, but not in denial. "Lacedaemon does not claim command at sea. Athens, Corinth, or Aegina—"

"Not Aegina!" Themistocles warned. "We officially built the fleet to teach Aegina a lesson. No self-respecting Athenian will fight under Aeginan command. As for Corinth, their navy is one-third the size of ours. They should be willing accept Athenian leadership at sea, just as they accept Spartan leadership on land."

"You'll have to talk to Adeimantus about that. I speak only for Lacedaemon."

Themistocles shook his head. "No false modesty, my friend. Where Sparta leads, other cities follow."

"Only as far as it is in their self-interest," Leonidas cautioned cynically.

"You underestimate your influence," Themistocles assured him gruffly—but then they were both distracted by a commotion among the men in the lower rows. Apparently some men had just entered, and soon no one was listening to the speaker. Annoyed, he broke off his monologue, and at once the president of the session (which rotated daily) brought down his gavel and announced the speech ended.

"But I haven't finished!" the speaker protested futilely.

Themistocles tapped Leonidas on the shoulder. "Those are the envoys we sent to Syracuse. Let's go hear what they have to say."

Themistocles was already on his feet again, moving down the steps, but Leonidas was slower, straining to see if this was true. Sparta had sent two of this year's ephors to Sicily along with two Athenians; one of Sparta's envoys had been Alkander. When Leonidas finally saw his friend, hemmed in by more and more delegates, he jumped up, signaling Sperchias to follow.

Inevitably, it was the Athenian envoy who was speaking. "... a tyrant! A self-important tyrant! No one in all Syracuse dares speak their mind. He's surrounded by sycophants who fawn and flatter! It was hardly better than the Persian court."

"But will they come to our aid?" a representative from Thebes called out impatiently.

"Aid? Not on your life! Gelon lectured us for failing to help him against Carthage!"

Alkander had caught sight of Leonidas at the back of the crowd, and he shook his head slowly and helplessly. The crowd, realizing Leonidas was behind them, parted enough to let him through. Alkander spoke to Leonidas, but the others fell silent when he spoke. "He admonished us for failing to avenge your brother Dorieus' death. He is, as my Athenian colleague says, a man of ruthless ambition. Utterly untrustworthy."

"He sold into slavery the very people who helped him to victory in Sicilian Megara," the Athenian spoke up again, outraged.

"He won't send any help *at all*?" someone from the crowd asked in a voice laden with despair. "Not even a score of triremes or a thousand hoplites?"

"Surely he could spare *some* men?" another took up the argument desperately.

"Spare them?" the Athenian asked back indignantly. "He claims to command two hundred triremes, twenty thousand heavy infantry, and two thousand horse, but he will not spare us even a tenth of it! He would come, he said, only if he is supreme commander of all Greek forces. That is like driving out Xerxes for the sake of serving under Gelon!"

"That's right," Syagrus, Sparta's other ephor, agreed. "He wants not to liberate but to enslave us. We had no choice but to turn down his offer."

A groan swept through the crowd and someone wailed, "We are lost! Lost!" The sentiment spread like wildfire, and other voices could be heard bemoaning and lamenting.

"Don't be ridiculous." The Aeginan tried to silence the swelling defeatism. "Corcyra promised sixty warships and marines to man them," he reminded them.

"And we've yet to hear from Crete," someone else pointed out.

"Crete? Didn't you hear? They received an oracle from Delphi warning them to keep out of this war! They were reminded that Theseus had abducted the daughter of Minos—only to abandon her on Naxos!"

"What about Argos?"

"They will come only if they are given command parity with Sparta."

Suddenly all eyes turned again to Leonidas. Fortunately, Leonidas had learned earlier in the day about the Argive response. He had no need to consult the Assembly on this: Sparta would not accept Argive parity in command. It wasn't just a matter of pride or principle. The Argives had not yet recovered from their defeat at Sepeia and could field barely five hundred hoplites. There were a dozen other cities in the Confederation that brought forces that size or greater. Argos had some eight to ten triremes, but again that hardly justified a position of prominence, much less command. Leonidas saw no reason to explain himself or Lacedaemon, however, and asked back instead: "How many commanders do you want? Syracuse and Argos and Athens and Aegina and Corinth and two Spartan kings? At this rate, you will soon have more commanders than soldiers." Then he nodded curtly to the stunned audience, took Alkander by the elbow, and left the theater.

As they walked away they could hear voices arguing behind them. Alkander and Sperchias looked over their shoulders, but Leonidas did not look back. "It's good to have you with me again," he remarked to Alkander. "I've missed you."

Alkander considered his friend and did not like what he saw. Leonidas had aged noticeably. He looked more worn down than when they had parted a little over six weeks ago. His once so candid and cheerful face was marked by lines that traced a frown. "What is it, Leo?"

"What do you think? They'll still be talking while the Persians burn down the stadium right there!" He gestured to the stadium that stood closest to the Isthmus, now deserted and sprouting flowers along the starting line. "Half of them are still talking about going to the Olympic Games—as if the Persians will respect our Olympic peace! They may be running around like chickens with their heads off, Chi," he responded to his friend's earlier comment, "but they still don't grasp the urgency of the situation." He stopped in his tracks and turned to face Alkander. "I need to talk to you in private." With a nod in the direction of the guesthouse, he added, "Two other ephors are with us here, not to mention our attendants and twenty guardsmen. Let's go down to Helen's bath." He referred to a cave on the coast below the sports facilities.

Although Leonidas had not been explicit, Sperchias sensed that Leonidas wanted to be alone with Alkander. At one level, even after all these years, it hurt, but Sperchias had learned to live with disappointment. He saved face by saying, "I want to talk to Syagrus about Syracuse, and you need to fill Alkander in on what has happened here and in Lacedaemon since he sailed."

Leonidas was grateful for Sperchias' tact. He smiled at him. "Thank you, Chi."

Sperchias turned and headed back to the theater, while Leonidas and Alkander took the partially overgrown path that skirted the stadium and palaestra before striking out across a field of scrub brush toward the lowest point on the shore. Here the path turned sharply to the right in order to angle down the steep incline. It then zigzagged its way to the shore, crumbling in places. It was lined with thistle and thorn and ended on a narrow beach.

A light breeze rippled the waters of the bay stretched out before them. The water was deep blue in the distance and turned gently turquoise and finally aquamarine along the shore. The waves licked at the beach, rolling the little stones as they swept inwards, before retreating to leave a line of frothing bubbles that dissolved almost instantly.

Leonidas bent to remove his sandals, and Alkander followed his example without exchanging a word. They tied their sandals by their straps, hung them around their necks, and began to walk in the shallows. The water cooled their feet as they followed the shore. Behind them the pebbles rolled into the footprints they left, so that only faint indentations marked their passing, and even these were quickly erased by the waves. They headed in the direction of a cave sculpted out of the limestone in the curving coastline, almost six hundred yards away.

Two-thirds of the way to their destination, the beach was cut off by an outcropping of black volcanic rock that sliced down from the shore and straight into the sea. Without a word the friends helped each other out of their clothes, left their linen corselets, chitons, and sandals in a heap under a rock at the foot of the outcropping, and slipped into the water to swim the rest of the distance.

They swam straight to the little cave. The water was crystal clear and the color of aquamarine. Looking down, they could see schools of fish feeding on the waving seaweed between the rocks on the bottom ten feet below; crabs and shells nestled in the sand. The gentle waves slapped against the sides of the cave and the clap of water on rock echoed overhead, but the sound of the seagulls and the wind outside were hushed. Here, with the cave protecting them from the heat of the sun and the eyes of others, Leonidas started to talk.

"You remember that the same week you sailed for Sicily, we sent to Delphi again."

"Yes," Alkander agreed cautiously.

"It was the turn of Leotychidas' representative to consult with the oracle, and he brought the message back to Sparta personally."

"Yes," Alkander waited.

"The oracle he brought read as follows." (Leonidas recited the oracle verbatim, because he had memorized it.) "*Hear your fate, O dwellers in Sparta of the wide spaces: Either your famed, great town must be sacked by Perseus' sons—or, if that be not, the whole of Lacedaemon shall mourn the death of a king of the house of Herakles. For not the strength of lions or of bulls shall hold him, strength against strength; for he has the power of Zeus, and will not be checked till one of these two he has consumed.*"

Alkander did not respond at once, but Leonidas waited until Alkander felt compelled to ask, "You think you are that king?"

"That's what everyone thinks. The entire Council—including Leotychidas himself—turned to look at me."

"It doesn't matter what the Council thinks; it only matters what the Gods intend. You had a very different oracle when you sent to Delphi three years ago," Alkander reminded him.

"Paraphrased, that oracle said: Even a small boy can break a single reed, but the strength of a mad bull cannot break a bundle. Clearly that referred to the need for all Greek cities to stand together—but it does not contradict this more recent oracle," replied Leonidas.

"No, but this one sounds suspiciously like Leotychidas'—or Brotus'—voice dressed in Delphic poetry."

"Perhaps," Leonidas admitted, and then took a deep breath to add, "but Sperchias says Persian ambassadors have made frequent trips to Delphi to assure the priests of their safety under Persian rule. He thinks the oracle has been corrupted by Persian gold."

Alkander nodded vigorously, commenting, "I'm not surprised—and that makes it even more likely that this latest oracle was fake and that the Gods do not want your death!"

"Alkander, if the oracle was a fake, then we can't be sure Sparta will be spared—whether I die or not," Leonidas reminded him, adding, "I don't *want* to think that."

Alkander thought about that a moment and then reasoned, "Leo, the oracle didn't say how the king had to die—or who it would be. For the oracle to be fulfilled, a dead Leotychidas would do just as well as a dead Leonidas."

"Gorgo said the same thing," Leonidas admitted, with a smile at the memory.

"You used to say that Gorgo was the brightest of all living Agiads," Alkander reminded him.

"She still is," Leonidas agreed, pulling himself up on a ledge and sitting with his feet dangling languidly in the luminous aquamarine water, his upper body hunched under the curve of the cave. "But she wasn't in Kastor's grave with me, and she's not impartial when it comes to divining this particular oracle."

"No, she's probably not," Alkander agreed, resting his elbows on a ledge but preferring to stay in the water for the moment. "What do you mean about Kastor's grave?"

Leonidas hesitated and then confessed, "At the feast of the Dioskouroi, right after Chi returned from Persia alive, I had a very odd experience. I had made the final sacrifice to Kastor, and then went into the temple over his grave, as I often do, just to think. Only someone else was there."

"Who?"

"I couldn't see anyone."

"So how did you know they were there?"

"A voice spoke to me. At least I think it did."

Alkander seemed to think about this for a moment before asking, "What did it say?"

"That I could choose immortality. I protested that Brotus would never rescue me from the dead as Polydeukes did Kastor, but the voice said that my immortality did not depend on my brother, only on me making the right choice about my life—and death."

"What do you mean?" Alkander persisted.

"The voice said—Kastor said—that I had to live for those in my care—which I have tried to do—but also that I would have to die for a good purpose. He implied I would have to die not for my own sake, not for my own fame as Achilles did, but for something greater."

"You think that something greater is Lacedaemon," Alkander concluded with a sigh.

"Not just Lacedaemon," Leonidas corrected him, "but all of Greece: our language, our culture, our unique belief in the value of each individual."

"Is that what Greece is? Isn't Gelon part of Greece? And Brotus? And the men who drove Miltiades to his grave? You have always idealized what we are, Leo, but the reality is: if you sacrifice yourself in this conflict, not only will you no longer be able to help those in your care, you'll be dying as much for the petty, greedy shopkeepers of Athens, the fat and selfish oligarchs of Aegina, and the cheating, whoring merchants of Corinth. You'd be throwing away your life, and your chance to do more good, for the likes of Brotus and Alcidas and all the others who have fought you tooth and nail over the last decade."

"Yes," Leonidas conceded, clearly shaken by Alkander's words, "but what else can I do? There isn't any way to separate the good from the evil. The only way to save that which I love most is to do what the Gods demand of me."

Alkander could think of a thousand objections, but they counted for little if Leonidas' mind was made up. "You believe, then, that the oracle was true, and that you are the sacrifice the Gods demand."

"By all the Gods, I wish I didn't!" Leonidas cried out, with such strength of feeling that his words reverberated on the walls overhead and seemed to frighten even the minnows swimming under their feet. More gently he added, "Alkander, Pleistarchos is barely twelve. He's still small and fragile—as I was at his age. He's got potential. He's quick-witted and he's bright, but he's still—I don't mean this pejoratively—soft. His personality is still unformed—like young bones that are not hardened yet."

"You don't have to explain to me how vulnerable young boys are, Leo. Have you forgotten I spent the best years of my life as deputy headmaster for the little boys?"

"Alkander, if I'm killed in this coming campaign, they'll yank Pleistarchos out of the agoge and lock him up in the royal palace with Brotus as his guardian. Brotus! What did we *not* do—short of killing him outright—to prevent Brotus from coming to power in Sparta? How can I go to my death knowing that he will win in the end?"

"The oracle didn't say you would die alone. If we are to fight, you won't be the only casualty. Brotus, for all his faults, is not a physical coward."

"I don't *want* to die," Leonidas cried out in a renewed burst of emotional pain. He dropped back into the water with a splash, and sank below the surface to overcome his embarrassment at this confession. When he resurfaced, he pushed his long hair out of his face with his hands and then braced himself against the side of the cave, as Alkander did. Then he spoke softly and slowly, his eyes deflected from his oldest friend in shame. "There's so much I haven't achieved yet. The land reform I wanted to enact to ensure poor citizens don't lose their citizenship is still little more than a raw concept! There are so many details that need to be worked out before I can submit it to the Gerousia, much less the Assembly. The law prohibiting parents from selling their children into slavery is only a draft. The legislation about the emancipation of helots who serve in the army is not even drafted—it's still all in here!" He tapped his head. "And then there's Agiatis, changing from child to maiden before my eyes. She gets prettier by the day, and her childish impudence is softening into alluring coquettishness. How can I turn her future over to Brotus? Brotus would take pleasure in finding the man *least* suited to her high spirits! I wouldn't put it past him to marry her to Pausanias, or even a brute like Bulis!"

"Then you must contract her marriage before you take any risks. Whether the oracle is genuine or not and whether you're interpreting it correctly or not, it would be irresponsible to go into battle against Persia without ensuring Agiatis' future. All you need do is arrange her betrothal before you depart."

Leonidas looked at his friend gratefully. Alkander was right: it was that simple. If he had already betrothed Agiatis to another Spartiate, Brotus would have no control over her marriage. "And Gorgo?" he asked next.

"More difficult," Alkander conceded. "I don't believe a husband can make disposition of his widow before—or after, for that matter—he's dead. On the other hand, Spartan law gives widows considerable freedom. Gorgo certainly won't be poor, and she cannot be forced to remarry. I think Brotus, assuming he survives any longer than you do, would have a hard time trying to make Gorgo do anything she doesn't want to. Nor should you underestimate her—or Agiatis'—influence on Pleistarchos. If you should die, Pleistarchos wouldn't be totally under Brotus' or Pausanias' influence, no matter what his legal status."

"And Sparta?" Leonidas asked next. "Talthybiades is now a councilman, and Alcidas has never stopped scheming to take over the agoge again. Orthryades and Lysimachos and Bulis and his friends—they're all lurking in the wings, waiting for a chance to feast upon my carrion." Leonidas' fears echoed from the roof of the cave like a chorus of alarm.

Alkander shared his fears, but he recognized that his duty was to comfort his friend, who clearly believed he was destined to die soon. "Leo," he said calmly, "you've been in power ten years, and the impact of your policies is increasingly tangible. Lacedaemon has a small but respected fleet that already deters attacks on our merchantmen. Trade has increased noticeably, while all across Lacedaemon ambitious helots are opening new shops and cottage industries. Every perioikoi town nowadays is enlivened with carpenters, smiths, lampmakers, and every other kind of craftsman necessary to produce our daily needs. Because Lacedaemon is broad and patterns of settlement dispersed, our craftsmen aren't concentrated in the metropolis as they are in Athens, where they compete with one another until half of them starve. The result may be more pedestrian products, but also wealth that is more equally distributed."

"Thank you," Leonidas answered this long speech, unsure how much had been said just to comfort him and how much was real.

"Leo," Alkander read his thoughts, "you don't have to take my word for it. Look at the response of the perioikoi when we told them we were sending troops to Tempe. Did they haggle or protest? Whine or drag their feet? Not for a moment. You asked for two thousand troops, and you had them three days later—first-rate troops, too, I might add. And do we have any shortage of volunteers for our triremes? You know we don't. That is thanks to you, Leo."

"And when I'm dead?"

"Men who have known greater freedom and prosperity will not accept new restrictions on either. I don't think your successors will find it easy to revoke your reforms."

That, too, was a comforting thought. Leonidas felt some of the tension easing, but he still did not want to die—not even for the sake of immortality. In fact, immortality seemed worthless beside the beauty of a warm, sunny day. And what was the point of being immortal alone, without friends like Alkander, without Gorgo, without his children....

As if reading his thoughts, Alkander remarked, "We don't *know* what lies beyond the grave, Leo. Just because our bodies go into the dankness of the sunless earth doesn't mean our spirits do."

"When I first heard the oracle, I walked across Sparta in the noonday sun, and I saw little boys running around in their herds, and I thought: if just by dying, I can ensure that they won't be castrated to become Persian eunuchs, then I will do it gladly. When I saw Simonidas with his unit on the drill fields, again I thought: if I can stop these youth from being chained together and driven underground, to die hacking gold and silver out of the earth to make Persia rich, just by sacrificing my own life, then I will do it smiling. When I saw Agiatis coming home from the agoge with a self-made garland of wildflowers in her hair, I knew that I would rather let them torture me than surrender her to be ravaged by men who think women less valuable than cattle. If my death can prevent all that...."

"The oracle must be true—and you must be the king it refers to."

They swam back to their clothes and lay on the beach to dry off. When they could postpone it no longer, they dressed, put on their sandals, and toiled back up the trail toward the sporting complex.

At the point where the trail crested the cliff, reality hit them. Four Spartan guardsmen were drawn up across the trail to prevent men from descending the path. Although he could not see beyond his bodyguard, Leonidas heard men arguing loudly. One of the guardsmen was insisting firmly, "King Leonidas is not to be disturbed! Tell us where he can find you, and he will come to you when he is ready."

"It's all right, Lakrates," Leonidas told the guardsman as he topped the incline. The guardsmen made way for him, and he found himself facing five men: the representatives from Mycenae, Tiryns, Aegina, Troizen, and Thespiae. The sight of Demophilus drew a smile from Leonidas. "Demophilus! When did you get here?" He embraced the Thespian before acknowledging the rest.

Demophilus held Leonidas' arm and looked him hard in the eye. "I came as fast as I could. We heard about your oracle.'"

"'Yes, and what of your own?"

"*Send your children and your wives to the halls of Fair Helen, for the Muses have fled before the horns of Hektor's avengers and the harvest of Helicon will soothe the wounds of Perseus' sons, even as the lions of Thespiae live forever beside the Divine Twins.*"

"Your wives and children are welcome. Spartiate families will each host a family of Thespians, and your children will play with ours on the banks of the Eurotas. We, my brother, will pit our strength against the bulls of Persia with the courage of lions."

"And what of us?" the Aeginan asked indignantly. "Will you abandon us?"

"Of course not! Why would we?" Leonidas asked back. "Our position at Thermopylae and Artemisium provides as much protection to Aegina, Mycenae, and Tiryns as to Thespiae."

"The position, yes, but not the command!" the Aeginan retorted hotly. "We will not fight under the Athenians. Athens, with their brand-new fleet manned by amateurs, has no right to command the rest of us. Indeed, they do not even have enough men to man their fleet. They have asked Chalcis to provide oarsmen for twenty of their triremes, and have requested the poor of Plataea to bring up to strength the crews of the rest of their fleet. Put an Athenian in command of the fleet, and you don't know *where* it will end up—maybe plundering Aegina before continuing on to take Kythera, or simply running away to Sicily like the oracle told them to do!"

Leonidas was shocked by two facts: the bitterness of Aegina's opposition to Athenian leadership, and the fact that his casual assurance to Themistocles about Sparta not claiming naval command was already known. "And what does Corinth say?" he asked, starting back toward the theater and forcing the others to accompany him in an agitated group, trailed by his guardsmen.

"Corinth is as outraged as we are!" the Aeginan assured Leonidas.

This sounded too self-serving to be accepted at face value—except that the other men were nodding, including Demophilus.

"Megara is outraged, too," the Mycenaean added. "They have threatened to withdraw from the coalition altogether if Athens is given command of the naval forces."

"And Troizen agrees," the Troizen representative asserted emphatically.

"How many ships do these cities represent?" Alkander asked.

"Megara and Aegina have twenty triremes each, and Troizen five; Corinth has forty. Together it's nearly a hundred."

"Would Aegina accept Corinthian command?" Leonidas asked the Aeginan.

"Adeimantus? No. He's a tile-maker, not an admiral. Put him in command and the whole fleet will soon be cowering behind the Isthmus."

That had been Leonidas' impression, too, but it was one opinion he would have preferred not to have confirmed. Why couldn't the Corinthians have given their command to the experienced and unshakable Erxander? How could they let internal rivalries get in the way of sound military decisions? As it was, the second-largest contingent of ships was commanded by a man who was only partially committed to the fight. A stand at Thermopylae would be totally pointless unless the Greek fleet held the Persian ships at Artemisium. If the fleet failed, the Persians would simply bypass Thermopylae and land their troops somewhere south of the Hot Gates.

"Who, then?" Leonidas asked the Aeginan. They were rapidly approaching the theater, where a lively debate was evidently in progress—at least, there were a large number of catcalls, boos, and hisses being hurled at the speaker.

"Sparta, of course," the Aeginan answered without hesitation.

"Sparta's fleet is also young—and much smaller than Athens'."

"Not as young as Athens', and you did not build it with the declared intention of crushing us!" the Aeginan reminded Leonidas.

Although Leonidas personally believed that crushing Aegina had only been a pretext to convince the Athenian Assembly to build the fleet, he could not deny that Themistocles had *argued* his case by promising the humiliation of Aegina.

"We will not accept Athenian command!" the Aeginan reiterated emphatically, seconded by his colleague, who declared, "Nor will Troizen."

Leonidas nodded and stopped. He could see into the theater and noted that the speaker was from Kos, an island bringing just two triremes and two penteconters to the coalition. The speaker had clearly tried the patience of his audience with his long-winded defense of Athens' claim to naval command.

Leonidas turned to the Aeginan. "Sparta will provide an admiral, if that is the wish of the majority of the coalition members that have naval assets, but we will not actively claim command at sea." Turning to Alkander, he requested of his friend, "Please go in and tell Sperchias that. Bring me word of the decision, when there is one."

Leonidas returned to the simple but solid guesthouse built to house athletes and trainers during the Isthmian Games. During the games, as many as forty men slept here in two rooms, but the entire Spartan delegation numbered just twenty-six, including the two men returned from Sicily. The ephors were apparently attending the debate along with Sperchias, while the attendants had gone in search of food.

Ever since the second oracle challenging him to lay down his life for Sparta, Leonidas had slept fitfully. Each time he lay down, his thoughts and feelings had plagued him like the Furies themselves. He had conducted full-scale debates within his head about what he must or must not do. His fears for Gorgo, Agiatis, Pleistarchos, and Sparta had fought with one another in his head. The less he slept, the more exhausted he became, and his very exhaustion made him nervous and tense.

But the swim and the talk with Alkander had done him good. He could feel a pleasant sleepiness, totally different from the raw exhaustion of yesterday, flooding his veins and weighing on his eyes. He lay down on the stone bench, on which Meander had spread out a thin straw mattress and a woven linen covering, without taking time to remove his sandals. He noted fleetingly that his hair was still damp; then with a sigh, his eyes rolled back in his head and he fell into a deep sleep.

They had to shake him awake. It was Alkander, and he could see flames and smell pitch and smoke. For an instant he was transported back to the Great Fire, and to the nightmarish reality in which Alkander had brought him word that Eirana and his twins had been incinerated in the flames. He reared up from his sleep and the memory. "What is it? What's wrong?"

"It's all right, Leo," Alkander calmed him. "There has been a vote. The ephors cast Sparta's vote. You have been named sole commander of the combined land and sea forces of all freedom-loving cities of Greece. Furthermore, the decision was taken to hold Thermopylae and Artemisium with maximum force at the earliest opportunity."

Leonidas' first reaction was to exclaim, "Truly? At last?" But then he realized, "I can't be two places at once. I'm not a naval commander."

"No, so you will appoint as your deputy whoever you think best—as long as he's Spartan."

"Eurybiades," Leonidas answered without hesitation. Eurybiades might not be the most senior trierarch in Lacedaemon's fledgling navy, but he was the most audacious, and as a former mercenary for Aegina, he would be the most suited to keeping Aegina loyal. Leonidas' brain moved on. "Then all that remains is for us to go home and ask the Assembly to vote for a full call-up and immediate deployment."

"Leo, by the time we return, it will be impossible to call an extraordinary Assembly before the Karneia, and once the Karneia starts, we won't be able to march for ten days."

Leonidas stared at Alkander, stunned. How could he have forgotten the Karneia? It was Marathon all over again. Sparta was going to respond too late! Only this time there was no Athenian army ten thousand strong to halt the Persians in their tracks. The Confederation had excused Athens from providing a single hoplite for Thermopylae, because Athens was providing two hundred triremes for the combined naval forces. With the Persian army ten times what it was at Marathon, and no Athenian army, Sparta's delay could prove fatal to all of Greece—including Lacedaemon.

Memories of the Great Fire that had devoured his first wife and his twins merged with images of the Farm of Horrors on Kythera. What if the oracle was right, but he wasn't given a *chance* to make his sacrifice because Sparta's Council and Assembly were too busy "honoring the Gods" while the rest of the allies attended the Olympic Games?

"We leave for Sparta immediately!" Leonidas announced, striding out of the guesthouse to tack up his own horse. The others looked at one another in exhaustion before following him.

CHAPTER 19

FAREWELL, LACEDAEMON

"I HATE YOU!" AGIATIS SCREAMED. "I hate you, and I'll never forgive you! Never!" She grabbed her skirts to hike them above her knees and ran out of the house, raced across the terrace, and plunged into the orchard. In moments, the white figure of the girl was obscured by the foliage of trees in full leaf.

Leonidas was left standing in the hall, his heart pounding in his chest, at a complete loss. Pain and incomprehension lamed him for several seconds before he managed to croak out, "What did I do wrong? I honestly think Lakrates is the best of the younger bachelors. I know the age difference is still significant, but it's not a great as between you and me—"

Gorgo put her fingers to his lips to silence him—and to touch him. She had the need to touch him as much as was seemly in these last hours they would be together. "My love, it wasn't anything you said, and it has nothing to do with Lakrates."

"Does Agiatis fancy someone else?" Leonidas asked, frowning, as he tried to understand his daughter's irrational and cruel outburst. For two days he had fought fiercely with the Spartan Council—first to call an extraordinary Assembly despite the approach of the Karneia; then, when that failed, to let him take the active army north. Finally, when they refused him that as well, he had to settle for taking an advance guard three hundred strong. Once that decision was made, he'd had the emotionally wrenching duty of selecting this advance guard, while calling up a perioikoi force and coordinating the march north with the allies of the Peloponnesian League and the Confederation. Yet despite these burdens, he had given much thought to which of the eligible bachelors would be best suited to Agiatis. He had looked for a man who would both do her credit and make her happy. When Lakrates came to mind, he had felt a sense of inspiration and relief, and when he talked obliquely with the young man about his daughter without hinting at his motives, Lakrates' response had convinced him completely. And now this.

"This has nothing to do with teenage fancies one way or another," Gorgo gently tried to explain.

"Then what is it about? Doesn't she realize that if I don't designate a bridegroom, Brotus will? Does she really think she'd prefer Brotus' choice to mine?" The strain of the last few days, combined with the pain Agiatis had inflicted, was making Leonidas angry, and Gorgo felt justified in putting her arm around him, reveling in the feel of his warmth, the hardness of his muscles, and the softness of his skin. How was she going to live without ever feeling this again? Maybe for decades and decades....

"That's not what upset her, Leo," Gorgo explained softly.

"What, then?"

"I don't think she understood—until you brought her news of her betrothal—that you were serious."

"What do you mean, 'serious'? Does she think the Persian invasion is some sort of joke? A—"

Gorgo again put her fingers to his lips to silence him, then took one of his hands in hers and kissed the back before putting it against her cheek. Leonidas watched her, moved by her gestures but still confused and unable to understand what she was trying to say. "She didn't believe, until you announced her betrothal, that you would not be coming home."

"How could she not understand? She's not a child anymore! Why, even Pleistarchos, at just twelve, understands! He spent all afternoon asking me how to be a *good* king."

Gorgo shook her head. "You're wrong, Leo. This isn't about understanding—they both do that in their heads. It is about *believing*—and being able to imagine what it will *mean*. Pleistarchos could spend the afternoon talking about being king, promising to carry out your Land Reform and the like, because he was focused on the superficial facts. He's too young to appreciate what he is losing. He isn't conscious of how much he depends on your advice, your approval, your support. To him it is as natural and as certain as the sunrise or the chirping of birds in the early morning. Who of us has ever stopped to think what it would mean if the sun did not rise or the birds were silent? So it is for Pleistarchos: he has been told he will be king, so he asks *you* what he should do—the most natural thing for him to do—without realizing that when he needs your advice most because he *is* king, you won't be there to give it to him. He can't think that far ahead. But understanding reached Agiatis this afternoon, because she knows how reluctant you are to see her wed. To bring her a bridegroom was like laying your corpse at her feet."

Leonidas didn't have an answer to this. He could tell that Gorgo was very close to breaking down herself, and he knew that he couldn't bear it if she did. He *needed* her to be strong now.

Gorgo sensed what Leonidas was thinking, and she backed away from the abyss one more time. She took a deep breath. "Leo, please try to forgive Agiatis. Accept that what she said and how she said it was really only a tribute to how deep her feelings for you are."

Leonidas nodded slowly. He wanted to believe his wife, but his own nerves were raw. If his daughter truly loved him, surely she would have understood that he was doing his best for her under extremely difficult circumstances? Surely, she would have trusted him and shown him more respect?

A shout from outside indicated that already the next visitor had arrived. A glance out the window revealed Phormio, clambering awkwardly down from a heavy chariot. Leonidas sighed. "I must see him, Gorgo. The perioikoi have responded with more alacrity—more loyally—than my peers and alleged subjects. I am still ashamed that the perioikoi are sending *their* best young men—they offered the full two thousand men of their active units—while the Gerousia begrudged me even three hundred!"

"But those three hundred are the very best that Sparta has to offer," Gorgo reminded him, adding, "Besides, you'll have the entire Spartan army, with a full, fifteen-year call-up, just six days after the end of the Karneia. If Xerxes continues to move as slowly as he has in the past, you may have the entire army—five thousand three hundred Spartiates—before you even engage."

"Assuming the Council submits the proposal to the Assembly as promised, and assuming the Assembly votes for it."

"I understand your bitterness, Leo, but you aren't being fair. The Council has summoned the Assembly for dawn on the day after the Karneia. They ordered the lochagoi to be prepared to march out the same day. Every able-bodied man in Sparta is preparing to fight. They *will* be there—*all* of them. All *you* need do with the advance guard is hold Thermopylae for ten days—"

Phormio was knocking at the door. Leonidas pulled Gorgo to him and kissed her hastily on the forehead. "Thank you," he murmured. "I needed that reminder."

She nodded and withdrew as Meander opened the front door and let Phormio in. She slipped out the back and through the orchard, following the direction in which Agiatis had disappeared. She reached the river without seeing her daughter and stood bewildered, looking for some sign of the girl. Agiatis was nowhere to be seen—not among the trees, not at the paddock fence or in the walled kitchen garden.

Gorgo noticed a rickety wooden pier that Pelopidas had built years ago to enable his children to fish and swim in the deeper part of the Eurotas without wading through the snake- and rat-infested mud of the shallows. It was almost obscured by tall river reeds that towered twelve feet high. A little uncertainly, because she feared the wood was rotten and might give way under her, Gorgo stepped on to the pier and moved hesitantly forward. The wood creaked and the supports shifted slightly under her weight, making her pause. Then the sound of sobbing penetrated to her ears, and she pressed forward.

Agiatis was sitting at the end of the pier, clutching her knees and holding her face down on top of them. Gorgo eased herself down beside her daughter and pulled Agiatis into her arms.

"Why?" Agiatis burst out instantly, coming up for air, then burying her face again, this time in her mother's lap to wail like a little child.

Gorgo held her close. Agiatis' sobbing shook her whole body and her tears soaked through Gorgo's skirts. Gorgo started to rock back and forth in an age-old gesture of motherly love. "Hush, sweetheart, hush."

"But why does he have to do it? Doesn't he love us even a little? Why does Sparta always have to come first? Why?"

"Oh, sweetheart! Do you really not see?" Gorgo was genuinely surprised by her daughter's misunderstanding. "This isn't about Sparta at all—it *is* about us."

"Then let Leotychidas die! No one would even miss him!"

"Of course not, but no one would follow him, either," Gorgo reminded her daughter.

"The army has to!" Agiatis spat back furiously. "He's a king, too!"

"Many of our citizens think he's not. They think Demaratus is the rightful king. And even if they obeyed Leotychidas out of respect for our laws, the Confederation would not—and so everyone would fight alone and would be defeated alone, and then the Persians would keep coming, unstoppable, to destroy us."

Agiatis sat upright, revealing her puffy, red face. She wiped her running nose on the back of her arm—as if she were four rather than fourteen—and argued, "But if Leotychidas were killed fighting up north, then Dad could lead the defense here *successfully*, because the prophecy would already be fulfilled."

"Oh, sweetheart, why do you think Leotychidas would die just because he went north? He is far more likely to accept a Persian bribe or just run away. And if he's not Sparta's rightful king, then even his death would not appease Zeus. Either way, your father would be left to rally what is left of our forces in a hopeless situation, and his life would *still* be forfeit—or we would be destroyed. Maybe both. Surely you see that he needs to make his sacrifice militarily meaningful to ensure his death brings us safety and freedom?"

Agiatis stared at her mother stubbornly, unwilling to admit that she could see her mother's point.

Gorgo understood her silence, and pulled her daughter back into her arms to hold her. They clung to each other for a few moments in silence; then Gorgo loosed her hold a little to stroke her daughter's soft, slender arms and comb her tangled, tear-wet hair out of her face. "Agiatis, you have to apologize to your father."

Agiatis didn't answer, but she squirmed defiantly in Gorgo's arms and shook her head. She pressed her face into Gorgo's lap again.

"You have to," Gorgo insisted gently but firmly, "not for his sake—he knows how much you love him, and he will forgive you whether you ask it of him or not. You have to go back and tell him how much you love him because if you don't, you will hate yourself for the rest of your life."

Agiatis went dead still.

"You do not want to live with the memory that the last words you said to your father before he died for you were, 'I hate you.'"

"My last words were, 'I'll never forgive you. Never,'" Agiatis corrected her mother.

"Is that better? Is that what you want to remember as your last exchange with your father? Do you want your last memory of him to be his wounded face when you flung those words at him?"

Agiatis sat up again and looked straight at her mother. Tears were brimming in her eyes. "Oh, Mom, it's not fair!"

That was too much for Gorgo. Her own throat was already cramping from trying to hold back tears, and suddenly she couldn't anymore. She pulled Agiatis back into her arms and surrendered to her own emotions, sobbing almost as hard as her daughter had only a few moments earlier.

Gorgo's self-indulgence did not last long. After a little while she drew back, wiped the tears from her face, and turned Agiatis to face her. "We have to pull ourselves together and make sure that your father's last memories of us are comforting ones—images to warm and cheer him not only as he marches into battle, but into the darkness of the underworld itself."

This time Agiatis nodded. In fact, she took a deep breath and announced, "You're right, Mom. We will. We will be better than Andromache for Hektor, because there are *two* of us—and Dad's going to *win*. Sparta isn't going to fall like Troy. You will never be a foreign prince's slave, and no Persian will rape me and make me serve him like a whore! And no one would dare mutilate Dad's corpse, because the Guard will defend it and bring it home, and he will be buried right here on the banks of the Eurotas he loved. And we'll put up a monument to him, like the one over Kastor's grave, and we'll visit him there, and talk to him, and tell him how happy we are. How good Lakrates is to me—he is a good man, isn't he?"

"He's a delightful young man," Gorgo assured her. "With a wonderful sense of humor, as well as being a brilliant armed runner and javelin thrower."

Agiatis nodded, satisfied. "All right. Then we'd better go fix ourselves up so Dad can't tell we've been crying."

"Exactly," Gorgo agreed. They helped each other up and, hand in hand, walked down the pier and headed back for the house.

Hilaira had made a feast, and the sound of voices from the terrace was more beautiful than the winning chorus at the Gymnopaedia. She was surrounded by everyone she loved, and to a woman of forty-five that was the most important thing in the world.

This being the eve of the Karneia, the agoge was closed and the young men were released from barracks. That meant that both Thersander and Simonidas were home for the holidays. Thersander had brought the maiden he was courting, Gnathaena. She was a pretty, dark-eyed girl, shy in the presence of her future mother-in-law and family, but she seemed very fond of Thersander. Hilaira was a little disappointed in her not for any fault, but simply because she knew Leonidas had considered asking Thersander to marry Agiatis. He had backed off as soon as he learned Thersander already had a sweetheart; it wouldn't work, he said, to make him marry Agiatis if his heart was engaged elsewhere. Hilaira was sorry about that. She liked Agiatis, though she could be a handful, and she liked the idea of having official ties with the Agiad house now that the protection of the Eurypontids was gone.

She looked out the kitchen window and leaned over to get a glimpse of her sister-in-law, Percalus. The once-famed beauty was now fat, and her face was puffy. She drank too much strong wine, and her temper had not improved in the dozen years since her husband had abandoned her. At least with so many others at the table, it was easier to ignore her.

Hilaira's eyes fell next on Simonidas. He had recovered remarkably well from the fever, not just physically but psychologically. Even the scars no longer seemed to worry him. His self-confidence came in part from the fact that he was not the only Spartan to wear them, but also because as an eirene he'd been given charge of a class of fourteen-year-olds, which was better than he'd expected. Last but not least, it had been wise of Leonidas to take the youth with him to Corinth; many of his comrades envied him the trip abroad, and it had given him greater status among his peers as well as more self-confidence. The latter was reinforced by his enduring friendship with the Corinthian youth Kallias.

The young Corinthian had come down with a delegation from his city to coordinate the coming campaign with Leonidas, and was staying here at the kleros for the holidays. Simonidas and Kallias were in a world of their own, exchanging news, remembering past adventures, and planning future ones. Simonidas kept saying, "If the war lasts just one more year, we can fight together!"

Men! Hilaira thought in exasperation. She could not understand the appeal of fighting together. She most certainly hoped this war would be over before Simonidas came of age and received his cloak and shield. It was bad enough that Alkander and Prokles were both part of the advance guard and that Thersander would follow with the rest of the army at the end of the Karneia. The only men left in Sparta would be the youths twenty and younger and the old men, like her father.

Hilaira's eyes lingered on her father. He looked very fragile. Hilaira's mother had passed away years ago, and her father had not been the same since. To Hilaira he seemed to be withdrawing more and more from the world. That made Hilaira sad, and she looked around the kitchen to find the candied lemons she had made especially for him; they were his favorite sweet and could still bring a smile to his face. But moving was increasingly difficult for him, and he visited Hilaira and Alkander at their estate only rarely.

He was here today out of respect for the fact that Alkander and Prokles had both been selected for the advance guard, and that had already become a mark of coveted honor. Although the initial selection had been made by Alkander, Dienekes, and Oliantus, everyone knew that the men who marched north in the advance guard all met Leonidas' personal approval. Just yesterday he had gone through the list one by one and made some discreet substitutions. The men who made up the advance guard represented the men Leonidas thought were Sparta's absolute best from among the married men with sons. To be one of "Leonidas' Three Hundred" already had the same prestige as membership in the Guard or the legendary Three Hundred that had fought the Argives at Thyrea.

Of course, some men grumbled that Leonidas' choice was colored by personal friendship—which was true. Some men, for example, had scoffed at Sperchias' inclusion—until Bulis, hardly one of Leonidas' supporters, acidly retorted to the critics: "I didn't see you stand up to Xerxes!" Bulis' defense of Sperchias had induced Leonidas to invite him to join the Three Hundred himself, an offer he accepted instantly.

Even more men had objected to Temenos, saying that he was unmarried and had no legitimate sons, a standpoint Leonidas shared. Leonidas had, therefore, approached Temenos to notify him he was not qualified. Temenos had looked Leonidas straight in the eye and retorted, "You said *living* sons, not *legitimate* sons. You, who know my boys so well, cannot deny that they are splendid boys."

Leonidas had capitulated.

And men criticized the selection of Prokles, too, saying that the former exile was not really Spartiate anymore. He'd spent too long abroad, outside the discipline of mess and barracks, living by different customs, wearing his hair short and drinking his wine neat. Leonidas had cut the criticism short by saying, "He has more battle experience than the rest put together. Why should I deny myself such a resource?"

That Prokles qualified to march with Leonidas was due to the fact that on his return to Lacedaemon three years earlier, he had immediately taken a bride, who produced a son within their first year of marriage and was now pregnant again. In fact, she was due any day, and sat proudly on the terrace with her hands resting contently on her swollen belly.

Hilaira did not like the girl much. She thought she was lazy and self-satisfied. But Hilaira knew that Prokles, exile and self-made outcast that he was, would have had a hard time finding any bride at all if Leonidas had not, as king, had control over several heiresses.

Hilaira leaned a little farther forward to try to get a better look at her sister-in-law.

"If you lean out any farther, you'll fall right out!" her brother observed, coming up behind her.

"Prokles!" Hilaira admonished. "What are you doing sneaking up on a woman in her own kitchen?"

"Just wanted to be sure you weren't holding the best things back," Prokles retorted, reaching out to snatch a fresh-baked raisin roll and sink his teeth into it before she could stop him.

Hilaira made a face, and started to put the cooling rolls into a basket to bring them to the table. Prokles hemmed her in with an arm that blocked her into the corner between oven and counter. "I just wanted to tell you I'll keep an eye on Alkander. I won't let anything happen to him."

"Alkander's perfectly capable of taking care of himself!" Hilaira defended her husband instinctively. "He's not a little boy that you need to look after anymore!"

Prokles grunted. Hilaira might be right that he still saw Alkander through the lenses of their joint childhood, when Alkander had been the weakling—but Alkander, unlike Leonidas, was not a born soldier. "Yeah, well," he answered his sister, "I won't let his devotion to Leo mislead him into any unnecessary heroics. Leonidas might try to unduly expose himself to danger in order to ensure the oracle is fulfilled, but Dienekes and I have agreed not to let him get away with it. The oracle could damn well be a fake, and we aren't going to take any chances with losing Leonidas to his own idealism just to be stuck with Leotychidas as our commander. That bastard couldn't command a troop of goats!"

Hilaira found this declaration comforting. Prokles spoke as if he were motivated purely by self-interest, but she knew better. Prokles didn't really give a damn about Lacedaemon as a whole; he was fighting for Leo. As for Dienekes, his priorities might be reversed, but he had long since decided that Leonidas was best for Lacedaemon, and he would do all he could to preserve Leonidas as long as possible. As for Alkander, he loved Leonidas—but, she thought, not more than he loved her and their sons. To her brother she said simply, "Thank you, Prokles. Now, let's go back outside before your bride suspects me of seducing you."

Prokles threw his head back and laughed heartily, before remarking with a satisfied smile, "She does have a jealous streak, doesn't she? But then," he shrugged, "she's got every reason to wonder who got the little kitchen maid pregnant."

"Oh, Prokles, you didn't!" Hilaira exclaimed in shocked disapproval.

Prokles shrugged, "She was so tempting—and not unwilling. What did you want me to do? Stay celibate until after the next delivery, or make love to a woman in Cassy's condition?"

"Other men wait!" Hilaira told him firmly.

Prokles laughed. "What you don't know can't hurt you, I guess. Come on!" Snatching another roll from the basket, he turned and headed back outside, leaving Hilaira torn between anger and uncertainty. She mentally ran through the helot births on her own kleros. Could any of the helot children have been conceived when she was pregnant? And what if they had? That didn't make Alkander the father. What was she thinking? How could a single remark make her doubt Alkander's fidelity after all these years? Oh, Prokles! It was just as well he was going away again.

But no sooner had she thought this than she felt guilty. She reached over, took a pinch of salt from the wooden bowl where it stood ready for kitchen use, and rubbed it between her fingers before scattering it on the floor. "Hades, I didn't mean it. Don't take him yet."

Pulling herself together, she took the basket of raisin rolls and went out onto the terrace to join the others. She took her seat beside Alkander and took his hand in hers. Mentally she was saying a second prayer, "But if you must take one of them, take Prokles, not my Alkander."

They didn't get to bed until quite late, and they were both very tired. As Hilaira let down her hair, she saw that it was more gray than brown these days, and when she unclipped the pins at the shoulders of her peplos, she looked down at big but sagging breasts and sighed. Below them, her waist was thick and her hips wider still. She certainly wasn't the slender, agile young maiden Alkander had married. Where had the twenty-six years gone? It wouldn't be long before she had grandchildren. It was odd to think of herself and Alkander as grandparents, when in her heart she still felt like that lithe young filly who had eloped with her childhood sweetheart.

She glanced over to Alkander. He was already naked and climbing into the bed. He was heavier, too, and his hair had receded halfway across his skull. Drill and the rations at the syssitia had kept him fit, but even so, he was clearly an "older man." The boys of the agoge never forgot to call him "father" as they had in his younger days.

Hilaira climbed into the bed beside him and laid her head on his chest. "Please don't take unnecessary risks, Alkander. Let the younger men prove their valor and compete to be a modern Achilles. You're too old for that."

"I know. And I never was the type, anyway. But I would be a slave now—and could never have married you—if Leonidas had not sponsored me in the agoge. The least I can do for him is to be with him now."

Hilaira drew a deep breath. "I *do* understand that, Alkander. I've never said you should stay here." At age forty-eight, both Alkander and Prokles would have been assigned garrison duty if they had not elected to march north with Leonidas. They could have been *safe* if they had chosen not to volunteer. But she would have respected them less. "All I'm asking is that you don't take unnecessary risks."

"Don't worry. Not even Leo is going to take foolish risks. This will be a defensive engagement in which we let the terrain fight for us. Our position is much more defensible than Marathon—and don't forget, despite the fierce fight at Marathon, only about two hundred Greeks fell."

Hilaira nodded. "I'm sure you're right. But to me, two casualties would be just as terrible as two hundred—if you and Leonidas are those two men."

Alkander's answer was to pull Hilaira to him and kiss her protectively, thankfully, and passionately.

The march-out was set for the middle of the morning watch—

later than usual, but a concession to the priests, who wanted Leonidas to publicly make the sacrifice and receive positive signs in favor of his (in their view) risky campaign during the Karneia. Leonidas and his family therefore returned to the palace very early in the morning. After ensuring that his personal belongings were long since packed on mules and ready to follow in the train, Leonidas had Meander and Taiwo help him into the armor they had spent much of the previous day polishing. This was one battle in which Leonidas intended to be recognized for who he was: a king of Sparta. In place of his usual modest and functional armor, he had allowed Arion to create greaves with snakes that climbed up from the ankle toward the kneecap, symbols of the Dioskouroi. His new breastplate had the ancient coils on each breast. His helmet had reinforced eye sockets and cheek-pieces with lion's claws. The crest itself was taken from chestnut horses, stiffened with wax and reinforced with gold wires. The combination of bronze and red, from crest to the skirts of his chiton, was dramatic.

Gorgo, meanwhile, was dressed by Uche (whom she had bought and brought back from Athens as Taiwo's bride) in a white peplos made of silk purchased in Athens. It had a broad border of purple and gold embroidery. Her himation was made of an even sheerer lavender-colored silk that shimmered in the sun. She wore a diadem and collar of gold and rolled amethysts. Even the Athenians would have approved, she thought wryly.

Agiatis was dressed in blues and turquoise, the colors of the Aegean, with a turquoise necklace and earrings. Gorgo let her wear a little rouge on her cheeks and lips as well, because that seemed to give the teenager courage.

Pleistarchos was given a fresh white chiton. His head was shaved, his nails clipped and cleaned, and his feet scrubbed with pumice stone until the last traces of dirt were gone. He was very subdued and said almost nothing—making Gorgo suspect that, as with Agiatis the day before, the meaning of what was happening was starting to sink in.

There was no time left for discussing things with him, however, because the sound of the crowd out in the street could no longer be ignored. Agiatis glanced out the window and exclaimed, "The whole city is out there!"

"What did you expect?" her mother answered.

From somewhere came the whine of a salpinx. The advance guard was moving into position. A moment later, Leonidas was at the door. "Ready?"

"As ready as we'll ever be," Gorgo told him, signaling to the children.

They descended into the private peristyle and through the hall to the front entryway. The palace seemed utterly deserted. Leonidas opened the door and abruptly the sunlight streamed in, glancing off his polished bronze as the wind caught at his red cloak. Gorgo followed, with Agiatis to her left and Pleistarchos on her right, into the sunlight. Halfway down the palace steps the ephors were waiting, flanked by the twenty-eight non-royal members of the Council. They parted to let Leonidas, Gorgo, and the children pass, and then the ephors and Council closed ranks behind them and followed the king and his family to the temple of Zeus the Leader.

Here an even larger crowd was gathered, including the professional priests and heralds. At the exterior altar, a young man held a magnificent black ram that waited docilely, oblivious to impending danger. Leotychidas was nowhere to be seen, but Brotus and Pausanias stood near the front where they had an excellent view, Gorgo noted.

Leonidas took the ram expertly between his knees, clasped it by its horns with his left hand, and pulled the head back to expose the shaved throat. He held his right hand out, and a temple attendant handed him a sharpened knife. It glinted briefly in the morning sun like a flash of lighting. Leonidas slit the ram's throat expertly. The ram sank down onto his knees. Leonidas bent and lifted the dying animal onto the altar with the ease of a man who still had great strength in his arms and shoulders. As he did so, the ram's eyes met his. The ram's last look was so full of reproach that Leonidas recoiled slightly.

The seer Megistias sliced expertly into the belly and let the innards spill out onto the polished marble of the altar. A moment later, the seer nodded and announced in a loud voice: "We march!" He smiled broadly to Leonidas. Megistias was going north with the advance guard.

A tall, blond helot, selected for this purpose, stepped forward to collect coals from the altar, placed them with metal tongs into a bronze pot, and prepared to carry these flames to the border. At the border to Lacedaemon, an altar would be built to Zeus and Athena and a new sacrifice made. Only if the signs were again auspicious would the army proceed beyond the borders.

Meanwhile, Leonidas laid down the knife he'd used to kill the ram and dipped his hands in a silver bowl containing water to clean the blood away. He shook the water from them before accepting the clean linen towel offered. He dried his hands, then started down the steps, with Megistias trailing him.

The men of the advance guard came to attention as Leonidas reached the bottom of the steps. He needed only to turn to the right to start marching at their head.

But Gorgo met him face to face. "Do you have any final instructions for me, Leonidas?"

Their eyes met. Leonidas bent and touched his lips to hers, but far too briefly for her to respond. Then he looked her straight in the eye and said, loud enough for others to hear, "Marry a good man and have good children."*

Then he turned to the right and started walking northeast out of the square, the city, and Lacedaemon, with his hand-picked advance guard of three hundred Spartans in formation behind him.

---

* This exchange between Gorgo and Leonidas is recorded by Plutarch.

CHAPTER 20

THE PASS

THEY WERE SIX THOUSAND ONE HUNDRED heavy infantry, not counting support elements, by the time they reached Thermopylae. Tegea and Mantinea each brought five hundred hoplites, Corinth four hundred, and the smaller Peloponnesian allies had mustered a combined force one thousand two hundred strong, including the smallest contingent of eighty men from Mycenae. These League troops, together with the three hundred Spartiates and the thousand perioikoi Leonidas had selected to bring north, made the Peloponnesian force three thousand nine hundred strong.

Leonidas was not displeased with this turnout by the Peloponnesian League, all of whom had a second line of defense at the Isthmus of Corinth. Sending so many troops north, far from their own homes, was a significant, indeed surprising, gesture of solidarity. He had, however, expected more men from Boiotia and from Phocis and Trachis, the regions north of the Isthmus most directly threatened. For these cities, the Pass at Thermopylae was the last defensible position. Yet mighty Thebes produced a paltry four hundred men, leaving Leonidas to suspect they planned to capitulate to the Persians.

In contrast, little Thespiae turned out with an astonishing seven hundred hoplites, virtually every man who could afford panoply of one sort or another. They were commanded by Demophilus and included the mason, Dithyrambus, who had lost his bride to Theban raiders and had endured a summer of Spartan training almost a decade ago. Leonidas recognized the man, now gray at the jowls, and welcomed him and the others with genuine pleasure. The enthusiasm was reciprocated—if cheers, back slapping, and smiles were anything to go by.

As the force moved closer to Thermopylae, however, the countryside became increasingly deserted. The last twenty miles presented a landscape that was eerily abandoned. The advancing troops of the Confederation encountered no refugees such as those that had flooded and partially blocked the road further south. The fields were empty of workers, and many gates swung, unlatched, in the wind. The houses were boarded up or simply left with doors and shutters open, their contents exposed or already plundered by passers-by. The only domesticated animals were strays. These either ran away or forlornly tried to befriend the transient strangers. The Phocians and Trachians, the natives of this region, seemed to have disappeared—taking their heavy troops with them.

Fortunately, this proved a misunderstanding. The natives of this region calculated the months differently from the Peloponnesians, and when the defensive force promised by the Confederation failed to arrive on the date expected, the locals had taken to the mountains. The sight of five thousand men marching up from the south, however, brought the Phocian and Trachian troops down from their hideouts. These increased the Greek army by roughly a thousand heavy troops.

Leonidas had been told about the Pass at Thermopylae by representatives at the Confederation Council—most specifically by Themistocles, who had passed through it on his way to Tempe and back—but Leonidas had never seen it himself. On arrival, therefore, he ordered the troops to set up camp near the town of Alpeni, just short of the Pass, but proceeded forward to conduct a thorough reconnaissance in person.

The coastline here ran almost due east-west, and the approach from the north by which the Persians would come lay at the west end of the Pass; Leonidas and his troops were camped to the east. He asked the Phocian commander to lead him through the Pass to the so-called West Gate, and took Dienekes, Oliantus, the perioikoi commander Isanor, and Demophilus, as commander of the largest allied contingent, with him.

The Phocian led them through the so-called East Gate, a track between the mountains and the sea barely wide enough for a cart. To their right the Malian Gulf was a vivid blue, lying about one hundred feet below the level of the road at the foot of a sheer cliff. Beyond the East Gate the steep shoreline continued, but the mountain on the left retreated somewhat to the south, forming a broad field almost a hundred yards wide. This was flat except for a lone hillock standing like a sentry before the steeper, stony slopes of the mountain. The lush green vegetation betrayed water reserves beneath the surface of the field.

Not more than a thousand yards ahead of them, the mountain curled back toward the sea, almost completely enclosing them with its sheer, barren slopes. The mountain ended in a broken cliff that dropped almost straight to the level of the field, just fifty feet short of the seaward cliff. Spanning the ledge between the mountain cliff and the drop to the shore were the ruins of a wall.

"We built that wall generations ago," the Phocian explained, "to protect ourselves from the Malians." He gestured to the west, toward Thessaly. "A bunch of cutthroats and thieves!" he dismissed the Malians.

Leonidas gave no thought to the Malians, who could not be defended and so had submitted to the Persians. Instead, he closely considered the wall at the point where it joined the mountainside, squinting up at the thousand-foot cliff with satisfaction. No cavalry in the world could cross this barrier. Meanwhile, Oliantus and Dienekes walked to the other end of the wall to look down at the sea. The drop-off here was almost equally sheer and the fall was a good eighty feet, an excellent anchor for their right flank. The Phocians had picked a good place for their wall. Leonidas nodded to indicate they could continue.

They scrambled over the ruined wall and found themselves in a yet wider field. To the left, nestled against the base of the mountain, were the hot springs that gave the Pass its name, Thermopylae (Hot Gates). The springs were dedicated to Persephone, the Phocian explained, but there was also an altar to Herakles. The hero had died not far from here, continued the Phocian, gesturing vaguely toward the northwest. That was appropriate, thought Leonidas; as a descendant of Herakles, his dying here would be like a family reunion.

This wider area gradually narrowed to a small passage which, like the East Gate, was little more than the width of a cart and formed the West Gate. The flank of the mountain that hemmed in the road here was comparatively gentle and covered with scrub brush, by no means as formidable an obstacle as the cliff behind them or even the mountain that formed the East Gate. From here it did not look suitable for cavalry, but foot soldiers, particularly men from mountainous homelands, would have no trouble scaling or descending this particular slope.

Beyond the West Gate, the countryside opened up into a broad plain fed by three rivers: the Spercheios, the Melas, and the Asopos. Here the Persians would have room to camp several hundred thousand men, grass to graze thousands of cavalry horses, and plenty of water for both man and beast.

As the small party moved beyond the West Gate to gaze into the still empty valley, Leonidas' gaze followed the road until it disappeared into the haze before the mountains in the distance. He stared in this direction for a long time. It was too hazy to see much of anything.

"And this is the *only* road into Phocis from Thessaly?" Leonidas asked casually, just for confirmation.

"Unless you count the Anapaia track," the Phocian replied with a shrug.

The others spun about, almost in unison, to gape at the man in disbelief.

"What did you say?" Leonidas demanded. "What track?"

"The Anapaia track," replied the Phocian, gesturing toward the mountains to their left. "It's not anything to worry about," he assured the southerners in answer to their shocked looks. "It's not wide enough for more than two men, in many places only one, and it climbs over very rough terrain—more of a goat track than anything—until it reaches the cornice between the mountain ridges. The Persians could never get their whole army over it. It's totally unsuitable for horses, let alone a baggage train with carts and wagons."

"They don't have to put their *whole* army across it!" Leonidas snapped. "Just an elite force of troops that can take us in the rear! Where does it start?" His heart was racing in alarm, and he was fighting to get control of his emotions. This was Tempe all over again! The locals had demanded assistance and assured everyone the Pass could not be turned—but it could.

"To reach it, the Persians would have to cross the Asopos gorge," the Phocian assured them, pointing.

"And can they? Can *you*?"

"They'd need a local guide. The gorge looks impassable."

"But it *is* passable?"

"Yes, in two places, although the better—"

Dienekes was cursing colorfully, and Demophilus looked outright sick. Leonidas waved Dienekes silent and looked so hard at the Phocian that the latter took a step backward. "You're saying there are *two* ways to outflank us?" Leonidas asked with barely contained fury.

"No, no! There are two ways across the Asopos gorge, but they meet on the other side at the foot of Kallidromos. From there it is a very steep, difficult climb—as I said, better for goats than men, and sometimes only possible single file. After that it follows the mountain ridge as the Kallidromos curves around, and then descends by a steep but good track into Alpeni."

The perioikoi Isanor was wiping his mouth with his hand in a gesture of subconscious distress, while Demophilus' face had turned into a rigid mask to disguise his emotions. Dienekes wasn't trying to conceal his feelings; he was cursing again. Oliantus, however, asked calmly, "Is there any place along the path that is defensible?"

"At the top of the steep track, where it comes out of the woods, would be one place. Right before the path levels off for a bit."

"How many men could be positioned there?" Leonidas asked, following Oliantus' logic.

"I don't know. A couple hundred." That was obviously a guess.

"Dienekes!" Leonidas snapped. "Go with this man and follow the trail to the point where the two trails coming across the Asopos meet. From there, follow the trail back until you find a strong defensive position. Then report back to me."

"Yes, sir!"

"You want to see the trail?" the Phocian asked, still uncomprehending.

"Yes. Immediately!"

The Phocian still hesitated, but Dienekes gestured sharply. "Let's not waste any time. I don't know about you, but I'm hungry, and neither of us is going to get a bite until we've seen this trail."

With a shrug, the Phocian turned and led Dienekes back through the West Gate, while Leonidas continued looking out in the direction from which the enemy would come. His companions waited until the Phocian was out of hearing, and then Demophilus risked the question: "Does this mean we have to abandon Thermopylae? That it is not defensible?"

Leonidas considered the Thespian nobleman, noting the desperation in his eyes. There was literally no place between here and Thespiae where the Greeks, with their inferior numbers, had a fighting chance against the overwhelming might of Persia. For Thespiae, a successful defense of Thermopylae was the last and only hope of retaining their freedom and independence. They had already sent their women, children, and aged parents to Lacedaemon for safety, but the city itself, their homes, temples, shops, and fields—the basis of their livelihood and their identity—would certainly fall to the Persians if Thermopylae were abandoned.

Leonidas shook his head and said firmly, "No. This does not make Thermopylae indefensible—only more *difficult* to defend. We will have to detach troops to guard this mountain trail, and that will reduce the number of men we can deploy here in the Pass. We'll have to await Dienekes' assessment of what size force is necessary up there. Meanwhile, let's work out how we want to organize our defense here." Leonidas gestured for the others to retrace their steps through the West Gate, but lingered and cast a final look over his shoulder at the empty plain before following them.

At the ruined Phocian wall, they encountered the commanders of the other allied contingents conducting a reconnaissance of their own. These men were noticeably impressed by the terrain—and already squabbling over the best strategy for stopping the Persians. Some of the men argued that they should fight as far back as possible, forcing the Persians to first file through the West Gate, then clamber over the wall, and finally file through the East Gate—by which time, these strategists suggested, they would be so disorganized that the Greeks could just pick them off.

"How many of our hoplites can we deploy in the East Gate at any one time?" Leonidas asked.

"Oh, five or six," one of the advocates of this theory answered readily.

"So against a million Persians you want forty men to stand alone?"

Those who had opposed this strategy immediately picked up on Leonidas' implied criticism. "That's just what I was saying!" "If we let them walk through the West and Middle Gates, then we have no second line of defense!"

The Corinthian commander started arguing, "We should meet them right at the West Gate! It's just as narrow as the East Gate, but if it's breached, then we have two more fallback positions."

"And you'll be in the front rank, I presume?" Leonidas asked. "You and four of your best friends to face a million men? While the Persian mountaineers climb easily over that hill and outflank you?" Leonidas' tone was soft and polite. He did not mock or sound sarcastic. He didn't have to. The Corinthian caught his breath. Leonidas continued, "Or did you think that was my place? That the Spartans should stand up there while the rest of you waited in the fallback positions? If that is your notion, then consider this: we would not last five minutes up there, and then it would be you and your friends after all, wouldn't it?"

"So what *do* you Spartans propose?" the Mycenaean commander asked in an exasperated tone. As a city that had sent only eighty hoplites, he did not expect his own opinion to carry any weight. His city was allied to Sparta to keep the Argives away; in exchange they followed wherever the Spartans led and took their orders from Spartan officers.

Leonidas pointed to the wall. "We'll take our stand here, at this wall." The others looked at the ruins a little dubiously, so Leonidas expounded. "We need to rebuild it first, of course, and shore it up, but six thousand men should be able to manage that in half a day. We can keep our reserves behind the wall, out of reach of Persian archers, and fight in relays in front of it. The need for the Persians to funnel through the West Gate will, as you noted correctly, both slow their advance and disrupt their formations, but by fighting in front of the wall in the wider area," he gestured, "we can bring more of our own men to bear." He paused to size up the field, his head swinging from side to side. "Either one hundred twenty-five by eight or one hundred by ten." He paused to let the others look back and forth across the field, squinting and making their own mental count of possible ranks and files. They started to nod.

"That means we'd only deploy a thousand men at a time?" the Mantinean asked.

"Correct," Leonidas agreed. "The Persians will never tire. Their dead, wounded, and exhausted men will be replaced from their inexhaustible supply without pause. Only the hours of darkness will force them to suspend fighting. We, on the other hand, need to husband our strength, because we'll have no relief here until the sixth day after the full moon, when the full Spartan army will arrive. If we fight in relays of one thousand men at a time, each unit fighting for one hour at a time, no unit will need to fight more than two hours a day—three at the extreme—with time to rest, drink, and dress wounds in the intervals."

The others grunted approval, nodding and looking around themselves and the battlefield. Leonidas thought he detected greater confidence in their expressions than a few moments earlier. "Let's post lookouts, rotating among the units just as we'll rotate the burden of fighting, and put the rest of the men to work on rebuilding the wall."

"But we only just got here!" someone protested, while another objected, "The men are exhausted from marching!" And someone added, "We all need a meal."

"And that," Leonidas turned and pointed behind him, "is the dust of Xerxes' millions blowing across the mountain face. You rest now, and you'll rest in Hades tomorrow!"

Even Oliantus started and looked over his shoulder in alarm, as did Demophilus and Isanor.

"Are you sure?" one of the others protested. "It looks like haze to me."

"Are *you* sure?" Leonidas countered. Then he walked away, giving orders to Oliantus and Isanor to put the troops to work repairing the wall near the coast where it was most ruined.

By dusk it was clear that Leonidas was right. The "haze" had increased all afternoon, and the plain darkened, like a blanket slowly soaking up water from the far edge. Then as daylight faded, pinpoints of light started appearing, not only on the plain but on the flanks of the mountains beyond. Work on the wall became correspondingly energetic and continued at a fevered pitch until it was completely dark. Instead of returning to their camp at Alpeni, however, many of the men spilled through the West Gate to stare in wonder at the multitudes mustered to destroy them.

The enemy fires were still multiplying. "There are more fires than stars in the night sky!" a young man exclaimed in amazement.

"And each fire represents what?—Ten or twenty men?" an older man grunted.

Leonidas, too, was trying to mentally calculate the enemy numbers. He chose a single square of blackness, counted the dots of light, and then attempted to calculate how many such squares were lit by distant fires. It was too much for him.

Dienekes came up behind him, smelling of sweat-soaked linen and leather. Leonidas turned to him with an unspoken question. Dienekes shrugged. "As the Phocian said, it's rugged terrain. Impossible for horses. But good foot soldiers can manage it easily—especially troops from the mountainous regions of Xerxes' empire. The good news is that it should be possible to hold a raiding force of, say, two thousand men with a defensive force of four to five hundred. We could send some of the Arkadians. They're mountaineers."

"And not defending their homes yet," Leonidas countered. "Furthermore, the Persians never do anything by half. If they send a raiding party, it's more likely to be five thousand than two thousand strong."

"That's assuming they find the trail at all," Dienekes pointed out. "After seeing it, I think it unlikely they'll discover it on their own."

"They don't have to. It only takes one traitor."

Dienekes had no answer to that.

"The Phocians have the most to lose in a defeat here," Leonidas noted. "They are also the most familiar with these mountains. I think putting all one thousand of their men on the track would be the best means of defending it—provided a thousand men can deploy effectively?"

"They could, but if we position all the Phocians up on the trail, we'll not have them here. Can we afford to reduce our force here by one-sixth?" Dienekes countered, with a telling glance at the hundreds of thousands of fires lighting up the plain.

"We won't deploy more than a thousand men at a time. If each contingent of a thousand fights an hour, they have four hours to rest before they are on the line again. It should be enough."

Dienekes nodded slowly, but he was frowning, evidently not convinced. "What about sending the perioikoi to hold the trail? We know their quality. We've never seen the Phocians fight."

"True," Leonidas agreed, thinking the plan through a second time, "but we also don't know they will *have* to fight. Maybe no one *will* betray the path. The Phocians are essentially a trip wire. Their job is to hold the Persians long enough for us to reinforce them. How long would that take from here?"

"Three to four hours," Dienekes judged.

"If the Phocians have good forward scouts, they should be able to detect an approaching Persian army at least one, possibly two, hours before contact is made. They would only have to hold their own for an hour or two."

"Assuming we can spare troops from here," Dienekes pointed out.

"If we're about to be outflanked, we'll have to spare them. But until there is some indication that the Persians have found out about the trail, I'm reluctant to deploy some of my best troops. Except for the Thespians, Tegeans, and perioikoi, I don't know how *anyone* will fight." He looked at the men around them, who were still mesmerized by the Persian forces.

"Well," Dienekes gestured toward the increasing number of lights spreading in the darkness, "I guess we'll find out soon enough."

The two Spartans looked again at the men jostling one another, pointing and discussing the awesome Persian force. They overheard a man remark in a loud voice, "There are so many of them, when they shoot their arrows, they will darken the sun."

Before Leonidas could respond, Dienekes called out, "Good! Then we'll fight in the shade!"*

---

* This exchange is recorded by Plutarch, and the Spartan retort is attributed variously to Dienekes or Leonidas.

Everyone within hearing turned around and strained to see who was speaking, belatedly realizing that the Spartan king and one of his officers were standing among them. They laughed nervously, from discomfort rather than amusement. Leonidas and Dienekes exchanged a glance; they could feel panic spreading.

Within two hours, several allied commanders were demanding a conference to "make a command decision before it's too late." Leonidas had been taking a meal around his own fire with the other Spartan officers and the seer Megistias. When the request for a council reached him, Bulis at once muttered contemptuously, "Cowards!"

"Watch your words," Leonidas warned Bulis. "Or do you want to find yourself here alone with the perioikoi?"

Bulis swallowed down his reply. Leonidas got to his feet. He stepped over his kit, which he had been using as a seat, and headed toward the wall where the other commanders had gathered.

As he moved, Leonidas became aware that two men were flanking him. He stopped. They stopped. He looked to his right and left but could not identify the men who were shadowing him. The campfires disrupted night vision by providing only small circles of unsteady light between which stretched greater darkness. Leonidas guessed, "Maron?"

"Yes, sir?"

"I don't need an escort. These are our allies."

"Yes, sir."

Leonidas took another step. The guardsmen kept pace on either side.

"That's enough."

"We have our orders, sir."

"From whom?"

"Dienekes, sir."

Dienekes had been given command of one of the three companies of the advance guard. His company was composed of the eighty-seven guardsmen who had living sons, plus men like Bulis and Alpheus who had been absorbed into the company to bring its complement up to one hundred. Leonidas was perfectly aware that—oracle or no oracle—they were determined see that he died at the last possible moment, so that the command did not fall to someone less competent.

"Then be more discreet about it," Leonidas advised and continued.

When he reached the other commanders, he heard the Corinthian commander arguing passionately for a withdrawal. "This is madness! No one can withstand such a multitude!"

Demophilus countered hotly, "Medizing already? Why did you bother to come at all? To try to destroy the morale of the rest of us?"

"What do you Thespians know of war? Do you think the Muses will help you here?" the Corinthian sneered.

Leonidas clamped his hand on Demophilus' arm before he drew his sword. He pulled Demophilus back forcefully, stepping between him and the Corinthian. "We can use all the help we can get—from the Muses, too. Surely you know we Spartans honor the Muses second only to Athena? So. You wanted to talk to me?" He looked around the circle of allied commanders.

"Look." One of the Arkadians gestured vaguely to the headland visible across the Malian Bay. "There are more men out there than I can count! How can we possibly fight them?"

"I don't think that looks like more than a million men," Leonidas retorted. "Didn't our intelligence talk of a million and a half? Or was it two million?"

"This is no laughing matter!" the Corinthian protested indignantly.

"Am I laughing?"

"You only brought three hundred men!" the Mantinean burst out. "How do you expect to fight all that with so few?"

"If we are to rely on numbers, then all of Greece is not enough to stop the Persian foe. But if *courage* is what counts, then we are enough."[†] Leonidas looked around the circle, forcing each man to meet his eyes or look down ashamed.

At last the Megaran remarked uncomfortably, "No one is questioning Spartan courage, but let's face it: that force out there is more than we can manage. We need to fall back on the Isthmus and—"

---

† This quote is attributed to Leonidas in Plutarch's collection of "Sayings of Spartans."

"Fall back on the Isthmus?" The outraged question erupted from Phocian, Trachian, Theban, and Thespian throats in a single roar.

"You would abandon half of Hellas just to save your own backsides?" the Phocian demanded furiously.

"Is this all your promises are worth?" Demophilus demanded, red with outrage. "I was present at the Confederation conference where you vowed to send as many troops as possible to hold the Persians here! Are you going back on your word?"

"We're here, aren't we?" the Corinthian pointed out, "And out there! We aren't just providing hoplites, but triremes as well!"

"Yes, and what would the Athenians think if they learned you Peloponnesians want to turn tail and scamper back behind your Isthmus?" the Phocian demanded angrily.

"This is pointless chatter," Leonidas cut the recriminations short. "We knew before we came that we would be massively outnumbered. That is not the point. We chose this position because the terrain here favors the defenders. I am far happier standing here, with you, than I would be in Xerxes' shoes with all his millions." He paused to let that sink in. Then, ignoring their skepticism, he announced bluntly: "Lacedaemon stays." He looked pointedly at the Phocians, Trachians, Thebans, and Thespians. "We are honored to fight with free men defending their freedom here, and—" he pointed out to sea, "at Artemisium." He turned and walked away.

Behind him there was some muttering, but that was all. The other commanders returned to their own troops. There was no more talk of abandoning the Pass.

As always when in the field, the Spartan army kept a watch that patrolled the perimeter of their camp. Every four hours the watch changed. Half an hour before dawn, the watch woke Leonidas and the other officers. While they combed out their hair and put on their arms and armor, their attendants fetched water and helped their masters with their hair. The helot in charge of the sacrificial animals in the baggage train brought forward a kid. Leonidas performed the sacrifice and Megistias read the signs as the other men started to wake up around them.

"Well?" Leonidas asked.

"Totally unremarkable. As if today will be a day like any other," the seer announced, sounding baffled.

"Maybe it will be. So far Xerxes has shown himself a methodical man of careful planning and dogged determination—but not exactly a man marked by audacity and unpredictability. I expect he'll settle in and try to get our measure. He'll reconnoiter as far forward as possible, maybe even send a herald demanding earth and water." Leonidas paused and looked around until he spotted his deputy. "Oliantus, who has the watch on the wall at the moment?"

"The Tegeans."

"Good. We'll go forward for our morning gymnastics."

Leonidas led all three hundred Spartiates forward from their camp, leaving it to the helots to guard their equipment and supplies. At the wall, they stripped out of their armor and arms, left them behind the wall, and went naked into the broad field between the wall and the West Gate to exercise. Leonidas set the tone by challenging Bulis to a wrestling match, and others followed his example. Alkander and Sperchias jogged side by side around the perimeter of the field. Maron and Alpheus started informal sprinting races. Prokles found some javelins and started hurling them in the general direction of the Persians, but so casually that it did not seem threatening. Soon the wall was lined with their allies, staring at them in disbelief.

"I think we're causing a sensation," Alpheus remarked to Maron, as the brothers sat catching their breath and rebraiding their hair.

Maron twisted to look over his shoulder. The sight of the other allies staring and pointing made him smile sidelong at his brother. "They must think we're crazy."

"We probably are," Alpheus retorted.

"Not just them," Temenos remarked, dropping beside the brothers after lapping the field twice. "Look over there!" He pointed to the crest of the hill that sloped down toward the West Gate. Something was clearly moving on it. When Maron realized it must be Persian scouts, he felt his skin creep. He jumped up and looked frantically for Leonidas. He was somewhere out here—naked as a newborn babe! A single, well-aimed arrow....

Maron caught sight of the grizzled exile Prokles, a man he did not like and did not trust, sprinting across the field, and realized that several other guardsmen were likewise converging on their king at all speed. Maron ran to join them, only to hear Leonidas growl, "Until you started hovering around, they didn't know which naked man was Sparta's king. Disperse!"

The guardsmen hesitated, glancing over their shoulders. Prokles planted himself between Leonidas and the Persians, his back to the enemy, and stood his ground. "Leo! You have no right to expose yourself to risks like this! I'm escorting you behind that wall. The rest of us are enough to make the point."

Leonidas glanced past Prokles' shoulder to the mountain slope ending at the West Gate. He could make out three Persians. He didn't think he or the other Spartans were in range, but Prokles had a point. He was taking an unnecessary risk. "Agreed."

The other Spartans continued their exercises for an hour without incident, and then returned to their camp beyond the wall. The sentries on the wall and the lookouts, however, reported a steady stream of Persian observers who came forward to get a look at the Greek position and then went away again.

Midafternoon an Athenian triaconter landed on the tiny beach of the fishing village below Alpeni. The triaconter took up almost the whole of the little cove and attracted a large crowd of idle soldiers. The young, elegantly dressed Athenian captain came ashore asking for Leonidas. By the time he reached the Spartan camp, he was grinning widely.

Leonidas was playing backgammon with Alkander. They were in armor with their hoplons, helmets, and spears ready at hand, but sat on folding stools, resting their elbows on their knees. A flurry of voices and the phrase "Over there!" alerted Leonidas to the new arrival. He looked up, then stood.

"King Leonidas?" the Athenian asked.

Leonidas nodded. "I am he."

The Athenian grinned more widely. "Abronichus. Themistocles sent me to report that the fleet has gone into position at Artemisium without mishap or loss, my lord. We're 183 ships strong, of which 174 are triremes. I am to remain here with my triaconter to serve as your courier. If you have any message to send to the fleet, I'll take it for you. A Phocian galley has been dispatched to Artemisium to serve the same function in the reverse direction."

"Excellent. Have a seat and join me for some wine. Meander?" Leonidas looked around for his attendant.

"Sir?"

"Bring wine for the captain."

"Yes, sir."

"So, how is the morale in the fleet?" Leonidas asked.

"Ah," Abronichus grinned, "what would you expect? Some men got a little weak-kneed at the sight of the Persian fleet and suggested Artemisium wasn't such a good place to fight after all."

"I can imagine," Leonidas observed. "And then?"

"Themistocles and Eurybiades convinced them otherwise, though we did move to a more protected anchorage. You wouldn't have a message you wish to dispatch at once, would you?" the captain asked. "I'd rather like to report how you strolled around naked in front of the Persians this morning."

Leonidas frowned. "I didn't *stroll around* naked; I was exercising."

"In full view of the Persians. I hope you bummed your ass at them!"

Alkander couldn't help laughing. Leonidas frowned at him, but then broke down and laughed himself, admitting, "I didn't think of it. The display was more for our allies than for the Persians. My intent was to convey nonchalance—not contempt."

"Yes, my lord." The captain tried to look chastised, but couldn't. He burst out laughing again. It proved contagious.

When the laughter died away, Leonidas observed, "You seem in extraordinarily good spirits."

"Why shouldn't I be? There hasn't been a fight like this since the Age of Heroes, and I will have a front-row seat. One day, I hope to tell my great-grandchildren that I personally shared a skin of wine with King Leonidas at Thermopylae. The only catch is, I have to live that long."

"That is a problem, isn't it?"

"My lord!" The shout came from farther forward. "Persians!"

They all looked sharply toward the Pass. A commotion had seized the men loitering near the East Gate, but it hardly looked like panic.

No one was rushing to get their arms. On the contrary, they seemed to be pressing forward, flowing through the gate in an agitated mob, but without their weapons.

Leonidas guessed it was some kind of envoy even before word was relayed back, "An ambassador!"

"Brave man," Sperchias, who had been watching Alkander and Leonidas play checkers, observed dryly, his thoughts far away in Persepolis.

Leonidas grabbed his helmet, with its chestnut cross-crest studded with gold wire, and got to his feet, muttering an excuse to the Athenian as he set off in the direction of the East Gate. By the time he reached it, word was being passed for him, and his own men parted to let him through. Men were speculating in a rumble of agitated voices, "Do you think they'll offer terms?" "Yeah, earth and water or death." "How do they know Leonidas is our commander?" "They had spies at the Confederation conference, stupid—all the cities that have since capitulated." "Yeah, they probably know how many men we have here, right down to the last water boy and the fleas on the goats."

Leonidas reached the wall and mounted it, by one of the ramps they had built to enable troops to deploy rapidly along its broad back. In front of him the Mantineans, who evidently had the watch, were lined up in a phalanx on the field with their shields locked and helmets down, but their spears sloped. A hundred yards beyond them, a Persian envoy waited on a magnificent white stallion, flanked by two heralds with flapping pennants proclaiming his mission. The envoy's horse was unnerved by the Mantinean hoplites, but the man himself exuded not just calm, but disdain. Leonidas thought he looked like the Persian interpreter that Sperchias had saved from the mob in Sparta more than a decade ago.

"Your king has a message for me?" Leonidas called out.

"King Leonidas of Sparta?" the question came back.

Leonidas descended by one of the three ramps on the front of the wall. He passed through the Mantinean phalanx but stopped in front of it. The horseman hesitated, but then dismounted. They approached each other, one step at a time, to meet halfway. Leonidas had been right; it was Zopyrus.

The Persian bowed slightly, as if to say he knew his manners but did not think Leonidas deserved the courtesy of kings. "We meet again, my lord."

"Sperchias told me you had made Persia safely. I'm pleased."

Zopyrus smiled coldly, conveying disbelief. "I am not here by choice," he started. "If I had my way, I would meet you with a bow, not a staff, in my hand. But His Magnificence, Xerxes son of Darius, the Great King, Lord of—"

"I'm familiar with his titles," Leonidas cut Zopyrus off. "And none of his minions can hear you here, so let's just get to the point. Your master has a message for me?"

"The Great King is a man of infinite mercy. He sees this pitiful band of men, sent by heartless or foolish cities, to fulfill a task no mortal can fulfill, and, being a civilized and compassionate man, he refrains from mocking or humiliating you. Clear the Pass and let him continue on his way unhampered, and he will hold no grudge against you."

"That is very generous of him," Leonidas observed. "But we did not come here to withdraw. We are here to fight."

"With this?" The emissary gestured with his long, beringed fingers toward the Mantineans.

"There are more men here than meet the eye," Leonidas assured him.

"How many? Ten thousand? A hundred thousand? Not all of Greece has enough fighting men to stop the might of Persia. Your cause is lost, and if you fight, your lives are lost as well. Why?"

"We prefer an honorable death to life without honor."

Zopyrus raised his eyebrows skeptically. "What is honorable in throwing your lives away in a foolish gesture?"

"We won't know how foolish our gesture was until you take the Pass," Leonidas pointed out.

"Is this your last word?"

Leonidas hesitated, wondering if he could drag the negotiations out until the full Spartan army arrived. Maybe not, but each day they talked was a day they didn't fight. Then again, if he put this offer to the allies, Leonidas feared they would start fighting among themselves again. He nodded slowly.

Zopyrus bowed his head with a slight smile. "I'm pleased. I

have waited a long time for the opportunity to show you just how arrogant—and stupid—you pig-headed Spartans are. Mind! This is not what Xerxes told me to say, but what I, Zopyrus, say. This is the second time you Spartans have rejected the Great King's generous clemency and insisted on blood. Last time we were three unarmed emissaries surrounded by a mob of barbarians. This time you are as outnumbered as we were then. This time, the blood you spill will be your own—and you will choke on it!" Zopyrus spun about and strode back in the direction of his horse. He vaulted on in a single leap, spun it around on its haunches, and galloped away.

The others surged forward and swarmed around Leonidas. "What did they want? What did they want?"

"Surrender."

"You turned them down?"

"Of course. We'll fight tomorrow."

Chapter 21

THE EMPIRE STRIKES

Leonidas was wrong. Xerxes did not attack the next day. The sun rose from the sea, oozed its way across the late summer sky, and slowly sank below the mountains to the west without the Persians making any move to threaten Thermopylae. The Spartans (without their king) exercised provocatively in front of the wall, and the sentries from each allied contingent took their turn on the wall in rotation. In the camp the men gambled, groused, told tall tales, and cleaned their already pristine weapons and armor. They visited the hot springs or ventured down to the shore to buy fish from the locals and cool themselves in the refreshing waters of the gulf. The Persians appeared to do the same, while Leonidas watched the moon. Another day of the Karneia had passed. And another.

Early on the morning of the fifth day, however, the sentries observed a great deal of agitated movement in the Persian camp. Dust blew in large clouds and unintelligible shouts wafted on the morning breeze. Word was passed back from the sentries, and Leonidas went forward to the West Gate. It took him only a moment to be convinced: they were coming at last.

At about this time the sentries spotted what appeared to be a half-dozen carpenters, the sound of their hammers ringing out in the morning air, working in great haste to complete a broad wooden platform on the flank of the mountain that formed the West Gate. The platform commanded a view of the Pass between the West Gate and the wall. Next, a score of Persians could be seen dragging and wrestling a large, awkward wooden object up to the platform. The Greek sentries speculated it must be some kind of massive arrow or sling that would hurl death at them, but then brilliant cloths were draped over it and cushions scattered around, and the sentries realized it was a large throne. They looked at one another, dumbfounded, and then sent this news back to Leonidas as well.

Meanwhile, Leonidas ordered the deployment agreed upon days earlier. The perioikoi took the field first, positioning themselves at the head of the wall, with the Spartans and Thespians drawn up in full panoply on the wall behind them, to reinforce if necessary or relieve them after one hour of combat.

The decision to let the perioikoi engage first had been made at Isanor's initiative. Leonidas had planned to take the field with the Spartans and Thespians, but Isanor requested the honor, arguing, "We'll show the allies it can be done." Leonidas had taken this wise advice. The perioikoi, although independent, had absorbed a great deal of Spartan training and ethos. Isanor was a veteran of countless border clashes with the Argives. Leonidas knew the perioikoi were up to the task, and Isanor's point was good: the allies believed the *Spartans* could hold the Persians, but they secretly doubted their *own* ability to do the same. Leonidas had to convince the allies as soon as possible that other Greeks, not just the Spartans, could beat the Persians. It was an ideal task for the perioikoi.

All they had to do, Leonidas reminded Isanor as the commanders dispersed to give the orders to their troops, was hold the Persian onslaught for one hour. Then, Leonidas promised, the Spartans and Thespians would move down from the wall and take the field to replace the withdrawing perioikoi. Meanwhile, the Tegeans and Mantineans would move on to the wall, ready to relieve the Spartans and Thespians. They would be followed by the Arkadians, then the Corinthians and Thebans, who in turn would be relieved by the then rested perioikoi, and so on until the Persians gave up. That, at least, was the plan.

Leonidas' greatest worry was that at the first sign of weakness, the relieving forces on the wall would panic and run the other way, rather than reinforce the fighters when they were needed most. To discourage this, Leonidas planned to keep one hundred Spartans on the wall at all times under his own command. That way there would always be some troops ready to spring into any breach and restore confidence and morale if panic threatened.

The noise from the Persian camp was getting louder, and the clouds of dust were like fog billowing up from the sea. Leonidas looked around at his companions. They were armed and upright—except for Prokles, who was leaning against a cart full of extra spears with his legs crossed at the ankles. Leonidas was vaguely aware of the other commanders in their respective camps calling their men about them and haranguing them, but it seemed rather pointless for him to do the same. There wasn't a man here, Spartiate or helot, who didn't know how important it was to hold this position until the full army arrived in what was now just seven days. So he just nodded and set his helmet on his head, cocked back on his neck. He looked for Meander. The young man caught his glance and nodded once, indicating the two extra spears on his back and the water skin. Leonidas noted the medical kit, too. "Let's go," he said, and led the Spartans forward.

The perioikoi were mustering just behind the wall when the Spartans arrived. "We'll be right behind you, and we'll reinforce you at the slightest sign of trouble," Leonidas paused to reassure Isanor, noting without looking the white faces and trembling hands of some of the perioikoi men.

"Don't worry about us," Isanor replied in his rough, gravelly voice. "We're not going to disgrace Lacedaemon."

On the wall the Thespians were forming up, too. Leonidas smiled at Demophilus and then Dithyrambus. The latter grinned back and asked, "You don't think there's any chance they'll turn tail and run before we can get a crack at 'em, do you?"

"Unlikely," Leonidas laughed.

"Did you see that?" Demophilus asked, pointing to the brightly cushioned throne on the slope beyond the field. It had now been provided with a footstool and a side table and was surrounded by smaller chairs, likewise draped with cloth. The distance was too great to see the details, but a dozen men were fluttering about, apparently slaves preparing snacks, refreshments, and what looked like documents. Xerxes expected pleasant entertainment, Leonidas concluded, while recording which of his captains fought most bravely and deserved the greatest reward.

Leonidas gazed at the scene for a moment, then turned to Demophilus and advised, "No need to keep your men on their feet while we're in reserve, and keep water circulating. No man should engage the enemy thirsty." He reiterated the best way to move the men down the three ramps onto the field and the way to file them forward. Although he had helped train the Thespians ten years ago, that had been for warding off raids and hit-and-run attacks, not for a fixed-phalanx battle of this nature. Still, to their credit, the Thespians appeared to be bearing up well. Leonidas' gaze ran along their front rank and recognized with a start not just Arion's brother, but the bronze master himself.

He strode over. "What are you doing here, Arion? I thought you were in Sparta making shields for my countrymen!"

"Sir? I, well—"

Leonidas regretted his question. The bronze master had never been a man of quick words and clearly didn't know what to say, but his sentiments could hardly be faulted. It had been unfair to single him out. Leonidas grabbed his shoulder and overplayed the awkward moment by declaring, "Well, now I know who'll fix my shield if it gets damaged." Leonidas held up the flashy aspis with the roaring lion that Arion had designed and made for him more than a quarter-century earlier. Today was the first time he was carrying it in battle.

A flurry of shouting drew attention to the front again, and the enemy was pouring through the West Gate. They came on the double, anxious to deploy as many men as possible through the bottleneck fast. The perioikoi responded by filing rapidly up the ramps on the back of the wall and down the ones on the other side. They formed up as Leonidas had recommended, one hundred across and ten deep, stretching across the field roughly eighty feet forward of the wall. Leonidas watched with approval as the men took up their position, and Isanor prowled up and down along the front rank. He was talking to them, but Leonidas was more interested in the way the rear rankers braced themselves with their legs about two feet apart, their left feet leading slightly. He was also watching the steadiness of their spears. The perioikoi were damned near as good as Spartiates, he concluded, with some surprise and a great deal of pride.

A flurry of exclamations erupted behind him, and Demophilus grabbed his arm and pointed. A figure in a tall headdress wearing glittering gold cloth covered with jewels had just emerged over the curve of the mountainside. He was accompanied by several men almost equally well dressed, and took a seat on the waiting throne. The attendants bowed low and backed away. Xerxes' companions appeared as relaxed as he. They took their seats, but then started signaling irritably for something. A moment later a gigantic parasol with a hanging fringe was rushed up the slope and adjusted several times until it shielded the Great King from the morning sun that glistened off the Malian Gulf, without blocking his view of the battlefield.

Meanwhile, his troops (identified by Sperchias as Medes) continued to pour through the West Gate until they numbered about four thousand. Those weren't bad odds, Leonidas thought, especially given the Medes' wicker shields and lack of body armor. The men deployed were archers. Some of them went down on one knee, their shields before them; others remained upright, the ranks staggered. After some last-minute orders and redeployments, an eerie stillness fell on the sunny field.

"I could use a little shade," Dienekes remarked to Leonidas, who laughed appreciatively. They glanced at one another, sharing the joke.

Xerxes raised and then dramatically dropped his arm. The Mede officers, who had been watching for this signal, shouted. The first volley whistled into the air.

The arrows did not darken the sun—there were too few Persians inside the West Gate for that—but the volleys were impressive nevertheless. For a start, they came at intervals of every two seconds, which meant they were reloading in eight seconds, Leonidas calculated. Men were bobbing up and down in perfect timing to ensure that the rear ranks got off their arrows in good order. All in all, very good shooting—except that it didn't have any impact on the Greek armor. Either the range was too great or the bows too weak; the arrows bounced off the hoplons rather than sticking in them, much less piercing them.

The Mede archers kept up the barrage for about ten minutes, and then, with the Greeks responding as if they'd gone to sleep, the Medes realized they would have to move forward. As they reduced the range, the arrows started to thump into the hoplons, and the first cries of wounded came up from the phalanx of perioikoi. Leonidas leaned forward and shouted, "Clear them out, Isanor!"

"Yes, sir!" Isanor answered, and then with a single command the perioikoi phalanx started advancing, just like a Spartan phalanx, at a slow but steady pace. The closer they got to the archers, however, the more deadly the barrage became. Remembering Marathon, Leonidas shouted, "Jog!"

Either Isanor heard him or he came to the decision on his own. In any case, the perioikoi doubled the pace, and a few seconds later they crashed into the Persian archers. They rolled right over them. The Medes had never before encountered anything like this wall of moving bronze. They didn't stand a chance. The perioikoi front ranks knocked them down without even stopping to stab with their upraised spears, and the rear ranks stabbed and gutted, kicked and trampled.

Leonidas didn't bother watching the perioikoi. He focused on Xerxes. The Great King had leaped up from his throne, knocking over the refreshment table. He clearly hadn't expected this, Leonidas registered with a slight smile of inner satisfaction.

Of course, the satisfaction did not last long. The perioikoi hadn't even reached the last rows of archers before reinforcements were pouring through the West Gate. Now it was Leonidas' turn to catch his breath and worry. Isanor's phalanx, unhinged as it was in the forward position, could be outflanked on either side, surrounded, cut off, and slaughtered.

But just when Leonidas was getting truly alarmed, Isanor signaled withdrawal. The perioikoi, with admirable discipline, disengaged neatly, stepping back sharply but in unbroken formation for a good ten paces before turning and sprinting toward the wall so rapidly that the Medes barely got off a dozen arrows before they were in position again, shields in front of them. "Well done," Leonidas remarked under his breath, and Oliantus nodded.

The Medes pouring into the field now were not archers but spearmen, and they came in greater numbers. Archers need space;

spearmen don't. Leonidas could hear Isanor shouting, "Steady! Steady!"

"They really are endless," Alkander murmured.

"This is a drop in the ocean," Leonidas answered.

Isanor was holding his men in position, making the Medes come to him, but that meant that with each second the odds were worsening. Leonidas found it hard to watch, but then, this was the best way to learn. He glanced up at Xerxes. The "Great King" had reseated himself and was sipping something from a vessel that glinted and gleamed in the early morning light.

The Medes collided with the perioikoi, and the battle was truly joined. Leonidas glanced along the front ranks beside him and could read its progress from the faces of his men—and from the sounds. He closed his eyes for a moment, experiencing the battle as if he were a middle ranker again, unable to see anything but the back of the man ahead of him, who had to guess at progress from the sounds, smells, and pressure of bodies packed together.

The Medes were howling, shouting, and screaming. Not knowing their tongue, Leonidas could not know if they were cursing, praying, or shouting insults. It didn't much matter. The screams of the wounded had their own unique note. Just listening, he thought he could distinguish between mortal wounds and merely disfiguring, mutilating, and debilitating ones. The perioikoi were killing.

Then something changed. It was like a collective grunt. And then another. Grunt. Pause. Grunt. Pause. The perioikoi were advancing again. Leonidas looked at the faces of the men in the front rank. The Spartans looked pleased, the Thespians amazed and elated. Yes, the perioikoi were clearing the field again.

"Time?" Leonidas asked.

"A quarter-hour still," Oliantus answered.

Leonidas came to life now. He walked over to Demophilus, warning him that it was almost time to relieve the perioikoi. The rankers, seeing their commander in motion, got to their feet, stretched and wriggled their muscles, then took up their shields.

Ten minutes later, taking advantage of a temporary lull in the fighting, Leonidas gave the order to deploy. The Spartiates went down the right ramp and took up their position on the right-hand side of the formation, while the Thespians went into position to their left. At a signal, they moved forward fifty paces and paused. Leonidas nodded for the trumpet signal that ordered the perioikoi to open gaps between their files for the relieving units to file through.

Several of the perioikoi rear rankers looked over their shoulders in apparent amazement; others had been looking over their shoulders every few seconds for a long time already. Both kinds of rear ranker passed the word forward, and a moment later the perioikoi compressed their files into columns of four men, providing gaps that the Spartans and Thespians could file through to the front. Leonidas was too close behind the perioikoi to see the enemy, but he could hear increased shouting, and guessed that the Persians thought the Greek line was breaking.

As he led the way through the central gap, Leonidas noted that the perioikoi were panting, sweating, and bloody—although Leonidas gathered that most of the blood was from their enemies.

He had reached the front, and guardsmen were going rapidly into position on either side of him, their shields clacking on one another, while behind him he felt the reassuring pressure of the second ranker already at his back.

Ahead of him a ragged mass of men was struggling to clamber over the bodies of their dead and dying comrades in order to engage the Spartans—a mass of men that quailed visibly when they realized the enemy was not fleeing in panic, but had been replaced by a new line of bronze. The moment of confusion lasted only a couple of seconds, however. Then the Mede officers shouted, the spears were raised, and the Medes rushed forward more furiously than before.

The crash of the Medes with the Spartan/Thespian line was sickeningly soft. Instead of the heart-stopping crash of bronze on bronze and the deep-throated echo of wood on wood that the Greeks knew from their own battles, there was only a whisper of breaking wicker and a mushy sound of flesh colliding with wood and bronze.

The eight-footers of the Greeks could kill three, even four ranks deep, but the Medes' spears were much shorter and connected only with the front rank of the Greeks. As far as Leonidas could see, the Greeks were killing without taking any casualties at all. The problem, he rapidly recognized, was that the bodies of the enemy were piling up dangerously high in front of them. The more the Medes climbed up onto their dead and dying comrades, the more they could stab downward. This forced the Greeks to raise their shields higher and higher.

That was not good. Hoplons were far too heavy, and a man's shoulder could not hold his hoplon high for long. The Greeks had to push the Medes back onto the level field.

Leonidas gave the order and set off, stepping forward onto the pile of human beings. His footing gave slightly and his foot slipped on something slimy, causing a queasy feeling. He felt warm liquid on his calves; something warm and slimy covered his toes. "Clear the bodies!" he shouted back over his shoulder, hoping the message would get relayed to the helots, one man at a time.

The Medes were fighting with a mindless, desperate courage. They howled in outrage as much as in pain. Leonidas could make out their faces, wrapped in their cloth turbans, and saw the bright colors of their sleeves and trousers turn a dull, dark tone as they soaked with sweat, urine, and blood. They fought as if deranged with their spears and, when these broke, with their curved swords. Leonidas noted in a detached part of his brain that the butts of the Medes' spears had round balls on them, apparently for balance but useless in battle.

Since he was fighting men without body armor or effective shields, Leonidas took a man out with each thrust of his spear. With a horrible, methodical rhythm he brought his spear down again and again, severing a man's neck, smashing through another's teeth, breaking clear through the chest of the next.

At last they were back on the level, but the field was also wider. Leonidas checked anxiously to see whether the Medes were swarming around the ends of his phalanx. He was alarmed by movement on his right, before he realized it was only the bodies of the dead falling to the sea as they were pushed, shoved, and flung over the cliff. The helots were feverishly at work.

A second later a spear tip connected with the side of his helmet, knocking his head back and blinding him briefly as his helmet shifted. He turned back sharply to eliminate the threat, but already Maron had thrust his spear so deeply into the Mede's armpit that he could not pull it out again. The man fell at Leonidas' feet, vomiting blood and defecating, while Maron called for a new spear. Leonidas killed the next Mede when the man slipped and fell on the liquids of his comrade before he could even get in a good thrust.

Leonidas felt nothing for the men he was slaughtering. There were too many of them. He was too preoccupied with wondering how much time had passed and how long they had to continue this before they would be relieved. He found himself wondering if they could keep this up two to three hours a day for six or seven days until the full army arrived. Then his thoughts drifted to the fact that so many dead would attract vultures, dogs, flies, and disease. If this slaughter went on for days, he calculated—without stopping his trained, methodical killing—the putrefying bodies of the dead would make the air impossible to breathe. They would poison the ground water. He was starting to realize that his own brain was incapable of imagining what this Pass would look like even tonight, much less tomorrow or ten days from now.

This thought, the sense that this couldn't go on forever, made him give the order to advance. Like the perioikoi before them, they moved forward just one step at a time, in the same slow push, pause, push, pause. The rear rankers carried the burden of the advance, their heads down and their shoulders against their shields. Each led with his left foot, bringing the right up and bracing on it before reaching out again with his left foot.

Leonidas found the advance easier than just holding ground. The Medes had no phalanx with which to counter the advancing Greek line. They crowded together but had not learned to fight together, in unison as a block. The pressure of a thousand trained and disciplined heavy infantry against a disorganized mass of men is immense. Within moments the pace was picking up and the killing was being done by the rear ranks. Leonidas sensed, more than saw, the wall of the mountain closing in on them again, and felt the men to his right pressing in to avoid falling into the sea. The West Gate was only fifty feet away. The Medes were screaming so loudly that his head ached. If he hadn't known that there were hundreds of thousands of the enemy beyond that Gate, it would have felt like victory.

They continued to the Gate itself; then with a shout, they turned on their heels and marched on the double back toward the wall. Here they reversed again and stood, gasping for breath and dripping sweat, while the Medes mustered enough men for a new assault.

Leonidas had a moment to survey the field. The helots had done a remarkably good job of clearing away the corpses—and at the moment, the Persians were helping them. They were flinging their own men, the ones nearest the West Gate that the helots had not yet reached, over the cliff. To judge by the screams of terror, some of the men were still alive.

Leonidas spared a glance for Xerxes. He was still sitting on his throne, surrounded by his courtiers. It was impossible to tell whether he was distressed by the slaughter and the summary execution of the wounded. After his initial surprise, he appeared rather to have become accustomed to it.

Leonidas also looked back toward the wall, and saw with relief that the Tegeans and Mantineans were preparing to descend on to the field. The Spartan/Thespian hour wasn't quite over, but it made sense to swap out the tired troops with fresh ones before the Medes could attack again.

Once the Spartans were back on the wall again, Leonidas sent two companies back to camp to refresh themselves, but waited with his guard to see how the Tegeans and Mantineans fought. Oliantus, serving as usual as his quartermaster, was tasked with reporting on casualties. Meander was beside him almost at once with a skin of water, which Leonidas half drank and then poured over his face. As he handed it back to Meander he remarked, "Good work clearing the corpses."

"Thank you, sir. We had some help from the slaves of the others, too. We couldn't have done it on our own."

"You're going to have to do it again—and again," Leonidas warned.

"I know, sir." Meander looked significantly toward the sun. It had not yet reached the zenith.

Leonidas looked out onto the battlefield. The Tegeans and Mantineans were doing just as well as the perioikoi, Thespians, and Spartans had done before them.

"You can't fault the Medes' courage," Dienekes observed.

"No," Leonidas agreed. The Medes, despite the obvious disadvantages of their armor and arms, were still fighting furiously.

"They must be mad to keep fighting like this," Dienekes thought out loud.

"Earlier this morning, they thought we were mad to defy them," Leonidas reminded him.

"War is madness," Alkander remarked softly.

Oliantus was back. "No serious casualties, sir. Sprained ankles and wrists for the most part, wrenched shoulders, a dislocated elbow, one bad puncture wound in the biceps. What is odd is that both Aristodemos and Eurytus have come down with some eye illness. Their eyes are streaming and so red and swollen they can hardly see."

"What caused that?" Leonidas asked, astonished.

"Apparently their eyes started itching after visiting the hot springs yesterday. They went together and bathed in the springs, then stretched out on some towels they found there to dry off."

"Idiots," Leonidas exclaimed angrily. People came to these hot springs to cure all sorts of illnesses. Spartiates should have known better than to use discarded towels.

"They were ashamed to say anything and thought it would go away, but during the fighting today they both found it increasingly difficult to see."

"Have the surgeon look at them and, just in case it's infectious, send them back to Alpeni, away from the others."

Oliantus nodded approval, his eyes wandering to the field, where the Tegeans and Mantineans were killing efficiently. Meanwhile, the Arkadians were forming up on the wall. Leonidas didn't like the nervous looks on many of their faces and the way they were jostling one another. They kept changing their positions as if they didn't have fixed positions in the phalanx. He glanced back at his guardsmen, and then asked Oliantus, "Are the others rested enough for one company to relieve the guard here and let the guard refresh themselves?"

Oliantus nodded and went back down from the wall. Ten minutes later the Kastor Company, commanded by the experienced lochagos Diodoros, relieved the guard. The Arkadians were still dressing their lines and were dragging their feet about going into position, even when one of the inevitable lulls in the fighting occurred, caused by the Medes waiting for more troops to deploy through the bottleneck of the West Gate. Leonidas felt compelled to give the order himself.

"We're going! We're going!" came the irritated answer.

Leonidas glanced at Diodoros, who just shook his head.

The trouble started almost at once. The Tegeans and Mantineans failed to open wide, straight gaps; as a result, the Arkadians were getting bunched up and deploying very slowly. When a shout went up from the west indicating that the Medes were advancing, some of the Mantineans panicked and started pushing and shoving their way to the back. The Arkadians responded by huddling together in city units, leaving large gaps into which the Medes poured wildly. In just minutes the Medes had turned the flanks of the most exposed units, and almost before Leonidas could grasp what was happening, these panicked. Men were trying to run back to the wall, exposing their backs to the Medes. They collided with men still standing fast. Men lost their footing. Men started fighting with other contingents or even their own comrades. If he hadn't seen it with his own eyes, he would never have believed it. Leonidas was not prepared for so much incompetence.

But he had little time to reflect on it. He exchanged a look with Diodoros, and they both pulled their helmets down simultaneously, then took the Kastor Company down the central ramp on the double. They waded straight into the fight, pushing aside anyone still trying to retreat and killing any enemy in their way. Around them, the sight of Spartan scarlet, the immaculate ranks and files, and the calm and silence of the Spartans quelled the panic. On both flanks men started to attach themselves. Later Dienekes, who came running in response to a message from Meander, claimed it had been like "rubbish sucked into the wake of a ship," but all that mattered to Leonidas was that the panic had dissipated and the semblance of a phalanx was restored.

The Medes, meanwhile, had smelled blood, and for the first time had seen that the Greeks were vulnerable after all. They redoubled their assaults. It was obvious to Leonidas that with the Arkadians, he could not advance and clear the field. That meant they were stuck here, just slogging it out, until they were relieved. But maybe that was enough, he told himself: maybe it was enough that the Arkadians saw that they, too, could kill the Medes.

When they were finally relieved, Leonidas was nearing the end of his strength, and he didn't protest when Dienekes announced he was taking over command of the reserve. "Go get something to eat and lie down!" he ordered his king unceremoniously.

"Eat?" Leonidas asked.

"It's past noon. There's a good stew on the fire, almost as good as black broth at home," Dienekes assured him.

Leonidas returned to the Spartan camp. It was surreal to find this area perfectly calm and ordered while little more than two thousand yards away the slaughter continued. Leonidas sank down on a stool, propping his helmet upright on the ground at his feet, leaning his shield against his knee, and thrusting his spear butt-end into the earth.

Sperchias handed him a bowl full of thick stew. Leonidas looked at it. Was he hungry? Human body parts, rather than chunks of meat, appeared to be floating in the brew. He shook his head sharply to clear the hallucinations, then drank the lamb and onion soup.

Around him the men of the Herakles Company were preparing to take up their position on the wall, but the men of the Kastor Company stayed where they were. Leonidas lay down to rest, certain he wouldn't be able to actually sleep. Meander offered to massage his calf muscles, and he agreed gratefully. Meander bent and removed his greaves; he rolled on to his stomach and closed his eyes. Meander was an absolute magician when it came to calf massages....

Prokles shook him awake. "The Medes have pulled out."

Leonidas sat bolt upright. "What?"

"The Medes have been pulled back. We can hear new troops mustering, but can't see them yet."

"What time is it?" Leonidas looked at the sun even as he asked. Although past the zenith, the sun was still quite high. Diodoros and the Kastor Company were already gone, apparently in position on the wall. Leonidas looked at Prokles with a slight frown.

"The perioikoi are on the field. Their hour isn't up but we thought it would make sense to swap them out now, during the lull in the fighting."

"Of course," Leonidas agreed. He grabbed his greaves, bending them back into place around his shins, and then got to his feet. Prokles handed him his helmet first, then the aspis. They walked side by side back to the wall in silence. From here, Leonidas could see the helots and slaves again clearing away the dead.

"What do you think their casualties have been so far?" he asked.

Prokles shrugged. "Easily five thousand men, maybe six."

"That's as many men as we have altogether."

"That's right—and it means no more to that man up there," Prokles jabbed his thumb in the direction of Xerxes, "than six or seven individual men mean to us—probably less. They aren't his friends dying, just his subjects."

Horn signals from beyond the West Gate were getting louder. Leonidas saw Xerxes and his entourage turn to look back at the mustering area behind the West Gate. He saw Xerxes nod and raise his hand as if in greeting. Leonidas looked over at Demophilus; the Thespian commander nodded.

Leonidas reached up, pulled his helmet down by the nosepiece, and descended the right ramp to the field. Here at the base of the ramp there was still some grass. Ten feet farther out it had been torn up and trampled under by the phalanxes as they mustered. Fifty feet away there was nothing but a morass that was starting to stink vilely, despite the work of the slaves and helots. Pieces of human bodies littered the field, while blood, sweat, urine, and feces had soaked the earth to create a revolting mire.

The new hordes started pouring through the West Gate. "Cissians," Sperchias identified them, and passed the word. They were brightly clad, and their pennants fluttered gaily in the offshore breeze. These were tall men armed with axes and javelins, but they, too, had no proper shields and no body armor.

Leonidas drew a deep breath and looked left and right. Around him men flexed their shoulders and shook out a wrist here or a calf there. Maron was circling his head to get the stiffness out of his neck. They were tired, and it was blisteringly hot. Let's get this over with, Leonidas thought, and gave the order to advance before the Cissians had even finished mustering.

They met about halfway across the field. The Greek phalanx was not as wide as the battlefield, and some of the enemy slipped around the left end, but this did not concern Leonidas excessively. There were too few of them, and he trusted the Tegeans and Mantineans to come off the wall and eliminate them. His objective was to convince the Cissians that they were no more invincible than the Medes.

The Cissians were throwing their javelins rapidly, and the sound of these missiles close at hand was unnerving at first, but the hoplons were holding up well. Leonidas' arm was jolted twice in succession as javelins clanged against the bronze, and he winced for Arion's artwork, not from fear. Then they had closed the distance, and the killing started again.

This time, however, Xerxes had planned a surprise for them. Shortly after they had engaged the Cissians, horsemen started pouring through the West Gate. Leonidas caught a glimpse of a white stallion, and he knew intuitively that it was Zopyrus. The Cissians, his brain registered, had just been bait, luring them deeper into the field where their wings were unhinged. Unlike the Cissians themselves, the cavalry could pour around the edges in sufficient numbers to be dangerous, and then they could either take them in the rear, or employ the Persians' preferred tactic of riding around them while firing their bows.

Spartans were not invincible—they were as vulnerable as any armed force to the surprise of novel tactics—but rarely did Spartans suffer surprise more than once. Leonidas' brother Cleomenes had suffered a humiliating defeat at the hands of Thessalian cavalry during his first attempted invasion of Attica, before Leonidas was even out of the agoge. Leonidas could still remember the heated debates in the syssitia on how to best confront cavalry. Now he was ready for it.

Leonidas passed the order, first to Demophilus and then to his own wings, for both units to form squares. The ranks were ordered to pack in close, each man brandishing his spear forward. Horses were either more cautious, or simply saner, than men. Again and again in drill, the Spartans had found that if they made their ranks look like a solid wall hedged with bristling blades, horses would shy away before contact. It was a maneuver they had even practiced with the Thespians, because Thebes had superior cavalry. Leonidas was confident that Demophilus could manage this well.

Meanwhile the Cissians had parted to let the cavalry through. The cavalry rushed forward at a gallop and started circling the two Greek formations with great élan. Their arrows made a huge racket as they clattered on the faces of the hoplons, but they rarely bit into the wood, much less found flesh. The horses, however, were going crazy, terrified as much by the smell of slaughter from the first half of the day as by the sight of the strange domes of metal. They kept trying to spring over the bodies of the dead and dying, swerving and leaping so abruptly that even these magnificent riders were sometimes unseated.

Leonidas had his eye fixed on Zopyrus. The Persian cavalryman was shouting and pumping his bow in the air, firing up his troops. He rode like a centaur, Leonidas registered, his legs clamped around the body of the horse so firmly that he seemed one with it. He pulled three arrows at a time from the leather case on his back and fired them in rapid succession, first aiming forward, then directly to the side, and then twisting in his saddle and firing to the rear as he rode around the Spartan formation. When he had done this three or four times, however, his expression darkened with frustration. Leonidas could imagine what was going through his mind. Xerxes was watching, and the Persian cavalry was riding circles around the Greeks but without any apparent effect whatsoever.

Leonidas saw Zopyrus raise his arm again, and with the bow still in his fist he made wide, circling motions. At once the cavalry drew off toward the West Gate, but Leonidas knew instinctively that this was no retreat. Zopyrus was too angry.

He was going to try to drive through them. The Persian cavalry was already formed up in a tight pack and gaining speed. Leonidas would have thought this madness, but the Persians rode huge, heavy-boned horses—significantly heavier and stronger than the Greek breeds. These, packed in as close as they were and maddened by the fever of their riders, might just stampede into his ranks of spears. A smile was spreading across Zopyrus' face.

If they stayed as they were, Leonidas feared the Persians would ride right over them. Men would be trampled, and the Persians would fire straight down at point-blank range. His only alternative was hardly safer, but it had the advantage of surprise. Leonidas gave an order that was unheard of except against light infantry, an order that no group of men but Spartans would have followed. He ordered runners out to meet the oncoming horsemen. The fleetest of the mid-rank men, men identified for this task long ago so that no one had to think about it now, jostled forward between files without hesitation. They ran toward the mass of horse. Just before they clashed, they formed into clusters, islands of spears, and then dropped down onto one knee.

The tactic worked even better than expected. The horses were frightened into confusion. They tried to jump over or run between the hedgehog-like formations of hoplites. They reared up, swerved, and collided with one another, and all across the field Persian cavalrymen were dumped on to the blood-soaked mud. The charge collapsed into a melee.

As soon as the impetus of the cavalry was broken, ranks of Spartans and Thespians sprang forward. A horse is far swifter than a man, but anyone who has run hounds against rabbits knows that a smaller animal can accelerate much faster. Before the Persian horse could turn to disengage and mass for another charge, the hoplites were upon them. Eight-foot spears cleared men from their mounts or sank deep into the flanks of already fear-maddened horses.

An engagement such as this had nothing to do with phalanx warfare. It was every man for himself, with the Greeks stabbing at horses as well as men. The wounded and terrified horses whinnied and reared. They kicked, bucked, and trampled friend and foe alike. The Persians flung themselves from their dying horses. They tossed away their bows and used their javelins like spears until these broke, and then they drew their swords. It was impossible to tell which side had the upper hand.

By now, the rear and middle ranks of the Greek phalanx were as much at risk as the front ranks. From two hundred yards away, Leonidas watched helplessly as a still-mounted Persian spurred up behind Euryleon as he struggled with a dismounted Persian. Leonidas wanted to shout a warning, but it was too late. The javelin thrust was so powerful it went clear through his friend's bronze armor and deep into Euryleon's back. The choral master dropped to his knees, vomiting blood, before falling face down into the foul mud, and Leonidas lost sight of him behind the other fighters.

Leonidas looked for Zopyrus. He was still mounted and almost alone. His horse was trying to bolt, but he held it by turning it hard so that it circled and circled. Around him Spartans and Thespians were killing the cavalrymen who had been thrown and were pulling those still mounted from their horses so they could be stabbed and gutted. Men and horses were screaming.

Zopyrus spotted Leonidas. His eyes narrowed as he lifted his bow and drew the string back to his ear. Leonidas could read the thoughts on his unprotected face: he no longer expected to triumph or even survive, but he intended to take Leonidas with him. Twelve feet separated them. Zopyrus was beyond the reach of Leonidas' spear. The bow Zopyrus carried was heavy, and Leonidas was certain the arrow it loosed could shatter a hoplon at this range—assuming he didn't put the bolt right through the eyehole of his helmet. The arrow flew and Leonidas raised his shield at a slant in the hope of deflecting the arrow, which he knew could not miss him. A second later the impact of the bolt almost unbalanced him. Leonidas heard it scrape on the bronze facing, and his arm was numbed. When he lowered his shield Zopyrus was nowhere to be seen—only Prokles standing where the Persian had been, beating the butt of his spear into something at his feet with an almost demonic hatred.

Later, Leonidas learned that the sight of the Spartans attacking the cavalry had brought Xerxes to his feet for the second time that day.

Late in the afternoon, another long lull descended over the battlefield. After the defeat of the Persian cavalry, the Cissians had fought for four hours, only to be slaughtered in even greater numbers than the Medes. At one point their ranks broke. They tried to flee back the way they'd come, only to be driven forward again by a fresh squadron of Persian cavalry. By the time the perioikoi were back onto the field, it was clear that the Cissians were no longer fighting willingly. Leonidas noted some men lowering themselves over the edge of the cliff toward the sea, apparently able to slip and slide away. Or perhaps the heap of corpses below had become so great that they could let themselves fall, sure of a soft landing? Whatever their fate beyond the cliff, they preferred it to fighting the Greeks.

Xerxes must have noticed this, too, because the Cissians were withdrawn. The Greeks waited for almost an hour, the perioikoi pulling back to sit on the comparatively clean grass in front of the wall, refreshing themselves with water.

"Maybe they've had enough for today," Alkander suggested hopefully as the waiting dragged on.

Leonidas just looked at him.

"How long until sunset?" Dienekes asked.

The sun had slipped behind the mountains and clouds were creeping over the sky, making it hard to know how long until darkness would put an end to today's slaughter. Suddenly an Arkadian lookout, who had been posted on the mountain flank around Xerxes' throne, came sprinting headlong across the killing grounds and pounded up the southern ramp to shout hysterically, "The Immortals! The Immortals are coming!" The panic in his voice was impossible not to overhear—and with every breath, he was spreading it.

"Good!" Leonidas called out to shut him up.

The young man gaped at Leonidas. "But, my lord, the Immortals! They can't die!"

"Don't be ridiculous. They're as mortal as you and I. The unit is only called that because it gets replenished immediately, like the Spartan Guard. They are the Persian elite. The best unit they have." The Arkadian stared, as did men from all the other allied contingents, collected at the wall just to see what was happening. It was for the latter that Leonidas added, "We should be honored. Up to now, Xerxes thought he could defeat us with slaves. At last he acknowledges we are Persia's equals."

Then he signaled Demophilus, Dienekes, Diodoros, and Kalliteles, the commander of the Herakles Company, to come to him. He drew them aside, but their men crowded around, too, elbowing out the other allies not due to fight just yet.

Leonidas raised his voice to be heard even at the back of the crowd. "These are Xerxes' best men—and they are an important prop to his throne. They can't afford to break, or the subject peoples will lose respect for their masters. But nor can they afford to take too many casualties, or Xerxes might find himself poorly protected in a sea of armed men whose loyalty is doubtful. When we stop them in their tracks, it will have a profound impact on enemy morale." Leonidas paused to let this sink in.

He continued: "The Immortals will have been thoroughly briefed on all earlier engagements. Their commander has probably been up there beside Xerxes all day." He gestured in the direction of the throne on the mountainside. "He will expect us to take up the same position as before and will have given his archers, who will take the field first, that range. What I propose is to take up a position farther forward, but thin our line so that it still stretches across the field, to give the illusion of being in the same place. That way the barrage should fall long, behind our ranks."

"They'll adjust fast. They can see everything we do," Dienekes pointed out.

"Yes, but we'll be able to close faster. As soon as the barrage is falling amongst us, we advance into it. No jogging. No running. Just slow and steady, as if the barrage were completely meaningless. But this time, as soon as we encounter the spearmen—who are the elite of the elite and Xerxes' own personal bodyguard—rather than engaging, I want every man to turn around and run as if we hadn't expected them."

"They've seen us reverse and re-form at the wall a dozen times already," Prokles protested.

"A half-dozen," Leonidas corrected. "And up to now we have only reversed and regrouped after pushing the enemy out, or nearly out, of the West Gate. What I propose is to break as if terrified—not just counter-march, but really break and run like panicked men—and to do that as soon as we encounter the spearmen. My bet is that they are so sure of their own aura of invincibility, and so certain we are afraid of them, that they will believe we are terrified, even if it is not logical."

Prokles shrugged. "There's something to that."

"The point is to act like we're terrified."

"I don't know if we can do that, sir," Alpheus spoke up, shaking his head dubiously. "We haven't drilled 'panic.'"

The Spartans laughed.

"Where do we draw up to fight again?" Demophilus asked anxiously.

"At the backward position: one hundred across, ten deep. When we reach the mark and turn, the main burden will be on the rear rankers." Leonidas' eyes sought men who were not front rankers, men like Temenos and Sperchias, men who were here not because they were the best fighting men Sparta had, but because they were his friends. He spoke directly to them. "You're going to have to dig in until you're up to your ankles in mud. The pursuing Immortals will be running, and they're going to collide with us. The front ranks will lose their footing and will have a hard time staying upright if you don't give us the support we need. Third and fourth rankers"—again Leonidas looked specifically for some of the men in these ranks, including Alkander and Oliantus— "you'll do the most killing at first. The first and second ranks, most exposed when we break and run, are going to take casualties. Make no mistake about that. There is nothing so dangerous as turning your back on the enemy and running away from him."

Addressing the front rankers now, Leonidas admonished, "When we break and run, keep your hoplon raised over your head, if you can, or even behind your head. I know it's awkward, but it could save your life."

They were nodding, but their faces were grim.

"They're not immortal," Leonidas repeated. "But they think they are. Let's prove to them just how mortal they really are."

At that, he pulled his helmet down and took up his shield.

Rather than pouring or spilling through the West Gate in a disorganized mass as the Medes and Cissians had done, the Immortals marched. They wore the same cloth turbans as the other barbarians, with long ties that were wound around their necks before hanging down their backs, but their uniforms were a particularly brilliant blue and yellow, with horizontally striped trousers and tight-fitting striped sleeves. Sperchias warned, however, that beneath their cloth tunics they had vests of leather scales that offered considerable protection for their heart, lungs, and stomach.

As the Immortals marched in, they expanded their front evenly and in an orderly, practiced manner. With each new man who marched in from the left of the Persian line, those already deployed stepped to the right. The whole rank advanced exactly one step forward only after it was full. It was an impressive piece of marching drill, and Leonidas gave the order for the Greeks to start moving their spears slightly, as if they were getting agitated. With satisfaction he saw Xerxes point to their lines. Xerxes had been taken in by their ruse; the question was whether Hydarnes, the commander of the Immortals, was taken in, too.

The first barrage of arrows, as Leonidas had predicted, soared well over their heads, and Dienekes remarked, "Shade at last!" to raise a chuckle from his commander.

It took the Immortals only five minutes to find the proper range, however, and as soon as the first arrows thwacked home into the hoplons of the front line, Leonidas ordered the advance. Although he had ordered a slow advance, the rear ranks were clearly nervous about what was to come and pushed the front ranks to a faster pace. Leonidas chose not to countermand their instincts, but let the battle take its course.

The arrows came at them ever closer to the level, ever more deadly. Three men to his left, one of the Spartan rankers took an arrow in the eye and dropped with an animal shriek of pain. The man behind took his place without missing a step, but gasps and other short cries indicated further wounds. Glancing along the line of the front rank, Leonidas was amazed by the number of arrows embedded in the bronze faces of the hoplons. His own lion had a mouthful of arrow shafts.

At last they were on top of the archers and, as Leonidas had hoped, these just seemed to melt away, pulling out to the sides to make room for the Persian spearmen.

Intentionally, Leonidas gave no order. Panic does not grip a unit in unison. It starts with the weakest link. The Thespians broke first, then the Spartans. Leonidas waited another couple of heartbeats, certain that the Persians would expect him, as king, to be the most determined to stand his ground. Prokles hissed, "Enough!" but still Leonidas counted to five before he turned and ran as fast as he could.

Leonidas was forty-eight years old, and he had never been a sprinter. The battlefield was littered with dead and dying. The footing was terrible. He tried to leap over a body, landed on the man's knee, and lost his balance. The man wasn't dead. He shifted, startling Leonidas even more. Leonidas began falling over backwards.

A hand grabbed him roughly under the left armpit and yanked him forward. A second later Prokles had him in a brutal grip by the right as well. Two men were pulling him forward, while someone else landed a kick in his backside to make him move faster. Behind him,

Maron and Alpheus locked their shields. "No!" Leonidas screamed at them futilely.

Twice Leonidas slid on the slippery, evil-smelling morass and would have fallen to his knees except for Bulis and Prokles, who still had hold of him by the armpits. Leonidas' lungs were giving out, and still he was running—almost flying, it seemed—on the stronger arms of his companions.

Behind them the Persians were shouting and hooting—part mockery, part triumph, part battle cry. It rose and reverberated into a melodic cry, a kind of "Wohuhu! Wohuhu!"

Leonidas collided with his own men, and spun around so fast his vision dimmed. The shields cracked into position. He looked for Maron and Alpheus, but there was nothing but a mass of Immortals, hundreds deep, rushing forward. Before he could catch his breath, the Immortals crashed into them. Leonidas was certain he would not have stayed upright if someone hadn't been crushing a shield into his back so fiercely that he literally had no room to fall down.

Some of the Immortals were trying to stop themselves, leaning backward and flailing with their arms. Many lost their footing, slipped and slid, or skidded in the stinking mud. Others tried to turn aside or around only to collide with the men behind them, who had not realized the Greek line had re-formed.

Leonidas never knew who gave the order—he didn't have the breath—but all at once the rear rankers were pushing and someone was calling out the time. "Left! Left! Left!" On each shout, the front rankers were pushed forward into this chaos by the men behind them. The spears of the second and third rankers thrust forward past the front ranks into the wall of still-confused Immortals. Slowly, the Spartan/Thespian line advanced with relentless cadence. Thrust, step, thrust, step.

They rolled forward for at least fifty feet, the rear rankers drawing more blood with their lizard-stickers than the front rankers, who were pushing their opponents down with their shields as much as killing with their spears. As the Immortals receded before them, two hoplites standing back to back and fighting doggedly with blood-drenched swords came into view. Maron and Alpheus! Leonidas could hardly believe it.

The sight of the brothers still upright, still fighting, brought a spontaneous cheer and then a surge along the length of the Spartan line. They almost jogged the last five paces until they had enveloped the brothers, and then slowed again to recover their cohesion as Maron and Alpheus were sent to the rear.

This pause, slight as it was, gave the Immortals time to recover from their shock. The resistance stiffened noticeably, and within seconds all forward momentum came to a grinding halt. What followed was the most vicious fighting of the entire day. The Immortals refused to give up another inch of ground, and although their spears were shorter, they could still find their mark.

Leonidas was aware of men going down all along the line; he could feel it, as if each man of his advance guard were a part of himself, as if each casualty were a wound to his own body. He was bleeding now from several wounds, cuts to his arms and calves, bruises to his feet and thighs. Any one of these would have been temporarily crippling in other circumstances. And each time one of his advance guard crumpled and fell, it was a new wound, draining his strength.

Leonidas noticed with horror that he was also slowly losing his eyesight. He could not longer see the enemy clearly. The colors were all blending together, going gray, while the sound of the battle was fading behind a louder, hideous roaring sound. He was completely soaked in something cold. Cold blood? Was he dying? Was he already dead?

He shook his head in disbelief. It was pouring rain, raining torrentially on a gale-force, southerly wind. Men on both sides were losing their footing as the rain saturated the already slippery morass under their feet. Men started to go down not from enemy action, but because their feet were swept out from under them as little, bloody rivers formed. At the far right, men screamed hysterically as they were swept off the edge of the cliff.

Leonidas shouted for the Spartans to drop to one knee with their hoplons in front of them. It was a posture most commonly used for withstanding arrows and javelins in positions where they could not advance, such as aboard ships. Now his concern was just to keep together. He wanted to avoid the risks of movement on this suddenly treacherous ground.

The wind was howling around the face of the mountain, and Leonidas spared a glance in the direction of Xerxes' throne. It was abandoned, the pretty cushions and cloths flying away or tumbling down the slope, the footstool and tables overturned. Lightning flashed and thunder followed right behind. The next bolt was even closer, and men flinched involuntarily. But the Immortals had faded away.

The Greeks were huddled in the middle of an empty field.

The other allies were wild with jubilation. They were jumping up and down, clapping one another on the back, and singing paeans to the Gods. Some had formed lines, arms on each other's shoulders, and were dancing despite the rain. They had not only survived the day, they had held the entire might of the Persian Empire to a draw. They had stopped the invincible Immortals in their tracks. The Pass was still in Greek hands, and the Gods were clearly on the Greek side. How else explain that Zeus himself with his thunderbolts had driven Xerxes from his viewing platform? How else explain that when the Greeks were in the moment of greatest danger, the rain and wind had forced the invincible Immortals to withdraw?

Leonidas was too tired to join in the rejoicing. He was far more concerned about bringing their wounded and dead off the field, and anxious that every man still alive was properly treated. Meander was hovering around him, anxious to bind up his wounds, but Leonidas wanted the names of the dead. "Where's Alkander?" he demanded, abruptly noticing the absence of his closest, dearest, oldest friend. No sooner did he miss Alkander than he felt instantly and helplessly lost. He was a little boy again, in that horrible storm during the Phouxir—only Alkander wasn't with him. He couldn't survive without Alkander! It was a moment before he remembered he wasn't supposed to survive.

Prokles pointed to the bloody field and growled, "He's out there looking for Sperchias."

Sperchias? That was almost as bad. He and Sperchias had been together on Kythera...just like Euryleon. Only now did it sink in.

"Sit down, Leo!" Prokles ordered. "Let Meander look after you. You're losing a pint of your god-damned royal blood, and for all we know it's the only pint left from Herakles." As he spoke, Prokles pushed him into the imperfect shelter of his tent to at least get him out of the drenching rain.

As he sat, Leonidas caught sight of his hoplon. With horror, he registered that the beautiful bronze work was torn, bashed, punctured, and clogged with clotted human remains—a hideous wreck. Only one eye of the lion was recognizable for what it had been. The rest, once so lifelike and defiant, was just junk, beyond repair. Leonidas felt a rush of shame. How could he have been so irresponsible as to take a work of art into battle? Why hadn't he left the shield at home for Pleistarchos? Men were mortal, meant to die, but art—art was meant to be immortal and transcendent. Something as beautiful as this shield should never have been subjected to this kind of violence! It should never have been violated by war. He wanted to weep for what was irretrievably lost to all mankind.

Prokles' voice snapped him out of his spiraling grief. "You'll need one of the spare hoplons," he commented matter-of-factly, and before Leonidas could even answer, Oliantus ducked into the tent to announce, "Fourteen confirmed dead, sir. Five still missing. Twenty-two seriously injured, plus Eurytus and Aristodemos. A total of forty-three casualties."

Leonidas stared at him. "At that rate, we have just five more days before we're wiped out." For the very first time since he had arrived at Thermopylae, Leonidas seriously wondered whether they *could* hold the Pass until the Spartan army arrived.

"Our casualties were disproportionately high today because we took the field against the Immortals. The other allied contingents have less severe casualties."

"What about the Thespians?"

"I don't have the exact numbers—"

"Get them. Or wait," Leonidas tried to stand, but Prokles and Oliantus both shoved him back down. Prokles signaled for one of the helots to fetch Demophilus.

Meanwhile Oliantus continued, "The helots have managed to get a fire going in a long pit behind the hillock and have rigged up canvas covers to protect it from the rain. They are roasting four pigs. The Gods alone know where they found embers and dry wood. As soon as

Meander gets you patched up, we should head over. The others won't start without you."

"Tell them not to stand on ceremony at a time like this. They can start without—"

"*Precisely* at a time like this," Oliantus corrected, "we need to remember who we are and who *you* are, my lord. At no other time is a Spartan king more important to us than on the eve of battle."

Leonidas bowed his head in silent acknowledgement, but then asked anxiously, "How badly wounded are Maron and Alpheus?"

This brought a smile to Oliantus' tired face. "If I hadn't seen it with my own eyes, I wouldn't believe it. They swear the Twins appeared and stood on either side of them, fighting with them and protecting them with their divine shields. Alpheus lost an eye, and Maron's ankles are bloated up like the fetlocks of a plow horse, but they aren't going to die."

Demophilus arrived, and Leonidas shook off Meander and Prokles to get to his feet. They gazed at each other silently; then Demophilus put his arms around Leonidas and murmured, "Thank you."

"Whatever for?"

"Without you, they would have run; they would have let the Persians just flood across Boiotia without even trying to stop them. Now they know it can be done," he continued, gesturing toward the men singing and dancing around other campfires. "Now *I* know it can be done. We can beat them!"

Leonidas was ashamed of his own moment of doubt. He nodded, but then asked, "What were your casualties today?"

"Close to seventy. And yours?"

"Half that," Leonidas lied. No need to alarm the allies. "Will you join me for dinner? I understand there is roast pork."

"No, I'll eat with my own men. Arion asked if you need him to make any repairs to your shield."

Leonidas looked at it, the sense of loss welling up again, but not quite so intensely as before. He shook his head. "Tell him his lion sacrificed its immortality to give this mortal another day."

Demophilus nodded. They clasped hands briefly, and then Demophilus withdrew.

Leonidas turned to Prokles. "Please. Help Alkander find Sperchias. Bring him here." He pointed to the corpse of Euryleon, which was already stretched out in his tent.

Prokles nodded and started in the direction of the wall.

Leonidas sat down again and let Meander finish bandaging his open wounds and firmly bind his swollen right wrist in linen. It felt much better that way. Then he pulled himself to his feet and hobbled out of his tent. The rain had eased to a gentle drizzle.

Dienekes met him as he approached. "We've just elected Maron and Alpheus the bravest fighters for today," he announced.

That pleased Leonidas and he nodded, adding, "I understand the Twins were with them."

"The Twins were with us all!" Diodoros remarked as he joined them, handing Leonidas a kothon brimming with wine.

Leonidas poured a libation, "To the Twins and Fair Helen!" Then he lifted his voice and took up the paean to Kastor. Around him the other Spartiates and even the helots joined in reverently. They were all acutely conscious of both their own mortality and the divine grace they had experienced this afternoon. As the song died on their lips, the wind and rain seemed to ease a little, and Leonidas was fighting back a new rush of grief as he registered that Euryleon would never lead another chorus, never teach another generation how to dance....

Leonidas' eyes fell on Temenos. He looked utterly exhausted. His hair had come loose from its braids and hung about his sagging shoulders, one of which hung lower than the other. "That's dislocated, Temenos," Leonidas diagnosed at once. "You need a surgeon."

"Oh!" Temenos looked down at his left shoulder, his shield shoulder. "Is that why it hurts so much? I just thought I was tired."

Around him the others laughed, and one of the men offered, "Come here! I'll pop it back for you." Leonidas caught his breath and watched in amazement as the others pressed around to help Temenos. Weren't these the same men who year after year heaped ridicule on him because he refused to take a Spartiate wife? Weren't these the men who called him "helot lover" and told their sons not to stand for him or show him other gestures of respect?

Diodoros moved closer to ask Leonidas in a low voice, "Can we keep this up until the main army arrives?"

Today was the last day of the Karneia. Tomorrow the Spartan

army would start marching north. If they held for just five more days.... Five more days like this? "We don't have a choice," Leonidas answered Diodoros, and continued toward the long, canvas-covered pit, in which a fire smoldered.

As he approached he looked around for Oliantus and signaled the quartermaster over to him. "What is the chief cook's name?"

"Eudios," Oliantus answered at once.

Leonidas smiled, thanked him, then raised his voice and called out, "Eudios!"

The helot was giving instructions to some of the youths turning the spits on which the pigs were slowly roasting. His face and forearms were streaked with smoke. The hair around his face was wet with sweat rather than rain. His face was bright red. He didn't hear Leonidas' call, and did not realize the Spartan king was addressing him until other helots started gesturing, jostling his elbow, and pointing.

The chief cook looked over, dumbfounded, then hastily wiped his hands on the grimy skirts of his chiton and tried to wipe the sweat from his forehead with the back of his forearm as he asked anxiously, "Is something wrong, my lord? We're doing our best, but the wood was wet. I could cut you—"

"Hush, man!" Leonidas ordered. "I came to thank you for getting such a good fire going. Dinner smells delicious. And, all of you," Leonidas raised his voice, and his eyes sought the helots hovering in the background—the helots who had herded the sacrificial beasts and meat-on-the-hoof, the smiths and wheelwrights, the coopers, surgeon's helpers, and assistant cooks—all the helots who kept the army moving, fed, and armed from the obscurity of the train. There were almost four hundred of them. Counting the attendants of the Spartiates, the helots outnumbered the Spartans more than two to one.

"All of you!" Leonidas raised his voice to be heard even in the shadows, where many of the helots hovered uncertainly. "You did an outstanding job clearing the field today. It made our job easier—indeed, possible. Without you, we might not have succeeded today. So this is as much *your* victory as ours. We trust you to do the same tomorrow."

For a moment there was stunned silence. Helots weren't used to getting public praise from anyone, much less a king. Then after a moment, one of the bolder youths risked calling out, "We're almost out of room to dump 'em, sir. The bodies are stacked up right to the edge of the road."

"Seriously?" Leonidas asked, shocked.

Several voices answered, all confirming the youth's report.

"Someone's going to have to go down to the beach, then, and start shifting the bodies into the sea," Oliantus muttered in Leonidas' ear.

Leonidas looked over his shoulder at his quartermaster; that was a revolting task. The men were exhausted, wet, and hungry. He didn't even want to give the order.

"Don't the Persians honor their dead?" one of the helots asked. "Won't they come and collect them?"

Leonidas shook his head. "Apparently not. I saw them toss their wounded over the cliff...."

"Sit down, sir," Eudios suggested. "I'll bring you some crispy pork and fresh bread, and we'll clear the beach later."

"First, a sacrifice for the Gods," Leonidas reminded him, squinting to see into the darkness beyond the pit toward the pen with the sacrificial animals.

"What do you want, my lord?" a voice asked from that direction.

"A cock. Just a cock. Anything larger would be inappropriate, since this battle is far from won."

It was too dark to see properly. The fires across the Greek camp were dying down, and the sounds of merrymaking had long since given way to snores. It was too dark to distinguish the fatal wound, or even how much blood was his own and how much was the blood of his enemies, but it was not too dark to recognize him.

When did you get to be so old? Leonidas asked Sperchias' corpse. *Do I look as old you? Gorgo never told me....*

He sank on to his heels and reached for Sperchias' hand. It was limp and chillingly cold. He laid it gently on his friend's chest.

Was it really a quarter-century ago that they had fought side by side on Kythera? Sperchias had kept him sane just by sharing the horror, the self-doubts, the nervousness, and the grief. For an instant they were floating together in the gently undulating, aquamarine waters before the Kytheran coast, struggling helplessly with the senselessness of cruelty. He closed his eyes and heard Sperchias' laughter as he teased Laodice out of a honey cake. But over the years that laughter had become rarer, the lines on his face deeper....

Leonidas reached out and traced with his thumb the vertical lines that split Chi's high forehead. His skin was clammy, almost clay-like, and sent a shiver up Leonidas' spine.

Like Cassandra, Leonidas thought, Sperchias had foreseen much, but no one had heeded him. He had known the consequences of rejecting Persian demands. He, more than anyone, had saved that arrogant ass Zopyrus, who had died only a few yards away from him today. In death their blood had mingled like brothers—the eternal fraternity of fighting men, Achilles and Hektor.

But Sperchias had been so much more than that. He had been willing to sacrifice himself to atone for the murdered ambassadors. He had been prepared to be slaughtered like a lamb, without a weapon in his hand. He had faced the prospect of being tortured, ridiculed, humiliated, unburied. That took a kind of courage Leonidas wasn't sure he had. Yet his fellow citizens had never seen, understood, or valued Chi as he deserved. Chi had wanted nothing so much as to be a public servant, but the public had not wanted his service. At least Euryleon had found respect as a choral master, Leonidas thought, his eyes briefly shifting to focus on the other corpse. Euryleon had enjoyed a good marriage, a happy family life. Sperchias had not been so lucky. His wife had never appreciated him, and had sought another man's bed as soon as Sperchias left for the Persian court. That was a hard fate.

"He was living on borrowed time," Alkander murmured at his shoulder.

Leonidas started and looked up in alarm. Alkander was no different from Chi or Euryleon! He, too, had virtues far beyond the simple ones of a soldier. Alkander's skill at coaxing the best out of young boys was far greater than his skill with a spear. He had no business being here!

Leonidas pushed himself to his feet, groaning unconsciously at the aches in his thighs. "I have an urgent dispatch that you must take to Gorgo tomorrow," he announced.

Alkander shook his head. "No, Leo. You don't, and I won't."

They were face to face, only a couple feet apart. "Alkander, listen to me. We lost almost fifty men today. Thermopylae may hold until the main army comes up, but there won't be many of us left. I want you to be one of them."

"And so do I—but not by running away."

"If I order you—"

Alkander kept shaking his head. "I'm not a helot messenger boy, Leo. I'm not, because *you* made me go back to school and learn to be a Spartiate. You made me what I am, Leo. You have only yourself to blame for where we stand tonight."

"He's right," Prokles' ruined voice sounded out of the darkness. "If it weren't for you, I'd be counting my pay in some tavern in Sicily now."

"Is that where you'd rather be? I can—"

"Stick it up your ass! I'm no more a messenger boy than Alkander. I'm here because I volunteered, and I'm here to fight."*

Leonidas looked from one friend to the other, then down at Sperchias and Euryleon lying side by side, thinking: "You won't be alone for long. Whatever Hades holds, we'll be sharing it together soon."

---

* Plutarch claimed that Leonidas tried to save the lives of some of the older men, but they "saw through him" and told him they were not heralds, but soldiers.

Chapter 22

CREATURES OF NIGHT

Late on the afternoon of the next day, Xerxes pulled his troops back out through the West Gate, and an eerie calm descended over the Pass at Thermopylae. The Corinthians and Thebans had just deployed for their second turn ahead of the wall that day; abruptly the Persian emperor stood up, turned his back on the Pass, and walked away from his throne, growing shorter step by step as he descended the hill on the far side. There followed frantic horn signals and shouting. The troops fighting for the Persian king turned and trampled one another in their haste to retreat.

Helot goatherds, who had scaled up the high bluffs to get a view into the Persian camp and mustering ground, had reported earlier in the day that Xerxes had positioned Persian cavalry behind the deploying troops with the apparent task of "motivating" them. Once or twice the helot scouts reported that the cavalry pressed forward, effectively herding the subject troops through the West Gate and into the killing grounds. In short, the morale of Xerxes' army left something to be desired.

Greek morale, however, was also sagging. When Xerxes pulled his troops off the field on the second day, the Thebans and Corinthians did not pursue. Isanor sent a runner to Leonidas complaining, "The only dead the Persians left during their withdrawal were the men that got trampled underfoot by their comrades!"

Leonidas, limping badly from a thigh wound, calmed the perioikoi commander. "A score of dead more or less makes no difference at this point in the slaughter. Persian casualties must already top ten thousand."

"It's indicative of poor morale!" Isanor insisted indignantly.

"Correct, and I am confident that the perioikoi would not have been so lax," Leonidas assured him. "But the Thebans and Corinthians are amateur soldiers, and they've had enough. We've all killed too many men already." Leonidas felt the throbbing in his spear arm and wrist as he spoke; he had no idea how many men he'd killed these past two days, but it felt like hundreds.

Vultures had circled constantly throughout the day, and they now swooped down onto the field to start tearing at the fresh bodies left behind. Lesser scavengers—crows, flies, canine and feline strays—were in almost continuous control of the field, except where the fighting was ongoing. The sound of beasts snarling in defense of carrion had punctuated the night before, and surely would again tonight.

The Theban commander pushed his way back through his troops and mounted the ramp, exhaustion evident in his every step. He addressed Leonidas. "Well, what now?" he wanted to know.

Leonidas was watching the West Gate, where the last of the Persian forces were disappearing in unseemly haste. He shook his head. "I don't know, but my guess is that the Persian king will try to buy us off."

"What do you mean?" the Theban frowned in confusion. "Negotiate?"

"I think Xerxes has had enough fighting for today and will try to get his way with a bribe."

"A lot of good that'll do him!" the loyal Isanor snorted, but the Theban looked alarmed. Leonidas could guess what he was thinking: if Xerxes offered the Spartans enough, they might abandon the others, and if the Spartans withdrew, the defense of Thermopylae would collapse. The Peloponnesians would make a dash back behind the Isthmus, and the remaining troops were too few to hold the Pass alone. In short, the road to Thebes would lie open to the Persians.

Leonidas told the Theban, "Stand your men down. We'll have time to deploy if they send in troops after all." The Theban gladly passed this order to his own men and the Corinthians, while Leonidas told Isanor to let the perioikoi relax as well. He then dropped down on the edge of the wall with his feet dangling and waited. His ankles, like those of every hoplite here, were swollen and inflamed with the excessive strain. He also had some bad bruises on his toes and the backs of his feet and the painful thigh wound, but it was his wrist that caused him the most concern. He couldn't afford a weak right wrist yet.

After about a half hour, a flourish of trumpet signals announced a flashily-dressed herald brandishing a long white pennant. He tried to ride on to the field on a white horse, but his horse was having none of it. The stench and the sight of the vultures triggered instinctive fear that no amount of horsemanship or even brute force could overcome. The herald withdrew to return a few moments later on foot.

Leonidas just waited, but word of the herald spread. One by one the other commanders joined Leonidas. Behind them came their officers and as many of their men as could squeeze on to the wall. Diodoros, Dienekes, Kalliteles, Oliantus, Alkander, and Prokles had to push their way through the crowd to reach their king. Leonidas reached up a hand, and Prokles and Dienekes together hauled him onto his feet.

The Persian herald came within shouting distance. "I have a message for King Leonidas of Sparta!"

"He's listening!" Leonidas shouted back.

"This is for his ears alone!"

An uneasy stir swept the crowd, and men started to push and shove to see Leonidas and how he was reacting. Leonidas knew that if he went out onto the field and spoke to the Persian herald where no one could hear him, the allies would start to question what secret deal had been struck—no matter what he told them. Even if he took one or two men with him as witnesses, those not present would assume the worst of those who parlayed: they would suspect a deal had been cut to their own advantage and the detriment of the rest. Exhaustion was already wearing away at morale; tomorrow or the next day men would reach the point where they didn't care about anything but rest, peace, and an end to this horror. They would then be willing to take any deal offered—and would assume that he was no different.

Leonidas took a deep breath and called out so that not only the herald, but the troops around and behind him, could hear: "I have no secrets!"

A rustle of approving grunts and nods from his own troops rewarded him.

"The Great King sends a message from monarch to monarch, not to the rabble!" the herald protested.

"The 'rabble' has stopped the Great King's armies; it can hear his words."

The herald was clearly disconcerted. He seemed on the brink of breaking off the parlay and returning, but then he lifted his head and shouted again: "The Great King Xerxes, son of Darius, offers to King Leonidas, son of Anaxandridas, of Sparta the following: If he gives up this pointless resistance against the forces of Civilization and the true God Ahuramazda; if he takes the hand outstretched in friendship by his most gracious Majesty, the merciful and generous Great King; if he puts his arms in the service of His Magnificence, the Joy of Ahuramazda, joining the invincible multitude of a thousand nations; then Xerxes, King of Kings, will make Leonidas, son of Anaxandridas, King of all Greece."

This offer provoked a collective gasp from hundreds of Greek throats, although Prokles muttered, "I'll bet Demaratus spews up his dinner when he hears this."

Leonidas spared Prokles a quick smile, then took a deep breath and called back as loudly as he could: "Tell your master that if he understood honor, he would not lust after what does not belongs to him. I, Leonidas of Sparta, would rather *die* for the freedom of Greece than rule it in subjugation!"*

The excited response among the men on the wall drowned out the answer of the herald. Leonidas thought the man said something, but he wasn't sure, much less able to decipher it over the noise around him. When the herald turned his back on the Greeks and started toward the West Gate, the crowd on the wall started cheering and hooting. Then someone started to chant: "Le – o – ni – das! Le – o – ni – das!"

"Get me out of here!" Leonidas ordered in a low voice to his countrymen, and they obligingly cleared a way through the crowd for him.

---

* This exchange is recorded in Plutarch's "Sayings of Spartans," although worded slightly differently.

The night was warm and dry, the moon just a day past full. If all had gone as planned, there had been an Assembly this morning that declared a fifteen-year call-up and approved the deployment to Thermopylae of all five lochagos at their maximum strength of a thousand each. If all had gone as planned, five thousand Spartiates, with their support troops and an additional thousand perioikoi, had started marching north by noon. Other cities that had held back because of the Olympic peace would not be far behind. In six to seven days, the Pass would be so full of defenders that they would have a hard time finding a place to camp and fresh water for them all. Once they were here, Xerxes would have no means of dislodging them. His only hope would be to break through the Greek fleet and outflank the Pass by sea.

The news from Artemisium was also good. The Greek fleet had sailed out yesterday afternoon to do battle. The Persians, taken by surprise by such audacity on the part of a fleet much smaller than their own, had launched their triremes at a leisurely pace. The Greeks had managed to capture or sink a number of these ships before Persian numbers started to overwhelm them. They then pulled into a defensive circle with their sterns together and their rams pointing outward at the circling Persians. The Persians again made the mistake of believing the Greeks intimidated and cowed. For the second time on the same afternoon, they were taken by surprise. At a signal from Eurybiades, the Greek fleet exploded outward, each trireme choosing a different target. In the ensuing fighting, which lasted until darkness, the Greeks sank or captured over a score of Persian ships for no losses of their own.

Leonidas invited the Athenian captain of the penteconter sent with this news to join him for a meal, giving the Athenian the "second portion" due to Leonidas as king, then sent the Athenian back to Eurybiades and Themistocles with the news of the second day at Thermopylae. Although Leonidas made no mention of Xerxes' offer of the crown of "all Greece," other members of the captain's crew heard the story from the still excited allies.

After the Athenian departed, Leonidas limped over to the field hospital that had been set up beyond the East Gate. Spartan casualties had been much fewer today than the day before, just five killed and seven wounded. The perioikoi had lost twenty men, however, so he visited them first, then stopped to speak to every wounded Spartiate, especially Alpheus and Maron. Alpheus had a wad of wool in his eye socket and a patch over it; he claimed he was not in pain. Maron insisted, less convincingly, that his ankles were much better. "I'll be back on the field tomorrow," he promised.

"That's for the surgeon to decide," Leonidas answered, and was about to say something more when Meander burst into the little field hospital breathlessly.

"Sir!" He could hardly talk for being out of breath. "Come quick!"

"What is it?"

"Deserter! A Greek deserter! From the Persians. He's—he has—intelligence."

"I'm coming."

A crowd had collected in front of Leonidas' tent. All three company commanders were already there. Likewise Isanor, Demophilus, and the Theban, Corinthian, and Tegean commanders hovered anxiously, as did Alkander and Prokles. Of his closest companions, only Oliantus was missing—he was still beyond the East Gate, checking the inventory of spare spears, hoplons, helmets, and greaves.

Leonidas didn't like the expressions on any of the faces before him, nor the tenor of their talk. "What is it?"

The other men looked over sharply, and then parted slightly. A half-naked man knelt on the ground with his arms tied behind his back. "This man was brought in by the sentries, sir!" Dienekes reported. "He claims to be a deserter from Xerxes' army, an Ionian from Cyme, impressed against his will."

"For such a patriot, you have given him a rude welcome," Leonidas commented dryly.

"Sir, he's just as likely to be a spy! He says Xerxes is offering a coffer full of gold to anyone who can show him a way around the Pass," Isanor protested hotly.

"I see. And has anyone come forward?" Leonidas directed this question to the deserter.

"I saw a man, a Malian calling himself Ephialtes, being escorted to the Great King's tent. He clearly wanted to claim the reward."

"What time was that?" Leonidas asked sharply, his heart pounding so frantically in his ears that he spoke unnecessarily loudly.

"Late this afternoon, shortly after you rejected the Great King's offer."

"Bloody, f**king hell!" Prokles burst out. "If they—"

Leonidas gripped Prokles' forearm so fiercely that even the battered marine felt the pain and shut up. Leonidas was staring at the deserter. "What happened then?"

"I don't know. Nothing that I could see. He wasn't a very reliable-looking man. Maybe the Great King didn't believe him."

"Why are you here?" Leonidas asked.

"Isn't it obvious?" the Theban burst out. "He's trying to sow panic and alarm. He's trying to make us betray ourselves!"

"Maybe," Leonidas conceded without taking his eyes off the man.

"I say we torture him and see if he sticks to his story," the Theban suggested next.

The Tegean shifted uneasily at this suggestion, and Demophilus sneered, "Now, that's a Theban suggestion if ever I've heard one. When you're not attacking virgins, you—"

"That's enough!" Leonidas cut the Thespian off. He turned again to the deserter. "Who sent you here?"

The man glanced nervously at the others, then up at Leonidas and looked him straight in the eye. "Demaratus."

"With what message?"

"Just what I said. That the Great King is offering a huge reward, and that at least one man has stepped forward to claim it. If there is a way around the Pass, the Great King will find it—if not today, then tomorrow or the next."

"I'm going to warn the Phocians," Dienekes decided on the spot.

"No! I can't afford to have a company commander chasing around in the dark. Find someone to go in your place. Someone reliable, fit, and fleet—a helot goatherd, for example, who hasn't been fighting for two days, isn't wounded, and is as comfortable on a mountain slope as his charges. Oliantus will be able to recommend someone. Go ask him, send the boy on his way, then return here."

Dienekes left at once.

"Shouldn't we reinforce the Phocians at once?" Demophilus asked anxiously.

"That may be exactly what Xerxes is trying to get us to do," Diodoros warned. "He may *suspect* there is a trail that outflanks us. He may be offering a reward for being shown it, but that is *not* the same thing as being on his way. He may hope that by sending this man here with this report, he can induce us to siphon off a substantial portion of our forces to defend a trail he has not yet found. If we are too weak here, he won't *need* to find that trail: he'll be able to break through. The weaker we are, the sooner we'll break."

Leonidas looked at the older man, who had once been his company commander. He could not dismiss his concerns out of hand, even if his own first instinct was to reinforce the Phocians at once. The Arkadians had been weak fighters from the start, and today the Thebans and Corinthians had started to show serious deficiencies as well. The Tegeans and Mantineans weren't much better. Under the circumstances, what Diodoros said made sense: before weakening their defenses in the Pass any further, they first had to be certain that the Persians had found the Anapaia track. Leonidas nodded agreement with Diodoros, adding, "Now, let's give this patriot something to eat and drink and treat him like a guest."

Dienekes found Oliantus beside the unhitched wagons with the extra spears. They had brought three thousand spares on the assumption that each man might go through a spear a day, and what they didn't use would be waiting for the main army when it arrived. They had, in two days, gone through just over eight hundred.

"Oliantus?" Dienekes called to him.

"Dienekes! What brings you back here?" It was a valid question. Dienekes led from the front and took little interest in supplies and support.

"A deserter, allegedly sent by Demaratus, claims that in exchange for a huge reward someone may have betrayed the mountain track to Xerxes, just as we feared."

"Already?" Oliantus was shaken. "But the main army can't get here for another four to five days."

"Leonidas wants to warn the Phocians to be on the alert and send for help at the first hint of the enemy."

Oliantus nodded and remarked, "Of course." He did not understand what this had to do with him.

"Leonidas suggested sending a helot goatherd, who is bound to be in better shape than any of us at this point and is used to climbing in this kind of terrain. He thought you might have a suggestion."

"Oh. Yes." Oliantus thought about it. "Gylis. He's seventeen, half-goat by the way he moves, and he's keen. He was the one who dared speak up to Leonidas yesterday. Come with me."

Oliantus led the way from the supply wagons to the improvised pen in which the livestock, including the sacrificial animals, were kept. The goats and sheep were all hobbled, but otherwise they moved around freely, nibbling at what grass they could find.

The herd boys were bedded down around a small fire at the edge of the pen. There were about a dozen of them. They were sharing the leftovers from the Spartiate meal in shallow wooden bowls and passing a skin around that was presumably watered wine. They wore their chitons pinned at only one shoulder and had never known sandals in their lives, but they exuded health and energy.

Their conversation was lively, because several of these youths had found a way up the shoulder of the mountain to look down on Xerxes' throne and into his mustering area. They had seen the Persian cavalry force the subject peoples to fight, and they had heard Leonidas reject Xerxes' offer of a pan-Hellenic crown. They were very conscious of witnessing history, and were inured to the bloodshed because they were used to slaughtering animals.

At the sight of two Spartiate officers approaching, their conversation and laughter died, and they waited warily. It wasn't fear. These youths had been serving with the army from the age of thirteen or even younger. Army helots enjoyed more independence and respect than the helots on estates, precisely because they were part of Sparta's prestigious military apparatus and because they were not subject to the whims of any one master or mistress. There were arrogant bastards that could make their lives difficult, but there were other officers, like Oliantus, who were fair. Furthermore, they were all volunteers. Not one helot was here against his will. Unlike the Spartiates, however, the helots on this expedition were not required to be fathers of living sons, because they would not be at risk. In consequence, most of the helots were the young and adventurous, youths without wives and children.

"Gylis!" Oliantus called out.

Gylis stood at the sound of his name. "Sir?"

"King Leonidas needs a volunteer."

"What for?" Gylis asked warily.

"Does it matter?" Oliantus asked back.

Gylis shrugged. "I'm sick of dumping bodies in the drink, if that's what he wants."

At so much impudence, Dienekes caught his breath and frowned. "Are you sure he's the right youth for this task?" he hissed at Oliantus.

"You're right," Oliantus answered loudly, so Gylis and the others would hear him. "Maybe he's not good enough. Do any of you others want to undertake important reconnaissance on Kallidromo?"

"I can do that!" Gylis protested hotly, overriding the voices of more than one of his colleagues. "I've got the best sight of anyone. I can see in the dark. Let me go!"

Oliantus gave Dienekes an "I-told-you-so" look, and Dienekes shrugged. To Gylis, Oliantus simply said, "Come with us."

Gylis handed his bowl to one of the others, wiped his greasy hands on the skirt of his short, ragged chiton, and combed his long hair out of his face. "Yes, sir!"

They moved out of hearing of the others.

Dienekes took over. "There is a track that leads up from Alpeni, over Kallidromos, and down to the Persian camp."

The youth's mouth dropped. He understood the significance of this fact.

"The Phocians are up there guarding it, but Leonidas wants them to be particularly alert tonight. Do you think you can get that message to them?"

"Yes, sir!"

"Good. Follow me, and I'll show you the start of the trail."

By the time Dienekes and Oliantus reached Leonidas' tent, a heated argument was raging among Leonidas' closest friends. "For all we know, he's a fake, a plant, a traitor," Alkander was arguing.

"So what? He came out of Xerxes' camp, and he knows where the bastard's tent is."

"But why should he lead you to it?"

"Because I'll have a sword up his ass!"

"So he'll lead you to Hydarnes' tent, and when you're surrounded by Immortals, he'll squeal."

"So what? Then I die sooner rather than later. What the hell difference does it make? But if I can get him to lead me to the Great Asshole himself, there's a chance I could cut off the snake's head. If Xerxes is killed, that whole anthill won't be able to take another step!" Prokles was gesturing contemptuously toward the Persian positions. "They'll be headless—or rather, all Xerxes' brothers will be so busy fighting one another for the throne, they won't have another thought for us. That's the real advantage of their harems, you know: they produce packs of royal whelps who hate one another more than anyone else in the world."

"And what do you propose to do? Stroll through the West Gate by the light of the full moon and say 'cheers' to the Persian sentries as you walk past?"

"You're still a stupid little—"

"Prokles!" Leonidas cut him off and turned to Dienekes. "Everything all right?"

"Yes, an eager young lad by the name of Gylis is on his way right now. What's this all about?"

"We have in the form of this Tyrrhastiadas of Cyme," Prokles answered, "a man in our midst who knows the exact location of Xerxes' tent. He could lead me to it. All I need to do is slip inside—"

"The unguarded, isolated royal tent—" Alkander mocked sarcastically.

Leonidas clapped his hands once sharply to shut Alkander up, and Prokles continued, "And cut his throat. Then the whole war, let alone this battle, will be over."

Leonidas looked straight at Dienekes without a word.

"It sounds like a good idea to me. I'd say six men. No more and no less."

"Why so many? They'd just attract attention!" Prokles protested.

"The idea is too good to put all our hopes on the likes of you!"

Dienekes retorted bluntly. "We should send in two teams of three men each. One can take the path that leads up from the Hot Gates over the spot where Xerxes had his throne. The helots can show the way up, and our deserter can show them the way down. The other three can take a fishing boat around to the back of the camp," he gestured vaguely toward the lights that dotted the dark stretch of coast beyond the Malian Gulf. "From there they can ask their way to Xerxes' tent, which will hardly be a secret. Given the number of Ionian troops with the Great King's army, no one will take any note of a trio of Greek hoplites. We should have thought of this days ago."

"Choose the men, Dienekes—anyone but yourself," Leonidas warned.

"For the three men to go over the mountain: Mindarus, Labotas, and Gallaxidoros. They're all born mountaineers, used to hunting in the harshest parts of Taygetos. For the sea route: Prokles here, Bulis, who speaks some Persian and has seen Xerxes face-to-face, and..." he paused for a moment, thinking carefully, before deciding: "Temenos."

Leonidas started slightly at this last choice, but he had told Dienekes to make the selection and had no grounds for calling his decision into question. "Fetch them," he ordered Meander.

The three fighting men hid in the bows of the little fishing smack as it danced across the waters, lit by the waning but still almost full moon. On deck the air was refreshingly cool. The sail strained happily against the rigging, bloated with wind, and the fisherman braced himself against the leeward side with the satisfied look of a mariner whose craft is sailing at her best. Below deck, the bouncing of the bow and the stink of dead fish made Temenos and Bulis so violently ill that they forgot their hatred of each other in their shared misery. They were puking on empty stomachs long before the boat came into the wind in the shelter of a tiny cove and the fisherman called out, "Fresh fish! Fresh fish for sale!"

The Spartiates were surprised by how readily the enemy splashed down to the shore and started bargaining with the fisherman. They were even more astonished by the outrageous prices he was able to charge. The Great King's army evidently had plenty of spare cash, and Prokles quickly concluded that the fisherman's offer to transport them across the bay had been prompted less by patriotism than by self-interest. In fact, he suspected that this was not the fisherman's first trip over.

"Wine?" the fisherman asked.

The customers, who spoke Greek with the heavy dialect of the Black Sea colonies, nodded and pointed back toward the camp. The fisherman answered, "Help me beach this boat and I'll come along." He flung a line ashore, and a half-dozen men took hold of it. They pulled the fishing boat up onto the beach until it was halfway out of the water. Then the fisherman, his two crewmen, and the crowd of customers moved away, leaving the boat leaning on its side on the sand.

Prokles waited a good quarter-hour before he decided it was safe to slip over the side of the boat and make their way up the beach. The moon was shining down far too brightly for Prokles' liking, but there were clearly no sentries of any kind, and once they reached the shore they stopped amid the pines to catch their breath and survey the scene.

Their landing beach was roughly two miles northeast of the West Gate. The bulk of the Persian force was camped on the plain ahead of them and along the coastline stretching back to the east. Xerxes' tent, the deserter had assured them, was at the far western end of the encampment, beside the clean, cool waters of the Asopos. This was to ensure that the water used for his bath and cooking was not yet fouled by thousands of troops and horses. (His drinking water had been transported in amphorae all the way from Susa.) The first task of the assassins was to head west until they reached the part of the camp nearest the head of the Asopos, and then reassess the situation.

The three Spartiates, their hoplons slung across their backs, their spears at the slope, and their helmets shoved back, walked boldly through the camp as if they belonged in it. As full citizens, they carried shields faced with personal blazons; not one bore the lambda of Lacedaemon. Nothing distinguished them from the Greek allies of Xerxes, certainly not in the darkness.

They soon passed beyond the campfires of the Greeks, however, and the babble of the other peoples was unintelligible to them.

Laughter, of course, is universal, but that was scarce in Xerxes' camp on this second night of the battle for Thermopylae. Once they came close to a group of men nursing a variety of wounds and looking irredeemably glum. Prokles gave them a wide berth—not for fear of being recognized, but out of a feeling similar to guilt. Although neither he nor his companions regretted causing so much injury, they nevertheless respected the grief these men were suffering.

After about an hour, the three Spartiates found themselves in a part of the camp where the tents were bigger and more luxurious. The smell from the cooking fires was overlaid with spices unfamiliar to them, and slaves moved about between the tents carrying water, tossing away rubbish, cleaning pots, and performing other chores. The sound of music—and laughter, too—spilled out of more than one tent.

Prokles paused in the shadows of some trees and cursed under his breath. "Too many damn princes! According to that deserter, Xerxes is here with three or four of his brothers. We'll never be able to tell them apart."

"I learned how to say in Persian, 'I have a message for the Great King' and 'Take me to the Great King,'" Bulis announced. "If we tie Temenos up, we could pretend we are escorting him to the Great King because he was caught trying to desert."

Before Temenos could protest, Prokles shook his head. "No, tie me up instead. That way, if they buy the story and I am taken to him by Xerxes' bodyguards, I'll still have a chance to kill him." Even as he spoke, he pulled off a small cord he wore tied around his waist and handed it to Bulis.

Bulis secured Prokles' hands together behind his back at the wrists, but rather than tie a knot, he handed the end of the cord to Prokles, who held it balled in his fists.

They stepped out of the shadows, Bulis leading and Temenos pulling a "reluctant" Prokles after him by the elbow. Bulis approached the first slave he saw watering a horse and recited in his stiff Persian, "Take me to the Great King. I have a message for the Great King."

The slave pointed and babbled directions that they could not understand. So they followed the direction of his gesture, and Bulis asked the question again and again, until they stood before a massive tent flying many different pennants and lit by scores of torches. There were evidently many lamps burning inside as well, because the tent seemed to glow in the darkness. They could see shadows moving about inside, and music wafted out of the tent. More significantly, important-looking men were coming and going. It looked like the right place, but Bulis hesitated. "No Immortals," he murmured.

"What do you mean?" Prokles growled back.

"I mean, the sentries here aren't Immortals. Xerxes is always guarded by a company of Immortal spearmen. This can't be his tent."

"Ask again," Prokles insisted.

Bulis had no intention of asking one of the men with curved swords at their hips or bows on their backs. He waited until he spotted a eunuch with a clutch of wax tablets and other writing utensils. Bulis approached him and tried his worn Persian phrases. The eunuch answered in Greek. "This is the tent of our Great Master, may Ahuramazda grace him with long life!"

"But where are the Immortals?" Bulis challenged him.

"They have other duties tonight. Why do you want to know?"

"I have this deserter here," Bulis waved a hand contemptuously in Prokles' direction, "that I was ordered to bring to the Great King."

The eunuch looked Prokles up and down. "Why?"

Bulis shrugged, "Damned if I know. My captain told me to take him to the Great King and no one else. The officers were in an uproar when they got him in the firelight and they saw who he was." He looked back at Prokles as if he were reassessing his prisoner. "I gather he is someone important."

"No doubt from your perspective," the eunuch told him condescendingly. "But the Great King has many more important matters to attend to tonight. I'm sure he won't see the likes of *you* now! You'll have to wait until tomorrow, after we've swept these vile Spartans and their slaves out of the Pass."

Bulis shrugged. "See if I care!"

The eunuch hurried away and Bulis returned to Prokles. "Now what?"

"This trick has got us as far as it's going to," Prokles announced. "Take me to the copse of trees over there."

Bulis did as ordered, and here in the shadows, Prokles unwound the cord from his wrists. His hands free again, he tied the cord around his waist again and then suggested, "Let's walk around to the back and see what sort of sentries are there."

The three Spartans slowly circled Xerxes' great tent, discovering that it was not so much a tent as a complex of tents—some smaller, some larger, some taller, some lower, some lit on the inside, some dark. Sentries paced slowly back and forth across the front and back and on one side, but the fourth side of the complex abutted the river Asopos. There was no evidence of sentries here.

The Spartans crossed to the far side of the river and walked along the far shore. They were directly beside another large tent from which mouth-watering scents wafted. Music and laughter escaped, muffled by the canvas. Someone sang in a very high voice, either a woman or a young boy.

"Some of the bastards obviously don't give a damn about the losses of the last two days," Temenos commented.

"What did you think?" Bulis snapped back. He hated Temenos and felt demeaned to be on this mission with him. "We're among the Persians here; the dead were Medes and Cissians, Lydians and Armenians, Egyptians and—"

"We get the point. We're not idiots!" Temenos snapped back.

"You act like it!" Bulis insisted.

"Shut up!" Prokles ordered. "Look over there! That tent nearest the water. That's where we go in."

The other two stared at it. Temenos guessed first. "It's the latrine."

"Exactly, and since the Great King probably doesn't like being watched by mere mortal slaves while shitting, the sentries probably have orders to look the other way. We'll go a couple hundred yards upstream, wait for the moon to set, then drop into the river and come downstream with the current until we're beside that tent. We scale the bank into the latrine and from there we just keep going as far as we can, killing anyone we meet."

Abruptly Temenos recognized how futile their mission was. He had allowed himself to be excited by it, even honored. After all, no matter what others thought of him, everyone knew that Leonidas loved Prokles. It had seemed obvious that Leonidas wouldn't send Prokles on a completely senseless suicide mission. And so far things had gone well. The ease with which they had moved around inside the camp had given Temenos a sense of security so complete, he'd hardly felt nervous.

But when Prokles said they would just kill everyone until they were killed themselves, Temenos realized that Prokles didn't have any plan for getting out again. Prokles expected to die here, very soon. That was chilling.

Temenos looked over at Bulis. Bulis looked as arrogant as always. Apparently he, too, expected to die tonight, and didn't care. Why should he? He'd been prepared to die four years ago when he went to the Persian court. His family was already dead. Technically, he shouldn't have been allowed to come, because Leonidas had said only the fathers of living sons....

Temenos felt his stomach lurch. Technically *he* shouldn't have been here either, because his sons, living though they were, weren't Spartiate. And Prokles was an exile, a mercenary....

Temenos was beginning to understand Dienekes' choice. They were all dispensable, all pariahs in their own way.

Prokles had found a grassy knoll near the river to wait out the setting of the moon, which hovered close to the top of the mountains behind them. It wouldn't be more than a half-hour before it sank from view and the night lost the illumination that had made movement relatively easy up to now. Meanwhile, a thin film of cirrus clouds diffused the light a little.

Bulis lay back and closed his eyes as if he were napping, but Temenos looked up through the long, limp needles of the pine trees and thought of his kleros. It had lots of pines that were always filled with crickets. The crickets screeched day and night. He had a helot woman who made honey that tasted of pine needles. His boys loved that honey. Just a week ago he had brought some over to Chryse's mother so she could use it for cooking, but Kinadon had nipped in under his mother's arm and managed to reach out an index finger. He wiped his finger along the rim of the jar and then inserted it into his mouth with an expression of defiant satisfaction. His mother had cuffed him, but his expression said clearly: "It was worth it."

"Moon's down," Prokles announced, getting to his feet.

Bulis sat up instantly.

They followed a track made by water bearers to the edge of the river and stepped off into the running stream. The water was cool, mountain-fed. Prokles sloshed ahead of them, finding his footing carefully on the rocky bed of the river. Temenos found himself in dialogue with his sons. He was telling them how much he loved them, how proud he was of them. It wasn't his fault that the laws were so harsh. If he could have sponsored them in the agoge, he would have. He'd talked to Alkander about it, and Alkander wanted to help—but he'd resigned as Paidonomos, and Ephorus wouldn't hear of it. He'd hoped that Leonidas….

"Here!" Prokles pointed. They had reached the point where the royal latrine sat over the river.

Prokles started up the steep bank, and the others followed. It stank of shit, and Temenos knew with inner revulsion that the black goo on his hands was as much feces as mud.

Prokles paused to listen, but the latrine above their heads appeared empty. He took his shield off his back and onto his arm. With it he shoved upward against the wooden seat, which had a large round hole in it for the royal bottom. The seat was nailed down, and his first push produced nothing but the dull thud of wood on wood. Prokles cursed, adjusted his stance, and tried again, this time with more force. To Temenos, the thuds sounded so loud that he was amazed the entire camp wasn't in an uproar. But no one came running. At last Prokles broke through. A moment later, Prokles had hauled himself up into the chamber housing the latrine, with Bulis and Temenos close behind him.

They paused to get their bearings and looked around in some amazement. The royal toilet had carpets on the floor and a big basket with dried rose petals and sprigs of lavender. There was also a pitcher of water, towels, and a stack of square linens too small to dry one's hands on. "I'll be damned," Prokles muttered, "they must be to wipe his ass!"

Temenos picked up the pitcher and poured water over his hands to clean them.

"Too sensitive for shit, are you?" Bulis mocked.

"No, I just prefer to have a firm grip on my spear shaft," Temenos retorted.

Prokles took the pitcher and poured water over his own hands before handing it to Bulis. They dried their hands on the Persian king's towels. Then Prokles pulled on his helmet, and Temenos and Bulis followed his example.

Temenos' heart was galloping in his chest. This wasn't like battle. In battle he was in the line, in his place, and he could feel, smell, and hear the men to his left and right, in front and behind. Now he felt utterly alone. "Chryse, thank you for all the love and understanding you gave me," he was thinking. "I'm sorry I can't help you anymore, but your parents and Gorgo will look after you."

With the tip of his spear, Prokles slowly pushed aside the curtain that shielded the royal latrine from the rest of the tent complex. They were in a kind of corridor, a canvas tunnel leading to another tent. Prokles slid into the tunnel on silent feet. He moved very slowly. There was no rush. It was the darkest hour of the night, and most men were asleep. The tent ahead was dark but not empty. They could sense that more than they could actually see or hear. Then, suddenly, very close at hand, came a little cry.

It was high-pitched. A gasp, really. And it came again. Higher. Sharper. Then it was smothered. A deeper grunting replaced it. The three Spartans looked at one another, flabbergasted.

Prokles recovered first. Using his spear, he reached toward the next curtain and pushed it aside. They looked into a chamber of rich carpets, silken cushions, gleaming hangings—everything threaded with gold, so that the diffused light from the chamber beyond glinted here and there. And there, in the midst of all this luxury, was the white body of a man fornicating with a woman, who lay on her back with her feet in the air. She had little bracelets on her ankles with baubles that dangled and danced as she was shoved back and forth in time with the man's grunting. The man had a rich mane of curly dark hair and a thick, full beard, pointed in the Persian fashion.

Temenos was awestruck with their luck. Helen herself must have led them here! They had got themselves into the royal bedroom, and here was the Great King, not only unprotected, but completely naked and distracted. They could kill him and return the way they came! They could be back in the Spartan camp before the Persians even knew their "Great King" was dead!

Prokles took two strides into the chamber, his spear raised. His footfall made a slight noise, but Xerxes was lost in his sexual ecstasy and heard nothing. Prokles rammed the spear down with all his might, aiming to put it through his back beside the spine and right into Xerxes' vital but unprotected internal organs below the rib cage. The spear easily broke through Xerxes' soft, white back. It pierced clear through him and came out his belly, burying itself in the intestines of the woman under him. A hard metallic clack told them the point had bitten into the ground beneath.

Xerxes emitted a croak, while the woman howled. Then Bulis' sword flashed through the night to decapitate the Great King, and the blood that spewed out of his neck covered the face of his concubine, flooding her windpipe even as her life fled from her punctured innards. Her gasping and moaning sounded like a woman in climax, and no one in the surrounding rooms of the tent took fright.

But Bulis was staring at the face, which had rolled two feet across the floor to stare up at him. "That's not Xerxes!" he gasped.

"What?" Prokles spun about, instinctively drawing his sword. "Who else would dare f**k the Great King's women?"

A voice from the next chamber was raised in alarm. It asked a question in a challenging tone. The Spartans could neither understand nor answer. They went dead still. The question came again and then a third time—sharper now, and obviously alarmed. A hand reached for the curtain, pulled it aside. A eunuch stuck his head into the chamber to see what was going on. His eyes widened in horror and then his head hit the carpet, bounced dully, and rolled to a halt beside the skewered corpses of the lovers, whoever they were.

But the eunuch had not been alone in the next room. Behind him were others, and they were awake and aflutter. Prokles plunged into this next chamber, killing everything he met as fast as he could. The fact that they were evidently inside Xerxes' harem and killing nearly-nude women made no difference. Only when they had killed all five of the women and two more eunuchs did Temenos notice that Prokles' and his own swords were dripping blood, but Bulis was just standing in the entry, his sword and spear pristine.

"What's *your* problem?" Temenos asked his white-faced tormentor. "Don't tell me you could rape Chryse but have a problem killing a Persian whore?"

"Shut up!" Prokles hissed at them, and prepared to advance to the next chamber.

Here their luck ran out. This chamber was full of eunuchs; they had heard the noises and cries and were already in a state of panic. One of them screamed, another started shouting for help, and a third got out the far exit.

Prokles started after him, shouting at Bulis and Temenos to follow. "Don't waste time with these geldings!" he ordered.

By now the entire tent complex seemed to be in an uproar. Not only was the escaped eunuch running through the wide room beyond, but somewhere farther away something metallic was knocked over and seemed to set off a chain reaction. Some men shouted in fear, others shouted orders. Someone gave a blood-curdling scream that was then choked off by blood bubbling up and overwhelming his vocal cords. Somewhere a horn was blowing, but closer at hand someone said "In there!" in Doric Greek.

They had met up with the other assassination team, or almost. They appeared to be one or two chambers away—still invisible—and between them was their quarry. A moment later men poured toward them. These were armed men, not guards but officers. They were in fine robes with heavy rings, bracelets, and collars, but they were trained fighting men and they had gleaming swords in their hands.

Prokles hurled himself at one of these, using his shield to knock him down, and spun to take the second with his sword. A third sprang on him and Temenos raised his spear, ready to take this man out.

Before he could deliver the blow, however, he heard Bulis gasp beside him: "Xerxes!"

A man had just entered from the far right—a man in long, flowing robes dusted with golden embroidery and wearing a tall headdress. In amazement, Temenos recognized that it was the same headdress he had seen from a distance on the man on the throne. This handsome young man was indeed the Great King!

But turning to look had cost him a vital second. With a grunt, Prokles crumpled up at the feet of the third assailant, and his shield dropped and rolled away from him. Two men were hacking at him, cutting him to pieces.

Bulis and Temenos locked shields and advanced on Xerxes. They were shoulder to shoulder, spears raised, all enmity forgotten in their common purpose. Xerxes' eyes widened, but he neither flinched nor fled.

Behind him, the wall of the tent seemed to just come apart. Temenos saw three men in crested helmets struggling with a line of Persian guards. The Persian guards were two deep. Even as he watched, one of the Spartans went down under an ax blow that smashed right through his nosepiece and sliced off the top of his head. Suddenly limp, his body sank down.

They were just three feet from Xerxes. Temenos drew his breath and cocked his spear. He had time to think: "If I kill Xerxes, they can't treat my sons like slaves." Then a volley of arrows slammed into them. One pierced his neck, another his eye socket, and the third caught him in the armpit of his raised spear arm. They extinguished Temenos and Bulis together in the same moment.

CHAPTER 23

ΜΟΛΩΝ ΛΑΒΕ!

(Come and Take Them!)

THE SUN HAD NOT YET COME up over the Malian Gulf, but the sky was pink, and the contours of the land were emerging from the darkness. A light breeze ruffled the purple waters of the bay. From this hillock—far behind the Phocian wall and the killing fields, beyond the stench and flies—it was still beautiful, Leonidas registered, and it had the makings of a fine day.

The night had been quiet. That was both good and bad. It indicated that the Persians had not yet found the Anapaia trail, or the Phocians would have raised the alarm. On the other hand, the silence from the Persian camp suggested that neither assassination team had been successful. If they had come anywhere near Xerxes before being discovered, there would surely have been some sort of commotion in the enemy camp.

The tinkling of a goat-bell drew Leonidas' attention away from the distant view and down to the foot of the little hillock. A helot youth was dragging an unusually reluctant black ram up the path. The ram twisted its head from side from side, reared on its hind legs, butted, kicked, and tried every conceivable trick to get free.

Leonidas watched the helot boy struggling with the goat, saw him lose his temper and kick it hard with his knee. Sacrificial animals were supposed to be treated with respect. They were also supposed to be willing....

At last the youth wrestled the ram up to the top of the hill. He brought it to Leonidas.

"Is your friend Gylis back yet?" Leonidas asked, causing the youth to start.

"My lord?"

"Gylis. That's his name, isn't it? The helot goatherd we sent to warn the Phocians?"

"Warn the Phocians?" The youth looked wide-eyed at him. Then he remembered his manners and looked down. "Gylis was sent on reconnaissance yesterday evening, but we haven't seen him since."

Leonidas didn't like the sound of that. He took the ram between his knees and pulled its head back. The goat looked at him with light blue eyes filled with hatred and fury. Leonidas had his knife ready, but the ram was too defiant. He stepped back and let it go, harvesting a shocked protest from the helot, before the boy remembered who he was and who Leonidas was.

"Bring me a cock," Leonidas ordered. "There's no need to kill a ram so early in the day."

"My lord," Megistias said softly. "I was the one who sent for a ram. On a day like this, we need to pay particular attention to the Gods."

"Can you not read a cock as well as a ram?"

Megistias hesitated, but then he bowed his head. "As you wish, my lord."

The first sliver of sun was over the horizon, rolling out a carpet of glittering gold upon the surface of the sea. Somewhere out there, Leonidas thought, were two hundred Greek ships holding back a thousand Persian triremes.

Panting, the helot boy was back. He handed Leonidas a black cock. The cock was limp because the boy had carried it by the neck all the way here, half choking it to death. Leonidas took it to the improvised altar, laid it on the flat surface, and dispatched it. Megistias gasped, and his face froze in a mask of horror.

"That bad?"

Megistias licked his lips nervously, stepped forward, and pulled apart the skin of the bird to take a closer look. He closed his eyes and his lips started moving. The bird's belly was completely invaded by worms.

"We are lost, my lord," Megistias murmured, while on the side of the mountain something was moving and shouting.

Leonidas looked up and searched the nearly barren face of the slope until he found it. Something small was coming straight down the face of the mountain, falling more than walking, yet it zigzagged a little, too, and it kept making a sound, a high-pitched human sound. As he got nearer, the sound seemed to coalesce into words. Was it saying "Awake!" or "Alarm!"?

"Gylis!" The helot youth recognized him first.

Leonidas looked again. The boy was closer now. He was sitting on his bottom and sliding down the rocks, scrambling over scrub brush, hobbling around boulders. Leonidas felt compelled to meet him partway, so he walked down from the hillock and across the broad gully separating it from the face of the mountain.

"My lord!" the helot wailed from a hundred feet away. "My lord! They broke! The Phocians broke! The Immortals are coming down the track! The Phocians broke!"

The boy reached him, sobbing for breath and from terror. "I tried, my lord. I swear! But in the dark, I lost the track! By the time I reached the Phocian position, the Immortals were already upon them." Leonidas just stared at the helot youth. He was covered with cuts and scratches. The soles of his feet were raw, his hands bleeding. If he had wanted, he could have just disappeared into the mountains—with or without warning the Phocians—let alone bringing word to him here. No one would have ever known. "You can kill me if you want, my lord, but I wanted you to know...."

Leonidas nodded numbly. They were all going to die. Today.

It had always been a possibility. He had taken that risk. Now it was a certainty. Chi, Euryleon, didn't I tell you you wouldn't have long to wait? But why Alkander, too? Why Oliantus? Why Maron and Alpheus?

The camp was waking up to a new day. Gylis' approach had attracted the attention of others. Men started to converge on Leonidas. Men were asking Megistias what was wrong, what the signs had been. Isanor was beside him. "Do we need to reinforce the Phocians?"

Leonidas shook his head. "It's too late. The Immortals have broken through."

"What? And the Phocians didn't even send for us?"

"They were asleep," Gylis gasped out, still panting, "caught sleeping. I don't think they—"

Demophilus arrived with several other allied commanders. "What has happened? What's the matter?"

"The deserter was telling the truth," Leonidas told them.

They stared at him blankly for a second. Then Demophilus echoed Isanor: "Then we must reinforce at once. I'll have my Thespians—"

"There's no need, Demophilus." Leonidas was utterly calm. In his heart he was already dead, and that made it easier. "The Phocians broke. The Immortals are already in our rear. The Pass has been turned. We must send word to Themistocles at once." Leonidas was looking around for the helot boy who had brought him the ram, while around him the other commanders were cursing and questioning, doubting and denying. "Boy!" Leonidas had caught sight of him. "Fetch me the captain of the Athenian triaconter at once!"

"We must withdraw immediately!" the Corinthian demanded, seconded by the Mantineans and Tegeans and some of the Arkadians.

"Cowards!" Demophilus countered furiously. "The Pass is still defensible—we just have to defend it at both ends! We can hold the West Gate as we have up to now with a thousand men, and put another thousand inside the East Gate."

"Yes, exactly!" the Theban supported him.

"What? All of us crushed together between the two Gates? We have nothing to eat in there! Nowhere to rest! No fresh water!"

Leonidas was thinking it through for himself. If they had two thousand men fighting at any one time, every man would be on the line every other hour. They might hold out for one day, but not the four they needed. He raised his hand, and the others fell silent at once.

"The bulk of the army should withdraw at once. The Immortals will close off your retreat in a matter of hours. You must pull out now and put as much distance between yourselves and Thermopylae as possible—enough so the Persian cavalry can't overtake you. Abandon anything you can't carry."

His words were met with stunned silence. No one had ever

expected the Spartan king to order withdrawal. But after they recovered from their shock, the Arkadian commanders did not wait to be told twice. The Corinthians and Mantineans were close at their heels. Isanor, Demophilus, and the Theban Leontiades, however, didn't move. They stared at Leonidas, horrified, until Demophilus asked softly, "What about you? What about the Lacedaemonians?"

Leonidas felt weak, yet detached. His emotions were numbed. Kastor had told him he would know when his time had come. It had come. "Someone has to hold the Pass long enough to give the rest of you time to withdraw. Otherwise, as I said, the Persian cavalry will overtake and slaughter you out in the open, where you won't have a chance."

"But you have a city you can still defend," Demophilus countered with dignity. "We do not. My Thespians will hold Thermopylae. Take the Lacedaemonians south so they can fight in the days and weeks ahead."

Leonidas was moved by this offer. He reached out a hand in gratitude, and Demophilus took it. "You did your best, Leonidas," the Thespian continued. "No one but you could have held them this long. But if Thermopylae is lost, so is Thespiae. We *have* no home to return to. We might as well die here."

"And so will we," Leontiades spoke for the Thebans as well.

Dienekes and Diodoros ran up. "The allies are spreading rumors and threatening to pull out!" Dienekes announced in evident outrage.

Leonidas shook his head. "They're under orders to pull out—"

"What?"

"The Phocians broke. The Immortals are just hours away from closing off the road south. I've given the order to withdraw."

Diodoros and Dienekes gaped at him, while Kalliteles and Oliantus trotted up. "Sir! Have you heard? The allies are packing up and pulling out. It's total panic out there! We must..." He fell silent and looked at the stunned, lifeless faces of the men standing around his commander. "What is it?"

This time Diodoros provided the explanation. Leonidas was staring at Oliantus. "I'm sorry," he mouthed. "I'm so sorry."

"What are you waiting for, Leonidas?" Demophilus urged. "There is very little time. Take your Lacedaemonians out, and we'll make the

Persians fight for the Pass and pay dearly for each of us. We'll delay them as long as humanly possible."

"There's no hurry," Leonidas answered with a glance toward the sun, which was now a copper disk already a hand's breadth above the horizon. "I'm not going anywhere—and whether I like it or not, my Spartans are not going to abandon me."

"You're damned right, we're not!" Dienekes confirmed.

"That doesn't apply to the perioikoi," Leonidas pointed out firmly, turning to Isanor. "Take all your men, the helots, and Megistias back to Lacedaemon."

Isanor hesitated. "We're still over eight hundred strong, my lord. We'd almost double your force."

Leonidas was shaking his head. "Whether we're one thousand or five thousand, we're about to be crushed. Take the perioikoi home with my blessings—I'll put it in writing, if you like, to ensure no one at home tries to twist facts. I'll also send a messenger to Brotus and Leotychidas to halt the march north at the Isthmus. Have we got a good long-distance runner?" Leonidas looked automatically to Oliantus.

"Yes, I have two runners we can send."

"Good. I'll write and seal the dispatches. And pass the word to the Spartiates," he added to Diodoros, Dienekes, and Kalliteles, "to eat a hearty breakfast, as we'll be dining in Hades."*

It was astonishing how fast the allies managed to pull out, but it was not until the sun had lost its copper sheen and was starting to burn away the freshness of the morning that the perioikoi were formed up for departure. Leonidas was on the wall, watching for some sign of a Persian advance, when Oliantus sought him out. "Leo, Isanor requests you come back to Alpeni."

"What's the problem?"

"The wounded are refusing to go."

Of course. He should have thought of that. Leonidas nodded and descended the rear ramp at a measured pace. He was stiff, his muscles hurt, his wound throbbed, and he needed to conserve his strength

---

* This quote appears in Herodotus.

for the battle, which could start anytime—unless the assassins had succeeded after all?

He glanced at the sun again. It was higher than it had been on either of the previous days when the attacks began. Maybe something was wrong in the Persian camp that they could not see or hear from here? Or maybe Xerxes was just giving the Immortals time to get into position.

The perioikoi had formed up neatly in companies of one hundred, followed by the supply wagons containing the wounded. Isanor, recognizing Leonidas from a distance by his cross-crested helmet, trotted over to meet him halfway. "Sir! We have our wounded in the wagons, but all the Spartiates refused." Isanor pointed to nearly a score of men standing in a bedraggled group beyond the wagons.

Leonidas walked over to them. They stood up straighter, squared their shoulders, and lifted their heads. The Spartans had buried thirty-one men here at Thermopylae; twenty-four had been killed outright, and the others had died of their wounds in the little field hospital. Before him were seventeen men with serious but not fatal wounds: Alpheus had a missing eye, Maron's ankles were still massively swollen, Exarchus had lost his right hand and half his forearm, Naucles had a shattered left elbow, and Pantesiadas had taken an arrow through his knee....

"Listen to me," Leonidas spoke to them collectively. "Losing Thermopylae does not mean losing the war. The Peloponnese is still defensible, and Lacedaemon will continue to oppose the Persian invasion with our allies from the League. We will need every trained Spartiate we have. I'm staying here for two reasons. First and foremost, I'm staying because we have to delay the Persians long enough for the bulk of the defensive force to escape to fight in the future. Secondly, I stay because it is my destiny. My death here, today, is the sacrifice Zeus demanded in exchange for sparing Sparta itself. I will make that sacrifice. No one else's life is forfeit. Your duty is to return to Sparta and raise your families to love our laws and our freedom as much as we have done."

"With all due respect, my lord," Pantesiadas spoke up, "our duty is to obey our laws unto death."

"What law says you should throw your lives away here?" Leonidas countered.

"The law says we must follow our kings wherever they lead. What sort of example would we be to our sons if we abandoned you here? Who would even listen to us if we slunk home, leaving a Spartan king to die alone?"

"I have two hundred and fifty Spartiates out there," Leonidas pointed to the East Gate and what lay beyond, "not to mention a thousand Thespians and Thebans. I don't need a bunch of cripples. You'll only get in the way of the fit men. Now get in those wagons and stop delaying the perioikoi! You have no right to stop them from getting out of the trap." With these words he turned his back on them, to signal that this was his last word and he would tolerate no further discussion.

But he did not get far. Immediately behind the wagons with the wounded was one laden with cooking utensils, cauldrons, and tripods. It was driven by the helot cook Eudios.

Leonidas paused to smile up at the old helot. "That was an exceptionally fine breakfast this morning. Thank you." He paused, thought about it, and added, "Thank you for everything."

That was too much for the old cook. Tears started spilling down his round cheeks, and after another second he broke down altogether and started sobbing. "How did it come to this? Why? Where's the army? Why do you have to die?"

Leonidas was surprised by this outpouring of emotion. He didn't know what to say, and before he could think of an appropriate response, the other helots were pressing around him. Some seemed to want to touch him, others to bless him, still others were weeping openly, and here and there he heard someone call out reproachfully, "What is to become of us?"

"No one is going to blame you for what happened here," Leonidas assured them, failing to understand that they feared not the immediate but the more distant future. They were afraid of a Sparta without his influence, of a Sparta dominated by his brother, his nephew, or Leotychidas.

Behind him he heard Isanor give the order to march, and the perioikoi set off smartly. He heard the crack of the teamster's whips and the creak of wagons with the wounded as they started to roll away.

He stepped back and signaled for Eudios to follow. "Go! May the Twins guide you safely home!"

Eudios slapped the reins on the rumps of the draft horses, tears still running down his cheeks and soaking his graying beard. Behind him the cooks, cobblers, herd boys, and other support helots started filing past until only a handful remained, standing stubbornly with their arms crossed, looking sullen and defiant.

Leonidas went up to them. He recognized Gylis. "What is it? What do you want?"

"We're not cowards like the Phocians and Corinthians. Don't we provide the power that drives Lacedaemon's triremes? Haven't we stood by you here, tending your wounds and bringing you water at the very edge of the battle? You look down on us because you think we are farmers, not fighters. But if you would just give us weapons, we would prove you wrong!" Leonidas heard echoes of Mantiklos, his first squire, in the youth's voice, and he hoped Pleistarchos would have the sense to harness—not repress—the spirit that lay latent in such young men.

In answer to Gylis, however, he replied by opening his arms and gesturing toward the field around them, littered with the rubbish left behind by the retreating army. "There are arms and armor everywhere. I cannot stop you from taking what you like and using it as you like. I only hope it won't be to stab us in the backs." He paused and added, "As for you, Gylis..." The use of his name surprised the youth, who had never dreamed the Spartan king knew his name, nor expected to be addressed personally by such an exalted personage. "If you are determined to stay, you would help me best as a lookout, above the West Gate where you were yesterday. If you are there, you can signal when the Persians are coming, in what numbers, whether by horse or by foot. That would be more use to me than one more hoplite."

Gylis looked down, fighting with his own emotions. He knew that the course Leonidas offered was one that would make him both a witness to history and a survivor. Part of him wanted to prove he was just as brave and selfless as any Spartiate, but the temptation to take the role Leonidas offered was great.

"Think about it," Leonidas urged, and continued back through the East Gate, making a point not to look back and see what the helots decided to do.

Beyond the East Gate, the Spartiates were making their final preparations. In the warm morning air, they stripped down and changed into their best chitons, combed out their hair, and rebraided it firmly. Leonidas noted that many of his soldiers were having their hair combed and braided by their attendants, but there was no way of knowing whether these helots remained voluntarily, or out of fear of returning home if they abandoned their masters.

A moment later he caught sight of Meander, waiting patiently for him near his tent. Leonidas signaled for him to come inside.

Meander followed nervously. By staying, he had disobeyed orders, but when so many of the others had declared their intention to stay with their masters, he felt that departing would have been both craven and an insult to Leonidas. Ever since his father had chosen to pull him out of the agoge and let Aristodemos remain, he had doubted himself. Sometimes he defiantly insisted he was as good as everyone else; sometimes he sank into near-suicidal self-pity. Today, he didn't know what to feel. His stomach was tied in knots. He was afraid of what was coming, but even more afraid to run away. He knew his brother Aristodemos, blind as he was, had been sent home with the rest of the wounded. He would survive, but how would he treat Meander, who was not disabled in any way, if he, too, scuttled for safety? Wouldn't he say: "Our father was right. You would never have made a Spartiate! Other helots stayed. Why, even a goatherd like Gylis stayed, but *you* ran away!"

"Don't I have a clean himation in that chest over there?" Leonidas' voice brought Meander back to the present.

"Yes, sir," Meander answered numbly, hastily going to the chest and opening it. His hands were shaking, which shamed him.

"Is there a chiton as well?"

"Yes, sir."

"Good. Then strip down and put the chiton on."

"Sir?"

"Put one of my chitons on," Leonidas ordered over his shoulder. He was already bending down to pick up Sperchias' breastplate. Sperchias and Euryleon had been buried with the other dead in their cloaks, but he had kept their armor to take home to their wives and sons. It wasn't going to get that far. It would fall into Persian hands one way or another, but first it could clothe Meander like a proper hoplite.

"Sir, you only brought red chitons with you."

"I know. Hurry up. The Persians are overdue already."

"But..."

"Meander, if you're going to fight with me today, then you will do so as the Spartiate you are. So hurry up and put that chiton on. I think Sperchias' breastplate will fit you well enough, and Euryleon's sword is in good condition. We'll get you a standard-issue shield and spear, and you can wear my spare himation—or take this one," he pulled it off his back, "and I'll wear the clean one."

Meander gaped at him, dumbstruck, until he at last managed to whisper, "Are you serious?"

"This is no time for joking," Leonidas answered, but he laughed nevertheless at the look of wonder on Meander's face. It struck him as absurd that Meander was so pleased—as if dying in Spartan scarlet would be less terrible than dying in the clothes of a helot.

Then, because the other man was still stunned, he reached into the chest and grabbed one of the chitons himself. "Put it on!" he ordered, thrusting it at Meander. But because this was the last hour of their lives, he changed his mind, and pulled Meander into his arms to hold him for a second.

Meander clung to him, trying with his arms to express the gratitude and admiration he could not put into words. Then he nodded and pulled back.

Leonidas ducked out of the tent, leaving him to change into the clothes and armor of a Spartiate.

By the time Gylis, who had taken his post far up on the cliff above the Middle Gate, signaled that the Persians were mustering again, Meander was not the only helot in Spartiate armor. As Alkander made his way back to Leonidas' tent, he recognized scores of other attendants moving about awkwardly and a little dazed in their new, if tattered, finery. His own man was not among them. Alkander's man had a young wife and two small children. He had hesitated a seemly moment, but Alkander's sincerity in urging him to go home had overcome his scruples. It gave Alkander a small sense of victory to know he had saved at least that young life, and he had taken the opportunity to send a last message, scratched on a shard of broken pottery, for Hilaira and his sons. That, too, was a comfort. With the departure of his attendant and that message, he had taken leave of home. All he had to face now was the short future that remained—starting with Leonidas.

He reached Leonidas as the latter emerged from his tent, jamming his helmet onto his head. Alkander knew Leonidas was angry with him for insisting on coming to Thermopylae and for insisting on staying. He knew he had miscalculated. His heart ached for Hilaira. He was sorry he could not be the surrogate father to Agiatis and Pleistarchos that Leonidas wanted him to be. But he could not regret his decision. His place was here. He met his friend's eyes, bracing for the fury he expected to see in them, and was taken aback by a look of sheer affection. Leonidas had forgiven him. Alkander felt his tension dissolve in the morning air.

They had no need for words. They walked together through the abandoned camp and mounted the wall.

Leonidas called the commanders to him: Demophilus and Leontiades, and the Spartiates Diodoros, Dienekes, and Kalliteles. They formed a little circle, and he searched their earnest faces. The shock of what had happened was wearing off, and reality was sinking in. These men were starting to think about what their death would mean, not just to them but to their families, their friends. It was good that the Persians were mustering at last, because waiting could be far more demoralizing than fighting.

"We need one phalanx inside the East Gate, facing east to meet the Immortals whenever they arrive." He paused and then looked at Leontiades. "Would you and your Thebans assume that position?"

Leontiades nodded, glancing back toward the East Gate. It was quiet now. Empty. No bodies rotted on that side of the wall. The earth had been torn up by thousands of men passing to and fro, but not by fighting. It did not stink. At the moment, theirs was the easier task. But the Immortals were Persia's elite troops. When they came, it would be a brutal fight—and an honorable death.

"Good. Then between us, Thespiae and Sparta, we have just short of a thousand men. What I propose is to—"

A commotion behind him made Leonidas stop and look over. Hobbling up the rear ramp, supporting one another, were seventeen wounded Spartiates and Eurytus, his eyes bound, led by his helot. Aristodemos was notably absent from the little group.

The sight of the walking wounded made Leonidas forget what he was about to say. He scowled. "I ordered you to return to Sparta with the perioikoi!" he growled.

"No one—not even a Spartan king—has the right to order a Spartiate to dishonor himself," Pantesiadas replied calmly, leaning heavily on Exarchus' shoulder. "Have you forgotten the answer you gave to me when I was serving in your syssitia as a boy?" Leonidas couldn't remember the incident at all, but Pantesiadas reminded him, quoting: "Life is a gift of nature, and a natural death overtakes even the vilest creature. An honorable death, on the other hand, is something only an honorable man can choose."†

There was no answer to that, and no time, either. A chariot was rushing toward them. It was a magnificent one, pulled by two matching bays groomed to gleam in the morning sun. The charioteer was dressed in tight-fitting striped trousers and a striped long-sleeved tunic, over which he wore a quilted corselet. The stitching of the corselet was gold, and the diamonds of the quilting were alternately yellow and green. He wore a tall turban of matching colored cloth embroidered with gold, which also covered his mouth—apparently against the stink. Beside him was a man in a tall headdress, wearing armor over bright purple and yellow cloth that was much baggier, looser, and finer. He wore gold bracelets on his wrists, gold cuffs on his arms, and a belt encrusted with coral. He had a long, curly beard and a staff of some sort. Unfortunately, with both Sperchias and Bulis dead, Leonidas had no one with him who might have cast more light on who he was or where he came from.

The charioteer pulled up and shouted: "King Leonidas of Sparta!"

Having watched the chariot's approach, Leonidas turned back to his commanders and ordered, "Demophilus, deploy your Thespians

---

† A saying to this effect is attributed to Leonidas in Plutarch's collection of "Sayings of Spartans."

to the left; we'll stand on the edge of the cliff to the sea. Kalliteles, your company to the far right. Diodoros, your company next to the Thespians.

"Leonidas of Sparta! Are you still there? Or has the Spartan king run away?"

"Follow me down onto the field," Leonidas ordered his troops. Then he turned and started down the central ramp onto the field before the Middle Gate.

The field had, as usual, been cleared of the dead during the night, by pushing the bodies of the enemy off the cliff into the sea and burying the allied dead. The vultures and other scavengers had followed the feast to the shoreline below. Nevertheless, Leonidas had to tread carefully, because broken pieces of equipment littered the earth. Broken spear and arrow shafts, broken swords and body parts, and—most dangerously—arrowheads and spearheads made the footing treacherous, although much improved since yesterday morning.

About a hundred paces ahead of the wall, Leonidas stopped and waited with his hands on his hips. "I'm Leonidas of Sparta. What does your master want now?"

"You have been betrayed. You will soon be surrounded. You have squandered any opportunity for an honorable place among the Great King's subjects. But the King of Kings is benevolent beyond measure. While your cause is lost, your lives need not be. The Great King offers you your naked lives, if you surrender your arms."

"*Come and take them*!"‡ Leonidas flung back at him—loud enough for the words to reverberate beyond the Pass and into history.

The chariot wheeled and raced away, and immediately the sound of shouting erupted from beyond the West Gate. Dust started wafting up and blowing toward them, but still no Persians came through the West Gate. Leonidas looked over his shoulder, wondering if Xerxes

‡ This is probably Leonidas' most famous line. It is recorded in Plutarch, but it probably has a much older and wider tradition. Its popularity is reflected in the modern monuments to Leonidas. In modern Sparti, the monument to Leonidas does not consider it necessary to identify him by name—only by this one phrase.

was hoping the Immortals would take them in the rear and eliminate the need for another frontal attack altogether.

The waiting was wearing on everyone's nerves, and then Leonidas had an idea. "Dienekes, let's try something different."

"Different?"

"What if, rather than just driving them back toward the gate, we intentionally force them into the sea?"

"Pivot the line on the right hinge?"

"Yes."

"Can the Thespians manage that?" Dienekes asked skeptically.

"If we take the Thespians between our three companies, it should work."

"It might, but we'll have to redeploy fast. The Persians will come at any moment."

Leonidas left his position and walked rapidly along the front to Demophilus. He explained his plan, and Demophilus agreed at once.

Leaving Kalliteles' company in position on the edge of the field by the sea, the other two Spartan companies pulled back. Demophilus split his Thespians into two units, and one closed with the left of Kalliteles' company. Leonidas inserted his own company between the two halves of the Thespian force, and Diodoros took his company to the far left wing.

The redeployment was completed before Maron, who had insisted on taking his old position on Leonidas' left, nudged him gently and pointed to Gylis on the slope above Xerxes' throne. Gylis was waving wildly, giving the signal for "archers."

Up to now the Greeks had waited with their helmets tipped back, their spears stabbed in the earth by their butts, and their shields at their knees. Leonidas pulled his helmet down over his face, picked up his shield, and took up his spear. The men to his left and right followed his example—so that without an order being given, the gestures rippled outwards and backwards until the entire phalanx was standing armed and ready.

Leonidas glanced along the front rank. By all the Gods, he thought, it was beautiful! Despite all the battering they had withstood. Despite the wounds, the aches and pains, the shallow breathing and twisted stomachs of the men behind the wall of bronze, it looked magnificent. Nothing moved except the horsehair crests. The shields, although dented, scratched, and torn, still caught the morning sun upon their battered surfaces and reflected it back, not in a blaze of polished glory but with a fractured yet quiet defiance that echoed his words. Come and take them, indeed, he thought with pride. Come and take them from us!

Then he ordered the advance. Leonidas had only one objective today: to sell their lives as dearly as possible. If he could push large numbers of the enemy over the edge of the cliff, so much the better. It would save his aching spear arm for the fight that was bound to engulf them when the Immortals arrived.

In order to carry out their planned maneuver, however, they had to spread their line thinner than usual. The objective was not a phalanx that could withstand a pushing contest, but a net. Furthermore, the left flank had to be in a position to connect with the far wall of mountain and then drive the enemy before it.

Leonidas considered Xerxes singularly unimaginative to have again sent in archers, but it made his task easier. As soon as the archers had gone down on one knee to start their barrage, Leonidas gave the order for his line to pivot. The burden fell on Diodoros and the Thespians to Leonidas' left to cover the greatest distance, hitching up to the slope of the mountain at Xerxes' feet, while the rest of the line adjusted to retain a single, straight front.

It was, Leonidas thought as he swung his head back and forth to assess progress, a ridiculously difficult maneuver. He was mad to try it at a time like this. At the same time, it was exactly what they all needed: something different from the senseless, mindless killing of the days before. It was also visibly throwing the enemy into confusion. Their targets were moving in a manner that appeared illogical. Some Greeks were getting closer and some receding, all without actually breaking formation. More and more archers stopped shooting altogether and kept looking around for orders, while their officers apparently argued with one another.

It helped that these subjects of the Persian king were armed with weak bows and wicker shields. They could see that their arrows had no effect on the men of bronze, who kept moving methodically in their ranks and files without even bothering to cower behind their shields. At the order to fire, the archers resumed the barrage furiously, but the Greeks responded as if the enemy weren't even there. Leonidas could see archers wetting themselves, and it was only a matter of time before total panic seized them.

The moment he ordered the advance, the nerves of these woefully underarmed and poorly led enemy troops broke entirely. The men at the front sprang to their feet and tried to run away. The Persian cavalry deployed on the far side of the West Gate, however, were driving yet more archers onto the field. The fleeing archers collided with these reinforcements and were pushed back onto the field.

Because the Greek line had pivoted, the only open space on which these increasing numbers of troops could spread out was along the edge of the field by the sea. Here they rushed forward almost to the wall in sheer animal panic, like terrified beasts fleeing into a trap.

Leonidas ordered the Greek line forward. They advanced with heads down to reduce the risk of arrows finding their eyes or necks, and they did not raise their spears in order to avoid the risk of arrows to their armpits. They could kill without touching a weapon. All they had to do was push with their shields.

The screams of the panicked enemy reached a fevered pitch. Frantic, they wailed and faded as one after another fell off the edge of the cliff, sometimes scores at a time. Leonidas was reminded of the screams of the Persian ambassadors as they were tossed down the well. It was a chilling memory, but the men today weren't unarmed, accredited diplomats. They were fighting men abandoned to the slaughter by indifferent and incompetent commanders.

By the time the killing ended, the sun was halfway to noon, and Leonidas was streaming sweat. Every man was desperately thirsty, but there were no helots to bring them water. They pulled back before the wall to re-form, catch their breath, and see what the Persians would send in next.

Leonidas asked if there was any sign of the Immortals yet, but the Thebans sent back word that all was still quiet at the East Gate.

Ahead of them, however, the Persians were again deploying through the West Gate. These weren't archers. Indeed, they were dressed far less flamboyantly than all the troops Xerxes had fielded up to now. Neither bright colors nor turbans adorned them. They wore leather caps with earflaps. They also wore leather trousers and boots and leather vests, but their arms were bare. They appeared to be javelin throwers.

Leonidas took one look at the way they were deploying and knew it would not be possible to carry off a pivot again. "We're going to shorten and deepen the line, then go in straight," he decided, and the word was passed along the line.

"Do we wait for them?" Dienekes asked.

"No," Leonidas answered. It wasn't a rational decision. He just had the feeling they had to get this over with. The Immortals were bound to arrive any minute now.

For Maron, walking was less painful than standing, and he was relieved when Leonidas took them forward. It helped to be in the front rank, too. Behind him seven men were pushing him forward, and that took some of the strain off his ankles. He glanced just once at Alpheus; his brother caught his look and answered with a smile. At some place in his brain, Maron felt sorry for his wife, his son. But neither he nor his brother had any choice. Maron had been Leonidas' man since the day Leonidas had stepped in to stop the senseless flogging of Alpheus during Artemis Orthia.

The javelins started coming in furiously, and Maron shouted at his brother, "Keep your head down! One blind man in the phalanx is enough!" An instant later, an axe was somersaulting through the air straight at him. He jerked his shield up to try to stop it, but the axe was too heavy and had too much momentum. With a horrible crashing scream, the hoplon shattered and the axe sliced through Maron's forearm and then his neck. His brother howled in agony, but Maron didn't feel a thing anymore.

Alkander stepped over Maron's body and was shield to shield with Leonidas.

The axe that had killed Maron was not the last. They had come up against a whole body of men armed with them, and each thrown axe meant a dead Greek. Alkander felt as if men were dropping all around him. The line was staggered as one hole after another was torn in it so fast that the second and third ranks could hardly move into place. The line came to a halt and was on the brink of collapse.

"Forward!" Leonidas shouted. "Close the distance!"

Alkander put his head down and felt as if he were cowering in the shelter of Leonidas' shield, just as he had when they were boys and only Leonidas' determination had made him keep going.

Somehow they managed to close with the axemen, but at close range the axes were still lethal. They sheared the Greek spearheads from the spear shafts or snapped the latter in two like twigs. Alkander found his spear worthless before he could even deploy it. He reversed it to use the butt end and called for a replacement, but there was no time to wait for one. He drew his sword and used it to parry the next swing of an axe. The sword held, but it left his arm numb. Ares! Alkander thought. These men are monsters.

Leonidas, too, was fighting with his sword—a bad sign. Alkander was close enough to him to hear him grunting with each thrust. Or was he cursing? Leonidas had never hated his enemies, yet Alkander thought he could hear him snarling things at them with each blow. Alkander had to advance to keep up with him; alarmed, he looked left and right. Leonidas was getting ahead of the line, creating a small, dangerous bulge in it.

"Steady!" Dienekes shouted from the other side. "Wait for the line."

Leonidas didn't appear to hear him. Alkander and Dienekes had no choice but to try to close up on him, and Alkander turned to his left to make sure Alpheus was with him, but Alpheus was no longer there. He had been replaced by a man Alkander hardly knew.

Someone thrust a spear into Alkander's hand from behind, and he plunged it into the nearest enemy at once. From behind him came more spear thrusts. The rear ranks had apparently managed to pass their spears forward, and the first two ranks were adequately armed again. The Spartan line started to surge forward. Alkander killed three men with as many stabs of his spear, and beside him, Leonidas was killing so fast that a mound of dead was building up in front of him.

But then Alkander's second spear broke. They were only seven deep. There were no helot attendants ready and able to fetch reserve spears from the supply wagons. Each broken spear was irreplaceable. Alkander sensed that this time there would be no replacement. He took up his sword again.

Were they getting close to the East Gate? The mountain seemed so close upon their left. Alkander risked looking up to Xerxes' throne. He didn't have time to focus. Sweat was stinging his eyes, but he thought he saw something golden and glittering. The Great King was watching the slaughter, just as he had yesterday and the day before.

"Prepare to withdraw!" Leonidas shouted.

Dienekes passed the order to his right, Alkander to the left. Leonidas counted to three. They had done this before; he hardly thought they needed the order. They were counting in their own heads.

"Now!"

They started stepping backward in unison at a brisk pace called to them by the enomotarchs of the rear ranks. These officers called off ten paces. Then, at a shout, they turned and started running as fast as they could.

Leonidas' lungs were laboring. His wounded thigh just wouldn't answer the orders of his brain. He was less aware of pain than of simply losing control. He was aware of something being very, very wrong, but he couldn't figure out what it was. Something was missing. His right was open, exposed. He was stumbling. His legs were collapsing under him, and there was no one to pick him up.

Alkander!

Alkander was not beside him anymore. Leonidas almost turned to go back, but Dienekes pushed him forward brutally with his shield, and a second later Meander was on his right—filling the gap left by Alkander with the strength and urgency of a young man who had not stood in the line for the last two days. With Dienekes pushing and Meander pulling, Leonidas staggered back to the re-formed line and turned around, still dazed and breathless.

The Persians were not in hot pursuit. No one was chasing after them. The Persians—or rather, whichever of their subject peoples had been fighting for them today—were falling down in exhaustion where they had fought.

Leonidas squinted at the field, littered again with bodies, some of which still writhed in agony or even tried to drag themselves to safety. Maybe one was Alkander, still alive as Maron and Alpheus had been that first day? But Alpheus and Maron were both dead now. They would all be dead soon. What did an hour more or less matter?

But he missed Alkander. He missed him.

"Drink this!" Dienekes ordered, handing him a skin with warm water.

Leonidas obeyed without asking where it came from.

"Do we await them here?" Dienekes asked.

"I don't think I have the energy for a new advance."

"Then we await them here," Dienekes concluded, paused, and then broke the bad news. "The Thespians have been decimated. Demophilus is mortally wounded."

"Who has taken command?" Leonidas asked, alarmed.

"Dithyrambus."

"A good man."

"They're all good men. Every single one of them."

"Every one of *us*," Leonidas corrected.

Dienekes smiled gently and glanced at the sun. "We could use some shade."

Horn signals warned them that the latest force of Persian subjects was taking the field against them. Through the West Gate new legions were deploying at a jog, their clothes bright and billowing and free of blood. A new troop, a new nation, fresh and ready to show off their courage before their Master.

But not archers. These appeared to be spearmen. Leonidas hoped they didn't have axes, too, like the last troops. Still, without arrows, there was no need to close the distance rapidly. Leonidas was content to let the enemy come to them—until they started throwing their spears.

These were heavier and more deadly than arrows, and the problem was aggravated by the fact that many of the Greek shields had been damaged and weakened over the last two days of fighting. Leonidas was aware of men cursing violently as their shields were pierced, and then he stopped a javelin with his own aspis and heard an ominous crack.

A glance confirmed that the tip of the javelin was pointing clear through the inside face of the shield. Worse: the bolts holding the metal frame together had worked loose. Because the shaft of the javelin still extended on the outside of the shield, each time it was shoved one way or the other it acted like a wedge, wrenching the wood farther apart.

The hoplon was the quintessential component of hoplite warfare. It was the line of overlapping shields that rendered a phalanx effective. A hoplite derived his strength, his sense of invulnerability, and his identity from his shield. Earlier this morning, Leonidas' men had killed with their shields alone. Spears were throw-away weapons, swords were often broken or lost, but shields were passed down from father to son, and the loss of a shield was a disgrace and a disaster. So the feel of his shield going soft, starting to bend and come apart, was as disorienting to Leonidas as the earth giving way beneath his feet.

Desperate to stop the extended shaft from weakening his shield any further, he lowered the hoplon in order to shear the shaft with his sword near the point of entry. It was a fatal mistake.

He had exposed his chest. The next javelin took him hard in the center of his breast with enough force to pierce through his breastplate and knock him over backwards. It took away his breath and all pain. He saw the sky, and registered that the sun was almost directly overhead, blindingly bright. It dimmed as a vulture with outstretched wings passed in front of it. He'll soon be eating my entrails, Leonidas thought calmly, already detached from his corpse. The blood, stench, and filth all seemed to be receding. The warmth of the sun was no longer burning, but soothing. Is this immortality? Leonidas asked in astonishment, feeling weightless and disoriented. It was as if the vultures were all beneath him now.

"Didn't I tell you it might not be all darkness beyond the grave?" a familiar voice said.

"Alkander?"

"Yes, and the others. Nikostratos and your father, too."

"My father?" Leonidas had a great deal he wanted to discuss with his father.

Behind him, all hell broke loose.

Leonidas was dead before he hit the ground, but the enemy knew who had fallen; his gold-studded, cross-crested helmet had been pointed out to them before they took the field. It was a prize worth a thousand gold darics.

The enemy swept in, hooting and howling in triumph.

Dienekes and Meander were caught off guard; they briefly closed their shields over Leonidas' corpse, but the enemy shoved them back in a burst of jubilant energy. One of the enemy grabbed Leonidas' body by the foot and started dragging it away.

Meander screamed, broke out of the line, and ran forward. It was an undisciplined and un-Spartan thing to do, but Meander had been forced out of the agoge at age fifteen. He fought not with the discipline of decades of drill, but with the emotions of his overburdened heart.

In a moment he had caught up with the men trying to drag away Leonidas' remains, and he was slaughtering them like a berserker. The madness of his attack terrified the enemy into pulling back long enough for Meander to wrest the corpse away from them.

Before Dienekes could bring up the rest of the Spartan line, however, the enemy recovered. In the next instant they were all over Meander. In a few seconds he was hacked to pieces. The enemy again seized hold of Leonidas' body. The men who had killed him, determined to claim the reward Xerxes had promised, started to drag it away again. Meanwhile, others pressed forward to stop the advancing Spartan line, confident that without their king the Spartans' fighting spirit would break.

The Spartan line was not stoppable. Fully closed up and reinforced with willpower born of blind emotion, it rolled over the men that got in its way until it had reclaimed the body of its king.

Now, however, the enemy had also been reinforced. From the rear, Persian cavalry was rushing in. They funneled through the foot soldiers, riding some of them down in their determination to seize the prize. The cavalry rode like a spearhead straight at the men trying to pass Leonidas' body to the rear of the Spartan line. They pierced the line by knocking one man down and forcing others back. They rode right over Leonidas' corpse in their determination to take control of it—then, whirling their horses and fighting with swords when their javelins broke on the Spartan shields, they managed to clear a space for one of them to jump down and fling Leonidas' body over the back of a horse.

The Spartans had recovered from their initial surprise. From all sides they attacked the Persian horsemen in their midst, killing with their swords and their shields, then kicking and trampling with a savage if silent anger rarely known in Spartan history. Not one of the Persian cavalrymen got out alive, and Leonidas' mortal remains were again in Spartan hands. Moreover, the enemy had become intimidated by the determination with which the Spartans defended even a dead king. Xerxes' troops knew that the battle was almost over. They hesitated to die *now*. They hung back—and from the east, horns started blowing.

The word spread through the ranks as if carried on the very wind: "The Immortals! The Immortals!"

"Back!" the Spartans said. Maybe someone had given the order. Maybe it was just an instinctive, collective decision. They had Leonidas' corpse, and they were not being pressed by the enemy. They pulled back warily at first, but when there was no pursuit they started jogging as fast as their weary, wounded limbs would take them. Four men had Leonidas' body on their shoulders. When they reached the ramps leading up to the wall, they were all gasping for breath. It was noon.

What was left of the Thespian-Spartan force, a thousand men strong this morning, streamed up the three ramps onto the wall and down the ramp on the far side. Here they fell on their knees or collapsed against the back of the wall. They were gasping for breath and bleeding. No one was in command anymore.

Oliantus walked along the back of the wall, searching for Dienekes, Diodoros, or Kalliteles. They were not here. He searched for any Spartan who had fought in the front rank, but there were none. Nor were there any Spartan second rankers left.

He found Dithyrambus holding the corpse of Demophilus in his arms and weeping. He found Arion holding a rag to the stump of his arm. He found Eurytus, the bandages torn from his eyes, squinting up through swollen lids, apparently able to see light and shadow.

He looked over his shoulder. The sound of battle was carried on the wind. Not just the horns and shouts, but the clang of weapons. The Thebans were engaged. They couldn't stay here. Here they would be slaughtered like game driven into a blind canyon. He looked around.

Behind him was the hillock where Leonidas had made the sacrifice each morning, and where Megistias had read the signs. Was that really less than six hours ago? It seemed a lifetime.

Oliantus tapped the man nearest him on the shoulder and pointed. "Up there." The man nodded and struggled to his feet. Oliantus moved on. "Up there. Up there. On the hillock." One by one or in pairs holding each other up, with the four men carrying Leonidas' body in their midst, the Spartans straggled across the field to the hillock and struggled up the gentle slope. They were so exhausted, they felt as if they were scaling Taygetos.

From here, Oliantus could see the Persians pouring through the West Gate and see the Thebans giving ground before the East.

"Form up!" he ordered, registering with astonishment that he was in command. He signaled for the maybe six score survivors to form a circle around the altar on which Leonidas had sacrificed a cock at dawn. The body still lay inert in its drying blood, covered entirely by flies.

The men with Leonidas' corpse staggered to the altar, roughly shoved the cock aside with the backs of their arms, and then gently laid their dead king upon it. Megistias emerged from a little copse of trees and came to gaze down at the lifeless remains of Leonidas.

"I thought Leonidas ordered you home," Oliantus addressed the seer.

"He tried to save as many men as he could," Megistias answered, "but none of us can escape our destiny. I am an old man. I sent my son home instead."

They were distracted by an eruption of hissing and growling from the men around them. Oliantus looked back toward the field below. The Immortals had broken through the East Gate. With their captains apparently dead, some of the Theban rear rankers were throwing away their weapons and raising their hands in surrender. The sight astonished Oliantus. It made no sense to him that men would throw away freedom and honor at a moment like this, when they were so close to immortality. But his eyes were his witness. They will regret this, he thought with detachment.

Meanwhile, the Persians were pouring over the wall. Their eagerness and enthusiasm to take this object, the goal of two and half days of bitter and costly fighting, was so great that some chose to scale the wall rather than wait to file over one of the three ramps. Once over the wall, they spread out on the field before the hillock, shouting and pumping their bows in the air over their heads in triumph.

The last of the Thebans were either dead or had been taken captive. The Immortals were marching through the East Gate in good order. Hundreds of them, thousands of them, Oliantus registered. Xerxes must have sent the entire ten thousand over Kallidromos, he calculated. Xerxes had taken no chances.

Orders were being shouted. Cavalry was clattering over the ramps of the wall. The horses whinnied and fretted, and the banners of the leaders streamed in the wind. A chariot was galloping in through the West Gate, flashing in the sunlight.

For a moment Oliantus thought the Persian king was going to make another request for surrender, but then he realized archers were forming up facing them while the chariot drove far behind the archers, following the road next to the sea. Oliantus wasn't sure if the man in the chariot was Xerxes or just another high-ranking Persian, but he was intent on meeting up with the commander of the Immortals.

A moment later Oliantus understood: the Persians were securing control of the Pass while leaving their subject archers to finish off the remnants of the defeated. Ah, yes, Oliantus thought to himself with a cynical smile, the Great King Xerxes did not negotiate with the likes of us—mere rabble in his eyes. With the death of Sparta's king, there was no one among the Greeks he was willing to even acknowledge.

The first barrage of arrows soared into the sky. Whoever had said Persian arrows would darken the sun was right. They did dim the light of even the noonday sun.

Oliantus took up his shield and moved to the front rank of the crouching phalanx. With a sense of inner wonder, he realized he was now in command of what was left of Sparta's elite, the remnants of her royal guard. It was an honor he had never aspired to, yet it made him proud. He, the eternal "second best," had stepped into Leonidas' shoes. For the next few minutes, maybe for a whole hour, he would endeavor to follow Leonidas' example as well. It was, he realized, an uplifting thought.

Epilogue

THERMOPYLAE

478 BC

The invading hordes were gone. They had dissolved into memory like the morning mist or the clouds of dust with which they had smothered a parched countryside. They had gone back whence they came—beyond the Bridge to Greece, beyond the Hellespont.

But evidence of the havoc they had wrought still scarred the countryside from Thrace to Attica. The charred remains of farmsteads, the shallow graves, the felled forests, the trodden fields, and the bleached bones of slaughtered livestock marked the passing of a million men come to trample Greece into submission. It would take years, maybe decades, to recover.

But the invaders were not just gone—they had been defeated. And not just once, but twice: by sea at Salamis and by land at Plataea. They would not return again anytime soon.

Today, on the second anniversary of the last day of the battle, dignitaries from all city-states in the anti-Persian Confederation had gathered to pay homage to those who died at Thermopylae by dedicating monuments marking the battle that had taken place here. It was not common to commemorate a lost battle or to honor the defeated, but the defense at Thermopylae had struck a chord in Greek hearts. Already, and dangerously, the dead heroes here were more revered than the men who had led the allies to victory: the Spartan Pausanias, the Tegean Chileos, and Themistocles, of course, who headed the Athenian delegation.

The Peloponnesians had erected a joint monument that boasted: *Four thousand here from Pelops' land, Against a million once did stand*—an exaggeration, Themistocles felt, considering that the bulk of them had fled in the end. Nevertheless, Themistocles reflected, the Peloponnesian monument was more seemly than the oversized one of a hoplite that the Thebans had put up for the four hundred of their men who had fought with Leonidas; its extravagance was apparently a futile effort to distract future generations from the fact that Thebes had switched sides afterward and fought with Persia at Plataea. That made Thebes the only city in Greece that had managed to be on the losing side in both battles, Themistocles reflected spitefully.

The Thespians had chosen a lovely marble frieze showing the Muses weeping around a corpse on which the names of all seven hundred men were inscribed. But it was the Spartan monuments that aroused the most comment.

"Have you seen what the Spartan monument says?" one of the Athenians asked his fellows in a low, scandalized voice.

"*Go tell the Spartans, stranger passing by, that here, obedient to her laws, we lie,*" Themistocles quoted easily.

"That sounds more like a complaint than praise!" the first Athenian remarked.

"What is it supposed to mean? Do they have a law against retreating?" another asked back.

"Hardly. They retreated from Athens four times in my lifetime alone!" Themistocles cut short the stupid speculation. "This refers to the law that says Spartan guardsmen never abandon their king in battle. Only Leonidas could have given the order to retreat. When he decided to stay and die, the three hundred had no choice but to stay with him. That is why there is a separate monument to Leonidas. To him goes the credit for the decision to fight here, with other Greeks, rather than cower behind the Isthmus. And to him goes the credit for remaining here, and covering the retreat of the others at the cost of his own life – and that of his companions. It was a noble thing to do," Themistocles conceded, nodding with satisfaction.

Themistocles had liked Leonidas, and he was also glad the Spartan king was out of the way. Leonidas would undoubtedly have challenged Athenian dominance of the coalition, insisted on putting forward his own ideas, and pursued Lacedaemonian interests. In short, he would have stood in Athens' way. Even his admiral, Eurybiades, had proved far more troublesome and independent-thinking than Themistocles had expected – or appreciated. Yes, things were much better the way they were, with Leonidas a dead hero rather than a living leader.

"The Spartans made the wrong choice," young Kimon declared, shaking Themistocles from his thoughts.

"What do you mean?" Themistocles demanded irritably.

"The oracle gave the Spartans a choice: their city or their king. The Spartans, who pride themselves on building their monuments in flesh, should have valued their finest soldiers more than their pedestrian public buildings and old-fashioned monuments. You would have thought they would have scorned the material Sparta for the spiritual one: the Sparta embodied by Leonidas."

Themistocles found Kimon's admiration for the Spartan king a bit excessive. He snorted and remarked, "Yes, well, that's what comes of so much Spartan virtue." He nodded his head in the direction of the marble lion lying on his side, pierced by a score of bronze arrows. "Meanwhile, we have to deal with men of a different caliber altogether." He nodded toward Pausanias, who was making an ostentatious display of sacrificing at the monument to Leonidas.

Kimon nodded. "You can tell a great deal about a man by his followers. Leonidas' friends were good, honest men; Pausanias' are sycophants. Leonidas' simplicity of speech and dress were not an affectation, but incarnated Spartan reverence for emotional honesty, intellectual integrity, moral incorruptibility, and humility."

"His example will live on," Themistocles promised patronizingly.

"Perhaps, but how long before nothing is left but the notion of death rather than retreat—regardless of circumstances? How long before senseless sacrifice becomes a sacred code that no man dares defy? How long before suicide is raised to a virtue—if only it is done in the name of some larger cause? Leonidas was not an idiot who mindlessly obeyed orders, nor was he a simpleton who equated senseless death with courage. Rather, he was a man who loved and understood freedom as only a Spartan can—not as a license to self-indulgence, but as an opportunity to be greater than one's self."

HISTORICAL NOTE

THE HISTORICAL RECORD FOR THE PERIOD of Leonidas' life covered in this novel is notably more complete than that for the first two books in this trilogy. The assassination of the Persian ambassadors, the Battle of Marathon and Sparta's role in it, the suicide of Cleomenes I, the dispatch of two Spartan sacrificial envoys to Persia, Leonidas' election to command the combined Greek land forces and the appointment of Eurybiades to command the combined Greek naval forces in 480, and, of course, the Battle of Thermopylae, are all recorded historical events. (Readers familiar with Steven Pressfield's *Gates of Fire* may be astonished to learn that there is not a trace of historical evidence for the more than twenty wars he describes Sparta fighting against her neighbors during the reign of Leonidas. Sparta was, in fact, at peace with all her neighbors, including Argos, for the entire decade of Leonidas' reign.) Last but not least, almost all the quotes attributed to Leonidas come from this period of his life and provide substantial insight into his personality.

Likewise, four of the key events involving Gorgo—the deciphering of Demaratus' message, her rebuff of an importunate admirer with reference to "not being able to play even a female role," her remarks about Spartan men and women, and her leave-taking from Leonidas—are recorded in history.

Based on this skeleton of facts, I have developed the substance of this novel. The novel weaves a logical story out of the isolated facts, but it is also an interpretation of the known facts. Furthermore, the interpretation is one based on knowledge of Spartan history before and after Leonidas. Given the sharp contrasts between archaic Sparta, with its international orientation and artistic flowering, and classical Sparta, with its declining population and xenophobia, I have consciously made Leonidas' death a turning point in Spartan history. My Leonidas is conceived as the incarnation and advocate of Sparta's archaic traditions and virtues; his domestic opponents, including his twin brother (completely unfairly and without historical basis, but for the sake of literary effect), foreshadow the degeneration of Sparta into a bigoted and militaristic state.

This interpretation is not arbitrary. There are a number of indications in the historical record that give credence to my thesis that Leonidas was well traveled and open-minded. First and foremost is the fact that Leonidas was elected commander of all Greek land forces by the independent representatives of all Greek states that chose to defy Persia in 481. This was not merely an acknowledgement of Sparta's military primacy. Three years later, the same cities rejected his nephew Pausanias, who had just won the battle of Plataea, and his co-monarch Leotychidas, who had commanded the Spartan forces at another victory, Mycale.

The sacrifice of the Thespians at Thermopylae, which represented a much higher—indeed devastating—loss compared to population size than the sacrifice of the three hundred Spartans, is likewise best explained in terms of personal loyalty to Leonidas. Thespiae had no alliance or other form of affinity with Sparta. It was not any more threatened than were other city-states in Boiotia. Thespiae did, however, demonstrate after Thermopylae a powerful ethos of "victory or death"—as was notably demonstrated at the Battle of Delium during the Peloponnesian War.

Other historical events too often ignored or viewed only in isolation have contributed to my interpretation of Leonidas as well. Key among these is the Spartan response to Marathon. A great deal has been written and speculated about Sparta's curious delay in responding to the Athenian plea for aid. Too little attention has been paid to the fact that what amounted to the entire active Spartan army (two thousand men) marched north in 490 *without* a king in command.

Certainly no king is named. At the time, this was very much against Spartan tradition and requires an explanation. Speculation about helot revolts (for which there is only the barest of inferential evidence) does not explain this fact. A domestic leadership crisis (Cleomenes was either still in Arkadia or already raving mad, and Leotychidas was in exile) would explain both the delay in responding and the eventual dispatch of an active army without a king in command. Leonidas, an Agiad prince, who was by this time a mature man and experienced in war and would shortly afterward became king, is the most likely candidate as Sparta's commander.

This in turn would explain how Leonidas won the respect and trust of Athens and Plataea. The Athenian leadership would have been very frustrated by Sparta's refusal to respond immediately, but they would have been thankful to the commander who turned up—ahead of expectations—after marching an army 120 miles in less than three days. Furthermore, if Leonidas had commanded the troops Sparta sent to Marathon, it would explain why ten years later he was obsessed with getting to Thermopylae in time—even if he had only an advance guard of three hundred men.

Insinuations that Leonidas played a part in his half-brother's death are almost unworthy of comment. There is not a shred of evidence to support the thesis beyond the naked fact that Leonidas succeeded his brother. But he could have done that at any time after Dorieus' departure from Sparta. Why, if Leonidas was a power-hungry man capable of fratricide, did he serve his half-brother loyally for thirty years before suddenly deciding to murder him? And where was Gorgo while her husband killed her father? Are we to assume that she suddenly turned patricidal? Or that she kept her mouth shut? Gorgo? Ancient historians blamed Cleomenes' madness on either a curse of the Gods or excessive drinking. Modern historians ought to be familiar enough with paranoid schizophrenia to realize that Cleomenes' behavior—including his self-mutilation—is completely consistent with this serious mental illness.

There is no evidence that Leonidas' ascension was challenged by his other brother, his twin Cleombrotus. The rivalry between the brothers is an invention of my own for literary purposes. That said, we do have a curious quote attributed to Leonidas that inspired my interpretation. According to Plutarch, "When someone said to him: 'Except for being king, you are not at all superior to us,' Leonidas, son of Anaxandridas and brother of Cleomenes, replied: 'But were I not better than you, I should not be king'" (Plutarch, *Sayings of Spartans*, 225). For a man who had not been heir apparent to his father and had gone through the agoge, it seems unlikely that Leonidas was referring to his royal blood alone. I think the response suggests confidence that he had proved himself superior to others. That, in turn, hints at some kind of a domestic power struggle. By making Leonidas a twin who had to convince the Spartan Assembly that he is the rightful king, I do justice to this exchange. My Leonidas is king not just by virtue of his bloodlines (Cleombrotus has the same bloodlines), but because he has demonstrated superior capabilities that induced his fellow citizens to raise him up above his twin.

Tellingly, another quote attributed to Leonidas is his refusal to accept the crown of "all Greece" from Xerxes with the argument: "If you knew what is honorable in life, you would avoid lusting after what belongs to others." This response does not suit the kind of man who would have killed for the throne—most especially not a man who would kill his own brother and father-in-law for the throne. If Leonidas had been ambitious and greedy (like Pausanias or Lysander after him), he would have accepted Xerxes' offer! Certainly his answer underlines the fact that he believed himself entitled to the Agiad throne—not something he would have felt if he had stolen it, by murder or otherwise. I believe a combination of legitimacy through birth and popular acclaim based on his achievements fits best with the known record of Leonidas.

There is no historical basis for the smallpox epidemic I describe. However, there was apparently a considerable delay between the murder of the Persian ambassadors and Sparta's decision to send two men to Persia as human sacrifices. I felt this delay could best be explained by some kind of catastrophe that could only be interpreted as divine displeasure. An epidemic had the virtue of being drawn out—and so, in contrast to an earthquake or flood, it would likely lead the Spartans to believe their envoys' offer to the Gods would still be relevant by the time they reached Susa. The names of the Spartan envoys are recorded, as are the verbal exchanges between them and the Persian satrap Hydarnes and with Xerxes himself.

Although not explicit in the historical record, it also seemed logical that if envoys went to the Persian court, they would encounter Demaratus there—and thereby become the means of bringing Demaratus' message back to Sparta. The delivery of that message, scratched on the wooden back of a folding wax writing tablet, is described in Herodotus (7:239). Herodotus states that at first no one could make sense of the blank tablets, until Gorgo suggested that the message was hidden under the wax. That she was present when the significance of the tablet was being discussed reinforces my interpretation of Gorgo as a partner to Leonidas, not just his brood mare.

Eurybiades is also a historical figure. He really did have command of Sparta's small contingent of ships (twelve at Artemisium and twenty at Salamis), as well as being appointed commander of the combined fleet of ships fighting the Persians in 480-479 BC. He was not personally elected as was Leonidas, but the allies refused Athenian leadership of their fleet—despite the fact that Athens provided by far the largest number of ships (nearly two hundred).

The allies specifically asked Sparta to provide a naval commander. This is highly significant, because it suggests that at this time Sparta was considered a naval power capable of providing competent leadership at sea. It is important to remember that Athens was *not* a significant sea power in the sixth century BC, and it did not build its massive fleet until the discovery of silver in Laurium in 483 BC. In short, in 480, Athens was a parvenu naval power. The naval powers of the sixth century had been Corinth and Aegina. They preferred Spartan command to Athenian command, probably out of deep-seated suspicion of their trade rival Athens, but they would not have accepted Spartan naval leadership if Sparta had been perceived as utterly incompetent and incapable. This is what led me to hypothesize a Spartan fleet-building policy under Leonidas.

Except for his role at Artemisium and Salamis, Eurybiades appears to play no role in history. It is important that he was Spartiate, which supports my thesis that under Leonidas, if not before, there were opportunities for Spartiates to gain experience in naval warfare. The fact that he was replaced as naval commander by Leotychidas the following year further suggests that at least briefly, in the post-Salamis era, naval command attained exceptional prestige. Then again, Leotychidas never distinguished himself with military valor, and so he may simply have preferred to face the Persians at sea, where the bulk of the fighting inevitably fell to the far more numerous Athenians and other allies, than to face the Persians on land, where he would be expected (but unable) to live up to the reputation of Leonidas.

The other reforms I have attributed to Leonidas tie in with this hypothesized naval policy. Triremes required oarsmen, and rowing a warship is notoriously back-breaking, tedious, stinking work. It was so unpleasant that it was seen as punishment in later centuries, when criminals would be condemned to "the galleys." The image of slaves chained to the oar-banks is one we carry around with us from films like *Ben-Hur*. In fact, however, in the ancient world, particularly in ancient Greece, the crews of warships were predominantly *citizens*. This was because no city could afford to entrust the maneuverability and speed of their fighting ships to anyone who did not have a stake in the outcome of an engagement.

This clearly raised a problem for Sparta. We know that Sparta's population was in sharp decline in the period after Thermopylae, probably due to a combination of a devastating earthquake in 465 BC and attrition in the brutal war with Athens that began in 459. Although Spartiates commanded ships and fleets during this war, eventually defeating Athens in the naval battle of Aegospotami in 405 BC, Spartiates did not man the oars of Lacedaemon's (eventually victorious) ships.

The most probable source of competent seamen was the perioikoi residents of Lacedaemon, many of whom were probably merchants and could have had a seafaring tradition going back centuries. Perioikoi towns, unlike landlocked Sparta, were often located on the coast (Epidauros Limera, Boiai, Kardamyle, Asine, Pylos, and, of course, Gytheon, to name only a few). On the other hand, perioikoi hoplites were an important component of Lacedaemonian land armies. The perioikoi element equaled that of the Spartiates at Plataea. This suggests that the perioikoi elite did not greatly outnumber the Spartiates themselves. However, there might have been poorer perioikoi who, like Athens' poorer citizens, manned the Lacedaemonian fleet. Given the fact that Sparta's fleet never reached the dimensions of Athens', it is conceivable that all manpower for the Lacedaemonian fleet came from the perioikoi. This would explain the trustworthiness of the crews, and would fit the notion that ancient Greek warships were manned by free men.

But we also know that revolutions do not occur when people are generally content or when they are most oppressed and exploited. On the contrary, revolutions or uprisings are most likely to occur when a long period of rising living standards and political expectations is abruptly ended by economic or political crisis. No more than fifteen years (and possibly as early as ten years) after Leonidas' death, the only documented helot revolt in Spartan history occurred. It occurred before the start of the Peloponnesian War, and so cannot be attributed to the impact of that conflict. The timing of that revolt needs to be explained. While the confusion and loss of Spartiate life caused by the Great Earthquake might have been the *opportunity* that the helots seized, their dissatisfaction—and the period of rising living standards and expectations that had been sharply disappointed—had to predate it.

My hypothesis is that during Cleomenes' reign the helots had enjoyed a slow but steady increase in living standards, which accelerated under Leonidas and was combined with rising political expectations. We know that later in Sparta's history, various popular leaders played with schemes to allow some helots to earn or buy their freedom. Some of these measures were eventually implemented. There is nothing inherently absurd about Leonidas entertaining such notions. Any Spartan politician with the foresight to appreciate naval power might also have looked to the most numerous class in the Lacedaemonian population for manpower. If Leonidas had introduced laws that opened opportunities for helots to earn their freedom, he would almost certainly have enjoyed huge popularity among the helots—which would in turn explain how a Spartan army could risk mobilizing her entire citizen population and deploying it outside of Lacedaemon, with a force of thirty-five thousand helots in attendance as light troops, during the Plataean campaign. If these thirty-five thousand helots had been in any way untrustworthy, they would have posed a greater risk than the Persians themselves, and they would never have been taken out of Lacedaemon.

In the post-Leonidas era, however, helot hopes and expectations must have been abruptly shattered, leading to the explosive situation that culminated in the revolt. This is another reason why I have postulated a conservative faction in Spartiate society that, after the death of Leonidas and his closest companions at Thermopylae, takes control of the Spartan government. We certainly know that Pausanias was not a paragon of virtue nor popular for long, while Leotychidas' performance was consistently dismal.

The historical justification for including a chapter with Gorgo in Athens is found in Plutarch's "Sayings of Spartan Women." On the one hand, Plutarch records that "a stranger in a finely embroidered robe" made advances to her, earning the rebuke that he "couldn't even play a female role." While a stranger might have been in Sparta and (somewhat incredibly) risked making advances to the Spartan queen, Gorgo could hardly have retorted with a reference to "playing a female role" based on experience in Sparta alone. Sparta had no theater at this time. If Gorgo rebuffed an importunate stranger by implying he looked like an actor playing a female role in a play, her remark implies that she had seen drama performed elsewhere—presumably in Athens, where theater was becoming popular at this time.

More convincing, however, is the fact that Gorgo's famous quip about Spartan women being the only ones who gave birth to men was, according to Plutarch, in answer to "a woman from Attica." Since women from Attica weren't supposed to be seen outside the women's quarters of their own homes, it is far more likely that Gorgo was in Attica (Athens) than that an Athenian woman was in Sparta. Together, these quotes gave me the courage to add a chapter with Gorgo in Athens, because I think it is important to remind readers about the deplorable status of Athenian women. The misogyny of ancient Athens is one of the most despicable of its qualities, and should not be brushed aside or ignored.

The account of Thermopylae in this novel is based first and foremost on Herodotus. I follow his very explicit statement that Leonidas and his three hundred were sent "in advance of the main army" (*Histories*, 7:206), and I have seen no convincing evidence that Leonidas was abandoned or betrayed by his home government, as many modern accounts suggest. According to Herodotus, "The intention was, when the Karneia was over (for it was that festival that prevented the Spartans from taking the field in the ordinary way), to leave a garrison in the city and march with all the troops at their disposal" (*Histories*, 7:206). He explicitly states that the only thing that prevented the planned deployment of the full Spartan army was the fall of Thermopylae much sooner than expected.

Herodotus tells us about the four-day delay before the Persians attacked, during which a Persian scout observed the Spartans exercising naked and combing their hair, which Herodotus claims induced Xerxes to send for Demaratus. Allegedly, Demaratus explained that this was "normal" for the Spartans when preparing to fight. Note that Herodotus' Demaratus says the Spartans were preparing to *fight*, not to die. There is absolutely no evidence in Herodotus that Leonidas or his men viewed their deployment as a suicide mission that would inevitably end in death for all.

Herodotus records that Xerxes waited four days before attacking and that, losing his patience on the fifth day, he sent the Medes in to clear the Pass, in expectation of easy victory. Herodotus claims Xerxes sent the Cissians in after the Medes failed, and then ordered the Immortals into the Pass late on the first day, after the Persian troops had suffered very serious casualties in heavy, all-day fighting. The tradition that Xerxes had a throne set up so he could watch the battle and that he jumped up three times in the course of the day "in terror for his army" also goes back to Herodotus' account (*Histories*, 7:212). Herodotus states explicitly that the Spartans "had their losses, too, but not many." He also describes the fighting in relays by city-state, and provides no details of the second day beyond that it was like the first, with heavy losses for the Persians.

Notably, Herodotus claims the Spartans employed various "feints" to outfight their "inexperienced" enemy. Unfortunately, the only one he describes is that the Spartans would "turn their backs in a body and pretend to be retreating in confusion, whereupon the enemy would pursue them with a great clatter and roar, but the Spartans, just as the Persians were on them, would wheel and face them and inflict in the new struggle innumerable casualties" (*Histories*, 7:212). While experts on hoplite warfare doubt that this maneuver is possible, I prefer to follow Herodotus, who wrote his account in the same century that Leonidas died and after interviewing survivors of the Persian wars.

Herodotus explicitly states that Leonidas fought further forward on the third day than on the two previous days, but the wheeling motion I describe on the third day of the battle is not explicitly described. It may well be too complicated for hoplite warfare at this time. On the other hand, it is only when describing the third day of battle that Herodotus explicitly mentions that many Persians "fell into the sea" (*Histories*, 7:223). This inspired me to imagine a slightly different tactic than used previously—if only to enliven the storytelling.

Herodotus also makes no mention of the night raid, but other ancient sources refer to it. It seemed a very logical thing for Leonidas to order, once he realized that his position was at risk and that he might not be able to fulfill his mission of holding the Pass until the full Spartan army could deploy. More important, it makes for a great story. I couldn't resist including it.

According to Herodotus, "There was a bitter struggle over the body of Leonidas; four times the Greeks drove the enemy off, and at last by their valor rescued it." This account has been challenged by modern historians, who feel it is too reminiscent of the *Iliad*. Maybe. But Leonidas' men were raised on the *Iliad* and saw themselves as the heirs of the Iliad's heroes. I think that as Leonidas' friends and subjects, they would have felt compelled by the tradition of the *Iliad* to retain control of his corpse for as long as they had breath in them.

Herodotus records the fate of Aristodemos (the only survivor) and Eurytus, who fought blind. He says the bravest Spartans, after Leonidas himself, were Dienekes (who is sometimes credited with the remark about "fighting in the shade") and the brothers Alpheus and Maron. The bravest Thespian, he says, was Dithyrambus, but the Thespians were commanded by Demophilus (*Histories*, 7:222). The fact that Xerxes ordered Leonidas' head displayed on a stake for his entire army to see as they marched past is also a detail provided by Herodotus. There would have been hundreds of thousands of witnesses of this fact (unlike many other details Herodotus includes), and so this detail can be considered verified history, more than almost anything else in his entire account.

GLOSSARY OF GREEK TERMS

Agoge The Spartan public school, attended by all boys from the ages of seven through twenty and by girls for a shorter time–probably from seven until they had their first period. The agoge was infamous throughout Greece for its harshness, discipline, and austerity, however, not–as many modern historians would have us think–for the exclusion of literacy, the arts, or intellectual training from the curriculum. On the contrary, ancient commentators claimed that "devotion to the intellect is more characteristic of Sparta than love of physical exercise." Furthermore, although the children lived in barracks, they were also introduced to democracy early by being organized into herds, or packs, which elected their leaders. Nor, as many modern sources suggest, were the children attending the agoge completely cut off from their families. They probably went home on holidays (of which there were at least twelve, each lasting several days), and would have been able to see their parents in the city almost any day. Sparta was a small society, and the agoge was in the middle of it.

Andron The chamber in a private house where symposia were held. It was often provided with permanent benches or shelves built against the walls for the guests to recline upon.

Aspis The round shield used by Greek heavy infantry. Often also referred to as the *hoplon.*

Chiton The basic undergarment worn by both men and women. It could be long or short, belted or unbelted, sleeveless or sleeved, and bound at one or both shoulders. Slaves usually wore it clasped only on one shoulder, and short chitons for mature men were also associated with "unfree" status.

Cithara An ancient stringed instrument.

Eirene A Spartan youth, aged twenty, on the brink of citizenship and serving as an instructor in the agoge.

Ephors Executives of the Spartan government elected from among the citizen body for one year. Any citizen could be elected ephor, but no citizen could serve in this capacity for longer than one term.

Enomotia A unit of between thirty-two and forty men in the Spartan army, commanded by an enomotarch.

Gerousia The Council of Elders in Sparta. This body consisted of twenty eight elected members and the two kings. The elected members had to have attained the age of sixty and were then elected for life. Although this institution was highly praised by commentators from other parts of Greece, who saw in the Council of Elders a check upon the fickleness of the Assembly, the senility of some Council members and the "notorious" timidity of the Council were often a source of frustration among younger Spartans.

Helots The rural population of Lacedaemon, descended from the original settlers of the area. Helots were not slaves.

Hetaera In Athens, an expensive whore, patronized by the very rich. Hetaerae were the only women allowed to take part in symposia. The majority of hetaerae were slaves, pimped by their masters

Himation The long, rectangular wrap used by both men and women as an outer garment.

Hippagretai Three men appointed each year by the ephors as company commanders in the royal guard. Each of the three men selected one hundred men to serve in their respective company.

Hippeis The "Knights" or Guard, a three hundred strong unit of young Spartiates (aged 21-30), chosen by the hippagretai. They served as the personal bodyguard of the Spartan kings when on campaign and appear to have also fulfilled certain police functions inside Lacedaemon. Appointment to the Guard was very prestigious but not permanent. The appointments were made annually, guardsmen had to maintain their reputation throughout the year to ensure reappointment. Presumably a change in commander might also result in a change in Guard composition.

Hoplite A Greek heavy infantryman.

Hoplon The full kit of a Greek heavy infantryman, including armor, greaves, aspis, spear, and sword. Often used interchangeably with aspis, however, to refer to the round shield only.

Hydria A pitcher for water.

Keleustes The officer aboard a Greek warship who commanded the rowers, watching for problems, relaying orders, and the like. These men held a very important position requiring a great deal of skill, and were in some ways more "professional" than the captains, who were simply men drawn from the upper classes, often for their ability to finance the construction of a ship. The keleustes, along with the helmsmen and bowman, were the "mates" or "officers" of ancient ships.

Kleros The land allotment granted each Spartan citizen on maturity as a result of the Lycurgan reforms. A kleros was allegedly large enough to provide for a man and his immediate family, and according to tradition there were originally six thousand of these allotments. Another three thousand were added in the sixth century as the population grew. Since not all kleros were equally productive and since property could apparently be bought and inherited, increasing inequalities of wealth were inevitable.

Kothon A drinking vessel similar to a modern mug, distinctive to Sparta. In most of Greece, drinking cups had two handles; in Sparta, just one.

Krater A large jar of pottery or bronze for mixing water and wine to the desired level of alcoholic content.

Kylix A drinking vessel with a low, shallow bowl on a short stem. These could be quite large, requiring two hands to hold, and were often passed around at a symposium.

Lacedaemon The correct designation of the ancient Greek city-state of which Sparta was the capital. Lacedaemon consisted originally of only the Eurotas valley in the Peloponnese, Laconia. In the late eighth century BC, the valley to the west, Messenia, was captured and remained part of Lacedaemon until the fourth century BC. There were a number of other cities and towns in Lacedaemon, but the bulk of these were inhabited by perioikoi rather than Spartiates. The Spartiates were concentrated in Sparta, because of the requirement of attending the messes (syssitia) on a nightly basis.

Lochagos/ Lochagoi The commander of a lochos; lochagoi is the plural form.

Lochos The main subdivision of the Spartan army, variously compared to a battalion, regiment, or division. It had an estimated peacetime strength of four hundred men and a maximum strength (full call-up of fifteen classes of reserves) of one thousand men.

Meleirene A Spartan youth, aged nineteen, about to become an eirene, and two years from citizenship.

Metoikoi/ Metics In Athens, free men living in the city but not enjoying citizenship status. They were subject to special taxes and were in need of an Athenian patron in order to be registered. Anyone living in Athens more than a month without being registered was liable to be arrested and sold into slavery.

Mothakes In Sparta, youths from families too poor to pay the agoge fees, who were sponsored by other Spartiates. The status carried no stigma after attaining citizenship, and many famous Spartans, including Lysander, were mothakes.

Paidagogos In Athens, a man, usually a slave, responsible for looking after school-aged boys–essentially escorting them daily to the grammar master, the singing master, and the palaestra or gymnasium.

Paidonomos The headmaster of the Spartan agoge.

Palaestra A public place for exercise, particularly wrestling.

Penteconter A single-decked, fifty-oared Greek warship, predecessor of the trireme.

Pentekostus A unit of one hundred to two hundred men in the Spartan army; similar to a company in the army today, and hence often referred to as such in this series of novels.

Peplos The most common indoor garment worn by women in Sparta at this period. It was basically a single rectangular cloth, folded vertically in half and sewn up the open side. It was held up by clasps over one shoulder or–if a hole for the second arm was made in the folded side–by clasps at each shoulder. Spartan women continued to wear this garment after it was out of fashion elsewhere, and the fact that it was left open from the thigh down for greater ease of motion earned them the (derogatory) epithet of "thigh throwers."

Peristyle A courtyard surrounded on all sides by a colonnaded walkway.

Perioikoi A non-citizen resident of Lacedaemon. Like the helots, the perioikoi were descendants of the non-Greek native population of the area prior to the Dorian invasion of the Peloponnese in roughly 900 BC. The perioikoi enjoyed free status and ran their own affairs in their own towns and cities, but had no independent state, military, or foreign policy. The perioikoi–like the metics in other Greek cities–were required to pay taxes to the Lacedaemonian authorities. They also provided auxiliary troops to the Spartan army. Since Spartiates were prohibited from pursuing any profession or trade other than arms, the perioikoi had a (very lucrative) monopoly on all trade and manufacturing in Lacedaemon.

Phouxir The "fox time," a period during a Spartan youth's upbringing when he was required to live "off the land" and outside of society. I have chosen to place this period at the end of boyhood and before youth and to fix the duration at forty days. Some historians believe it lasted as long as a year. It was during–and only during–this period that stealing by the boys was tolerated by society. Otherwise it was considered demeaning, although obviously a skill once learned could be used again if detection was avoided.

Pilos A felt cap worn under the Greek battle helmet or as a head covering against the cold. It was often worn by helot attendants without helmets.

Polemarch A military commander.

Spartiate A full Spartan citizen: that is, the legitimate son of a Spartan citizen, who successfully completed the agoge, served as an eirene, and was admitted to a syssitia on coming of age.

Stade The length of the Olympic stadium, used to measure distances in ancient Greece.

Stoa An open, roofed area supported by columns. In its simplest form, it is little more than a portico built against a building. More elaborate structures, such as Pausanias describes in his travel guide to Greece, might have several rows of pillars. They could be round or rectangular in shape.

Symposium A dinner or drinking party, popular in Athens. They could include intellectual discourse or be characterized by erotic entertainment and excessive drinking—or both.

Syssitia Spartan messes or dining clubs. Adult Spartiates were all required to join one of the many existing syssitia when they attained citizenship at age twenty-one. Thereafter, they were required to dine at these messes nightly unless excused for such things as military duty, athletic competition, or hunting. The existing members of each syssitia had to vote unanimously in favor of an applicant before he could be accepted. Recent research suggests that membership in the various syssitia may have been based on family ties or clan relationships, but this is not certain. They were not, however, merely military messes based on military units, and they were explicitly designed to encourage men of different age cohorts to interact. Each member was required to make set contributions in kind (grain, wine, oil, and so on) and was expected to make other gifts, particularly game, in accordance with their means. Failure to pay the fees was grounds for loss of citizenship, and failure to attend the meals without a valid excuse could result in fines or other sanctions.

Thetes The lowest class of Athenian citizens. Although freemen, thetes generally owned no land and could not afford hoplite panoply, let alone horses. They manned Athens' fleet of triremes, receiving pay for this service, and also made up the majority of the men voting in the Athenian Assembly or serving as jurors in trials. At the start of the Peloponnesian War there were an estimated sixty thousand thetes in Athens.

BIBLIOGRAPHY

Aeschylus, *Persians*.

Aristophanes, *Birds*.

Aristophanes, *Knights*.

Aristophanes, *Lysistrata*.

Aristophanes, *Frogs*.

Aristophanes, *Peace*.

Baltrusch, Ernst, *Sparta: Geschichte, Gesellschaft, Kultur*, C.H. Beck, Munich, 1998.

Baumann, Hellmut, *Greek Wild Flowers and Plant Lore in Ancient Greece*, Hirmer Verlag, Munich, 1982.

Blundell, Sue, *Women in Ancient Greece*, British Museum Press, London, 1995.

Bradford, Ernle, *Thermopylae: The Battle for the West*, Da Capo Press, New York, 1993.

Carroll-Spillecke, Maureen, *Wohnen in der klassischen Polis III: Der antike griechische Garten*, Deutscher Kunstverlag, Munich, 1989.

Cartledge, Paul, *Sparta and Lakonia: A Regional History 1300-362 BC*, Routledge, London & New York, 1979.

Cartledge, Paul, *Spartan Reflections*, Duckworth, London, 2001.

Cartledge, Paul, *The Spartans: The World of the Warrior-Heroes of Ancient Greece*, Vintage Books, New York, 2002.

Chrimes, K.M.T., *Ancient Sparta: A Re-Examination of the Evidence*, Manchester University Press, 1949.

Dalby, Andrew, and Sally Grainger, *The Classical Cookbook*, British Museum Press, London, 1996.

Davidson, James, *Courtesans and Fishcakes: The Consuming Passions of Classical Athens*, Fontana Press, London, 1997.

Dettenhofer, Maria, "Die Frauen von Sparta," in *Reine Maennersache?* Deutscher Taschenbuch Verlag, Munich, 1996.

Euripides, *Andromache.*

Euripides, *Electra.*

Euripides, *Iphigenia.*

Euripides, *Medea.*

Euripides, *Trojan Women.*

Figueira, Thomas J., "Population Patterns in Late Archaic and Classical Sparta," in *Transactions of the American Philological Association,* #116 (1986), pp. 165-213.

Finley, M.I., *The Ancient Economy*, Penguin Books, London, 1973.

Forrest, W.G., *A History of Sparta 950-192 BC,* W.W. Norton & Co., New York, 1968.

Grant, Michael, *Die Klassischen Griechen: Die Bluete der hellenischen Kultur von Miltiades bis Aristoteles,* Gustav Luebbe Verlag, Bergisch Gladbach, 1994.

Hale, John R., *Lords of the Sea: The Epic Story of the Athenian Navy and the Birth of Democracy*, Viking, New York, 2009.

Hamilton, Edith, *The Greek Way*, W.W. Norton & Co., New York & London, 1930.

Hanson, Victor Davis, *Hoplites: The Classical Greek Battle Experience*, Routledge, London & New York, 1991.

Herodotus, *The Histories.*

Hodkinson, Stephen, and Anton Powell, eds., *Sparta: New Perspectives,* Duckworth, London, 1999.

Hodkinson, Stephen, *Property and Wealth in Classical Sparta*, Duckworth, London, 2000.

Homer, *The Iliad.*

Hornblower, Simon, *The Greek World, 479-323 BC,* Routledge, London & New York, 1983.

Jones, A.H.M., *Sparta*, Barnes and Noble Books, New York, 1993.

Kennell, Nigel, *The Gymnasium of Virtue*, University of North Carolina Press, Chapel Hill & London, 1995.

Kennell, Nigel, *Spartans: A New History*, Wiley-Blackwell, Chichester, 2010.

Link, Stefan, *Der Kosmos Sparta*, Wissenschaftliche Buchgesellschaft, Darmstadt, 1994.

Morrison, J.S., J.E. Coates, and N.B. Rankov, *The Athenian Trireme*, Cambridge University Press, Cambridge, 2000.

Mueller, Werner, *Architekten in der Welt der Antike*, Koehler & Amelang, Leipzig, 1989.

Murray, Oswyn, *Das fruehe Griechenland*, Deutscher Taschenbuch Verlag, Munich, 1982.

Musiolek, Peter, and Wolfgang Schindler, *Klassisches Athen*, Koehler & Amelang, Leipzig, 1980.

Ogden, Daniel, *Aristomenes of Messene: Legends of Sparta's Nemesis*, The Classical Press of Wales, 2004.

Pausanias, *Guide to Greece*.

Peridou-Gorecki, Anastasia, *Mode im antiken Griechenland*, C.H. Beck, Munich, 1989.

Plutarch, *Lycurgus*.

Pomeroy, Sarah, *Spartan Women*, Oxford University Press, Oxford, 2002.

Powell, Anton, *Athens and Sparta: Constructing Greek Political and Social History from 478 BC*, Routledge, London & New York, 1988.

Rich, John, and Graham Shipley, *War and Society in the Greek World*, Routledge, London & New York, 1993.

Richter, Gisela, *A Handbook of Greek Art*, Phaidon, London & New York, 1959.

Roberts, J.W., *City of Sokrates: An Introduction to Classical Athens*, Routledge, London & New York, 1984.

Sealey, Raphael, *Women and Law in Classical Greece*, University of North Carolina Press, 1990.

Sophocles, *Oedipus Rex*.

Stibbe, Conrad M., *Das Andere Sparta*, Verlag Philipp von Zabern, Mainz, 1996.

Thucydides, *History of the Peloponnesian War*.

Vandenberg, Philipp, *Das Geheimnis der Orakel*, F.A. Brockhouse Verlag, Leipzig, 1979.

Whitby, Michael, *Sparta*, Routledge, New York, 2002.

Wycherley, R.E., *How the Greeks Built Cities*, W.W. Norton & Co., New York & London, 1962.

Xenophon, *A History of My Times*.

Xenophon, *Erinnerungen an Sokrates*.

Xenophon, *On Horsemanship*.

Xenophon, *Spartan Society*.

Xenophon, *The Anabasis*.

Zaidman, Louise Bruit, and Pauline Schmitt Pantel, *Die Religion der Griechen: Kult und Mythos*, C.H. Beck, Munich, 1994.

HELENA P. SCHRADER

HISTORIAN, NOVELIST, DIPLOMAT

www.helenapschrader.com

HELENA PAGE SCHRADER IS A CAREER diplomat who earned a Ph.D. in history from the University of Hamburg with a ground-breaking dissertation about the mastermind behind the Valkyrie plot against Hitler, General Friedrich Olbricht. She has published nonfiction works on the German Resistance, women in aviation in WWII, and the Berlin Airlift. Her novels on the German Resistance, the Battle of Britain, and ancient Greece have won praise and awards.

List of Principal Publications:

Nonfiction

- *General Friedrich Olbricht: Ein Mann des 20. Juli*, Helena Page (Schrader), Bouvier Verlag, 1993/1994
- *Sisters in Arms: British and American Women Pilots During World War II*, Pen & Sword Books Ltd., 2006
- *The Blockade Breakers: The Berlin Airlift*, The History Press, 2008/2010
- *Codename Valkyrie: General Friedrich Olbricht and the Plot Against Hitler*, Haynes Publishing, 2009

Fiction

- *The Olympic Charioteer*, iUniverse, 2005
- *Are They Singing in Sparta?*, iUniverse, 2006
- *The Lady in the Spitfire*, iUniverse, 2006
- *Spartan Slave, Spartan Queen*, iUniverse, 2007
- *Leonidas of Sparta: A Boy of the Agoge*, Wheatmark, 2010
- *Leonidas of Sparta: A Peerless Peer*, Wheatmark, 2011
- *Where Eagles Never Flew: A Battle of Britain Novel*, Wheatmark, 2011
- *Hitler's Demons: A Novel of the German Resistance*, Wheatmark, 2012

ALSO BY
HELENA P. SCHRADER

Nonfiction Works

***Codename Valkyrie:** General Friedrich Olbricht and the Plot Against Hitler*

Haynes Publishing, 2009, 288 pages

The objective: to kill Hitler and end his reign of terror. The means: a coup d'état disguised as a legitimate General Staff plan approved by Hitler himself. The mastermind behind it all: General Friedrich Olbricht. Olbricht's plan would have changed the course of history if only Colonel Claus Count von Stauffenberg had not failed.

***The Blockade Breakers:** The Berlin Airlift*

The History Press, 2008, 2010, 304 pages

The Berlin Airlift, one of the largest and most ambitious humanitarian efforts in history, began practically without aircraft and aircrew and without sufficient airfields. Yet once it began, the Berlin Airlift became an inspirational feat of organization and international collaboration. Soon ordinary people, from cooks to controllers and from loaders to pilots, had made it more successful than even its originators ever imagined possible.

Sisters in Arms: *British and American Women Pilots during WWII*

Pen and Sword Books Ltd., 2006, 298 pages

During WWII, a few carefully selected women in the United States and Great Britain were given the unprecedented opportunity to fly military aircraft. Yet while the British women were awarded equal pay to that of their male colleagues and could even attain command authority over men, their American sisters were denied both. This book explores why.

Fiction: World War II

Hitler's Demons: *A Novel of the German Resistance*

Wheatmark, 2012, 557 pages
(Originally published as *An Obsolete Honor,* iUniverse, 2008)

Hitler's demons were those Germans who opposed his diabolical regime on moral grounds. They sought to defend human dignity and restore the rule of law. This novel is a tribute to the brave men and women of Germany's resistance and tells the true story of the Valkyrie plot to assassinate Hitler.

Where Eagles Never Flew: *A Battle of Britain Novel*

Wheatmark, 2011, 623 pages
(Originally published as *Chasing the Wind*, iUniverse, 2007)

This is the novel RAF fighter ace Bob Doe called "the best book" he had ever read about the Battle of Britain. According to Doe, Schrader got it "smack on the way it was for us fighter pilots." Retired US Air Force fighter pilot Kencil Heaton called the book "hard to put down ... and perfect for a follow-on Hollywood cinema production."

The Lady in the Spitfire

iUniverse, 2006, 315 pages

Returning from a mission over Berlin with a badly damaged B-17, Lt. Jay Baronowsky, USAAF, almost collides, while landing in bad weather, with a British Wellington. When he discovers the pilot of the British bomber is a woman, the near-crash becomes a clash of cultures—and a love affair.

Novels of Ancient Greece

The Olympic Charioteer

iUniverse, 2005, 408 pages

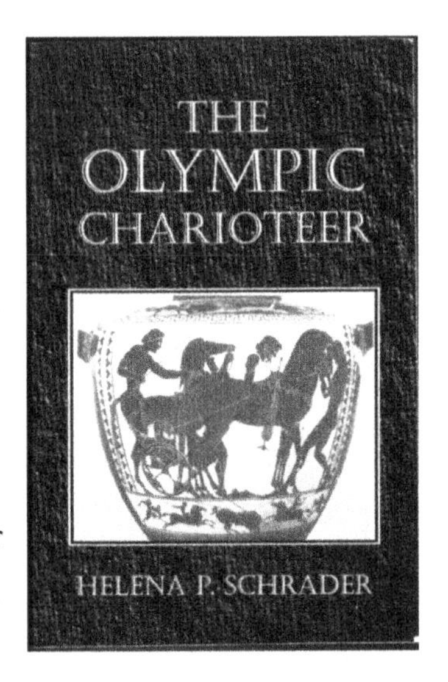

Two cities at war…

Two men with Olympic ambitions…

And one slave - the finest charioteer in Greece…

Set in archaic Greece and based on incidents recorded in Herodotus, this is the tale of a young man's journey from tragedy to triumph, and the story of the founding of the first non-aggression pact in recorded history: the Peloponnesian League.

Are They Singing in Sparta?

iUniverse, 2006, 414 pages

Sparta is losing the war in Messenia when the Delphic oracle orders a lame Athenian schoolmaster to become Sparta's reluctant supreme commander. But the schoolmaster-poet soon discovers there is more to Sparta than Athenian propaganda led him to believe. Before long the lame Athenian and a young Spartan commander are moving Sparta in a new direction—under the influence of a young widow they both admire.

***Spartan Slave, Spartan Queen:** A Tale of Four Women in Sparta*

iUniverse, 2007, 309 pages

Two women, one beautiful and one ugly, are enslaved in the same Spartan raid against the rebellious Messenians. This novel follows their different fates, and in so doing explores the nature and effects of beauty on human interactions.

The Leonidas Trilogy

Leonidas of Sparta: A Boy of the Agoge

Wheatmark, 2010, 250 pages

Leonidas of Sparta—destined to lead the 300 at Thermopylae—earned his citizenship, kingship, and fame by force of personality, but Schrader is the first writer to produce a biographical novel of the Spartan hero. Schrader combines historical research with a novelist's skill to tell Leonidas' compelling personal story and create a refreshingly unorthodox portrayal of Spartan society. This is the first book in her Leonidas trilogy.

Leonidas of Sparta: A Peerless Peer

Wheatmark, 2011, 523 pages

King Leonidas of Sparta lived for half a century before his defiant death at Thermopylae. This, the second book of the Leonidas trilogy, traces Leonidas' evolution from ranker to commander as he develops his leadership skills, grows into his civic responsibilities, and finds the woman he needs in Gorgo, the precocious daughter of his half-brother Cleomenes.

Lightning Source UK Ltd.
Milton Keynes UK
UKOW04f0608211117
313079UK00001B/230/P

9 781604 94830